P9-BAW-584

RAVES FOR
Michael Malone's
DINGLEY FALLS

"*DINGLEY FALLS* IS A WONDROUS ACHIEVEMENT. IT IS FULL OF THE THINGS THAT BOOKS SHOULD BRIM WITH: HUMOR AND SUSPENSE AND WIT, AMONG THEM. . . . THE BOOK IS BEAUTIFULLY TEXTURED, SUPERBLY STRUCTURED. . . . AS LUSTY, WHIMSICAL, TRAGIC—EVEN AS BIZARRE—AS LIFE ITSELF. IT IS A TRIUMPH OF THE HIGHEST ORDER, AND READERS WHO HAVE YET TO DISCOVER IT SHOULD DO SO POST-HASTE."

—*The Atlanta Journal-Constitution*

BEANIE DINGLEY ABERNATHY: At age fifty she is a shy scion of Dingley Falls, statuesque, athletic, elemental—and about to become the town's Junoesque goddess of love . . .

JOY STRUMMER: While Beanie falls in love for the *last* time, the exquisite blue-eyed sixteen-year-old is ripe for her *first* love. And it's speeding toward her in a maroon Jaguar, straight from the venerable Dingley Club . . .

"WHAT AN EXUBERANT NOVEL FOR THESE TROUBLED TIMES! IF NOT THE GREAT AMERICAN NOVEL . . . *DINGLEY FALLS* IS SURELY THE GREAT AMERICAN COMEDY. THE TWO MAY JUST BE SYNONYMOUS."

—*St. Louis Post Dispatch*

(more)

"A WILD ORIGINAL—FUNNY AND PASSIONATE AND WISE—AND MICHAEL MALONE IS ONE OF THOSE RARE WRITERS WHO CAN SLOWLY UNCOVER THE HEART OF AN ENTIRE TOWN. MALONE IS A WONDERFUL STORYTELLER, AND *DINGLEY FALLS* IS A MARVELOUS JOURNEY INTO ABSURDITY, HUMOR, AND COMPASSION."

—Alice Hoffman

"DINGLEY FALLS IS A MARVELOUS, CHARMING, INTELLIGENT, AND ABSORBING BOOK WHICH WORKS ON MANY LEVELS. THE BOOK HAS BEEN COMPARED TO *OUR TOWN* AND THE COMPARISON IS VALID."

—*New York Newsday*

"A PLEASURE TO READ AS FEW MODERN NOVELS ARE. . . . *DINGLEY FALLS* IS A TONIC."

—Marilyn French

———

FATHER SLOAN HIGHWICK: A shoo-in for heaven—should there be one—the rector of St. Andrew's Episcopal Church is gifted with happiness rather than self-reflection. God knows he hired his highly desirable curate Jonathan Fields simply for his good looks—but Father Highwick doesn't . . .

A. A. HAYES: The transplanted Southerner and alcoholic editor of *The Dingley Day* dreams of publishing the town's true news—"Dingley Heiress Beds New York Poet on May 31, Husband the Last to Know;" "Elderly Tea Shoppe Owner Fears Death;" "Local Editor Fears Life"—stories universal in their particularity of pathos and passion . . .

———

"DELIGHTFUL . . . MALONE HAS AN IMAGINATION LIKE KAFKA'S—MIXED WITH THAT OF ERNIE KOVACS."

—*The Raleigh News & Observer*

MISS RAMONA DINGLEY: The town's oldest resident and 1927 tennis champion is anxious to learn her ultimate destiny. ("Must I be resurrected? Couldn't I simply turn into fertilizer and help out, don't you know, a few nasturtiums behind Town Hall?") But she's even more concerned with the strange lights—falling stars? flying saucers?—beyond the marshlands outside Dingley Falls . . .

POLLY HEDGEROW: Dingley Falls' brainiest teenager is old enough to weep over Russian novels, but still too young for passion. On a sleuthing mission for Miss Ramona Dingley, she's approaching the town's most dangerous secret . . .

Books by Michael Malone

Dingley Falls
Handling Sin
Uncivil Seasons

Published by POCKET BOOKS

Most Pocket Books are available at special quantity discounts for bulk purchases for sales promotions, premiums or fund raising. Special books or book excerpts can also be created to fit specific needs.

For details write the office of the Vice President of Special Markets, Pocket Books, 1230 Avenue of the Americas, New York, New York 10020.

DINGLEY FALLS

Michael Malone

For Ann
with warm regards
Michael Malone

POCKET BOOKS

New York   London   Toronto   Sydney   Tokyo

For a singer
"Dodie"
John Darwin Penland
1950–1979

Song's a good prayer.
So is laughter.

POCKET BOOKS, a division of Simon & Schuster Inc.
1230 Avenue of the Americas, New York, NY 10020

Published by arrangement with Harcourt Brace Jovanovich, Inc.
Library of Congress Catalog Card Number: 79-3529

ISBN: 0-671-67180-4

First Pocket Books printing June 1981

10 9 8 7 6 5 4 3 2

Map by Paul J. Pugliese, G.C.I.

POCKET and colophon are trademarks of
Simon & Schuster Inc.

Printed in the U.S.A.

ACKNOWLEDGMENTS

I've never understood why those who write fictions should not acknowledge debts as publicly as those who write facts. I'd like to thank Mrs. Arthur E. Case for her generous friendship, and Dr. Barbara Otto and Dr. J. J. Quilligan, Jr., for consenting with such kind cheer to diagnose the peculiar symptoms afflicting Dingleyans. During the four years it has taken to finish *Dingley Falls*, numbers of readers, both in and out of what is for some odd reason called "the industry," have given me good criticism, wise advice, and warm support. My heartfelt appreciation to them all.

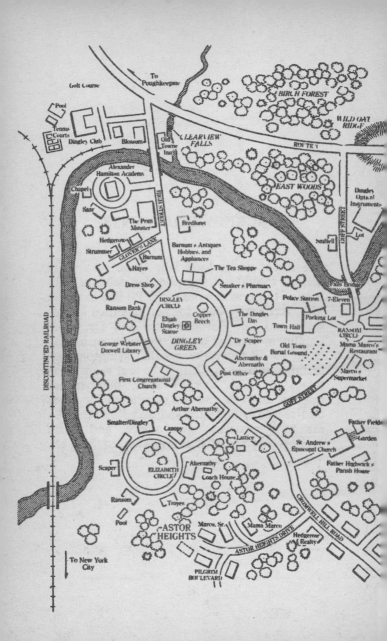

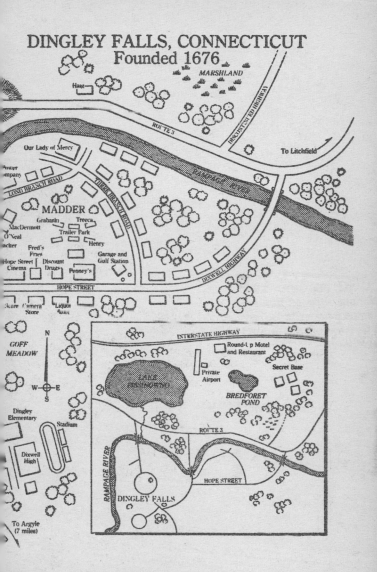

DINGLEY FALLS, CONNECTICUT
Founded 1676

MARSHLAND

Hall

ROUTE 3

DISCOVERY HIGHWAY

To Litchfield

Our Lady of Mercy

Power
Company

RAMPAGE RIVER

LONG BRANCH ROAD

THREE BRANCH ROAD

MADDER

Grabaski   Treeca

MacDermott

O'Neal

Trailer Park

acker   Fred's
Fries   Henry

Hope Street   Discount
Cinema   Drugs   Penney's

Garage and
Gulf Station

DIXWELL HIGHWAY

HOPE STREET

kare Camera
Store   Liquor
tore

GOFF
MEADOW

N

W   E

S

INTERSTATE HIGHWAY

Round-Up Motel
and Restaurant

Secret Base

LAKE
PISSINOWNO

Private
Airport

Dingley
Elementary   Stadium

BREDFORET
POND

Dixwell
High

ROUTE 3

RAMPAGE RIVER

HOPE STREET

DINGLEY FALLS

To Argyle
(7 miles)

*"On the Rampage, Pip. Off the Rampage, Pip.
Such is Life!"*

PART
One

CHAPTER
1

There was something the matter with Judith Haig's heart. That was why she had to quit her job at the post office where she had sorted the lives of Dingley Falls for eleven years. Mrs. Haig was only forty-two years old. She didn't drink or smoke, and she was slim enough to have worn her daughter's clothes if she had had a daughter. So it seemed to be simply bad luck that her heart murmured. She was in Dr. Otto Scaper's office now, waiting to be told how careful she needed to be.

The post office wasn't really the problem. All she did there was raise, then lower the flag, weigh packages and sell stamps, slip into their slots the rare letters and regular government checks that sustained those (very few) too indigent to have homes to which the postman, Alf Marco, could take their mail. The problem was the dogs. Mrs. Haig was afraid of the dogs that lived in the trailer park and gathered in packs to wait for her when she left her home north of the Rampage to cross the bridge into downtown Dingley Falls. Waited to tear out onto the bridge and snarl at her ankles. They never quite bit her. But they scared her, and troubled her heart.

Her husband, John "Hawk" Haig, police chief of Dingley Falls (and the neighboring borough of Madder), did not believe his wife. The one day he had walked with her to work, there had been no dogs at all on Falls Bridge. They knew that she was afraid of them, and that her husband wasn't, and so they hadn't bothered to come. Mrs. Haig was most afraid of horrible thoughts that she couldn't keep out of her mind. Among them, unavoidable premonitions that these dogs wished and planned to ravage her. This fear, and her belief that the dogs knew she understood what they wanted, she did not tell her husband.

For years Chief Haig had wanted her to quit her job anyhow. Everyone knew there was no reason for her to be working, not with his salary, and with no children to support. And they had their house of flat new bricks shoved up against the shoulder of the highway above Dingley Falls and Madder. She might as well stay there and enjoy fixing it up.

Now Mrs. Haig watched huge Dr. Scaper come out of his office with the lawyer Winslow Abernathy and pat the patient on his long, thin back. "Well, you never can tell about the heart," roared the seventy-four-year-old physician. "How long you plan to be up in Boston then?"

"Just three days. Meanwhile, I'd rather not let Beanie know about this, I think. I'll give you a call, Otto, thank you." Abernathy nodded his vague, frowning smile at Mrs. Haig, whom he knew from the post office but failed really to see. The door closed quietly behind him.

"Be with you in one minute," Dr. Scaper yelled at Mrs. Haig. "Got to use the facilities." He shuffled over to whisper, "Call of nature, go in there to smoke. Ida here's against it."

Through the sun-splintering window next to her desk, the doctor's nurse saw Polly Hedgerow pedal past in a rush of red on her bicycle. "Fifteen years old," sighed Ida Sniffell, "and I don't believe she's thought to buy herself a bra." Judith Haig tried to reply with a smile, but returned to the magazine she wasn't really reading—so she didn't learn that in this Bicentennial year Betty Ford, and other rich and famous women in America, had their problems, too.

Without hands, in a private bravura performance, sixteen-year-old Polly Hedgerow cruised the freshly tarred rotary that circled the little town green. In its center a granite Elijah Dingley sat stiffly in his marble chair, and in the stone arms of the statue snuggled Joy Strummer, languidly reading a movie magazine in the shade of a giant copper beech.

Elijah Dingley had founded the town on which he imposed his name three hundred years ago, when he banished himself from Providence, Rhode Island, in disgust at the emotional displays of Roger Williams and on his way to New York, got lost. Dingley Falls was in Connecticut, east of the Hudson and west of Hartford, in low mountains and beautifully situated on the Rampage River, a branch of the Housatonic. Joy Strummer was Polly's best friend.

"Joy!" she yelled as she flew past. Joy's little spaniel jumped up and barked at her.

The pretty town of Dingley Falls was well-off and white-bricked. Dingleyans had watched the riotous sixties on television and were happy to have missed them. They were proud that in 1976, as all around Great Societies puffed themselves up and blew themselves away, here in Dingley Falls the true America had been safely preserved, like an artifact in a time capsule. They had lost nothing but their elms. Here there were no disaffections, no drugs or delinquency, no pollutants or impoverishments to trouble repose. The town's politics were Republican, its income private, and its houses Federalist. Some of these homes had black shutters, some had gray, and Mrs. Ernest Ransom had painted hers bright orange. Priss Ransom was Mrs. Vincent Canopy's best friend. "Priss has always insisted on defining herself," explained Tracy Canopy.

This morning Polly Hedgerow happened to be on her way to visit the man who, twenty-seven years ago, had married Tracy to Vincent Canopy. He was Father Sloan Highwick, Rector of St. Andrew's Episcopal Church and Polly's sidekick. Together they spied, like an unfallen Lear and Cordelia, on who was in, who was out, in their little town. First she circled the green three times, not only to avoid annoying powerful forces, but also to check things out for the Rector. As she pedaled, she panned the white brick and gray slate buildings, the civic and mercantile Stonehenge of Dingley Falls. As far as she could tell, nothing much was going on. The lawyer Mr. Abernathy stood on the sidewalk as if he couldn't remember where he was supposed to go next. Across the green old Miss Lattice scurried to Ransom Bank, probably to get change for her Tea Shoppe. In the doorway of Barnum's Antiques, Hobbies, and Appliances that creepy Mr. Barnum was ogling Joy Strummer, smacking his lips. *The Dingley Day* office still had a broken window; Mr. Hayes, the editor, didn't seem to care. And at the far end of the green the bespectacled Mrs. Vincent Canopy was driving the right front wheel of her Volvo up onto the curb, where she left it. Mrs. Ernest Ransom got out of the passenger door and laughed.

Leaning into a left turn, Polly sped away from the town center and gathered speed to climb Cromwell Hill. At its top, in his Irish country hat, Father Highwick was pestering his gardener, Sebastian Marco, who was trying to transfer Red Sun isc dahlias in the solitude an artist deserves. The Rector had nothing to do, and for sixty-six years he had never been able to bear being alone. So while Sebastian grimaced when the girl suddenly rattled into his garden, her wheels scattering his combed gravel, he forgave the barbarity, because as long as she kept Highwick company the gardener could work without having to rebut an erroneous homily on the gardenia or listen to an off-key "Cantate Domine."

With the lovely smile of one who has never troubled himself over life's perplexities, the Rector put an avuncular arm around his young friend; poor only child of a widowed agnostic, he sighed to himself, *and* with glasses and that unfortunate hair. His own hair, luxuriant and nicely brushed, looked as white and soft as angel's hair on a Christmas tree, and his eyes looked

as bright as blue china cups. "Yes, Polly, dear?" he
asked.

"There's something the matter with Mrs. Haig's
heart," she told him. "That's why she has to quit her
job at the post office."

CHAPTER
2

If anyone had asked Dr. Scaper's nurse who were the
best-housed, best-bred, best-off women in Dingley
Falls, Ida Sniffell would have given the same answer as
Father Sloan Highwick, or anyone else familiar with the
town's social register. They were "Mrs. Winslow
Abernathy. Mrs. Ernest Ransom. Mrs. Vincent Canopy. And oh, yes, Mrs. Blanchard Troyes." Unlike
Judith Haig, these ladies did not go to Dr. Scaper with
their problems, though Dr. Scaper had, as a very young
man, seen three of them into the world. Instead they
went to expensive doctors in New York. They went
shopping in New York, and they were all best friends.

Mrs. Winslow Abernathy had once been Beanie
Dingley. She was still big-boned and buxom with
generous features, thick, curly hair, and a rich roan
coloring. Mrs. Vincent Canopy had once been Tracy
Dixwell. She was still short, trim, and square-faced,
with green-apple eyes and owlish glasses. Beanie and
Tracy had grown up very pleasantly with petite, pretty
Mrs. Blanchard Troyes when she had been, decades
ago, petite, pretty Evelyn Goff. "The Three Graces of
Dingley Falls," *The Dingley Day* had called them when
they had been photographed embracing one another in
their white dresses and huge horsehair hats the day the
paper announced their coming out. The Three Graces

had since moved through their lives together: Beanie at
a healthy stride, Tracy at an efficient clip, and Evelyn in
a dreamy float.

Beanie was a Dingley, but the ancestry of Tracy and
Evelyn was more broadly distinguished. Beanie's fore-
bear Elijah had, after all, simply founded a little town
on the Rampage, while their thrice-great-grandfathers
Goff and Dixwell had been regicides, and there were
still streets in New Haven honoring them for having
had the audacity to lop off the head of Charles I and the
perspicacity not to be in England when Charles II
returned home. Dingley, Dixwell, and Goff were
among the best names to grow up with in Dingley Falls,
where the girls happened to grow up, so they were
invited everywhere, and they went everywhere together. That is, until college. For then, to Tracy and
Beanie's sorrow, Evelyn Goff had not come to Mount
Holyoke with them. Instead, overcoming familial objections with the deadly tenacity of the fragile, she had
floated off to the Peabody Institute in Baltimore, where
she dreamed of singing Mimi at the Met. "Evelyn has
always confused life with an opera," explained Tracy at
the time. "But oh, gosh, Tracy, we'll miss her," said
Beanie.

At Mount Holyoke an elegant Bostonian had been
drawn into the gap of the Graces. Her name was Priss
(Priscilla) Hancock. Soon, with her tall glamour (all
chic and sharp angles) and her ironic festiveness, Priss
replaced the absent moony Evelyn as Tracy's confi-
dante. And though the lacrosse-playing Beanie was not
exactly Priss's type, one could not be Tracy's friend
without taking along her childhood companion, rather
like—as Priss said to someone else—dragging out in
public a shy St. Bernard. So for four years Tracy,
Beanie, and Priss majored in French together and
danced the fox-trot and did their hair like Ann Sheridan. They all got married to men who had been officers
in the war. First Beanie eloped with Winslow Abernathy, to her mother's disappointment (she'd hoped for

a big wedding) and relief (she'd feared Beanie was too
big to catch a man). Then Priss, in a moment of spite
against a professor with whom she was infatuated,
accepted the third and probably final proposal of
Ernest Ransom, who had been Winslow Abernathy's
roommate at Yale. Finally Tracy married Vincent
Canopy of Manhattan, with Beanie and Priss as ma-
trons of honor. The romantic Evelyn had already
surprised them again by running off with her Italian
violin instructor at the Peabody Institute, Hugo Eroica.
He went to fight in the war, too, but, apparently, on the
wrong side, leaving Evelyn alone and unwed in Paris,
where, before her parents could rescue her, she met
and married Blanchard Troyes, a French industrialist.
Only after Troyes's death had she finally floated home
to Dingley Falls.

There she found that her old friend Tracy (Dixwell
Canopy) was also at home alone, because her husband,
Vincent, had died and it made no sense to maintain a
townhouse in Manhattan too. She found that her old
friend Beanie (Dingley Abernathy) was home as well,
because she'd made Winslow the lawyer for her
railroad and her Optical Instruments factory. And
there Evelyn found a new friend, Priscilla (Hancock
Ransom), because Ernest Ransom, a native Dingleyan,
was president of the Ransom Bank and the most
influential man in town. So the Three Graces (with
Priss added) were back together. They lived on Elizabeth Circle, they gave each other dinner parties, they
played bridge and a little golf and tennis at the Dingley
Club, they took one of Beanie's trains into Manhattan
every Wednesday to see shows and shops and occasionally doctors. They had numbers of projects and belonged to many organizations. On Mondays, like today,
they held meetings of the Thespian Ladies Club.

Now, over daiquiris at The Prim Minster, their
efficient club president, Tracy Canopy, was reading
aloud: " 'The Stabbo-Massacrism Band, which in the

last year has frenzied young British audiences with its filthy talk and spittle, found their entire tour canceled Thursday when towns throughout the United Kingdom learned of their having vomited on a member of the Royal Family during a private performance following the marriage of the Earl of Swithorne's daughter to the son of Sheikh Qārū of Grosvenor Square. "Rock and roll is all very well," commented the best man, George St. George-Albans, "but really!" The bride's mother, Lady "Babs" Howard, wearing a quilted evening gown of embroidered pink and mauve roses, appeared a picture of composure as she was carried to her waiting limousine midst the enthusiastic cheers of loyal onlookers. Many of the hostile villagers then stayed at the estate gates to boo the first American superstars of thug-rock, who defiantly pantomimed sexual perversities at them until removed by local constables.'

"Now really, indeed." Mrs. Canopy paused indignantly, looking over her glasses, then took up another clipping. "And just yesterday." She gave them now news closer to home. "In Argyle, listen to this: 'An elderly vagrant, who gave his name as Old Tim Hines, was arrested and held without bail Sunday, charged with molesting five suburban preschoolers, having first gained their trust by tap-dancing for them with beer-bottle caps tacked to his loafers. "Old Tim's nice," maintained one of the alleged victims, whose name was not disclosed.'

"Art is being sexually abused," concluded Mrs. Canopy, who, since her widowhood, had given her heart over to Art.

"Art who?" asked the playful Priss Ransom.

"Oh, dear, I hope not," sighed Mrs. Blanchard Troyes, née Evelyn Goff, briefly of the Peabody Institute.

"I don't know what," confessed the president, her jaw as stubborn as Woodrow Wilson's. "But something must be done to save Art for future generations. Here

we are in the most idealistic country in the world, but
how can we hold up the torch to other nations if the
torch is covered, well, if it is covered with spittle?"

The heart of Mrs. Canopy had been before jostled
but not dislodged from its place in line before the ticket
booth of Art, where she had faithfully stood alone since
the main curtain of Life, as the Rector put it, had fallen
on Vincent seven years ago. After Mr. Canopy had
died in the reception line of their twentieth wedding
anniversary celebration, Tracy had lent out to homeless
painters their townhouse in Manhattan, that city to
whose insatiable Art she and her husband had fed so
many thousands of unearned dollars. Nor, to this day,
could mistrust of her faith disabuse her: the masterpiece of Habzi Rabies, a Pakistani painter who had
hocked her car for hash and then set fire to the summer
house on Lake Pissinowno that she had lent him, the
masterpiece for which she had provided both the
money and the medium, continued to hang over
the mantel of her Dingley Falls living room. *Fingerpaint
on a Widow's Fur* was its title. "The primitivism of a
child. So unspoiled," said Mrs. Canopy. "Sad the same
is no longer true of your Russian sable," joked the
sarcastic Priss to Beanie Abernathy with a wink.
"What?" asked Beanie, who never got a joke.

"Artists are different from you and me," Mrs.
Canopy always explained. She herself indulged in a
little pot throwing and even wrote poems, which she
placed in the finished pots and left on the Dingley Falls
doorsteps of her many acquaintances. But she made no
claims to Art and was not given to those excesses she
allowed the Gifted. Nor did her concern today about
this "sexual abuse" of Art derive from a squeamishness
that might seem compatible with her age and heritage.
Mrs. Canopy went staunchly off to be raped by Art
once a week. *She* was not afraid of Virginia Woolf, and
while *Oh! Calcutta!* had cost her an involuntary
struggle, she'd never let out· a scream. Neither was
violence any less supportable. Ushers had carried away

far younger than she when Porko Fulawhiski disemboweled himself with a palette knife in *Dead on Red: Final Appearance of a One-Man Show in SoHo*.

What was it then that so disturbed her now about these clippings of Old Tim Hines and a relative of the Queen, the latter of whom she planned to lunch with this summer at the Waldorf across a crowded room of some seven hundred other Bicentennialists? "Mr. Hines may or may not be; but that band just simply isn't *sincere*. Or maybe I'm just getting old," she suggested with a brisk sigh. The cutouts describing the cutups of Hines and the Stabbo-Massacrism Band introduced today's topic, "Sexuality and the Arts." Their guest speaker was Mr. Rich Rage, an obscene poet hailed by *The Village Voice* as "The Baudelaire of the Bathroom Wall" who was also a visiting instructor of creative writing at Vassar College, where he had been obligingly seducing his class in roughly alphabetical order. By the term's end he had progressed as far as the *R*'s, which is how young Kate Ransom had persuaded him to come overnight to Dingley Falls—both them mildly anticipating her capitulation. Mrs. Canopy did not know of this private inducement; neither, for that matter, did Priss Ransom, who had lost track of her daughter Kate's maturation some years back.

Rage swallowed a roll whole, rose to his feet, and spoke from his heart. "Ladies, look, you gotta spread your legs, raise your knees, and open your cunts to art. Fuck the brain. Until art comes inside you so hard, the come shoots out your nose and ears, you haven't had art, and art hasn't had you. Now that's what Wordsworth and Coleridge said, and that's all that needs to be said, you follow me?"

"I *think* so, Mr. Rage," said the valiant Mrs. Canopy, whose memory searched in vain through a college course for anything resembling such startling remarks by the Lake Poets. Beanie Abernathy bit through the toothpick in her chicken club.

When Rage finished his brief but vibrant "Stare Up

the Asshole of Art," he tossed all the half-eaten
sandwiches and fruit cups forgotten by the ladies in
their attentiveness into his green canvas bag and flung it
over his broad tweed shoulder. "Nobody ever finishes
their food! The freedom to waste, that is definitely one
of the glories of America!"

"Are you a Socialist then?" asked Mrs. Canopy, her
eyes behind the round glasses as bright as flags. She was
ready to bear it if he were.

"Oh, hell, no. I'm a monarchist. Love the House of
Hanover and especially the hemophiliacs."

"No, please," said Beanie Abernathy, slipping her
long feet back into her low-heeled shoes. She had just
been told by Tracy Canopy to escort Mr. Rage on a
tour of the town until time for him to meet Kate
Ransom at the Dingley Club. Tracy herself had to take
to the Argyle bus station, seven miles away, a visiting
Lebanese music student who had seen America for
ninety-nine days and was now going home. Tracy asked
Beanie to drive Rage first to the post office, where he
needed to mail some student grades, and then guide
him through as much of historic Dingley Falls as he
cared to see.

"Tracy, Prissie, Evelyn, don't leave me alone with
him," Beanie bent to whisper at her friends. She stared
at the poet in his warm brown turtleneck that was the
color of his eyes. From across the room, where he was
selling copies of his book, he grinned at her. His hair
and beard looked like curly wheat.

"Oh, Beanie, don't be silly." Priss laughed. "Winslow
won't mind. And you're bigger than Mr. Rage is
anyhow." Indeed, Beanie was Juno-esque of face and
figure. Her form had been a drawback at twenty, except
for her serving as goalie on the Mount Holyoke lacrosse
team, but thirty-two years later, age had finally caught
up with her features, and now Mrs. Abernathy was
quite something to see, though she'd never seen it. She
still hunched over at cocktail parties to shorten herself,

just as she had shrunk into a corner at birthday parties in the sixth grade.

"You take Mr. Rage then, Evelyn," Mrs. Canopy instructed the wispy Mrs. Troyes, as the group followed her into The Prim Minster's parking lot.

"Oh, I am so sorry, Tracy, but really I can't because I've already arranged to drive Father Fields to Argyle for his new contact lenses. Beanie, please, forgive me, I'm sure it will be fun, but I'm already late." And without waiting, Evelyn rushed to her Chrysler New Yorker. They saw her lovely prematurely blue-gray head peering through the steering wheel as she shot out of the parking space and sped to an assignation with Reverend Highwick's beautiful young curate, Jonathan Fields.

"Fuck, that broad can *drive!*" whistled Rich Rage, who appreciated talent wherever he found it.

"Mrs. Troyes lived in Paris for twenty years," Tracy explained.

The lot emptied, except for Mr. Rage and Mrs. Abernathy and a stray dog, whose head Beanie scratched as she stalled for time. The dog, one of the pack that frightened Judith Haig, pushed his head up under Beanie's hand.

"Looks like they stuck you with me, huh?" Rage smiled. "Sorry," he shrugged. "Looks like we'll have to make the best of it."

"Yes. I guess if you'll follow me," mumbled Mrs. Abernathy, the unwilling guide, as she led him to her car.

"Love it!" grinned the agreeable poet.

CHAPTER
3

The Rector of St. Andrew's and Evelyn Troyes were fighting over young Father Fields, though none of the three knew it, least of all the nearsighted object of passions no less tumultuous for being unconscious. Tracy and Priss had long since analyzed this cerebrally erotic *ménage à trois* in their mind-control group and elsewhere. Now, after their Thespian Ladies' meeting, they synopsized.

"Evelyn has always confused the spiritual with the sensual," said Mrs. Canopy, as she lurched her Volvo into Elizabeth Circle. "That's why she ran off with a violinist."

"*Bien sûr.* And was so inexplicably unabused by life with Hugo Eroica that after he abandoned her for Mussolini, she married Blanchard, another foreigner! Of course, Jonathan Fields *is* pretty. God knows that's the only reason Sloan hired him."

"Priss!"

"I said God knew it, I didn't say Sloan did."

Tracy, who admired her friend's wit and sometimes jotted down her remarks to remember them, smiled appreciatively. "I'll just drop you off here, Priss. I must get Babaha to the station by four-thirty. Extraordinary amount of luggage for a student to accumulate in so short a stay in this country. Souvenirs for her family, she said. She tells me the Lebanese have very few conveniences. Toilet paper has been such a delight for her. Oh, I hope Beanie's all right; perhaps I shouldn't have asked her to go with Mr. Rage, she's so shy."

"Don't be silly. When in h. is she going to grow up and stop gawking around like a huge teenage horse? Before you rush off; I got one, my dear, one of the letters." Mrs. Ransom snorted. "Remember, like the one Beanie got, but she threw hers away and said she couldn't recall what was in it?"

"Oh, read it!" begged her friend. "If you don't mind."

Priss already had the sheet of cheap typing paper unfolded in her gloved hand. "It's most vilely intriguing." She laughed. "Mrs. Ransom is spelled *s-u-m*. 'Think you're sharp as tacks? You don't know the half.' "

"Slant rhyme," said Tracy automatically.

" 'There's baby doo-doo up your tushie,' "

"My!"

" 'You need a big dong to clean it out, you Lezzie.' "

"Lizzie?"

"No. Lezzie. *L-e-z-z-i-e*."

"Ah. Lesbian," explained Mrs. Canopy, who knew these expressions from off-Broadway productions.

"Well, my dear, that's all. 'Half' is spelled *h-a-f*. Fascinating, *n'est-ce pas?* What do you make of it?"

"I believe he, whoever wrote it, feels you may be a homosexual. Latently, of course."

"*Ha!* And who in h. is 'he'?" demanded the skeptical Priss. "If Wanda hadn't found it wadded among the milk bottles a week before he arrived, I would think it more than likely that your poetical Mr. Rage had sent it. There's a certain similarity of tone."

"Who could it be?"

No one knew. But somebody in Dingley Falls was writing hate letters, accusing people of harboring uncommitted crimes in their hearts, vividly detailed crimes that they would never have the "balls" to carry out. Limus Barnum of Barnum's Antiques, Hobbies, and Appliances had written to the paper to call for action against what the editor, Mr. Hayes, facetiously called "this mailiac out somewhere at night, defiling

our boxes and slits with his misspelled smut." The
letters were not stamped, were not entrusted to Mrs.
Haig or Alf Marco at the post office, but were
hand-delivered; were on two occasions, in fact, left
next to the poems inside Mrs. Canopy's gift pots. Not
even Polly Hedgerow knew who the anonymous author
was, and neither did Father Highwick, unless he was
holding out on her.

Oh, boy, thought Polly as she coasted down Cromwell Hill, after trading the Rector word of Mrs. Haig's
heart for news of an assault by an unemployed construction worker named Maynard Henry on one Raoul
Treeca up on Wild Oat Ridge—not that a Madder
hardhat was worth the Dingley Falls postmistress. Oh,
boy, thought Polly. Here comes Mrs. Troyes after
Father Fields again! The gray Chrysler roared past her,
sucking the bike into its wind tunnel so that Polly was
forced to grab the handlebars to keep her balance.
Then down the hill she flew into a fantasy, on her way
to speed the precious serum through enemy lines just in
time to save the stricken village. Mortar whistled
around her fearless head.

At St. Andrew's Episcopal Church, Evelyn Troyes
tapped girlishly on the window of the young curate's
stone cottage behind the parish house of Sloan Highwick. The snowy-haired Rector was watching her
through his open door. "Jonathan's not home yet,"
he called with satisfaction across the garden. "The
headmaster asked him to pay a visit at Hamilton
Academy."

Startled, Mrs. Troyes spun around with a dainty leap.
"Oh, it's only you, Sloan." She floated to his side,
oblivious of either his or her own raging jealousy.
"Poor Jonathan, I expect he forgot his eye appointment. Always thinking of himself last. People make
so many demands on him, and he takes their problems so to heart, he's simply too good to say no

and there are those who will take advantage of his thoughtfulness."

"Exactly," Highwick hurled out at her with what he intended as a smile. "I'm just making tea now. Will you?"

"No, no." She fluttered away. "I'll see you tonight at the Ransoms', won't I? But now I think I ought to trot down to High Street and wait there in the car for Jonathan." Her voice sang out. "I'm driving him to Argyle. His tinted lenses came in, you know."

"I know. *I* took the call," fired back the Rector while waving a blessing at Mrs. Troyes. His heart was heaped with coals of fire, but he had, as it were, no smoke detector.

In his delightful study at Alexander Hamilton Academy for Young Men, the handsome headmaster, Walter Saar, swept with his binoculars the playing fields, where his boys sported in white shorts. Ray Ransom was humping Charlie Hayes again, grabbing between Hayes's tan thighs for the football. The headmaster had a hard-on. He also had a hangover and was worried about himself. He lit his fifteenth cigarette of the morning. Sunday he had waked up nude and alone in a very unattractive hotel room with rope burns around his wrists and his wallet missing. He had stayed in the filthy shower for as long as he could bear to, and then had left New York vowing never to come there again, at least not to the Village, at least not to bars in the Village where merciless young men with sullen eyes waited. Now he had wasted his entire morning sending telegrams to cancel his credit cards. And he would need a new driver's license. He couldn't afford to drink anymore. He was thirty-eight years old. One hint of this incident and Ernest Ransom would tell him that the board of trustees would be pleased to accept his resignation. Worse, perhaps, one of these days he might be killed. The headmaster, an excellent teacher, had been asked once before, years earlier, to resign voluntarily from a school; in exchange for his doing so he had received excellent recommendations to this excellent academy. Such an incident could not be allowed to recur. He vowed again to get on top of life and ride it.

Meanwhile, in Saar's tasteful bathroom, his guest, Father Jonathan Fields (who had indeed forgotten about his eye appointment), was masturbating as quickly as he possibly could, so as not to keep his host waiting. Without seeing his own face (a face like a Raphael, the Rector had told him) reflected in its amber glass, Jonathan gazed at the beautiful carved oak mirror. Whatever had possessed him? What had forced this urgent visit to the toilet before he simply came all over his clerical pants while sitting in the headmaster's Chippendale chair with his Royal Doulton teacup jingling in its saucer on his lap? Either Walter Saar, or Saar's exquisite furnishings (each piece of which he longed to own himself—awful, awful envy), had unignorably raised the curate to a turgid height of desire. Visualizing the Holbein over the Queen Anne lowboy in the study, Father Fields ejaculated into the toilet bowl, returned his still twitching member to his shorts, and, having washed his hands, pulled the chain on his passion.

"Jonathan. Ahem. Good." Saar coughed. After having noticed Mrs. Blanchard Troyes parked in her enormous Chrysler across the lane from his house, he had placed his binoculars back on the window seat beside an unopened *Birds of New England*. The two men had been planning for two months a choral concert to be performed at St. Andrew's Church by the Alexander Hamilton Academy Choir on Whitsunday, when Father Fields would accompany the boys on the magnificent organ that Timothy Dingley had ordered from London just before the Revolutionary War.

"I've heard you play it only once," said Saar, as he mournfully sipped tomato juice. "The Evensong when your Almighty pulled me inside by the ear like a child and sat me down in a corner pew. Bach! Here, I'm subjected to hours of amplified howls bellowing out of every dorm, sounds that make me feel old and fragile and approaching the climax of a nervous breakdown."

Startled by Saar's use of the word *climax* (had he been overheard, overseen, in the bathroom?), Fields stuttered, blushing, "Maybe, you know, if you like, I could play for you sometime, though I'm not really very good."

The truth was that Saar agreed with this modest appraisal. He knew music. The curate played with no self-esteem, and so without conviction. But he couldn't say that, so he said, "Jonathan, you should modify your *mea culpas*, really. All afternoon I've listened to you lacerate yourself as an unworthy priest, an unworthy counselor to the many, many people who insist on your help, an unworthy son, an unworthy friend. Really, your unworthiness is becoming a megalomania."

"I'm sorry. I guess I've been monopolizing the conversation."

"There! Again. Now, how about Thursday here in the chapel? You play for me. Lights out at ten, and I'll let old Oglethorpe beat the boys back into their beds alone—though it is my favorite duty of the day, of course." The headmaster smiled. His headache throbbed, and he was deeply suspicious of his motives in not mentioning to Father Fields that Mrs. Troyes was parked outside, apparently awaiting him.

"I'd like that," Jonathan murmured. "Thursday." His heart leaped against his ribs.

The headmaster and the curate had been in love for almost a year. Their erotic feelings (unlike those of Evelyn Troyes and Sloan Highwick) were more or less known to themselves, but not to each other—at least not with sufficient certainty to warrant a declaration. Each, fearing the other's disapprobation, offered no clues whose meaning could not be denied. That it should not require two months to plan a quarter-hour recital was such a clue, one that forced itself upon the attention, finally, even of the innocent Rector, who terrified his curate one evening by observing, "Jonathan, I would bet you anything you like that all this choir business is nothing but a sham. It's you Walter wants. Yes, I can always spot it. He's on his way to God and is afraid to confess it for fear of looking like a fool. So many intellectual fellows are, poor things. But that man is seeking conversion, and you, dear boy, are the tool of our Lord."

Finding that the Dingley Falls post office was for some reason locked, Beanie Abernathy had no idea what to do with Rich Rage, who sat contentedly in her Seville munching on Mrs. A. A. Hayes's tuna salad on toast and asking her questions about her life. Should she proceed with the architectural tour? Should she take him immediately to the country club, where his original hostess, Priss Ransom's daughter Kate, was playing tennis with Evelyn Troyes's daughter Mimi? Rage told her he had no desire to do either, so she drove him to Argyle, seven miles south, where she knew there to be a bigger post office. Unless Monday, May 31, was a national holiday commemorating something neither she nor Mr. Rage could recall, it was sure to be open.

Dreary, dirty Argyle made Rage want a drink. He took her to a macho bar. "Love 'em," the poet told his guide. "Saw a merchant marine in a place like this in the Battery; downed a pint of hooch on an empty stomach; his capillaries closed up on him and he keeled over dead, right at the feet of the guy that had challenged him to do it. Checked out, *whap*, on the floor, like that! That's life."

"And death," said Beanie, who did not know what either *hooch* or *capillaries* meant. She shrunk her ample form against the corner of their greasy booth, for Rage was rubbing her leg with his lively tweed knee.

Three blocks away, Beanie's friend Evelyn sat in the ophthalmologist's waiting room, waiting for the young curate whom she had brought there after collecting him from Walter Saar. In the interim she memorized the danger signs for glaucoma, unable to decide whether she had all or none of them. In the office itself Jonathan Fields, itchy in his still-gummy jockey shorts, spotted the appropriate letters on cue from Carl Marco, Jr., whose chest pressed briefly against the curate's face and evoked, to Fields's dismay, an unconscionable fantasy of being fellatioed against his will after having been shackled to the examining chair by the virile ophthalmologist.

"'Scuse me, Father, let me just get in here a sec and lower this gizmo," said Dr. Marco, who had sexual problems of his own, as he took this confessional proximity to explain, for he was going to have to marry his receptionist before the end of her first trimester. "My father's just about to bust a gut, Father. You know? Maybe I shouldn't have told him, just gotten it over with. Tie the old knot. What do you think?"

What was he supposed to think? "I think it's always best to be as open as you can. Do you, well, love her?"

"Oh, sure, yeah, sure, I guess so. She's okay. But the thing is, she's not Catholic, so, well, you know. My father is. Real gung-ho. So he's in a bind, you know. I mean abortion is no go. Well, hell." The young doctor's grin looped above his white tunic. "I got out of Vietnam, I guess you can't get out of everything. You know? Don't blink."

"Jonathan! How terribly nice," cried Mrs. Troyes when the trim, curly-haired cleric burst upon her like a night in Reno with his tinted contact lenses. Yes, he had time to share a quick cocktail with her at Dingley Falls's Old Towne Inn. So Evelyn's heart was full as she floored the Chrysler and left behind Argyle and Beanie Abernathy, unseen at the intersection, in the blur of her rearview mirror.

CHAPTER
4

Dingley Falls's own Dr. Scaper, big as a bear and deaf as a post, telephoned Judith Haig. She wasn't at home. "Wonder, by God, if something isn't poisoning folks in this town. Those tests on that woman don't make sense," he boomed at his nurse, Ida Sniffell, who ignored him. She was reading a book on how to pay more attention to yourself than to others. "Call Sam Smalter," he boomed again. "Tell him to get this prescription made up for Mrs. Haig. Okay? Hell's bells, you listening to me at all, Ida?"

He got a nod, which was all the book allowed her to give.

Mrs. Haig wasn't at home because she was standing in the checkout line of the Madder A & P. West of Goff Street (which, as precisely as Marxism, scissored Dingley Falls into class sectors known as Dingley and Madder) everyone had his groceries delivered by Carl Marco, Sr. Those who lived east of Goff in Madder had to shop for themselves. Mrs. Haig's clerk at the A & P was Sarah MacDermott, who would have also been her best friend had Judith allowed herself one. For though Mrs. MacDermott had plenty of other people to absorb the volubility that bounced about inside her like popcorn against a pan lid, she had chosen Judith in the eighth grade and would not give her up. And, since Sarah's husband, Joe, was Chief John "Hawk" Haig's assistant, the two women shared the law as in-laws. That such was the full extent of their commonality was

22

an abyss over which Sarah MacDermott could leap fearlessly because she had never noticed the gap.

"Men and women, Jesus bless us." The gum-chewing Mrs. MacDermott now began, with her typical preamble, to put Judith in touch with the day's gossip. "Chinkie Henry was just in here with a black eye, proud as the Pope she was of it too, if you ask me. A black eye on a Orientaler, if you can picture that! She told me, I had to ask her, that Maynard did it. Her own husband. *And*, what's more, he rammed Raoul Treeca right over Wild Oat Ridge, broke both his legs and totally destroyed his Chevy pickup."

Judith Haig glanced up from her canned goods to the cash register as Sarah, without once looking at either, flawlessly rang up her carefully chosen purchases. The man in line behind her ostentatiously juggled three boxes of frozen fish and glared irritably at Sarah for talking with a customer.

"Who?" Judith finally asked.

"Who what?" clacked Sarah as she shoveled an armful of cans toward the bag boy. "Watch the rice, Luke, hole in it. *Maynard* Henry. He caught Raoul Treeca trying to run off with his wife, with Chinkie. Chin. The Saigon girl that the Grabaski cousins, you know, brought back from Vietnam last year and set up in that trailer where they took turns with her or all went in together for all I know. We'll never get the nitty-gritty on that one, and of course you can't understand a word Chinkie's saying anyhow, even if she would tell you."

"That's all," said Judith palely, pushing a slab of meat toward Luke, then opening her purse. It was, in fact, too much. She remembered pictures. A highway of black-hatted bodies running in slow motion, like *Fantasia* mushrooms afloat in a flooded river. Televised race to escape torched homes, bodies running from one enemy to another, carts heaped high with grandparents and bicycles, some too old, too young, too unlucky, crumpled dead into ditches, the spaces they left in the crowd gone in an instant. The black-and-white picture pushed its way across Judith Haig's eyes as she tried to listen to what Sarah was saying. Such pictures (images seen on television, stories told her) often assaulted her mind without warning and were, she suspected, among the causes of her heart condition. She dreaded their coming, as epileptics dread the look of light that foreshadows seizure.

Still talking, Sarah jabbed out a final sequence of buttons, and the drawer binged open. "Look at that! Forty-eight forty. People should refuse, just refuse to pay these prices. It's criminal. They're strangling us."

"Yes."

"Well, what can we do, we have to eat."

"Yes."

"Anyhow, let me finish. Maynard found out about it, he'd been overseas too—haven't I told you this before?"

"No, I don't think so."

"Joined the marines in Argyle. Anyhow, they say he beat up both those Polacks, took Chinkie off, and made her Mrs. Maynard Henry that very month. A year later, *this* happens. Well, I could have warned him. Stick to your own." Sarah counted out change. "Sorry, honey, but that's it, not enough silver to hold down the eyes on a dead man. My boy, Jimmy, he saw Raoul hitching Maynard's trailer to his pickup, ran over to Fred's Fries, and told Maynard he'd better come see. Maynard caught up to them slowing down for the ridge—just outdrove them—run them into the shoulder, jerked Chinkie out, unhitched the trailer, and *then* just shoved Raoul, still sitting like a fool in his pickup, wetting his tight pants." Sarah took a breath with gusto. "And, like I say, *right* over the top. Both legs and three ribs snapped like wishbones on a chicken. Right near your house."

"I don't know him," said Mrs. Haig. She watched the boy organize her groceries into their bags; he chose among possibilities like an artist with collage materials. Sarah helped him squeeze the bags into the pushcart.

"Oh, *Judith,* you went to school with Maynard's big brother, Arn. Arn Henry? Scored twice for Dixwell in the playoffs our senior year?" Exasperated, Mrs. MacDermott blew a puff of air up to her yellow bangs. "We were *standing* right there in the bleachers when Hawk threw him the pass!"

"I'm sorry, Sarah, I don't remember."

"On the Blessed Virgin, Judith, it amazes me you can remember who *you* are sometimes."

Sometimes it amazed Mrs. Haig, too. And sometimes she couldn't.

"Why, Hawk and Joe arrested Maynard for assault this morning. . . . What's come over you? Wait a minute, where are you going?"

"I'm sorry, I'm afraid I'm not feeling well. Dr. Scaper seems to think there may be something the matter with my heart." Having offered this information in order to placate her friend, Mrs. Haig then disappeared while Sarah MacDermott, who had turned to the fuming customer, called over her shoulder, *"What?* Jesus bless us. Judith! Judith! Wait a minute, what did you say? Your *heart?* Listen, honey, I'll call you! And Coleman Sniffell, *you* just keep your pants on!"

Judith Haig walked quietly home to fix up her house for her husband, Hawk, who apparently had been out arresting someone she should have known. She had no trouble on the way. The dogs did not know that the post office was always closed on Memorial Day and were not expecting her to cross Falls Bridge until after five.

CHAPTER
5

"What's your real name? No mother names her beauty 'Beanie.'" Rich Rage was trying to get to know his bewildered guide, Mrs. Abernathy, who, pointing out points of interest as they drove back through Dingley Falls, referred to each simply as "That's an old house over there to your left," or "There's an old house on your right." Mesmerized by the bumpy-road rhythm of Beanie's ample bosom, Rage looked at none of this history. Both he and she had left behind the stiffness of sobriety in the macho bar, where, on top of the Thespian Ladies' daiquiris consumed earlier, they had drunk three Scotches each, while discovering that Beanie liked shelling peanuts, driving cars, playing most sports, baking bread; liked children, animals, colors, cloth, and walking in the woods. She had never said so before; the questions had never been asked. She liked wood shavings, dancing, the mountains, the ocean, fire, and clouds; she had loved to feed, rock, diaper, and play with her twin sons when they were babies; she had waited for them to come home from school when they were older so that they could do things together. She liked to hammer, cut with scissors, polish silver, and fix broken things. She liked to sink in leaves or snow or goosedown. She liked, he summarized, physical sensations. And, she thought to herself with surprise, she liked Rich Rage.

"Your name, stand for Sabrina?" he asked the buttons on her cashmere blazer.

"Beatrice," admitted Beanie.

"Hell, that's even better. Dante tears the balls off Milton any day. Mine's really Richard Rage, I mean it's not a personal statement. They called me 'Dickie.' So Beatrice, meet snivelly, scared little Dickie Rage from St. Louis. Acne left not a trace on my face, for the scars went deeper."

"Richard," said Beanie.

"I like the way you say it."

"Richard," said Beatrice again.

Having filled over fifty bags for Sarah MacDermott and then signed out at the A & P, Luke Packer was following Joy Strummer home. He kept his distance by staring intently at the sky whenever the girl, her movie magazine rolled in her hand, dawdled to coo at her stupid cocker spaniel or to strip a hedge branch of its leaves in one swift upward pull. Half a block behind, he was uncommitted but ready to rush forward if danger should assail her, which Luke despaired of its ever doing in this stupid dump of a town.

Down Glover's Lane they strolled on opposite sides of the street where Joy lived with her family next door to Polly Hedgerow. And it was now not her own but Polly's house (like hers, newer and so less affluent than the houses on Elizabeth Circle) that Joy Strummer entered. Across the lane from the Hedgerows', Luke sat down on the Hayeses' front porch, patiently spinning on one finger the basketball that his friend Tac Hayes kept ready beside the door. Basketball bored Luke. "You got the height. You got the hands," the Dixwell coach had blurted in front of the entire gym class one day. "But you don't got it up here." Tap to the head. "Or in here." Thud to the heart. "That's where it counts, Packer, up here and in here." "Yes, sir." "Get your tail in gear, Packer." But he knew he wouldn't, though Joy had gone out at least six times with Tac, who had nothing to offer but the letter on his sweater. Sports would not be Luke's ticket out of town and into the world.

Sooner than he had hoped, the two girls came down the Hedgerows' broken porch steps. Round, creamy, blond Joy, and that sarcastic bloodhound, that freckled wire, Polly Hedgerow. They dawdled back up Glover's Lane toward Dingley Green. Behind them padded Joy's doting spaniel. Behind him, with a preoccupied look, strolled Luke.

"Luke Packer's following you," Polly whispered, placing her copy of *Anna Karenina* on her head. "He's been doing it for days."

"I know," replied Joy dreamily.

"He's a jerk."

"Maybe."

Circling the green clockwise, as they had always done on odd-numbered days, Polly and Joy tried to hurry past Barnum's Antiques, Hobbies, and Appliances store before slick-haired Mr. Barnum, who was holding the door open to let old Miss Lattice out, could get up close and breathe his mouthwash on them.

But, "Hi there, girls," he gurgled, so they had to stop. "Guess they gave you a break from school today, huh, Joy? I saw you taking it easy up there on the statue."

"There's never any school on Founder's Day, Mr. Barnum," Polly answered for her friend. "And besides, all that's left is exams tomorrow. A dog just got into your store."

As Barnum charged back inside, Polly sneered, "Wouldn't you hate it if he tried to cop a feel? I bet he'd love to get next to a girl and cop a feel. That's what guys call it. Ray Ransom is always trying."

"On you?" Joy smiled with tolerant disbelief.

"Don't be sick. No. Suellen Hayes told me."

"Oh, her." Joy watched herself reflected in the glass windows of The Tea Shoppe; as she floated by, her silvery blue, starry T-shirt shimmied with light. "Listen, I don't want to stay too long, okay? I feel rotten."

"You don't look like you feel bad."

"I look awful," sighed Joy, who knew otherwise.

Joy had changed, Polly thought, puzzled and a little sad. She no longer said, "Oh, vomit!" when the boys from Alexander Hamilton Academy invaded Miss Lattice's restaurant like a Wall Street panic of under-aged stockbrokers in their striped ties and gray blazers. She no longer wanted to ride her bike or explore Birch Forest. No, now she lingered at her locker, happily penned there by a lanky circle of long arms and legs. She stayed in her room listening to records endlessly repeated. Now she sighed and daydreamed, her phone was always busy, her grades were even worse than before. Polly was losing her best friend to a genetic mechanism that had pulled the switch on the dam and let loose a lake of hormones in which Joy now floated placidly but inexorably to a destiny that in Polly still elicited a defiant "Oh, vomit!"

The two girls nodded politely at Prudence Lattice in her lilac dress as she shook the lock on her Tea Shoppe "to be sure." They passed the pharmacy and *The Dingley Day*, where through the broken window they saw Mr. Hayes twisting his hair as he read. They passed the cream brick building where both Dr. Scaper and the two Mr. Abernathy lawyers had their offices. Then, just as they reached the post office, Polly wheeled around, yelled, and flung a flamboyant wave at Luke Packer half a block behind them. Caught off guard, his composure deserting him, his body broke loose and hurled him through the door of Sammy Smalter's pharmacy. Joy laughed without looking back.

Around the circle, beyond old Town Hall, and next to the older but newly painted First Congregational Church, was George Webster Dixwell Library. The dungareed girls climbed its smoothed stone steps, Joy pausing to rest on the way, and interrupted Sidney Blossom, the successor to Miss Gladys Goff, who had finally died, to most people's relief, seven years ago.

Mr. Blossom, in his early thirties, always pretended not to notice that off in a corner of the second floor, adolescents were reading Henry Miller's works and other books that the sour Miss Goff had banned in the old days, when she had tyrannized over the literary habits of Dingley Falls. Now he turned from Mrs. Canopy and welcomed the girls with a wink. Polly liked Mr. Blossom, who told her stories of the great rebellions of the sixties, and he liked her.

Driving home from Litchfield, where he had retrieved from a bridal shower his fiancée (the impishly christened Emerald Ransom), Arthur Abernathy, Winslow's son and partner, slowed down for Wild Oat Ridge. He was happily ignorant of the fact that five hundred yards away his mother, Beanie, lay under an oak tree with an obscene poet.

Beatrice and Richard had been wandering, lost, through Birch Forest for more than an hour. Now they rested beneath the oak to eat the rest of the Thespian Ladies' leftovers. It was not his female guide but the city dweller, Rage, who confessed himself "totally wiped, *whap!*" by their exertions. Beanie indeed was a woodswoman of long standing, a blue-star trailmistress in East Woods and a weekly hiker around Lake Pissinowno just north of town, where she collected mushrooms for her marvelous stews.

"Gosh, I'm sorry. I guess I shouldn't have suggested a walk. I've never been lost before," sighed with chagrin a climber of Cadillac Mountain, mortified that she had failed one whom, for some reason, she wished to be proud of her.

"Vice versa," sighed Rage as Beanie slipped off his loafers and massaged his soft, pink, blistered feet with her long, strong fingers. Circulation returning, he was tingled into composing an ode in her honor, and attempting to stroke her shapely calf like a lyre, the Bathroom Baudelaire extemporized in a gravelly

talking croon copied off record albums from Johnny
Cash:

Your cream coming
Is cleaner I know
Than snow hidden below
That old lost road
That old goat thug
   Frost
Chose against choosing.

Great jugs jiggle loosening.
Squat, squat your holy twat
Hot on the dick of human Dick Rage.
Free falling unfallen Beatrice.
To Dante Unaged.
I'm in love, I'm in love, I'm in love, I'm in love,
   I'm in love
With a wonderful gal.

Except for the last line, which had a kind of ring to it,
this poem was as Greek to Beanie as Mount Holyoke
French had been. It was nothing like the verse that
Tracy Canopy, the only other person ever to write
poetry to her, had left only last week inside a lopsided
blue jar perched atop the Abernathy mailbox like an
overweight jay:

Dear Beanie remember, how once in December,
We shopped for a pot in Poughkeepsie.
Here's one to betoken the one that got broken.
(You dropped it because you got tipsy.)
                 I'm only teasing, Tracy.

"What do you think?" Rage asked the once again
tipsy Beanie.

"I like your voice," she said.

"The idea's to take the dirty words, you see, and

show that they're the ones saying the most sacred things, you see? They're the cleanest."

"Oh."

"Poem stinks. All right, you don't have to tell me. I've got no traditions, no background. That's it. I'm a monarchist deep down. So how can I be a poet without any background? Tell me that."

"I don't know. Use somebody else's." Beanie had more than enough background for them both. She had, in this country alone, three hundred years of lineally recorded past that she had never even touched and would have been glad to lend to Rage, had she known how. "Look at the sun over there to your left," she said, turning the conversation from Art to Nature. "So round and bright. I don't know why, but it makes me want to bake you a lot of big red apples."

I don't know why either, but I think I love this broad, thought Richard Rage, baffled.

CHAPTER
6

The Ransoms were giving a party. Dinner at eight for sixteen. It was now 6:30 and two of their list (Beanie, one of them; Richard Rage, their guest of honor, the other) were missing. From the pale oak secretary in her off-beige bedroom Priss Ransom called Evelyn Troyes. Mrs. Troyes was home listening to a recording of *Manon Lescaut,* having, an hour earlier, returned Jonathan Fields, with his now dazzling aquamarine eyes, to the impatient Father Highwick.

"Where in h. is Beanie?" Priss wanted to know. "What's she done with this scatological Rage?"

"*Mais je ne sais pas!*" gasped her wispy friend.

"When I picked up *ma* Mimi *et ta* Kate, they seemed to think Mr. Rage was supposed to join them for a swim *ou quelque chose* at the Club. But then he never came, *et je . . .*"

"There's no need to say 'my Mimi' like that. It's been twenty-one years, Evelyn. I ought to know by now which child is whose," snapped the frazzled Priss, who was further irritated by Mrs. Troyes's unconscious lapse into intermittent French when first startled or upset. It was struggle enough for such a Francophile as Mrs. Ransom to forgive her friend for having lived twenty years in Paris, without hearing that lilting luck sung in her ear over the phone.

"Yes, it's just a habit, I'm sorry, Priss. Oh, I do hope they'll be along shortly. I have to tell you, I have just now received the strangest letter, *quite* unsigned and most obscure. I found it pushed under my wipers and of course jumped to the conclusion that it was another silly parking ticket from that terrible Mr. Haig. I've told him I simply cannot remember to put the coins in those meters he keeps sticking up all over town. We never had to before, did we, and . . ."

"Evelyn . . ."

"Then I thought, but no, it must be one of Troy's cunning little notes, but I'm afraid it isn't that at all, not at all."

"Evelyn! My dear, I haven't time to hear about it now, I'm completely at my wits' end."

"Oh, I am so sorry, why?"

"Everyone's expected at eight and now Beanie seems to have misplaced Mr. Rage. What's worse, Pru Lattice did not send me one of her regular girls from The Tea Shoppe to help Wanda serve. She sent a refugee called Chan or Chin or something, a Vietnamese with a black eye."

"A Vietnamese, here in Dingley Falls? You mean someone struck her in the eye?"

"How in h. should I know? I don't think she speaks a word of English. That asinine war!"

"But wasn't President Ford trying to be helpful, taking them all in?"

"I can't argue politics with you now, Evelyn. But someone with a little experience would have been *more* helpful tonight."

"Oh, dear, shall I send you Orchid? I could call her, should I?"

"No, no, we'll manage. Just try not to be terribly late, will you, Evelyn? And be sweet and take over the Rector for me. Try to keep him from telling everyone for the thousandth time about the g.d. jewels the Romanoff duchess dropped in his pocket while the *Lusitania* sank."

"Oh, Priss, I don't believe Sloan ever said it was the *Lusitania!*" protested Father Highwick's rival, always fair to her foe.

"Evelyn, *à bientôt.* I haven't dressed, and Ernest is home. I hear his golf bag thudding in the foyer."

Ernest Bredforet Ransom trod heavily up the steps to his wife's room. He had lost the light step but kept the face and much of the form of an unusually handsome man. Had sexual self-consciousness ever illumined his looks, he would have been irresistible to women. As it was, he continued to resemble Tyrone Power—for whom, many years ago, he had twice been mistaken, once by Priss Hancock, who first saw him at a Mount Holyoke VJ Day dance to which the wounded war hero, now back at Yale, had been invited by his childhood friend Beanie Dingley.

Now Ransom almost kissed his wife's high cheek as she went by him to her closet. "Wanda tells me," he said conversationally while emptying his pockets onto the dresser top, "that there's an assaulted Chinese girl in her kitchen crying, and she adds that it makes her feel 'creepy.'"

"Oh, for God's sake, I'll go down. After your shower I'd love a martini. How was your game?"

"Poor. My leg." He rubbed it. There was a steel pin

in Ransom's thigh for which in 1944 he had received a silver star.

"People are coming at eight. You want to see about the wine and check the cabinet."

"Yes. Where are the girls? Is Kate home?"

"Who knows? I hope Arthur picked Emerald up. Kate is probably out somewhere looking for that moronic poet she dragged here from Poughkeepsie for Tracy."

"Is he lost?"

"Beanie took him on an educational tour of Dingley Falls. If you can imagine our monosyllabic Beanie in that role."

"This late?"

"I know. Unless she's teaching him lacrosse in the dark, I can't imagine what they're doing."

Spread beneath the oak tree, on her hands and knees, her soft plaid skirt wadded around her waist, her splendid buttocks glazed in the setting sun, Beatrice Dingley Abernathy was being, as her ancestor Elijah would have phrased it, "rogered" by an inspired Richard Rage. First slowly, then with abandon, with one hand on pine needles and the other on Beanie's mossy firmament, he thrust lustfully home, at last believing, after thirty-nine nihilistic years, that, sure enough, home *is* where your heart is.

"Funny . . . but nice," decided Beanie, grasping the trunk of the oak tree as Richard shot a shower of sperm into her with such a jolt that a less sturdy woman would have toppled. Pulling out, he slid under her backwards, reverent as a mechanic under a Rolls-Royce. His beard twined in her vagina, Rage then did something Winslow Abernathy had never done.

Below her head, like a stalagmite, his glistened organ dripped beads on its shaft. From down where he was doing the something he mumbled at her. It sounded like "I'm your mother, you're my mother, suck each

other (or utter) (or udder)"—all of which was peculiar.
But she did feel a brand-new urge to put that shiny flesh
in her mouth, so when it sprang away from her, she
grabbed it without thinking, pulled the head inside, and
sucked.

Something funny was happening to her, something
she thought she ought to get away from.

"No," she said. "No, I won't." But "yes"—he
laughed—"yes, you will. Yes."

CHAPTER
7

Along the low, tidy shelves of Sammy Smalter's
pharmacy, whose entire stock the boy had long since
memorized, Luke Packer scuffed his tennis shoe. Just
now that stupid Polly Hedgerow had scored on him,
had spooked him into the clearly uncool move of diving
through the screen door of a drugstore while Joy was
there to see it. Gable would have stood his ground and
grinned.

Luke Packer had sought a self in the movies for half
his sixteen years. He watched the old ones on television
and went to the new ones at the Hope Street Cinema,
which Mr. Strummer owned. He liked the old ones on
television better, because he sought a large self, heroic,
romantic, magic in its self-possession, and only the old
stars had size enough to carry such definitions. Still,
because Mr. Strummer was Joy's father, Luke had
recently given the Hope Street theater faithful attend-
ance, even sitting at some Saturday matinees like a
sulky Gulliver among rows of swarming brats who,
shrieking in relentless delight and terror, screamed at
dumb werewolves and giant mutant Venus flytraps.

Most of all, like many of his fellow Americans, Luke liked violent crime. Taking his native folklore from films and television, he had concluded that the only vocations that mattered (or, indeed, existed) were the commission and solution of violent crimes. Detective films had led Luke, in secret, to books. Now, near the dusty crutches and artificial limbs that all the kids in Dingley Falls tried to walk with until Mr. Smalter caught them at it, he stopped at the revolving stand of paperbacks. Most of these books wanted to change your life into something better, or to expose the author's own. Others had pictures of frenzy-eyed girls racing away from blue moon castles in the doors of which stood cruel-eyed men holding riding crops. Luke's sister read them. (So did Prudence Lattice and Evelyn Troyes; Sarah MacDermott had started one last Christmas, but had never found time to finish it.) Slowly turning the stand, Luke looked to see if the new Ben Rough was in. *Heather Should Have Died Hereafter.* There it was, with Heather dangling stiffly over a water bed, a pair of panty hose tied tightly around her neck. Luke skimmed the blurb on the back; sometimes they put new jackets on books he'd already read. Political graft, mob syndicates, police corruption, brutal beatings; fast sex, cars, and guns—that was all familiar. But the private eye, Roderick Steady, jilted by a quiet librarian? That was new.

Suddenly, from behind the counter Sammy Smalter appeared, with a quick jerk at his yellow bow tie. You always thought you were alone in the pharmacy until the diminutive owner came out at you. Strangers sometimes jumped, but Luke was used to Mr. Smalter, and to the yellow tie and the three-piece suit the midget always wore, summer or winter, and to the baby-fine yellow hair circling his bald crown like a wreath of duckling feathers.

"I saw you were still open. Is this new Rough book any good?"

"Hello, Luke. How are you this evening?" Mr.

Smalter insisted that even the young observe the few civilities of life.

"Fine. How about you?"

"Well, thank you." Now he answered the question. "I'd say, not up to *Die Quickly,* but at least better than the last two. Rough was in a slump. Just for a handful of silver he left us." One of Smalter's few self-indulgences was his constant conversational use of quotations from Victorian poets. Since almost no one ever caught his allusions, and no one was impolite or interested enough to ask him what he was talking about, most Dingleyans classified the pharmacist as a nut or an egghead (terms nearly synonymous), though the majority agreed that his mental peculiarity was understandable given his physical one: despite painful surgery as a child, he had never grown taller than he had been at eleven.

Luke shook his salary from its A & P envelope. "I'll take the book, okay? And about that job, I tell you, school's out tomorrow, you know, and then I start part-time for Mr. Hayes at the *Day.*"

"Ah, well, the lure of journalism."

"But, see, with the groceries, well, I get the tips, so, I mean it was nice of you to think of me, but I think I'd come out ahead."

"I see." The bespectacled blue eyes stared up at Luke. "Your drive is admirable."

"No, I just want to get out of this stupid dump."

"Outside this dump, Luke, are dumps just like this one, just bigger. Here, no charge on *Heather.* You let me know how you like it. Yes, the world's not very different from Dingley Falls. Of course, Life insists that you not believe me for an instant; Life wants you to leap before you look. It's how she does her magic trick, the illusion of progress."

"I guess so."

" 'Therefore I summon age / To grant youth's heritage.' "

"Well, thanks for the book." Mr. Smalter was pretty

weird; Luke could see why he made some people nervous. But at least he was interesting, which was more than could be said for most of the stupid jerks at Dixwell High.

"Ben Rough still your favorite?" The pharmacist asked this every time Luke bought a book.

"Sure, next to Chandler."

"Ah, *well*," agreed Sammy Smalter.

The bell on the screen door chinkled. Luke turned. But it wasn't Joy. It was the post office lady whom Mrs. MacDermott had been blabbing all about Maynard Henry to in the checkout line. He noticed that she looked tense. She was a tall woman with her hair twisted around the nape of her neck the way nobody wore her hair these days. And she had remarkably blue eyes without anything done to fix them up. Her clothes looked different, too, as if she didn't much notice what she (or other women) wore. They looked good on her, though, because she had that kind of body, nice breasts, and a straight way of standing. Sort of an Ingrid Bergman look to her, he decided. Not sexy, nothing of course like Jean Harlow, who reminded him of what Joy Strummer was going to look like in a few more years.

"Mrs. Haig. I was waiting. I have it ready." Mr. Smalter vanished behind his shelves.

Mrs. Haig didn't nose through the store like most people; she just stood there. It annoyed Luke to think of her being married to a police chief, for almost all of them were stupid and corrupt like the guy in *Killer in the Rain*. That bully Haig, pulling you over at night when you were just out on your bike, minding your own business, waving you over and yelling out of his car, "Know what time it is? Let's head on home now."

The woman gave Luke a funny look, and he realized he'd been staring at her. "Hi," he mumbled, then called over the counter, "See you, Mr. Smalter."

The pharmacist pulled himself up on his stool. "Listen, I'll go another seventy-five cents an hour,

okay? Think it over." The adults watched the boy run
out. Smalter smiled. "More energy than we need when
we have it, and always gone when we finally discover
something worth using it on. *They* burn up, and *we*
burn out. . . . Here. Ida Sniffell called this in for you.
Four times daily, and Otto gives you, it says here,
unlimited refills."

"Yes."

"I," he mumbled, "have heart trouble myself." Mrs.
Haig's head jerked back as if he had slapped her. For
Mr. Smalter hurt her enough already, simply by the
fact that he was occasionally grinned at by another
customer as he stood with his packages at the post
office counter and raised them up for her to reach over,
take them, and relieve him of their weight. That should
be a fair share of suffering.

"I'm sorry to hear that." She felt she had to offer him
something, some knowledge to match his. "I just found
this out, about my problem, a few weeks ago."

"Ah, well. I've known for years," said the pharmacist.

As soon as the sun went down, but not before, it
began to rain on Dingley Falls. The Ransoms' first
guest arrived at 7:55. Jonathan Fields escorted the
Rector, Father Highwick, up the walk under an umbrella. Fields himself had not been invited. In any case,
he had a call to pay on Miss Ramona Dingley, an
elderly shut-in imprecisely known in the town as
Sammy Smalter's aunt. (They were second cousins.)

"Tell poor dear Ramona to keep up her spirits," the
Rector briefed his curate. "Don't encourage her to
carry on about those flying saucers. It agitates her, I'm
sure."

The insomniac Miss Dingley, an otherwise sharp and
cynical person, had for years reported UFOs to whoever would listen. She claimed to have observed these
beaconing visitors descending to land somewhere north
of the Rampage beyond Wild Oat Ridge.

"Tell her I'll pop by someday soon," the pastor added. At seventy-three, Ramona Dingley was only seven years Highwick's senior, but she had aged while he had not. And now her ill health was an unbridgeable gap between them. The Rector was happy only in the company of the young and the physically well-to-do.

Once the door was opened to his superior, Jonathan Fields hurried back through the rain to St. Andrew's new black Lincoln, a gift to the church from Ernest Ransom. He wondered if Walter Saar had been asked to their party, if he were already inside there, or if he might come walking around the corner. Would he walk, would he drive? The young curate drove as slowly as he could through Elizabeth Circle to Miss Dingley's, but he saw no one along the way.

"You see, Ernest, it did not begin to rain until the sun went down. Elijah Dingley must be quite a friend of our Lord's. They say it has never rained *once* on his day in a hundred years." Father Highwick had decided on this opening observation as the Ransoms' maid, Wanda Tojek, took his raincoat. He delivered the remark first to her, then to his host, who, inserting a gold cufflink, had come immediately downstairs to greet the Rector in the off-mauve living room.

"Yes, Otto lost faith this afternoon because of those clouds, but I guess heaven stays on our side. A little humid on the back nine, that's all." With this reply, Ransom took Highwick's hand and shook it in welcome, though they saw each other nearly every day.

The evening's party was given, according to Priss Ransom's handwritten invitations, to toast the fact that there was a Dingley Falls in existence for them to have the party in. "Join us for flounder on Founder's Day," she'd said. Today was the day formally established in Dingley Falls during the Gilded Age to commemorate the fact that on May 31, 1676, Elijah Dingley (sick of wandering around lost) had sat down on what was now the town green and had refused to budge a step farther.

He had dated his decision in a diary bequeathed
generations later to the Yale archives, where it was
periodically read by excited graduate students who
chanced upon the scurrilous document—most of which
consisted of detailed accounts of Elijah's sex life with
his wife, Agatha, their indentured servant, Mary, and a
female Indian possessed of considerable physical agili-
ty. This year's Founder's Day festivities had taken place
on the green yesterday, Sunday afternoon. They had
included a close drill by the Argyle Fife and Drum
Corps, short speeches by civic leaders beneath the
copper beech, a pantomime by the elementary school
depicting Elijah's treaty with the Indians (not including
his lady friend), six cannon shots, a band concert
featuring Victor Herbert melodies, free balloons printed "Buy Barnum's," and a benediction by Sloan
Highwick.

"And this summer the Bicentennial Festival and a
parade with the Governor's Horse Guards," said
Highwick happily; he loved parades. "Imagine, Ernest.
Here we are, a hundred years older than this wonderful
nation itself."

"We? I feel I may well be older, Sloan, but I can't
believe you've said good-bye to your forties." Ransom
smiled. "Care for a drink?"

"Oh, perhaps a little martini; would that be incon-
venient?" proposed the Rector, who invariably drank
at least four before each of the many Dingley Falls
dinners to which he was invited.

Upstairs, Priss (slipping the zipper up her off-beige
gown) interrupted the serene trance of her beautifully
boned elder daughter, Emerald, who sat on her bed
staring at the polish on her fingernails.

"Emerald, did you tell Arthur to phone his mother?"

Emerald combined the nod of a yes with a quick
series of gentle puffs on her nails.

"Where in g.d.h. could Beanie be?"

Emerald raised her handsome eyebrows to denote
her ignorance of Mrs. Abernathy's whereabouts. She

added for emphasis a shrug of those fashionably thin shoulders that gratifyingly mirrored her mother's.

"Is Kate still in the toilet? . . . Emerald! Is Kate still in the toilet, dear?"

By a languid shake of her hair, which she was now ready to brush, Emerald gestured her unfamiliarity with her sister's schedule.

On her way out Mrs. Ransom picked up a lace slip from the floor; she put it on a pale green chair and gave it a pat—it was one of hers. "Please try not to be *too* long. Emerald? Try not to be too long. As usual the Rector has come early and is undoubtedly down there already, lapping up the gin like a dipsomaniacal kitten. Chang Chow or whatever she calls herself has sobbed Wanda's consommé quite soggy and I feel like standing out in the middle of the rain howling like the call of the wild."

Her head curved sideways into her dark, glossy curls, Emerald frowned simultaneously at her mother and a split end.

Downstairs, Priss interrupted her imminent son-in-law, Arthur Abernathy, who stood alone in the library staring at a photograph of the infant Emerald.

"Arthur, did you call your mother again?"

"Yes," said the lanky, unsettled merger of Winslow Abernathy's bones and Beanie Dingley's flesh. "There was no answer."

"Where in g.d.h. could Beanie *be? Pardonne* my French, Arthur dear, but I am so frazzled I feel like standing out in the middle of the rain howling like the call of the wild."

Standing out in the middle of the rain, somewhere in Birch Forest, Richard Rage and Arthur Abernathy's mother were making love for the sixth time in half that many hours.

"We can't go on like this," gasped Beanie, shiny wet and naked as the day, in 1924, she was born. "It's not possible."

"I *know* it's not possible. It's fucking amazing!" agreed Rage, who had never felt so undeflatable before in his life, not even with Cerise Washwillow, the majorette to whom he had given his love and virginity and with whom he had made love, sobbing, the night before she married the future pediatrician instead of the high school's senior poet, class of '55.

Now years were sublunary and time itself had stopped for Dante and his Beatrice. They swayed, they buckled, they bent and quivered like a single oak tree storm-tossed among puny birches.

"Fucking in the rain!" Richard exclaimed. "What a glorious feeling."

"Oh, Richard," moaned Beanie. She was coming again.

"Don't think."

"I'm not thinking, I'm not thinking at all."

"Don't."

"I won't, I can't, nothing makes any sense."

"Darlin'," he laughed, "there's all kinds."

CHAPTER
8

Dinner at the Ransoms' was always elegantly spare, permitting the guests to study the design on their dinner plates. "Lovely china," said the very old Mary Bredforet, who had often said the same to Ernest's grandmother, her sister-in-law, fifty years ago. She smiled benignly around the circle of lyre-backed Duncan Phyfe chairs, two of which had been removed.

"So peculiar really," said Tracy Canopy to Sidney Blossom, the librarian, who had been invited because he played the piano. "My clock radio, electric coffeepot (and coffee), pocket calculator, some personal garments, a great many toilet articles, several record albums, two assorted packs of cereals, and a rather valuable diamond brooch that belonged to Great-Aunt Dixwell. I searched everywhere. All missing."

"Like Beanie," sighed Evelyn Troyes. "*C'est dommage.*"

"I can't imagine," Mrs. Canopy continued, "how the burglar managed to break in. Without disturbing a single lock."

"What *I* can't imagine, Tracy," scoffed the cynical Priss, "is how that Babahaba of yours is planning to slip through Lebanese Customs with half your household belongings in her duffel bag."

"Oh, for heaven's sake, Priss, Babaha didn't take them. She's not a thief. She's an artist."

"Ha!" her friend concluded. "Asparagus, Walter?"

"Has your exchange student left us then?" asked Father Highwick as he wistfully watched the wine bottle sit near his host across the wide table. "Tracy," the Rector explained with inebriated liveliness to Mrs. A. A. Hayes, "is a kind soul, always taking in these foreign students that come riding around on buses to taste the feel of America. Charming girl, Baraba, though not, of course, Christian. Muslin, I believe. Worships the Koran. Fine book in its way, had it in divinity school. All to the glory of the Lord, whatever we do. Oh, thank you, Ernest, yes, just a touch more then." Ransom refilled the Rector's glass.

"Is Vassar treating you right? Kate?" asked Sidney Blossom of the girl on his left. "Is Vassar . . ."

"I hate it," replied Emerald's dispirited younger sister with a glare at the air where Rage should have been sitting, trying to seduce her.

With half their soaked clothes held next to their bodies, Rich and Beanie, after having tasted the fruit for quite a while, were finally being driven from the Garden by inclement weather. Like their original parents before them, they headed east.

"I know you'll find a way out for us," said the poet, trustfully following his long-striding love through a pathless maze of fallen birch trees. "I've got a lousy sense of direction."

"I've got a good one" was the reassuring answer. But suddenly Beanie stopped and came to a point. Far off, far north of Wild Oat Ridge, greenish lights vaguely loomed from where there should have been nothing but the marshlands beyond Bredforet Pond. "What in the world is that?" the native pathfinder puzzled. Had she gotten completely turned around?

Behind her Rage slipped on a soppy mass of moss and tumbled down a tiny ravine. "Help!" he screamed.

Leaping from boulder to boulder, Beanie descended after him. With a long, strong arm she pulled her golden lover from the rising river in which he was helplessly flailing. Rescued, he immediately began to chant:

> Like some great randy she-goat
> You came bounding,
> Teats swung out, to save
> A Shelley drowning.

"Hush, Richard, your lip's cut open." Beanie looked about her. "Good, this is the Rampage. And there, look, there's the highway. Can you move? Let's get out of this rain." Relieved, she helped him up.

"It isn't raining rain," he laughed. "It's raining violets."

"Hush, Richard."

Coffee and after-dinner drinks at the Ransoms' were served in their living room.

"One lump or two?" asked Priss.

"Five," said aged William Bredforet, who was too old for moderation.

"My dear child, is there something in your eye? It looks so inflamed." Father Highwick peered down at the pretty Oriental maid, who thrust a large tray of apricot wafers into his hands, then rushed tearfully out of the room. "Heavens," he said to his host. "Your girl seems upset, Ernest."

"Yes, I'm sorry. She's only temporary. Some B and B, Sloan? Here, I'll take that tray."

"Somebody got her pregnant, that's my bet," said old Mr. Bredforet loudly. "I had an Asian girl myself once. In Singapore. Limber as a rainbow trout."

"She was a swimmer?" asked Highwick sweetly. Ransom led his great-uncle William away with a whisper. "Now don't kid Sloan tonight."

"I wasn't kidding," growled the roguish octogenarian. "Was *he* kidding?"

Walter Saar was appraising a Louis XVI settee when Evelyn Troyes floated down on it and addressed him. *"Mister* Saar! Our Jonathan tells me he's been playing with your boys. And that they're coming along beautifully. You both have worked so hard. Don't you think he has real reverence for music?" She paused, posed, for a response.

"Oh, yes, indeed; in fact, I hope to have him play on our organ someday, without the boys." Saar here indulged in a game of verbal risk at Mrs. Troyes's expense. Such self-amusement was a trait he greatly disliked in himself.

"Have you a nice one then?"

Good God, he thought, was she playing the game too? "Small compared to the one he has at St. Andrew's, naturally, but the *timbre* not bad, we think." Saar knew he was drinking too much again and couldn't seem to stop himself. "Will you excuse me a second while I guzzle every drop of booze on the bar and then rape myself with the bottles?" Oh, my God, had he said that? No. There still sat Evelyn in a halo of blue hair, with a smile like Lillian Gish's. She was saying, "I don't think Ernest smokes, but Priss will have some, won't she?" What was the matter with him? Of course what he had really said was "Will you excuse me while I borrow a cigarette from Ernest?" If he kept on, he was going to lose his job.

A. A. Hayes, former North Carolinian and currently graying editor of *The Dingley Day*, couldn't seem to stop himself from drinking either. He, however, had no desire to do so. Sighting down the length of his glass, he glanced at his attractive wife, Junebug, off by herself in a corner, where she fondled a collection of Steuben glass birds. Everyone in Dingley Falls thought June Hayes to be pitifully shy, whereas her husband knew her to be pitilessly hostile to them all, himself included. He looked away when she sensed his watching her, before she could pretend to almost drop the small object in her hand. He knew she wanted to leave. Hayes wished the Abernathys were here, so that he could talk with Winslow while Beanie moved quietly around the room, pruning the Ransoms' ferns and cacti. But for some reason they weren't. Turning to their son, Arthur, who was leaving the room with the exquisite Emerald Ransom on his arm, Hayes said to the junior Abernathy, Dingley Falls's first selectman, "Shouldn't I start printing up your banns, keep up the old-fashioned traditions here in our little town?" The editor strove for a Village Elder chuckle, but heard his words elide into a smirking leer. Fourteen years in New England, and still the expatriated southerner felt he *just* missed the proper tone, the decorous distance, appropriate among these socially parsimonious Yankees.

"Truth is, we haven't exactly decided on a date yet. Officially," said Arthur, while Emerald brushed a manicured hand through her black curls so that a diamond winked out of darkness at Hayes.

"Well, then just let me congratulate you privately. I'm sure you'll be very happy." Hayes did, indeed, consider the young couple well suited, for he thought them both polished into perfect vacuity. After they hurried out, he returned to the ebony liquor cabinet, where he knew his host would offer to refurbish his Scotch.

"Refurbish your Scotch, A.A.?"

"With pleasure. How, as they say, is the bank?"

"These are not the best of times . . . as your editorials remind us."

"No. What your last man in the White House hadn't time to impound or inflate before his stonewall caved in on him, his more genial apologist, Mr. Ford, is flummoxing nicely. No, no water." Hayes realized he was quoting next week's editorial and would now have to rewrite it. "Why not get a Democrat back in there?"

"These are not the worst of times either." Ransom smiled equably and turned to speak to Tracy Canopy. Hayes finished his drink alone. Why had the pompous ass invited them then?

"Where did the children go?" Mrs. Troyes asked Priss, who really wished Evelyn would not refer to a twenty-seven-year-old woman and thirty-one-year-old man as "the children."

"I sent them over to the Abernathys'. I want Arthur to look around the house. It occurred to me that poor Beanie might be lying in a pool of blood with her head bashed in by that leftover hippie."

"Oh, dear, I hope not! You don't think, do you . . . ?"

"For God's sake, I was being hyperbolic. But something must have happened to them. And with Winslow away in Boston. Beanie has never been particularly worldly."

"Did you notice how heavy the air was today?"

"What?"

"Well, I heard something on the 'Today' show this morning. Whole areas have their moods just like people. It's cosmic energy or vibrations like weather patterns but affecting lives by biochemistry or the stars or something. Do you think there might have been terrible ozones over Dingley Falls today? Tracy's burglary. And Beanie's vanishing. And did I tell you I received the strangest letter?"

"Evelyn. Don't be silly. No concoction from some celestial chemistry set forced Beanie to skip this party without a word of notice."

"Well, there is a book and the man who wrote it was on the show and apparently it's doing quite well . . ."

From near the french windows the Reverend Mr. Highwick's amiable voice floated toward Mrs. Ransom: "Not until I was back in my stateroom did I dare reach in my pocket. There, right there in the pocket of my dinner jacket, or rather Quince Ivoryton's which he'd very nicely lent me, right there where she must have stuffed them as we stood on deck, the duchess's jewels were wrapped in a brocade window sash. I saw that royal monogram stitched in happier times . . ."

Priss clapped her hand loudly.

"Oh, Priss," whispered Evelyn. "He's only telling it to the Bredforets, and they're both, dear things, practically deaf. See how Mary's smiling?"

"Rubbish!" yelled old Mr. Bredforet at the Rector. "A duchess stuffed her hand in your pocket? Then I bet it was *your* jewels she was after."

Priss clapped again. Faces obediently turned.

"Everyone," their hostess announced. "Evelyn here has kindly agreed to sing for us. Of course you will, Evelyn, don't be silly. And Sidney," she informed Mr. Blossom, "will accompany her on the piano."

"Splendid!" called out the Rector, who had no idea he detested the very sound of Mrs. Troyes's voice.

"Well, sing something with some snap to it, Evelyn. I can't stand that lilimimiheehee shrieking. It would send a dog under the house," bellowed Bredforet, and "Oh, shut up, William," said his tiny wife.

So Sidney Blossom asked the moody Kate to turn his pages, and her mother stared her into acceptance. Then, with hand posed Peabody Institute-style on the

Steinway, Evelyn began "Ah, Sweet Mystery of Life," swept up to Schubert, and crashed to a halt with "Un bel dì" when June Hayes dropped the glass robin that had belonged to Ernest Ransom's grandmother. It shattered on the polished floor. Mrs. Hayes screamed, her husband winced, Mrs. Troyes slid off her note, and the room came to a full stop.

"Oh, Priss, I feel just *awful*," gasped Mrs. Hayes breathlessly. "I'm nothing but a clumsy, a terribly clumsy old fool. I don't suppose you can *ever* forgive me." She sank to her knees among slivers of glass. Both Ransoms came hurrying over. Ernest helped his guest to her feet while his wife gathered the broken bird into a silent butler. A. A. Hayes refurbished his own Scotch.

"For heaven's sake, June, it's nothing," said the fifth generation of Ransom hosts in this house. "Tell you the truth, I detest those silly things, always have."

"I'm surprised they didn't all fall off this rickety table. I've been meaning to have that leg fixed," said the host's wife.

"I'm always breaking things," threw in Tracy Canopy.

"This society is patched with the paste of lies," said A. A. Hayes to Chin Lam Henry, who was refilling the ice bucket. She smiled and nodded. "Don't suppose that's exactly news where you come from," he added. She smiled and nodded again.

Walter Saar handed Mrs. Hayes a glass of sherry. "Much more dramatic way of finishing off poor Madame Butterfly anyhow. Euthanasia," he murmured. Saar was very sensitive to the humiliations of others. Rubbing alcohol on his empathy only inflamed this exposed nerve, and in his urgency to soothe he often miscalculated. As now; for June Hayes (mother of one of his students) looked at him with what, had he not thought her incapable of it, he would have called murderous hate. "Let's play a word game," he tried again.

"I love games," said the Rector.

William Bredforet yelled from the settee, "Thought they said somebody was going to read his poetry."

"He couldn't come after all," explained Evelyn.

"Good. I don't like poetry."

Mrs. Ransom handed the broken glass to the Vietnamese girl with the black eye, Chan or Chin or whatever her name was.

CHAPTER
9

Arthur Abernathy returned from his parents' house visibly shaken. Emerald sent Priss and Tracy to him in the library, as Priss preferred to call what everyone else in the family called the den. The other guests were still playing word games.

"Read this," said Beanie's son.

Priss drew her glasses from her dress pocket. " 'May twentieth. A final reminder. From Vassar Library. To Richard Rage. Our records indicate that the titles listed below were due on January third. If . . .' "

"Other side," said Arthur, sinking into a chair.

" 'Dear Arthur. I'm writing this to you because you'll be *c-o-m-m-i-n-g* home after the Ransom party.' " Priss looked at Tracy. "It's from Beanie. She can't spell worth a damn. '. . . after the Ransom party and please say I'm sorry for missing it and my *r-e-g-r-e-t-t-s* for not calling. Your father won't be back from Boston til Thurs. You'll have to explain this to him, Arthur, and I'm sure you'll do a better job than I would. You *t-o-o* are awfully alike. But I'm leaving now with Richard here, you haven't met him though I hope you will someday, but only if you want to. His name is Richard Rage. Tracy invited him, and we met each other.'"

"Oh my, oh my, oh my," said Tracy.

"'. . . met each other. I'll be gone for a while and I guess that means the same as forever. We have fallen in love *against our wills*. Please believe this.'" Priss read faster and faster, no longer pausing to point out spelling errors. "'I know your father will be hurt and it's the last thing I want to do but I really *can't help* doing this. I've never felt like this and I have to find out. And after what has happened, it wouldn't be right if I stayed.'"

"Oh my, oh my, oh my."

"'Tell him to try to understand (or if not possible, put me out of his mind). I don't know where Richard is going but feel I have to go too. I know you will think this is crazy and I guess it is. I will write him. Or call. Tell him I took the Seville. All the rest is his with all my heart. I have Big Mutt with me. Love, Mom. P.S. I love you. Tell Lance I love him. I'm sorry. P.P.S. Please, I hope your father won't let the plants die. Chicken salad in fridge. Don't worry about me. I love you.'"

Mrs. Ransom looked with shock at her son-in-law-to-be. She removed her elegant glasses and passed the piece of crumpled paper to Tracy. "This must be a joke." She frowned.

"My mother never told a joke in her life," groaned Arthur, his head in his hands.

"Well. Beanie has . . . surprised me," said Mrs. Ernest Ransom.

By 11:40 the last guests were leaving the Ransoms' dinner party. An hour earlier the ancient Bredforets had been reclaimed by a sharp rap at the door from their equally ancient and irascible chauffeur: "Already haf-pass they bedtime this minute, Mistuh Ransom," the tiny old man had shouted down the hall, ignoring Wanda, who attempted to block his path.

"Stop embarrassing me, talking like that," yelled his employer. "Everybody already knows you're black."

"Thank you for a lovely evening. Pay no attention to either of them." Mrs. Bredforet had smiled sweetly.

Now the others were gently ushered out by their host. Ransom was particularly helpful to the lethargic A. A. Hayes, who had slipped into a trance halfway into his raincoat.

"Ernest, I'm sorry but could you help me with Alvis, please?" Hayes heard his wife sweetly ask for this assistance, and in retaliation he leaned back against the doorjamb and offered to write campaign speeches for his host. He knew he was annoying Ransom and didn't care. "You *should* run, you know. You could be governor. You're a perfect candidate. I think it's your cufflinks. Or maybe your rhetorical flair. 'These are not the worst of times either.' I liked that."

"I'll keep it in mind." The banker smiled. "Now, I believe that June is waiting, A.A.; it *is* raining. . . ."

On the walk Hayes's wife stood in the rain, her eyes patiently downcast.

"Ah, yes, the missis." Hayes grinned. "Burning pits in your bricks with her acid eyes. Coming, Junebug honey." He tilted down the steps.

"Hayes is incorrigible," said Ransom to his wife after they had closed the door. "I feel sorry for June. I only asked him because Winslow gets along with him so well, and then Winslow takes off for Boston. While Beanie . . . ! Well, I'm sure there's been some misunderstanding about that note."

News of Mrs. Abernathy's letter had traveled like a final party game through the living room, since Arthur and Priss, clinging to the hope that there was an alternative explanation, had more or less played "Beanie, Beanie, who's got our Beanie?" with several of the guests. But no one had seen her since Tracy (now crushed with guilt) had left her with that unpardonable poet in The Prim Minster's parking lot. Had Tracy not introduced him with the topic query "Is art being sexually abused?" . . . Recalling the incident, she said to Priss sadly, "It seems such a dramatic irony, doesn't it?"

"Ha. Ha," said Priss.

Evelyn Troyes had taken Walter Saar home. It was important to her to understand those with access to Jonathan Fields. Saar was not a walker; but having lost his driver's license, and feeling what he suspected was an excessive fear of the police, he had asked Sidney Blossom for a ride to the party—and when Sidney went home early, he had accepted Evelyn's offer for the return trip.

"I know this road," she promised, gunning the motor as she went into the wet blind curve at the bottom of High Street.

"A little knowledge is a dangerous thing," blurted the headmaster, who was almost as frightened as he'd been the night the two Puerto Ricans had taken him back into the kitchen of His Fancy Club, where they had demanded his watch, sports coat, and cash. He had to stop drinking.

After Ernest Ransom thanked and paid and placed in the town's only taxi Mrs. Maynard "Chinkie" Henry, after he complimented Wanda on her dinner and his wife on her dinner party, he swung open his french windows onto a starry night. Across his landscaped lawn the full, wet trees gleamed like coal. On the other side of Elizabeth Circle, lights were on in the third floor of Ramona Dingley's monstrous Victorian house. Sammy Smalter, who lived there with her, stayed up until all hours. Ransom considered this habit unorthodox, and therefore suspicious.

He decided on a walk. Something troubled him. It had nothing to do with Beanie Abernathy's love flight, behavior so aberrant that the banker simply rejected the reality of the news. Something else was on his mind.

An image was still stuck there that had for no reason pushed its way into a conversation he'd had earlier that evening with Dr. Otto Scaper at the golf course.

Scaper had come shambling toward Ransom's golf cart from the small practice green where on sporadic afternoons the bearish old physician took what he claimed to be all the exercise his body would put up with. Ransom had stood politely by, his very good leather golf bag shouldered over his perfectly fitting knit shirt, while Scaper lumbered interminably closer in baggy suit pants, wearing a soiled white shirt with its sleeves rolled tightly up his huge arms and an unfashionable tie flapping loosely around his enormous neck.

"Ern, a second, hey," he had puffed out around his cigar. "Got a minute?"

Of course Ransom had.

"Something's pestering me," the old doctor growled. "I want to come see you at the bank, tomorrow maybe, see what you think. I know there's no sense bringing it up officially unless I do. Arthur and the rest of them just do whatever you tell them anyhow."

Ransom smiled to shake away this presumed power over Dingley Falls's selectmen, while Scaper pawed at the ground with his putter and mumbled, "Something, well, doesn't make sense. Now I know I never was much of a diagnostic man, no eye for fancy guesswork, just fiddle and fix, and I'm not denying I haven't kept up; who could, working the way I do?"

Ransom nodded. "Of course. Just what is . . ."

"But I've poked around in a lot of insides and sent out a lot of tests. I'm not going to get you balled up in a lot of lingo, Ern, but the situation is I'm getting all this endocarditis, and it's not responding the way it ought to. And awhile back that goddamn fluky brucellosis costing me Pauline Hedgerow before I could turn around! You know? *No reason.* . . . What? What? You say something?" Scaper turned his right ear to the banker. A hearing aid was looped there.

Ransom looked bland and blank, but not at all impatient. "No, but tell you the truth, Otto, I don't see . . ."

"Look here." Gripping his putter hard, Scaper stared out across the lush fairway of the country club. "I swear I'm starting to think some . . . pollutant's gotten loused up, maybe in our water, or produce; or we got ourselves some kind of industrial poisoning, or some such goddamn thing is going on. Now I went ahead and sent out a water sample."

"Let's not get any rumors started now that are going to get people upset, Otto. I mean, people do die."

"I know that. Die as sure as the sun shines. I know that. But you just get a feeling after all these years. This is different, it's unnatural, it's wrong. Ever seen a bird that died from oil slick? Another bird that dies a regular way is just as dead, but it's different."

It was then that the image still troubling Ransom even after his party had suddenly surfaced in his mind. He had suddenly remembered a gash of burned-out earth covering a lot the size of a football field. He had come upon it four years earlier, when he had hiked out near the marshland to look at some land of his he intended to sell. He remembered how he had been so surprised, so surprisingly sickened, to see it blasted and seared into his former property. The image had jammed in his head as the doctor spoke, so that instead of hearing Scaper's words, Ransom heard the crackle of leaves on an autumn Sunday back in 1972 when he had worked his way through the marshes alone, setting out from an unfinished strip of highway. Instead of seeing the safe, rich green of the Dingley Country Club's golf course, he saw that black, scorched, pitted earth onto which he had stumbled out of thick foliage. That image was stuck in his head today, like, he thought, a slide caught in a projector, the same slide appearing click after click on the screen. Through tonight's dinner party, and now after it, as he walked along the rain-polished flagstones between the rain-shiny flower beds, that image kept flashing, of land as wasted as the moon and black as oil slick.

The banker stooped to pull up a grass clump shoving through a cracked flagstone. A threshing noise of snapped branches lashed into the night. Then loud grunts and labored breath. Ransom felt his heart jerk. He ran around a curve of clipped shrubbery and saw across the smooth, dark lawn a female shadow who swung something over her head. The sight startled him again, then she turned and he realized the female was Kate, his second daughter (first in his heart). She was pummeling an azalea bush with a tennis racket. Ransom walked over and caught her arm. "Hold on, now." He smiled. "What would Sebastian Marco say if he saw you beating on his flowers like this?" His tone was smooth, calm, and habitual. All the Ransoms, but Kate, lived formally and had no forms for fury. Only her manner, like her looks, was so unruly. Her parents had been appalled by her temper tantrums since she had been a baby. Grown, she was a handsome, disheveled copy of both their good looks, but her face still, at twenty-one, could twist into lines of tantrums no one had ever seen on Ransom's face, or his wife's.

"Hold on, now," he said.

"I hate him. He's a pig!"

"Who?"

"Rich."

"Rich?"

"*Rich, Rich Rage!*"

"Mr. Rage?" Ransom assumed that Priss had told Kate, then, of Beanie's extraordinary good-bye letter. "Well, yes, I'm sure there's been some mistake, but of course it is embarrassing. And dreadful. But Beanie, Mrs. Abernathy, will come to her senses, and I don't think you need to . . ."

Kate wasn't listening to him. "He came here to be with *me*. I'm the one that brought him here!"

"Yes, I understand that you must feel a little . . ."

His daughter flung his hands away. "Oh, Daddy, you don't know anything about it! For crap's sake."

"Now, no need. No, I suppose I don't. It doesn't matter. Shouldn't let things upset you like this. Hold on now."

"Thank God that's over," sighed Priss Ransom, dramatically dropping into an armchair. On the settee with Arthur, Emerald was studying her smart beige pumps. "Arthur, perhaps you ought to call Mr. Haig about your mother. Don't you think, darling? Emerald?"

Emerald shrugged her Indian shawl off her shoulders.

"Well, this isn't like Beanie. . . . That sounds silly, considering, doesn't it?" Priss frowned. "And there's the rain. A car accident?" But she was really not very hopeful. "Or phone Vassar about this moronic Rage? Where is Lance?"

"Where else? He's in Forest Hills playing tennis. There's nothing he can do to help." In fact, Arthur Abernathy thought there was nothing his twin brother, Lance, could do to help any situation.

"Really, someone *should* call Winslow. At least. Are we just going to sit here and do nothing?"

"Frankly, I'm reluctant to tell Dad," confessed the son as he sadly wound his pocket watch. "No cause to upset him needlessly. I mean, I'm sure Mother will have some . . . explanation. The problem is, I guess it's all right if I tell you, Dr. Scaper told me this afternoon to try to keep sort of an eye on Dad to see that he takes it easy for a while. He's afraid there might be something the matter with Dad's heart."

CHAPTER
10

Chief John "Hawk" Haig had built his house upon mud, having bulldozed his way through everything that lay on top of it. Now a light red brick ranch house squatted like a solitary hog in the newly landscaped clearing at the edge of town, on Route 3 south of the marshlands and not too far east of Wild Oat Ridge. What the hell was he doing there? his former Madder neighbors wanted to know. If he was going to build, why not be sociable and build in Astor Heights along with everybody else who could afford to get out of Madder? The truth was that Haig did feel like a fool out there in the wilderness. Listening to rumors, he had outsmarted himself; rather he had outdistanced the rumors.

There was to be a highway, a big one with excellent connections. That dead stretch along Route 3 which Haig now owned (or, more technically, for which he now made monthly payments to Ransom Bank) would bloom like yuccas in the desert then, and when it did, the police chief, of course, would have the last yuck on them all.

And as Rumor promised, the state did begin construction of a big connector heading north off Route 3, east of the marshlands, on land Ernest Ransom had sold it—and, no doubt, Haig was certain, had made a killing on. Workers collected in Madder, crowded a trailer park with the tawdry household goods of their transient households; among the workers Maynard Henry and the two Grabaski cousins, heroes home from the evacuation of South Vietnam.

But then, as Rumor neglected to mention, at least she said no words in Haig's ear, construction abruptly stopped, half a mile after it started. Ernest Ransom bought back the land and, no doubt, came out ahead. It was always the little guy, Haig was certain, that got screwed. Now the highway connector connected with nothing but weeds and broken trees, a short black tongue stuck out at Nature, who ignored it. Yucca Boulevard never blossomed, and the last yuck was on John "Hawk" Haig, who owned a house and thirteen acres of pine needles on a thirty-year mortgage.

So he became a sportsman, a hunter of small game on his useless preserve, wiping away with shotgun blasts the smug satisfaction of his victorious tenants, the squirrels. People decided Haig had always been the outdoors type and had bought the land to shoot at. He let them think so.

Meanwhile, his modern house sat as unembarrassed by its incongruity as a Burger King on the moon, serene in the certainty that the future was on its side, and eventually so would be Texaco and K-Mart.

His house sits and Judith Sorrow Haig sits in it. There is nothing else to do. The rooms are clean. All the furniture, which, since she didn't care about furniture, her husband had purchased by the roomful from places where it was sold by the floorful, sits in precisely those arrangements in which the store had chosen to display it. The kitchenette with sliding doors to a (future) patio. The dinette/living area with its contemporary cone fireplace and five-piece matching living module in brown velveteen. The master bedroom with bath. The family room, where she is now. It is midnight, and her family (John—they have no children) is off in Madder cruising for disorder. A policeman must keep late hours. So must Mrs. Haig, because she has difficulty falling asleep and is reluctant to be flung there by the pills Dr. Scaper has given her.

Judith is a good housekeeper, though she cares nothing for her house. She is a good wife, for she cares for her husband, not merely by being his caretaker, but by taking on herself all the cares that trouble him, and all the caring that he neglects to feel. When John's father died, Judith wept. When John is thoughtless, she feels guilty for him.

She feels too much. Indeed, she is so assaulted by feelings that she walks around stunned, and her acquaintances (apart from Sarah MacDermott) think her cold, or stupid. Whereas the truth is that Judith is stupefied. She is deafened by screams she hears shrieking from closed mouths, she is blinded by tears she sees swollen in dry eyes, she is numbed by shame she feels in cool, sweatless palms.

Judith Haig is too sensitive. She cannot watch television, where once she saw a terrified pig stuck twisting with spears, a terrified soldier hanged twisting from a wire; or even all those fictional heroes, unterrified, who in night after night of violent crime eliminate their enemies, hour by hour. She cannot look at magazines, where bloated children stretch bowls out at her from the page, flies on their hands. She cannot listen to the anger or the ache of those who would be her friends. It hurts her to think of the pharmacist, Sammy Smalter. She wants no plants in her house for blight to shrivel, no pet to lie twitching from the blow of a car, no love for life to rack her on.

For years she has waited, paralyzed, her heart stopped, for it all to go mad. For old men and old women to run howling from their unheated rooms, to throw slop pails of acid in the indifferent faces of young passersby. For starving children to leap like rats at nourished throats. For the dispossessed to rape and pillage, for the betrayed to take revenge, the unloved to hurl grenades from windows down on lovers. For wild dogs to overrun the earth and avenge it.

It was foresighted of the Sisters of Mercy to name her Judith Sorrow, though perhaps not merciful, for she had suffered in the Madder orphanage the inevitable jokes. Now, of course, everyone calls her Mrs. Haig. She is an attractive woman (as even Luke Packer, brutalized by youth, realized), handsome enough to have married the handsome Hawk Haig, the football hero, who was to have gone places, but who, as things turned out, wênt a little too fast, led on by Rumor.

People like her, at least in theory. They admit she is not very good at canasta, being unable to concentrate on her cards, or much fun at the bowling alley, or a backyard barbecue, or a *tête à tête* at the A & P. Still, they say she is a nice woman, always thoughtful.

Judith Haig has no hobbies; there is nothing Limus Barnum can sell her. She has no outside interests at all, other than the post office. Enveloped emotion is as much as she can bear. But taking such careful care of the mute appeals and unseen responses that her fellow humans make to one another, make through her hands, has been, she believed, something to offer. In her eleven years there she has never lost a letter. Today, by doctor's orders, she lost her post office. He had said that she needed to take it easy, that her heart might be in a little trouble. That her heart should be troubled was no surprise to Mrs. Haig. It was an old complaint.

Dressed for sleep now, she sits in the family room in a stuffed chair of bright green plaid still protected by plastic. What the doctor ordered to ease her heart is on a table beside her, a new table that happens to be an imitation of a two-hundred-year-old table in Mrs. Vincent Canopy's living room.

John Haig's house sits there and Judith Haig sits in it. She sits next to an oversized picture window that pictures now only that it is midnight. She is waiting for the glass to shatter and the dogs to leap through the jagged hole.

CHAPTER
11

At 1:00 A.M. Sammy Smalter was awake, typing. Polly Hedgerow was awake, studying her American history notebook with a flashlight propped under her chin and a pillow propped under her neck. Tracy Canopy was awake, reading *Poetry Sucks!*, a collection of poems by Richard Rage.

Beanie Abernathy was awake, driving in silent, scared faith toward New York City and away from her past. Beside her, Richard Rage was even more awake with shock and terror, for he had never dreamed that a woman so modern as to leap into the sack (as he termed it, though it had actually been moss and pine needles) with a stranger could also be a woman so traditional as to assume that her doing so forever abnegated her marriage vows by committing her heart and hand to this stranger till loss of love did them part. Awestruck by his attraction and her absoluteness, his grin had turned to stone, and then the stone had crumbled. The poet was stunned into silence by her announcement that she planned to go away with him, as she termed it, then and there, or wherever he chose. And so this easy lay led him away as if his accidental plunge into the Rampage had proved a baptism, and he—driven through the night in his still-damp clothes—a convert to her newborn faith.

Back in Dingley Falls at the academy, Walter Saar was awake with an old desire.

In the trailer park Chin Lam (Mrs. Maynard Henry), whose husband had been arrested by Hawk Haig, was awake because she was frightened to sleep alone. On

Cromwell Hill Road a cat with one eye oozed shut sprang at the screen door behind which Miss Lattice's Siamese, Scheherazade, wailed another of her one thousand and one nights of song, and out walking alone through Elizabeth Circle, where everyone had it easier than he did, Limus Barnum was irritated by the noise. Along the high window ledge of Town Hall a rustle of feathers shook each pigeon in turn. The rest of Dingley Falls slept.

Mr. and Mrs. Ernest Ransom slept under queen-sized Marimekko sheets without touching. Still intoxicated, A. A. Hayes slept, at his wife's request, on the couch in the den. In her sleep the oldest Sister of Mercy died of heart failure. Beside her spaniel Joy Strummer—about whom Luke Packer was dreaming—slept with her arms outflung, two buttons of her pajama top sliding open. Evelyn Troyes dreamed, smiling, of Hugo Eroica and of Father Fields, who was dreaming of Walter Saar. Sidney Blossom's dream, Kate Ransom, tightened her fists between her crook'd thighs and groaned aloud in her sleep. The sound woke her father. He alone of her family always heard her nightmares and always hurried to stop them for her. He did so now.

"Daddy. Was I dreaming?"

"Yes. Everything's all right."

That question, that answer, all these years. Why should his Kate be troubled by dreams?

After sitting awhile by his daughter's bed, Ransom had always returned to his own, where he always fell almost immediately back to sleep. Tonight, however, he put on his robe and slippers—both were monogrammed presents from Priss—and felt his way down the carpeted stairs into the kitchen, where after some searching he found the V-8 juice he had asked Wanda to order. In his den he turned on the television: men in cars were chasing each other up and down city streets. On another channel men on horses were chasing each other in and out of valleys. On a third, young bearded men with hair longer than Kate's leaped up and down

as they beat on guitars and contorted their faces into
yowls. Ransom turned the set off. Why did that
memory of the burned land stay stuck in his mind
tonight; now, when four whole years had passed since
he had seen it; now, when he and everyone else had
pretty much forgotten about what A. A. Hayes's
editorials had called "The Abandoned Highway Scandal"? The banker sat down in his recliner-rocker.
Across the room the wall was lined with photographs of
his family. One of Kate frowned at him. That slide in
his head kept clicking, and he closed his eyes against
the following memory:

During the time when the state had first expressed
interest in building a highway connector on his property, Ernest Ransom had decided that he ought to go
look at land, even useless land, that had been so long
his family's inheritance, before relinquishing it. He had
not explored the woods and marsh of the acreage he
owned north of Route 3 since his boyhood. He had
gone there and found again, after a search, the old
Indian trail that led westward toward Bredforet Pond.
And setting out, his thoughts, his senses, had suddenly
rushed back forty years. Back to a time when the
woods he then hiked through, when the flat, high-
grassed marsh had been a field for tests of courage
more vital to his sense of who he was than those more
dangerous tests in later fields like the beachhead near
Caen in Normandy, where he had won his silver star
and steel pin. Back to a time when with his father and
his great-uncle William Bredforet he had stood silent,
thigh-rooted in damp, still sedge, until a dog, now long
since dead, had rushed the silence, changed it to a whir
of ash-brown wings. "Get it!" Uncle William had
shouted. It was a Canadian goose Ernest had shot, a
goose with white breast and black crown, the long black
neck limp like a dead snake. His reward had been the
burn of brandy from Uncle William's initialed silver
flask. "The best part, you ask me, best part of any fool
sport, drinking after it." The small handsome man had

grinned, his moustache lively, his eyes like flowers in the cold sunrise. On their way home through the woods they had flushed a deer with white breast and black crown of nubby antlers which spun leaping, then turned, half hidden in close pines, to watch them, noisily and speedlessly, go by. "Young buck!" whispered his great-uncle Bredforet. "About your age, Ernie. Joke to think of some creature out to make a trophy of *your* knobby head. . . . By God, women *will*, in good time. Scalp you pretty close, and charge you for the haircut." And his father had laughed and Uncle William's bright laugh had skipped like a pebble down the path.

That memory, so long undisturbed, of hearing his father, now long since dead, laughing with William Bredforet had made the sight seem all the worse when he saw it, the sight that was keeping him awake now in his den four years later. The sight of that black burned-out waste someone had made of his father's land. Like a nightmare twist to a nostalgic dream, the sight had scared the past away and sickened him. It did not look like land cleared by fire for future planting, but like land annihilated forever. It looked unnatural. And angry, though the anger had no focus, he had cursed aloud, then hurried on northwestward through the now ruined beauty of the day.

He had kept walking for hours, harder physical exercise than any he had done since the war, had hiked all the way out of the marsh that afternoon four years ago, until he came upon a large artificial clearing beyond Bredforet Pond. And there he found his land was plowed and packed. It was cordoned with steel-link, barbed-wire fencing. At intervals metal signs warned trespassers to keep out of Restricted U.S. Government Property. At some distance, stark in the denuded earth, two big aluminum buildings had glared at him. Senselessly substantial, they stood where there had always been nothing but the land over which the geese flew. Around the buildings, in bulldozed earth

gutted with tire tracks, craters of red mud puddled the
ground. Flowers and baby pines had been planted in an
attempt at landscaping. Stumps of trees, still oozy from
the saw, stuck up everywhere. Beside the longer
building, dozens of unboxed crates and barrels rose in
orderly piles. There was even a red Coca-Cola machine
and a basketball hoop. A young man in a white coat
walked out of a side door and across to the second
building. He was eating a sandwich.

It made no sense, but it had to make sense. Ransom
decided that there must be an entrance to this compound from its northernmost point, farthest from
Route 3 and Dingley Falls. It meant there had to be
another way into the marshland, from the north or
west, though he had never heard of one, and there were
no towns in those vicinities. It meant that except for the
unlikely chance that someone, like himself, might
stumble on the clearing by accident, no one need ever
know the compound was there. It meant those who
built it intended that to be so.

As he stood there, he saw something to which old
instincts reacted before he had consciously assimilated
what he'd seen. He dropped to the ground with a grunt
at the pain the unaccustomed quick movement caused
his leg. From the far corner of the compound two
young men in fatigues had walked toward him, laughing at a third who jerked at the chain of a black German
shepherd. All three men had rifles. Ransom crawled to
a covert of bushes, where he hid until the soldiers and
the dog moved north out of sight. He'd felt in danger;
he'd felt, though he could not have said why, guilty and
caught in complications.

He had pushed himself too hard. His face and arms
bled with cuts from brambles he had to shove through
at a run in the fast-darkening woods as he worked his
way back to Route 3 and his automobile. He sat in his
car a long time, feeling nauseous and faint, before
starting home. His soft leather shoes were ruined,
caked in mud. A sole had torn loose. His soft wool

trouser leg was ripped and snagged with brambles. Staring down at his leg, Ransom remembered mud-thick boots and a khaki pants leg shredded and his thigh unbelievably bright red, wrong-looking, with the bone sticking out of it. He remembered how he had stared at the leg, there at the beach in Normandy in 1944, propped up where a medic had dragged him. As then, he stared now at his torn clothes and muddy shoes as if the messy disorder he saw could be no part of him.

When he reached home that Sunday, Ransom threw the shoes and pants away and in response to Priss's shock at his condition, said only that he'd gone out to walk in Birch Forest and had gotten lost. He did not tell Priss, or anyone else, what he had seen. Nor had he ever told anyone that in 1969 (three years before negotiations with the state about the highway began) he had leased that northwesternmost part of his land to the federal government, whose purposes, of course, were none of his business—if they chose to restrict them.

In his recliner-rocker tonight, Ernest Ransom had not retraced much more of this memory than his setting out on that autumn walk. It was late, and he was an early riser who tried to be in bed by eleven and invariably got out of it by six. He had fallen asleep almost as soon as he had leaned back in the chair, had waked up disoriented half an hour later and returned to the queen-sized Marimekko sheets.

In her aviary of a bedroom on the fourth floor of the tallest house in Dingley Falls, old Miss Ramona Dingley abruptly sat up. It annoyed her to find herself awake. More and more each night, sleep escaped her an hour or so after it was seized, as if, in anticipation of imminent endless rest, her body could not be bothered with nightly naps. Her brain was too anxious to learn its ultimate destiny (if āny) to want the reprieve of dreams. Young Father Fields, who had spent that evening offering her Pascal and Paul Tillich, had not come up with any answers that satisfied. A sweet boy, but a fool like most men; men, who can't give birth, giving birth to gods in order to have gods to love them.

Miss Dingley's collapsible cane flicked open like a switchblade. She poked at the darkness with it. One floor bleow her relative Sammy Smalter had finally turned out his light and gone to sleep. Slowly, down the hall, the old woman walked, angered by her turtle pace. Wasted by time, she couldn't afford to waste time. Then, out on her widow's walk—though, in fact, she had never wed—she stared at the star closest to her. The star stared back. But not at a fat, stooped lady in a white nightgown leaning on the balcony rail of a Victorian house. No, the star had no idea, yet, that Miss Ramona Dingley was ever born. It saw backwards in time, saw a forest in which an Indian hid and spied on Elijah Dingley, who sat exhausted in a little clearing and remarked to a bonneted woman in a cart words he later preserved in a diary: "Here is as farr as I ride, dear Yokefellow. That the Lord is no longer perswaded we should continue in this toilsome Journie, I judge from the bloodie Blistering of my great Toe. Some ale from the Hogshead, good Agatha, here be our Home!" The star saw three hundred years ago the founding by the Rampage of Dingley Falls. And farther stars saw flood across America, and farther still saw ice.

"What do You care?" asked Ramona, looking up at the star-bright sky. "You or Your Son either?"

Much closer, off beyond the marshlands, a quick flick of light spiraled down to Bredforet Pond. Falling stars are much more haphazard, thought the old woman. It had to be methodical man. But why, she wondered, should flying saucers be so persistently fascinated with a Connecticut marsh? Maybe the idea of UFOs was nonsense, after all. Her eyes were still as good as a hawk's. If only she had her legs and her wind back. She would find out. Perhaps it was smugglers. From Canada. Perhaps somebody was smuggling something to America. Through her town. Well, she would send a spy whom life had not yet crippled. She would borrow young legs. With that plan in mind, Miss Ramona Dingley returned slowly to bed.

And now all Dingley Falls slept, on a Founder's Day that the closest star would finally see three hundred years from now.

CONCERNING PLOTS

We are all premeditators, plotting one thing or another. Hawk Haig is plotting to be rich, Chin Lam Henry is plotting to free her husband, Limus Barnum is plotting to be accepted or avenged. No one can return to spontaneity. Language will not let us go, but bars with its sword our return to that wordless, thoughtless Eden. Beanie Abernathy wishes there were no words, yet even she must write a letter. Even Sloan Highwick must have some plot in mind, if only how to persuade his host to offer him a martini.

There are those, like Walter Saar, who actively plot against themselves, and those, like Ernest Ransom, whose indifference becomes a plot against others. There are those whose plots are mysteries to themselves. Judith Haig is such a person; so is Richard Rage. So entangled are we in our own designs that the concurrent and often conflicting plots of our families, friends, and enemies may come to us as surprises suddenly unraveled or traps suddenly sprung. Our show of surprise is our way of protesting the injuries done us, or denying that we have offered bribes for the gifts bestowed. If no one can see into another's heart, Beanie tells Winslow, it is probably because no one comes close enough, or stays long enough, or "listens loud enough over the thump of their own," to see and hear.

Spiders fast in the centers of our own webs, we are

busy creating the world in which we live. But as we spin out of ourselves our private universes, in the end the webs tangle, and we become flies to one another, caught for good or evil. Caught by surprise.

The certainty that there are larger plots, Byzantine and diabolical webs in which a few are spiders and the rest witless flies, is a popular faith among paranoid atheists like A. A. Hayes, who is very fond of the spider metaphor. Once they had condemned God for what He did to humanity, people like Hayes fled immediately to the sanctuary of conspiracy. The editor admits they only changed the words, but would argue that language is everything. Hayes clings to meaning, and words have definitions. Better, he says, to believe in conspiracy than in nothing; better to believe that the big spiders of the world secrete from their corrupt entrails a complex web whose interconnections can be traced and plotted, than to accept that all of us, flies and spiders both, dangle in a webless void.

A. A. Hayes thinks a great deal about evil, for which—as humanists do—he blames God. His faith in evil is ecumenical; he sees its causes everywhere: our homes, our hearts, our heads, our hormones; in short, our Fall. We are all guilty of merciless possibilities. But Hayes worries less about the evil of the individual heart, which is, after all, so garishly dressed and loudly spoken that it is not very hard to spot it in the crowd, and is almost comforting, it's so old-fashioned: Like evil in a melodrama, a villain with a waxy moustache. Like Hitler, against whom personally and with such a clear sense of rightness Ernest Ransom had fought World War II. What, thought Hayes, would people like Ernest Ransom do without Hitler? Faith in Hitler's insanity kept the modern world sane, as faith that the plague was God's visitation helped to keep the Middle Ages from going completely mad. Hitler's was the easy face of horror both to bankers like Ransom, who saw peril in Communist hippies like Sidney Blossom, and to populists like Blossom, who saw peril in Fascist capitalists like Ernest Ransom.

Yet Hayes, too, clutched at a faith in evil still human. For the editor's enemy was organized crime, of which the Mafia was the least dangerous. Hayes meant crime organized so blandly and on such a big scale by bureaucracies like ITT and U.S.A. that none of the victims ever realized crimes were being committed. While he believed in an impersonal conspiracy, he believed it to be under the conscious control of evil persons. A boardroom of waxy moustaches.

But Hayes's imagined conspirators, those military and industrial men, can no more weave beyond their own private webs than he can, though their threads may be stretched farther than his. There is some conspiracy. It has spun us all together. It has fixed each of us in our strand of the radiating web, our places chosen for us, or chosen by us, or unchosen. The question, Ramona Dingley's question for Jonathan Fields, is, of course, which? If the conspiracy is not God's, if He has not woven the web and does not sit in its center, is there nothing there to hold the pattern in place?

Is the labyrinth itself the center? Programmed so long ago it can program itself now, wholly self-sustaining, does it sit in the center insentient, paradoxically omniscient because it perfectly knows nothing at all? Does it weave the world, paradoxically omnipotent because it is perfectly random? Are we chosen by the chance computations of the Minotaur's machine? At whose mercy, by whose grace, do we plot?

We who rarely understand our own petty plots, and more rarely look into the mystery of our neighbors, who have no way of knowing (and spend little time wondering) whether our lives are governed by divine design or a complex of technology and bureaucracy or by nothing at all, should not fault Dingleyans for seeing no more than we do. The same heart beats in every human breast and is as little listened to. Even less should Dingleyans be expected to have explored the plot north of the marshlands, when life has given them so short a time and so slight a skill to explore themselves.

But the plot is there. North of the marshlands is a secret base, which began Operation Archangel in 1969 and which, in the preoccupations of an unlucky administration's fall, was never told to stop. So it never did.

The secret base happens to be, in 1976, that Bicentennial year, the unseen antagonist of Dingley Falls, Connecticut, but the townspeople, though some have heard rumors and some have seen lights, know nothing about it. Suppose they did know what was up there, outside their limits? How could they, any more than we would, think that a government base (a collection of orders, buildings, formulas, men, and test tubes) was a chief plotter against them? And was only one of unknown numbers of plots? In melodramas there are heroes to unveil the villain; in Dingley Falls there are only people like the rest of us.

The secret base is plotting to bring peace in our time and make the world safe for democracy. It is plotting to put a stop to the aesthetic absurdity of military armaments, the technological naiveté of crude and mostly nuclear missiles. The secret base has known for a long time how to end wars before they start, before they waste national resources like time, energy, money, and the human race. The secret base is not susceptible to jingoism, is indifferent to the paranoiac political gobbledygook about the Communist menace that so worries Ernest Ransom and the paranoiac political gobbledygook about the Fascist threat that so worries Sidney Blossom. The base has always known that it is silly to spend a great deal of money training and equipping people like Maynard Henry to travel ten thousand miles to kill people like Chin Lam. The secret base has gone beyond neolithic man, who has heaped up mounds of yellow metal in vaults beneath the earth and called it power, who has hauled huge, bullying ships across water and over clouds and called it defense of honor. Ernest Ransom's little silver star on a rag of ribbon is an absurdity to the secret base.

North of Dingley Falls near the marshlands beyond Bredforet Pond, there is a compound of disinterested, dispassionate equipment, including personnel, that believes that knowledge is the only gold worth shoring up, worth hiding, and worth setting a guard around to keep off the descendants of the mindless mob that plagued Galileo, burned Brahe, and, ever the foe of science, feared and fought the future. Knowledge and peace and quiet, a good lab and the men to work it, are all the secret base wants. The men don't know from how high up the orders came down telling their director, Dr. Thomas Svatopluk, to proceed with Operation Archangel. Some say the orders came from the very top, some say not. They don't really care. It matters little to these scientists who sits in the presidential chair, who snatches the seal for a few silly years in an oval office. They are dedicated to the operation, and the plots of their own careers, and are tangled in the webs of their own lives.

Scientists who are pure care little for implementation. But in this Baconian world, theory must lie down—for money—with technology. Science must test things out. Testing things out is the way Ford, Wright, and Edison gave so much to so many, the way Bell discovered the telephone and Columbus discovered America. It is the way the secret base discovered that in the tip of an eye dropper, in the tip of a speck on a microscopic dot, lay power to conquer the will and the heart of the world. Not that they made their discoveries for the federal agency that had given them the code name Archangel, nor for the Pentagon's intelligence divisions, who were 100 percent behind the potential in the operation. Not that they were doing it for whoever first told them they could do it, for they don't even know who that was. They were not doing it because they were members of a conspiratorial web. They were doing it to find out if it could be done.

The secret base was plotting—theoretically—conquests beyond Alexander's dreams.

It was testing them out on Dingley Falls.

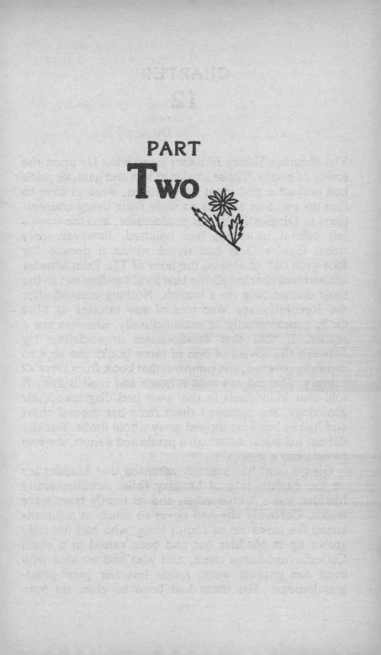

PART Two

CHAPTER
12

The librarian Sidney Blossom loved what lay upon the leaves of books. Those stories of loss and gain, of pride and prejudice and great expectations, were as alive to him up on their shelves as were their living counterparts in Dingley Falls. His predecessor, and the town's last official historian, had honored, however, only trees. Gladys Goff had dated within a decade the foot-wide oak boards on the floor of The Prim Minster inn and had charted all the best local families out to the most distant twig on a branch. Nothing created after the Revolutionary War was of any interest to Miss Goff, genealogically or architecturally. She was not a reader. If told that salaciousness or socialism lay between the covers of one of those books she kept so carefully covered, she removed that book from Dixwell Library. She did not take it home and read it first. If told that individuals in the town had disgraced their genealogy, she removed them from her mental chart and had in her time lopped away whole limbs. But she did not tell tales. Although a prude and a snob, she had never been a gossip.

Gladys Goff had scarcely admitted that Madder lay on the eastern side of Dingley Falls. Architecturally Madder was a hodgepodge, and its family trees were weeds. Certainly she had never so much as acknowledged the existence of Judith Haig, who had not only grown up in Madder but had been raised in a small Catholic orphanage there, and who had no idea who even her parents were, much less her great-great-grandparents. For there had been no clue, no note pinned with a gold brooch, no monogrammed lace handerkerchief left with her in the cardboard box that Father Patrick Crisp had found beneath a Station of the Cross one Good Friday night forty-two years earlier. This morning the pastor had heard, from Sarah Mac-Dermott, that there was something the matter with Judith's heart. It did not appear that God had made her lucky. Her story, sighed Father Crisp, continued to be a sad one.

Before Mrs. Haig retired to fix up her house, she had to make final arrangements at the post office. Tuesday morning at 8:50 her husband, Hawk, left the police station, where he had sat since 7:00 A.M. to protect Dingley Falls. He drove across the rickety bridge and returned with his wife. The dogs returned to the trailer park, but they watched her go by.

At 9:05 Sammy Smalter came to her post office window, where he handed up one of his usual packages addressed to New York.

At 9:20 Prudence Lattice, who had nothing else to do, opened her Tea Shoppe.

At 9:21 Limus Barnum went in there for a cup of coffee. He brought his own doughnuts in their cellophane wrappers and a magazine for men.

At 9:30, after the jog around Elizabeth Circle and the light but fibrous breakfast whereby he maintained a form trim enough to don, if need be, the World War II captain's uniform boxed up in his attic, Ernest Ransom arrived at his bank, where he learned he had sold three hundred shares of United Chemicals at a considerable profit.

At 10:30 Polly Hedgerow, having already scored at least 98 on her history final and having decided that 98 was good enough, was pedaling full speed along Cromwell Hill Road. She had raced out of Dixwell High without bothering to turn down the hall to see if her friend Joy Strummer was at her locker yet. A team of ball-dribbling boys would have surrounded Joy anyhow. Swinging dangerously onto the gravel path,

Polly entered the courtyard behind St. Andrew's.
Father Sloan Highwick was out there, clipping the roses
all wrong and humming the Nicene Creed, "He suffered and was bur-i-ed."

"Guess what?" she called.

"Yes, terrible. I already know."

"How?" Polly dismounted.

"I had dinner last night at Mr. Ransom's. Everyone
was there. Very pleasant. Except, of course, for poor
Mrs. Abernathy. And poor Mr. Abernathy. And that
poor misguided fellow who has apparently, I say
apparently, um, gone away with her." The Rector
sighed. "Such is Life, Polly dear. Not all roses." He
returned to clipping his.

Polly was chagrined. Elation over her now worthless
scoop deflated like a bike tire. She kicked her kickstand. Her age was such a rotten handicap—while she
was forced into an early bed, the Rector ran about
getting invited to parties and slurping up information
right and left.

Sloan Highwick, however, never understood the
gossip; he simply collected it, just as Petrarch collected
the Greek manuscripts of Plato long before he found a
tutor to teach him how to translate them. Polly
Hedgerow was, in a way, the Rector's tutor. But being
so young, her translations were sketchy at best, even
when news did come her way. For it was the "why," not
the "what," that intrigued her. Gossip to her was
simply a book (some of whose words sent her to the
dictionary) for whose hidden meaning she read between the lines. This intellectual superiority to Highwick consoled her now, for Polly was in that regard a
bit of a snob. And so she decided again not to share
with Highwick the biggest fact in all Dingley Falls, a
fact that she assumed no one but she had discovered
(and she by accident while digging for Indian arrowheads east of Birch Forest). The fact that beyond the
marshlands somebody had built some kind of a U.S.

government compound—she wasn't sure why, but imagined it might be to store atom bombs in—an installation surrounded by high electric fences and guarded by soldiers with dogs. She had never heard anyone in town mention such a place. She wasn't sure such a place should be in Dingley Falls, Connecticut.

The telephone call from his son and partner reached the attorney Winslow Abernathy as he drank coffee and stared down from the window of his staid hotel to the pond in Boston Public Garden where the docked swan boats floated empty together.

Abernathy was surprised by Arthur's revelation about Beanie's departure. Had any local gossip reached him of his wife's involvement with another man, he would have dismissed it without thought. So he was surprised, but his composure was not shattered. It was his habit, or nature, to take hurt inside and smother it there. He asked Arthur if they were sure it was Beanie's handwriting, if there had been further news, if Lance (Arthur's twin) had heard from her in Forest Hills, if the hospital had been called, if the highway patrol had been called, if she had provided herself with clothes and money. He asked who had seen her last and what was her presumed state of mind. He and his son were lawyers.

Abernathy could think of no friends or relatives to whom his wife might have gone. Apart from old Ramona, Beanie was the last of the Dingleys. Her friends, her life, were all there at home. But, indisputably, she was gone, and it was not in her nature to joke or to lie. The senior partner said he would leave immediately and should be back by three that afternoon. His business in Boston had been to protect Beanie's interests— her factory that made periscopes and telescopes and microscopes, yet seemed to make less money each year. In the letter Arthur had read, Beanie had given her husband that factory. With all her

heart, she'd said. He knew she didn't think he would
want it as a recompense for losing her. He knew she
hadn't thought at all, if, in fact, she had left him.

What Winslow thought as he continued to drink his
coffee and noticed that his window was gullied with the
aimless path of last night's rain, what he *felt,* at first,
was not so much a sense of loss as a sense of wonder at
Beanie's revealed intensity. What must so precipitous
an emotion be like, to blot out domestic and social
habits, to cut through the easeful inertia of *that* many
years? It must be frightening to be caught in such a
passion. Beanie must be frightened. No, that wasn't
true. Physical things had never scared her. Letters and
numbers scared her, in their (to her) arbitrary manifes-
tations—like cocktail party invitations or bank figures.
He and she were quite opposite in that, in most ways.
Abernathy had no fear of anything that could be
written down. He was, on the other hand, made queasy
by the darting approach of a cat, or Big Mutt, the dog
Beanie had so named because he was simply that, a
large mongrel. She was not given to metaphor.

The lawyer worried about how his wife must feel
about how *he* must feel. How must he feel? Betrayed?
He could not visualize this absurdly named man (this
poet?) with regard to whom his wife had written that
she had never felt this way before. He could not feel
betrayed, because he could not believe it. Arthur was
right: Beanie would be home before he got back. That
was the only thing that made sense. And perhaps Otto
was right, perhaps he should tell her about his checkup,
that he might be slightly hypertensive, might be putting
a strain on his heart. Maybe he should share the
worrisome things with Beanie. Perhaps she was right,
that he should not hold himself in so much. Yes, Beanie
would be home when he got there, and he would tell
her he was afraid to die. But if she had left him, if she
wanted to be released from their marriage? Then he
would not tell her; for out of charity she would stay,

even against her desires. While, for three decades, Winslow Abernathy had not probed to discover just what his wife's desires might be, he would never—should they be made explicit—bribe her to deny them.

A line was forming beside the first swan down in the Public Garden; a sailor and his girl were ·in front, waiting, in no hurry. On leave in his officer's uniform, over thirty years ago, Winslow had sat in such a boat, perhaps in that same boat, and had rewritten Beanie's French composition so that she could eventually graduate from Mount Holyoke, so that he could finish the war and finish law school and marry her. She had held out her hands to the ducks. "They'll bite you," he warned her. "Not unless I hurt them," she said. Then she had snatched up his hands in hers and said, "Oh, throw that book in the water. We could just get married now, couldn't we, before you go back?" "Yes," he'd told her. "All right."

He had wanted to marry her for a long time, perhaps since the afternoon they were introduced by Ernest Ransom at a game in the Yale Bowl. A cautious, careful young man, never before had Winslow made a decision with so little regard for the evidence, so brief a review of the relevant facts, before entering his plea. But Beanie had seemed to him at once to be an absolute fact, like the war, to be so tangible that connected to her reality, he could stretch out a tentative hand toward a world he otherwise ignored, and sometimes found frightening, and often misunderstood. Within a year of their wedding they had the twin boys. Two more tangible facts, like Beanie. And for a long time she tried to have other children. When she didn't, she drove to the pound in Argyle and brought back Big Mutt. Now, Arthur had said, she had taken the blind old dog away with her last night. Had she loved the dog too much to leave behind, or feared he loved the dog too little?

The sailor helped his girl into the trembling swan.

And up in a window of the stone hotel, Winslow
Abernathy noticed that the coffee he drank was now
cold. It was past time to take his pill.

The First Congregational Church, which looks down
on Dingley Green and is physically the largest church in
town, should be, by New England tradition, also the
church to gather into its fold the largest number of
Dingley Falls's big sheep. Three hundred years ago,
however, Elijah Dingley, revolting against his father's
Puritanism and his mother's Evangelicalism, had gone
so far—from Providence—as to found Dingley Falls on
the Rampage and to build there a High Anglican
Church, of which St. Andrew's was the third stone
replacement; and to confirm in it his firstborn, Thomas
Laud Dingley, whom he had named after that very
Archbishop of Canterbury who had driven Elijah's
father out of England in the first place. Where the
founding family worshipped, most of their immediate
court inevitably followed, and so, down the centuries, a
rivalry for the souls of the social circle (generations of
Dingleys, Goffs, Dixwells, Ransoms and Bredforets)
continued to be waged from the pulpits of First
Congregational and St. Andrew's Episcopal. The more
indifferent (or ecumenical) townspeople went to whichever church was closer, or boasted more of their
friends. For these, the later service, shorter sermons,
richer gossip, and more alcoholic coffee hours of St.
Andrew's may have played a part in its greater
popularity. No Dingleyan proper, as opposed to Madderite, had been a Catholic since 1925, when Ramona
Dingley's father had died in that faith. A few (like
Ramona, A.A. Hayes, Sidney Blossom, and Polly
Hedgerow) attended neither the Low Church on the
green nor the High Church on the hill, nor any other
church anywhere else. And the more indecisive (or
passionate) felt called first by one bell, then another:
Evelyn Troyes had become an Anglican three times and
a Congregationalist four. Even after she concluded that

Sloan Highwick never was going to marry her, Prudence Lattice had faithfully appeared at even Evensong, though she worried that her ancestors would have writhed in their graves had they known a Lattice was receiving Communion out of a gold chalice in front of a gilded choir screen.

"Miss Lattice likes to make things for you," said Polly. "She wants somebody to need her."

Father Highwick had given his young friend two of the dainty pâté sandwiches that Prudence Lattice had brought him in a calico napkin from The Tea Shoppe.

"She's a good soul," said the Rector with an easy smile.

"Nobody would marry her, I guess."

"Quince Ivoryton wanted to. I think it was Quince. But God calls us all to different altars, and Quince fell in France, poor fellow. Or Italy."

"Don't you want to know how I found out about Mrs. Abernathy so fast?"

"Poor lady."

"Suellen Hayes told me this morning. She heard her parents talking about it when they got home. Her dad was stinko." Polly checked to be sure the Rector had heard that tidbit. "And Mr. Hayes was laughing out loud. 'I never would have believed it of ol' Weanie-Beanie' (he called Mrs. Abernathy that). 'Who in hell would have thought' (I'm just telling you what Suellen told me in homeroom), 'who in hell would have thought that ol' Weanie-Beanie had the imagination to commit adultery?' "

"Hum."

"He said that news ought to really shake up the old town, except he was sorry because he liked Mr. Abernathy and he liked ol' Weanie-Beanie, too. He said he wished they'd find out Mr. Ransom was a dope peddler and Mrs. Ransom was a fiend or something."

Sloan Highwick frowned. He had, after all, his pastoral duties. "That was not very nice of Mr. Hayes, perhaps. Hum. Do you know what adultery means?"

"Of course I do. It means a sexual affair." Polly pursed her lips primly.

"Hum. It means being too intimate, hum, with someone to whom you're not married, if, hum, you are married."

"I know," said Polly. "Like Anna Karenina."

"It's a sin."

"Not anymore, is it?"

"Heavens, a sin's a sin. It's not like narrow lapels, you know, or wide ones, which really I think have gone too far. There, then." He laughed his benevolent laugh, and pedagogic duty discharged to Highwick's satisfaction, they walked back through the garden.

Polly looked at the erratically clipped rosebush. "Sebastian Marco's going to kill you when he sees that!"

"That Sebastian! He thinks himself a genius, which he may indeed be." The Rector glanced at his gardener's perfect striped tulips. "However, it's all very well to *be* a genius, but when you start to act like one, it's a different matter entirely. When you can't even bother to answer a few civil questions!"

"He quit again?"

Highwick forlornly nodded.

"Oh, he'll be back. He's scared you'll ruin his garden." Something flashed at Polly as the door to Jonathan Fields's cottage opened. "Gosh! What happened to him? His eyes are all different."

"Those are his new contact lenses. Poor fellow, so young," sighed Highwick, who had perfect sight and never troubled it with much reading or writing. The lithe Jonathan came toward them now with two huge sapphires twinkling in his face. He carried a stack of library books, for he was on his way to visit Ramona Dingley again, after he made all the church calls at the hospital near Argyle, where Evelyn Troyes was driving him since it happened to be on her way to wherever she told him she was going that happened to be along that way. "Mrs. Troyes is a little lonely, I don't like to say no," he told the Rector. "I have to eat dinner with the Rector, he gets a little lonely if he has to eat by himself," he told Mrs. Troyes.

"I have to go to Miss Dingley's," he now said to his superior. "I don't think I'm much help though. She asked for some books on the historicity of Christ. 'Tough ones,' she said. She said the gospels were nothing but gossip. Maybe, Rector, I'm not really sure how, maybe if *you* could . . ."

"No, no, no, you're doing a marvelous job. I shouldn't interfere. But dear, dear Ramona. First flying saucers in the marshes. Now this, this greedy curiosity. The elderly sometimes get that way. Suspicious. Poor old thing. Discourage her, discourage her gently. It never helps to poke and prod into the Mystery, to spoil the bloom on the bud," counseled the Rector, who was, in that sense, completely unspoiled.

The curate hurried away, laden with books that Gladys Goff had selected for the townspeople's edification, though whatever missionary impulses Father Fields may have had were dampened when he noticed that most of the tomes had last been checked out in 1935. Doomed to failure, Miss Goff had devoted her life to attempts to improve the minds and preserve the lineages of Dingley Falls families. It's just as well she died when she did and was replaced by that more charitable reader, Sidney Blossom, while the house of Dingley itself, whose fireplaces and forebears she had so carefully catalogued, was still standing. For now there was gossip about the last direct lineal descendant of Elijah the founder, stories going around about Beatrice Dingley Abernathy that—even if untrue—Gladys Goff would have never allowed on her shelves.

CHAPTER
13

Ernest Ransom was driving out of town to visit that former property of his. He was a man of many holdings—most of them handed him, as each ancestor finished his life's run and passed the stick forward, handed him in a lineal descent of bonds and a bank, of glass birds and dishes, land, houses, and attitudes. One such holding was fifty swampy acres just north of Dingley Falls, property no one had ever thought usable, but simply something in the family, bequeathed along with keepsakes like Charity Bredforet's embroideries of national landmarks—which no one wanted either.

Ransom, however, had found a buyer; rather a buyer had found him. In early 1969 someone representing someone who represented something governmental had presented himself at the bank with a letter of introduction from one of the congenial Washington acquaintances whom Ransom had met as a result of his reliable, if unenthusiastic, support for the Republican ticket the previous fall: reliable, because Bredforets and Ransoms had always been dutiful citizens whose substantial contributions to the GOP they considered as morally obligatory as their donations to the Episcopal Church—both those institutions being, in the family's inherited judgment, as fundamental to the social order as gravity is to the well-running of the universe. Nevertheless, Ernest Ransom had not been enthusiastic, because in 1968 he could not bring himself to believe that either of his party's national candidates were what he could really call "gentlemen." Eight years earlier, in fact, he had taken the unprecedented, and unrepeated, step of secretly voting for a Democratic president, who, if reprehensible in all other ways, undeniably had been schooled to dress, play for Harvard, sail, and get himself injured for his country— as a gentleman. But that brief infidelity, like an affair with a dangerously seductive foreigner in wartime, clearly could mean little in the pattern of one's life, and Ransom had never committed adultery again.

In 1968, therefore, he had contributed time and money to Republicans. And in return he had been invited to meet Republicans of time and money, those who made decisions, or who had heard decisions in the making, knowledge that proved useful to have in the banking business when mixed casually with a drink and handed to Ernest Ransom at gentlemen's luncheons. And so, approached by his government about the leasing of mostly marshy land that no one had ever thought of using anyhow, he was happy to oblige. Profit was not at all his motive, though profit was, naturally, all to the good. He understood the representative to say something about possible ornithological research into migratory cycles. Possibly in the future there might be something on the order of a national wildlife refuge. Possibly it might bear the Ransom family name. All to the good. Since William Bredforet was now too old to stand holding a gun for hours in sodden rubber boots down among sedge and gnat-thick rushes, and since Ernest preferred golf, there was no family objection he could see in the preservation of any mallard or woodcock that might be left in the area. So the land was leased, and the banker kept the fact, as he had been asked, under his hat. That had been more than seven years ago.

Today, his sunglasses filtering out the bright summer glare, Ransom drove his sedan a little too fast around Ransom Circle, up Goff Street, and out onto Route 3, out to that suddenly sliced-off carpet of superhighway rolled out, it had seemed to Police Chief Hawk Haig, to herald the future—a future that had declined, after all, to make an appearance. At the road's abrupt end, Ransom squatted in his tailored suit to pull out a few clumps of sprawling weeds that leeched forward on all sides to reclaim the land. He felt ill at ease there. Accustomed since a very pleasant childhood to everyone's regard, Ernest intensely disliked being disliked. And the problem of the discontinued connector had caused him the unpleasantness of alienating a number of people. Not that he had done so deliberately, but things had, as he generally phrased it, gotten rather complicated.

Three years after his dealings with the nation the state (still in what all Ransoms considered the disturbingly itchy hands of Democrats) had proposed to connect Route 3 to the Interstate that ran twenty miles to the north. As a result (the result upon which Hawk Haig had bought his land and built his future), vacationers would have driven right by Dingley Falls to Lake Pissinowno or farther west into other lovely scenery, rather than entirely bypassing the town to the northwest (as members of Dingley Falls's Historical Society hoped they would continue to do). And after the confetti of red tape had settled over the State House, an engineering report appeared. It proposed a route through the southeast corner of Ernest Ransom's land, which, since the site in question did not directly overlap the land he had leased earlier to the federal government, he was happy enough to sell. Construction began. Construction workers praised the union and the union praised the Democrats and Ransom invested the money and Hawk Haig purchased his acres and, except that the Historical Society had neon nightmares about Tastee-Freez and motels with names like Bide-a-Wee, everyone was content.

But things had gotten complicated. Soon after his negotiations with the state, Ransom received a disturbing visit from a disturbed representative of a federal agency. It seemed to this Mr. Palter that Mr. Ransom hadn't caught the signal right when he'd leased the federal government that land. It seemed there were too many players on the field, and the coach thought the team ought to huddle and come up with a better game plan. In the end, it seemed that the nation thought it counterproductive for the state to be plowing up earth even within a fifty-acre radius of (leased) federal property. Mr. Palter explained that once the offensive line had knocked out Congress, that possible Ransom National Wildlife Preserve was on the theoretical assembly line. And though the ball of a bill had not yet been passed over those hard-line congressional committee fuckers, excuse the term, still indications were in the affirmative. Meanwhile, let's get a few strings pulled on this end and get the state the hell off the field. So Ransom understood this Mr. Palter to say, though he was not completely certain they were speaking the same language.

Soon after Mr. Palter's visit, a speedy investigation by another federal agency demonstrated to its own satisfaction that the state had indeed left dangling a few dirty strings. Such as, the state's construction contractor and the state assemblyman who had first proposed the connector were related by marriage. Such as, the contractor and the engineer who had drawn up the first report were both alumni, twenty years back, of a secret teenage social club called the Hartford Hellions. Such suspicious connections behind the connector clearly indicated, at least to the federal investigators, that there was dirt to be dug up before the state dug up any more of Ernest Ransom's dirt. Ransom was persuaded that he agreed. He advised Dingley Falls's first selectman to push for a second surveyor's report. The federal agency even volunteered army engineers, who, with the same impressive speed, discovered, at least to their satisfaction, that the route already under construction was *far* from sound. In fact, so dismal were geological and soil conditions found to be, by this second report, that it expressed frank astonishment that the first report should ever have proposed pouring the state's concrete, unloading the state's gravel, into a substructure so highly acidic and upon soil of such poor drainage that, as a Republican friend of Mr. Palter's exclaimed on the floor of the State House, in his quotable way, a mere ten years would suffice to *sink* that connector into a bog of treachery where misguided motorists might, for all the Democrats cared, drive in their swimsuits with snorkels clenched between their teeth, since that would be the only way of getting across the damn thing. And what kind of a "social club" had that been, anyhow?

Privately, Ransom was surprised. Business dealings in the state over a number of profitable years had occasionally brought him in contact with the president of the original engineering firm, and nothing in the man's past seemed to prefigure so gross a miscalculation, and nothing in his character seemed to make likely the deliberate malfeasance that the federal findings called the only explanation possible. But Ransom had been schooled never to doubt federal findings. So, though privately surprised, and somehow ill at ease, publicly he condemned that original engineering firm.

The vehement protests of the backers of the state report over such "unfounded insinuations" by the backers of the federal report were overruled by the long, loose strings of litigation, after which, in a quiet act of good citizenship, kept under his hat, Ransom agreed to act as agent for the purchase of that land from the state by the nation. With the help of the cooperative banker the federal government came into possession of the entire fifty acres. Ransom took no fee for his service, but had the pleasure within the year of an appointment to a board of twenty advisers to a trade committee, and of an invitation to a dinner given by state leaders in order to raise money for their party's national leader, who came personally to thank them, and from whom Ernest Ransom sat only a flattering seven seats away. All to the good.

Except some people weren't happy. Not that Ransom had the slightest personal regard for Hawk Haig, or for Maynard Henry and the rest of the out-of-work construction workers, or for the union, or for Hartford Democrats. Still, he disliked being disliked. He disliked too certain unfounded insinuations about the abandoned highway. He disliked these rumors even more after it became all too apparent that both those national officeholders to whose election in 1968 and 1972 he had given so much time and money had not behaved as gentlemen during their abbreviated tenure in office. Ransom heard unsavory phrases (whose inapplicability to his own motives did not entirely mitigate the uneasiness he felt at having such words in verbal proximity to the words *Ernest Ransom*). These phrases (payoff, kickback, hush money) were the more galling when his own party's folly, taped and televised like some interminable soap opera, had made the words so delectable to mouth-watering liberals like A. A. Hayes. Had *The Dingley Day* (whose cryptic editorials on "The Highway Scandal" had momentarily increased its circulation) still been owned by the Highwick family—who, however, had sold it fifty years ago to a chain of western New England papers that now belonged to a television network that belonged to an oil company—Ransom would have insisted that the Highwicks oblige him by firing A. A. Hayes immediately.

But the highway business was over now; even Hayes had dropped it. Everyone had grown accustomed to that disconnected asphalt strip. It was part of the landscape now, no more noticed than the banks of the Rampage. Still, the place made Ransom uncomfortable, and it had been four years since he last saw it. He would not have come now except for that image, wedged in his mind by the conversation yesterday with

Dr. Scaper, which last night had almost kept him awake
past his bedtime. Of course, what he had seen four
years ago would be gone by now; once he proved that,
the uneasy image ought to go as well. That he should
get rid of it as soon as possible, even if it meant wasting
his morning, was important to the banker, for he
disliked (and was unaccustomed to) having anything
uncomfortable in his life, or mind.

Stooped down now, he worked his way through
brambled hedge growth, westward, away from the
aborted road, west to where, beyond a tangle of thick,
dark conifers, the old Indian path led to the marshland.
Until yesterday, when Otto Scaper's chance remark
had called back up that devastated stretch of earth that
looked so uncomfortably like the pictures of bombed
terrain ten thousand miles away which, in the 1960s,
obsessive liberals had broadcast over and over, with
such unfortunate results; until yesterday Ransom had
really almost forgotten about the land. He'd sold a
great many things since 1972, and talk about scandals
had died away after the new president had pardoned
the old, leaving him to repent in private as he would.
The country was absolved of guilt. A decent man,
promising to awaken those troubled from their nightmares, enjoined his fellow citizens to think of themselves as decent men. Ransom already did so.

Privately, the banker had long since assumed he must
have come upon a testing site for military hardware—
some experimental flame-thrower. He had assumed the
information to be classified, the installation to be a
military secret. Faith in one's superiors, orders without
explanations, the importance of security, all these were
a part of Ransom's heritage. In his time as an army
officer, he had obeyed without asking questions, and he
had ordered, without answering them. So while he felt
ill at ease, he had never queried the representative
about his government's objections to the proposed
highway; there could be, he assumed, no legitimate

reason for discomfiture—since whatever they had built there obviously had its purpose, all to the good. And obviously, now that its purpose had been served, it would be gone. The war was over. He told himself today that he was wasting his morning only to confirm what he already knew.

Ransom slowly worked his way through the matted wilderness. He felt ridiculous, a fifty-four-year-old man, a bank president, spying as if to protect himself against a government in whose capacity to protect him and his he had always placed absolute faith. Finally he climbed out of undergrowth into the clearing. It was still there. What he had told himself he would not see, and had feared that he would see, was still there. That cold black plot of unnatural earth seared into his inherited land. Why, in all that time, had no grass, no weed, thrust through the cracked soil? What weaponry could kill the earth forever?

In his tailored suit Ransom stood there. He stood there until his breath was quiet. Then he looked away, looked past it, looked toward the marsh grass, alive, yellow, and moving, looked beyond the marsh to woods, green and moving. Sweat felt cold in his hair and in his hands, and he took out his handkerchief to wipe it away. He knew now that he wouldn't go into the woods. He was too old and too busy to put himself through hours of hard hiking through the woods and marsh to where he had seen that compound. The buildings wouldn't still be there anyhow. But if they were, he could only not know it by not going. But, of course, they weren't. But if they were, they would have some new purpose all to the good. He turned and walked back the way he had come.

A big rotted elm had fallen years ago across the old path. Ransom sat there in the shifting speckled light and smoked a cigarette. He very rarely smoked, but kept the lighter and gold case because it was his habit to keep things that had been given to him.

The banker told himself that he had been silly to come there again. He really should get back to work. It was none of his business anyhow, and everyone else had forgotten. It wasn't his land anymore.

CHAPTER
14

Unlike Sloan Highwick, through whom the evils of gin (like the evils of life) passed without the slightest effect, A. A. Hayes had a hangover. Even when Hayes felt his fittest Limus Barnum gave him a headache, and today, before noon, his quarrel with his wife after last night's party as unpatched as the Ransoms' glass robin, Dingley Falls's editor could scarcely bear the sight of Barnum. Indeed, he prayed that the gym-muscled merchant would miraculously drop dead in the office doorway where he now stood, baring his shiny teeth in a smile. But Barnum didn't, and Hayes remained the atheist he had become in high school.

"How's it going, A. A.?"

"All right."

"Whatcha up to? Anything going on?"

"Just gathering the news of the Dingley day."

"Guess there's not much of it, is there?" The emigrant from Worcester, Massachusetts, snickered at the emigrant from Thermopylae, North Carolina. "What a hole this place is."

"No, I guess there's not much." But as a matter of fact, Hayes guessed just the opposite, guessed that among Dingley Falls's few thousand human souls was all the news the world could bear. Of course, it was not news fit to print. *That* common news, the mutually agreed-upon mass communiqué of which *The Dingley Day* was the local medium, that news was now being copied off the wire service and slipped from syndications in the back room by Mr. Coleman Sniffell, who with Hayes himself comprised the entire staff of the town journal. That public news everyone in Dingley Falls already knew, since they saw it on television, quite often, mused Hayes, as it was happening. *Ford Falls Down Gangplank. Rape Gang Falls Upon Grandmother of Twenty. African Government Topples. Stocks Topple. Prices Soar. Consumers Sore. Former President Seen Alone on the Beach.* These were not the "goings-on" that Barnum wished to know about.

Could Hayes, as he occasionally imagined, publish the town's true *acta diurna*, he felt there were broadsides enough to topple Dingley Falls, too. News universal in its particularity of pathos and passion: *Dingley Heiress Beds New York Poet on May 31. Husband the Last to Know. Local Banker Admits, "These Are Not the Best of Times." Town Midget Mocked by Local Owner of Antiques and Appliances Store. Elderly Tea Shoppe Owner Fears Death. Local Editor Fears Life. Wife of Local Editor Longs to Hatchet Family; Claims They Have Stolen Her Life. Local Banker Adds, "These Are Not the Worst of Times Either."*

"So, how you doing, A.A.?"

"All right."

"Family?"

"Fine." (Civilization is a lie.) "You?" There was no "yours," for Barnum was, natch, a bachelor. At least that's what Hayes thought. In fact, the merchant had been divorced by his wife just before he moved to Dingley Falls.

"Can't complain," said Limus, but found he could for about ten minutes. Business was nothing to shake a stick at. The editor knew no one who might want a great deal on a Jap color TV that was slightly scratched, or a turn-of-the-century brass spittoon in the same condition. Nor did he know where all the damn tourists were hiding.

"If you want to know what's going on, I'm the last person you ought to come to," said Hayes. "Nobody ever tells me a thing." He instantly regretted having made this remark; it gave Barnum the opening he had pushed his way through for the past ten years—that as they were both outsiders they should stick together and show the snotty locals what was what. Nothing irked Hayes more than hearing Limus Barnum say things that he himself had felt. He had never been able to decide whether he cared if hc were an outsider or not; but he did know he didn't want to be out there looking in with Limus Barnum.

"These snoots wouldn't tell you if your coat was on fire, A.A. No way they can hush it all up about the Abernathys though. Huh? You hear about that? I hear she skedaddled with some hippie college prof. That's the kind of guy we got teaching kids in college these days. Make you sick, doesn't it? Guess old Abernathy wasn't giving her enough of what she wanted, huh?"

"Couldn't say." (Society is a sewered conduit.)

"You could tell that lady was hot to trot, couldn't you, huh?"

Cornered, Hayes broke out from behind his desk on which the appliances dealer was seated, by one buttock, a tasseled loafer swinging to and fro like a shoe store sign. He felt asphyxiated by Barnum's presence. "I'm a little pressed for time," he said, though it was space really. "Something in particular, Lime?" Hayes offered the nickname as compensation for wanting to pitch the man out a window. "Something about your ad?" SPEND TIME WITH LIME, AND SPEND LESS.

"No, guess I'm going to go with it. Can't reach a fly without honey, and honey costs money." Lime snorted. Suddenly he snapped his face into solemnity as if he were going to salute somebody. "It's those damn dirty letters, A.A. What's being done about them? Zero, goose egg, that's what. Now women and children are being scared out of their ever-loving minds by all this filth."

"Oh, I don't think so."

"Hell, yes, they are. *Hell,* yes. Lives are being threatened, did you know that?"

"Like whose?"

"Like mine, old buddy" was the triumphant reply.

Hayes was surprised. "You got one of the letters?" Frankly, he had thought the anonymous scandal monger who had begun a few months ago to address accusatory notes first to the town's public officers, then to its private citizens, was interested only in Dingley Falls's civic and social leaders—neither of which Limus Barnum could claim to be.

"You're damn straight I got one." Barnum had it ready in the breast pocket of his short-sleeved shirt which sported red stripes vertical against the red stripes horizontal of his tie. The cheap paper and awful typing were the same as those on the letter Hayes had found for himself a month ago, lying in the bottom of the tin mailbox in his office.

Barnum's letter read in part (that is, the part Barnum read to Hayes), "Somebody ought to put you away for good, you scum, and I'm the kid to do it. Nobody's going to stop me. Nobody gives a shit."

An irrational connection sparked in Hayes's brain where it was almost regretfully recircuited: maybe *he* had sent Barnum that letter while intoxicated. Of course he had not. Nor was he to learn what the preceding (unread) part of Barnum's note said. It said, "Fuck cunts," typed a dozen times in punctuationless succession, followed by: "All of them stupid cunts. Can't get it up, can you. Your too dirty for a good woman. Think your so nuts about your mother. You hated her dirty guts. And that other bitch too."

"Maybe it's some kid with an unfortunate sense of humor," suggested Hayes.

But Barnum swiped this possibility away with his red

fuzzy arm. "Listen, don't kid yourself, we're dealing with a maniac and I'm getting tired of waiting around. Now I think we ought to get a committee together. The selectmen are dragging their asses as per usual. Arthur Abernathy couldn't be bothered, and that old biddy Ramona Dingley ought to be put to sleep. You know we can't even count on Hedgerow to wipe his own butt. Now why don't you get with me on this, A.A.? Get the paper behind it."

"Limus, it's nothing but a bunch of silly letters."

"You don't know *what* it could be. Get on that ass Haig. Can you believe having a wife looks like that and he spends all day in the woods shooting at birds and all night over in Madder pestering a couple of old whores too lazy to get out on the street anyhow! Now if we had the kind of government that we ought to have in his country, we'd have some police that we could count on. How do you know this guy isn't going to stop writing someday and start shooting, huh? What about your window there? Who broke it, Haig checked into that? Some cop!"

"I broke it." (Actually, Hayes had no idea how the window had gotten smashed. Nor was he certain why he was being so perverse as to lie about the fact.)

"You're crazy." Barnum's eyes narrowed. "Why don't you get it fixed?"

"Too stuffy in here."

"You're really nuts, Hayes. You ought to go see somebody."

"Probably."

Barnum then shoved across another of his letters to the editor criticizing the federal government. The editor agreed to print it. Why not? Wasn't this a free country large enough to tolerate Limus Barnum's condemnation, and besides, who apart from Barnum and Tracy Canopy ever bothered to write *The Dingley Day?* The ass, thought Hayes, simply wants his name in type, identifies himself by his echo, exists only when reflected. It was known that Limus Barnum took such pleasure in the duplication of his image that he spent nearly all the proceeds of his Antiques, Hobbies, and Appliances store to advertise himself in the paper, on balloons, and even on television, where he had played the main role in six thirty-second commercials long familiar to local insomniacs. He was Dingley Falls's only screen star. How could he have so missed his calling? It was clear, thought Hayes, the gods had meant Barnum to sell used cars in Los Angeles, but had set him down by mistake too far to the east.

"Now Lime," he cautioned. "If I were you, I wouldn't let the FBI in on this letter scandal just yet. You know how they are, they're liable to get it all wrong, probably infiltrate your committee and arrest *you* for being an agitator."

"I'm no agitator."

"For being agitated then."

"Very funny."

The editor walked his concerned citizen toward the front door and with a neighborly pat privately hurled him through it into oblivion. But before dropping off, Barnum jerked his head in the direction of Kate Ransom, who had just walked sulkily past them, having circled the green in anticipation of an accidental confrontation with the perfidious Richard Rage, who she refused to believe was gone.

"How'd you like some of that?" Lime grinned.

"Some of what?"

"That!" His auburn hair, blown dry and sprayed, bounced stiffly at the retreating anatomy of Mr. Ransom's younger daughter.

"No, thanks," answered Hayes, and closed the door. He didn't even much want some of what he did have.

Back at his desk, the editor picked up the folded newspaper that Barnum had left there. He threw it in the trash can without looking at it. He knew what it was and had seen Barnum leave it and had known Barnum left it on purpose. For in addition to wanting Hayes to join him in rebuffing the slights of native Dingleyans,

Limus Barnum had for years wanted the editor to join
him in reading the news that the American Nazi party
considered fit to print.

Two buildings down, at the Lattice Tea Shoppe, Mrs.
Vincent Canopy and Mrs. Ernest Ransom were anato-
mizing "Beanie's behavior."

"Inexplicable," Priss concluded, keeping an eye on
the window, for she continually expected something
more from life, though she had no particular anticipation in mind. "My God, there goes Kate again. Why
does she have to slouch like that?"

"Shall I stop her?"

"I wouldn't dare! Kate hates to be seen with me in
public. Apparently it defines her or represses her or
something unforgivable." They watched Kate wander
by. "Inexplicable," Mrs. Ransom continued. "Leaving
Winslow in a rush of menopausal madness. Unless that
poet of yours forced Beanie at gunpoint . . . No, she
would have knocked it away and broken his arm."

"Priss!"

"Ah, Ching Chang!" called Priss to the woman she
had employed last night, Mrs. Maynard Henry, now
one of Miss Lattice's girls.

In her colonial bonnet and long, ruffled calico skirt,
with her purple bruised eye, the young Vietnamese
looked, thought Mrs. Canopy, dreadfully unhappy.
Still, she assumed, it must be better than Saigon.
"Chinkie," war-orphaned only child of a minor bureaucrat who had made a killing on the black market before
being killed by a bomb, had been brought to Connecticut without being asked whether she would prefer it to
Saigon or not.

"Ah, yes, some more coffee, please." Hieroglyph-
ically, Priss held up her cup. "And I think a pastry."
She pointed to the tray of desserts on a side table, then
elaborately stuffed an imaginary cake in and out of her
mouth. "Pastry? Yes. You, Tracy? No?" She touched
her breast with a single index finger. "Just one then.

One pastry. Thank you." The ladies waited until their novice waitress quite cleverly returned with the tray and the coffeepot and the pastry. Tracy smiled in encouragement as Chin poured, and thanked her exuberantly when she left.

"Wherever does poor Prudence find them?" Priss wondered. "Remember years ago the loud woman with that gazebo of dyed yellow hair? I think Evelyn said she was Orchid O'Neal's sister. The middle of lunch that day she bellowed out that William Bredforet had his hand up her skirt while she was clearing his table."

"Didn't she hit him with her tray?"

"Yes, yes, and then poor Prudence flung herself between them and was knocked to the floor. Hordes came running from all over the circle, hoping somebody'd been killed. Of course, I'm sure that little old goat *was* pinching her!"

The ladies laughed.

"I'm sure William has spawned litters all over the place in his time."

"Oh, Priss."

But such remembrances were not solving Beanie's problem. "It won't be the same tomorrow without her," Tracy said. On Wednesday a few of the Thespain Ladies were taking the train (her interest in which Beanie had left with all her heart to Winslow) into Manhattan. There they would see the premiere of an avant-garde film sponsored by PATSY—an organization titled Protect Artists Through Saying Yes that supported creative people offensive to the Establishment, an organization to which Mrs. Canopy had said innumerable *yeses*, one of them the summer home on Lake Pissinowno that Habzi Rabies accidentally had set on fire with an acetylene torch; another of them her townhouse in the East Sixties where the sculptor Louie Daytona was now staying after his release from prison.

"Really, Tracy." Priss laughed. "You know Beanie never gave a good g.d. about our Wednesdays. She slept straight through that wonderful revival of *Candi-*

da, and last time we heard a lecture at the Metropolitan, she wandered out in the park and joined a Puerto Rican softball game."

The ladies laughed. "Oh, our Beanie!" Tracy sighed. But then, Beanie wasn't theirs anymore, was she? Strangely enough, the only time their prosaic friend had ever stayed (at least stayed awake) through an entire poetry reading, she had wandered off with the poet.

"Winslow will find her," said Tracy.

"Will he look?"

"Of course he will. What do you mean?"

"I mean," said Mrs. Ransom, "my dear, they are so utterly *insympathique* and have been for thirty-odd years. Winslow is, like me . . . and you," she added expansively, "an observer of the circus. And Beanie is a . . ." She first thought "elephant" but set it aside as uncharitable. ". . . seal. Life is to Winslow, and me, and you, a silly, sweaty melodrama, in response to which only the deodorant of irony seems sensible, or bearable."

"Well, oh, irony? I've never thought I . . ."

"Yes, yes, yes, it's quite true," interrupted Mrs. Ransom, who did not want her phrasing meddled with. "On the other hand, as Walter Saar said to me on the phone this morning, Beanie will leave a rather *large* hole in Winslow's life. Rather like overlooking the Grand Tetons not to notice she was missing. Now, I imagine that if someday Ernest misplaced *me,* like a golf ball, he might briefly scan the grass with his shoe, but he wouldn't want to hold up the game and would soon decide he could simply get another."

"Priss, you always joke!"

Tracy's friend had to agree that when looking Life in the face she had some difficulty keeping her own straight. "Though Ernest doesn't lose things," she added. "I've lived with him thirty years. He's had the same cigarette case longer than he's had me. A methodical man."

"I don't know why Ernest doesn't go into politics," said Tracy, apropos of nothing, except that all anyone had ever been able to think of to say about Ransom was that he should go into politics. "Why doesn't he?"

"*Qui sait?* He never says anything to me he wouldn't say at a dinner party. I prefer that," Priss quickly added. "Intimacy doesn't appeal to me. I like Ernest because his surface is so deep."

"I *think* I know what you mean. Oh, my, it's late. I must go take Vincent some flowers."

Priss's chiseled upper lip twitched at the edge of her coffee cup. She rather disapproved of Tracy's increasingly frequent visits to the grave site of the late Mr. Canopy. The act smacked of, what? The Pre-Raphaelites. Or worse, Elizabeth Barrett Browning. Of their foursome, she and Tracy had always played the roles of the enlightened sophisticates, cynics and critics, whereas Evelyn Troyes had been cast as the moonstruck romantic. And Beanie as (what was her son Ray's term?), as, yes, the jock. Now, not only was Evelyn burning a tank of gas a day in pursuit of that pink-cheeked curate, Jonathan Fields, but Beanie had run sexually amok, and Tracy was off twice a week scattering roses on her husband's tomb. Mrs. Ransom began to wonder if perhaps she were missing something, if something were missing. Annoyingly, a phrase from that anonymous letter bullied its vulgar way into her mind. Did she, after all, have whatever it was up her tushie? Could one be a Lezzie and not notice? She thought it unlikely. Even if the big dong had never much appealed either.

Today was the seventh anniversary of Vincent Canopy's completely unexpected death while discussing golf clubs with Ernest Ransom during the celebration at the Dingley Country Club of Vincent's twenty pleasant years with Tracy Dixwell.

"Excuse me, Ernest, been feeling a little off," he had said, and gone to the men's room. There they had searched for him when time came to toast the couple's long life and happiness.

"I'll never forget it," Father Highwick often remarked. "Vincent there in the booth, the door open, seated on the bowl, a carnation in his lapel, his head lowered nearly to his knees like a man in deep thought, or perhaps looking for a key. 'Something troubling you, Vincent?' I asked. Poor fellow, he toppled right over, dead, though I didn't know it, and gave himself a nasty crack on the head."

Despite being on the spot, there had been nothing Dr. Otto Scaper could do. Others at the festivity also became ill, though none as critically. The rumor raced through town that Carl Marco, Sr., grocer and caterer, had poisoned Dingley Falls's entire upper class. Dr. Scaper said it looked like old Malta fever to him, but admitted that brucellosis didn't usually kill people like that. Everyone then decided that Mr. Canopy must have imported a bug from New York City, which was known to be full of germs. A week later, however, Mrs. Cecil Hedgerow (Pauline Moffat Hedgerow—Dr. Scaper's own god-daughter, and Polly's mother) had died, and three days after that Joe MacDermott's mother in Madder had died, both with the same symptoms as Vincent Canopy. Neither woman had shopped at Marco's, neither had traveled to New York, and neither had been in contact with Mr. Canopy, who commuted to "the City" during the week—and undoubtedly would have wished he had not made an exception to stay home for his twentieth wedding anniversary. Yet these three people, among others who recovered, had suddenly died of apparently the same disease. Gossip said it was very peculiar. Then Gossip forgot it.

Today Vincent's widow went to visit him. She took with her a memorial bouquet and a sonnet whose final couplet read: "Seven years, seven long and lonely years, since last/We spoke, and oh, so pokey time has passed." Vincent was sleeping with his Dixwell in-laws

in a sunny corner of the Old Town Burial Ground that
rose above the green behind Town Hall and the
Congregational Church. By climbing an incline of
Bredforets, Ransoms, Goffs, and of Dingley Falls
judges, babies, generals, and beloved wives, by turning
left at the statue of Charles Bradford Dingley IV—a
full figure in Quincy pink granite by Daniel Chester
French—the largest sarcophagus in the cemetery and
the only one without a body beneath it (the body, the
bones by now, were presumably somewhere near the
Argonne), finally and a little breathless, Tracy Canopy
joined her late spouse.

She unfolded a low canvas stool and sat down beside
a high sphere of flattened panels made of crushed
automobiles, an abstract rendering of *Victory over
Death* which the widow had commissioned from the
subsequently unjustly imprisoned sculptor Louie Daytona. At its base was a bronze plaque:

VINCENT TYLER CANOPY

1908–1969

HERE RESTS A LOVING MAN WHOSE HEART
WAS GIVEN FREELY TO HIS FRIENDS, AND ART.

"Oh, Vincent, Vincent, I wish you were here," said
his wife to the side door of a maroon Buick. "More and
more I wish you hadn't died."

By talking over her concerns with her husband, by
reading him her cutouts from the world of the arts and
sharing the news of her life, Tracy had become very
good friends with Vincent in the years since his death.
Actually, even before that they had gotten along nicely.
Having met at the Met (as they afterwards joked), the
couple had married over the protests of no one. Being
both well named, well taught, wealthy, and healthy,
they were declared to be well matched. Personally,
Vincent had been slightly more . . . physical than she,

but the passion that had not passed him by while he was away in the City all week making his investments was with time safely in the past, where it could not leap out at Tracy, who frankly confessed finally that she "would rather not." Their basic compatibility had been solidified by Canopy's demise and was now as solidly welded as his tomb.

"Vincent, you'll never guess. Beanie's gone, oh, my, well, I don't know what to call it. Who could have known? She eloped with a poet last night," Mrs. Canopy explained as she always had, for her husband had never kept up with Dingley Falls gossip. "With one of *my* poets. What can I say to Winslow? He'll wonder why I didn't try to stop her. I think I'll write him first, before I see him, not just that I'm sorry but just to let him know . . . oh, my, let him know what? I wish you were here to take him off somewhere nice for dinner and be his friend. But Beanie, too, what can she be feeling?"

With a sigh, Tracy arranged her husband's jonquils in the candelabra of polished tailpipes atop the metallic sphere. "I was robbed, too. Priss, you know her cynical mind, Priss thinks Babaha did it, stole everything and put it in her duffel bag while I was at our Thespian Ladies lunch. Where Beanie met him. Mr. Rage. But I can't believe she would do such a thing. Babaha, I mean. Or Beanie. Really, so many strange things seem to be happening. Mr. Hayes, you never liked him, told me Otto thinks our water's been poisoned. And I met a nice young girl from Vietnam, beaten up by her husband, and he's in jail. How can things like that be happening in Dingley Falls? Remember how we never even used to lock the front door, and we used to think how different it was here from Manhattan? Was it so long ago?"

It should not be assumed that Mrs. Canopy addressed her deceased husband in a way that suggested mental disturbance; perhaps it would be fairer to say that while her conversational tone might have suggested to a casual passerby some such problem, she was quite capable of distinguishing reality from fantasy. She needed a vehicle to receive her thoughts, and Vincent's Buick had come to serve that purpose. She did not, necessarily, assume that he lay listening beneath it. For that matter, he had rarely listened when he had sat across from her at dinner, or before the living room fire. The change was that he no longer got up and went to bed before she finished.

Mrs. Canopy stretched out her legs and recrossed her ankles with a sigh. How ridiculous not to be able to sit on a low stool without cramps, creaks, and mottled skin that had lost its circulation. How annoyingly unavoidable aging was. She had been right never to become too involved with her body. It only betrayed you in the end, deserted the highest Olympic jumper as well as she, who had only trotted, swatted, swum, and touched her toes for the four years she'd been obliged to do so by a college gym instructor. And the worst of it was that when the body finally did collapse of its own puniness, it dragged *you* right along with it. You had no choice but to follow it down into the grave. It was really maddening, after all.

"Now, stop it!" Mrs. Canopy told herself sharply. "Sometimes you have to just not think." And so she sat for a while and watched two thoughtless bobolinks. But mind, despite ten lessons, would not be controlled. "You know that letter I found? Priss got one, too, terribly ugly. I didn't tell her about mine. Being called a fool is worse, I think. Perhaps I am one, after all. I feel so . . . expendable. I've never worked in all my silly life, well, except for those two years for the USO, I suppose I could count them. But my charities and my poor artists. Remember we used to call our artists our children? Maybe we were wrong not to have any children, except I did know, I thought, I wouldn't be very good at it. But what a waste I am. Poor Beanie. You know, nothing has ever been really the matter with me or really horrible happened, except, you know, of

course, when I lost you. But they advertise late at night
the most pitiful souls, deformed or starved and dying
day after day. And I can't even claim to understand it.
How could I say I did?" She straightened a flower.
"But I'm watching, and the funny thing is I keep falling
asleep and I wake up, well, in tears without warning.
Sometimes I wonder if I shouldn't *see* somebody about
it. Suddenly I wake up in tears, and quite a bit of time
has simply vanished. Isn't that funny?"

Mrs. Canopy wasn't at all certain she thought it was
funny, but she had always tried to look at life, if not
with Priss's derisive snort of laughter, at least with the
smile she now gave her husband's tomb.

CHAPTER
15

No man can escape the detection of his housekeeper,
whether a paid one or his wife. Sammy Smalter was not
married, but his rooms on the third floor of Ramona
Dingley's house were cleaned every Wednesday by
Mrs. Orchid O'Neal, who therefore knew more about
the druggist than anyone else in Dingley Falls, Fortunately, she was not a gossip, or at least she did not
grasp the significance of those clues which he preferred
to keep secret, or at least she had no one to tell them to
but her sister, Sarah MacDermott. Mrs. O'Neal had,
however, made a discovery today, by cleaning on
Tuesday rather than Wednesday, that she thought she
should share. To her amazement, Mr. Smalter kept a
machine gun under his bed and could have been
dreaming of destroying them all.

There was another gun the town already knew about.
This was Limus Barnum's .357 Magnum, with which he

had shot himself through the heel of his bedroom slipper while chasing a, he said, black burglar across his front lawn and through June Hayes's herb garden. The burglar had allegedly escaped with a tape cassette and a vicuña jacket, and Limus had subsequently appeared in a photograph in *The Dingley Day* pointing at the pistol with which he had protected his home.

The right to bear arms was one thing, but what did a pharmacist need with a machine gun? If it was not for the drug addicts he supplied in his drugstore, it was, decided Orchid's sister, Sarah MacDermott, for mass murder. She was not unique in considering Mr. Smalter an eccentric anyhow—his most evident eccentricity being the fact that he was only four and a half feet tall. "The dwarf's an oddball," Lime told A. A. Hayes. "He gives me the willies." "Poor Sammy, but I do think wearing a *yellow* bow tie in the winter is going too far," Father Highwick told Jonathan Fields. "He could be dreaming of murdering us all in our beds," Sarah MacDermott told her sister, Orchid. But Sammy Smalter was not a dwarf and hated to be called one. He was a midget, or he was somewhere, depending on the textbook consulted, between midgethood and low man on the totem pole of height. No one in town knew exactly why he should have been so afflicted; he had simply stopped growing. Gladys Goff suspected it was because his maternal great-grandfather, Charles Bradford Dingley III, had married a servant girl. That servant girl, Bridget Quin Dingley, was sure the boy was a midget because her daughter had married a cornet player out of a Chautauqua tent, who, losing his lip, had taken her money to open the Smalter Pharmacy right on the Dingley Green. Whatever the cause, this man's grandson, Samuel Ignatius Dingley Smalter, was extremely short, though certainly not a dwarf.

"As perfect proportioned as you or me," Orchid O'Neal told her sister. "And Sarah, you should see his little sink and toilet Miss Dingley ordered in just his size when he first came there to live, and cute as a dollhouse. And socks and boxer shorts no bigger than your Francis's, stacked up in his drawers neat as a pin with all his pills. He orders his T-shirts, I've seen the packages come in, from Saks Fifth Avenue in the children's department. Quite a savings, he says too, in his joking way, buying in boys' sizes, menswear being so overpriced. Well, you know how that's a fact better than most."

Sarah MacDermott did indeed know it, for she had five weedy sons and an overweight husband. "Joe, Jr." She grimaced in agreement. "You remember the blue herringbone I almost got him at Penney's last April? Well, the exact same one is on sale now for twenty-three ninety-nine *more* that it was *original*-priced a year ago."

"Mr. Smalter's suits have his name hand-stitched right into them."

"Yes, it can't go on. You work all your life and year after year you can afford less and less. People won't stand for it one of these days, Orchid."

"We're better off than any other country, though, that's certain."

"People just ought to refuse to put up with it."

Orchid O'Neal and Sarah MacDermott, the former O'Reilly sisters and granddaughters of the Madder patriarch Francis O'Reilly, whose freckled progeny filled a dozen pews at Our Lady of Mercy, were arguing economic revolution at the A & P. Meanwhile, Sarah was ringing up the groceries Orchid had purchased for Ramona Dingley and Sammy Smalter, whose housekeeper she was until two o'clock, when she became Evelyn Troyes's housekeeper until six o'clock, when she became her own. Orchid lived next to her sister in a four-family blockhouse across the Rampage from the Dingley Optical Instruments factory, where Orchid's husband had worked until his death. After the widow's own children had fled Madder for a better life in California, her squabbling young MacDermott nephews kept her empty apartment filled with the sounds of the past. They gave her somebody to love, just as the people on Elizabeth Circle gave her "somebody to do for." To clean for someone had been her life's work, and she was quite proud that she did it so well.

Sarah, however, took offense at her sister's profession. The time had been, a century ago, when everybody kept an Irish girl indentured in the kitchen, offering her in exchange for her service a drafty attic room and time off to rush to early Mass. Sarah maintained that the Irish had served America long enough and, having risen even to the presidency, deserved servants themselves—hired from among the less tenured minorities. "Well, I guess Francis O'Reilly clambered and climbed out of a peat bog to sail to New England and open his own liquor store so his granddaughter—" Sarah grabbed a jar of mustard. "Seventy-nine cents! Can you believe that? Sixty-nine just yesterday! Orchid, remember how I told you, don't buy the name brands. They put the exact same junk in A & P cans— Climbed out of a bog so you could pass your mornings washing out a dwarf's socks." She rang up the mustard and backhanded it to Luke Packer. "And why that Mrs. Troyes couldn't make do with a nice colored girl instead of sitting on her fanny while another white woman vacuumed her floor is something she'll have to try explaining to her Maker. These tomatoes are green on the bottom, don't buy anything you can't see all the way around. I guess Granddad's up in heaven pulling out his hair by the roots to see you a servant still, while Grandma and the angels watch in pity. Baby clams?!"

"If it's salary you're talking about, Sarah, I'll have you know I make more than you do."

Mrs. MacDermott laughed. "Jesus bless us, the holy blind nuns with their begging cups make more than *I* do." She ate three of Sammy Smalter's grapes, then dropped them into a plastic bag.

"Just tell me why shoving about other people's food is more high and mighty than tidying a decent home, I wouldn't mind knowing?" asked Orchid.

"Scrubbing the ring on his 'cute little' sink!"

"I like Mr. Smalter. He's a good man for all his affliction, and very considerate to me. 'Rest your feet, Mrs. O'Neal, have you had a bite of lunch yet?' He always has a decent word."

"A bite of lunch? Watch he doesn't have a bite of your legs one of these days while you're bending over his cute little tub! Didn't you just now tell me how he's got a machine gun under his bed?"

"I don't mind saying it gave me a shock seeing that ugly thing poked out from under the dust ruffle. But he *is* the sole protection of his aunt."

"A machine gun? I guess he thinks the Russians are sailing up the Rampage after his aunt?"

"Could be it's a war souvenir of his dad's."

Sarah filled her eyes round with incredulity and then rolled them. "Mind yourself. That's all. Dwarfs can turn vicious without a minute's warning."

"He's not a dwarf, and if God made him a midget, He has His own reasons, and if Jesus Himself didn't mind eating supper with prostitutes and washing the smelly feet of fishermen, I bet He don't mind me washing Mr. Smalter's sink." With that rebuttal Orchid ended, for today, a six-year argument and changed the subject. "Well, that's too bad what you say about Judith being sick. Right on top of the poor Sister with her heart giving out, passing away alone like that in the night with no chance for the Last Rites."

"Well, it don't mean Judith'll be gone in a week. Like I told her last night on the phone, 'Honey, sometimes people live their whole life long with a bad heart, so don't you let it worry you.' I told Hawk the same. Him and Joe got on the phone about Maynard Henry. Did I tell you that the people in Argyle locked Maynard up with that crazy old man, the one, you remember, that was out shaking his black dingle in the innocent faces of little white children? Joe said Maynard was just about foaming at the mouth, he was so mad being shut up with that old Negro. Put in with a *loco,* like *he* was a loco. When everybody knows that Raoul Treeca has had it coming to him a long time, and just lucky it was only his legs and ribs and his Chevy, and not worse."

"Well, I don't care. Maynard had no business hitting that poor little wife of his in the face. I don't believe for a minute she knew what she was doing getting in that truck with Raoul Treeca. But Maynard's quick to hurt. He always was."

"Wouldn't surprise me if he shoved *Hawk's* car off a cliff when he gets out. After this latest." Mrs. MacDermott slid a pencil in and out of her yellow topknot. "Well, come and eat with us tonight. I grabbed a real nice London broil right when the truck pulled in. *If* your society folks let you off in time."

Outside Luke Packer loaded Mrs. O'Neal's groceries into Ramona Dingley's Pontiac Firebird. The elderly shut-in bought a new car every year—each one racier than the last—as if she thought she could outdrag death if she only had the horsepower.

"I sure would love to have this car," Luke sighed. "I'm going to work for Mr. Smalter in the drugstore."

"Well, that's nice." Orchid smiled.

"Listen, did you happen to ask him what he had a machine gun for?"

"Oh, not for the world. I'm scared to death what he'll do when he finds out I was in his room on the wrong day. Oh, no, I didn't ask him. He would have snapped my head off for sure."

The social circle of Dingley Falls was named Elizabeth, and on it lived, clockwise, the Abernathys, Mrs. Troyes, the Ransoms, Dr. Scaper, Ramona Dingley, and Mrs. Canopy, each with a few acres' privacy. All the houses had their birth dates discreetly displayed near their doors. Unlike the rest of them, Ramona Dingley's home was not an eighteenth-century one. It was Victorian, a festooned wedding cake of a house that had in fact been a wedding gift. It was frosted with

gables, gambrels, a mansard roof, and a widow's walk.
It was a scrolled and gewgawed hobby-house personally
designed by Ramona's grandfather, Charles Bradford
Dingley III, when—to the horror of his neighbors—he
had wantonly torn down the perfectly good Federalist
house of his forebears to replace it with this Taj Mahal
for his Irish bride. "Waste not, want not" had been his
neighbors' philosophy with regard to so much as a used
soup bone, much less a used house. They said it was
lucky that Charles III had already sent his mother,
Augusta, to her grave by eloping with her parlormaid,
because this demolition of the family homestead would
have struck her down even more cruelly.

Inside, the house was as dark as the outside was
sugar-white. Its rooms were somber and muffled with
thick sofas and drapes. All over the enormous parlor
perched stuffed wild animals and religious icons: taxidermy and Catholicism having been the two pastimes of
Ramona's long-dead father, Ignatius, second son of the
architectural Charles Bradford Dingley III and of
Bridget Quin, that wily parlormaid who (according to
Charles's mother) had tricked the sensitive youth into a
misalliance (marriage) by telling him that the Virgin
Mary had visited her in the pantry where she had
announced that Bridget and Charles were destined to
give birth to another St. Francis. As things turned out,
their son, Ignatius, though obsessively religious, had
failed to found an order. He *had* loved animals, but had
preferred them stuffed. Now, like the rest of the house,
his collected passions belonged to his only surviving
child, Ramona. On the mantel an owl flapped open its
sooty wings beside a crimson bleeding heart, and a
scrawny otter hid among St. Sebastian's brass arrows.
Two bobcats leaped out from the window ledges at
guests already distracted by a life-sized German wood
carving of Christ crucified on the wall.

Unlike her home, Ramona was very eighteenth-
century. She had left the house furnished just as her
father had left it to her, not out of sentiment, but as a

raffish decorator might stick a Picasso satyr in the middle of a Dutch Colonial boudoir. So, wryly, Miss Dingley placed herself in her father's mansion.

"Awful, ain't it?" she asked, for even her grammar had an eighteenth-centry flavor—once an affectation, now a habit. Miss Dingley was speaking to Father Jonathan Fields, whose bright, plastic-covered eyes stared at the bright glass eyes of a racoon that clung to a bookshelf.

"Oh, no. They're very well done. Is taxidermy your hobby?"

She guffawed as rudely as Dr. Johnson. "Don't be an idiot. And don't think I'm one. They're my father's. Loved graven images. Stuffed ones, too. One of those types of Catholics enraptured by anything killed in an unpleasant way. Have some port."

"No, thank you. I'm sorry. I don't drink." The curate sat in his immaculate black clerical suit in a high-backed chair with claws carved into the arms. Across the tea (or port) table Ramona Dingley perched, also in black, on a motorized wheelchair which, to her visitor's disconcertion, she kept starting and stopping in little jumps as she talked. She liked motion. A private elevator brought her plummeting down each morning from her fourth-floor bedroom. Her housekeeper drove her briskly around Lake Pissinowno in the Firebird, but never fast enough. Ramona was a thin person whom age had annoyingly loaded down with weight. Her hawk face jutted strangely out of the fat—hawks are rarely obese—and her plump arms ended strangely in strong, thin hands.

"Oh, yes, you said so last night." She poured two hefty goblets of port. "You should drink though." She held the goblet out until he-took it. "Do you a world of good. *In vino veritas*, and that's what we're here for."

"Yes, I brought you the books, Miss Dingley."

"Don't be literal. I meant here on earth. We're put here on earth for a piddling span in order to learn the truth. And do you know what we learn?" She drank up her port. "That we're here on earth for a piddling span. Absurd, ain't it?"

"Life?"

"Death! Life's not absurd. Not unless you try to make sense of it. Notice, young man, your Rector don't. He's a happy man, Sloan Highwick. A shoo-in for heaven should there be one."

"But you don't think there is?" Father Fields, at a loss, tried to lead Miss Dingley toward those problems for help with which he was, he assumed, being asked.

"Don't talk shop right off the bat. I don't get many visitors. And Sammy's forever up in his room at his typewriter. No evidence, but I suspect he's a blackmailer. Got barrels of money. Went away for a weekend once right after my heart attack. Brought me back a case of my favorite wine."

"That was thoughtful."

"It certainly was. Bought it in Paris for me. Knocked me over. Found it hard to believe."

So did Jonathan Fields.

"Yes, barrels of money. I don't grudge him. Compensatory, don't you know, for being a tad on the short side. One of God's little lapses of concentration. Too proud to ask a woman out. Hard for an Adonis like yourself to imagine, no doubt, but Sammy thinks he'll be rejected. Probably right."

But then the curate himself, six feet tall and with (according to Father Highwick) the face of a Botticelli angel, was afraid to ask anyone out. That is, afraid to ask Walter Saar.

"*So.*" His hostess grabbed a Chinese ivory walking stick out of the paws of a stuffed bear that reared up beside the couch and, as she spoke, swatted the air with it. "Who can I talk to? I turn to the church. They *got* to come. May get a recruit. Neighbors won't, any more than they have to to be decent. People are scared of the old. Scared they'll drool down their chins or have fits and die right in front of them. Feel guilty because the old bore them. Embarrass them. And because they're

so glad they're not tottering into six feet of wormy dirt
any minute now. I know *I* gloated when I was young.
Whenever that was."

The swinging cane whisked by Jonathan's head.
"You were," he said, "I think the Rector told me,
weren't you a professional tennis player once?"

"Yes. I was. Hard to believe now, ain't it? God could
lob me for the moon, round and pasty as I am now."

Jonathan found this image so unnerving that he
laughed, then blushed, then mumbled an apology.

"Why? Don't be sorry. Always laugh when folks
joke about themselves. Always encourage sanity. It
helps. That'd be a better job for the church than trying
to figure out whether that idiot, God, exists or not. Yes,
I played tennis. Too rich to do anything worthwhile.
Family wouldn't have stood for it. Would have cut me
off without a nickel, then where would I be now? Off
with a bedpan in the state home without my elevator,
or *this*. My wheels." She slapped her wheelchair with
affection. "Yes, all the old were young and had a life
they cared about, and a body someone paid attention
to. But the young can't see the first and get sick
thinking about the second. Tennis was my passion. Not
that the family didn't cringe when I stopped playing a
prissy game in the backyard on Sundays and took off to
the tournaments. With a sheer *lust* for victory. Won a
lot of them, too, got the trophies up in my room.
Lance, Beanie's boy, you know him? He gets it from
me. So did Beanie. A sportsman in every generation of
Dingleys. I was better than Lance'll ever be. I had the
killer instinct. And at least a few brains. Now I hear my
niece has vamoosed." (Beanie Abernathy was not Miss
Dingley's niece, nor was Sammy Smalter her nephew;
they were both, to different degrees, her cousins.
Nevertheless, each of them called her "Aunt," though
they never seemed to consider that they were consequently also related. They scarcely knew each other at
all.) Ramona poured more port. "Good healthy lust is
a fine thing. Sorry I was too wrapped up in the game to

get a man. Back then you had to choose. Life or marriage. Too late now, of course. Shock would kill me. Sex at this late date."

The curate was increasingly alarmed. What should he say to any of this? Her words and her wheelchair jumped at him in the same fast jerks.

"That idiot Winslow," she went on after a long drink. "Good, decent man. No killer instinct though. Knew he was bound to lose Beanie if a man in the market ever got within striking distance and gave her a shake to bring her to. But. None of my business. Tell me now." She raced her chair abruptly forward at the startled priest. "That girl. Skinny girl with the frizzy hair. You know her. Hedgerow. You know her. The one that flies all over town on the red bicycle, with all the books."

"Polly Hedgerow?"

"Get her for me."

"Get her?"

"Tell her to come see me. Tell her, do a good deed, call on the old dying shut-in, don't you know. Tell her my house is full of unheard-of things. She'll be curious. I would have."

"Of course, all right, I'll be happy to. She comes to see the Rector a lot and I'll ask her."

Miss Dingley made a spitting noise. "Comes to see Sloan? What for? Not one of those moony adolescent religious fanatics, is she?"

"Oh, no, I don't think so. I believe she and the Rector, well, I gather they just, well, exchange news, sort of, about people in Dingley Falls. From what I've overheard, I mean."

"Gossip! Sloan always did. Oh, don't look shocked. I don't mean malicious. He hasn't got the brains to be malicious. Well, ask her."

"All right."

"Now. You're eager to save my soul as quick as you can and get on with your own affairs. So tell me, Jonathan—absurd for me to call a baby like you

'Father'—what do you think of this?" She poured him more port. "The idea came to me after our enjoyable quarrel last night. Be pleased I fix my mind on theology and ain't just luring you here to fix my eyes on you. Don't be modest. You know you're gorgeous. If you don't, your skull's even emptier than Sloan's. But. Now Christ is taken down from the Cross. Alive. That's my point. After all, it was Passover, wasn't it? So they only left him up there six hours. Without a bone broken, remember. Now I checked, what a pack of monsters, those Romans, and it often took two, maybe three days to kill a man by crucifixion. The human race, well. Jesus wept, but I suspect somebody was laughing. So! Here's your Christ, a young man, no bad habits, healthy, in his early thirties. Probably simply lapsed into a coma, I should imagine. Wakes up at Joseph of Arimathea's—rich fellow, had a previous arrangement with the soldiers. Paid them off to take away the body, didn't he?"

"Yes," said Father Fields weakly. Port fumes and Miss Dingley's theory crashed in his head.

"All makes sense. Jesus wakes up, goes back to His carpentry shop in Galilee. No doubt by now He's sensibly concluded He never should have left it in the first place. Those moronic disciples of His find out from the women they left at the tomb, too scared to stick themselves, that Christ is gone! Ascended! Naturally, they don't believe a word of it at first. Would you? Then gradually the notion dawns on them. The Messiah! If He beat death, they've got a miracle worth the world. They head home to spread the good news. Who do they spot on the road but Jesus Himself, nail holes in His hands and fed up with trying to talk idiots into salvation. Of course, they can see that their whole religion is going to be laughed off the map if their risen Christ is seen tapping out cabinets in Nazareth. So! *They* kill Him! How about that? Find a flaw."

Passion and port drove the shy curate to his feet. "But no, you see, no! You're talking about it from the

wrong . . . I mean the mystery isn't whether . . .
Christ was the Son of God, Miss Dingley. That's *my*
point. He was God. *God* died. God chose to suffer the
ugliest, most sordid death the most wretched of us
could die. Public execution! Think of the shame. God
felt it. To free you! I'm sorry, I don't mean to yell."

"You're not yelling. Don't apologize, even if you
were. You believe it, don't you?"

"Yes."

"Well, stick to it. Now how exactly is God's public
execution supposed to free me from anything?"

"Well, because it does. It frees you, you see, the
moment you fully and, well, freely believe that it
does."

"Does what?"

"Free you."

"And that's faith, I suppose. Quite a trick. Too easy,
you ask me."

"Oh, I don't agree. Almost too hard. As hard for us
as it is to, I guess, allow ourselves to be happy."

"Pah. Now what's to keep me from believing any-
thing· I want to? Suppose I said, I don't know,
Eichmann's execution set me free?"

"The point isn't that God *died*. It's that *God* died."

"Well, young man, it's a question of temperament,
ain't it?" She frowned, then grinned. "And then He
ascended into heaven and sits at the right hand of His
Father, and all the believers are up there too? Am I a
daughter of God?"

"I feel quite sure you are."

"Well, Mr. Fields, I sat at the right hand of my father
long enough. In there." She jabbed the walking stick at
the door to the cavernous dining room. "And he was a
relentless believer. I hope you're not telling me I have
that horrible experience to look forward to again. Must
I be resurrected? Couldn't I simply turn into fertilizer
and help out, don't you know, a few nasturtiums
behind Town Hall?"

CHAPTER
16

From behind her iron grille, Mrs. Haig saw the pink circle ringed with yellow tufts as Mr. Smalter moved across the foyer over to the wall of post office boxes. Later than usual he had come to check his mail. With a spin of the lock, he removed the letters, turned, and waved the white envelopes in her direction. "Thank you."

Judith raised herself on the stool to lean over. "Hello, Mr. Smalter."

He came closer. "You didn't mention yesterday that you'd be leaving the post office. Otto told me. I'll miss seeing you here. I'm an old creature of habit, and you see, you're a part of my day."

"Thank you," she said without looking at him. "But it will be easier for Alf, for Mr. Marco, here in the office. He's really getting too old to have to do the deliveries, and someone new will do that."

"And you?"

She said nothing.

"Ah. You have your new house. A great deal to do there."

"Yes."

They fell silent.

He glanced through his letters. "Maybe you noticed, I've been putting a new address on all those packages. After 'a lull in the hot race'?"

"Oh?" Having for seven years seen the thick manila envelopes addressed to James Poe and Sons, the postmistress had of course been unable to avoid seeing a new name typed there instead.

"That relationship, with Jimmy Poe's sons, exhausted itself, Mrs. Haig." Smalter slid his letters into the pocket of his three-piece-suit jacket. It was striped blue seersucker, as it always was in June. "I got a little rancorous and then they got a little rancorous and so it seemed best to call it quits on my birthday. Forty-two!" He opened his hand in apology or resignation at that figure.

"Forty-two? So am I," she heard herself say. This conversation was the longest Judith had ever had with a man whom she had seen several times a day, through her bars, for close to a decade. It must be, she thought, because of our hearts that we can talk now.

"Our prime, they say," said Mr. Smalter after another pause.

"They do?"

"Don't they say life begins at forty? Let's not give up hope. No, James Poe and I have parted company. You know, you've never even asked me why I have some letters sent to this box and others sent to Elizabeth Circle."

"I don't like to pry."

"Of course not. Yes, you must know all our secrets, all our lives passing through your hands day after day."

She frowned, blushing. "It's very impersonal. I mean, I don't look at them."

"No, of course not. But wait, wait, *we* are surely old friends?" His overlarge blue eyes stared up at her through the grille with an odd mixture of wryness and expectation.

Mrs. Haig's mouth very slowly formed her serious smile. "Yes," she answered. "Yes, we are."

"Then don't you wonder? Ask me something."

There was nothing she wanted to know. She already knew two things about Sammy Smalter. Because she was the postmistress, she could not avoid knowing that he sent packages and letters to publishers, that he received packages and letters back. For the same reason that she felt her husband John's pain before he felt it, she could not avoid knowing that Mr. Smalter was, hard for her to say the phrase, in love with her. It was unavoidably present in his eyes, as was his effort not to reveal it. Her duty was not to give him the pain of realizing that she saw it and pitied him for it. So there was nothing she needed to ask him. But he stood there and needed her to speak. "Ask away," he said again.

"All right. You're a writer?"

He laughed; he had small, white teeth like a child's. "Ah, well," he said. "*Not* in fact the question most people are shy about asking me. Yes, I'm afraid it's true. Just popular pulp though." His smile went to his eyes and shut out the other look. "But no one in Dingley Falls knows, and you mustn't tell a soul. When I came back home I decided not to mention my hobby. But you were bound to know. No, no, I'm glad you finally asked me. Well, I won't keep you from your work. But I'm glad somebody knows, and I'm glad that it's you. Have a good day now. In our prime, you know." He patted the counter top briskly, turned, and left the post office.

In front of The Tea Shoppe, Luke Packer leaned his old bike against Polly Hedgerow's new one, as Mr. Abernathy got out of his son Arthur's Audi, which Arthur then drove away.

"Hi, Mr. Abernathy." Luke waved. But the thin, graying man walked right past him, and, embarrassed, Luke lowered his hand to pull his ear.

Then the lawyer turned. "Oh, sorry. Hello, Luke. Wool-gathering, I guess." His voice was muffled with preoccupation as he searched through his pockets. With a nod he hurried on, finally having found the key to open his office door.

Luke's face was pressed against Miss Lattice's window when Mr. Smalter poked a short finger in the boy's spine. " 'You're covered, Shades,' " the druggist quoted. " 'Let me see all nine of those fingers point at the Big Dipper.' "

Luke spun. "Hi. I know. Ben Rough, *Murder by Machine Gun*, right?"

"Absolutely. Well, tomorrow then, we start in together, waiting for someone to buy something. We'll get a lot of reading done. Glad you changed your mind."

"Sure, I'll be there, nine o'clock."

"Going in for a late lunch?"

"Just messing around. I've got to be over at Mr. Hayes's at three. Just looking for a friend now."

The little man straightened his yellow bow tie. "Like us all. 'Love is best,' Luke. Good luck."

The friend Luke sought was, as he expected, inside The Tea Shoppe. The place was crowded, but not with the clientele its proprietor would have preferred. To Miss Lattice's horror, the dread day had come again; school vacation was upon her. Gathered to slouch in her cane-backed chairs were not only half the "townies" at Dixwell High School, but all the stray boys cutting class from Alexander Hamilton Academy. Miss Lattice's Tea Shoppe had fallen on younger days, which was not at all what Prudence Lattice had intended to happen.

At Joy Strummer's table, Luke saw to his chagrin not only Joe MacDermott, Jr., and Tac Hayes, but the academy hotshot Ray Ransom and one of his nerdie roommates. And with them sat Polly Hedgerow—ostentatiously reading a book.

"Hiya."

"Hiya."

Luke dragged over a chair, bumping it along the floor. (Miss Lattice winced.) Ray Ransom was shooting off as usual. "So I said, 'Who, me shoplift? You think I need to steal a stupid tube of airplane glue from this dump?' Then I charged a new amplifier to my mom; man, that shut him right up. That jerk Barnum."

"That's right." The nerd nodded. "Then he walked right out with a whole box of the glue right there under his raincoat!"

"Oh, everybody does it," modestly admitted Ray. No one had a comment. Ray Ransom was the only local boy to board at Alexander Hamilton. The academy had obliged Ernest Ransom, chairman of their board of trustees, by making an exception for his son, and for the same reason Walter Saar restrained himself from expelling the young man who had absolutcly nothing to offer but looks, wealth, and a quick tongue. It was enough to get by on, though not enough to get Joy Strummer.

Luke poked Polly too hard in the arm. "Whatcha reading, dope?"

"A book."

"Thanks a lot."

The young men crunched ice cubes and wolfed cheese sandwiches brought them by Chin Henry. Miss Lattice had turned a deaf ear to all requests for hamburgers, french fries, and pizzas. Let them petition McDonald's to come to Dingley Falls, she said. Let them leave her alone.

The young men devoured pastries and tried to outwait one another, though the victor—the last one left with Joy—would then shuffle away, too, no troth plighted other than "You be here tomorrow, huh, Joy?" The instinct herding them with their rivals was as yet still stronger than romance.

And in their midst Joy reposed. Her pink scooped jersey was imprinted "Keep On Trucking." Her pink shorts were embroidered with rainbows and comets. Wooden clogs enclosed her pink feet. Her blond hair curled, her starry eyes shone, her stung lips blushed. "Boy, now that is one foxy lady," Ray Ransom informed his roommate, who replied, "Sure. But if you get caught off limits with a townie, Saar will put your dick through a meat grinder." "Up yours, you'd love it." "Up yours, you've done it." And so on and on until sleep silenced them. Joy did not know how centrally she figured in the nightly *débats* of Academy Hall, but the news would not have surprised her. The pleasant discovery that she was unusually beautiful had been verified in the past year beyond the need for further testimonials. She knew she was gifted. Now she had only to give the gift away. Had only like pollen plume of the spring-blooming birch to float. To float until wind, fate, choice, swept her down to where, of all possibilities, earth was rightest and ripest for her.

And, tapping time to "Let It Go All Over," by the Stabbo-Massacrism Band, his U. Mass. ring click-clacking on the steering wheel of his Jaguar, Lance Abernathy was riding into town. Up the pike he tooled in his birthday present from his mother, Beanie. Every few miles he tossed a quarter into the state's collection plates with the flip unpremeditation of a cardinal throwing pennies at Parisian peasants in June 1789. For Lance was soon to be overthrown.

His less handsome, more methodical twin, Arthur, had never gotten through to him at his Forest Hills motel; Lance, when not on the courts, was out courting in sporty bars. Actually, Arthur had rarely in their thirty-two years (thirty-one *ex utero*) gotten through to his twin brother. So this time, as had always been his habit in the past, he left a message. Like "Get your junk out of my closet!" "Return my pullover!" "You owe me ten dollars!" this one was exclamatory and might have been rephrased "What did you do with my mother?!"

Of course Lance didn't have her. The news that a stranger did, he found, in retrospect, less of a gas than he had originally remarked to Notta Choencinhelska, a curvy Ukrainian on whom in last night's mixed doubles he had scored. And by the time Lance downshifted on Wild Oat Ridge, the thought of Beanie's abduction made him mad as hell. Perhaps some ultrasensory effervescence of Rage's outrage lingered there, in the forest, and wafted onto Route 3. At any rate, the son's nostrils flared and his fingers stopped tapping.

Mom was out of her mind, he decided; Jesus God, pretty damn humiliating for the rest of the family. Poor old Dad. And this punk poet, this pig, this prof, he was about to get his teeth knocked down his throat. A hell of a nerve, an egghead like that making off with an old lady (making out with her, too, but that part of the picture Lance promptly threw a drop sheet over). When he spun into Dingley Circle, Lance was so choked up that his Jaguar spit to a stop in front of Ransom Bank. Just as well. He'd go there first. He leaped out of the sports car, and, three at a time, up the stone steps he bounded, swung past the Doric columns, and jumped into the quiet, cool interior of the bank. Clerks looked up, their eyes pulled in his direction by the magnetism of outdoor energy in so indoors a place. Ernest Ransom, in conversation with his secretary, followed her glance.

"Help you, Lance?"

"Hey there, Irene; what's the word, Ernest? Just got in. Is my mom, you know, back?"

"No, I don't know. Haven't you been home?" Ransom tried to pinpoint when it was that Lance had begun, uninvited, to address him as "Ernest."

"Nope, thought I'd drop by town first. Seen Dad? How's he taking it?"

"Lance. Really, I think it would be better if you . . ."

"Okay, okay, I'll go over to the office. Wouldn't mind putting it off though. It's going to be rough, you know what I mean?"

"For Winslow, yes, I expect it will." Ransom was annoyed. Lance's unfocused vitality (he almost shadowboxed as he stood there) rasped the banker's composure.

"Rough on a guy to see his folks fall apart. Gets to you. Well, see you around, I'm just here to bounce a check."

The banker lent him a smile. He watched this young man, this embodied cigarette ad, stride up to the young female teller with a grin. Tanned and tall in a white-ribbed body sweater and white pleated trousers, Lance needed only surf and sand to lope along while he inhaled some satisfying smoke in order to look as if he had been cut out of a glossy magazine and pinned above a young girl's bureau. Ransom had to admit that Lance was much better-looking than Arthur, his future son-in-law. Lance with his chestnut hair like Beanie's, with her warm brown eyes, most of all with her—Ransom searched for a word—her physicalness. Still, he preferred Arthur, who, like Winslow, was contained and containable, and who called him "Mr. Ransom."

Cecil Hedgerow entered the bank and joined them at the teller's counter. "What are you doing in here, Cecil? Trying to mooch a cabin cruiser?" Lance grinned.

"No, Ransom is too hard a trout to land. I'll stick to pike."

"And not pikers, eh?" joked Ransom, who matched his manner to his material if possible and was so inoffensive that he could refuse loans to people who then advised him to run for governor to make the state the kind of place in which they could get their loans approved. "Good to see you, Cecil." The hand swung out from the broad Brooks Brothers shoulder and shook Hedgerow's, then the banker returned to his secretary.

"How's life?" asked Lance.

"Hard work," answered Hedgerow, then each went about his own business.

Cecil Hedgerow was the town's third selectman; in other words, the loser in the race for first selectman; in other words, the Democratic candidate. Like the second "selectman," Ramona Dingley, he'd been in office for years, repeatedly elected by a coalition of workers from Madder, where he had grown up, and Dingleyans who did not choose to oblige Ernest

Ransom by voting for whomever the bank president had selected to run the town that term. Arthur Abernathy had been his most recent choice. Arthur had obliged Ransom not only by becoming his first selectman, but also by selecting Ransom's daughter Emerald to be his wife. Cecil Hedgerow did not like Arthur Abernathy, or for that matter Ernest Ransom. Ransom did not like Cecil Hedgerow either. But the antipathy made financial negotiations an agony to Hedgerow, whereas they affected Ransom's decisions not at all.

Like his only child, Polly, Hedgerow was thin and wore glasses; unlike her, the widower's hair, step, and personality no longer had much spring. Still, Madderites admired him, because he had married into a good Dingley Falls family when he married Pauline Moffat, and because they thought he owned Hedgerow Realty Company, which Carl Marco, Sr., really owned. Marco, in fact, who everyone assumed owned only a supermarket, even owned much of Hedgerow Realty's real estate. And Ernest Ransom's bank owned the Hedgerow home. Of major purchases all the Cecil Hedgerow owned was a very expensive violin, a car that he hated, and a motorboat that he loved. He was a religious fly caster; the grail that he worshipped and pursued was the smallmouth black bass, and every weekend in his aluminum boat he renewed his quest on Lake Pissinowno. In the past Lance Abernathy had sometimes swooped down, in the Piper Cub he rented on Saturdays, to buzz Hedgerow—a surprise attack that had never ceased to terrify the fisherman or to delight the pilot.

Hedgerow interrupted Lance's conversation with the now giggling teller to say, "You ought to come out and do some fishing. Been a long time."

"Sure thing. See you around."

The realtor then returned to the trailer near Astor Heights, Carl Marco's new development south on the road to Argyle that most people thought belonged to

Cecil Hedgerow. There he was only occasionally required to set aside *Field and Stream* in order to show a former Madderite, ready to come up in the world, a blueprint of the American Dream.

At The Tea Shoppe, while Miss Lattice kept her eyes fixed on the clock, Luke had persuaded Joy to laugh at his imitation of their stuttering history teacher, Ms. Rideout, who had announced today that she would not be returning in the fall because they had driven her, in a single year, to a view of human nature that was not only incompatible with the pacifism in which she had once believed, but incompatible with her personal sanity.

"I agree with Ms. Rideout," Polly said.

"You would," sighed Joy.

Luke had outlasted even Ray Ransom, but Polly Hedgerow would not leave. She kept on stubbornly reading as if she sat there alone. Finally with a pounce he grabbed the book away from her. "Okay, what's so fascinating?"

"Give that back!" she hissed.

"*Anna Karenina?*" Despite himself, Luke looked at the back cover. Even worse, he asked Polly a question. "Who is this guy, the writer?"

Polly gave him the sneer she'd seen last Saturday night on Bette Davis in *Dangerous*. Channel Six. Luke had seen it, too, but failed to recognize the replica. "Tolstoi is a very famous Russian novelist," she said in disgust.

"Yeah, well, is he any good?"

"Any good, ha, ha!" The Davis eyebrow went up into Polly's uncombed bangs. "He's not exactly Mickey Spillane, if that's what you mean."

"Oh, screw you." Luke could sense that Joy, blowing bubbles through her straw, was bored. Why was he doing this, wasting time over a stupid book with stupid Hedgerow? "Well, have you ever heard of Raymond Chandler?"

"Of course I have." This was a lie, and she felt compelled to modify it. "But I never read him."

"You like mysteries?"

She did.

And for fifteen minutes, Joy forgotten, they swapped murderous plots, women axed to pieces, men shot full of holes, greed, ambition, jealousy, hate, and all those passions that wade in pages of blood.

"Boy, this is really dumb," said Joy with a sigh. "Listen, you guys, I'm going. School's supposed to be over, in case you didn't know."

Miss Lattice, who still gazed at her clock like a novitiate at the Cross, now spoke in rapture. "Three-fifteen, ladies and gentlemen. I have to close. Checks, please!"

"Joy, wait. Damn. I'm late to work, do me a favor, will ya, Polly? Can you pay this for me? I'll pay you back tomorrow. I promise." Luke gave her his check as he ran out the door with a placating smile for Joy, who ignored him.

"Jerk," Joy said.

"I guess," Polly replied. They sucked on their straws a last time. "Hey, Joy, listen, want to ride bikes this afternoon? No, listen, this is serious. Really. There's something I want to show you," she whispered quickly, "out near the marshlands. It's some kind of *Two Thousand and One* kind of thing. Nobody knows about it. It's really spooky."

"All the way out Route Three? Forget it, it's too hot to ride bikes anymore. Anyhow, I don't know, I've been feeling rotten. My arms hurt. I'm tired."

"Oh, come on, you always say that."

But Joy had gone up to pay Miss Lattice, who waited with resignation as this newly perfected body somnolently approached her in pink slow motion. Polly scrambled after, spilling her books. "Listen, Joy, honest, it's something special out there, I'm not kidding."

But Joy was not listening. A warm ache poured from Polly's heart out to her cheeks and reddened them. Today, when she had offered the queen of her secrets collection, to be so treated! Joy wasn't even interested. Polly had lost her friend.

"Your change." Miss Lattice coughed. "Polly! You dropped your change."

"Gosh, I'm sorry, I wasn't paying attention."

None of them ever does, thought the little shopkeeper of sixty-five slender years, who had once, to cheers and whistles, danced the Charleston atop the captain's table as the *Queen Mary* sailed across the waltzing seas. And that girl had paid no attention to the frowns on old deadened faces.

CHAPTER
17

Fate is very old and tired. She leans more times than not now on those hackneyed tricks that cost her no imaginative energy. With the same trite scenarios she used on Sumerians, she indiscriminately joins and sunders us, destroys or saves us. She's done it so often, and it must be hard to tell us apart. Hollywood's screenwriters are far more ingenious than she in bringing together a boy and a girl. Movies had led Joy Strummer to believe that someday her prince would come in a blackout, or a flood, or on the Orient Express, or on horseback or at a masked ball or out of the sky in a parachute. But Fate works on a tighter budget.

So, down the bank steps danced Lance Abernathy, vaulted into his Jaguar, roared around half of Dingley Circle, and braked with a blare of horn as out of The

Tea Shoppe floated Joy Strummer, straight toward the front of his car.

"Hey!" he yelled, without looking, annoyed. "Hey!" he called in a new voice, seeing her.

"I didn't see you, I'm sorry," she said, then saw him.

"I wasn't watching, I'm sorry." He smiled in reply.

The truth was that, from time to time for a dozen years, they had seen but not looked at each other, or had looked but never seen. Lance was almost twice Joy's age, and so Fate had waited until that once vast difference had contracted to insignficance—as far as desire at first sight could see.

"I haven't seen you around here before." Lance leaned over the side of his open sports car, a crimson burning chariot. Joy had often seen herself riding in such a car, her hair tied in a sky-silk scarf, and wearing costly sunglasses. "Oh, I live here," she confessed.

"Me too. Poor us. What's your name?"

"Joy."

Lance never doubted it for a minute. And Joy still stood where he had almost run her over, and he still pushed at the brake. And the birch plume poised trembling in air, then chose, was chosen, and, floating downward, fell to earth. "Joy Strummer."

"Lance Abernathy."

"Oh. Well, your car's nice, even if it almost killed me. I've seen it around before."

"You're okay, right? You weren't hit?"

"Oh, no, yeah, I'm okay."

"Look, maybe you shouldn't walk, maybe I should give you a ride, two locals, right? That'd be okay?"

"Well, I don't know, oh, sure, I guess so. I was just going home, that's all."

"Hop in, Joy." He leaned to the right, in his costly white sweater; his handsome tan hand flung open a door for her. And Polly Hedgerow, foot at her kickstand, watched, astonished, as Joy (too shy to raise her hand in class or joke with the librarian, Mr. Blossom) not only conversed easily with a grown stranger, but sank easily into the leather seat of a foreign car, as if nothing could be more customary, utterly disregarding her mother's warning—never get into a car with a stranger.

Deserted by Joy (friendship can hold no candle to the flame of love), Polly returned to books. We bloom at different times. Joy's recreational petals were open, Polly's tightly bound in leaves. Polly's ideational blossom had flowered, while Joy's was but a bud. The spring of some is others' summer, and in winter a few (like Beanie) may still fall.

All spring, off in the library, while the slowed sun shadowed her chair, Polly had practiced the same faith as that expressed by an earlier New England young female: that for solo excursions a book is the best frigate. And on that voluminous ocean of print Polly had sailed, if not as far as Emily Dickinson, then at least all the way to London, Paris, and Moscow. And she had decided she preferred the people she met there to her fellow Dingleyans. For her, the garbled gawking of even the most popular suitors would be silly—had she not heard Mr. Darcy and Byron woo? For her, the clumsy clutchings in the lot beside the Falls held no allure. How could they, compared with the passion of Heathcliff and Aramis? Who at Dixwell High could love her like Prince André or Count Vronsky? Certainly not Tac Hayes, who was, okay, pretty handsome, but who loved only a netted hoop ten feet off the ground. Certainly not Luke Packer.

But Nature, marshaling summer for her assault, pursued Polly even across her sea of books. Nature has always had frigates of her own. Up in a dim corner of the library's second floor, where rare (and rarely read) books were moved only when dusted, Polly had hidden (behind shelves where Gladys Goff had gathered the lives of valiant missionaries) a few forbidden texts. There she went after Joy had left her, to begin *Lady Chatterley's Lover*. The place was dark. Apparently no one else was in the entire library, not even the librarian, Mr. Blossom.

Polly was wrong. As she saw when she flipped the switch and abruptly lit up Sidney Blossom and Kate Ransom on the floor in front of her secret shelf. They were wrong, too, for they had relied upon the (usually quite reliable) Philistinism of Dingleyans to keep them away from dusty learning on so lovely a June afternoon. The two now stared up from the rows of dusty theology, frozen as two rabbits caught in a headlight beam, caught, appropriately enough, in the missionary position.

The Fact, after so much fiction, was to one whose view of Romance had come largely from Victorian novels as unsettling to Polly as Norman Mailer would have been to George Eliot. Mr. Blossom's far too hairy buttocks jerked up away from an emphatically untanned width on the all too obviously female flesh of Kate Ransom, whose collegiate allure and modishly proletarian outfits Polly had often admired from afar. But now Kate's clothing was inappropriately high or low. Flowered panties like a wrist corsage dangled around Kate's ankle, her tennis skirt was up to her waist, her tennis shirt was up to her neck. Mr. Blossom's pants were down to his feet, and his far too white and skinny legs were squeezed between Kate's raised tan knees.

"Oh, excuse me, gosh, excuse me," blurted Polly. They could come up with no reply before the bulb flicked off—her finger had never left the switch. Darkness handed the lovers back their privacy as swiftly as light had snatched it away. And Polly's sneakers snuck quickly away down the steps into the main reading room and out the varnished oak doors and into a fat red sun that slid out of the sky behind Mr. Barnum's store.

Now she had seen It. Sex. So that was It. It was ridiculous. And the thing, Mr. Blossom's, a twitching red knob sticking out of the wet, curly hair around it.

For a fraction of a second before he sank down on Kate Ransom, she had definitely seen that too. It was really big. Was Joy destined to let Lance Abernathy push his into her?

Polly ran back into the green. She had left her bike there, leaning against the ancient copper beech known as Dingley Tree, when she had gone to sit beneath the Dingley statue to try to read *Anna Karenina* and had then gone to the library to try to read another book instead. Out of *The Dingley Day* sauntered Luke Packer with Coleman Sniffell, who went irritably to put a coin in a parking meter.

"Hey!" Luke yelled. "El Dopo! Wanna ride the bus over to Argyle with me?"

"*No!*"

"What's eating you?"

"Why don't you drop dead?" was her answer, as she jumped on the bike and rode off.

"Hey! How much do I owe you for my sandwich? Hey! What's bugging you?"

"Typical," muttered Coleman Sniffell. Luke shrugged.

Out of Dingley Circle, Polly pedaled home to Glover's Lane. Locked in her room, its haphazard eaves covered with posters of Spain, Al Pacino, Bella Abzug, and Snoopy, its high blue shelves stacked with the clutter of a past she could never bring herself to discard—unraveling bears, plastic camp trophies, a broken tower of popsicle sticks, rocks and shells now dull and dirty that had glittered in the sand once with such promise of treasure, children's books all bearing a card saying "POLLY'S LIBERRY. PLEASE RETURN IN A WEEK"—locked in there, she pulled to her window a wicker chair (also painted blue, as were the walls, the bed, and the dresser, and as would have been the floor and ceiling as well had her father not said, "Enough's enough, I'm seasick"). Just outside the window was Polly's maple tree, The Kublai Khan of her hermitage. Climbing through the window onto the roof, onto the big branch, among leaves in her favorite escape, she sat to think it over. Sex.

It was a funny thing, overrunning people's lives, driving them crazy, destroying them—like Anna Karenina or Mrs. Abernathy or *The Scarlet Letter* or the poor Great Gatsby. Not her, Polly determined. Passion was not going to ruin her mind, not going to make her act like an idiot, not make her slide about on a sweaty floor, tangled up in somebody else's arms and legs. Not make her put goop on her eyes as Joy Strummer now spent hours doing. She would not be Madame Bovary, but Madame Curie, dedicated to science (or something), her faculties intact, her limbs unentangled.

Of course, Madame Curie had had Pierre. It would eventually be nice to fall in love. Life, Polly decided, would give her a Pierre, a friend and colleague who would save the world with her; and she would incidentally have a few children (she'd always wanted brothers and sisters). Then when they brought her word that a bus, or something, had run over and killed her Pierre on his way to the lecture hall, she would remain beautifully calm, gather up his notes (or better, know them by heart), and so go to give that lecture on science, or something, in his place. Tears twinkled happily in her eyes as she heard the standing ovation burst forth for so brave and brilliant a young woman, who would now go on alone (her parenthetical children having dropped from the dream) to win the Nobel Prize, or something.

These thoughts made her feel immensely better about It. It would be different with her and Pierre. Much more noble. She brought back the sight on the library floor and looked it over. She had today learned something she wanted abstractly to know. She had seen sex. She had also learned something about Sidney Blossom. It appeared that he was not a pansy, as many people thought—simply because he was a librarian, was known to have ironed his own shirts, hung up his own curtains, and subscribed to a cooking magazine. According to Ray Ransom, Mr. Blossom sneaked up behind boys when they bent over at the water cooler in the library, and *wham bam*. It was just another of Ray's dirty lies. Now Polly was tempted to tell Ray about his big sister, Kate, the Vassar girl. Serve him right. Obviously she couldn't share this latest Dingley Falls scoop with Father Highwick without the embarrassment of describing how she had discovered it, and she would never, after the way Joy had spurned her for a sports car, tell Joy Strummer anything ever again.

It was good to find out, however bluntly, that the librarian was not a pansy, for she liked him and had worried that there was no one in town for him to be in love with that way: except possibly (and this was a new hypothesis of Polly's—also unshared with the Rector) Father Jonathan Fields, who was as beautiful as Dorian Gray (in another of Miss Goff's forbidden books), but whom Mrs. Troyes and the Rector already completely monopolized.

Coitus interrupted by a summer bookworm, the shaken couple had flung on their clothes to meet the citizens' committee Blossom imagined was on its way to arrest them for visually assaulting a minor. But there were no knocks or sirens, and no posse showed up as they smoked a cigarette off in the librarian's tiny office, where a portrait of his predecessor, Gladys Goff, frowned down at them as if she had witnessed their sacrilege in her cherished theology section. Gradually shock faded, and shame followed.

"Crap," began Kate. "She's probably done it herself by now. I know I had by sixteen." The worldly Miss Ransom, now twenty-one, here juvenilized (though only by one year) the loss of her virginity at seventeen to Bobby Strummer in the den of her family's summer house on Lake Pissinowno, where this local Apollo had reigned as lifeguard before going to Vietnam, where he had been for years "Missing in Action." "You should hear the stories Ray tells me about what goes on up at Alexander Hamilton and Dixwell High. Sidney, you're so naive. You've hidden yourself off in this hole so long, you don't know what's going on. Even Dingley Falls is out of the dark ages. Even Dingley Falls went through the sixties. They do *everything* these days. Drugs. Group sex. They do it in grammar school, for crap's sake."

"Well, I can still be sorry she had to see us like that, probably at least embarrassed her."

"Embarrassed *her!* She's the one that barged in."

"I know, I'm sorry about the whole thing, forgive me, okay?"

"*I* started it, Sidney. Don't think you raped me or something."

"But not like that, right on the floor in a damn library!"

Sidney Blossom was not a worldly man. In his thirty-two years he had had sexual intercourse twice with his mother's maid, four times with prostitutes in Providence during four years at Brown University, and twenty-six times with Beth Page, a fellow library science student, during a summer tour of Europe—once in England, six times in France and Germany, and the rest in Italy. On the way to Greece Beth had thrown him over for a friend of his and had so wounded him—by a detailed comparison of his own and his rival's sexual performance—that after his graduation there had been in his life only a rare commercial arrangement with the hostess of Fred's Fries Bar and Grill. And that arrangement had been only at the prodding of Lance Abernathy, to whom the shy librarian had finally turned for information about "where to go." It was really not much of a record.

When Blossom met (remet) Kate Ransom on his return to Dingley Falls seven years after he had left it, he had fallen in love with her sulky beauty, with the thick black eyelashes and brows that windowed the sullen blue eyes. She had her mother's stylish body and

her father's remarkable good looks—in her made
animate by an apparently inexhaustible annoyance with
what she called "the System." Her sister, Emerald, was
as cool as her name, but Kate seethed. She was cool to
him though. They spent a great deal of time together.
They went to movies and out to eat and to reminisce
about the sixties while listening to folk-rock records.
They analyzed the seventies and each other. But Kate
had told Sidney so often, "Stop trying to make me and
let's be friends; that's much harder," that finally—
though it was much harder—he had stopped. She
explained that she wouldn't sleep with him because she
knew he wanted to marry her, and she couldn't afford
to get involved with such a man. He was finally pressed
to pretend to casual lust, only to be told, "You must
think I'm really dumb if you expect me to fall for that."
Sometimes he worried that she went out with him only
to threaten her parents with the possibility that she
would marry him, for he knew he was not, in their
view, a suitable suitor for Kate.

So, today, when miraculously she had walked behind
the library counter and leaned over his back as he filed
the late cards, when she had pressed her unbra'd
breasts into his shirt, Sidney had lost his head. So lost it
that he did exactly what for years he had dreamed of
doing, and feared she would reject him for attempting,
and feared he would fail in accomplishing even if he
were not rejected. Still, he felt he should not have
gotten so out of control. "Let me apologize, okay? I
practically forced you."

Kate laughed. Today she had simply done exactly
what for years she had more or less planned on sooner
or later doing. "Forget it. It's no big deal."

"It is to me." Sidney frowned. The voice he heard
did not sound familiar. He sprang down from his desk
and pulled Kate out of her chair. "It is to me!" The
voice was thick and came from a different place than
Beth Page had ever gotten to know. "Kate," he heard
this voice say. She looked up, startled. He kissed her up

against the file cabinet, he kissed her to her knees, he kissed her, at last, to the floor—half under his desk, half under Miss Goff's baleful stare. He kept on kissing her. Down again to his feet went Sidney Blossom's pants. Out again came his thing. And soon into Kate. There it stayed, thick and full as his voice, for twenty uninterrupted minutes. Compared to years of waiting, twenty minutes really wasn't very long. But compared to Bobby Strummer, two Yalies, one U.Masser, and a Harvardian, Kate was impressed.

By now they had cleared the desk and were squeezed between a swivel chair and a dictionary stand. "There!" rumbled Sidney, finally, as he hooked his arms under her knees, raised her almost off the floor, and let go inside her a hundred nights of dreams. *"There!"*

"Damn!" panted the object of his dream. "Oh, goddamn!"

Soon out came the thing, hot, red, and nodding in triumph. Limbs disentangled, the way Polly Hedgerow preferred them to be. Both shiny lovers lay puffing for breath on the floor. Even Kate's tennis was not quite so strenuous, and as for the unathletic librarian, he fully expected immediate (though happy) death. Kate recovered first and asked for a cigarette. "Sidney," she said in a spiral of smoke, "I came twice."

"Marry me" is what Dingley Falls's librarian wanted to say. But he had learned to wait. So what he said was "Sid. I hate being called Sidney. Just Sid. Okay?"

"Okay."

At last, he was on his way.

CHAPTER
18

Frankly, Winslow Abernathy had found little consolation in the sonnet Mrs. Canopy had left for him in a terra-cotta bell jar outside his door. In it she had voiced a presentiment that Beanie would soon be home to change "the raven, Rumor, back to Truth's own dove/ Through heaven's magic trick—transforming Love." But Beanie wasn't back. The Seville was not in the garage, Big Mutt was not on the lawn, there was no note on the bedroom dresser, no telephone call, no telegram, no hospital, no police station, no apology, nothing forwarded from his Boston hotel, no repentant wife come into his office, where he had sat until 6:30, waiting. There was no Beanie.

Since his return at three, Abernathy had received five invitations to dinner for that evening. As if I were abruptly widowed, he thought, and judged helpless to care for myself. A solicitor in need of solicitude, of immediate transference to another female, lest I famish, go naked in rags, smother in dirt, die of neglect.

"You'll need to eat, Winslow," Tracy Canopy had added in a postscript to her sonnet. "Let me have you over, something simple."

"Dear Winslow, the house." Evelyn Troyes had stopped by his office to remind him. "Shall I send my Orchid over? And then your laundry?"

"It never helps to be alone," counseled Sloan Highwick, "and we could drive to a new Chinese place I heard about where your legs don't go numb from all that MSG, and honestly I've often thought I'd had a stroke from some of those dishes. But it's only twenty miles or so south of us. Or west."

"Priss thought," Ernest Ransom had phoned, "we could all have dinner at the Club tonight. Sound okay? Their scampi, you know."

"I gather the whole town has heard. Tell me, Ernest, were you having a town meeting at your house last night?"

"No need to take that tone. Just thought you might feel a little at loose ends. Never mind then."

Finally the lawyer accepted an offer by A. A. Hayes to share a Scotch at The Prim Minster. While he was too shaken to bear the solicitude of his wife's friends or of his old college roommate, he found he could not afford solitude just yet. With the newsman he could focus on news other than his own. Abernathy and Hayes were not intimate; neither had aspired to "friendship" for many years. But their minds had moved each toward the other's, so that at parties the two men usually found themselves off by the bar—by Hayes's request—alone in conversation. Abernathy and Ransom, on the other hand, had never learned to talk easily together, though they had lived during their undergraduate years in New Haven in the same bland room. Abernathy suspected he made Ernest uncomfortable because he knew so much about him. But with Hayes, Abernathy shared a professional interest, shared the luck of being paid (Abernathy much more handsomely) to do what each most enjoyed—working with words to find out truths. Not so much to right wrongs with their proofs, but more purely and simply to penetrate truth's secrets with the pin of language. They also shared the shame of feeling that they had betrayed the highest achievements of their callings—juristic and journalistic—by being, in their opinion, failures. They also shared, though had never discussed, an incapacity to communicate with their wives or their children, none of whom shared their love of pure language.

Now they were talking about national and not

personal failures. In the low-ceilinged "Churchill Room" of the inn, by the enormous summer-swept fireplace, they sat across the dark tabletop with its pewter ashtray and its matchbooks printed *The Prim Minster 1726*. From the Colonial perspective of these surroundings, the two men found fault with more recent American developments. Hayes savored the last swallow of a drink. "Believe me, you're wrong. Washington wouldn't blink at an assassination. They're all a bunch of trench-coat lunatics, like the Marx Brothers in a James Bond movie. Down there trying to blow up Castro with a cigar!"

"I suppose there may be a lunatic fringe."

"They're all alike, think alike, talk alike. Everybody in the government is working for the Godfather, and the Godfather in this country is organized money. One day we'll find out how those secret services are behind everything, and the everything they're secretly servicing is organized money. Good old oil and steel. Where's that waitress? Have another one with me, Winslow. Why, Texas and sheikhs bestride this narrow world like Colossuses while all us petty men walk under their huge derricks"—Hayes waved his glass at the bartender—"and get pissed all over. Yes, sir, Neiman-Marcus will be selling plaid mink coats in Cairo, and your old alma mater will be shipped, ivy and all, to an Arabian desert, you just wait and see."

Abernathy thought that Hayes ought to cut back on his drinking; maybe he kept a bottle in the office—surely he couldn't have gotten this drunk in the short time they'd sat here. "You're getting paranoid," he said.

"That's what they all say. I just see significance, that's all. I see the signs. It all signifies something. You call it paranoia; the old Church Fathers called it the Grand Design."

"Don't tell me faith in the powers of the CIA is sending you back to the church?" Abernathy smiled as he searched for his pipe.

"No, sir. Those old theologians thought it was all a *good* plan. I think the pattern's there, but I think it stinks. That bartender in a coma, or what?" Hayes shook his Scotch glass more vehemently. "Look here, Winslow, something I've been meaning to ask you."

Not him, too, thought Abernathy. Must I explain away the loss of a wife even to him? "What?" he asked. His pipe seemed to be in none of his pockets.

"You know that crazy smut mail folks have been getting, accusations and out-and-out libels? Have you gotten one?"

In his relief the lawyer laughed. "No. I was passed over. I know Arthur got one inviting him rather brusquely to resign as first selectman. Otto mentioned something about it. Probably some prankster, you know, like teenagers calling strangers on the phone."

"Well, that's what I told Limus Barnum; he seems to think we should ride out at night like vigilantes and string the guy up. Ah, sir, your child, I believe."

Winslow's son Arthur and Arthur's fiancée, Emerald Ransom, came through the bar on their way to The Prim Minster's dining room. Abernathy was embarrassed; he had only a few hours earlier (pleading exhaustion) declined his son's invitation to dinner.

"Well, hello, Dad. A.A. You decided to join us then? Kate and, I guess, Sidney Blossom are meeting us. Glad to have you."

Abernathy stood. "No, just on my way home, really. Just had a quick drink. Not really hungry. Pretty tired. Have a pleasant evening. How are you, Emerald? You look lovely." Emerald touched a bracelet on her wrist and then fleetingly offered Mr. Abernathy a lovely hand as she passed by into "The Queen's Room," where pewter pitchers of gladiolus were set out on cream linen tablecloths and engravings of Victoria's prime ministers crowded the walls.

As Emerald wafted away, Hayes stared at her through his empty glass. "Just one thing I want to know," he mumbled. "I just don't see how those two ever managed to get engaged. I swear I don't believe the woman has ever opened her mouth. Now I love quietness; an excellent thing in a woman, as the Bard says. Beanie has it, and I love it in her. But *that* girl's downright comatose." The editor realized, too late, that he had—as he told himself—slid his fat foot into his drunken mouth once again.

Beanie's name lay heavily in the air. Hayes could think of no words in which to ask his friend how he felt. And so the lawyer and the editor called for the bill.

CHAPTER
19

Of the people in Dingley Falls who now sat awake alone in their houses, Judith Haig was neither reading, like Tracy Canopy, nor watching television, like Evelyn Troyes, nor listening to records, like Walter Saar, nor writing a letter, like Limus Barnum, nor preparing a sermon, like Jonathan Fields. Judith, having long ago cleaned the little of her house that needed cleaning, was sitting in her robe by the window and trying not to think about what Sammy Smalter's life had probably been like. Had he gone to special schools, had he cried in his bed and begged not to be sent, not to be seen, not to be? Did he waken from dreams to feel himself once again shrunken beneath his sheets?

Judith stood. She had to close the curtains more tightly. Then she went to a closet. On its floor was a paper sack of yarns and needles. Years ago she had knitted things; the quiet discipline was one the Sisters of Mercy had taught her. For some reason she had packed this crumpled A & P bag in with the rest of her belongings (or Haig's belongings, rather, for she did not collect things) and had let the movers move them here from Madder, here to the outpost of Hawk Haig's yet unlinked chain of businesses, here on the highway shoulder.

Judith now decided to knit something. A scarf. She would knit Sammy Smalter out of her mind and into a scarf of her scraps of yarn. Until almost midnight she unraveled the knots of balled threads and began slowly to knit again. Into that beaded click without warning the screech of a telephone shrieked out at her. From Hartford, where he had gone that evening to meet a man who was "looking into something" for him, her husband was calling her. "Just checking," he said. Now that Dr. Scaper had warned him, Hawk Haig worried about his wife.

Her husband had been on her mind too. Just before he'd left, he had sat over his slab of steak in their new dinette in a kind of smug expectation. The cheerful mood startled her, after so many, many months of his bitter chagrin about the highway and the rotten luck of losing his one chance to make a killing, to make something of himself (and her), to "make it" (for her, for him). He said he was pleased because he had arrested the man at the trailer park. Except for an occasional drunk driver or exuberant adolescent, arrests in Dingley Falls were rare. As he ate, Haig had recounted jubilantly his incarceration of Maynard Henry: "A mean SOB. Just mean. Crazy, you know, Jude? Imagine a great guy like Arn having a kid brother like that. I've been waiting for a chance to put him away for good, he's a menace. Came at me with a knife once, over at Dixwell High, in the parking lot. I heard how over in Vietnam Maynard was always in trouble, got in a bar fight in Saigon and bit this guy's earlobe off. Now I'm talking about another American's! Can you believe that? Bit his *ear* off! So instead of locking him up, they give him a medal and he comes back here and marries a gook. You know? Joe and I already had two run-ins with him at Fred's Fries. Way

out of line. Now he thinks he can get away with shoving
some dumb spic's car off a cliff and busting his legs.
And you wouldn't believe what it took to get that dumb
Treeca even to press charges! That whole trailer park's
a cesspool, honey, any more coffee?"

Now, on the phone, Haig told her he'd had a chance
to talk to a guy in Hartford, and maybe he was onto
something about the canceled highway. He had some
real leads now, and if she wouldn't mind, he was going
to stay and check them out. He was convinced that
somebody had stopped the highway on purpose and
that the somebody was Ernest Ransom, and that
Ransom knew something about the land that made it
too valuable to sell. For a few days Joe MacDermott
could manage the station. Judith didn't mind. He told
her that later that summer maybe they'd take a trip
together, a real vacation, maybe even fly to Florida. It
would do her good. They deserved a rest, they'd
worked hard all their lives—unlike that crew over on
Elizabeth Circle. Judith did not think it would do her
good to see Florida, but she said, "All right," since
what desire did she have to set against his desire? After
he hung up, she finished a skein of blue yarn and
started a red.

She stopped. Something was outside, coming in the
dark toward the house. A deadened crunch of someone
stepping in the gravel. Then she heard the dog.
Staccato barks like pellets. And then a knock.

Judith waited. The knock came again. It was not
angry, not even insistent, a patient knocking. Pressed
inside the door, she asked, "Who's there, please?"

"Mrs. Haig?" The voice was a woman's, high and
unsure. "Chief Haig?" The pronunciation was careful
and unsure.

"My husband's not here. Can I help you?"

"My name is Chin Lam. My husband, Henry.
Maynard Henry. Your husband has inprisoned."

"Yes? I'm sorry, Chief Haig isn't here."

"Not?"

"No, I'm sorry."

"It is late now, I know. I was lost walking to look for you."

Judith had to open the door. "Just a minute, please." Turning on the hall light, she unlatched a chain. And with a guttural roar, a black German shepherd lunged up at the opening. A burning rip of terror (not surprise, but fulfilled nightmare) tore up Mrs. Haig's chest to her throat.

"No! No, no, no. Night! No!" A young, thin Oriental girl grabbed the dog by his collar and pulled him off the door; she stroked his head until, begrudgingly, he stopped growling. "Okay? It okay? My husband's dog. I was fear, frightened to come, just me. I leave dog outside. It okay?"

"Yes, I'm sorry. It's just that your dog startled me. Yes, come in."

The dog sat down on the front steps to wait. Chin Henry, with a large, frayed man's parka kept on over a summer dress, sat down on the edge of a plastic-covered chair in Judith Haig's family room. Urged, she accepted a cup of tea—a package Mrs. Haig found behind the spices in her new kitchen cabinets.

Her English, Chin apologized, was very poor. (And, of course, neither Mrs. Haig, nor anyone else in town, spoke much Vietnamese, though it had not occurred to them to ask Mrs. Henry's forgiveness.) Her arrival, Chin apologized, was very much an intrusion, but she hadn't found a phone, nor had she known the Haig's home was so far from her own home (trailer, rather) or she would not have walked this late at night. Having gone so far beyond the bridge, she had become very confused. "Sorry I'm coming too late. Very dark. No more houses here."

"No, there aren't. I'm sorry."

They tried to talk. They had to make do with very few words. Mrs. Maynard Henry spoke in intense frustration, robbed of her language, left in such poverty when her need was most imperative. Mrs. Haig strained to translate the message across their differences. That message seemed to be that the young woman had no one to turn to. Her husband had been arrested by the husband of her hostess. The police chief had even threatened to have Chin Lam deported as an illegal alien. She didn't know whether she was an illegal alien or not. Today, after work at The Tea Shoppe, she had ridden the bus to Argyle City Jail, where they had let her speak to Maynard behind a grille. She had found her husband furious that he was locked in jail, in a cell with an insane person.

Judith imagined (had not Sarah MacDermott said so?) that Maynard Henry felt that he was being kept in jail for keeping what was his: his wife. And that Chin was his, that she had been swept in panic with shouting people into a Saigon building, swept with yells into a helicopter, swept into a ship across a sea to a plane, to a bus, to a row of wood barracks in America; that she had had to submit to Victor Grabaski and been driven by him north to Dingley Falls, Connecticut, that her husband had spoken some words of her language, had saved her from Victor Grabaski, from law, from loss—had done so by marrying her, all this Judith imagined from Sarah's remarks to be Chin Lam's story. That Maynard had struck Chin because she had allowed herself to be swept away by Raoul Treeca, who had told her something she could not understand, but that she must go back somewhere, that the other refugees were somewhere else, and he would take her to them, all this Judith assumed had bewildered the girl. Forced to imagine the planes and buildings and people shouting, Judith Haig had felt, unavoidably, what those months must have been to Chin. She could not help but feel. She was too sensitive. "I'm sorry," she kept saying, "but what can *I* do?"

"You could ask your husband? He could let Maynard

go? Maynard is so. Angry. Angry all the time. He lose, lost job making roads." Chin danced with her arms her spouse's labor. "Sorry. So stupid. What is word? Construction."

"Yes, the highway." Both their husbands, then, had lost the highway.

"Yes. Now in jail. I have nobody. Chief Haig, he does, I am sorry, he does not like Maynard and tells him, 'You not coming out ever. Your wife must go back. Not a real wife.' What best for me to do now? Miss Lattice is so kind, I am working now. But at night, by myself? In trailer park, old man has died today. I am too afraid." Chin held her hands tightly to her chest, then let them fall like leaves. She had a round, childlike face. Life had not yet printed there the meaning of anything it had forced her to witness. Mrs. Haig poured the girl's tea as she tried to decide what was being asked of her. There was another bedroom. No one had ever slept in it, but, as she was a careful housekeeper, it was ready. "Has your husband," she asked, "a lawyer? Someone to put up the bail?"

"Bail? Bail?" Chin shook her head apologetically.

"Money. So he can get out. All right. I'll speak to my husband, but he's out of town just now, but in the meantime. Well, all right. You look tired. Tired. Yes. You should sleep. There's a guest room, the bed's already made." Only as she spoke did she decide to make this offer.

"No, no, I walk home now."

"I don't drive, you see, and it's so late. Tomorrow you'll feel better."

"No, no. All Maynard's things in the trailer. I watch them."

They looked at each other. "All right then," said Mrs. Haig. "Let me call Mr. MacDermott at the station, a very nice man, he'll come give you a ride home. Will that be all right?"

"You are sure it okay?"

"Yes. And tomorrow we'll talk again."

"You are kind. Thank you for my help." Chin stood up and held out her teacup to Judith.

"No, please, sit there. Let me call him. Try not to worry."

Mrs. Haig took the cup.

CHAPTER
20

Seated in her favorite armchair, Tracy Canopy was organizing the Bicentennial Festival, which the Historical Society was sponsoring and in which the Thespian Ladies were to play leading roles. As president of both these clubs, Mrs. Canopy had a million and one things to do. The Society had great hopes of buying from Carl Marco the town's early Victorian train depot, evicting Sidney Blossom, and then restoring it with the thousands of dollars that an endless stream of tourists would be happy to pay for such souvenirs as Bicentennial T-shirts, caps, pennants, balloons, and turtles—all printed with the Betsy Ross flag and with slogans like "DINGLEY FALLS 1676–1976" and "I WAS IN DINGLEY FALLS AND I LOVED IT" and "SHOP DINGLEY FALLS." Limus Barnum had gotten the ladies a great deal on the merchandise, and the ladies' markup was justified only by their worthy cause. The grand finale of all these festivities was to be ten *tableaux vivants,* each representing one Dingleyan event for every thirty years of the town's history, each starring a member of the Thespian Ladies. Even Beanie had been pressured into portraying her grandmother Lady Camilla Dingley as she charged on horseback into the Great Madder Strike and Riot of 1898. Everything had been planned for months. Everything ought to go well. Beanie would surely be back.

With a nod of approval, Tracy set her clipboard aside and turned to the stack of glossy catalogs on her cherry butler's tray table. Tonight Mrs. Canopy had also finished organizing Christmas, as she always did six months in advance, beginning on the day of her wedding anniversary, now also the commemoration of her husband's death. She felt the need on such a day to list all those who lived in her life, who kept her connected. Mrs. Canopy filled her life by giving to such decisions as much time as they could be made to consume. She was an indefatigable consumer and was much taken advantage of by those elitist catalogs that rob the innocently wealthy by overcharging them. Now she glanced over her list with satisfaction. For Beanie, that Audubon print. And a Dunhill lighter for Winslow; Beanie said he'd lost his. French perfume for Priss and her daughters. For Evelyn Troyes, something chinoiserie. For Prudence Lattice, Sloan Highwick, and other acquaintances, crates of Royal Riviera Pears, Alphonse LaValle Grapes, and Giant Kiwi Berries delivered monthly. Among her artists, Habzi Rabies would have the most practical gift, as he now had a commission to paint a mural on a section of the Alaskan pipeline and needed a warm coat. And for herself, as a treat, she would buy another piece of statuary by the young Cuban refugee Bébé Jesus. Perhaps the J. Edgar Hoover wastepaper basket done in tin, the one he had shown her last spring when she went to pay his landlord so that he could get back into his studio in Sullivan Square.

Mrs. Canopy already owned (and used) a toilet made by Bébé of Fidel Castro's affable face, with his army cap lifting off as the lid and his cigar a foot flusher. "My God in heaven," Priss had said when she first saw it installed in the bathroom. "I'm going to use the facilities upstairs, if you don't mind. I'm afraid I'm simply incapable of relaxing while squatted over the head of a Communist."

"That's the point Señor Jesus wanted to make. Political oppression. So witty, I think."

"Ha!" said her friend.

Tracy wished she could chat with Priss now. She went to her window. Sammy Smalter's light was still on. And perhaps that was Winslow Abernathy's study light across the landscaped circle. But of course she couldn't call men up at midnight.

She could refill her hummingbird feeder. She could think of a speaker for the next Thespian Ladies meeting and a new project for the Historical Society. Mrs. Canopy had already dusted Vincent's snuffbox collection in its oak curio cabinet. She had glazed and fired two clay pots, selected some clothing and antiques to donate to an auction given to raise money for a community theater in Argyle. It was still only 1:15 A.M. She wound her Ridgeway grandfather clock, glanced at *Fingerpaint on a Widow's Fur* above her mantel (obviously she needed to ask Habzi, before he left for Alaska, whether or not it would hurt to embed a few mothballs in the fabric of her former sable), and briskly climbed the stairs to her room. It was chilly there. From her heirloom trunk (where a photograph of Vincent holding his beloved terrier smiled up at her from pressed sheets and forlorn fashions folded away with the past) she took a lovers' knot coverlet. Having dressed for sleep, Tracy climbed with a sigh into her pumpkin pine four-poster canopied bed and began to read *Naked Lunch* where she had left off two nights ago.

CHAPTER
21

In his study Winslow Abernathy read again his wife's letter to his son. One flesh they were all supposed to be. Yet Beanie had simply driven away. And Arthur preferred to act as if nothing had happened. And Lance, Lance who had revved his engine to a stop in the driveway a few minutes ago, almost seemed to be blaming Winslow for the loss of his mother. "Couldn't you stop her? I mean, shit, Dad!"

Lance was now out in the old coach house in the backyard, where at sixteen he had insisted on fashioning out of attic furniture a bachelor hut. Naturally, Beanie had let him do it. Why didn't he get a job? Maybe both his sons were secretly gloating that their father had lost his wife. She had always loved them best, called them her little lovers, spoiled them irrecoverably, and they, the snot-nosed pricks—good God, what was wrong with him, why was he talking like this? Those couldn't be his words, not his emotions. He seemed to be turning into A. A. Hayes, paranoid and intoxicated. Winslow realized that the drink in his hand was his fifth; he remembered that he had failed to eat dinner, or lunch, nor had he slept well in Boston the night before. Obviously he was drunk and debilitated, and so not himself, for he didn't drink. Nor did he stay up until 2:00 A.M. It was after two by the rosewood desk clock, Beanie's gift. "You won't remember to wear your watch but you always want to know what time it is, so I'm putting a clock here and one on the office desk."

Abernathy looked around his study. Beanie had

157

decorated it; she had the gift of fabrics and forms, of
woods and colors. He loved the room, its three
windows opening onto seven pine trees and then the
meadow of green yard beyond them. He loved the mo-
saic of his books, the fine faded pattern of the Oriental rug, the Daumier and Hogarth engravings that
mocked his profession, so that as he searched for
precedents, sardonic attorneys winked down at him and
porcine judges snored. He loved most of all the
alabaster head, yellow with age, that sat by the
window. The head of Marcus Antistius Labeo, a
Roman jurist who had declared the decrees of Caesar
and Augustus illegal for the purely logical reason that
the authority of these two gods had been illegal.
Naturally, people had paid no attention to Antistius,
but apparently someone thought he deserved at least a
bust for his purity and simple logic. Now Abernathy,
who had once thought he would be such a jurist, owned
the bust, loving it the way Lance loved his Jaguar.
(Both had been expensive. Beanie gave expensive gifts
and dime-store gifts indiscriminately.)

The light went out in Lance's bachelor quarters. His
son would now fall effortlessly asleep. When the twins
were first born (terrifyingly small, squirming life bound
in blankets of less length and weight than the little
plush bears Tracy Canopy had given them), Abernathy
had kept awake, fearful that if he slept, Arthur and
Lance would simultaneously cease to breathe. Nothing
so small and unevolved could possibly sustain the
complexity of human life. Pressed beside the nursery
door, he had chosen squalls over silence, for silence
meant death, suffocation, or just a mysterious stop to
mysterious life, six pounds of life being in itself
obviously too fragile to last.

But he had eventually slept, and waked to find the
twins with him in bed, suckled by Beanie, though he
had warned her that to bring them there could be
dangerous. He had slept, worked in his office, appeared
in court, traveled in defense of (mostly) money; he had

studied in his study the laws, *ius civile*, of imperial Rome. And while he did so, the boys studied too—the turn to the side, the smile, the full turn, a seated position, a wave, a clap, a crawl, a creep. Then they stood in their cribs crying *"mamamamamama,"* afraid to sit down, afraid to fall, into what? For how could they know what might be back there, they who had yet to study gravity? So they clung to their bars, and when he came, they wailed louder, *"mamamamamama."* Time after time Beanie had gone to them, her robe a flow of color behind her. Juno descending to rescue her chosen little men, who howled and clutched at the rails of their tiny ships. Over and over again she went, for as soon as saved, they stood again—vain ambition of the human race. She never lost patience with them.

She had apparently now lost patience with him, for she had gone. Gone beyond the compass of *his* call, should he call. Winslow poured himself another Scotch and gazed with mild dismay at the white water circle he had allowed to stain his desk top. Well, he thought, why not get angry about it all? People were always telling him to get angry: "Say how you *feel*, Winslow," Beanie had desired. Why not then chase after her with a siren atop his car, force her by law, by physical bullying, to return? Why not pitch Lance out into an employment line? Accuse Arthur of moral and intellectual muteness? Yes, the snot-nosed pricks, Beanie had always loved them best. And they, hadn't they turned on him, hadn't they (in their heart of hearts) been trying to murder him from the moment they were ambulatory? Murder him in cold blood and pass their patricide off as a childish accident? Had not ambush stalked him, turned his home into a Theban road of subterranean explosives—an innocuous tricycle suddenly angled at the top of the basement steps, an escaped pet tarantula walking the tightrope of his steering wheel, an electric razor carelessly dropped into a tub he was just preparing to step into.

Could he not make a case that only by relentless

caution and cunning (or sheer chance) he had survived
their adolescence? Had not Lance, in that ruthless
time, brazenly shoved his superior musculature and
sexuality into Abernathy's face at every opportunity:
springing out of the bathroom with a towel pushed out
from his genitals, tossing the statuesque Beanie in the
air while she laughed like a five-year-old? Had the
father not survived the challenge of wrestling matches
and tennis bouts, the green bruises squeezed into his
flesh under the guise of affection? Survived the news
that Lance found the golden chambers of higher
learning "a total drag" and endured academics only at
the insistence of the air force, which he had joined
because "flying was his trip"? Had he not survived
never knowing which he feared most—the death of his
son, or the realization that his son casually agreed to
cause the deaths of others: "So don't worry about me,
Mom. I'm eighteen thousand feet up in the air. Got a
A-One pad here in Guam, good buddies, air conditioning, the works. We just fly them over, drop them, and
head back home. Nothing to worry about"? Had he
spent two years being bombed on a carrier in the Pacific
to make the world safe for someone who would write
letters like that?

And Arthur, Arthur, from whose studiousness
Abernathy had hoped to find a companion lover of
learning. Had not Arthur confessed himself a grind for
grades, who indifference to the content of his education
was masked by a stolid determination to gather from
his prominent university as many calling cards (knowledge the least of them) as time and diligent cultivation
allowed him? Arthur, who copied even Ernest Ransom's archaic fashion of wearing a gold pocket watch
on a chain, and who had followed the banker into golf,
Scotch with soda, hearty handshaking, football on
television, and had finally gotten his dual reward—
Ransom's daughter (and Hayes was right about Emerald) *plus* first selectmanship of Dingley Falls (and
Winslow wondered if he didn't almost agree with what

that anonymous letter writer had had to say about that)?

Arthur and Lance. The words themselves began to sound nonsensical to him. Who were these two men, these props of his age, branches of his root, flesh of his flesh? God knows. And Beanie, his Eve, his rib. There was the rub, his rib had broken off, had snapped like a wishbone—and gotten her wish. "I'm drunk. I'm really drunk," said Abernathy aloud. He stood, wiped the water from his desk with his jacket sleeve, and having turned out his desk lamp, felt his way through the kitchen. He thought he had better drink some coffee. But where was it, where was the grinder, and how exactly did this new automatic dripolator of Beanie's work? It was too much to cope with. There was nothing to do with intoxication except put it to sleep. He'd just take some aspirin, if there were any, and he could find them.

Someone screamed. A ululant animal sound that kept on and on and made no sense in Elizabeth Circle. A human moan that whined out from the house on his right, Prudence Lattice's house. Abernathy realized that he was running efficiently out the door, through thickets of pine, to his elderly neighbor's smaller yard, running successfully among all her boxes and buckets of summer flowers. Near her back door, by a garbage can, Prudence Lattice stood, spectral in the shadows. She clasped the lid of the can to her chest. Her wail, lulled now, had sharply sobered him.

"Prudence, are you all right? What's wrong?"

He had frightened her. Her thin arms in an old flowered bathrobe tightened around the lid; she held it against her like a shield. One slippered foot pressed quickly on the other, then switched, as if she ran in panic but was too panicked to move.

"It's just me. It's Winslow. I thought I heard a scream. Is something wrong?"

The small woman stared at him blankly. "Scheherazade," she whispered.

"Your cat?" Then, with sickening suddenness, Abernathy saw what lay at the top of the garbage pail. His old neighbor's cat, her Siamese. A stiffened reality of what had once been life, now hard fur and legs locked in a stretch. The crossed blue eyes gazed moronically ahead, indifferent to the night.

"My God, Pru." Abernathy pried her hands from the lid and covered the can. He had to ask her twice what had happened.

"She got out tonight, oh, Winslow, somehow, and then she didn't come home. I called her, called and called. I never let her go out at night, and she always comes when I call."

"Yes."

"I went to bed but then I woke up and came outside to look, I worried that . . . but I couldn't find her, and then there was a broken pot just there, flower pot."

"Yes."

"I just, not thinking, went to put it in the trash, but when I took off the lid . . ."

"I'm sorry, Pru. I'm so sorry."

"Someone"—she breathed the fact with a long shudder—"killed her and put her there."

"Let's go back inside, let's go now." Abernathy led Miss Lattice into her old, oversized kitchen which spare furnishings made appear even larger, and their owner even smaller and less substantial.

"Perhaps," the lawyer said, "someone thought to be . . . of assistance; I mean, perhaps a car struck her, and someone couldn't think where else . . ."

"No." She shook her head, "Don't tell me it was kindness."

No, Abernathy thought, probably not. Probably an unthinking act, a prankster, a stranger who did not know that Pru Lattice had nothing to love or be loved by except a Siamese cat romantically named for one thousand and one unattainable dreams. No, not kindness.

Her hands folded in her lap, her feet twisted under,

Miss Lattice sat silently in her kitchen chair. Her neighbor sat down across from her. "Shall I send someone over to stay with you?" If only Beanie were home. "Shall I call Otto over to give you something?" A woman or a doctor would know how to help.

"Thank you, but you go back home, I'm all right, you shouldn't have troubled."

"Well, try to sleep. I'm very sorry this had to happen."

"It didn't have to happen. But then, it did, didn't it?" She smiled too brightly. "But, if it wouldn't be too much trouble for you, I'm sorry, but I don't want her . . . left there, and I'm afraid I can't make myself . . ."

"Of course, of course."

"Thank you, Winslow." She let him out and locked the door of the house that was all her father had left her when, fallen on harder times, he had had nothing more to leave and no one else to leave it to.

Abernathy could not touch the cat. He found a shovel with which to lift it out of the garbage can. Even so, death's cold seemed to chill the shaft and ice his hands. The cat was heavy. Its skull, he now noticed, was crushed, and clots of viscous gelatin clung to broken pieces of bone. So much for the mystery of intelligence, thought the lawyer. At the end of the yard, by an oak tree, he dug a hole. It was not as easy as he had assumed. There were rocks he had to pry loose with his fingers in the dark. Still, he dug deeper than he needed to, for fear of dogs. Then he shoveled the cat down into the hole.

At least the animal had been dead when he found it, and not dying. Not like the cat-mauled blue jay that had once flown crazed around and around their living room until it killed itself, slamming against the window's illusion, before Beanie could catch it in her sweater to set it free. "I'll do it, if you'll just hold the door open!" Beanie had yelled, for Abernathy had backed away, nauseated by the bird's terrible frenzy. Into the new

world, padded with papers, muffled by machinery,
Life's old facts rarely come to stun us. That a wounded
jay should chance to fly in through an open screen was a
freak of nature, an unwanted intrusion by the old world
on the new. "It's not going to hurt you. It's frightened
to death," Beanie had yelled. "I know that, I know,"
he had hissed at her.

Cats killed birds. Cats were killed. With the flat of his
shovel Abernathy smoothed the dirt over the small
mound packed above Miss Lattice's pet. He tried to
replace the clods of grass carefully. A blister had
already raised on his thumb, and sucking on it, he tore
off a piece of skin. It tasted of dirt and grass.

When he returned the shovel to the garage, he
noticed a folded piece of paper taped to the side of the
door. Without thinking, he went over and read it.
There was one typed sentence: "Since you won't shut
that damn thing up, somebody has to. Serves you
right." Abernathy ripped the sheet from Miss Lattice's
door, balled it up, and jammed it into his pocket. Then
he walked home. In the northern sky he saw a star fall.
Another Lucifer, he thought; for pride and treachery
hurled down to damn the earth. Another one. And the
first archangel has done so well.

CHAPTER
22

The great truths are all truisms, having bred for a great
time in a great many that contempt with which familiarity is fertile. Among the trite and true notions about
human nature, none is more so than the fact that the
majority of people care more for what they do not have
than for what they do have. This legacy of our original

parents is the foundation of progress. It supports all such improvements in living as the discovery of the spear, America, and the garbage compacter. It subsidizes credit cards and divorce lawyers.

There are a happy few who through either consummate humility, stoicism, luck, or self-satisfaction want for themselves no more than what the gods have decided to give them. Probably only one of that graced minority lived in all of Dingley Falls. Father Sloan Highwick. At divinity school a poetical classmate whose procrastinating habit it was during study periods to sketch portraits in verse wrote perceptively of the future Rector:

> *Our Sloan's a man of bonhomie.*
> *So blithesome, so blessed in jollity,*
> *He thinks that the Reaper's grim*
> * scythe is a grin*
> *Inviting souls over for Heavenly gin.*

That death should be to Highwick an invitation to a grand cocktail party in the sky did not at all mean that with any *de contemptu mundi* distaste for his earthly lot he was eager to fling himself into the reception line where his eternal Host waited to welcome him. Quite the contrary. As he was always among the first to arrive and the last to leave any Dingley Falls gathering to which he was asked, so the good white-haired Father was in no hurry to rush from this party to the next. For Highwick was happy wherever he was. He was, for example, happy living alone in the rectory of St. Andrew's. That life would have been fuller had he taken a wife was, to Prudence Lattice's grief, no troublesome realization of his twilight years. That life would have been truer had he taken a male lover was (despite Walter Saar's disbelief) not an insight that had ever once crossed the Rector's mind. He delighted in the company of young men because he persisted in his own delighted young manhood.

Sloan Highwick's sanguinity derived from his lifelong incapacity for self-reflection. It is, as the gloomy John Stuart Mill noted, our brains that make us miserable. Of course, lacking inner resources, Highwick's mood depended upon continual stimulation from others. But that, given his calling and his character and his luck, he had never had difficulty obtaining. As a child he had once been read a story about a handsome rabbit who was the favorite of all the animals in the forest until one day a new, even more dazzling rabbit arrived, causing the first to be promptly dropped by his admirers. To this lesson on the slippery wheel of fortune little Sloan's response had been to ask, "Why didn't the first rabbit just get a bunch of new friends?" With such easy adaptability, Highwick had moved through life, alone only when he slept.

All the other solitary people in Dingley Falls were proof of that truism of human nature which the Rector chanced to avoid. For all of them thought they would be happier if they did not live alone. Indeed, they saw in their solitude the very source of everything that kept them from utter and lasting satisfaction with life. Among those on whom the untimed silence and unchanged space of lonliness weighed so heavily that they felt they must keep in continual motion to escape being numbed, the most frightened were Evelyn Troyes and Walter Saar. An odd pair, the elegant headmaster and the petite widow, though they shared the added coincidence of escaping solitude with music while wishing to escape it in the company of the curate, Jonathan Fields, who spent far more time with Father Highwick than with either of them. Of course, Jonathan was scared, too, and knew that Highwick was safer: he was demanding, but his demands could be met, for the Rector wanted time, not love, which costs more. Jonathan earnestly believed that his happiness lay in a life shared daily with a lover, but he deceived himself in this assumption, for his wiser self had actually chosen well for him. As a bachelor priest he

could give a little to a lot without giving the whole lot
(himself) to anyone, which was what he mistakenly
thought he longed to do—if only he were not so
insecure and so much in demand.

But Walter Saar and Evelyn Troyes were ready to
make such gifts. They were honestly unsuited to living
alone. Evelyn had managed to avoid it for more than
forty years, having proceeded directly from her childhood home to a conservatory dormitory to an elopement with Hugo Eroica to a marriage with Blanchard.
In fact, she had scarcely so much as slept in a solitary
bedroom and had never, until her daughter, Mimi,
abandoned her for college, lived in an entire house by
herself. She wasn't used to it and she didn't like it.
Evelyn knew best who she was through a man's
response; without the boundaries of a male surrounding her, her identity seemed to her to drift away into
vapor. She could not define herself.

Walter Saar, on the other hand, was quite used to
living alone, but he didn't like it either. Yet consciousness of his vast desire for love ("If unrestrained, I
would darn some dear man's socks with my teeth")
held him in check. Less conscious that he wanted, even
more than a chance to be loved, a chance to love, to
give away a heart that was too enlarged for comfort, he
played the profligate prodigal even to himself—
imprisoning with barbs of wit that "disgustingly domestic sensibility" of which he was so ashamed, fearing
rightly that if his heart got loose it would embarrass him
by espousing, in a loud, tacky voice, such unsophisticat-
ed clichés as monogamy, fidelity, hope, and, God
forbid, faith.

The loneliness then of Walter Saar and Evelyn
Troyes was singleminded. In that regard, it was unlike
the solitude of Dr. Otto Scaper, who missed a wife in
the past but was otherwise reasonably content, and of
Sidney Blossom, who missed a wife in the future but
was otherwise moderately capable of enjoying himself.
It was different from the loneliness of Tracy Canopy,

who would have been wretched on a desert island with
Vincent but without a phone to call her many acquaintances, or a post office from which to receive her many
catalogs, or a committee in which to exchange her many
ideas. It was different from the loneliness of Prudence
Lattice, who had lost hope, or of Sammy Smalter, who
had never allowed himself to have much, or of Winslow
Abernathy, who had had only one day to assimilate
solitude, or of Judith Haig, who found it impossible to
assimilate anything else, or of Limus Barnum, whose
need was so mammoth that no one person, no number
of people, could fill it, and whose anger at not being
filled was so naked that everyone looked the other way.
    All these people lived alone in Dingley Falls and
were convinced that happiness lived in more crowded
houses. They should have seen A. A. Hayes drive,
slightly intoxicated, enviously past the bachelor quarters of Sidney Blossom, on his way home to four
children he failed to understand and a wife whose
proximity was more painful because his love—which in
the beginning he had thought as enduring as marble—
had not yet entirely been worn away by the oceans of
rage that beat against it. They should have heard Sarah
MacDermott long for the silence of Judith Haig if only
for the two minutes it would take her to remember
what her name was. They should have noticed Priss
Ransom hurriedly suppress the thought that while
Ernest was for the most part agreeably unobtrusive, he
would be entirely so should he join Vincent Canopy
and leave her, like Tracy, her own woman. They should
have listened to the awe with which many of Walter
Saar's students spoke of his wit and style and courage to
stay free. They should have eavesdropped on Coleman
Sniffell.
    But they didn't. And besides, knowledge is no cure
for envy. The incontestable proof of history that wealth
and fame and youth are no sole source of happiness in
no real way lessened Hawk Haig's desire for wealth or
A. A. Hayes's desire for fame or Ramona Dingley's

desire for youth, and for the same trite and true reasons
no evidence of their neighbors' misery could stop
Dingleyans from envying one another. "Such is Life,"
Sloan Highwick would say, and return to his roses.

CONCERNING LETTERS

The power of the post office is awful. There stands
Judith Haig, sorting lives, collecting decisions, distrib-
uting possibilities. In the hands of a satanic humorist,
or even a careless carrier (Mrs. Haig is neither), futures
could be randomly redistributed, happiness returned to
its sender, undelivered. Mail that is government-
inspected (and microfilmed, too) has always seemed
scary to A. A. Hayes. But now he has also begun to
worry about Dingley Falls's anonymous letters. As he
told himself, when slightly intoxicated: "Some sadistic
bastard is hand-stamping on the scribbles of the human
heart. And we can no more escape what's being said
about us than we can escape that bully the telephone,
or that SOB the IRS."

None of the townspeople have reported these written
slanders officially to Chief Haig in order that the culprit
might be legally pursued, though gossip about the
letters has been rampant. Few people prefer to have
even a maniac's analysis of their psyches read into a
public court record. Particularly when the analysis is so
compellingly negative, and at least possibly true. A. A.
Hayes, for example, could easily have written his to
himself: "You chicken-snot snob. You loser. Why don't
you kill your wife? She's killing you. You like that?
Hard to kill a dead man, right, pal? No-ball liberal."
Hayes could go even further: "As Lime says (nobody's
all bad), someone ought to get on the stick. Am I so
morally lackadaisical, so stripped of ambition, that a
scoop can be flung in my face like a chocolate pie and

not arouse in me even the curiosity to comment, 'Ah, chocolate'? Apparently so. Some paranoid! I have let drop the dropping of the highway, the breaking of my window, the smashup of my life, without so much as a who, what, when, where, or how. Not to mention why. Some journalist! Some spy! Don't I care? Apparently not. My whole life could go by while I sat on the pot reading *Journal of the Plague Year* with the door locked to keep the world away."

The editor knew of a half-dozen other Dingleyans who had received the letters. But there were still others he had not heard of: Priss Ransom, who had said "Ha!" to it all, had said so only to Tracy Canopy. Tracy had not shared with a living soul the anonymous accusation that she was a fool. Evelyn Troyes was still waiting for an opportunity to ask Priss or Tracy exactly what she should make of the following: "Your Juicy Fruit Father Field's a fagot. You bore him stiff. He'd like to get sucked stiff. Not by you."

Sammy Smalter had laughed at his—he'd heard worse. And Beanie Abernathy had thrown hers away without brooding on its evidently prophetic advice, which was: "You itch, Mrs. A. Lawyur can't reach it, can he? I'd like to suck those big tits. You got a itch. You got to scratch it."

While Hayes was starting to worry about these letters, there were, of course, other letters threatening Dingley Falls, just as anonymous and far more dangerous than those smutty misspelled ones that dispensed both with the post office and with the postmistress, who had never received one. There were literal letters far more harmful than words. Words, a child knows, can break no bones.

The secret service behind the secret base is abbreviated. (No country ever spells its secrets out). Here in the U.S.A. we have whole anonymous alphabets to save us from the KGB of the USSR, and from one another. Operation Archangel is thought to be run by the DDT—the Department of Dirty Tricks division of the CIA division of the OSS. DIA says NIC threw them some money. NIE has them on record. The INR and the AEC have the OSS under surveillance, and the FBI has the INR and the AEC on file. Despite this sticky web of connections, the continued operation of Operation Archangel has escaped the notice of those responsible for it.

The most outspoken enthusiast of new experiments in deterrent virology had been from the beginning the big former tackle of Rose Bowl renown, Commander Hector Brickhart of NIC. He shot from the hip and said everybody else should, too. With regard to the Virilization of Defense, as he misheard the phrase, he saw a great future in it. "This stuff is a damn sight bigger than all the nukes in the sea. This thing gets out of hand, and, let's face it square in the face, we can kiss the whole shithouse adios amigos." By "the whole shithouse" the commander meant the world as we know it. By "this thing" he meant, of course, Operation Archangel.

In its first year the secret base was able to report a few practical tests. The facts, as Commander Brickhart asked for them on a personal visit to the base, and as the chief of staff, Dr. Svatopluk, gave them to him, were these: Bacterial and viral pathogens of intensified virulence can be produced, preserved, and safely transported to their destination. Some pathogens, for example, are airborne, so that a man on a subway with a nasal decongestant atomizer could (theoretically) easily release into the crowded air, for example, *Mycobacterium tuberculosis,* or *Neisseria meningitidis,* or *Streptococcus pyogenes,* or *Diplococcus pneumoniae.* All of which Viralization of Defense came down to what Commander Brickhart thought he might as well call "pretty damn mean medicine." All of which, Dr. Svatopluk told him, were "crude," "obvious," and "uninteresting," very much like (he told his staff) the military mind. "My word above," snapped Dr. Svatopluk, "those missile-happy jock brains have got bomb releases for their sphincter muscles! TNT or toxins, it's all the same to them. Fly low and drop a load!"

The commander had been very impatient with the head of the operation. He wanted something that worked, and he wanted it now! Svatopluk tried facetiousness: "Don't you think it might be a teensy bit suspicious, Commander, if all of Moscow woke up one morning with meningitis, and every Commie in Indochina simultaneously dropped dead of TB?" Facetiousness had no more effect on Hector Brickhart than had an Ohio State offensive guard. He got a little hot under the collar, he tried bribery, he tried insults of a crude and obvious sort. Nothing would induce Dr. Svatopluk to mass-market his product until it was ready.

Frankly the scientific team found the notion of viral and bacterial saturation a primitive one. They had tried a little salmonellosis and a little brucellosis, and they knew they worked. It is easy, but uninspired, to food-poison a given population, or fever a control group.

On the other hand, what if a virus could be developed by modifying the very DNA by which we live, and what if that virus could imperceptibly alter the human heart? And what if no diagnostic test could detect it? And no antitoxin could arrest it? And no one need ever know it was being done?

Now that, thought Dr. Svatopluk's team, would be interesting; that would be worthy of the chief of Operation Archangel.

PART
Three

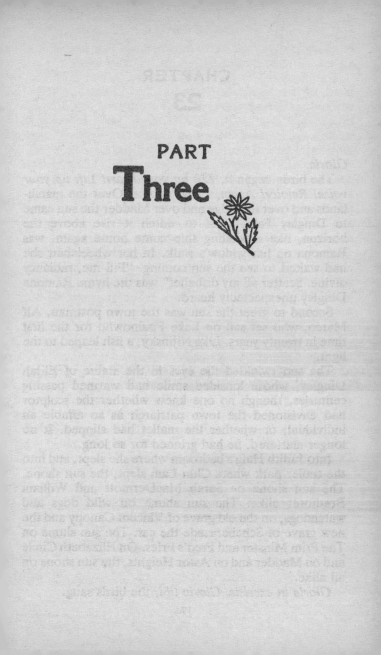

CHAPTER
23

Gloria.

The birds began it. *Lift up your heart! Lift up your voice! Rejoice! Again, I say, rejoice!* Over the marshlands and over the ridge and over Madder the sun came to Dingley Falls. First to watch it rise above the horizon, like a whaling ship come home again, was Ramona on her widow's walk. In her wheelchair she had waited to see the sun coming. "Fill me, radiancy divine. Scatter all my disbelief" was the hymn Ramona Dingley unexpectedly heard.

Second to greet the sun was the town postman, Alf Marco, who set sail on Lake Pissinowno for the first time in twenty years. Like Nijinsky, a fish leaped to the light.

The sun twinkled the eyes in the statue of Elijah Dingley, whose lopsided smile had warmed passing centuries, though no one knew whether the sculptor had envisioned the town patriarch as so affable an individual, or whether the mallet had slipped. It no longer mattered, he had grinned for so long.

Into Judith Haig's bedroom where she slept, and into the trailer park where Chin Lam slept, the sun shone. The sun shone on Sarah MacDermott and William Bredforet alike. The sun shone on wild dogs and watchdogs, on the old grave of Vincent Canopy and the new grave of Scheherazade the cat. The sun shone on The Prim Minster and Fred's Fries. On Elizabeth Circle and on Madder and on Astor Heights, the sun shone on all alike.

Gloria in excelsis. Gloria tibi, the birds sang.

Along the garden walk to Morning Song came the sun, and with it Father Highwick, who sang St. Stephen's hymn with a smile. "'The King shall come when morning dawns, / And light triumphant breaks.'" The Rector's shoe slipped off, and he stooped to tie it. Then away he hummed. "'When beauty gilds the eastern hills, / And life to Joy awakes.'"

And on Glover's Lane, Joy to life awakened, for Lance Abernathy was coming to take her for a swim at the Club. On Monday Joy had never ridden in a sports car; on Tuesday she had never been to the Dingley Club; and now on Wednesday, Lance and life and maybe love waited for her outside her room. Anything, everything could happen. Maybe now she would stop feeling so tired and sick all the time, and maybe her mother would stop treating her like a baby, and maybe she would tell Lance she was only almost seventeen— instead of the nineteen years she had claimed for herself when he asked.

Next door to Joy, Polly Hedgerow bounced with an arch of her back out of bed. Today was vacation's first day, that first vacant day undefined by the bells of Dixwell High School. The beginning of time when anything, everything could happen. She pulled on the jeans and T-shirt that she had thrown last night over her wicker chair. Perhaps she would ride her bike alone up to the marshlands. Perhaps she would walk along the Rampage, though not up as far as Sidney Blossom's little depot. The thought of Mr. Blossom was still embarrassing. Perhaps Miss Dingley, who had asked to see her, would be like Miss Haversham in *Great Expectations* and tell her a horrible tale of blighted love.

Polly was slicing bananas onto a bacon and mayonnaise sandwich when her father stumbled downstairs into the kitchen. Clumsy and snappish with sleep, Cecil Hedgerow squeezed his tie tighter around his neck as if he were trying to hang himself. He looked healthier than he felt. Because his weekdays were spent selling houses in the sun, and his weekends spent chasing the smallmouth bass, Hedgerow's face, neck, hands, and arms to the edge of his short-sleeved shirt were a leathery brown; the rest of his body was gray-white.

"That's not a breakfast," he said, as he fumbled to remove the twisted wire that sealed the bread.

"Sure it is. Did you know there're tribes in the Pacific that don't eat anything but yams?"

"That's not a yam. And you're an American. Eat an egg."

"Did you know Americans are having heart attacks from eating too many eggs?"

"Did you know that until I drink this cup of coffee, *anything* you know is knowing too much?"

"Coffee's a drug."

"You think I'd go to the trouble to make it if it weren't? Haven't you been wearing those clothes for a week?"

"Go ahead, why don't you tell me I didn't comb my hair, and my fingernails are dirty, and my room's dirty, and you can't manage all alone with no cooperation from me, and maybe I *should* have gone to live with my aunt. Boy, what a grouch!"

"Well, it's all true." Hedgerow sighed and broke three eggs into a pan. "Maybe *I* should have gone to live with your aunt. You're the grouch."

"You started it." His daughter opened the back door, and light raced through the room like a two-year-old. "Look! Cheer up, it's a great day outside."

"Be in the high eighties by noon, and muggy."

"You ought to think positive, Cecil. You're what they call a melancholy personality."

"Hmmm," mumbled her father. "Don't call me 'Cecil,' call me 'Daddy.'"

"Oh, vomit, I'm too old."

"Well, how 'bout Pop, or Dad, or Sir, or Mr. Hedgerow?"

"I'll call you *papa*, like Natasha calls Count Rostov."

"Fine." Hedgerow sat down at the brunch counter

with his breakfast and bent open his *National Geographic* to a photograph of anglers in the River Tweed. He wished he were with them.

"I'm going."

"Well, don't slam the door, babe."

"Father Fields said Miss Dingley wanted to see me today."

"What for?"

"I dunno. Mysterious."

"Aren't you goint to school?"

"Oh, Daddy! School's over."

"Fine."

The widower watched his only child pedal past the kitchen window, her sandwich clamped in her teeth. She needed a mother. Someone who understood female things, like Peggy Strummer, or Evelyn Troyes. She was getting too old for him. Her clothes just didn't look right, her hair wasn't right. Obviously Mrs. Strummer next door explained things to Joy, about appearance and other things. Of course, Polly would never look like Joy, no matter what advice she got, but she had a good head on her shoulders. It was just her bad luck that she'd taken after him and not her mother. He ought to talk to Polly, but he kept putting it off. They just made do day by day, postponing serious cleaning, serious shopping, serious conversation. So the dishes got done, but the sink was grimy; the floor got swept, but cobwebs floated in the corners of the ceilings; their clothes got washed, but not ironed; the lawn mowed, but not seeded; his wife's flowers grew, if they would, without gardening. Father or daughter usually had to make an extra trip to Marco's supermarket halfway through fixing a meal.

Polly needed a mother, and he needed a wife. But they only wanted the one they had lost in one fevered night seven years ago. Lost with such incomprehensible speed and with such absurd finality, lost so wrongly, that they both waited to learn there'd been some mistake, waited for Pauline Hedgerow to come back into the room where she belonged, to open the door and call as she always had, "Anybody home?" They waited, and postponed things.

I am a melancholic, thought Hedgerow; how could I not be? Still, the sun came easily through the kitchen window. And untended, the hawthorn outside the window blossomed, and there unending was the song of blackbirds and sparrows. *Lift up your hearts. We lift them up unto the Lord,* sang the birds.

Limus Barnum had a motorcycle. Gravel spat like bullets in the sun when he spun it out of his driveway to scare Polly Hedgerow. She swung her bike away from his approach. His machine skidded sideways, and, embarrassed, Lime skipped off to run beside it, as if he had planned all along to walk it down the lane.

"Hey, watch out!" Polly yelled, to be sure he knew she knew he had fallen.

He knew. "Where's your pretty friend?" he asked.

"I couldn't presume to say," she replied. "Did you get hurt falling off?"

"You're the one that's gonna get hurt, riding that bike in the middle of the street like that." Barnum tightened his helmet, popped his clutch, and jumped away like a racetrack rabbit.

Sleepers wake. "That asshole Barnum," said one of them, roused to consciousness by the roaring motor-cycle. A. A. Hayes, Lime's next-door neighbor, hid his head under the pillow. His wife left their bed.

Sleepers wake. Coleman Sniffell, who worked for A. A. Hayes, said to his wife, Ida, who worked for Dr. Scaper, "Ida, don't tell me I have to like my life. I *don't* like my life. I have to live it, but I don't have to like it. And I don't like my job either, but I'd still like to get there before noon." At the breakfast table, Ida was reading aloud from *Like Your Life!,* now in its sixteenth week on the best-seller list—a good reason, thought Sniffell, for the author to be pretty fond at least of his own.

"All I'm saying is, make a list," prescribed Ida, "of seven little things you could do that would give you pleasure, then do one of them today, and one more every day after that. Learn the habit of happiness."

The first little thing that came into Sniffell's mind was the thought of spooning arsenic into his wife's cereal; the habit of happiness was obviously too dangerous for him to cultivate. So he just said, "Pass the sugar." He scooped it out despite the news that it was a serious health hazard and that the cereal was 90 percent sugar already. "Who cares?" he told Ida.

Sleepers wake. Sidney Blossom woke when a phone sang into his cottage, the reconverted Dingley Falls train depot. "Sid? This is Kate. I bet I woke you up. Can you have lunch with me? I'll bet at the Club playing tennis." Melody poured out of the librarian's shower. "No ear hath ever caught such rejoicing."

Kate Ransom's parents woke and stepped out on opposite sides of their expansive bed. Each went into his or her bathroom.

Tracy Canopy woke when her book fell off the bed. Evelyn Troyes woke to catch "Today" on television. So bright, so light, so right as a song was the sun that Dr. Otto Scaper woke when his radio told him to. Walter Saar woke and put on a record; the headmaster, who knew he should prefer the late sonatas, put on Beethoven's Ninth instead. *Freude, schöner Götterfunken, Tochter aus Elysium* sang out the deaf old dead man in a hundred voices, and with him Walter Saar sang. He revenged himself on his students' midnight stereophonic gibberish in this way. Late to dining hall, Ray Ransom galloped past the master's house. "I bet Saar's on drugs," the senior decided. "Blasting that junk out at eight in the morning."

Prudence Lattice woke and waited for Scheherazade to insist on breakfast. Orchid O'Neal woke and was driven by her sister, Sarah MacDermott, over to Elizabeth Circle to wait on people. Judith Haig woke at the very same minute she had always been awakened

by the nuns. Winslow Abernathy, who always woke
early, slept late. Lance Abernathy, who always slept
late, woke early. He sat up and yawned, he stood up
and stretched, he did a dozen sit-ups, push-ups, and
chin-ups. He slipped into French jockey shorts of a
bold design. He slipped into a blue leisure suit, and at
his leisure drove to the Dingley Club for breakfast.
Old Mr. Bredforet was already there at the billiard
table, waiting with a Bloody Mary for anyone else to
arrive.

The sun to Lance was a golden girl. The sun to his
brother, Arthur, was a pocket watch that warned him
not to be late for his meeting with Ernest Ransom. On
his way to the bank, the sun to Ernest Ransom was a
giant coin. The sun to Father Highwick, on his way to
church, was a glad Communion wafer. And to Tac
Hayes, soaring toward the hoop, the sun was a yellow
basketball, while to Luke Packer, bicycling to work, the
sun was a globe mapping paths to shiny foreign places.

To Sammy Smalter, the sun that morning, for no very
good reason, seemed to change from glory into glory,
as he leaned against the porch rail of his aunt's white,
white house, lost in wonder, love, and praise.

And the birds kept on.

Gloria.

CHAPTER
24

Father Jonathan Fields was awake, but still lay in the
single bed which pressed its white coverlet against the
white wall of his little bedroom. Across the dark oak
floor was his desk and on the desk, vows in a gold
frame: "Thou did'st give Thyself to me. Now I give

myself to Thee." St. Andrew's stone cottage had only
three rooms—study, bedroom, and kitchen. Each was
furnished with simple but good pieces (gifts of Father
Highwick's, to whom they had been given by parishioners). The curate had himself bought only a few things (a
secondhand upright piano, a copy of an engraving by
Burne-Jones), and he thought he owned too many, and
he wished to own many more. And he feared that if
Christ had come carrying His Cross past him down the
street, he would have fled up a side alley hugging his
puny desires under his coat. Jonathan hated himself
because he did not labor in a leper colony, did not carry
stones to build a Harlem schoolhouse, lay not on iron
but on ironed sheets, lay there with an erection he
could not will away. Though not purposely evoked by
thought or deed, though raised in a dream, still, might
not the dream itself be unforgivable?

Indulgence in remorse was rarely an early morning
opportunity for the curate, to whom had fallen nearly
all the impersonal church duties. The Rector's delight
was to officiate over Sunday Solemn Mass; he loved a
crowd. Today, however, Highwick had offered to take
Morning Song service, despite its unpopularity, since
he was leaving that afternoon for two days in Manhattan, and therefore leaving Jonathan to draft the financial report, pay the sick calls, listen to confession and
conversions, and celebrate Communion, alone.

On the other side of the garden from the curate's
cottage, now before the altar, Highwick was intoning to
Prudence Lattice and three other early risers: *The Lord
is in His holy temple. Let all the earth keep silence
before Him.*

Sliding away the sheet, Jonathan looked down on his
risen demon. He let his mind haul up the cannon of its
constant war: had his calling been active desire, or had
he, as he had once painfully confessed in an anonymous
church, run to God so that he could not hear the call of
active desire? Was he gay? (He certainly wasn't
happy.) If he could not marry, was it then better to

burn in holy fire? That anonymous confessor (had *he* been gay?) had claimed that Christ, indifferent to the particulars of whom we love, just commanded us *to* love. Let us love one another as *ourselves*. The hardest part of that, thought Father Fields, would be to love himself.

Let us humbly confess our sins unto Almighty God, said the Reverend Mr. Highwick with a broad smile.

Jonathan clenched his pillow. How could he have been so ashamed of his mother's shabby dresses, so ashamed of the sores on her legs, that he had refused to walk beside her anywhere his friends might see them? He had been ten.

We have followed too much the devices and desires of our own hearts, the Rector told the four people in the pews, who would agree that they had followed their desires, but add that they had never caught up with them. *We have left undone those things which we ought to have done and we have done those things which we ought not to have done.*

Jonathan pinched his arms. How could he have been so careful in high school to shun the unlucky ones, the unhandsome, the ungifted and uneasy, all those whom no one else had liked? He had been sixteen.

He pardoneth and absolveth all those who truly repent, said the Rector, nodding reassuringly.

Jonathan winced and prayed, I will be kind. I will not envy my classmates who got assigned to rich, alluring cities. I will not be impatient with Father Highwick. I will go back to Miss Dingley's and try again to help her. I will be careful, I will care. I will not waste my time—I will not waste Your time, Lord, in trying to make Walter Saar like me.

Let us heartily rejoice in the strength of our salvation. The celebrant laughed across the garden.

Does Walter like me? Why should he? But he seems to want to be around me. Don't, don't, stop it. Forgive yourself. *Is* he gay? How can I be sure? How do people know; is there a signal? Should I say something? Talk about Rimbaud, or Benjamin Britten? Suppose I said I loved him and he just said I'm sorry?

As it was in the beginning is now and ever shall be . . .

Jonathan's hand circled the outward and visible sign of his inward spiritual disgrace. The warmth was wonderful.

O ye Fire and Heat, bless ye the Lord: praise Him, and magnify Him forever.

Jonathan looked on at his hand caressing him. A deeper rose was rising and the sweetness of the feeling caught his breath.

Father Highwick hurried happily on. *The Peace of God, which passeth all understanding, keep your hearts and minds . . .* Faster and faster. Highwick longed for a cup of tea. *And the Holy Ghost, be amongst you and remain with you always. Amen. Depart in peace, Alleluia.*

Too late now, Jonathan was sighing, as across the garden the Rector blessed his parishioners, shared with each a little private joke, and then returned them to the world. Too late now to stop, Jonathan went on. With thumb and fingers he rang the ring of up, down, up, down, root to rim, rim and root again. How *could* he, he who wore the black wedding band of Christ around his neck? How could he not now? Best not to think and so postpone the end. Get it over with and then get on with it. "Hey, hey, beat the meat!" Down the college hall the call had gone. Guys would yell it out, laughing, poking, easy joking. Jonathan would shut his door, disgusted, thrilled. Flong the dong, pull and push, pull and push the dang dong dick stick. Funny how the mind will never shut up. But here it comes, up and over. A jismy fountain of old faithless at last. O come all ye! O hell!

Someone was opening his cottage door. Someone was singing away with great good cheer: " 'Guilty now, I pour my moaning, / All my shame with anguish owning.' " The goddamn Rector. He never knocked.

"Jonathan! Lovely day! I hope I'm not disturbing. Still in bed? Ill? Quite flushed! You may have a fever, let me feel, well, all right, but you can't be too careful, you know. Health is all that stands between us and the grave. Some tea will fix you up. No, no, no, no trouble at all. Have you any though? Good, I'm all out. If it's bowels bothering you, tea will help. Did I ever tell you about my Alexandria dysentery? The trip to the Holy Lands? Yes. Runs you wouldn't believe. Oh, ho-ho-ho-ho! Quite literally, too, oh, ho-ho. I raced from water closet to water closet like the woman at the well. Maybe it was Baghdad, though. Was it? I couldn't keep *anything* down, not even bread or soup or . . ."

"Just let me get dressed," his curate replied.

CHAPTER
25

Sammy Smalter was not an outdoorsman; he hadn't the stature for climbing or the stamina for hikes. But today, as soon as he walked into his pharmacy, its shades unraised, the dark, closed space felt stifling. So, in a rare disordering of habits, he relocked the store and stepped back into the sunshine. He even took his car top down to spin off for a quick ride around Lake Pissinowno. Just as he reached the Falls Bridge on Goff Street, he saw a half-circle of large, scrawny dogs baying a woman up against the wood rail of the bridge. The woman was Mrs. Haig. Braking quickly, Smalter called to her, then yelled at the dogs. Unable to make himself heard over the pounding rush of the nearby waterfall, he slammed his hand down on his horn. The pack turned toward the blare, finally broke, and fell back to the vacant lot near the Optical Instruments factory. Mr. Smalter crawled out of his roadster and chased after the dogs, crying, "Scram!" Most of them were big—a gray, brown, and black mottled progeny of half-breeds; mongrels in whom only a few signs of past heritage were scattered: a shepherd's coat, a weimaraner's milky eye.

The pharmacist reached for a rock, but following some undecipherable message from somewhere, the pack, tails twitching, loped away. Mrs. Haig's face was gray. "A mean-looking bunch," he said. "Underfed. Aren't they almost wild?"

Judith let out a slow breath. "Some of their owners left them behind. They scavenge at the trailer park."

"Ah, they've really frightened you."

Judith made herself take ordinary breaths.

"Something like that would scare me to death." The midget smiled. " 'Nature red in tooth and claw.' Let me drive you to the post office; were you headed there? No. I insist. I'll turn around. Then my playing hooky is transformed into a good deed. Come on now, if you think you can squeeze into this little sewing machine case of mine." Mr. Smalter opened the door for Mrs. Haig. She folded herself into the little seat of his MG. She was a tall woman, and her legs made a long curve to the floorboard; she clasped her hands over her dress at her knees. The car, even open, smelled of leather and of the pipes that stuck out of its ashtray. There was an intense intimacy in the smells, and in the act of entering this car, this private space long familiar to a stranger. The feeling startled Judith. Had the top closed over them, the invasion would have been worse, indeed, impossible for her.

"I hope you're not too uncomfortable," said Mr. Smalter. "Have you a scarf? Ah, well, we'll go slowly then."

At the intersection of Goff Street and Cromwell Hill Road, the yellow roadster stopped to let a black Lincoln pass by. In that car Father Highwick exclaimed to his driver, "My goodness! Isn't that something,

Jonathan? Poor little Sammy Smalter out driving about town with the postmistress! And with his top down like a teenager. Peculiar. Shouldn't they be at work? Now, let's not stay too long with poor old Oglethorpe. When people are feeling *that* ill, it's really unkind to put them to the trouble of conversation. And don't mention religion to him. Just a quick word of cheer, then let him get his rest. Chills in June! Well, such is Life." They motored on to call upon the oldest teacher at Alexander Hamilton Academy. Jonathan was wondering if Walter Saar would sense his presence on the premises and appear around some corner at some moment during their stay. He might, if only Jonathan could maneuver the Rector into staying more than two minutes. Or if only the Rector had ever learned how to drive so that he could leave his curate behind to sit by those sick beds so antithetic to Highwick's untroubled disposition. Jonathan felt that he could deal with illness, with tragedy, even with death. It was the life in between that was giving him trouble.

The Tea Shoppe kept irregular hours. This morning it was closed when Sammy Smalter helped Judith Haig out of his car. She had decided to go in to speak with Chin Henry and was relieved not to have to. Luke Packer, sitting on the curb with a book, stood up to wave at the embarrassed pharmacist, who had, in fact, completely forgotten about his new employee. Together they watched Mrs. Haig walk up the street to her post office. "She seems like a nice lady," said Luke.

"Yes," said Smalter. "I've always thought so. Well, to work, Luke, such as it is. My apologies for keeping you waiting. Too bad Prudence isn't around; we could go get a cup of coffee."

"Shouldn't we open the pharmacy?"

"Might as well, I suppose."

Luke thought that while Mr. Smalter might be interesting to talk to, he was certainly not much of a businessman, and that the key to his store was not going to unlock the gate to golden opportunity. Luke was in a hurry.

Behind the post office counter, Judith Haig helped Alf Marco pack into his cracked, worn leather bag her careful arrangement of Dingley Falls's communications. The two worked, as usual, without conversation. Alf, the second of Mama Marco's sons, was a slow, thickset man in his late fifties. He was a reticent, resigned man caught between his grocer brother Carl's energetic drive and his gardener brother Sebastian's moody artistry. Alf had grown up in the middle of his family—and worked now in the middle of Dingley Falls—largely unnoticed by anyone. As a result, he had no sense of how it would feel to be singled out for special attention. He felt no lack of, or need for, unique gifts or unique recognition. He carried the mail for Dingley Falls. That was all. When Mrs. Haig retired, he would be postmaster of Dingley Falls. He would have refused had he not thought his doing so would have caused trouble.

"Nice day," he suddenly said.

"Very nice," said Mrs. Haig. "How are you today, feeling better?"

" 'Bout the same, I guess. Well, not so good, tell you the truth."

"Why don't I call Argyle and get somebody to take the mail around for you? Just for today."

"Naw. There's not much, don't worry about it." Marco shouldered the bag and rubbed his neck. "So long."

"If you . . . Alf? Alf. If you start feeling tired, come back, will you?"

He nodded without looking around.

Judith now made three telephone calls, thereby breaking in one day an eleven-year weekly record. They were hard for her to make, and she wasn't sure why she felt she had to make the effort. First she was told by an operator that there was no phone in

Maynard Henry's trailer. Next she was told by Prudence Lattice that Chin Henry was there with her at home, where Prudence was staying because she had had a bad night. But Chin had asked for extra work, and so the shopkeeper had asked her to come help with the baking. "The child looked so exhausted, Mrs. Haig, that I just now insisted she lie down awhile. May I take a message?" Judith said she had only wanted to know if the girl was all right, since last night she had seemed upset. "Oh, I didn't realize you knew Chin," Miss Lattice replied. "Yes, of course, it's an awful situation. What can we do?" Mrs. Haig said she didn't know. Then she made her third phone call, asking for an appointment to speak with the senior partner of Abernathy & Abernathy.

"Yoo-hoo, day off today, Lord love me," caroled Sarah MacDermott as she thrust open both big wooden doors at once so that the sudden sun made the postmistress cover her eyes. Sarah was, she said herself, in a fantastic mood wholly unsupported by reality. "But every time I get out of that stockyard at the A & P, it makes me so damn happy I feel like going over there and peeking in the window, just to watch somebody *else* punching those buttons all day long. They'll bury me and my ears'll still be ringing. *Ping!* Two for ninety-nine. God rest her soul. *Ping!* And those crazy bra burners are out screaming how women have the right to get out of the kitchen and go to work! Every one of them ought to be forced to work at the A & P, that's all I can say."

"Good morning, Sarah." Mrs. Haig made her effort to smile.

At her leisure Sarah wore slacks and a sleeveless blouse of slick orange synthetics. It had blue stripes that nearly matched her blue straw sandals with strawberries painted on them. Her yellow topknot nearly matched her big yellow plastic handbag with the Golden Gate Bridge painted on it. She clopped over to the counter and dropped a sloppy package down in front of Judith. Wrapped in an old A & P bag, taped erratically, and tied with five feet of string, the box was addressed in giant chartreuse letters. "A pair of pj's for my brother, Eddie. I guess they still wear them, even out in California, you think? Better make it Special Delivery, I totally forgot him and he's real touchy about his birthday. Orchid said it was tomorrow. What can you do? He's out of a job, too. Went out there because there was nothing here, and then there's nothing there. Makes you wonder where it is. See, his plant lost all their army contracts and, anyhow, they just slammed the doors in everybody's face that didn't have whatdoyoucallit, longevity. But I told him, 'Eddie, if you got to be laid off it might as well be where the sun always shines so you can at least get out and get a tan and not be here freezing your fanny off.'"

"I suppose so."

"But, hey, anyhow, I hear you had a visitor last night. *Honey*. What in the world was she doing out at your place? Chinkie. Joe says it was after midnight when you called him to come and get her. Jesus love us!"

"She was upset about her husband."

"I guess so! I'd be upset too if I'd come all the way and sneaked into America and ended up with a jailbird. Men and women! Arn always did say that Maynard would turn bad. He was always too dead-set on things; sort of, you know, fixated. Anyhow, what's it all got to do with you?"

"She thought I could help her. I don't know why."

"Help her! I guess you *don't* know why, 'cause there's not a blessed reason. America is just too nice, that's all. Honey, you take my advice, don't get mixed up in any funny business. Joe just couldn't believe she'd gone over there, bothering you, with you sick and all. 'Wait'll Hawk hears.' That's what Joe was saying this morning. How much is that package? Are you kidding? That's more than the pajamas cost! I might as well buy a ticket and fly them out to Hollywood myself. Maybe meet a movie star, have a little fling for myself!" Sarah rolled her eyes and popped her gum with cheerful lasciviousness. "Heaven help us, Judith, if they keep on with this inflation, there's not going to be a thing left that ordinary folks like me and you can afford to buy. Can't afford to mail a package, can't afford to turn on the furnace, can't afford to put gas in the car. But what can you do? Judith, Joe and I are buying a house. Finally we just said, it's now or never. The way things are going, in six months they'll double the price and leave off the roof. But we got to go, my boys are hanging from the beams where we're renting now."

"Yes, I know you're . . ."

"Crowded? Honey, we might as well, all seven of us, be Siamese twins, we're so mushed up together! So I'm seeing Cecil Hedgerow about one of those nice new Cape Cods over in Astor Heights. The one on Pilgrim Boulevard. Did I tell you this? With the green dutch doors? I sure wish you two'd bought down there instead of building out in the middle of nowhere. 'Course, I mean, you got a gorgeous house. But we could have been neighbors again, like on Long Branch."

"Well, John wanted . . ."

"Say no more! What can a wife do but grin and bear it? Now, you know me, I wouldn't trade Joe and the boys for all the coffee in the A & P, but not a day goes by when I don't wish one or the other of them would get eaten by a bear and save me the trouble of buying a gun to shoot them. Lord, you've ruined me; that ten was supposed to lay away Tommy's overcoat. Once you break a ten these days, it's like a dollar used to be, you might as well flush the change down the john. Come over and take pot luck with us tonight, no sense to cook just for yourself what with Hawk away. Liz Taylor's going to be on Channel Six, too; I can't help it, I'll just watch anything she's in. Well, anyhow, you call me if you change your mind and get lonely. And you tell

Chinkie Henry there's not a thing you can do. You got to take care of yourself now, Judith. *I* know. You scared me so bad yesterday, I went over and made Dr. Scaper listen to my heart. He said I shouldn't have bothered, said I'd live forever. But my father, and his father before him, both died of their hearts. 'Course, you don't drink, but still."

If the allotment of heartbeats to glasses of alcohol was inevitably predetermined with arithmetic precision, and if A. A. Hayes had kept count of his daily drinks in his thirty years of daily drinking, he could now calculate his own demise and scoop Death for his paper. But in that time Hayes had lost count of much more than bottles. He drank in order to lose count; not like Walter Saar, to get in touch with who he was, but to stay out of touch with who he might have been.

Still, he congratulated himself that, as yet, he had not taken to antemeridian imbibing. Even this morning, with all four of his incomprehensible children home on three months' parole from school and already bored, with his wife, June, locked up with another migraine, with his colleague Coleman Sniffell in a (if possible) more than typically rotten mood—still, Hayes could boast, he was not drinking. He was smoking, gulping coffee, sucking cough drops, chewing pencils, and feeling all his fillings with his tongue. He was twisting his hair, biting at his cuticles, picking at his ears, and rolling his book pages between his fingers. But he wasn't drinking.

The Dingley Day was a misnomer; the paper had ceased daily publication in 1931. Even weekly now, it filled no more than two dozen pages. They included not only summarily treated national affairs, but those communal reports closer to the hearts and purses of Dingleyans—*Property Tax Hike Looms. Battle Waged to Save Falls Bridge. Volunteer Firemen Demand New Hoses.* And there were personals ("Please give me a home. I am a perky kitten with lots of personality and no tail"). And more than anything else, there were advertisements:

The Prim Minster. Since 1726 / Hedgerow Realty. Traditional Homes at Old-Fashioned Prices / Step into the Past at The Tea Shoppe / Happy Hour All Day Long at Fred's Fries Bar and Grill / Today Thru Thurs. ONLY. *Jaws!* Hope Street Cinema / Join Us in a Yard of Ale at Beautiful Old Towne Inn / SPEND TIME WITH LIME, AND SPEND LESS

Once A. A. Hayes had dreamed of the speech with which he would accept the Pulitzer Prize awarded him for toppling corruption in his government or laying bare the stinking fat carcass of high finance. Then for a while he daydreamed that the same prize might be given instead in recognition of his quiet decades as the editor of a small-town weekly whose muted clarion calls for all the right things had been always written with the style of Adlai Stevenson and the ethics of Eleanor Roosevelt. Those decades had passed. Now he daydreamed in the mornings of an afternoon drink, and in the afternoons he daydreamed of lives he might have lived and now was quite sure he never would. He had not made it. There were only so many mirrors in the house of fame, and he was never to see his face in one of them. Some people have better luck, or timing, or help, or skills, or fewer children, or none, and no wife, and so A. A. Hayes, reflecting, passed his sober morning.

A cricket call of key tapping glass caught his ear. Someone waved at him, then fluttered inside. "Alvis, I'm so sorry to bother you, I think one should never bother a man when he's busy at work." And she isn't even being sarcastic, thought Hayes, as he stood up from his daydream to welcome Evelyn Troyes. She swayed inquisitively toward him, slender as a jonquil in a green dress and yellow hat with matching shoes and purse.

"No bother." He smiled. "Not doing a blessed thing. Evelyn, we should do a list of the best-dressed women in town and you'd be first every time."

"Why, thank you. I always say you southerners are the only American men to take the trouble to notice the trouble a woman may have taken, you know what I mean, don't you? But I have one little question and then I'll leave you alone. We'll be in New York this afternoon, the Thespian Ladies will, and oh, I'm so sorry, I called your June earlier, and she has another of those awful migraines, doesn't she, and can't join us *again*. So awful for her, isn't it?"

"Yes, apparently they're very painful. Here, let me get you a chair."

"No, no, I'm already behind this morning. Alvis, I want to buy a signature for a friend, and I know you have so many yourself, famous signatures, so I thought you could advise me where I could get a Bach, or if not, perhaps a Mozart or a Beethoven, or even a Brahms would do. I did try Altman's, but they had mostly those presidents nobody ever heard of. Oh, and Napoleon's mother! They wanted two thousand dollars for her, *He* was only fifteen hundred, and his mother was two thousand, isn't that cunning?"

Hayes explained to Mrs. Troyes that even Brahms would not be cheap, but he wrote down for her some agents in Manhattan who handled names. She fluttered away.

It was true that the editor had in his den a collection of famous names, framed with engraved faces on velvet cloth. They were mostly signatures of Union generals—Grant, Sherman, McClellan, Polk—handwriting of the devil, as his southern relatives had called them; for each of those bold official scrawls might have, long ago, ordered the loss of an ancestor of theirs, or the burning of a town square. Hayes had collected them in his youth not merely because fame intrigued him, but in order to be perverse: "What makes you like to fly in every-body's face that way?" his family had asked him with sad and puzzled reproach. He'd answered, "I thought you'd be tickled to see all those Yankees dead and hung up before your eyes," and then he'd grinned at them with the superiority of his first year at college, which was one more year than any of them had had.

Later his collection had turned to criminals—a natural progression, his relatives would have said. To be made history, to be defined by one act, an act that might have taken no more than the minute needed to murder—that was fame, too. And besides, the existential *act* of crime, the willingness to choose the act and then perform it, fascinated Hayes with what he suspected was envy. Those who could concentrate rage or greed or madness (as a painter might concentrate skill) had the advantage of that distillation over those whose impulses were diffused into the ordinariness of normal compromise. Just as a nuclear bomb has an advantage over dynamite. Just as his wife, shut in inviolate darkness with the blind concentration of a migraine headache, had an advantage over him, with his simple hangovers that aspirin could cure. Just as Maynard Henry, the man whose story he had heard and now thought he would add to his collection, the man who had shoved someone's car off a cliff for daring to abduct his wife, had that advantage of absoluteness over Winslow Abernathy, who, when his wife was stolen, had allowed himself only a drink at The Prim Minster. The mad get away with murder.

Hayes's office door slammed. Well, at least it wasn't Limus Barnum.

"Got a match, A.A.?" bellowed Otto Scaper. "Why don't you fix that damn window, hey? The weather keeps warm, this place will be crawling with bugs."

"I want that hole there so you can blow your stinking cigar smoke into it. What have you been up to? Haven't seen you around for a while. Coming over to Cecil's for the game tonight?"

"Guess so, if folks give me a chance. Too much business, too much." The old doctor lowered himself, grunting, into a chair and licking his fingers, rubbed them against his eyelids. "Old fellow, Jim Price, remember, used to be a night watchman out at the factory? Had a coronary yesterday. Lived in the trailer park over there. One of the Puerto Ricans found him."

"Somebody told me you lost the old nun at Mercy House, too. She was the last of them, wasn't she?"

"Yeah. Monday. Endocarditis. Lot of it, too much. I'm beginning to wonder if every damn person in town isn't going to walk in with it. Well, I don't know. Overworked and ignorant. Overaged, too. Ernie Ransom told me flat out a couple of days ago that I ought to retire."

"Fat chance."

"Old folks die, I guess. Young ones, too. Well. Lucky, I had a birth this morning. Vacationers up at the lake; weren't expecting till July, they said. Had a girl. Sort of set me up. Things have been bad."

"Listen, Otto, I hear you went out and got our water supply checked." Hayes grinned. "Got a story for me? You don't still think somebody poisoned Pauline Hedgerow, do you?"

Scaper shook a vast paw at the editor. "Goddamnit, don't get facetious with me, Alvis, I won't stand for it. I loved that gal. Hell's bells, man, dying's more than a column in a damn newspaper. I swear I think you fellows would film them sweeping up your mother's brains off the highway if the wreck was big enough to make it onto the six o'clock news. What a verminous profession you got yourself into."

"I don't know that yours has got much luster left to polish either. But I'm sorry if I sounded facetious, I didn't mean it that way."

"Well, all that booze has soured your insides, that's all. Gimme one of your cigarettes. This goddamn thing tastes like a bedpan." The doctor threw his cigar butt across the room into a trash can.

"So? What about our water?"

"Pure as a baby's tears. Nah, there's nothing there. I've been thinking about something else. Dogs."

"Dogs?"

"Ever think about how Vince Canopy's dog died about the time he did, didn't it? And old Mrs. MacDermott went all to pieces about that yapper of hers going, then next thing we knew she was gone, too. And this fellow Price over there eating out of the same garbage just about as all those mutts."

"I don't follow you, what's the connection?"

"What?" Scaper turned his head and Hayes repeated the question. "I don't know. Just funny all of them being dog nuts, sort of. Pauline's old collie."

"Are you saying they died because of their dogs?"

"I don't know what I'm saying just yet." Scaper rubbed his huge arms.

The phone buzzed. Hayes listened, then held out the receiver. "It's Ida. Oglethorpe up at the academy just collapsed; they think he's in shock."

Scaper lunged from the chair like a whale. He grabbed the phone. "The nurse there? She got him wrapped up? On my way." He dropped the receiver on its hook. "A.A., that your car out front? Give me the keys, I walked in."

Fishing in his pocket as they hurried out the door, Hayes offered to drive the doctor.

"No, thanks, not if you pay as much attention to the road as you do to this machine. Why don't you clean your car up sometime? Looks like the goddamn inside of a goat's stomach."

"It's symbolic."

"Bull roar. It's sloth."

All Dingley Falls was awake now. Onto the track of the town circle at some point in the day came all the chariots known by their colors and styles to every local citizen. Green Audi: Arthur Abernathy. Old Rolls: old Bredforets. Yellow MG Midget: Sammy Smalter (a private joke). Blue Volvo: Tracy Canopy. White Mercedes: Ernest Ransom. Battered green Ford: Cecil Hedgerow. A blur of gray Chrysler meant Evelyn Troyes and a blur of red Firebird meant Ramona Dingley and Orchid O'Neal. All came but the Abernathys' copper Seville which was now being towed away from Bank Street in Greenwich Village, where Beanie Abernathy slept late with Richard Rage.

Here sped a maroon Jaguar out of the Dingley Club. Down High Street, past Alexander Hamilton Academy and then The Prim Minster, past Dr. Otto Scaper rushing in Hayes's dirty brown Plymouth the opposite way, past the Bredforet estate, it roared confidently to its destination. Lance Abernathy wheeled it into Glover's Lane. Here down the walk skipped Joy Strummer with her little golden spaniel. She came to meet the wave of a brown hand in a blue leisure jacket. Beneath her dress she wore a blue bathing suit, just the color of her dew-blue eyes. Out Lance leaped to seat her, and off they drove to float in blue pool water. The sun frisked and frolicked all over the shiny hood, caroming from chrome to chrome. All around her the wind whisked her sky-silk scarf. She smiled. He smiled. They laughed at the sun. O Love Divine, all loves excelling, Joy of Heaven, to earth come down.

And like gold scarves the little spaniel's ears fluttered against his mistress's fluttering heart.

CHAPTER
26

Out into a crisp noon sun (Cecil Hedgerow had been wrong—it wasn't at all muggy), Judith Haig walked from the post office next door to the cream Georgian building that the Abernathys' law firm shared with Dr. Scaper. Along Dingley Circle came a black and cinnamon Rolls-Royce; in its front seat beside his chauffeur, old William Bredforet sat puffing a Fatima while his wife breathed easier in the back. Bredforet swung his trim gray head along the line of Mrs. Haig's step as they drove past her. He nodded. "That's what *I'd* call a good-looking woman. Fine carriage. Fine form. Pride there. Bones," he added, staring back as they passed "Looks like somebody. Who? Looks like my sister that's it! Look at her. Amazing."

"Got no mind to be cranin' that old neck of your's out of a window at a lady, man as close to the cemetery as you is," snorted his driver.

"Damnation! Will you stop talking like a pickaninny in a minstrel show? That Amos 'n' Andy act of your burns the fire out of me. Why don't you just drive, i you can make out the road, blind as a bat."

"Why doan you . . ."

The glass behind them slid open. "William! Bill! Shu up, please." The glass slid shut. The Bredforets an Bill Deeds, in their eighties, had returned to th egalitarian effrontery of eight-year-olds. They live together in a huge house across the road from The Prin Minster. Strangers often confused the two buildings and once Bredforet had left a party of six waiting in hi

front hall for half an hour until he returned to tell them
the cook had murdered the dishwasher and there would
be no further service that night. William's practical
jokes were equally annoying to his wife and his
chauffeur, who had been in a conspiracy for years to
keep him reasonably decorous, reasonably faithful, and
reasonably sober.

Deeds, whose son was a CPA and whose granddaughter was a doctor at the Center for Disease
Control in Atlanta, refused to allow his family to retire
him and move him to Chicago. His passion was cars,
and he knew that if he lived with his son, he wouldn't
be permitted, at his age and with his eyesight, to get a
driver's license. His other passion was gin rummy, and
after a sixty-year tournament, William Bredforet now
owed him almost $9 million. Mary Bredforet told
people that the two men had enjoyed bickering together too long for anything but death to shut them up.

On Elizabeth Circle, Deeds slammed to a stop
behind Ramona Dingley's red Firebird. Its tinsel
modernity offended him. "Shantytown morning glory,"
he sneered at the car.

"You want to sit out here or come inside with us?"

"Whut do I want to sit in there for?"

"Well, stay out here then. Just keep your nose out
from under Ramona's hood."

"You s'pose' to take your nap at one o'clock. But I
bet I haf to come git you like always."

"I bet you better not," said William in a tone that
implied fingers waggled in ears and a tongue stuck out.

Because Ramona Dingley had been a boisterous girl
of ten when the Bredforets had married (in the social
event of 1914), the old couple continued to think of her
as she had appeared in a corner of their wedding
portrait—hanging in her lace dress from the porch
fence, one black buttoned shoe kicked out at air—to
think of her as someone far too young and agile to be as
ill as she now claimed to be: "Still fooling around in
that wheelchair, Ro? Here, let me take a ride in it."

"William! Let her have her own motor, for heaven's sake."

"Thank you, Mary. Be back in a minute. Don't let him set the house on fire." Miss Dingley spun her wheelchair in a tight circle, then putted across the hall to the dining room.

Wandering through her parlor, Bredforet poked a trim, manicured finger into one of the holes in the life-sized wood carving of Christ that hung on the wall. "Mary, the fact is that Ignatius Dingley was mad as a hatter. The Dingleys have always been dumb, but his screws were loose. Remember, I always said they should have locked him away the first time he saw John the Baptist on the steps of Ransom Bank."

"Lunch!" Ramona shot into the parlor, then backed out in reverse.

They gathered at one end of the dark, long table, where William instructed his wife to "tell Ro her niece has run off with a young stallion, bolted off in the night."

"Know it already," said Ramona. "Heard he was a professor, though. That's what surprised me. Used to think Beanie would marry a sportsman. Sometimes wish I had myself."

"Don't," old Mrs. Bredforet advised her junior, who was seventy-three. "Keep your independence, Ro. I always intended to see the world as a nurse and that was sixty-odd years ago."

"Who's stopping you?" asked her husband.

"Yes, I wanted to amount to something but I didn't have the courage. I just admired Florence Nightingale with a passion. I wanted to sit by the bed of men wounded in foreign places."

"Wounded in foreign places, aha! That's a good one, Mary!" Bredforet's trim gray moustache leaped up to his cheeks in a grin. "Worst place in the world to be wounded though. Ha. Ha."

His wife pinched the freckled skin on his hand. "I am

going to slap your head off one of these days," she told him.

"Too late for all of us now, ain't it?" sighed Ramona as she briskly poured the claret. *"Our* beds will be the ones for nurses to sit at now, sit there bored by our dying, reading romantic trash and dribbling chocolate candy on our sheets. Then with nothing much accomplished, down into the dirt we go. With that idiot Sloan Highwick to sing out a list of insipid virtues they've decided to pretend we had. Down they drop us, *thunk. Thunk!"* She slammed the crystal top into the decanter.

"Rubbish. You're too cooped up, isn't she, Mary? You know, Ro, there's nothing the matter with you. I bet you *had* that heart attack so you could get that machine. Your father was mad as a hatter, and living in this old curiosity shop with a passel of stuffed vermin and porcupine martyrs everywhere you look has turned you morbid. That's all. You're healthy as a filly, and so is Mary, and so am I. Where'd you get this idea about dying?"

"From life," said Miss Dingley. "Unfortunate but true, Willie. Hardly a soul seems to have managed to avoid it."

"Wait your turn then. Don't push."

"I don't mind death so much," said his wife quietly. "I don't *think* I mind death. It's probably very peaceful. But I just don't want William to go first."

"Neither do I," he assured her.

"I'm so used to him, it might be even more unsettling than dying, not to see him, and not to know where he was."

"You and Bill Deeds are probably counting the days until you can get your hands on my money and plow it all in that fool garden of yours. Don't let them put me in a hospital either, Ro. I wouldn't trust a nurse within ten feet of me unless I could keep an eye on both her hands and feet. All of them itching to pull my switch or trip over my cord and let me grind to a halt to make room for the next poor bastard. I hate doctors. Run in blindfolded with a butcher knife and hope they accidentally whack out the problem before they kill you slicing off everything else. No, thanks. Last time I wanted to die I was nineteen. I'm way too old for it now. Now hand me that pea soup," called William with gusto as out came Orchid O'Neal with the cat-faced china tureen that no one had ever liked, but that had perversely refused to be dropped and broken, and that had outlasted three generations of Dingley owners. Fragile as china is, it is less fragile than life.

For Winslow Abernathy, lunch was the last of the chicken salad on Beanie's pumpernickel bread. All he had to do was combine the two and place the sandwich in a bag. He put in a piece of fruit as she had done in the mornings for him and the boys. Three lunches taking shape while breakfast bacon cooked. Always surprises inside: black and green olives, celery, carrot sticks, flowered radishes, mushrooms filled with cheese, all in little glass jars. Sometimes quiche, wild blackberry muffins, marbled cake. When had she prepared them? At night when her family slept? In the morning while the coffee brewed? Where had he been while his daily life was being taken care of by someone who now proved herself a stranger? He had the chicken salad. When that ran out, he was on his own. Abernathy had never prepared more than one meal a year; he made oyster stew on New Year's Eve. Well, I can learn, he said. But, oh, she'll be back.

He pulled the pieces of bread apart and stared at what was spread on them. The thought of that food, all that thirty years of food ladled into him by Beanie, suddenly became nauseating. As a child he had always kept carefully separated with his fork each item on his plate. He had eaten each separately, too, believing that by completely finishing peas before he began potatoes, peas and potatoes would escape uncontaminated to

solitary compartments of his stomach. This habit
persisted, and, in fact, the sight of Beanie's casseroles
and stews had often made him queasy. Now Abernathy
imagined the sum total of cartons and cans, quarters of
cows and lambs and pigs, mounds of vegetables,
everything stacked in heaps up the walls of his office.
Then he imagined all of it, all ten thousand eggs and the
rest, mingled in a slimy pulp inside his body. Then all
the food he had ever eaten in his life pressed against his
bones and organs. Bloody meat slid in front of him by a
grinning navy cook. He wrapped up his uneaten
sandwich. He put it in the wastebasket.

The lawyer was awaiting Judith Haig's arrival. Had
he not spoken to Mrs. Haig on Monday at Dr. Scaper's
(when they had shared, by proximity, the vulnerability
of an examining room with all it implied of helpless
flesh probed for any unfortunate secrets), then he
might have told his secretary to postpone her until next
week. But he had not done so, and now the door was
opened and Mrs. Haig was ushered in. Could it be a
divorce? he wondered. He knew John Haig had his own
lawyer, a blustery Argyle youth who clearly hoped to
slide into the district attorney's job on the trombone of
his own self-esteem. Why should she want a lawyer of
her own?

"I'm afraid I'm upsetting your lunchtime. I could
wait outside."

"No, not at all. How can I help you, Mrs. Haig?
Please, have a seat."

Pulled back into the old leather chair, her eyes on her
white, still hands, Judith took a hesitant breath and
began so softly that the lawyer had to lean across his
desk to hear what she said. "My husband is out of
town. Last night a young woman, Chin Henry, who
works for Miss Lattice, came to see me. Perhaps you
know of her, she's a refugee, a Vietnamese?" Abernathy shook his head. "Oh, well, you see, she married
a construction worker here, but there may be a
question of the legality, I don't know. But there has

been some misunderstanding between them, and well, I
believe her husband assaulted someone on her behalf.
He's been put in jail. By my husband."

"Yes?"

"The girl is very frightened, and alone here, of
course. She came to me. Is there, would it be possible
for you to find out whether bail could be arranged for
him? I suppose that's the first thing. He's not employed
and I gather there is little money."

"What are the charges?"

"I don't know exactly."

"Yes. The court, Mrs. Haig, provides counsel for
those unable to make private arrangements. And there
are bondsmen."

"I understand. The circumstances aren't clear to me.
But I thought, if you wouldn't mind placing a call for
her . . . You see, she came to me, and I feel I should
try to help if I can. I'll be happy to pay for your time, of
course." Across the orderly artifacts on his desk,
Abernathy sat looking at the woman who sat there,
motionless but clearly nervous, pale and tall, dressed in
a white suit, unadorned except for the thin gold ring
and the tips of gold pins that held her hair. He thought
of Roman chastity, a Vestal Virgin, of a nun, of a
camellia. Suddenly she looked up, and he could see the
pupils of her light blue eyes widen with fear, then
quickly close down as she turned away from his eyes.
He understood her embarrassment. It always shocked
him too when his glance elided with someone else's.
It had often struck him as well how infrequent the
occurrence was; how nearly all the business of life can
be conducted without our looking closely into other
people's eyes.

At Abernathy's request, Judith described what she
knew about Chin Henry, and as was his habit he
surrounded her statements with hypotheses. What was
her motive? Marital hostility? She seemed to want help
in obtaining a release for a man her husband had

arrested. She seemed a very unlikely wife for a man like John "Hawk" Haig. Was it maternal impulse?

"Have you a daughter?" he asked.

"A daughter? No." His question had alarmed her.

"I only meant, perhaps you feel, very natural in you, a motherly wish to befriend this young woman. I assume she must be an orphan?"

"Yes. That is, I think she's not certain."

"Evacuations are not very tidy. Pardon me for prying, but have you a large family yourself? I mean, were you considering offering her someplace to stay?"

"I had not, no. But I have no family."

"I see."

"I was raised by the Sisters of Mercy in Madder."

"Ah. Ah, yes." That explained it—the formal diction, the reserve and quietness of her manner. Yet there was something in her quietness as intense as vociferous emotion would be in someone else. Something that confused Abernathy and led him into questions. Everything, every ordinary social inquiry, seemed to take on eerie tension with this woman. He felt flushed, as if he and she confronted each other, not about a phone call on behalf of a stranger, but at some much deeper level. Perhaps his acute, almost painful sensitivity (as if, he thought, he were under the influence of some consciousness-raising drug), his awareness of the weave of fabric in her white jacket, the slight muscle strain at the sides of her mouth, the movement of one of her hands against the other— perhaps all this resulted from his exhaustion after last night, from the shock of Beanie's departure. Whatever the cause, his response was perplexingly disproportionate to the context of their brief acquaintance and legal conversation. As Mrs. Haig continued to speak of the Vietnamese girl, the insight came to Abernathy with certainty that she *always* experienced this radical a relationship to life, that she was without defenses, without the padding of protective indifference that muffles out the world for others. And he felt, strangely, that to know it, to penetrate that secret, was to share an intimacy with her that imposed responsibilities. He felt, more strangely, that to respond to her attractiveness, when she apparently had no knowledge of it, was to put her at an additional disadvantage, in a way to imperil her, and so that too exacted his solicitude, his wardship. These reflections passed through Winslow Abernathy's mind as Judith Haig apologized for asking his help.

Now the lawyer stood. "No bother at all," he said. "I'd be very happy to help if I can. Her immigration and marital status will be simple to verify. Then we'll see what's best to do next. Tell her to try not to worry." He held out his hand, and Judith took it.

The chain on Polly Hedgerow's new bike had snapped. She was walking back through the Madder section of town, where the stores and working people noisily knocked up against one another. (As A. A. Hayes had once written in *The Dingley Day,* "Leisurely trees and grassy quietness have become costly; only the urban rich and the rural poor can afford time and space anymore." Reading which, William Bredforet had remarked to his wife, "Joke to think that your grandfather's paper is in the hands of a Johnny Reb Socialist drunk now." And it would have been a shock to Daniel Highwick, capitalist, abolitionist, and teetotaler.)

Here on Three Branch Road, near what had once been shacks and was now the trailer park, Polly's father, Cecil, had grown up in one of the crowded brick row houses. Since he'd first pointed his old home out to her, she had come to look at it a number of times. The narrow, cracked stone steps and grimy bricks held a sad magic for her—a sweet, sharp rush of pity to think of her father, skinny, unfashionably dressed, coming down those steps with his violin case on a cold morning to walk to school, where the other boys had once ganged up on him: they were Catholic and Cecil Hedgerow's mother was Jewish. His father had not been Jewish, nor had he raised his son in that (or any) religion. The Hedgerows' had been a love match—it had also cost them their respective families' love. Widowed, Miriam Hedgerow had remained alone in Madder, where she opened a seamstress shop in her living room and for twenty years took in and out the clothes of Dingley Falls ladies as fashion or flesh required. She had also played the piano and worn small silver earrings in pierced ears.

It was a special regret of Polly's that she had not known her grandmother, who, after a long illness, had died of cancer when her only grandchild was two. Grandma Miriam was nevertheless very real to the girl. She was a source of exotic beauty, folk wisdom, inherited courage and artistry and liberal ideology, of fascinating foreign ancestry on which Polly could draw to define her own uniqueness. Grandma Miriam stood for all those things that separated Polly from the others and would lead her to a Special Future.

Now, on the steps of that house, a fat child sat with a sucker. His white belly drooped over his shorts. Full of pity for her father's boyhood, Polly waved at the child, but he was lost in a sugar daze and only stared. She hurried along, turning left toward Dingley Falls at the Catholic Church, and realized that she was near where Luke Packer lived, though she wasn't certain which door led to his home. How strange to think of him outside the corridors of Dixwell High, outside *her* territory of downtown Dingley Falls and here in his own, where she felt like a trespasser. Funny, she had seen Luke nearly every day of the three years since he'd come to town, but had never thought of him as living anywhere in particular, or with anyone. How strange, too, to think of him as *poor*. Not just "not rich," like her and her father, but poor. "Wasn't it awful not to have *any* money?" she had once asked her father, and he had answered, "For me it wasn't too bad because I didn't have the responsibility. For your grandmother? It was a war that never let up. You couldn't win it, you could just keep day by day trying not to lose it. Holding on wears you down. For her it was awful, but I didn't know it then."

Polly wondered if Luke knew it, recalling now that, like her dad when he had been at school, Luke was always at work somewhere—bagging groceries, delivering papers, shoveling snow. Funny, she'd often envied him those male prerogatives, those victorious proofs of independence and self-sufficiency. Funny, she had never thought that he worked because he had to, that he was trying not to lose a war. Their history teacher, Ms. Rideout, who had lost heart and quit, had told them, stuttering, that America believed in a race up a ladder and warned you that if you weren't fit enough to grasp the top rung, you had no one but yourself to blame. She said this was a cruel myth, that some people had no time even to reach for the bottom foothold up; they were too busy scrambling in the ground for food. Polly remembered how Luke had argued with the teacher and reminded her of many heroes of the American Dream who had awakened like Carnegie, richer than fabled kings. And the teacher had reminded Luke that they had been, that Luke himself was, halfway up the ladder at the race's start. He was bright, he was white, he was hale and male. Poverty alone, she said, was a simple affliction. But more often than not it was a complication with many symptoms, some of them incurable.

Ramona Dingley believed that property should be inventoried. She readjusted her will annually and advised her relative Sammy Smalter to consider his estate—whatever it might consist of. But Smalter had given little subsequent thought to his first and only will, in which whatever he had was to go to Ramona if she were alive, and to Beanie Abernathy otherwise. Yet the pharmacist had much more than anyone in Dingley Falls imagined. He had more money than his aunt, more than Mrs. Troyes or Mrs. Canopy, though not, of course, as much as Ernest Ransom. Or Carl Marco. But he had more than he knew what to do with. Given that it could purchase neither ten more inches nor ten more years, there was little money had to offer him. It could buy love, or an excellent facsimile, since it is as easy to love someone for his money as for other such talents. It could buy the world, or at least rent it. But it could not give him Luke Packer's youth or size, and it could not change the past.

In the beginning, Sammy Smalter had not believed that. As checks had come in, first small ones, then larger, and finally ridiculously large, they had come like passports permitting him to leave his life behind, to take the vacation of vacating his past, the recreation of re-creating Samuel Smalter. On the stilts of that money he had planned to step over the slights and jokes and self-contempt that had crippled his earlier years. He had planned to climb so high, he could not even see the looks on faces below him. During those years, when Dingleyans assumed he had gone to try his luck elsewhere, Smalter had been more places in the world than Cecil Hedgerow had over longed for. He had seen more heaps of marble ruins and chunks of gilded rocks, more scaffolding left behind by the human race, than Tracy Canopy had ever heard of. He had bought longer random nights, paid more for them, wasted more, lost more, even hurled more futilely into the winds at the Cliffs of Dover, than Luke Packer had yet to earn. But he had bought experiences and pleasures without undoing a life's protective habit of keeping himself safely withdrawn, enclosed in what Ramona called his prissiness. Withdrawn, he had bought a box seat at the human comedy, had sat through the opera of foibles, intrigues, and dramatic pastimes. He had spied, from an excellent place in the house, on life and lives. He had observed interesting people do their interesting things. In the end, Smalter had only this regard for money—that it was better to have enough than not to. Like so much else in life (success, sleep, height), it gained its value in its absence. In the end he found he preferred work as a vehicle of vacation. He took pride not in the work he did, but in the fact that he did it diligently. He preferred the old New England values. And he preferred to live at home, where no one looked at him because they had seen him so long.

But, since his return to Dingley Falls when Dingley-ans assumed his luck had run out, the money had kept on earning money, and the earnings had earned money, and money overflowed like the buckets of the sorcerer's apprentice. In New York the corporation that was Sammy Smalter had lawyers and managers to find something to do with it. He made money because he gave money away; in the name of the corporation, his lawyers had charitably saved children, whales, clinics, theaters, alcoholics, paraplegics, nuns, lungs, and the birthplace of a Victorian poet. Ironically, he even made money because the pharmacy in Dingley Falls lost money. And that the pharmacy did lose money was the one fact of Mr. Smalter's finances that his fellow Dingleyans knew for certain.

"Poor little fellow," Father Highwick had said to his curate. "He hasn't a head for business at all. Really, it wouldn't be usurious to ask people to pay *some* little part of their bills, would it? A lady, I don't think you've had a chance to meet her yet, Jonathan, told me in confessional she owed Mr. Smalter three hundred and fifty dollars for insulin and allergy pills (poor thing) and hadn't paid a penny on her account in five years. I don't know how we got onto that subject because the point was she felt she was somehow losing her faith entirely (which was true, I was sorry to hear), but all the same it proves what I mean about Sammy. Fire sales up to ninety percent, and unprovoked by fires. It's all very well and good to be big-hearted, and Sammy always was because I remember he left two silver dollars in the plate on his confirmation day, dressed so nicely, too, though I do think now, at his age, yellow in the winter is a little flamboyant, but *de gustibus non disregardum*, as Quince Ivoryton always used to say to the cook at the dining hall in divinity school, and it was wretched fare. But Sammy's Three-for-a-Penny Days always struck me, and Ernest Ransom agreed, rather like a Baptist tag sale, though of course wonderful, and I'm sure the Baptists have the best intentions in the world. All to the glory of the Lord, whatever we do, Jonathan. But if it wasn't for Ramona though, I don't see how the little fellow could make ends meet."

Through the glass of his secretary's office Ernest Ransom watched his daughter Kate stride with a slouch toward him. Unconsciously, the banker straightened even further and filled his chest with air. "Well, you look nice and cheerful." He smiled, relieved to see her without a scowl.

"Hi, Irene. Daddy, stop it." Kate tossed her curls away from her father's hand.

"How can you see?" He frowned.

"Listen, Daddy, we're going to use the pool tomorrow night for a party, okay?"

"Who's we?"

"Well, you know, just whoever. Me and Sid and Lance and just some people, summer people. Anybody that wants to, that's all."

Ransom raised his eyebrows, a reaction of his wife's that he had acquired. "Sounds a little vague. Well, I think it would be polite to check with your mother."

"Oh, she doesn't care. I'll need to get something to drink, and I want to know if we could barbecue steaks."

"Tell Wanda what you want to eat, and here." He

took from his wallet three twenty-dollar bills. "Is that enough?"

"Thanks. I'll pay you back when I inherit all my money."

"Unfortunately I'll be dead, but I appreciate the thought. Now be sure to include your sister."

"Crap. I don't horn in on *her* junk."

"Kate, there's no need to feel that way. Emerald and Arthur will probably not even want to horn in on your junk, but you shouldn't give them the impression that they aren't wanted."

"Okay. I'll lie, if it'll make you happy. See you. 'Bye, Irene."

"She just gets prettier and prettier, doesn't she, Mr. Ransom?"

"Thank you, Irene. It's very kind of you to say so."

Polly Hedgerow, cutting across the cemetery from Ransom Circle, came out onto Dingley Circle and saw Luke Packer on the other side of the green. He and Mr. Smalter stood in front of the pharmacy; then the proprietor went back inside while Luke, pushing off on his bicycle, sped out into the street. Polly felt the same strange rush of feeling that had made her wave with such affection at the fat child on her father's steps. "Hi, Luke!" she yelled, flagging her arms. He pedaled over to her with a grin.

"Whatcha up to? Going to the library? Joy in there?"

At that moment Kate Ransom came out the doors of the bank and started down the stone steps. Hurrying along the sidewalk so quickly that Luke had to trot beside his bike to keep up with her, Polly answered, "I don't know where Joy is. Good-bye."

"Hold up. Come on, wait a minute." They walked a few minutes in silence. "I'm taking a prescription over to Elizabeth Circle. Wanta come?"

"No, thanks."

"Okay. No reason to be so nasty about it. How much do I owe you for the sandwich?"

"Nothing. Forget it."

"I don't want to forget it. Where's that new bike of yours?"

"Broken."

"Hop on then. I'll give you a ride."

"That's okay. I guess I'll walk."

"Come on, don't be a dope. You won't fall."

"I know that, I've ridden double a lot."

"Okay then, hang on to me."

"You hang on to me."

"Jeez, women's lib!"

This sarcasm made Polly smile. She'd always felt liberated, but couldn't recall anyone's ever having called her a woman before.

Orchid O'Neal had crossed Elizabeth Circle to clean up Mrs. Troyes's house, so Ramona Dingley answered Polly's ring herself. "Hello. Step in. Turning a bit warmer. May rain. Good of you to come. Must wonder what I'm up to." Then the wide black figure disappeared as her wheelchair took an abrupt left turn. Seconds later it shot backwards into the hall again. "In here." The chair vanished. With some trepidation Polly followed it into a room that far surpassed what Father Fields had described as "very interesting." She quickly decided that it would be less offensive to stare at the stuffed animals than at the religious statuary, and so she did.

"Creepy, ain't it?" her hostess asked with, Polly was glad to see, a warm smile on her face. "Gives me the spooks sometimes, if I'm especially fatigable. Even after all these years. Don't it you?"

Polly nodded ambiguously.

"Well, dear, take a seat. Oh, it doesn't matter. Take the one there that looks like a throne." High-backed, ornately carved, with a red velvet seat, it did make Polly think of *Ivanhoe*. "Be pleasant, now," Miss Dingley added, "to have your own smart throne, wouldn't it? I know I always lusted for one. A real one, I mean. Like one yourself?"

"No. Yes, I guess so." Polly had indeed made

numberless proclamations of a regal nature from a
hollow tree trunk rooted by the bank of the Rampage
in the woods behind Glover's Lane. One of her worst
humiliations had been being overheard, at age eleven,
in one of these ringing speeches by Tac and Charlie
Hayes, who had sneaked up on her and mercilessly
laughed.

"Why don't you take that chair home with you?"

"Excuse me?"

"The chair. Put it in your room. See anything else
you want? Place is claustrophobic. Time to get rid of it
all. Take whatever you like. Be a big help."

Too nonplussed to answer, much less chalk up her
choices, Polly looked politely around the room, hoping
she gave the impression that she longed for everything
she saw.

"Well, now," said Miss Dingley, wheeling a table in
front of her chair as she drove up to the girl. "I didn't
ask you here to unload my white elephants on you. Or
owls. What'll you have?" Bottle after bottle was held
up as if being auctioned. "Coke. Root beer. Ginger ale.
Seven-Up. Apple cider. Don't suppose you drink ale.
Milk."

"Oh, anything's fine."

The fat woman jutted out her strange hawk's face.
"*Never* don't ask for what you want. If you're lucky
enough to know what it is. Take charge!"

"Root beer, please."

"That's better." Miss Dingley had silver ice tongs,
which Polly had never seen before. She had silver bowls
of pretzels, chocolate bars, and nuts—red pistachio
nuts, which Polly had never before seen in such
quantities. "Like them," explained her hostess. "Takes
so infernal long to get at them. Too much trouble to
overeat. I've put on weight. In the last forty years.
Reprehensible. But still. Used to be as skinny as you."

Polly blushed.

"Better thin than fat. Stylish. Don't fret. Time will

be your revenge. Now. Want to know why I asked you over?"

Her mouth to her glass, Polly nodded.

"I've had my eye on you. You've got gumption, I should wager. Always accelerate on the curves, don't you? Took particular note of that."

As she pried open pistachios, Polly watched in wary fascination as Miss Dingley poured herself a goblet full of dark liquid from a crystal decanter. "Port." The invalid nodded and drank it down. "Assuasive. I find it supplies the want of other means of spiritualizing. Ha! So now, first let's get acquainted. Then I'll come to business. What have you heard about me?"

"Oh, nothing, really."

"Nothing? That's certainly a disappointment. Not that I'm lively? Rich? Tennis champion, nineteen twenty-seven? Mad? At death's door? Smell bad? Nothing? Your dad never told you I was a senile old reactionary and had no business on the selectman's board with my hands on the purse strings and my behind squatting on this poor little town? Never told you that? Told me that once, right to my face."

"I heard you hadn't been feeling well."

"True. Not since nineteen sixty." She poured out some more root beer and port.

"I'm sorry."

"So am I, dear. But such is the exorbitancy of that odious grudge, Life. He charges us too much for his cheap merchandise." Miss Dingley slapped her knees. "Useless, the human body. Shoddy parts, bad labor, worse design." She slapped her wheelchair. "This machine is better-made."

Out of a desk drawer Miss Dingley took an old almanac and a framed photograph. "Me. Hard to believe, ain't it?" A hearty, handsome girl stood laughing into the sun, a tennis racquet in her hand. The almanac fell open to a page upon which a star had been drawn in the margin beside the name *Ramona Dingley*,

Singles Finalist. "My quarter of an inch of fame. Nineteen twenty-seven."

"Gee, you're right there in the almanac."

"Right along with the worst drought. Always played singles. Never married either. Probably should have. Save a little time out to get married, dear. Don't forget. But I live here with my nephew Sammy now. You know him? Runs his grandpa's pharmacy?"

"Oh, yes. He gives me old magazines."

"Not surprising. Sammy's one of God's little lapses of concentration; did so much better on the plants and animals—got to humans late in the week and was too tired to keep His mind on what He was doing. That's my theory. No, Sammy's a marvel. Might have turned him sour. Just turned him a tad stuffy. What about you?"

"Me?"

"Took me awhile to realize who you were when I saw you on that bike. Pauline Moffat's girl."

"Yes. Did you know her?"

"She was a flower, your mother." Miss Dingley reached over to tap Polly's arm with a suddenly shy kindness. "Otto Scaper doted on her, did you know that? Never had any kids of his own. She was his favorite out of all he delivered. Yes, a rare flower. And your father!" She briskly thrust the chocolates at her guest. "Cecil used to bring me firewood. What a rascal. Practical joker. Sold me candles once you couldn't blow out. Made a fool of myself at the dinner table trying."

Her father, a "rascal," a "practical joker"? Polly tingled with information.

"Yes, dear. I can promise you this town was a tad surprised when Pauline chose young Hedgerow over Ernie Ransom. Her folks had a fit. But your dad, he *flared* up with love for her. She flew right at him like a moth. Anyone could see it. No, he wasn't much to set the world on fire before her, tell you the truth. And when he lost her, he just quit. Always used to talk about going to sea. Wanted to be a violinist, too. Never did either. People mostly don't. Don't have as much stomach as appetite, I mean. But he had her, and that's more than a lot get. Loving her was his success."

"Could you tell, what was he like when he was young?"

"He was shiny and couldn't stand still. Used to dance when he walked, danced up those steps with the logs. Pauline was the world to him, much less China. And when you finally made an appearance—and my opinion is you wouldn't come down until you were good and ready—Pauline was happy as a skylark. They both were. Bragged till even Otto got bored with what a marvel you were, how you could read at six weeks and fly around the room at ten."

How wonderful this was. To see the love story of her parents as if in a movie. To hear her own life from one who had seen her before she herself knew who she was. A pleasure better than the best book. Polly felt her mouth stretching into a grin. It was wonderful to know that her mother (of whom she had such a few, such a faded, fixed treasury of memories) was known in other, new ways, and that she could happen on these discoveries like Easter eggs. That Kate Ransom's father should have loved *her* mother! That her mother should have surprised the town and driven her parents to fits!

"Yes." Miss Dingley smiled. "She was a flower. Now, you. You remind me more of your grandmother Hedgerow. She did my sewing, you know. Too ham-handed to do it myself—I could do marvels with a racquet, but a needle! I wanted nothing to do with anything female. As a result of which, of course, I'm totally incompetent to take care of myself."

"I'm named for my grandmother and my mom. Miriam Pauline. But everybody calls me Polly. But when I go out in the world, like to college, that's what I'm going to tell people to call me. Miriam."

"Yes, you've got her eyes. Snappy bright little black eyes. She never missed a thing, not a stitch, not a word, not a truth of life. Ought to have let her run that factory where your grandfather worked until my uncle made such a mess of the business they had to lay everybody off."

"My dad says she worked very hard."

"Didn't have an easy life, I shouldn't imagine, but she fought back. Every match point. One time she said to me, 'Suffering, we pick and choose. Could be this, could be that in our lives we let break our hearts. A thousand kinds of misery, and only one word for happy. Happiness you don't choose. It chooses you, like luck. You look down, there's a quarter or a rose. You listen, somebody's singing.' Oh, something had upset me, can't remember what now, and she was trying to perk me up. She always had her radio on."

Polly's grin had contracted to a sad and tender smile for her grandmother's life, for the woman seated in a frayed armchair by a standing lamp, the radio next to her, for the woman repairing other women's clothes. In Polly's hand the warm chocolate was sticky. Then suddenly Miss Dingley raced her chair to the other side of the room, where she flipped a light switch that jolted the girl back into the baroque clutter around her.

"Idiot, I don't know when to shut up. Well, Polly, or Miriam, I should say, the old have nothing to give the young but the past, and the young don't want it."

"Oh, no, Miss Dingley, I love to hear it."

"Well, good, you'll learn something. Next time you tell me about the future and I'll learn something. But now to the point. I have a theory, and I want to borrow your legs to test it out. You know that stretch of marsh and forest up near Bredforet Pond, up north of the highway where people used to hunt?"

Polly gulped her drink as if she watched a magician.

"Something's funny up there." The woman fixed her eyes on the girl. "For a while I thought I was seeing

UFOs. You know, flying saucers. Nobody would listen to me, of course. Never will listen to old people. Sometimes wonder myself if I am senile. Read too many of those sordid newspapers Orchid buys at the A & P. Still think something's going on. Too embarrassed to follow it up officially until I get a fact. Let's find out there's nothing there, I'll get it off my mind."

Polly shook her head excitedly. "No, no, there *is* something there. I got lost up there, if this is the same place, and I saw a sort of government thing. Buildings. I bet it's bombs."

Miss Dingley set her goblet down sharply. "Are you telling the truth? Up near Bredforet Pond? There *is* something up there?"

"Yes. Yes. It's really weird, way far back beyond the marsh. I got lost looking for arrowheads."

"What makes you think it's the government?"

"It said so. It said 'Keep Out.' I was out there for hours and hours before I saw it. A big cleared space with an electrified fence. It says 'U.S. Government. Keep Out.' I saw a dog inside, but I didn't see any people."

"That land belongs to Ernest Ransom at the bank. Been in his family for eons."

"I saw it though. Maybe he gave it to them."

"For what? When? What makes you think it's bombs? See any silo whatchamacallits?"

"I don't think so. Just buildings."

"Nobody's said a word about such a thing! Don't know what the idiotic government would be doing up here on private property anyhow. Creeping into everything and taxing us for the trespass. I won't have them here in Dingley Falls. Without so much as a by-your-leave."

"I'm not sure I could find it again, but I did see it. I was going to go and look."

"I never heard a word about Ernie Ransom selling that land."

"I told a friend of mine, but she wasn't interested."

"Hard to believe he'd let them set up such a thing on his land. Well, Miriam. Let's go look. It's certainly nothing this town has authorized, I know that much."

"I could show it to you." Polly noticed the wheel-chair and then blushed.

"Yes. Wish I could. Absurd, ain't it, stuck in this thing? But I tell you what. Orchid and I will drive as far as we can. I want you to get somebody to go with you. Have you got a camera, much good at taking pictures?"

"No. But, well, I guess I know somebody who can. A guy in my class; he takes pictures for the paper. Do you think it's something criminal? I mean, maybe we'll get arrested."

"I think just about everything to do with the government's criminal. Give men the means for grand larceny and they'll commit it. Every other kind of atrocity you can come up with. They'll go at it happy as boys with slingshots in an abandoned glass house." Ramona poured another glass of port. "What you say you saw up there, very disturbing. I don't like it. I'm an old woman. The government's got the power now, and I'm used to the rich having it. When they did, they were all crooks too, of course. Well, we'll see. Take those nuts home. Yes. I knew we'd get on. First time I saw you on that red bicycle. Used to have one myself. Now, you see, I'm still on wheels."

CHAPTER
27

Gone were the ample, untaxing days when Beanie's grandparents, Charles and Camilla Dingley, had ridden to Knickerbocker balls and banquets in a private railway car stuffed with purple plush. A car of couches with its own potted palm tree. A car with a dining table over which hung allegorical oil paintings, heavily framed. A car with a big bronze Atalanta, interrupting her race to stoop for the golden apple and dreamily staring out the window at landscapes running the other way. Gone now were those plush, gilded days when trains went on pilgrimages to shrines of victors in Newport and Saratoga Springs, when so fast and deep the money flowed along the Hudson, the Housatonic, and even the little Rampage that it took a substantial traffic in railway cars to hurry owners to property, and guests to owners. Those days had passed when everyone knew who everyone-who-was-anyone was. Those thick damask days when Vanderbilts, Whitneys, and even Dingleys had passed their ample, untaxed time in paying calls on one another, in marrying one another, breeding money with one another, and heavily entombing one another.

All lost now—houses, horses, and purple plush. "Goddamn fool taxes and the goddamn Roosevelts," old William Bredforet had often told his great-nephew Ernest Ransom, when Ernest asked him, "Where did all *that* go?"

"It went down the drain," Bredforet told him. "Ignoramuses pissed it away. That grinning mous-

tached monkey Teddy squatting in the smut with his
muckrakers! Big stick, ho! Trust buster, ho! Him and
the worse ones after him. Threw it away in the Atlantic
Ocean, blew it across the sea with kisses. 'Take it, it's
free!' So people did. Let too many goddamn people in
the fool country, and every last one of them thought
they had a right to the moon.''

And so it was. The big cheese of the moon was sliced
into smaller and smaller shares, and mice began to
nibble on the rats' portions. Soon nearly everyone had
private cars and nearly no one had private railway cars.
In fact, those trains, in which the granddaughter of
Charles (Bradford IV) and Camilla Dingley still owned
shares though not coaches, no longer even stopped for
passengers in her hometown. The former depot now
belonged to Carl Marco and was rented by Sidney
Blossom. To catch her train, Beanie Dingley Abernathy
was obliged to make her way into Argyle, just as if ten
generations of Dingleys had never toiled, scrimped,
underbought, and oversold, never wrested land from
the Indians and income from the land, never risen by
their bootstraps and stamped out the competition,
never merged, cornered, and capitalized, never been
self-made at all, but in the mythic memory of a great
dream. For what remained of so much private enter-
prise? Only a pass. A piece of paper that entitled
Beanie (and her immediate family) to ride without
charge in a public compartment of those trains, to ride
to and from wherever the trains happened to be going
anyhow. That was all. She couldn't even treat by any
inherited *droit de madame* her best friends, Tracy,
Evelyn, and Priss, to a free seat on her train when they
took their regular Wednesday journeys to the market of
Art. No, the Thespian Ladies had to pay full fare. Had
to pay to ride on tracks that Beanie's great-great-
grandfather, Charles Bradford Dingley II, had sledge-
hammered through Connecticut rock, with, he used to
say, his own bloody hands. On a train that he had

shoved up hill, down vale, with his own sweaty shoulder to the wheel, Beatrice, his last heiress, had no privilege but a pass.

"What was it all for then?" William Bredforet wanted to know. "That sobbed-over common man! *He* never had the brains or intestinal fortitude or balls or vision to build the goddamn country. Then the little weasels come along and whine, 'You can't keep all this to yourself, it's not fair!' Well, there were too many of them in the end, Ernie. They ate it all the way crows can eat a stag if he's down. And it's all gone now."

The coach was gone. So too, it seemed, was the heiress. Gone and left her shares with all her heart to her immediate family. Like her ancestors, she had seized the moon, just a different one. Now she would miss the PATSY-sponsored premiere of the feminist film to which Tracy had invited her fellow club members. Now, when Evelyn screeched her Chrysler to a stop-on-a-dime (a dime's width away from the back bumper of Tracy's Volvo), Beanie had not been there waiting to go to the train station. Now, when Tracy and Priss, waiting by the curb for their tardy driver, scampered up the slope on seeing Evelyn's car tear at them like a huge, gray wounded elephant, Beanie was far away. Without her, then, they went to Argyle, paid their full fares, and entered, for Priss's sake, a smoker.

"Filthy," snapped Priss.

"People don't seem to care like they used to," sighed Tracy, as they shuffled through leaves of trash on the aisle floor. "Wait. My shoe's stuck in gum."

"We ought to *drive* to the City, I keep saying," said Evelyn again. "I've done it in thirty minutes less than the train, you know."

Yes, they did know, for they had been flattened against the backseat, their faces stretched into Mongolian contours by wind and terror the day Evelyn had set that record.

"No, this is fine," Priss insisted, as she pried used

Kleenex from her ashtray with a gloved finger. "You sit over there, Tracy. Put your bag down next to you. Here. Put Evelyn's coat."

But before they could secure the seat, someone claimed it. "Walter! How cunning," chirped Evelyn Troyes. "But I thought you'd be with Jonathan. I'd been hoping he and I might have a quick bite of lunch, but he said he'd promised you to work with the choir. What a nice surprise."

So, thought Walter Saar, he uses me for his alibi. Fair enough. I use him from time to time, in my thoughts. "Unfortunately," he said aloud, "we had an emergency today. One of the teaching staff suffered a heart attack. Mr. Oglethorpe. In fact, Jonathan had just been to call on him when it happened."

"Oglethorpe? My God. I've met the man," said Priss. "Well, he must be seventy. Homely and catatonically shy?"

"Yes, he's been ill a long time. He was in the infirmary with a virus, then suddenly . . ."

"Is he all right?" asked Tracy.

"He's in Argyle Hospital now. I called his sister. They say he's not critical."

"Thank God it was you on the train, Walter," said Priss. "You never know what odiferous sort will try to sit next to you and tell you how awful their lives are these days."

Had Walter Saar not been dazed with shock from the sight of Oglethorpe's eyes, pinpoints of panic in an old chalk face, he might not have found himself being driven into Manhattan. But there was nothing he could do for the man, the school carried on, the gap was filled. He needed his half-holiday. He needed to get out. And had Saar been watching where he was going, he probably would not have chosen to sit beside the Thespian Ladies to wherever (and he preferred not to predict his ultimate destination) he was traveling. Not that he disliked them: Mrs. Ransom was a witty bridge partner, and her husband controlled the trustees of

Alexander Hamilton Academy. Mrs. Canopy was, when you came down to it, a kind soul whose heart was in the right place—didn't he love Art himself? And Mrs. Troyes was simply very lonely. Well, God knows, so was he. No, he did like them, but he preferred, when transformed into Mr. Hyde, to ride alone. Certainly he would rather not be squeezed among the social acquaintances of the good Dr. Jekyll, headmaster and dinner guest. Mr. Hyde? Saar winced. In his attaché case at this moment lay cradled a cool can of Michelob, which he very much wanted to drink. But of course he couldn't pop open a beer can on a train in front of these ladies.

"What are you up to, Walter?" Priss blew her words across the aisle in a coil of smoke that tickled Evelyn's nose and made her miss Blanchard, who had also smoked Gauloises.

"Why, I'm . . . nothing definite. Into the city. Though I might, the new . . ."

"Oh, I know. The new rock ballet of *Riders to the Sea?*" guessed Tracy.

"Good God!" snorted Priss.

"I'm sorry, I don't think so," Saar said, his throat hoarse with wishing for that beer. He lit a cigarette, then realized he already had one in the ashtray.

"Oh, of course! You're the opera buff." Tracy wagged her finger as if he had deliberately thrown her off. "The new Houston opera. That's for you."

"Why, ah, yes," said Saar with a dry smile. At any rate, it would serve.

"Oh, is it *peut-être* Puccini?" sighed Evelyn. "I'd love some Puccini more than this movie."

"No, no, no," Mrs. Canopy explained. "Joe Tom Steeler. *Big D to High C.* It sounds very original. Perhaps we could all go next week. I *believe* I read that all the singers are cows, I mean costumed as cows. Mr. Steeler shows that life is simply one big dirty cattle drive, from Dallas up to Chicago, and in his last act he has everyone scrunched up in the stockyards, and while they sing (you knew it was atonal, Walter, didn't you?), apparently these giant mechanical axes representing oil derricks smash them over the heads until they're pounded beneath the stage floor. Oh, but perhaps I shouldn't have told you the end. (You knew the reviews have been almost vicious.)"

"Well, Tracy, they laughed at Wagner, too. Not everyone can be as generous and open-minded as you," said Saar politely, ignoring Priss's secret smirk.

"Yes! Yes! Give him a chance, exactly!" Mrs. Canopy's enthusiasm was not infectious, but it persevered. "Mr. Steeler has worked so hard and long, this is his *twenty-seventh* opera, and not one that you could really call a popular success. But I find reviewers almost enjoy being cruel, which is such a small, jealous talent, I think. I suppose it's easier to laugh at people, isn't it?"

"I'm afraid so." Saar felt heat run down his arms to his hands. God knows he had laughed at Tracy Canopy enough, had amused Priss Ransom at the Club, between bridge hands, with witticisms about their menopausal Maecenas and her eight-cylindered monument to dear, dead Vincent. Surely Tracy didn't deserve to be laughed at like that. Well, she did deserve it, but surely we ought to give each other more than we deserve. Was bitchiness the only fashionable gay style available? Was Oscar Wilde the only triumphant role model? Why not take Walt Whitman instead? Saar felt a sudden rage against Priss Ransom, and so also against himself, as she sat across the aisle telling Evelyn Troyes, "Stop feeling sorry for June Hayes! I have. How many g.d. migraine headaches are we supposed to ooh and aah over? How many years are we going to scrape her off the ceiling every time the *phone* rings, before we get an itsy bit impatient? Evelyn, really! Surely June knows what a g.d. phone sounds like after forty years."

"She's very sensitive."

"Indeed she is. So is a Chihuahua. For the same reason, too. It's cultivated."

"No, try to understand, Priss. People who have, who feel, who have artistic dreams for themselves, and then, you know, Priss dear, they don't come true, well, then, do you see what I mean? It's a terrible loss."

"Ha! Evelyn, I'm sorry, if she's that sensitive, let her, oh, how in h. should I know, let her retire to a padded cell or move to Alaska where there's nothing valuable to break. I just can't sympathize. And I don't believe in unsung Miltons either. If you had been meant to sing, you would have sung. If June had been meant to do whatever she thinks she was meant to do, she would have done it. Now I was smart. I never *had* to have anything at all, and so now I have everything I want. Walter! Our little Scarlett O'Hara has been assaulted once more by migraine. *Plus ça change, plus c'est le même chose.*"

"*La,*" corrected Evelyn without thinking. "*La chose.*" Fortunately she was looking out the window at the time and so was not frozen by the Gorgonian stare Mrs. Ransom gave her.

"Excuse me, is the rest room back there? Ah, yes, excuse me, Tracy." Saar bumped his way hurriedly to the back of the car.

"Why did he take his briefcase with him to the toilet?" asked Evelyn dreamily. Receiving no reply from Priss, she began to take the quiz on an advertisement in front of her to find out if she was one of the millions who didn't know they were suffering from alcoholism.

The toilet was engaged. Saar waited until finally, after much rattling, the bolt slid back to *Vacant*. And after further jiggling of the knob, the door opened. Out squeezed Father Sloan Highwick's affable face, rosy above the tight black collar and the stunningly white clerical suit he wore in the summer months. "Walter." He beamed. "Where are you off to? I'm going to see my mother. Wish I could join you, but I mustn't. The smoke, you understand. An old man's eyes."

"Here, let me," offered Saar. He slid back the compartment door that the Rector was tugging on.

"Oh," Highwick turned to add in his pleasant, whispery voice, "there's quite a mess in the bowl."

"Ah."

"It doesn't flush. What's happened to the railroads? Things used to flush." The Rector jerked his white shoe loose from the sliding door it was stuck in and was gone. He had someone newer to talk to: Carl Marco's son, Carl, Jr.—the very good-looking Argyle eye doctor.

"Praise God." Highwick continued his conversation where he'd left off. "I have the eyes of a hawk. My mother's eyes. She's ninety-two and she paints the entire Nativity on coffee mugs for the missionary Christmas box. She's an artist, always was."

"Gee, that's nice."

"But poor Jonathan. I liked those eyes you gave him, Carl, I told him so. Still, it's a shame. Nothing wrong with my eyes. Lately I have been wondering if I'm not getting a sore throat though. Scratchy. Take a look here, would you? *AAAAaaaahhhh*. Down 'ere . . . 'ee any'ing?"

"Gosh, Father, not really. Maybe you ought to see an ENT man if you're worried."

"Do you know one? We can't be too careful about our health. A gift of God, thank God."

That mess in the bowl did make rather "close" (as Saar heard his mother saying) the little cubicle in which he now stood, jostled with the train's movement, to drink his Michelob. He preferred not to think about what his mother (home alone in Concord) would have thought could she see her only son—her bright, shining Wally—hiding in a train john, guzzling a can of lukewarm beer, on his way to go stare at (if not worse) whichever male whores the city happened to throw out upon its dirty streets. Her concert companion, her valedictorian, her sole creation, driven into the streets of Manhattan by the Furies of what a college psychiatrist had called his deep-seated masochism and deeper-seated hatred of his mother. Poor Mrs. Saar—had she known what sins a series of counselors had ascribed to her while her son protested in vain, had she heard her psyche bandied about through rings of pipe smoke, had she learned she was frigid, castrating, passive-aggressive, and schizophrenogenic! She didn't even know that Walter was a homosexual, much less that it was her fault. She didn't even know that Walter had seen psychiatrists, much less that her second husband had paid for them. She was aware that Walter's stepfather had once given him a generous subsidy to his salary, but she thought this gift was merely natural. She, after all, would have given her son the moon, and in fact used to pretend when he was a toddler to take it down out of the sky and place it in his hands. But she was not a party to the gentlemen's agreement in which Walter, prior to his majority, agreed to be a circumspect and infrequent visitor to Concord, to try to overcome his disease, and to accept this disability pay as a spur to recovery.

Teeth bared, Walter Saar grimaced his Mr. Hyde's face into the mirror above the train's grimy sink. There had been a time when his power to create such ugly intensity had frightened him. Now the mugging was just a habit. He didn't even much hate his stepfather anymore, or hate himself for having once accepted money to try to "cure" himself, or seriously worry that he might lose control at a Concord Christmas party and kiss full on the mouth one of his stepfather's business associates. He did feel he had no right to go out of control in Manhattan. Unlike Oglethorpe's irresistible pain, Saar's pain was not, he chided himself, beyond the will's power to deny it.

Someone was trying to open the door of the toilet. Who could it be? the headmaster snarled at the mirror. Ernest Ransom? Both the old Bredforets? Everyone else in Dingley Falls known to the good Dr. Jekyll was obviously on this train. Why not those three? Why not the entire board of trustees? You deserve this, losing your driver's license to a hustler. Mr. Hyde grinned. The evil image cackled at the unfortunate Walter Jekyll's discomfort.

"Know what I did this morning?" Dingley Falls's postman asked his superior.

Judith Haig turned toward Alf Marco, who slumped forward in his chair beside the table where they sorted outgoing mail that the truck from Argyle would pick up at five.

"Know what I did?" he repeated. "I got up real early. I went up to the lake. And I went fishing." Marco's drawn, pinched face, so at variance with his fleshy torso, looked up at the postmistress with more significance expectant in it than his remark would have seemed to indicate.

"It must have been beautiful," Judith said.

He nodded slowly. "I hadn't gone, you know, for twenty years. I guess it's been. Maybe not."

"But you went this morning?"

"I don't know why."

Mrs. Haig tied the sack of letters and packages, then sat down across from the postman. Usually Marco left for Astor Heights immediately after completing his duties. Now he seemed in no hurry.

"I woke up real early, and I got to thinking, out of the blue, it'd be nice out on the lake right now. Quiet and pretty. I used to fish some when I was little, go along with Carl and his pals, tag along, kid brother. Not so much the fishing, you know, but I liked going on the boat. And being out there. I liked it the way everything was so green and quiet."

This, by far the longest and most personal remark Marco had ever made to Mrs. Haig, disturbed her for that reason. He was not himself. The man's eyes, which appeared to see the lake water as he spoke, staring somewhere beyond her, looked bruised, two smears of soot deep in the sockets. Rubbing his hands along his calves, her colleague now slowly blew out a sigh. "Well, what happens? To time, you know? You don't even notice. All those years. And I never went back. I don't know why. Never even remembered I'd forgotten it. The time just went." He gave a quick, uncomfortable laugh. "Funny, I guess. Reach over to turn the TV set off for the night. And you look at your hands. And you see you got old somehow." His hand, which he held out now, trembled.

"You're tired, Alf. You shouldn't have tried to do the route today, in the heat and all."

"It was a nice day though, wasn't it? Well, I ought to go on. Keeping you here past time." He stood, but his legs shook, and with a surprised stare he sat down again. "Guess I am pretty beat, huh?"

"Yes. Don't try to leave just yet. Just rest, catch your breath. Would you like me to call your brother?"

"Nah. Don't bother anybody, it's nothing." They sat silently for a while. "Carl's kid," he then began to speak again, almost at a whisper. "Carl, Jr.'s got a rowboat he keeps up there with the big boat. I took it out a ways. You know Matebesec Cove?"

"No, I'm sorry, I don't. Are you feeling all right?"

"It's just a little place. It's real pretty though. Lots of pine trees. The way the water sits quiet and clean, different colors. You know? You ever notice how when the new pine needles come out on the tips of the branches and they're a light-colored green and the old needles are a dark-colored green? I was noticing that this morning. Red pines. I think. Maybe. One time . . . I got a book of Sebastian's one time. We were little. Mama got him picture books. We thought he'd be something special. He could draw anything, anything there was, you show him something and he could sit down and draw it just the way it looked."

"Alf? Should I call Dr. Scaper?"

"This book though. It told all the names of trees and

showed their pictures. I got so, so I knew. Ash. Beech. Hemlock. Locust. I'd figure them out. Taking the mail. Red pine. Ash, and, and, and maple. Red pine."

"Alf! What's wrong? What's the matter?"

"I, I don't know. I guess I don't feel too good."

"Please, sit still, sit still. I'm going to call." Judith ran from the room to a small side office where there was a telephone. She pushed against the panic that was closing in on her as she dialed the police station, whose number she knew by heart. Finally Joe MacDermott answered. "Joe. This is Judith. At the post office. Could . . ." Then, in the mail room, she heard wood scrape against the floor. There was a sharp crash, then another crash, duller, heavy, and terrifying to her. The noise swept the panic up and swirled it through her voice. "Please. Quick. Help me. Alf's ill. Please call Dr. Scaper. An ambulance. Come quick. Please Please."

There was no noise anymore except her own voice whispering, "Please, please, please" as she ran back to where on the floor Alf Marco lay facedown beside the overturned chair.

CHAPTER
28

"Got anything for me today, Sergeant?"

"Hello, Hayes. Don't you have anything better to do with your time? Get them to lower taxes, give me a raise, something like that?"

"Like all Americans, you greatly overestimate the power of the press to do anything but jerk skeletons out of closets. Indecent exposure's our racket. So, men we can manage—even presidents. Money, we can't budge."

"No presidents in here just now."

"Well, jails are my hobby."

"It's not much different here from outside, just a little more clearcut, and smells worse maybe."

"You're a philosopher, Fred. That's another reason I come to Argyle. To sit at your feet."

"Sit in a bar be more like it."

"That's another reason, I admit. So, anything much?"

"Naw. The usual. Drunks. Disorderlies. Guy took a lug wrench to his wife; twelve stitches. Kid broke into the record store; a music lover. Couple of hookers, couple of pushers. Oh, we still got that old colored nut in here."

"Who's that?"

"Fellow named Tim Hines. Got caught out in Meadowlark Hills exhibiting himself to kids. So the charge goes. Pretty cheerful old bugger. In there all day, laughing, playing a harmonica, tap-dancing. Got these beer caps tacked onto his shoes. A nut."

"Yeah, he sounds too pleasant to be sane. Didn't actually harm anybody, did he?"

"Naw, too puny if he wanted to. But you never can tell. Talks gibberish. Could be senile. Couple of the women over in Meadowlark pretty up in arms about it, so they'll probably put him away for good."

"What about this guy Maynard Henry over my way? Rammed somebody's car over the ridge with the somebody in it."

"Aggravated assault. Maybe. Yeah, he's here. The D.A. may go for attempted homicide. John Haig's pushing for it, hard. Can't say I blame him. This guy's a real nasty bastard, believe me. A chip on his shoulder a mile high. Two arrests out in California, but dropped. He was over in Vietnam a long time, too long probably. Sometimes in the brig, sometimes getting decorated, what it sounds like. Don't guess you ever knew his big brother, Arn Henry? He was a kind of big football hero around here awhile back. High school. Then went to one of the Big Ten. Lives in Boston now, selling insurance. Never can tell. Good seeds and bad."

"Football builds character," said Hayes. "Think Henry'd talk to me?"

"Maybe. He's in there with Tim Hines, and he's not much of a music lover, so he might want an excuse to get away. Not much of a talker either, though, far as I can tell."

"Not like you and me, huh?"

"Takes all kinds."

"So they say. Problem is they never mention what it takes all kinds *for*."

"Keep God from getting bored."

"Fred, tell the truth, ever read Spinoza?"

"Never read anybody but Eric Ambler."

"Close enough. Well, show me your prize specimen."

He looked like, what? A caged animal? That was too easy. Prisoners always looked like caged animals. A cheetah, anyhow, Hayes thought. A thin meanness, and the wheat-colored clipped hair, the weak chin, and eyes that raced ceaselessly around the visitors' room, white-heat eyes running instead of the legs that twitched with impatience on either side of the straight wood chair. Legs much too long for the thin chest.

"Maynard Henry?"

"Yeah?"

"I'm A. A. Hayes, I'm the editor of the Dingley Falls paper."

"Yeah?"

No, Hayes decided, he looks more dangerous than a cat. "Appreciate your taking the time off to see me." Stupid thing to say, thought Hayes, as he looked up at the irony in the pale, humorless eyes. What's time to him?

"Got a cigarette?"

"Sure. Here, take the pack."

Henry took only one and slid the rest back across the wood table. His hand was wide but thin, rubbed a raw pink, so clean that Hayes assumed they must have him washing dishes or laundry. His blue work shirt and jeans were starched stiff, both as pale as his eyes.

"Got yourself a lawyer?"

"They sent some dipshit around. I figured you for another one."

"No, sorry. I just drop by here once in a while, talk to folks, see if anything needs reporting. Thought you might want to tell me your side of the story."

Behind the smoke Henry's eyes flicked past Hayes as they swept the room. Finally he spoke. "Fuck you." He said it flatly and quietly.

Hayes smiled. "Okay. I guess that means you *don't* want to. Who knows, though? I might be able to help."

"Can you walk me out of here?"

"You've been indicted. Bail set at what?"

"Enough to be too much. If I'd robbed a bank instead, maybe I could come up with it."

"Instead of what . . . Okay. Don't you want bail? You like it here?"

"It sucks. You can write that. It sucks."

"Been here before?"

"Look it up, you're the reporter."

"I did. You've been in the can before."

"No shit." There was hardly any interest behind the voice. An indifference that flattened the obscenities into ordinary words, devoid of their usual signals. They were almost not insulting.

"How 'bout your brother?"

"How about him?"

"Well, I hear he was a big honcho around here, star of the gridiron and all. Those things carry weight. Couldn't he arrange bail for you? Get you a good lawyer?"

Irony skittered across the eyes again, but Henry

didn't reply. He was pulling matches one by one out of the paper book, lighting them, placing them to burn in a symmetrical row in the ashtray. Hayes was reminded of photographs of western settlers—miners, ranchers, gunmen, workmen. Pale yellow and brown group pictures. All men, few of them old, posed or captured unposed in flat, raw settings. Dirt streets, pine storefronts, tents, sod huts. Men surrounded by the machinery and timber of unfinished mines, unfinished railroads, unfinished towns. At times a dozen men in one picture, each of them solitary and isolate even in camaraderie. Some in their dark bowlers and white shirt-sleeves, some with ties and vests, some collarless, some moustached, some beside lanky, stiff-legged dogs, some beside rifles, some squinting into pans for gold. Like this prisoner, all of them angular, rawboned, hard-eyed, and hard-lipped. In every face a pinched alertness and suspicion. In every body a skitterish readiness for hard work or hard drink and barbarically hard times. Cold chastity in their whoring. Innocent indifference to murder or death. Thin, alacritous male faces, turned westward, ready to move, accidental founders of states.

"You finished getting a good look at me?" asked Henry.

"Look, you were in Vietnam, right? I hear you got some medals over there, and then you ran into a little trouble. That true?"

"You ask a lot of questions."

"Guess I do."

"They gave me some fucking medals. Then they busted me. Then they gave me some more fucking medals. Then they gave me the fucking boot. I wasn't supposed to think it was funny either time." The voice was again disinterested.

"No, the military's never been known for its sense of humor."

"Some tough shit."

"Bounce you for drinking?"

"You got a sense of humor."

"Drugs?"

"You wanna know? Okay, I was trying to grease a guy but he had on the wrong uniform."

"Grease?"

"Kill, shoot, eliminate the cocksucker. He was a dink. They were on our side."

"I remember."

"Good for you." Henry tore into pieces the empty matchbook and stood, his fingers stretched on the table, his leg jerking against the table's leg. "Okay, okay, you here to do good, do me something, okay? They got me in there with a spade about a hundred years old, and the dude's flipped, I mean he's nuts, okay? I got to get him out of there. I can't hack that guy freaking on me in the middle of the fucking night." The voice accelerated, whirred higher. "I got to get things cooled out, I got to get back home."

"You married?"

The eyes dashed back to Hayes. This time anger rushed out. "You stay the shit away from her, you got that? She's none of your fucking business!"

"Sure. Sorry." Here was, Hayes thought, the quicksilver plunge he'd been precipitant in Maynard Henry's body the whole time he'd been in the room. The bolting of the horse. "Listen, I'll ask the desk about the old man. Seems like the smartest thing, though, would be to find somebody to put up bond for you so you could get out yourself."

"I'll get out, you'd better believe it. And you can tell that fat cop that I'm going to cream him. Okay? There's a story for you, you can write it because it's going to happen. I'm going to beat the crap out of him. He's been begging a long time. It's going to happen." Henry's hands sprang up from the table as if twitched by strings. He went to the door and rapped it with his fist.

"Sure, fine. Thanks for the chat. Sure you don't want my cigarettes?"

"Your brand's for shit." The door slammed behind the prisoner.

"I know what you mean," Hayes said to the empty room.

"You were wrong, Fred."

"How so?"

"He can talk."

"What'd he say?"

"Well, if you're the fat cop he had in mind, I got the feeling he's fixing to do you in."

"They all feel that way sometimes. It's mutual."

"He asked me to look into something, doesn't seem too unreasonable. Appears he's really bothered by his cellmate. Your harmonica player. He says the old man's insane."

"Probably is. Harmless though."

"Well, it upsets him. Couldn't you just move him? What's the difference?"

"I'm not running a Holiday Inn here. First come, first served. No place to move him to. It's just temporary anyhow. Christ, after all that time in Vietnam, you'd think he'd be pretty used to listening to people go nuts."

"True. Well, like you say, anything to keep *ennui* away from the Lord. Take it easy. I got to get back to work."

"Shit, I know where you're going. Drink one for me. I'm not an intellectual like you. I got to work for a living."

"Quit and write a book. *Words of Wisdom from a Small-Town Warden.*"

"I got nothing to say that hadn't already been said since the year one. Why should I write a book?"

"If you feel that way, you're right, you're not an intellectual, Fred. What'll I drink for you if I should happen to walk into a bar by mistake? Scotch or bourbon?"

"Just drink me a beer. I can't afford Scotch."

"Write a book, Fred. There's a book in you waiting, I can hear it hollering to have its sentence commuted. 'Let me out of here.' "

"You know, Hayes, I bet you and Hines would get along like a house on fire. You want to meet him, see him dance? Why don't you and him write a book?"

"Oh, we've written lots already—me and old black Hines. Ever hear of Faulkner?"

"Yeah, I've heard the name. Wrote Westerns, didn't he?"

"Well. There you go."

CHAPTER
29

Because Evelyn Troyes had searched everywhere without success for a Bach, Beethoven, and even a Brahms, the Dingley Falls ladies arrived at the loft in Sheridan Square only as the big event began. They found the whitewashed, bare-beamed room crowded with lovers of cinematography—and of the cinematographer, Marjorem Harfleur, feminist writer, director, producer, and star of *A Day in the Bed of an American Woman*, a film that the artist herself called *Elliptic Ellipsoid*. Tracy, Priss, and Evelyn had only a second to find throw pillows to squat on before the projector whirred and the Harfleur logos (a nude female corpse hanging from a garter belt to a meat hook in a supermarket freezer) flashed, then froze before them.

As her day in bed bounced on the screen, split in two, triplicated, sped up, retarded, inverted, negatived, and was otherwise subjected to psychic and filmic disorders, Ms. Harfleur herself swung upside down, dangled from a rope in front of the wall where her life was being shown. Dressed in black and white leotards, the live Harfleur inscribed with red chalk in both hands her emotional response to this particular screening of the filmed Harfleur.

"I had no idea," whispered Priss, "that American women were entitled to so full a day, or so full a bed! I feel quite deprived, don't you?"

"My!" said Tracy, who had just glimpsed (as Ms. Harfleur flew by on the outswing and cleared the screen) a giant poodle attempt to sodomize a man in a Nixon mask as he attempted to copulate with a woman in a Red Army uniform. They squirmed on the crowded mattress where the star, dressed in nothing at all, sat smoking a water pipe like the caterpillar in *Alice in Wonderland*.

After about an hour, the live Ms. Harfleur began to moan and spasm in her shackles. As her day fragmented on the wall, the screen filled with blood. It poured out of the eyes of a poster of Mary Pickford and soaked the mattress. All the bedfellows were washed away in a red tumble, the filmmaker herself went limp, and that evidently was "The End," for the lights came on and everyone began to talk.

"That blew my mind away!" said a young woman with a crew cut, dressed as a Russian peasant. "Didn't it yours? Washed in the blood of the lamb. Reborn! Wow."

"Why, thank you, no, I don't smoke," said Evelyn Troyes as she declined the rather smelly and messy (could it be Russian?) cigarette offered by her neighbor, who appeared to have at least six shawls tied around various parts of her body.

The girl gooed, "I just love your outfit, it's wild. Where'd you ever find feathers like that?"

"I think, yes, abroad, I'm afraid." (In Paris, in fact, where she had also bought the Chanel suit of raw silk Della Robbia blue that she now wore with the gray-blue pheasant-feathered cap. In Paris that summer when Blanchard had only months to live and they had thought they had a lifetime.) "A long time ago," Evelyn added.

Around the loft—someone's home, evidently, for those blue things Tracy said were chairs, and the orange ones, tables—conversation crackled to the crunch of dipped raw vegetables and the munch of slivered meats.

"I told Jer, 'Look Jer, if I *am* getting bent out of shape, it's because my play's getting bent out of shape by that hop-head hyena!' "

"Whuddah'd Jer say?"

"Said he and the hyena were having an affair. I could have torn out my tongue."

"But everybody knows that! He's really nuts about her. He sent her to Boston and had her dried out."

"*En pointe?* You're kidding! He must weigh two-ten!"

"First *she* horns in on my analyst, and now she wants Dr. Meddrop to see her lover too! Can you believe that, Charlie? She's got the apartment, the stocks, the kids. Now she wants Dr. Meddrop. You know what the rent was on that apartment? Only one-ninety a month!"

"Come on, Kurt, don't start crying again. Please. People are staring at you. You've had a little too much to drink. You'll find a new apartment, you'll see."

"I know. I'm sorry. I guess you're sick of me parking myself at your place. I'll get out. I'm sorry. Sorry sorry sorry. Sorry sorry sorry. But fuck, Charlie, I mean, Dr. Meddrop's all I got left."

"A ticket to that show Saturday? Your body wouldn't buy such a thing. When this town moves, it's like lemmings to the sea."

"Death is *in*. I'm telling you, it wasn't forty-eight hours after all those coeds died from the defective foam insulation in their dorm that Paul had a treatment slapped on a producer's desk. Forty-eight hours, and he got two hundred grand for it."

"I don't want to know, don't tell me. Greed and envy are eating me alive anyhow. My mother told me she tried, but she just couldn't read my novel. She wants me to write for 'Marcus Welby.' "

"I told you death was in."

"Marjorem's stuff is passé. Nobody cares about the stupid *screen* anymore. Now, my new film, people watch the light coming out of the lenses, see what I mean? Light! The meaning's in the shift of light, what it reflects."

"Smoke?"

"Form! Form! Form!"

"I was apeshit over that animal. I mean mentally he was a yo-yo. But, sweetie, he could ball! I was coming three and four times a night. But after his coach benched him, he just lay around my apartment all day in his well-hung glory, sucking Tootsie Pops and watching reruns of 'Gomer Pyle' on my tube. Besides, it was like feeding a St. Bernard. Finally, I had to throw him out."

"I admit it, I'm a workaholic, I don't have time for men. Four times a night? I couldn't fit it in. A woman can't take time off to go whoring around like a man can. But I'm so damn horny. Maybe I'll become a Lesbian."

"Forget it. Take it from me. That takes time too, and you end up going to meetings every other night."

"Told me she couldn't get me any big-name blurbs for my book because I didn't have any Reality Content."

"So what gives you Reality Content?"

"Having big-name blurbs on your book."

"I love it."

"All I'm going to say now is, we're talking six figures, and think of this: it's the gay *Death of a Salesman.*"

"This is Ralph Ang, he just had a one-man show in Leopold's, and this is Chauncey Cohen, Chauncey wrote that piece on the Pre-Rockwellites for *The New Yorker.* This is Olivia."

"Sorry, I didn't catch what you do, Olivia."

"I don't. I *am,* and I hate the way Americans define themselves by what they do. The whole *shmeer* turns me right off."

"I know what you mean. We're like those fish that push those mud balls along the ocean floor with their noses."

"Hey, I like that."

"So my bones have completely reknitted, and I'm back up to three miles before breakfast again."

"Great."

"Plus the racquetball."

"Great."

"And I'm down to a pack and a half a day."

"Great."

"Tried the punch?" asked a man in a jumpsuit with long gray hair and a beard like Moses. He was wrapping ham and roast beef in napkins and stuffing them into a shoulder bag.

"No, I haven't," replied Mrs. Ernest Ransom, who stood by the refreshments from some vague sense of social security in their proximity.

"Don't. It's sheep dip. . . . Who's the Oreo?"

"I'm sorry?"

"The Afro-Saxon in the gray stripe, you were talking to him over there by the pinball machine."

"Really, I'm a stranger here. He was simply discussing the film."

"You know, I figure him for a straight tush man. You know, wasp mink. No offense. I'm pretty ripped. Haven't eaten in about a week either. No offense."

"I beg your pardon?"

"Well, the guy trying to put the make on him now, the guy in the applejack cap and the platforms? Well, he's going to crash, isn't he? Maybe the Oreo swings both ways. I don't know; I was just wondering."

"Ah. Would you excuse me, I see my friend over there."

"No offense."

Mrs. Canopy was chatting with someone she knew (indeed supported)—the Apollo Belvedere of modern sculpture, Louie Daytona, now released on parole and residing in her townhouse. They were discussing a common acquaintance, the Pakistani painter Habzi Rabies.

"You see Hab's new stuff?"

"*Bent Void* One through Sixty-five?"

"Yeah, well, he's flushed it, Trixie."

"Tracy."

"Yeah, Tracy. Hab really had something, back, seventy-one, seventy-two. That *Kama Sutra* mural he did on your dining room ceiling at my place. Bootiful! But he's pissed it all away now. He's in a making-it bag, and that's always a bad scene. Sixty-five stretchers with no canvas in them, come on now! So the wood's warped, so what. I don't call that art. Do you call that art?"

"I don't mind telling you, Louis, I was a bit puzzled as to what Habzi might be getting at."

"Jack! That's what he's getting at, Trudie, jack and more jack. Painting all the presidents on the lousy Alaskan pipeline! Man, that's sad. Nobody can paint with their fists full of dollars."

Mrs. Canopy, who had paid Louie Daytona $3,500 for Vincent's funeral monument, defended Mr. Rabies in vain.

From across the room three handsome gentlemen

observed Mr. Daytona and Mrs. Canopy, while Evelyn Troyes, standing nearby, heard but did not catch what the gentlemen said.

"I have just flashed on heaven, girls. Look at the basket in those bells! The faunet over there making up to the kitschy fag hag in cashmere."

"Sweetheart, that's Louie Daytona. He's twisted, totally unglued. He just got out of jail for assault."

"I don't want to *marry* him, my dear. Just a sordid fling."

"Never happen, you're too ladylike. Daytona cruises the meat track, seafood, really rough trade."

"I think I'll join the navy then. Anchors aweigh!"

From across the room two handsome gentlewomen observed the handsome gentlemen.

"Will you look at Werner over there giggling with those two queens?"

"I know. Christ Almighty, I wish Werner'd never come out. He's gotten so enthusiastically campy, it's like having all three of the Andrews Sisters sit down next to you in one chair."

"Well, I love his blouse! Wonder where he got it."

"Looks Bloomie's to me."

From across the room the husbands of the handsome gentlewomen observed the world.

"It gripes my balls."

"Look, don't make noises. He's in the barrel. Ted'll fire him before the week's out. They got plenty of ammo against him."

"Fire him! They ought to ream his ass out. The whole lousy account he cost me! I feel like personally going over there and beating the royal fuck out of that joker."

"No need to make it into a big machodrama."

And all around the room, names were dropped like manna.

"And I was just wearing some old *shmatte*, so when she asked us to come backstage and meet . . ."

"And *he* was lying there in the buff and no makeup

when the cops showed; well, you know what they say
about him and pills . . ."

"And listen, this is straight, he's gay . . ."

"And listen, she tells everybody she slept with her
father . . ."

"Listen. It's all fake."

And into the loft walked Richard Rage and Beatrice
Abernathy. Heart hand-fast in heart the lovers stood.
Rage in his tweeds. Beanie in deep chiffon green with
fluttery sleeves. The poet was humming into her ear
that greensleeves was his heart of gold, as near them
Ms. Harfleur asked the host, "Who's *that*? With Rich.
She looks like a giant sequoia."

Rage was an old friend of the host, Charlie Rolfe.
Beanie, of course, was an old friend of three of the
guests. Unnoticed by the others, the couple had come
into the loft after the film started, had left for a walk
along Village streets before the film ended, and now
had returned so that Richard could again press Rolfe
for the $200 owed him, for he wished to find some
haven in which to shelter this woman, if possible,
forever. Last night they had spent at a painter's on
Bank Street, where, for the evening, they had left
Beanie's dog, Big Mutt, whom the painter wanted to
use as a model. He needed a bear and couldn't afford
one.

"My God, Tracy! There's Beanie!" said Mrs. Ransom.

"It *is!*" said Mrs. Canopy.

"With Mr. Rage," said Mrs. Troyes.

"What in the g.d.h. does she think she's doing?"

"She's eating shrimp salad at the buffet."

"Evelyn, for God's sake. I see that. Two days ago she
elopes with a middle-aged hippie after thirty years of
marriage and tonight she's happily eating a quart of
shrimp salad?!"

Over marched Priss. Tracy and Evelyn followed in
quick step. Beanie saw them come, remembered what

she had done to them, to her boys. She flushed and put down her plate.

"Beanie. Dear, dear. Is this true?" asked Tracy. "Did you *mean* what you said in your note? Forgive us, but Arthur read it to us. He thought we should know. It's just coincidence we're here, but are you really leaving Winslow?"

"Beanie! You have simply lost your g.d. mind. This is hysteria."

"Beanie. Did he, wait, Priss, let me, did he force you to come with him? Oh, my dear, think of Winslow," whispered Evelyn.

"Yes, I know, I do, and I'm sorry."

"We'll just walk out right now and go home and forget it."

"No, Prissie." Beanie had never said so flat a no to Priss before, and her obstinacy so disquieted Mrs. Ransom that she arrested her friend by the arm and led her off to the bathroom. Tracy and Evelyn came, too. Locked in with a purple tub and a toilet bowl in which cigarettes unhappily floated, the four women considered Beanie's future. She admitted she had not thought about it. She admitted she had not thought about her past either. Under Mrs. Ransom's cross-examination, Beanie was brought to further admissions. She admitted she was hurting her husband, her children, her unborn grandchildren, her friends, her neighbors, her community, her name, God and her sex and her country and the great chain of being. Seated on the edge of the tub, Beanie began to cry. From the rim of the toilet, so did Evelyn.

"You must do what's right, right for yourself, Beanie," said Tracy, handing her friend some toilet paper. "But have you really *thought*?"

"Of course she hasn't thought. The man has mesmerized her, she's under some kind of spell."

"Yes, Priss," said Beanie. "I didn't mean for anything like this to happen to me."

"Well, then, can't you see how absurd you are? Come home."

"No."

"Oh, my God, I cannot believe this. What are we going to do with you?"

"Please don't worry about me. I know it's crazy for you. It's not easy for you to understand."

"Not *easy?*"

"Not possible. But it's true. I *will* talk to Winslow soon. But I can't come back right now. I know he thinks he's hurt, but he'll be all right. He's never loved me *that* way. You see?"

"How do you know he doesn't love you *that* way, whatever *that* means, for God's sake?"

"I just know, Prissie."

"And this Rage of yours?"

"I feel like he loves me."

"Ha. What in the world do you mean by love?" Mrs. Ransom wanted to know.

There was a rap-tap-tap at the door. "Darlin', you in there?" asked Rich Rage.

"Yes," Beanie answered. "Just a minute."

"I think I found us a place to stay. Something the matter? You okay?"

"I'll be out in a minute. I'm all right."

"Okeydoke. I'm right by the table."

In the bright light of the bathroom the four ladies sat or stood in silence. Then Beanie dried her eyes on toilet paper. "Thank you for caring about me," she told them. "But I had to go because I had to find out. You know, I almost lived my whole life and never knew. Tracy? You know? Could you just leave me here alone for a minute now? Please?"

What could they do? Abduct her? So they unlocked the door and left her with Tracy's hug and Evelyn's kiss and Priss's warning.

The whitewashed loft floated in layered clouds of gray and blue smoke. The loft winked with a hundred icy glasses. The loft warmed with the heat of hype. The

Dingley Falls ladies had left, but the party stayed. The party laughed and leered and sneered and mooched and munched and stroked and quipped and tripped and never quit. For the flash-trash cash-bash of the Big Apple is open all night.

CHAPTER
30

Beanie was telling Rich that she could not breathe in his friend Charlie's apartment. That people here in Manhattan kept their lives in little squares, with more and more and more people on top of them, beneath, beside, behind, in front of them. That people here in Manhattan were penned like dogs in a pet shop, and some lay listless with the loss of hope, and some leaped about, manic with the chance of being bought. She could not breathe on these streets because earth could not breathe. The earth had been smothered in cement. Manhattan was a gray Titan's cemetery. And she felt dead here.

She did not say this in so many words, of course, for Beanie was a woman of very few words. She said, "Richard, please, I feel so cooped-up here with this kind of people. I guess I miss Dingley Falls. Could we go someplace green and quiet? Someplace living. Does that make sense?"

Richard Rage was saying that he loved it here. That the spires defied the sky and drew him up to their height, inspired him with their clean, strong thrust at possibility. Manhattan raised his head and quickened his heart. Mammon and Moloch doing their mighty things out of steel and glass and power. The mind of man electrifying a megalopolis, splintering with light-

ning bolts a mound of rock. "Let there be light!" said
no more than mammal man. And there was light! Here
at the source of power, Rage plugged into a trillion
electric sockets, he was sparked with all their energies.
Here he saw himself transmitted and projected into
twenty Richards, saw them simultaneously on twenty
television screens in one store window. He was magnifi-
able on millions of radios. He was sped through
subterranean mazes of a fantastic game, led from one
flash and spark to another like a pinball. He was
elevated and escalated. He was instantaneous. He was
high.

He was jazzed by a billion car horns, cop whistles,
shill spiels, cameras clicking, transistors, subway
screech, whoosh of wind, clatter of pushcarts, fiddles
begging, ferry bleating fog, sirens singing fire, church
bells ringing salvation. He was high with a thousand
lingos. All around him cantatas of multitudinous
accents and argots, tympanic, flat, sharp, glottal, nasal,
dental, twang, slang, jive, and jargon. Chatter and woo
and barter and curses in Bronxese, Blackese, Chinese,
and all the Babelites that worked to build the mighty
tower and called one another honkie, wasp, wop, spic,
mick, kraut, polack, kike, and jig. All their voices
amplified him. All the people dashing at him when the
light flashed go. Fat, lean, gay, straight, crooked,
hebephrenic, hale and hearty, melancholic, sober,
drugged, yellow black brown red and white, all zippy in
the dynamo of the giant power generator they call
Manhattan. And he felt alive here.

He did not say this in so many words, of course, for
love is a sparing translator of differences. He said,
"Darlin', New York's got *everything!* You want grass,
you got it. Trees? A fucking forest! A forest with seals
in it!"

With a wave he hailed a pumpkin-yellow coach for
his lady. The first cab that Richard called came at his
bidding. "Love it!" he shouted. "Look at this! You're
my luck, darlin'. I've got the world on a string, sitting

on a rainbow! Columbus Circle," he told his driver,
who was Armenian and a fan of the New York Yankees.
Out of the radio sputtered the cheers and jeers of fans
as the cab wove its wheeling way through the city lights.

"What's the score?" asked the affable poet.

"Nuddin', nuddin', top uh de tenffh. Tell me why I
bodder wid de bums?"

"Love," Rich told him. Love was in the air wherever
he and Beatrice breathed, love and luck were wed in
magic. And so there was one horse and carriage waiting
for them. And a grandly moustached chauffeur named
Curley McGuire who ate pieces of pizza from a
cardboard box as they shambled along the curves of
Central Park.

"Now. Ain't this a night in a million?" Curley's
question ambled back to the couple curled together
beneath a nappy blanket. Who better than they could
answer, "Yes"?

Beanie asked where the seals were.

"Lady," said Curley, as he chewed pepperoni and
peppers. "You talking about the zoo? They got those
seals locked up at night, long time ago. Drunks and
bums was sneaking in there at night and diving in, and
getting their fingers bit off. And nuts and kooks was
taking potshots at them seals and throwing beer bottles
at them."

"Why?"

"Why? Lady, this here is New York!"

Still, the grass was green. Horns were hushed and
cars no more than blurs of motion. Night breeze shook
awake the leaves on trees and shifted their patterns as
the hansom passed. Yes, there were trees, as real as
those rooted in East Woods and Birch Forest. Leaning
back on Richard's shoulder, Beanie looked up at a sky
luminous with phosphoric crystals like the stars of a
smoky ballroom. A sky haloed in the city's haze. In
Dingley Falls tonight, the sky would be ablaze with
candelabra on black velvet and each star would be vivid
with its own iridescence. Still, in this nimbus sheen,

there was a beauty. Beautiful to Beanie, though she knew that for her to be here at all made no sense. Just as love makes no more sense than magic.

Of course, they were right to tell her it made no sense. Priss was right to think it hysterics. She had thoughtlessly left, after thirty years of marriage, a good quiet man who thought he loved her for this strange, unquiet man who knew he wanted her, who had swirled her into his passion like wind and leaves. But they were right, she was being unfair to Winslow and could not for much longer refuse to think about that.

Still now Richard's pulse in his neck pressed the rhythm of his heart to her face. And his hand beneath her hand was vital. And for so long she had not been touched, except by words—Winslow was thoughtful and said kind things—for years somehow they had not made love, and even in the beginning her husband had evaded passion. It had been for so long that she had neither known herself to be a passionate woman, nor been aware that in passion's loss she was that much less herself.

But Richard knew, knew it the moment he brushed against her with his knee in that Argyle bar. He knew who she was. He saw it in each act of her body, in her hands on the wheel of her car, in her lips on the rim of her glass, in her eyes on star moss and cowslip almost hidden as they climbed through Birch Forest, in her teeth biting wild blackberries as they climbed. He had touched her, and her body, for so long husbanded, quickened. He saw, heard, touched, sensed, knew who she was, and that was as magical to them both as pink lady's slipper shining out of pine needles in the shadows. As sudden as the sun spilling into the evening lake.

He took Beatrice's hands like a prayer. She had touched him, and after all those diffuse and scattered years, Richard felt that perhaps he could be centered now, concentrated in her absoluteness. For she was, he believed tonight, the most holy (because the wholest) person he had ever known. He kissed her now, and red chestnut blooms like candles flickered down a hall of branches as they passed beneath the trees this night in Central Park. She kissed him now, and his breath was perfect to breathe, his beard was strange and perfect on her lips, his hair was yellow-red and perfect-feeling in her fingers. Leaned back against the musty leather, they kissed and that way translated all they had not said. With the ease of the evening air, they were reverent with each other. Like birds at rest in a wave, with only a halcyon sigh, they touched as Curley McGuire led his slumbery horse under the shadowed pavilion of trees in the park.

Back above Sheridan Square, the friends of Richard Rage were analyzing his peculiar behavior.

"I don't get it. Our Rich, and a town and country grandmother!"

"What the shit is he up to? Making an ass of himself hanging all over that aging Amazon?"

"Did you try talking to her?"

"Moronic."

"I asked her what she thought of Marjorem's film and she said the dog looked dehydrated to her."

"I love it!"

"It's obvious, isn't it? I mean, she's obviously loaded. She probably clips coupons the way I clip my toenails. Now she owns a piece of her very own living poet."

"And prick."

"The Roman Spring of Mrs. Stone."

"Stone Mountain."

"Then Rich must be a hell of a lot better in bed than he is on paper."

"He's not, not from what I've heard. I heard he was lousy."

"Well, sweetie, she's no Lady Chatterley herself."

"Did you see the *Review* last week? The Lawrence factory is turning it out like it was Ben Rough!"

"It's all hype. It's all a great big hype."

On the train home, the friends of Beanie Abernathy were analyzing her peculiar behavior.

"My God, that woman's more of a fool than I thought! What in h. she sees in that charlatan I simply cannot imagine."

"Oh, poor dear Winslow."

"It's absolutely apparent that all Mr. Rage is after is her money. We've already been told he can't even pay his g.d. library fines."

"Should we call Winslow tonight and tell him where Beanie is?"

"Oh, Tracy! *Fi donc!* To tale-tell against our Beanie?"

"Evelyn, don't be a g.d. fool. Our tale-telling is the last of her worries. Tracy's right. Winslow will have to take steps. She's lost her mind, and he and Otto can admit her someplace *sympathique* till she comes to her senses."

"Priss! I don't think, I didn't mean *commit* her, I meant tell Winslow so he'll know she's all right."

"You mean to say you think that woman's *all right?*"

"Isn't it the strangest thing, though?" sighed Evelyn Troyes. "The way she said he loved her, the way she knew. It was like that when I fell in love with Hugo."

"Yes, and you see where that got you. Abandoned in Montmartre with the Nazis at your doorstep like something in a B movie. Don't try to tell me that Beanie Abernathy is in love, really in love, with a ridiculous, penniless man who's shorter than she is, whom she met on Monday! Ha!"

"Oh, look," whispered Evelyn. "Isn't that Walter Saar up there in the next section, lying down with his head on a newspaper?"

"Yes! It *is* Walter," said Tracy. "I won't wake him, but I wonder how he liked the opera."

"Wait till he hears about *this* opera. *The Magic Loot!*" snorted Priss. "Brunhild and Sig-greed!"

"Oh, I don't think you should talk about it, do you?"

"Evelyn, it was the talk of the town five minutes after it happened."

He kissed her temples and moved his fingers slowly along her hairline. Bedded, unclothed, the marriage of their bodies illumined in the aura of a street light, each looked unashamed into the eyes of the other—that most naked intimacy that only a child or a lover can bear. Curving her long legs over him, she held him in her hands, and sinking down, made them, for that while, one flesh.

And both Richard and Beanie, and their friends, made to each other perfect sense.

CHAPTER
31

"Miss Lattice?"

"This is she."

"This is Judith Haig. I'm afraid I'm calling awfully late."

"Oh, that's quite all right. I'm rarely in bed before eleven."

"I called to explain why . . ."

"Oh, I heard! Poor Mr. Marco. You must have been so close after so many years. I think there's never anything anyone can say, but if these things have to happen, we can be grateful that it was so sudden and so little suffering, don't you think, Mrs. Haig?"

"Yes. That's true."

"You're probably calling about Chin Lam. She's still here."

"Actually I called to ask . . ."

"Sleeping now. I don't think she had slept for days before, I really don't. She talked to me this afternoon, more about this horrible situation with her husband, and I hated for her to be back in that trailer in Madder all by herself, so I just insisted she stay with me until things get straightened out. We locked it all up and arranged for somebody to keep an eye on it."

"This is all very kind of you, Miss Lattice."

"Oh, not at all. She's no trouble at all. I'm glad of the company. A sweet girl really, but terribly frightened, I'm afraid, by everything that's happened to her. Naturally."

"Yes. I spoke with a lawyer, with Mr. Abernathy actually."

"Chin told me how kind *you've* been, to involve yourself. What did Winslow say?"

"He was very thoughtful."

"Oh, he's as considerate as he can be. I'm very fond of Winslow."

"Yes. He, in fact he came by after we spoke to say he'd already been in touch with the people at the prison. The magistrate has set a rather high bail, I understand that's because of previous arrests."

"Do you know what those were for?"

"No, he didn't say. But he said he would go to Argyle tomorrow to look into it."

"Oh, that's wonderful, isn't it? But I don't mind telling you, Mrs. Haig, of course it's none of my business, but from what I gather from Chin, I'm not really sure she *ought* to go back to her husband. What I mean is, I'm not really sure the girl knew what she was doing when she married him. And frankly, her loyalty to him strikes me as a little misplaced, although I believe he did come to her rescue in a *very* bad situation. And loyalty ought to be admired, even if misplaced, I suppose."

"She was worried that there might be some question of her legal status. I thought you might tell her that Mr.

Abernathy says her marriage is perfectly legal, as is her entry as an immigrant."

"Yes, she has her green card. Her work permit. Thank you. I'll tell her first thing in the morning that you called. Maybe you could drop by The Tea Shoppe. You know, I don't think we've ever actually seen you in there. Please come let me give you a pastry. And I know Chin will want to thank you."

"There's no cause, but thank you, I'll try to come."

"And all my sympathy about poor Alf Marco. Will there be services tomorrow?"

"I'm sorry. I'm not really sure yet. I was not actually a close friend, I'm afraid."

"Well, I'd like to send a few flowers. I can hardly keep up with them in my yard, and maybe the family, well, yes, I'll see. Good-bye, then, thank you again, good-bye."

"Tracy, Winslow. Hope I'm not disturbing. I know how worried you've been, though, and thought I'd just give you a call to say I heard from Beanie just awhile ago. From New York. The phone woke me up, and I'm probably doing the same to you. No? Well, she's all right, I mean, not hurt or anything. And, well, I thought you'd want to know."

"I'm glad you called. Is she, well, never mind, I'm glad nothing's happened to her."

"Of course, as I guess you know, she has, ah, has felt that, ah, she needs some time to, ah . . ."

"Winslow, oh, I'm sure you two will work this out. I'm just sorry."

"Well, I won't keep you up. I just thought you'd be worried."

"Yes. Thank you. I'm glad you called."

"Ernest, have you ever had an affair?"

"What do you mean?"

"You know what I mean, slept with someone besides me."

"Of course I have, you know that."

"Help me with this necklace, will you? No, I meant, since we were married?"

"Why in the world do you ask? There, all right?"

"Have you? Thanks."

"Of course I haven't. You know that."

"Why not?"

"Where's my . . . Why not? What do you mean 'Why not?' "

"The thought never occurred to you?"

"Why should it?"

"No, don't empty that in there, just leave it. Well, it's natural, it usually does to most men, doesn't it?"

"Does it? Isn't Kate home yet?"

"She said she was going to a late movie with Sidney. In Argyle, I think. She seems to be seeing more and more of him; maybe we ought to give her the money to go to Europe next month. Have you ever *bought* a woman then?"

"Bought?"

"Yes, for the evening. A call girl?"

"For heaven's sake, Priss, this is ridiculous."

"Have you? Well, for all I know you might have a seraglio stashed away in the Waldorf. How would I know?"

"This is stupid."

"Isn't it the fashion for businessmen away from home?"

"I couldn't say, frankly. What is Emerald *doing* in there?"

"Oh, it's an electric face buffer. The wiring in this house is simply absurd. We'll have to have someone in."

"All right, make an appointment. Do you want this?"

"No, I don't think so. *Klute.* That's the name of it."

"You want your light on?"

"Yes, um, no, I guess not, New York has really exhausted me. Turn them both off. Want the coverlet?"

"I'm fine. Good night."

"*Klute*, the film. Jane Fonda played an expensive call girl. For men like you."

"Hmmm."

"But, naturally, she falls in love."

"Um-hmmm."

"You know, Beanie. Beanie says she's in love with this Richard Rage. She was quite eloquent on the subject."

"Hmmm. Beanie."

"Yes, I know, still, she did go off with him. Do you think she'll come to her senses?"

"Probably. I've got to get up at six, Priss. Sorry."

"Sorry. Good night. Sweet dreams."

"Hmmm. Sweet dreams."

"Your brown twill's back. It's in your closet."

"Hmmm. Good. Thanks."

"No, I didn't know *what* to say, Evelyn, it was perfectly awful! I just couldn't think. He said Beanie called. Yes, from New York. It must have been right after we . . . Yes. Oh, my, I feel terrible. I hope I made the right decision, *not* to say we'd just seen her. I couldn't, that's all. It just seemed disloyal to Beanie. Poor Winslow though!"

"Jesus bless us, poor Judith. Having Alf Marco drop over dead in her lap like that after eleven years. And after getting the news about her own heart just this week. *And* poor Sister Mary Joseph, after she helped raise Judith over at Mercy. Did I tell you? Judith didn't even know about Sister Mary Joseph until I told her today. I'm sure it gave her the creeps about Alf. Didn't it give you the creeps when you got there and saw him? It gave me the creeps just hearing about it. Joe? Joe?"

"Unnh-hungh."

"With Hawk away who knows up to what! *Eddie! Tommy!* Shut up in there and go to sleep! Hawk away, and Chinkie Henry banging on her door in the middle

of the night. I don't know what she thought Judith
could do about Maynard anyhow. Funny Chinkie didn't
come to me, after getting my old job at The Tea
Shoppe, and with you being an arresting officer and all.
'Course I would have told her and no bones about it,
the truth is she should have had more sense than to get
in a pickup with a dope fiend like Raoul Treeca. The
whole thing's her fault in the first place if you look at it
that way. But now Maynard's going to just have to pay
his debt to society just like the rest of us, veteran or no
veteran. Anyhow, Hawk always said how Maynard
ought to be put away for good, didn't he? Didn't
Hawk?"

"Unnh-hungh."

"Honey, don't jiggle, I just got polish halfway up my
toe. You know, Hawk ought not to have gone out of
town like this, with Judith having so much to deal with.
Sometimes, maybe this sounds funny and I love Hawk,
but I wonder if Judith and him are really meant for each
other. You ever wonder that? I'll tell you the honest
truth, Joe, sometimes I get this intuition, you know, the
way she looks at Hawk sometimes, that maybe she
doesn't even *like* him. Isn't that an awful thing to think?
'Course I don't like to pry and she always says, 'Oh, I'm
fine,' no matter what you ask her. But she worries me.
She will have a stroke, God bless her, just all nerves
anyhow, always was, remember that time you and me
and them, when Hawk ran over that dead dog just lying
out on Route Three, remember?"

"Un-ungh."

"Oh, you do too. She made Hawk pull over and then
she just ran into the bushes and by the time I caught up
with her she'd messed all over her nice wool jacket.
Tommy! Your father's getting up out of bed and coming
in there in *one* minute! Poor Judith. Anyhow, I just
wish she'd ridden along with me to look at our house
with Cecil Hedgerow. Then when Alf had his stroke,
she wouldn't have even been there to see it and get all
upset. So I was thinking, when Hawk gets back, let's

have them over, go out to Astor Heights and look at the new house, knock on wood. That'd be nice, wouldn't it, Joe? Joe? Joe? Joe!"

"Mrs. Haig?"

"Yes?"

"Winslow Abernathy. I apologize for disturbing you. I should have waited until tomorrow. I realize it's late."

"No, I was here knitting. Is it late?"

"Almost twelve, I'm afraid. You'll think I'm being absurd, but Otto Scaper just dropped by my house on his way home. I think he's been a doctor so long, day and night have lost their distinctions for him. Well, he mentioned the news about Mr. Marco, and naturally he was concerned about the effect, he did tell me you hadn't been well, and that you would naturally be feeling a little upset. And somehow, I just began to worry, this is so silly. I hope you're feeling all right. Mrs. Haig?"

"Oh. Yes. I'm fine. It's kind of you to call. But, thank you, I'm all right."

"Of course, I was sure you would be, but, suddenly, I just got this feeling of, well, worry, I suppose. You had mentioned being alone, and somewhat . . . isolated. Obviously, it was not necessary. Sounds irrational, I'm sure. My apologies. And my condolences about your employee."

"Please, don't apologize. I appreciate your concern. Miss Lattice told me earlier how grateful she was for what you've been able to do. Chin Lam, Mrs. Henry, was there with her, and I passed along your information."

"Ah. Good."

"I'll drop by to speak with them tomorrow at the shop."

"I see. It would probably help if I could speak with the girl, too. Would you mind if I joined you?"

"I hate to take up your time with this, Mr. Abernathy."

"Could you make it around one? We could have lunch while we talked. Would that be convenient?"

"Well, I'm not sure. No, all right, yes. One. Are you sure you have time?"

"All I've done so far is make two phone calls. Tomorrow then. And please, excuse my disturbing you in the middle of the night, but I'm glad to hear Otto's worries weren't warranted. Good-bye, then, Mrs. Haig."

"Good-bye. Thank you."

"That feels nice."

"Ummmmm."

"Your neck's a mess, Sid, you know that? Nothing but knots. You're too sedentary."

"I'm a librarian; what do you expect, Lance Abernathy?"

"He's sedentary from the neck up."

"Where'd you learn how to give massage? Never mind, don't tell me."

"My roommate taught me. You feel for the heat."

"Feel away."

"Here, take these off."

"Hey. Kate! Hey, cut it out."

"Hold still."

"Stop, stop, okay, yours too, then."

"You win, you win, wait, wait. Sid!"

"Oh, Kate."

"Here, move, wait, here, okay, now, yes, there."

"All right?"

"Yes, yes. Sid, I *love* fucking you."

"Well, that's a start."

In shadows the chariot waited, stars caught in the dew on its crimson leather seats. Stars caught in the spray of the waterfall. She should have been home long ago, but she saw herself caught in Lance's eyes, and he was caught in hers for as long as she didn't move. He should have nev   brought her her   ·here her fears

could seize him with a terrible tenderness he was
unaccustomed to feeling. Beside her, his cheek pressed
against a blanket that he had often before spread
beneath the stars in the lot near the Falls, he did not
know suddenly if he wished to take the gift or not.
Frowning, he touched her breast with his hand. Her
eyes never left him, they were open and he was in them
as she moved nearer. She kissed him. And he, who had
never noticed such things, saw that desire was new and
frightening to her, and so her moving nearer, placing
herself in his hands, made her braver than he was. And
he surrendered his desire to her newness, he felt it fade
away. He did not know which held him in check, the
undefendable courage of her innocence or the troubling
tenderness it made him feel. He took his hand away.

"I'll take you home, Joy," he said.

He took Joy home, drove to Madder, picked up the
hostess at Fred's Fries, took her to the Round-Up
Motel and Restaurant near the airport (she was a
divorcée with two children and a mother asleep in a
four-room apartment), had her perform fellatio on
him, brought her to orgasm with his hand, brought
himself to a second orgasm inside her, then dropped
her at her door with a wave and a wink.

CHAPTER
32

Prudence Lattice had never meant to own a tribal
meeting place for the aimless assignations of teenagers
who baited and dated one another while slouched in
her white wicker chairs. She had meant The Tea
Shoppe to serve afternoon teas to professional gentlemen and shopping ladies. But then, it seemed to

require so surprisingly many of them eating for her to be able to eat, and in a buyer's market one must live with the buyers who come. But Miss Lattice had not meant it to be this way.

She had meant to marry Sloan Highwick in 1928, when he was at Princeton and she was almost the most popular girl at Miss Whitely's in New York, and almost the most daring madcap of all her flapper friends. She had not intended to turn down two marriage proposals only to discover that Sloan Highwick planned to ordain himself a bachelor forever. And she had meant to travel through the south of France in a racer and to be a stage star on Broadway and to have a thousand acquaintances. She had meant to write poetry and to give birth to beautiful laughing children. She had meant to have romance, to be swept into mystery and adventure. She had dreamed of herself at sunrise flinging armfuls of roses out of an airplane down on ancient Delos in the blue Mediterranean sea.

Pru had never thought life would be cruel to her, would send a telegram to say a German grenade had killed her older brother, whose games and books, half a century old, still sat on the shelves in his bedroom upstairs. She had never meant for her mother to die so slowly and with such embittered complaint that pity died before she did. Never meant for her father to lose everything they had in 1929 so that she was called home from London before she had crossed the Channel for the first time. Called home to supervise his funeral after he blew a ragged hole through his head. She had not planned to watch helplessly as her own life lived itself out here in Dingley Falls, where all her father had left her (after the wealth that disappeared—like her father, her mother, and brother), all he had left her was the house on Cromwell Hill Road and the little building on the green which she had made into The Tea Shoppe in order to pay its taxes. All the rest was gone somewhere, or nowhere, without leaving behind explanation or excuse—like her father.

How had it happened? Somehow lives and time and chances sneaked away from her behind her back, when she had always intended to be brave and beautiful. How could she have dared so much in her dreams, but asked so pitifully little of life? She who had never meant to stop looking like Norma Shearer? She who had once, once, intoxicated, danced atop a captain's table, and had lived at that height in no other moment, and was now sixty-six years old?

"I really think you are the silliest old creature," Miss Lattice told herself, and sighed as she tied up the last box of the marzipan she'd made that night. She felt sorry for herself, and sorrier because there was no one but herself to pity her, and sorrier still because self-pity was such an unattractive quality, revealing, as it did, that very weakness of character for which she pitied herself. "I'm just overtired. I ought to go to bed. I'm just upset about Scheherazade."

Although Miss Lattice had gathered up all the possessions of the dead Siamese, she had found herself unable throughout the evening to throw away even her cat's food dish, which was now beginning to smell. Finally, with a sigh, she picked it up, washed it, packed the dish in a box with pillows, collars, and bells, and put them all on a closet shelf. It's all right to be a little low, losing someone close for such a long time, she told herself. Someone to talk to, that's all. The truth is, there was more: that Scheherazade's self-satisfied independence, her courage, and indeed her greed and foul temper had been the sole source for her mistress not only of admiration and envy, but of vicarious pleasures. Through this loud, demanding, smug, excitable Siamese, Prudence Lattice had indulged herself for years in motherhood, gluttony, promiscuity, bullying, torture, and murder. Now she would never wail seduction into the night again, or fasten her teeth in the throat of life.

"Oh, Pru, Pru, you really have no excuse," Miss Lattice sighed while checking locks and shutting off

lights. Then on tiptoe she walked up to the room where
her visitor, Chin Lam, slept. "I'll just see if she needs a
blanket." From the foot of the bed where the Vietnamese girl lay curled on her side in motionless sleep,
Night, the black German shepherd, raised his head
from his paws. "Shhhh," Miss Lattice told him. "Let
her sleep. Want something to eat? Food, Night? Come
on." The dog stood, stretched, jumped to the floor.
Chin Lam drew herself into a tighter circle.

No, no excuse for me, thought Miss Lattice. When I
think of that child. The things she told me! The things
that she has seen and gone through, and still going
through now. Padding down the stairs behind her,
Night followed the small woman into her kitchen,
where she fed him the ground beef she'd planned to
cook for dinner tomorrow. He devoured it in seconds.
When he whined for more, she gave him a pork chop.

Her arms crossed over her bathrobe, her hands
resting on her shoulders, she watched the dog snap a
bone in two. Then all at once he tensed to sounds she
couldn't hear but which she instantly assumed were
those of another dog, come to dig up the grave of
Scheherazade. Unable to see anything from the window, she took back out of the closet a red leather leash
that her cat had refused to wear, and having attached it
to the dog's collar, she opened the kitchen door. With a
single sharp bark, the shepherd lunged, dragging her
down the porch steps before she could pull against him.
A shadow, but a human one, seemed to be running
through the pine trees into Elizabeth Circle, toward the
back of Mrs. Blanchard Troyes's house. It disappeared
before she had seen it clearly. Nor could she think who
it might be out there at 1:00 A.M. Certainly not Evelyn
Troyes, whom Prudence envied for her European love
affairs, and for her daughter, and for the wealth that
allowed her to take trips into the bright carnival of
Manhattan theater and operas and fascinating artistic
people, but whom Prudence did not suspect of noctur-
nal assignations at this stage of her life.

It must be, she thought, some young lover returning home to Astor Heights, happy to walk miles in the star-sparkling grass, happy with the kiss still flush on his lips and the future as infinite and shiny as stars.

"Never mind, Night," Miss Lattice sighed. "Let's go back in." On her way up to bed, she picked up the new historical romance she had bought from Sammy Smalter's pharmacy. She would take to bed with her the latest of her Lotharios or Lovelaces or Rhett Butlers. She would spend the night with this virile bachelor, and in her dreams life would be passionate and she would look like Norma Shearer.

CHAPTER
33

When Benedick crowed, "I will live a bachelor," it is assumed that the groundlings cheered, for it has long been the whimsical fantasy of civilization that male bachelorhood is a blessed state, nobly sacrificed, like female virginity, to that necessary institution, the family. A paradise lost, and regained only at court costs. Not so, as Kate Ransom told Sidney Blossom. "Polls have proved that the happiest people in America are married men, and the most unhappy, married women." This forecast was protested by the bachelor Blossom, proposing yet once more in vain to Kate, who could not yet agree, with Millimant, to "dwindle into a wife."

Among Dingley Falls's other bachelors, imminent marriage loomed only for Arthur Abernathy, who had no objection to wedding Emerald, and for the ophthalmologist, Carl Marco, Jr., who had no way to avoid wedding his receptionist other than flight. Luke Packer

had never given the question any thought, and neither
(at almost twice his age) had Lance Abernathy, though
the question had certainly been posed to him by a
variety of individuals, some of them extremely indignant. It was apparent by now even to Prudence Lattice
that Sloan Highwick would never go to the altar with a
lady. It was not apparent to anyone but themselves that
Walter Saar and Jonathan Fields would never do so
either. Walter's mother still saved hand-knitted caps
and blankets to pass along to his bride upon her happy
pregnancy, and Evelyn Troyes (reconciled to her own
ineligibility) was ever on the search for that perfect girl
whom Jonathan had not yet chanced to meet.

Bachelorhood is a disposition, not a condition. The
truest bachelor in town was old William Bredforet, who
had been parenthetically married for more than sixty
years and during that time (despite the military recon-
naissance, stake-outs, and spy system of his wife, Mary,
and of Bill Deeds—maneuvers they might have forgone
had they realized what spice they added to Bredforet's
game) had enjoyed innumerable brief affairs among the
general delights of being a knight on the town. So much
a bachelor at heart was Bredforet that he had no notion
of fatherhood, despite the fact that he had parenthetically fathered three illegitimate children: one son in
Paris, another in Singapore, and one daughter, now
forty-two years old, right here in Dingley Falls.

A judge had divorced Mr. and Mrs. Limus Barnum,
at Mrs. Barnum's request, on the grounds of her
husband's mental cruelty and physical abuse. Lime had
had to pay the bitch alimony and figured that broken
nose he'd given her had cost him a good $15,000 (at
$400 a month for three years, plus legal fees) before she
got tired of milking him and married some other stupid
sucker. He'd never be sap enough to marry another
one, that was for sure.

Limus Barnum lived alone in the smallest and newest
house in Glover's Lane. He had bought it in 1961 at the
same time he'd bought the antiques store with all its

stock from a New York divorcée who had decided in
two years that she did not, after all, wish to retire from
the world to sell horse collars to weekending couples.
As Barnum often boasted to the realtor Cecil Hedgerow, he had not by a long shot given the woman what
she'd asked for the store. "No siree bob, I jewed her
right down. She was so hot to trot she never knew what
hit her. Come on, Cecil, what would you guess I got the
store and every damn thing in it for? Come on, take a
stab."

"Ten thousand in cash and a roll in the sack."

"Hah. Hah. Come on now, seriously. But if you
really want to know, sure, I could have had her. Easy as
that!" And Lime snapped his fingers with a grin.
Whether he had had her or not, he indisputably had the
store and the house.

"I mean I was just passing through this dump and I
saw how the land lay. Sure, I'd never thought about the
antique line, but what's to know? And, pal, who turns
it down when they're giving it away? Not this cookie.
Everybody's getting into antiques. Then I add on the
games and hobbies. Everybody's got hobbies. Then I
get into the big appliances. Everybody wants a TV.
Now, if you'd been on the ball, old buddy, you could
have had that store."

"I don't have your feel for the market," said
Hedgerow.

"You can sell anything to anybody; they don't have
to need it, or be able to afford it, or even want it, you
know that?"

"I've heard it said."

That was a long time ago. Everyone had assumed
then that Barnum would be gone in a few years—like
the divorcée. But fifteen had passed by, and now Limus
Barnum's feverish face leered at Dingleyans like an old
nightmare at least twice in the middle of movies on
"Midnight Cinema." Tyrone Power would kiss Loretta
Young, and then Barnum would yell at every insomniac
in town, "Spend time with Lime, and spend less!" They

were used to him. Still, they had no idea *why* he stayed, though they suspected he made a great deal of money by selling fake Tiffany lamps and oak-veneered pine ice chests to innocent New Yorkers on vacation, and by opening charge accounts for model airplanes and eight-track tapes and other amusements, chargeable to the parents of young gentlemen at Alexander Hamilton Academy. They assumed he had friends, he must do something besides buy and sell, but as to what he did, and with whom he did it, they hadn't a clue. They didn't like him.

Occasionally Lime gave way to the suspicion that they didn't like him. It made him hate them all. He spent some evenings at the Old Towne Inn (which thought it was better than he was), and some evenings at Fred's Fries (which was beneath him), and in both these barrooms he tried to strike up conversations with people who seemed to have it easier than he did at getting along. It was naturally difficult for Barnum to acknowledge that he had no talent for friendship, but he acknowledged that *something* was wrong, though he couldn't figure out what it could be: neither shyness nor physical impediment nor peculiarity of style or dress hampered him. It must be the people of Dingley Falls, then, who conspired against his happiness. All of Limus Barnum's life (a life that had taken him from Detroit to Cincinnati to Pittsburgh to Worcester to Dingley Falls) things had stood in his way, blocking his reach: Socialist teachers, Communist Jews, welfare blacks, and the female sex. Politicians, journalists, labor unions, the Supreme Court, and women strove to deceive and impede him. If he could only one evening turn Fred's Fries into a *Bürger-bräukeller* to start that *putsch* that would set America right, then he would show them. But nobody in Fred's Fries wanted to listen. Something was wrong.

At 1:30 A.M., Barnum stood in his upstairs room. The night had gotten hot and sticky, and his window was open though covered with curtains. Now from across the street he heard laughter. One-thirty lousy A.M., and they were still at it. Hedgerow's poker party. It made him hate them all. Especially that snot A. A. Hayes, who hung out not only with his neighbors on Glover's Lane, but with the lawyer Abernathy and the rest of the big snots over on Elizabeth Circle, people whom Barnum had invited into his store for fifteen years, but who had never invited him anywhere. He bet he could count on his fingers the times he'd been in Hayes's house, and Hayes lived right next door to him.

The upstairs room was the room where Barnum kept things. Things like his weight-lifting equipment. Things like his political literature and his pictures. Stacked in the corners with his weights were hundreds of muscle magazines and magazines of men with guns, and men being attacked by grizzly bears, and men fording rapids, killing Viet Cong, and having other adventures. All jumbled together were Nazi magazines and hobbies-merchandising magazines and hard-porn magazines and catalogs of antiques. Randomly taped all over the walls were photographs torn from magazines: women being subjected to sexual assault, body builders demonstrating particular exercises. On some of the latter, arrows pointed to the relevant anatomy to be improved; other muscle men posed in contorted stasis like Laocoöns of inflated flesh, their sinews twisted, their faces glossy, narcissistic blanks. Among the pictures of women chained to walls, roped to beds, bent under dogs, gagged by pasty, black-masked men was one of a handsome, sky-eyed Luftwaffe commander who was neither flexing his biceps nor brutalizing a woman, but was only staring indomitably at Limus Barnum. This upstairs room was, needless to say, a private retreat of its owner, locked against the conspiracy of the outside world to ignore him.

A barbell in each hand, Barnum stood in his jockey shorts before a full-length mirror. Thrown in the corner were pants and jacket, and tasseled loafers to which blades of wet grass from his night walk through

Elizabeth Circle still clung. His face was red from his
exercising, and the veins on his neck puffed out.
Raising first one arm, then the other, Barnum sped up
his rhythm and wordlessly talked to the straining
image. One-lousy-thirty A.M. Listen to them. Bigshot
poker players! Penny-ante! Fat lot they know about the
game. Boy, I could take them all for a ride. Like that
big shot in Pittsburgh that night. Two hundred big ones.
Bluffed him right out. He never knew what hit him.
What the hell they got against me? I've been right here
on this crummy block for fifteen crummy years. Isn't
that long enough for the snots? Bet I'm in a lot better
shape than Hayes, make a hell of a lot more, too. That
boozed-up Commie; rather go out drinking with a
dwarf than a man. Brushing me off about the letters
like that. So what if a killer drags his wife out of bed
one night and shoves it in her. Probably pay to get rid
of the bitch. "I wouldn't let the FBI in on this. They'll
arrest you!" Sure, pal, sure. You'd be surprised,
wouldn't you though? Forty-nine, fifty. Not bad, not
bad. Pretty damn good. He flexed his arms for the
mirror, then lay down in front of it and began a rapid
series of sit-ups.

Yeah, Hayes has got himself a real bitch. Women
don't want a man anyhow. They'd rather have that
pansy librarian. Finger-stuff with fairies, that's what
they all like. I showed her though. I showed her what it
was like to have a man in her again, no matter what she
said, whining and screaming. Hell, it was worth it to
see the look on her face, fifteen thousand dollars but it
was almost worth it. They're all Lesbians and fairy
lovers. That Troyes biddy goo-gooing at that faggot
priest in a public restaurant. Stupid cunts. I showed
them. You're damn straight. Boy, they'd be surprised
what I know. Don't live in this crummy hole this long
and not figure how the land lies. Not if you're on the
ball.

Breathing in short gasps, Barnum stood in front of
the mirror. He flexed the pumped-up pectorals with

satisfaction. Then, his eyes fixed on his face, he removed his shorts and threw them into the corner. He squeezed his testicles and penis.

From a closet in which hung garments that Barnum never wore outside this room he pulled out and put on gray military tunic, cavalry pants, and jackboots. He brought a belt and a German officer's hat and a wood chair back to the mirror. From a bureau drawer he took a leather-wrapped hammer handle. He put it beside the belt near the chair.

Barnum stared at himself in the mirror, patted down his hair, adjusted the hat in an exact line with his narrowed eyes. He smiled, then he frowned. "When I tell you to do something, do it," he snarled through tight lips. "Do you think it matters now? Do you think you can stop me? Bring her in here." Expanding his chest, he let out a slow breath and tossed the hat into a corner. "Tie her hands behind her back. Push her down. Do what I say. Hold her." The man in the mirror unzipped the pants. They fell down over the boots, and in the mirror his swelling penis jerked. He rubbed it roughly as he spoke. "You don't have any choice now, do you? Go on. Go on." He unbuttoned the jacket and pulled it open; sweat was shiny in the hair on his chest. Grinning, he threw his foot up on the chair. "Bring them in. Go ahead, you crummy bastards, get it up and do it to her. You're no different. Shitty, dirty scum. You all do it. She screams but she likes it. You're all going to be shot. When they finish, shoot them. Hold her down."

His pupils blackened the color from his eyes, eyes rapt on the mirrored eyes. Picking up the belt, Barnum bent himself over the chair and supporting his weight with one hand, lashed awkwardly back with the belt at his white buttocks. His mouth had fallen open and saliva filled it. He watched the black leather welt the skin in the corner of the mirror. Grabbing the wrapped handle, he bent again, reached between his legs, and with his breath caught, sweat like tears on his face, he pushed the stick up into his anus until it would stay there. One hand gripped the back of the chair, one hand pulled at his penis, as Barnum stared up at the man in the mirror.

"Clean him out," he told him. "Show them. Bastards. Cunt. Cunt. Make her do it. Make her." He stood, reached back, and jerked on the hammer handle. It clattered to the floor. He pulled faster on the red veiny muscle. Breath burst from his face. Sperm burst from his penis. The man was grinning in the mirror, and kept grinning till his eyes closed.

Before he went to bed, Barnum straightened the upstairs room, hung the clothes back neatly in the closet, restacked the magazines, and locked the door. He thought no further of the woman whose imagined presence had been subjected to his will. Different images of women had filled the role in this and other private rooms of Barnum's—some were women in magazine pictures, some strangers who had come into a store or a bar. This particular woman had never been in his store, or in Fred's Fries, or in the Old Towne Inn, though she was not a stranger. While she had never spoken to him except across a grille, he knew her name. Her name was Judith Haig.

At 2:30 A.M., as thunderhead clouds put out the stars and the weight of the air grew electric, there was only one light on in all of Dingley Falls. As usual, it was Sammy Smalter's. The flame of suspicion in Sarah MacDermott's mind about the man she erroneously called a dwarf would doubtless have been fueled had she seen him now, for Mr. Smalter (in pajama bottoms and one of the little T-shirts so appealing to Sarah's sister, Orchid O'Neal) was pacing his room and making hideous faces. He was also muttering aloud, though completely alone, and while Sarah was a monologist herself, she always insisted on an audience, even if she could find no one better than her sleeping husband,

Joe. Smalter, of course, was a bachelor and had no bed partner.

"It'll never work." He grimaced. "Sweetheart, look . . . Look, sweetheart. You'd never know if I was coming through that . . . through this door at night or not. . . . No." Smalter ran his hands through his wreath of hair, fluffing it out in yellow tufts. "No . . . You'd always be waiting for that call saying I was on a slab in some morgue with a card tied to my toe, and my face . . . a mess of blood and bones. . . . My face . . . shot away. . . . My face . . . a scrambled plate of spaghetti. . . . My face . . . Oh, to hell with it. Enough for tonight."

Mr. Smalter ripped a page from the typewriter on his desk. He brushed his teeth and took his pill and thought of Mrs. Haig taking hers. He bent over ten times, occasionally touching his toes. He flipped off the desk light, flipped on the bed light, slid under the covers, and opened his Browning to "Andrea del Sarto."

The light burned along after clouds had rolled over the moon and stars, long after the reader slept and dreamed whatever compromises, accommodations, or readjustments of reality his sleeping psyche thought it safe to allow him. Out of the third-floor window of the tallest home in Dingley Falls it watched like a lighthouse beacon over all the houses anchored nearby in a bay of night.

In Argyle a conscientious mortician, working until nearly dawn, studied more earnestly, saw more aesthetic possibilities in Alf Marco's face than anyone in his life had ever seen. Another mortician stroked gently into Sister Mary Joseph's withered cheeks the only rouge they would ever wear.

In Argyle, while Mr. Oglethorpe's elderly sister, exhausted by her long bus trip and the family crisis, slept on an unfamiliarly large bed at the Holiday Inn near the hospital, the oldest teacher at Hamilton

Academy slipped away from the nurses' intensive care and, to their surprise, died. If there are souls, he became one. If there are gatherings elsewhere, he went to one. If he could come back to earth and say so, Miss Ramona Dingley would be eternally grateful.

Seven miles away, Ramona sighed in her restless sleep. Gray, haloed clouds knocked against heaven. Rain burst out of them like tears. Summer rain beat down on Dingley Falls. The Rampage rose.

CONCERNING THE HEART

The heart of a spider is a single tube. The heart of man and dog, be it false or true, is a four-chambered double pump, simple enough in design and designed to work hard for a living.

The poets say there is no language but the human heart. The language of the human heart is *lub-dub, lub-dub, lub-dub*. Translations have made much of it. Over the ages the poets have massaged this hollow muscle into a flabby thesaurus of dead metaphors. A. A. Hayes once made a list of them. We may have a heart, or a change of heart, we may win a heart or lose one. We can cross our hearts, wear them on our sleeves. They may be in our mouths, they may sink, they may flutter, burn, warm, freeze, or throb. Our hearts may be whole or cold, or in the right places. Some hearts are bleeding, some are hard, and some are trumps. All this while beating time to the days of our lives. The post office is in the heart of Dingley Falls, for instance, and its postmistress seems to take life too much to heart. Such is the versatility of a double pump.

Out of Eden rushed grimacing into the world all the diseases of the heart which Hayes had diagnosed in himself: lust, gluttony, sloth, wrath, avarice, envy, and pride. All set loose when, reaching for the first big apple, our parents tripped and fell. We are told that the Lord experiments on the heart; He hardened Pharaoh's, and tested Job's and saddened Ruth's, and puffed up David's. We are told that where your treasure is, there will your heart be also. Such is the economy of desire, such is the universal language catalogued by A. A. Hayes that speaks in the hearts of every Dinglcyan when Dr. Otto Scaper hears *lub-dub, lub-dub.*

Dr. Scaper's concern is the damaged heart. But for most things that may hurt this organ he has no prescription. The doctor has to worry about other vital disorders. Such as murmuring hearts that go *lub-dub-dub, lub-dub-dub.* Such as heart block, heart arrest, heart attack, heart failure. Guardian of the human heart by which we live, Dr. Scaper must be on the watch for myocarditis, pericarditis, bacterial endocarditis, arrhythmia, thromboembolism, coronary occlusion, angina pectoris, arteriosclerosis, rheumatic valvular disease, mural thrombi, atrioventricular nodals, hypertension, and syphilis of the heart. It is, he says, too much work for a deaf old man.

"Hell's bells, we don't know what we're doing anyhow," Scaper had confessed to Winslow Abernathy. "Coronary X rays are pretty dangerous, and the damn things don't show up small lesions anyhow. Look here, forty percent of myocardial infarctions (it just means heart attack, like coronary thrombosis means an artery block lousing you up), *forty percent* of coronaries fail to cause symptoms. Somebody gets arrhythmia, blood supply drops, they go into shock, first thing you know the poor bastard's dead. Less than half even get to the hospital. And maybe there were no abnormalities at the exam, nothing on the test. All of a sudden you get balled up in a stress situation, you get a severe pain, heavy pain, a fist in the chest like a vise, it goes shooting down your left arm. Angina pectoris. Nausea, pallor, trouble breathing, crushing pain. All of a sudden congestive heart failure. Necrosis of the muscle—secret fraternity lingo for dead, gone, *kaput*."

"Just a minute, Otto, are you telling me to expect all this in the near future?" asked Abernathy with his mournful smile.

"No, no, no, 'course not. But it could, that's all I'm saying."

"Can you treat it?"

"Sure. Thump and listen. Diet. Digitalis for some things. Heparin for clots. Now we got heart valve surgery. Give you a stainless steel one. Give you a hog's. Give you a whole goddamn plastic ticker now. Sure, we got lots of stuff now. Nitroglycerin, cardiopulmonary massage, defibrillators. Trouble is this business does everything ass-backwards. Look here, I read in one of these damn journals over there on that shelf in that pile of mess that the *majority* of our boys in Korea and Vietnam—now, Winslow, this is boys, average age around twenty-four and supposed to be in pretty good shape—the majority of the autopsies on those soldiers show they had coronary artery disease. Had arteriosclerosis at their age! And of course they didn't know it."

"Otto. I'm sorry, let me just ask you, how serious is my condition? Are you trying to avoid telling me I'm going to die soon?"

"What? Die? Hell, no. You're not going to die tomorrow, not necessarily. Not unless Evelyn Troyes runs over you. I'm just talking shop. You've got to get this blood pressure down, though, and tell Beanie to cut out some of that rich food, how you keep on looking like a rail post instead of a boxcar like me, I don't know, the way she cooks for you. Well, at least you don't smoke. I don't count that pipe because you never remember to put any tobacco in it. Look, I bet I've got emphysema right this minute, headed for acute pulmonary obstruction. Massive embolus wouldn't surprise me. Well, I'll let you get on your way. Going to

Boston, huh? Got Mrs. Haig out there waiting anyhow. Hypertensive, same as you, Winslow. Ought to make you both take up watercolors or this yogi stuff or something. Well, you never can tell about the heart."

That had been Monday, of course. At that time Dr. Otto Scaper had not told his patients how peculiar he found their particular symptoms. How, given the results of all the tests he knew of, their symptoms made no sense to him at all.

North of the marshlands at Operation Archangel the team of dedicated, diligent young scientists worked cheerfully. Frankly, job security was a comfort, considering that the golden grant-filled days of Sputnik chasing were now, in 1976, as out of style as the Nehru jacket Dr. Svatopluk had bought in those old times to go drink cocktails with a liberal senator. The young men all knew of MIT graduates standing in un-Euclidean unemployment lines and even if this base wasn't Cape Canaveral, still, the pay was good, and the equipment was great. It was still science. It was research. They had a lounge with color TV, Ping-Pong, pool table, paperbacks, pornography, and vending machines. Sometimes, though rarely, a few were even given leave to come into the neighboring town for a drink at the Old Towne Inn or at Fred's Fries in Madder, or for a pizza at Mama Marco's, or a movie at the Hope Street Cinema, or to drop something off at the post office. Of course, the scientists purposely did not that often visit the town they called "the target." They stayed at the base and worked; they were good boys, their reports said. Race, Caucasian; marital status, single; average IQ, 135; average age, twenty-nine.

Their chief—known to his young staff as Dr. Splatterpuke, Dr. Faustus, Dr. Flatus, Dr. No, Tom the Bomb, The Archangel, and Herr Snotindernosen—Dr. Thomas Svatopluk had been all that Monday evening in conference with two government representatives who had, all on their own, borrowed a helicopter to come see what the secret base was up to. They had learned of its existence inadvertently and were determined now to take credit for supporting it, or take credit for stopping it, or stop each other from taking credit for one or the other of these actions; as yet, of course, they weren't sure which one, since they did not know yet what it was up to. One of these men was Bob ("Bucky") Eagerly of the executive division. He had on an expensive suit that didn't look it. He looked like the manager of a huge southwestern discount department store, but was, in fact, a media manipulator of preeminent capacity and one of the keys that turned the administration. With him was a man whom he disliked and envied, Daniel Wolton. Wolton was very moral and very handsome, both in a posh New England way, and these two qualities seemed to everyone, himself included, to be connected and dependent on each other. He had silver hair curling around patrician ears, he had an upper-class accent and a stiff upper lip. Moral superiority was what Wolton had to sell, and he had sold it so far to OSS (where he worked) and to INR at the State Department (where—unbeknownst to OSS—he also worked) and to the newspapers.

The object of Wolton's and Eagerly's inquiry, Dr. Thomas Svatopluk, was a brainy and sinewy naturalized East European, brought to New Jersey ("Of all places!" he afterwards protested) in the steerage of a boat in December of 1929 ("Of all times," he would add) at age three. He was small, sturdy, messy, arrogant, temperamental, full of energy, and congested—from a cold he'd been unable to shake for the last six months. Dr. Svatopluk had been cooperating with his visitors (walking them through his labs and offering them excellent coffee) because he assumed that they were his bosses, there in response to long-unanswered reports he'd written Washington asking them to stop the Pentagon from interfering with his work again. He feared, he said, that if those tinker-toy wood-head soldiers were given the go-ahead, they would go ahead until nothing was left in the world but dropsical cockroaches munching on TV antennas. "Gentlemen," Svatopluk warned his guests, "we cannot trust the yahoos. And why did you think you needed the military complex? You don't even need scientific research for viralization." He waved his arm around his gleaming white laboratory. "Not when you consider how well the *industrial* complex can massproduce deadly disease, apparently, if we are to take them at their word, without even trying." With a sardonic grin, the scientist counted on his fingers: "Leukemia from ionizing radiation; cancer from a hundred things, say, dust inhalation, say, nuclear reactors, say, H-bomb tests; sterilization from you name it; asphyxia from decompression; brain and kidney damage from lead, beryllium poisoning. Et cetera, excuse me, *ah-CHOO!*"

"Allow me, Doctor, please." Wolton passed the man his own linen handkerchief, and Svatopluk wiped his nose. "Now, Dr. Swätterplök, whom exactly in the military organization would you say you were talking about? Would you wish to call this an abuse of privilege by the Pentagon sphere of influence, for instance?"

"All *I* wish to say is Commander Hector Brickhart was a pain in the *tuchis*, and I don't want any more like him. He was always up here pestering me to 'slip him some stuff' so he could spray it down the Ho Chi Minh Trail. Can you believe that? He seemed to think we kept it in giant aerosol cans, like Windex. When those tinker toys started losing that war in Vietnam, Commander Brickbrain really took it to heart. My opinion is he went slightly freaky-fluky bananas. Flew up here in the middle of the night a half-dozen times and threatened my team and me. Talking nonstop macho nonsense about how we should hand over our experiments, *or else*, don't you know."

(This is what the commander had said to the doctor's scientific team: "Those dinks are losing that war for us,

boys. But it's never too late until the final whistle
blows. *Is it?* Now we know Charlie's all pissed out by
now. Why, we've shot the whole goddamn country
right out from under him, haven't we! But these pansies
in Washington, you know what they're like. They get a
little negative kill ratio incoming, and everybody starts
hollering uncle. Are you going to let that happen? Are
you going to sit on your butt and let the United States
go down on a TKO? Come on. Have a heart! Just give
me a little something. My boys can fly it over tomorrow
and drop those slopes in their tracks. Adios amigos. No
more Mr. Nice Guy. Let's waste those weasels, hey,
what do you say?")

"Then he tried to bribe me," Svatopluk told his
visitors.

"Would you want to go so far as to suggest actual
'bribery'?" asked Wolton, pinching his aquiline nose as
if the odor of possible corruption were insupportable.

"*He* did," replied the scientist.

(This is what the commander had offered: "Want
your country to thank you, Svatopluk? Maybe get a
medal, maybe get a carrier with your John Hancock on
it, U.S.S. *Svatopluk*, sounds pretty damn good, doesn't
it? Son of penniless immigrants comes to the aid of his
countrymen? I might be able to throw a little private
sector something your way. Squibb. Procter and Gam-
ble. I've got friends. How about a nice big fancy lab?
Women? I could fly in half a dozen by tomorrow night.
The best, too, nothing but the best. Booze? Boys?
Cash? . . . You know, you could disappear, Svatopluk.
Funny things happen, people disappear, turn up dead, I
don't have to tell a smart doctor like you. Listen, the
Chief would bring you in and give you his personal
thanks, now I can guarantee that, his *personal* thanks.
Good God, man! Two hundred years, we're *unde-
feated!* Are you going to sit there now, picking boogers
out of your nose, and watch a bunch of zipperheads
wipe their yellow asses on the Stars and Stripes?!")

"Hector Brickhart, hmmm." Wolton frowned. "He

was, I believe, with naval intelligence. But the reason you haven't seen him here lately is that—I assume I'm at liberty to divulge it—the commander has retired recently and has accepted a position as chairman of the board at ALAS-ORE Oil. Whose conservation policies may or may not be what you and I would desire," he added with a moral chuckle. "But of your, and I suppose we might as well call them 'accusations,' the only cause for alarm is the implied complicity of our, I guess we should say, nation in the commander's alleged, shall we call them 'inducements.' What would you say to this, Bucky? What did your people think about the commander's alleged visits up here?"

"Dan," said Bob ("Bucky") Eagerly, "if this guy Brickhart tried to illegally bribe a government employee, the White House never heard of him. When Dan here caught a look at your correspondence *vis à vis* Pentagon interference, it was the first we'd even heard that this thing is operational." Eagerly, by means of a tiny transistorized American flag in his lapel, took down everything they said for the record, on a tape recorder. He took down for the record what everybody said, even his wife. It was a habit.

"Why, that's bullshit! We've been here since nineteen sixty-nine," sniffed Svatopluk impatiently. "Working our buttsos off. You know that!"

"I don't," said Eagerly loudly.

"Dr. Swätterplök, let us get to the heart of the matter," urged the handsome Wolton, sitting down in a canvas-backed chair, crossing his legs, and revealing a trim ankle in a black silk sock without a sag in it. There are not many men who can, seated, be superior to other men standing right next to them. Wolton knew he was one of them. "Let us be open. Would you tell us exactly who authorized your assignment? Would you tell us what your assignment might be? Would you tell us what you think we should conclude about its merits? Would you tell us"—he changed legs and revealed the other trim ankle—"frankly, why are you, I might as well say, *hiding* here in a forest, like fugitives from the horrors of slavery?"

"I would have preferred MIT, myself," replied Svatopluk. "I don't know who authorized us. I think you did. DDT of CIA of OSS. But that's by the by now. And what we're working on is just what you told us to work on. Defense viralization research."

Asked to debrief them briefly, and in his own words, as to the meaning of defense viralization research, Dr. Svatopluk gave his guests a lecture on microbiology, terrifying Mr. Eagerly by grabbing up, and indeed twirling on his fingers as he spoke, test tubes of presumed lethal matter. The head of Operation Archangel explained that there were certain deadly germs that occurred so rarely that a widespread outbreak of one, the plague, for example, would be highly suspect. There were other pathogens that might be common and might spread rapidly, like measles epidemics, but (a) they couldn't exist outside a living cell, and (b) people built up immunity to them. "No getting around it," he confessed. The original mandate of the operation had been to study pathogens (he mentioned in passing some short-term tests they had done with brucella and salmonella) and to study commensals, that is, viruses and bacteria that exist harmlessly in our systems all the time, but then all of a sudden change and, in the doctor's phrase, "turn vicious." "One of our little projects was to learn how to trigger that shift, to learn why, for example, an inactive pneumococcus abruptly wants to become an active pneumonia, and to learn how to make it happen."

"I get your point there," interrupted Eagerly. "Obviously, science has got to prepare for the future by looking for answers to the big questions, whatever the cost. I keep thinking of those poor bastards that burned up in Apollo Five, somehow they stick in my mind."

There was a brief silence, and then Svatopluk resumed his explanation. "This is so so kindergarten you wouldn't believe it," he promised. His team had finally come up with a germ that was very rare, hard to diagnose, easy to transmit, and generally satisfactory. They called it "New Q." Q Fever. A rickettsia that could be passed through dogs, for example, though the hit ratio in that case would be inevitably slapdash. But it could also be transmitted in, say, straw you'd use to pack something in. Or in dust. Or in, say, the public mails. The best part of it was that humans rarely ever get Q Fever and if they did, it was usually no more than a bad fever, shakes, and nausea. However, Q Fever could do some interesting damage to the coronary valves. Assume, Dr. Svatopluk invited his guests, assume that interesting factor could be isolated and intensified, could be made resistant to the normal antibiotics like tetracycline. Assume that through experiments with DNA fragments that intensified factor, transferred through a bacteriophage from the host to a recipient cell, could result in a new kind of Q Fever, deadly, transportable, undiagnosable. A killer to which no one had built up any immunity. "A winner." The scientist grinned as he swept them out of his lab. "I don't mind saying that's when my gray matter began to gyrate. The rest was just, don't you know, old hat for us. Right through here. My office. Can you believe this dump? I wish you could have seen the suite they gave me at Cal Tech, back in sixty-three. More coffee? I could give you some Sarah Lee apple strudel."

Daniel Wolton graciously declined. "Let us be clear, shall we? I confess I remain a bit in the dark . . ."

"I'm completely in the dark, I think I said so before," said Eagerly again to the flag in his lapel.

"Are we"—Wolton stroked the dimple in his chiseled chin—"talking about theoretical research into germ warfare? Is that correct? Are we talking about analysis of those future conditions—assault by some power that abrogated the laws of common military decency, some new Fascist megalomaniac—in which we might find ourselves in a state of germ warfare?"

"*Ah-CHOO!*" replied the chief of staff. "Mr. Wol-

ton, we are *in* a state of germ warfare right now, always
have been. This puny planet is a hostile, nasty place
and every eensy-weensy inch of it is crammed with
submicroscopic killers. Now that was a point I never
could get across to Commander Brickbrain. I am
talking about so, so small. Take a guess at the size of a
poliomyelitis virus. It's twenty-five millimicron, that's
all. That's point zero zero one times point zero zero one
times twenty-five equals one-millionth of an inch.
Okay?"

"That *is* small." Eagerly nodded.

"How can you fight a killer that size? They keep
coming, coming, coming at us. They sneak in everywhere. Through our food, drink, air, water, through
our *eyes*. Our skins are crawling with billions of these
killers. Ditto our dicks and twats."

Dr. Svatopluk reminded his visitors that it had
always been the American way to make allies of
enemies. In the same way disease could fight for us
abroad the way it already does at home by killing off
the unsavory poor and helping us maintain ZPG. With
the proper immunodeficiency condition, *one* carrier of
infection could serve as well as any army. He gave them
an example from the Faroe Islands, where a man from
Copenhagen with the measles singlehandedly killed six
thousand natives out of a total population of eight
thousand. The survivors were over sixty-five and had
endured exposure to a previous European that many
years earlier. "Why," said the scientist, "gentlemen,
we could have *sneezed* on Hiroshima! We could spit in
Red Square and give Russia the plague."

"But would it be right?" Eagerly asked his lapel.

"I think not," replied Wolton with a lofty frown. "I
really rather think not. All nations who abide by
international codes have long agreed that disease is not
a civilized way to kill your enemies. I am in accord."

"Myself, I'd be hard put to choose," remarked
Svatopluk over his strudel. "Get me straight, I don't
advocate mass distribution of viralization. Implement-

ing it as a military strategy would be your business. I just make it."

"Why not simply let loose the plague?" Wolton asked with an arm flourish.

"It wouldn't be right," interjected Eagerly. "Of course, we wouldn't *use* it. But with a deterrent like that, you know, we could put a stop to the arms race. I bet we could bring peace to the world. Right, Dr. Sweaterpluck?"

"Exactly so," said the scientist, smiling. "Whatever."

"But just out of curiosity," Eagerly said, "what about this Q Fever stuff. How does that thing work?"

"It gives people heart attacks, if I follow the doctor's remarks correctly," replied the OSS executive (and secret INR liaison officer).

"Exactly so, very good." Svatopluk picked up a test tube on his desk. "To kill everyone in New York City, for example, would not require as much as could fit in this tube."

At the moment, confessed Svatopluk, New Q had not quite been perfected. Trial runs had been buried near the base, as they may have noticed flying in by the defoliation. But now he and his team were "onto something lethal as hell." Unfortunately it was decomposing after a half-hour out of a living cell situation. "Just let me get back in there, and we'll get it! Don't worry about a thing. This one's the whole *megillah*."

"I'm afraid I do worry," interjected Daniel Wolton. "I'm afraid I must worry. Are you performing experiments on living animals?"

"In a manner of speaking. We're working with humans actually."

"God Almighty," Eagerly gasped. "That's incredible. Where'd you get them?"

"Well, we don't exactly get them. We just work on them where they are."

Daniel Wolton stood, stiffening in symbolic protest. "Are you prepared to tell me you are performing experiments here in the United States of America? Here in one of its most distinguished regions? Are you testifying that you are murdering American citizens in the Litchfield Hills?" The government fact finder had forgotten that he was not appearing on one of the many televised investigatory committees upon which he was so popular.

"Are you bananas?" asked Dr. Svatopluk. "I'm not prepared to testify to anything. We're testing New Q here in our control site, this little town, and a little bit in Manhattan. Here and there. The way it's usually done. That's all I'm saying. We're doing what you told me to do."

"*I*, sir?" Wolton's silver-haired voice rumbled with righteous indignation, and with his palms he brushed down the passion in his handsome breast. "I told you nothing."

"Same here," mumbled Eagerly.

"Well, somebody did," snapped Svatopluk. "And I want you to tell them that if they don't like the work I'm doing, they can get in touch with me and say so. Because I haven't heard a word of thanks out of you tinker toys for years. Money, yes. Equipment, yes. But hello, good-bye, keep it up? Forget it. Bureaucracies! Geniuses of inefficiency. Ninety percent! It *has* to be on purpose, or I would slit my throat over the human race." The scientist had either lost his temper or was, as Mr. Eagerly assumed, jogging in place in his office. "I have to get back to work now!" he said. "I can't waste any more time. It must be midnight. I'm sorry, but we're right on the edge! You know how you get that feeling? What your people call the Big Enchilada."

"Yes, well," said Eagerly, "the important thing is, Sweaterpluck, will it work, and is it right?"

The three men stood in the dirt clearing of the compound while the pilot prepared the army helicopter for lift-off. "A nice machine," sniffed Svatopluk. "Remember those S-Sixty-four Skycranes, military transport helicopters? Huge, excuse me, *ah-CHOO!*

The Vietnamese have probably turned them all into restaurants by now. Yes, I admit, machines are impressive. But don't you forget, all the weaponry a Skycrane could carry would be nothing more than a bee's belch compared to *Pasteurella pestis* carried in the front stomach of a flea." The head of the base was worried. What would happen to his boys, not to mention his base, if Washington (lashed by Wolton) suddenly flung itself into one of its periodic flagellating spates of moral self-contempt?

Eagerly was equally uneasy. Word was that Wolton was looking for a seat somewhere—on the Hill, in the cabinet, on the bench. If he got on his high horse with this bit of news about germ warfare, so called, between his teeth, he could gallop it God knows where. With that kind of copy, he'd be all over the front page, he could stir up all the old nests—the pacifists, the environmentalists, the human righters, the right-to-lifers, the no-no-nukers, the SPCA, leftover Yippies, and the whole Mrs. Ralph Bunche bunch that patronized moral outrage.

Wolton was thinking the same thing. It was important, however, not to act too precipitously. He must be certain that when he kicked open the door, he would catch *in flagrante* something big. Though not, at least not prematurely, something *too* big. Wolton took Svatopluk by the arm and attempted to lead him away from Eagerly, who could not be shaken off but pressed his lapel even closer. "I will be presenting the information you've given me," intoned the OSS official, "presenting it, without delay and without distortion, to the proper authorities in Washington, at the very instant of my return."

"So will I," Eagerly said.

"What do you think you might say if I asked for your assurance that no further experiments will be carried out until the legality of your authority to test them on American citizens has been verified to my satisfaction?"

"Satisfactory verification," Eagerly said.

"Of course." Wolton's voice glided smoothly past the interruption. "Of course, you will want to continue your *research*. Keep everything going in the lab as before, until I return."

"What are you talking about? What's he talking about?" Svatopluk spun away from Wolton's grasp and wheeled on Eagerly.

"Well, it's just that Dan here thinks we ought to be sure we've got our wires straight before pushing ahead. Just take a little time out, check on our signals," the executive aid muttered while rapping his fingers on the flag in his lapel. He couldn't decide where his best position lay. Should he take Svatopluk aside, and warn him to blow up the base and destroy every trace of Operation Archangel, or should he take Svatopluk aside and ask him to blow up Daniel Wolton? Or should he throw in with Wolton and go the savior-stoolie route? Wolton, he noticed, was still orating, though it was hard to hear him over the helicopter: something about "perfectly willing to stand alone. Until I learn that some responsible branch of this government has sanctioned such an operation as you appear to be conducting against the inviolate rights of private individuals, I cannot believe it, I will not believe it, and, in such a democracy, thank God, I am honor-bound not to believe it. When the policies of Adolf Hitler . . ."

"Dan, hold off a second, we've got to board. We can talk about this later."

"Can we, Bucky, can we?" Wolton ran his Ivy League ring through his gray groomed hair. "Don't you frankly find this situation absolutely mind-boggling?"

"This guy's bananas," Svatopluk told the sky. "Listen, boggle your own mind. Tell me this, okay? If Operation Archangel isn't authorized, then who's sending us the Cokes? Huh? Huh?"

"He's got you there," Eagerly noted. But, without another word, Wolton pulled him into the helicopter and instructed the pilot to take off. Thomas Svatopluk,

M.D., Ph.D., winner of many prizes, prized only son of doting parents, now chief of staff, was unaccustomed to being ignored and discounted. More maddening than the blustering threats of Commander Hector Brickhart was the cool contempt with which Daniel Wolton had just now slammed the (helicopter) door in *his* face, *he* (so intimidating to his staff of Ph.D.'s and M.D.'s that they stammered when they spoke to him), *he*, a man of science, a man with the skill to transform the substance of life itself, a man who was the brightest man he had ever met, *he,* Thomas Svatopluk! "Come back here, you ivory-dick twat-head!" he screamed at Wolton. "Okay, tinker toy! Go ahead and tell on me, see if I care! Do they want to be number one, or don't they? Tell them to make up their minds!"

In an excess of feeling, Svatopluk smacked out at the tail rotor blade just at the instant when the helicopter began its ascent. He scrambled for a rock, picked it up, and hurled it into the night. It winged the blade. Then everything happened in a matter of seconds, the way such horrible things usually do. Tipped, the helicopter went out of control. Svatopluk was slammed, like a carpet, into the side of a tree. The tail rotor slammed against the side of his laboratory. A blade snapped off and flung itself, spinning, through the window. The machine looped and somersaulted up into night. And looking like—or so it had seemed to Ramona Dingley, watching miles away on her widow's walk—a falling star, the helicopter then spiraled down and dove headfirst toward Bredfort Pond.

The tiny American flag tape recorder on the White House staffer's lapel recorded these words: "Would you say something's wrong?" asked in a gasp by Daniel Wolton. Followed by Bob ("Bucky") Eagerly's exclamation, "Holy shit! God Almighty! Fuck!" And terminating with the unhurried, unmistakably American sign-off of the young pilot's "Come on, baby, come on, baby, hold it. Hold it, honey! All right, hang loose, down we go. Hello, Mama!"

Down fell the global machine like a smug and innocent Humpty Dumpty who never dreamed he could fall, or break into a thousand pieces that all the kingdom's men could not put back together in just that way again. Never dreaming that he wasn't more than the sum of his fragile parts.

PART

Four

CHAPTER
34

Like a Busby Berkeley chorine, Dawn sprang up to admire herself in the million mirrors shining on grass and flowers. The day, announced Sarah MacDermott, was a real production number, though she couldn't help supposing it would have been more fitting if it had kept on raining through the little services for poor Alf Marco and poor Sister Mary Joseph. "God's tears, Joe. That's what the Father said when it poured so hard the morning we buried Mama. I remember he came around the side of the grave and I was thinking how his nice shoes were getting all covered with mud and how Mama was down there in that box wearing her best shoes too, and he said, 'Sarah, this rain is God's tears for your mama.' "

But in the night, wind had hurried the rain along eastward, shirring toward the sea. And now Dingleyans were cultivating their gardens. Some did so only in a Voltairean sense, by renouncing unattainable desires (again). A. A. Hayes, for example, gave up a spasm of hope that on such a day he could "do something" to give his life significance. Sammy Smalter gave up a fantasy of love and Winslow Abernathy gave up a fantasy of marriage and Jonathan Fields gave up Walter Saar. Other Dingleyans, in the Virgilian manner, cultivated in the sun with hoes and humus. Of these, many had application and a few some talent, but only that floricultural archimage Sebastian Marco was a Merlin, and over the best gardens in town he held an inviolate suzerainty, which with unpredictable moodiness he periodically accepted, resigned, and reclaimed.

This morning Sebastian was supposed to be at work on the Ransoms' garden. His absence, however, was not temperamental: with his mother, his brother Carl, and Carl's wife and children, the bachelor gardener sat in the Church of Our Lady of Mercy, where Father Patrick Crisp said some prayers for the soul of Alfredo Marco. Without imposing long illness, expensive hospitals, or even an outing in inclement weather on his family, the postal assistant had died as undemandingly as he had lived.

By herself, across the aisle from the Marcos, Judith Haig knelt in black. She was watching the sun inflame the robe and face and outstretched hands of the Madonna painted on the stained-glass window behind the altar. Streams of crimson light seemed to reach out at her. She thought of having sat as a child near the plaster statue of Madonna and Child that still stood, chipped and yellowed, by the side chapel; she had pretended that the woman was her unknown mother and had imagined crawling up into her lap, displacing, pushing to the floor, the baby already there. Pushing aside Christ. She had never confessed this sin, not because punishment was unbearable, but because she could not then bear to repent the daydream of hugging herself to that warmth, of wrapping the arms of the Madonna around herself, alone. But guilt was stronger than desire finally, and the wish had died by her tenth year. Mrs. Haig no longer wished to be held.

After the prayers, Father Crisp stopped Judith on the steps of the church. He brought with him faintly the incense-mingled summer smells of Sebastian's and Prudence Lattice's flowers whose colors mocked the mourning they had been sent to grace. The old priest took Judith's arm to remind her that she had not been coming to Mass. Indeed, she had rarely been in the church in the past five years, but the fact that he spoke of her lapse as if he referred instead to an absence of no more than a few weeks struck neither of them as peculiar. Judith Sorrow had been raised to share in the

expanse of Father Crisp's temporal perspective, where
five years were no more than five weeks because both
were nothing. The whole world with its sad, sorry
history was nothing at all. To lose it, nothing at all.

Evelyn Troyes, however, who had just lost "Today"
on television, felt hopelessly adrift without it. "Today"
not only began, it explained her morning. Yet there on
the round white table in her breakfast nook, nothing
but meaningless static buzzed out of the gray blur of her
television screen. The automatic adjuster adjusted
nothing. Evelyn was upset, for if significance is to be
measured by time, television watching was the most
significant event in her present life. Her passion for it
had developed gradually, had begun only after Mimi
had left her for Vassar, but it had grown. Solitude
disturbed (more precisely, dissolved) Mrs. Troyes, who
had said of her first affair, "I never knew where Hugo
left off and I began," and had said of her marriage,
"Oh, Blanchard could read me like a book, he always
told me I was his favorite book." Bereft of anyone to
read and so make sense of her, she could now while at
home keep in touch with herself only by listening to
operas and watching television. She watched it, she
believed, far too much and was ashamed of herself for
doing so. For years she had made resolutions to quit
entirely, to cut back, to watch only after dinner, to
watch only documentaries, only PBS. But the truth
was, and she had never confessed this even to Tracy
Canopy, she watched more and more. She watched
during the day. She watched soap operas daily. They
provided her with a wide circle of people in whose
operatic dramas she immersed herself, to whose tena-
cious wrestle with life she attached her own quiet
existence. She liked to worry about these women on
television. Their problems seemed much more deserv-
ing than her own boring concerns, just as Jonathan
Fields's health (which was excellent) appeared to her to
require far more solicitous watchfulness than her own.

As if nature teased her through the wide, bright-curtained windows, sunlight sparkled all over the useless, silent mechanical box, that Pandora's box of a vicarious human race. Evelyn stared at the screen. It was rather like looking directly into a mirror and seeing nothing reflected there. When she hurried out her dutch doors to see if the rain last night had disconnected her cable, what she saw not so much horrified or angered her as bewildered her. Her beautiful summer garden had been vandalized. Someone had flung her plants everywhere, their roots dangling limply out of dirt clods. Someone had slashed the backs of her bamboo chairs. And along the wall her television cable had been neatly cut. A section of it lay like a severed snake on the patio bricks. Dazed, Evelyn walked back inside her house, where, her fingers to her lips, softly breathing, "Oh, oh, oh," she floated from one pastel room to another. Mimi had left at dawn for Cape Cod. What should she do? As she reached to phone Tracy Canopy to ask her advice, through her front window she glimpsed Ernest Ransom. In a blue sweatsuit he jogged methodically along Elizabeth Circle toward her house. Rushing down the steps, Mrs. Troyes beckoned him inside to take care of her.

"Typical," snapped Coleman Sniffell when his car radio announced that his car had been recalled because it was leaking carbon monoxide. "I wish I were dead and had done with it."

"Oh, you do not," said his wife, Ida, cheerfully.

"It's always me. Termites, rats, dog bites, clogged toilets, mail lost, get in the line that doesn't move; buy something, one tiny screw's missing. Life is a lemon and I want my money back."

"I'll tell you what it is about you, Coleman. There's a Mr. Healthy Self in us all, but you are what we call stifling yours with the Whining Child. Just using your Negativity as a pacifier. You're listening to a sick script. Listen to your healthy self!" she advised, as she held up in front of the steering wheel a rainbow-covered paperback. *Listen to Your Healthy Self!* it said.

The car swerved. A high, nasty horn bleated. Limus Barnum's motorcycle cut in front of the Sniffells as they entered Dingley Circle. It popped to a stop in the middle of the parking space in front of The Tea Shoppe, so that Coleman had to squeeze his car between the cycle and Hayes's dirty coupé—which was also poorly parked. "Typical! Has it ever occurred to you that Limus Barnum might be psychotic?" Sniffell asked his wife. "He has that sweaty, grinning look of somebody that might have an ax behind his back."

"Oh, Coleman, you just don't *like* people." Ida sighed as she stooped her white, starchy form to straighten her hose. "I don't see Doc's car. Poor old man, he was up all last night over in Argyle about Mr. Oglethorpe. Doc's just in a tirade lately over all these people getting sick and dying on him."

"He'll drop dead himself, at his age. Why doesn't he retire to Florida—eat himself to death instead, in peace and quiet?"

"Oh, Doc'll never retire, not with his psychosystem. Besides, who'd take his place? No, Doc thrives on what you call engagement. That means life and death just come naturally to him. Now when I . . ."

"Good-bye, Ida."

"Oh. Good-bye, honey." She held up the corners of his mouth with two fingers. "Now smile, and the world smiles, et cetera."

"Sure."

Coleman Sniffell had never considered the world a great grinner. If he tried to imagine earth a face, he saw a miserable sneer stretching from Africa to India. In his view, the irritating optimism of people like his wife could be sustained only by ignorance of a planet that Sniffell in fact did know more about day to day than anyone else in Dingley Falls, since his job for many years had been to summarize the public news for *The Dingley Day*. And the fatalism with which he tolerated

his private annoyances was rarely alleviated by anything he read in the reports of the world that lay in neat
stacks on his desk. Sniffell didn't know it, but he liked
his job. Everyone finds satisfaction in constant confirmation of deeply felt beliefs. What the apple was to
Newton, famine in Bangladesh and obstruction of
justice in Washington were to Coleman Sniffell. Every
day, news of new disasters, corruption, brutality,
greed, folly, and rotten luck added proof to his
hypothesis that what God did to Job was par for the
course. Not without a sense of humor himself, Coleman
tacked on a bulletin board examples of what he took to
be instances of God's not dissimilar wit: the family
whose house was demolished by a crashing airplane
while they were away in their car being run over by a
truck. The CIA's training dolphins to be spies and
assassinate enemy frogmen.

Sometimes A. A. Hayes came into the back room
and chuckled over these clippings with Sniffell. The
latter didn't know it, but he liked Hayes, too. Nevertheless, he felt superior to his editor because he sensed
that while A. A. shared his assessment of the human
condition, he was unreconciled to so pure a philosophy.
Indeed, Hayes's obsession with conspiracies simply
indicated a naive refusal to let go of meaningfulness. In
Sniffell's opinion, the southerner lacked the courage to
trek resolutely into the white wilderness of absurdity
or, at least, was unable to set forth sober. Sniffell
himself called on no St. Bernards to save him with
brandy. He had no bad habits, including that habit of
happiness espoused by his spouse.

Entering *The Dingley Day* at 8:30 sharp, Mr. Sniffell
slipped on the wet floor and got a sliver of glass in his
finger from the broken window through which last
night's rain had poured. Typically, Hayes still hadn't
fixed it. Nor was Hayes here, though they had agreed to
meet early so that they could write the obituaries of the
teacher Oglethorpe, Sister Mary Joseph, the watchman
Jim Price, and now of the town postman, Alf Marco, in

time for Friday's edition. He washed his finger under the bathroom faucet with no hope of avoiding infection. He opened *The New York Times*. In the Bronx an elderly couple, immigrants in terror of being mugged by minority youngsters, had hanged themselves by tying the rope to the closet doorknob and then lying down on the floor. Coleman Sniffell reached for his scissors.

From the gazebo where he drank a mixture of coffee and sugar with the consistency of molasses, the octogenarian William Bredforet watched his wife and chauffeur argue about whether it was too late or too early to thin out a section of their garden. "Neither one of you knows what you're doing; haven't managed to grow so much as a pokeweed in the past fifty years."

"No one's tried to grow pokeweed," warbled his wife across the emerald lawn. "Don't be such a dog in the manger."

"I got to go now." Bill Deeds eased himself to his feet. "You go ahead and ruin it if you got to."

"Go where?" yelled Bredforet. "I may need you to drive me to the Club."

"I can't help that," Deeds replied. "You doan wants to go to no club nohow; just currious. Scared you miss sumpthin'." He took a huge handkerchief from his pants pocket to wipe his hands. "Got to go pick up my granddaughter. She's showed up on the train on vacation from her hospital to come see me."

Recklessly Mary clipped an armful of jonquils by the clump. "Ruth? But that's wonderful! Why didn't you warn me? All the way from Atlanta! Oh, I'll love seeing Ruth again. Now you give her these. I always wished someone would hand me flowers when I stepped out of a railway car. But I married William instead. I remember seeing a gentleman hand a whole bunch of roses to Ro Dingley at the old Dingley Falls station when she came back from France in 1924, but that wasn't for love, just tennis. Oh, I wish I had a granddaughter.

Isn't that something, William, that Bill's granddaughter is already a grown woman, and a doctor, and I remember when Ruth was only eleven and outscored you and Ernie Ransom both at shuffleboard that Fourth of July?"

"Rubbish. She did not."

"She did so, I remember it too." Deeds nodded. He knew very well that Bredforet wanted to accompany him to the train station, but was too stubborn to invite him. Deeds chuckled as he waved from the car window at his bored employer, who had early on given his life over to hobbies, like lechery, that were fun for the short run but that could not go the distance, that lacked the stamina to jog along with time. As opposed to hobbies like gardening. Or raising a family who would give you grandchildren.

In his garden Ernest Ransom rested after a two-mile circuit of Elizabeth Circle that had been interrupted by Evelyn Troyes. Ransom had sent for Joe MacDermott and had mentioned to him the likelihood of the patio assault's being the mischief of juvenile marauders from Madder, only to be told by MacDermott (who lived in Madder with five sons) that it "could be rich kids raising hell for the hell of it, Mr. Ransom." "Entirely possible," the banker had agreed. He considered his own boy, Ray, as the hypothetical culprit, but found the notion ridiculous, since he could not believe that anyone as lazy as Ray would walk all the way into town from the academy in order to pull out poor Evelyn's buttercups. Evelyn, Evelyn, what should be done for her? Widowhood was a hardship for women, though of course another marriage at her age was preposterous. Well, he'd send Sebastian Marco over to replant things for her.

Where was Sebastian? It was after nine o'clock. Behind Ransom, in a house that announced its birth on a placard (1789), his wife and daughters still slept. He wished someone would wake up. Strange, because being alone had never bothered him in the past. In fact, his children had been so often reminded not to intrude on his work that now, he knew, none of the three had a habit of relationship with him, or the desire for one. I must be getting old, Ransom thought, grimacing as he pushed himself up from a white iron chair. His calf and thigh muscles were strained from his jog, and "the war souvenir," as he called the steel pin in his leg, was hurting. But Ransom approved of purposeful, respectful pain and enjoyed feeling the earned ache as he walked down the flagstone path to the in-ground pool set at the far end of his lawn in a circle of azaleas and rhododendrons.

He'd brought a drink out here last night, while Priss was away in New York; he'd sat in the dark and tried to think about his drive that morning up to the aborted highway. But soon, listening to the bubble of the mechanical filter, his thoughts had moved away from that troublesome image to more pleasant recollections. He remembered how he'd felt hearing all the living foreign and familiar night sounds the lake had made when as a boy he'd taken Pauline Moffat out rowing after dark. Pauline Moffat. He hadn't thought of her in years, and yet when she'd told him that she was going to marry Cecil Hedgerow, he'd felt physically ill. He wasn't sure he could remember what she looked like, and yet seven years ago when Otto Scaper had sat up all night drinking because he hadn't been able to keep Pauline Moffat Hedgerow alive, Ransom had gone next door to sit up all night with him. He'd gone to mourn the loss of a person he'd already lost years, years earlier, and to mourn the person he himself might have become in a life with her, though he had no sense at all of what that theoretical Ernest Ransom might have been like.

There were leaves floating in the pool water now; he scooped them into the net. This afternoon he ought to drop by Smalter's to buy some film for Kate's party. It had been awhile since he'd gotten any pictures of his three girls—as he called his wife and daughters when he showed people their portraits in his office or screened the home movies in which Priss, Emerald, and Kate, with the baby, Ray, skied or sailed or stood impatiently in front of natural wonders and historic relics. On film they silently mouthed, "Oh, Daddy, that's enough" and "For God's sake, Ernest, please!" as the camera zoomed from them to the Acropolis, St. Peter's, Mount Kilimanjaro. Ransom was a compulsive photographer, not because he particularly enjoyed the hobby, but because he was afraid that if he did not capture the moment, it would not exist. He felt compelled to collect his past and bank it, to preserve a record of experiences whose meanings he believed would someday come clear if they were only framed. The movie titled *The Ransoms* was therefore carefully shelved; short reels spliced together into long reels, slides labeled in carousels of baptisms, first steps, birthdays, presents, performances, trips, graduations, heights, weights, freckles, skills, fashions, moods, friends, and Kate's broken leg and Emerald's sunburn and little Ray's return from the hospital. All had been photographed. Ransom had lost nothing.

Dingleyans cultivate their gardens. Even Cecil Hedgerow shoved the lawn mower up and down a third of his backyard before giving up when foot-high weeds twisted hopelessly around the rusty blades. Lying in the sun, Joy Strummer's little spaniel did not move when the mower passed.

"Whatcha doing?" called Polly from the kitchen door.

"Nothing." He quit and walked to his car. "See ya, okay? The money for that bike's stuck behind the phone. Brand-new bike!"

She pushed her glasses up on her nose. "I told you. The guy at the filling station said somebody did it on purpose. It wasn't my fault."

"Fine. Nobody's blaming you." He pushed his

glasses up on his nose. "But do me a favor, change your clothes before you go over to Ramona Dingley's. And tell her I said hello." As Hedgerow backed his car out, he watched his daughter slide her bare feet (unfortunately resembling his) back and forth in the freshly cut grass. He wondered how many days she'd been in those same jeans and shirt. "I forgot," he called. "There's a mash note for you on the table. I found it stuck in the screen door. And listen, we *have* to work on this yard when I get home, okay?"

"A *what* note?"

"A love letter. Have a good day. Eat an egg."

Not a love letter. A note from Luke Packer, thought Polly, saying whether or not he could go look for the base with her and Miss Dingley. She hurried back to the door, stooped, and ran her fingers through the soft grass stubble. It smelled wonderful. "Summer summer summer summer summer," she whispered like a charm.

"And look over here. Here's where he just took a knife or something and gouged the backs out of my wing chairs that Blanchard bought me in Guadeloupe. Oh, *mon dieu,* it just hurts my feelings terribly to think someone must hate me so."

"Evelyn, I feel absolutely positive that this carnage is the work of a werewolf. A g.d. werewolf has contracted an inexplicable passion for you and is trying to get your attention." Mrs. Ransom laughed. "Tracy, did you happen to notice the moon last night?"

"Oh, don't tease her now. It's really very disturbing. Perhaps you don't understand because you don't live alone, Priss."

"Yes, please, Priss, I'm still so upset, you can imagine." Mrs. Troyes gazed thankfully at Tracy and Priss, whom phone calls had brought across Elizabeth Circle. She squeezed each of their hands. "I'm so lucky to have friends so close."

Tracy's hands were coated with clay; she'd been

throwing a pot. "Oh, my, I've got you gooey. I was at my wheel, and I just ran over. It's infuriating! And they say they don't have much hope of ever catching the person. Why not? What is the world coming to, what is *America* coming to?" Mrs. Canopy's spring-apple eyes stared at the black coil of cable on the red bricks, much as General Cornwallis might have looked at a "Don't Tread on Me" flag flapped in his face at Yorktown by one of Tracy's ancestors. "Things like this did not used to happen. Did they?"

"Not to people like us," said Priss. "Except every now and then when the Bastille got stormed." Careful not to lean her white tunic against broken bamboo, she sat down gingerly in one of the wing chairs and, lighting a cigarette, studied her slacks and sandals, which were both also white. "You know, Tracy, this whole scene does have a certain *je ne sais quoi* that reminds me of your Communist friend, the one that designed your toilet. Do you think he might have slipped into town and done it as a surprise for you? Baby Jesus, I mean."

"Bébé. My, really, Priss, I don't think this is anything to laugh at."

"Very little at any rate. But there *is* so very little that one is forced to be *un peu* indiscriminate."

Mrs. Canopy's square jaw jutted slightly. Mrs. Ransom, who was flicking an ash from her slacks, did not notice this very faint warning of revolutionary discontent in one who had for so long admiringly attended her court.

Polly found the letter first incomprehensible, then disgusting, and then very frightening. Just by reading them, the words had made her dirty and ashamed. She had the irrational feeling, too, that whoever had sent this letter knew she had seen Sidney Blossom and Kate Ransom together in the library—and that that was why he had sent it. Now the kitchen, the quietness, that had been safe a moment ago were suddenly scary. Someone might have gotten into the house already. If she looked up at the screen door, would she see his face there, watching her? Could she hear him breathe? Forcing herself to look at it, she latched the screen. Forcing herself to move slowly, she walked through the house. It was changed, and was ominous. Finally she reached the front door, locked it behind her, and ran.

In the backyard next door, the letter held behind her balled up in her fist, Polly asked Mrs. Strummer if Joy were still in her bedroom. She was. Joy had a yellow ruffled room arranged according to the instructions in a magazine. Little dolls in foreign costumes stood in rows on white shelves. Large dolls sat in a yellow rocker. Enormous stuffed animals sat on the floor. So did a record player. A young breathless male voice seemed to be singing from the bottom of a warm vat of syrup, "Make Mine You." Joy was in bed; she hung up the phone when her friend entered. Polly looked around the room and slowly let out her breath. Everything was the way it always was. There were the wallpaper and bureau and rug she'd seen a million times. She was all right. "Your mom says to turn that down. She can hear it out in the yard."

Her breasts pressed against the letters of a sweatshirt that read "U. Mass.," Joy reached slowly down to the floor and took the record off. "Listen," she said, "I need you to do me a big favor, okay?"

"Where'd you get that sweatshirt?" Polly replied. Two days ago she had sworn never to share another secret with Joy Strummer as long as she lived. But in the urgency of her need to exorcise the letter's power by exposing it to others, Polly couldn't afford to stay angry with her friend. She uncrumpled the moist piece of paper. "You know when my dad said some people in Dingley Falls had gotten some dirty letters? Well, I just did."

"*You* did?"

"Somebody left it in the door. Listen, this is serious.

Tell me what you think I ought to do, if I was you, I mean. Do you think, well, I just don't want to have to show it to my dad. Maybe we could ask your mom?"

"Give it here." Propped against pillows printed with daisies, her gold hair haloing a heart-shaped face, her lashes deepening shadows below her blue eyes, Joy read the smudgy typed sheet. It said, "Want your cherry busted? Somebody's going to knock you off that bike one of these nights and take you for a Real ride. How'd you like a trip around the world? End up with your cunt in the air, screaming for it like the rest. Smart kike kid."

Joy wrinkled her nose. "Boy. That's pretty creepy." She frowned.

"It's sick, isn't it? I ought to do something, shouldn't I? I mean, suppose somebody really, you know."

Joy shook her head. "No, I don't think so. No. Forget it. It's just sick."

Polly took the note back, stared at it, folded it. Then finally she nodded and tore the paper into tiny squares, which she dropped into Joy's flowered trash can. "Yeah, sick, I'll say! What does that mean, 'trip around the world'? Do you know what they mean by that stuff?"

"No, but I bet it's gross. Just forget it." Sitting up, Joy crossed her legs under the daisy coverlet. "Now, if I tell *you* something, will you swear you won't tell a soul, especially my folks?"

"Why should I tell your folks?"

"I just don't, double don't, want my mom knowing."

"What?"

"About Lance."

"Did he give you that sweatshirt?" Polly stared at the shelf of dolls. She turned a tiny can-can dancer to face a Buckingham Palace guard. "When?"

"We spent all day yesterday together."

Polly looked at her friend, but instead of giggling as she expected, Joy stared solemnly back and whispered,

"It's different with him, kind of scary. I think he's scared too, you know?"

"Scared of what?"

"I don't know."

"Isn't he awfully old?"

"That's why I don't want anybody to know."

Polly sat down in the yellow rocker, pulling a huge Raggedy Ann doll onto her lap. "You're acting pretty funny," she said finally.

"I guess. So look, that was Lance on the phone, he wants me to go to this party he's got to go to, and I'm going to tell my mom I'm just walking over to the library with you or something. So will you go there tonight and, you know, if she says anything later on, back me up?"

"You just said you didn't want anybody to know. If you go to a party with him, *everybody* will know."

"My *mom's* not going to the party!"

"Your mom's not going to let you go anywhere. She said you had a fever and chills last night and everything. You're supposed to stay in bed."

"Are you going to do me this one little favor or not? Jeez!"

"Say we're going to the library? I'll say we're *thinking* about going. Okay? But you better figure out what you're going to do if you get into trouble about this. I bet you will, too."

"Maybe." Joy sank into the hills of daisy pillows.

From the headboard of Joy's bed Polly took down a doll in a white dress. She tied the doll's sash, and then smoothed down its blond curls. "Remember when my mom gave you this? I remember when we picked it out, she said it looked like you, the hair and everything."

"Yes," said Joy sleepily. "The birthday we went swimming at the lake. And she made us the crowns of clover."

"Yes." Polly put the doll back. "You going to sleep?"

"Look, if my mom says anything, you tell her you

think I look fine. All right? Because I'm perfectly okay, it's just that she gets all bent out of shape if I get a little fever, or tired, or anything."

"Well, okay, but I hope you start feeling better soon. And, Joy, listen, okay, would you not mention about that letter to anybody?"

"Who would I mention it to?"

"Well, just forget about it, okay?"

"Jeez, I promise! I bet I know who wrote it," Joy added drowsily.

"Who?!"

Her eyes closed, Joy lay still beneath the daisy coverlet. "It's that creep Mr. Barnum. He wrote it," she said. "Who else?"

CHAPTER
35

Deprived for a while of his beloved garden, Father Highwick perambulated among the greenery of Central Park with his ninety-two-year-old mother, who moved with the aid of an aluminum walker. Mrs. Highwick was a happy little woman in orthopedic shoes who wore a straw sailor hat and an extra-large Aran Island sweater over her dress. Her son was elegant in white.

"Lovely morning, Ma. Beautiful blue sky. Fluffy clouds."

"But I don't like those fat hippopotamuses up there. Who let them waddle up there? Call the police before they pee on our heads."

"Oh, hoo-ho-ho. What a way you have of putting things, Ma. It's not going to rain! Not a chance."

"It rained on the Pope, didn't it? Yes. It rained on

the heathen Moabites in the Promised Land. Yes. It rained, rained, rained until their boots filled up with fishes. They told me it was awful."

"True, true. It rained forty days and forty nights. It *must* have been awful."

Along the path they slowly plunked toward a lake where boats bumped into one another and bottles without messages bobbed to the banks. Roller skaters, cyclists, joggers, pushcarts, and strollers raced past them. Along the path flowers bloomed through the litter.

"Narcissus." The Rector beamed. "We used to have them out beside the front walk, remember?"

"Nononono. Poison you. Everything in my cabinets is poisoned. Every can, every box, every box, every can. Poisoned through and through. Call the police."

"Exactly so, I know what you mean, Ma. It's those horrible preservatives and artificial ingredients they're putting into everything these days. Not at all like your cooking. Dreadful stuff *will* poison you. Cereal tastes just like the box, doesn't it? Such is Life. But then it's Progress. The stuff keeps forever, they say. Why, my goodness, look, Ma! There, rowing in the lake with a man with a beard. There's one of my parishioners. Beatrice Abernathy. The large woman at the oars. What a marvelous stroke she has! Really. Quite outstrips the rest of them. Too far off now to call after her. I'm sure she'd love to meet you."

"She stole my purse! Catch her. She stole it. It had a hundred silver dollars in it. She knows I see her. Look how she races away. She's the guilty one!"

"Oh, no, no, Ma. You forgot, remember? You left your purse at home. I saw you hide it up the chimney flue before the nurse brought your breakfast in, and in fact, now you mention it, I had intended to caution you that might not be the very best place for safekeeping, if you forgot and lit a fire. It isn't safe."

"Haven't got a safe."

"No, I know you haven't, that's why I'm saying it

worries me to hear you say you have all those silver
coins . . ."

"She keeps the pills in a safe. Fills them up with
poison and makes me swallow them so I can't remember. Throw her out the window."

"Miss Calley *is* a trying soul, isn't she? Short-
tempered, I'm afraid. But be patient, Ma. Nurses are
so hard to keep these days, fly off at any excuse. Now,
stop, Ma, wait a minute. Let me just look. Yes. That
must be the fellow they were talking about. Mr. Mr.
Wrath? No. Mr. Rage. Well, Priss Ransom must be
mistaken about them. That's all. He seems a perfectly
pleasant fellow. Talking a mile a minute. With really a
very nice smile."

"He's the Czar of Russia. They never killed him. The
bullets froze in the snow. She slept with horses,
Catherine the Great."

"Ma. I don't like to hear you repeat ugly rumors like
that, when you can't be really sure about the facts.
You're right, he does look Russian. It's the shirt. No,
those rumors about Mrs. Abernathy were really quite
wide of the mark. It's obvious they are *friends*. Out
here, on the lake for a row, after all. If they were what,
hum, they were accused of being, well, they wouldn't
be here outdoors!" That settled, Highwick smiled
happily. "I must, remind me, I must preach a sermon
soon on believing the worst. Susannah in the garden.
Joseph and Potiphar's wife. Motes in the eye. Cast the
first stone. Glass houses, throwing rocks. Ma! Ma,
come back. No, no, *don't* throw rocks! Oh, ho-ho, such
a clown." The clergyman laughed at a morose individual who leaped up from the rock where he'd been sitting,
staring at his cigarette, until Mrs. Highwick pelted him
in the back with a fair-sized piece of shale. "My
mother," explained the Rector. "Ninety-two! Always
joking. And talented! She paints. Every dish in her
house has a scene from the Bible on it beautifully done.
And on her walls, Creation, Exodus, and halfway
through to Paradise. That's why she won't move in with

me. Ninety-two!" The man snarled and slumped away.
"Good-bye now," called the Rector after him. "Careful, Ma. I wonder if you should try to do hills, you
know. Your walker doesn't seem to be made for them.
Let me help here."

"Who are you? Get away from me. You've got a
stethoscope in that pocket and you want to listen to my
secrets. Nononononono. You give me back my
womb and my kidney, *then* I'll tell you a secret.
Nebuchadnezzar is right in this garden and he's hanging
all the little fishes up to dry. *They* don't mind, they're
so glad to be here. The secret's not here. Nonononono.
The secret's in the Promised Land. He promised me,
but then he took my womb instead. I told *her* to let me
go there. She stole my pictures away from me and put
them in her pills. Lock her in the safe. I'll paint the
rowing lady, I'll paint her right into Paradise. Yes.
Naked and a banana in her mouth. There's a picnic on
the sky. Put down the blanket. Yes. The light's so
bright. We'll eat up the stars. Yes. We'll eat up the sun.
Yes. We'll all eat the secret. Nobody will rain. No.
Nobody will rain anymore."

Father Highwick gave his mother's cheerful cheek a
kiss. "Exactly so." He beamed. "The Promised Land,
the secret, yes. But I never would have thought to put it
that way. Ah, Ma, dear, what an imagination you
have!"

Down the path they went.

Having rowed as fast as she could out of sight of
Father Highwick exuberantly waving at her from the
lake bank, Beanie had hurried Richard back to the
apartment that a friend of Charlie Rolfe's had offered
them in place of the $200 Charlie owed Rage. The
friend wanted someone to sublet his place for a month
and love his plants while he studied at a Sufi center in
Marin County, California. They had agreed to do so.
But Beanie was ashamed and confused now. Didn't she

owe the Rector some explanation? In his beckoning arm she had seemed to see her past call her home to account for herself. Her husband, sons, relations, friends, generations of dead Dingleys in the town cemetery—all waved in Sloan Highwick's fluttering white jacket like smiling ghosts. That among all the millions of Manhattan strangers he should appear there and at that moment was a sign to her. "I have to go back," she said, and she saw that Richard's heart leaped. Yet he said, "All right, darlin'. Whatever feels right to you."

"There're more people involved than just me."

"Can I help?" he asked her, thinking, How could *I* help? Help her clear away her past for her? Now, when for the first time in his life, Rage felt with an ache the loss of his own past? Must love now cost the two membership just when he was eager to join the community club, the fraternity of generations? Unlike her, he had been long disconnected. He was as rootless as the plastic rubber plant he'd given a neighbor, along with the rest of his mother's furniture, soon after she'd died in Phoenix without disclosing in some whispered confession her son's heritage. There had been no mysterious past bequeathed him on her deathbed. She'd said only, "I'm so sick of feeling rotten," and then died. Long before that, a car had by chance killed his father. No relations, paternal or maternal, had traveled to Phoenix to mourn and eat and share the same memories.

Not that it had ever occurred to Richard Rage to ask where he came from anyhow. He came from St. Louis, and he grew up in Phoenix, where, having reached the age of exploration, he was more concerned with getting his own ashes hauled than with poking around in those of his ancestors. All he knew was that his paternal grandfather had hated St. Louis, had worked hard all his life, and had been married to a professional martyr. All he knew was that his maternal grandfather had sung sad songs happily when he drank, had drunk himself to death, and had been married to a saint who worked hard all her life.

There was never a need to know more. No one in Phoenix, no one at Colorado State, no one at *The Chicago Star,* no one in the Village, no one in America, had ever asked Richard Rage to show his past-port. He became a poet all on his own. No one said he couldn't. He could have become anything he wanted to. Success or failure was his for the making. Poetry was his family Bible, Emily Dickinson was his mother, Hart Crane his father. He wrote poems extolling pastlessness, he glorified the land where everyone could rise out of Phoenix, nothing but themselves, everyone an empty canvas on a stretcher, and free to paint whatever vision they chose there.

But now Rage sighed, now that he needed roots, and it was too late to find them now, now that the files were dead. It was all different today, today he was in love and wanted a future, and men who want the future also feel the need of the past. Richard wanted his Beatrice, radiant there by the window nuzzling Big Mutt, to nurse their future. But what (and the thought sent him to the refrigerator for three of the buttermilk biscuits Beanie had baked at dawn), what had he to offer a child, should it be their destiny to have one?

Milk glass in hand, Rage looked out the window to the sidewalk, where two small boys sat counting stacks of comic books, and imagined a son. His beautiful little Jacob, who would have no birthright to snatch, his son with a pastless father, an Isaac father who knew no more of Grandpa Abraham than that he had cracked peanuts with his teeth and had been run over by a '52 Studebaker. That was no heritage! Rage wished he were Jewish, or Amish, or Lithuanian; something with shared sufferings and joys passed down with recipes. Something instead of this bland mongrel new American-ness that built houses without attics. If only he were an old American, with his trunk with its Civil War

saber, its Rough Rider pistol, its Nazi bayonet. Where
were the flat yellow satin of a wedding gown, the thick,
scratchy phonograph recordings of Caruso and Al
Jolson? Where were the Happy Warrior button, the
tattered star for the Christmas tree; where were all the
ticket stubs and brown photographs and souvenir
programs that sum up lives? Could Rage give a son
nothing more than a newspaper clipping that called him
"The Baudelaire of the Bathroom Wall"?

Thoughtful, he munched the last biscuit. Beanie was
now upholstering an old chair she had carried up early
that morning from the trash pile on the sidewalk.
Happy green flowers spread over the castaway and gave
it life. "Darlin'," said Richard after a long silence, "I'm
gonna write an apology to the past." He laughed. "I'm
gonna say I'm sorry I asked the past to kiss my ass.
What do you think of that?"

Beanie smiled, her mouth full of tacks.

"I got to get my shit together. We got to get ready to
have a baby," he told her. "I'm thirty-nine, you
know."

The metallic taste in Beanie's mouth was suddenly
sour. "Richard, a doctor told me years ago that I
couldn't . . ."

"Oh, bullshit. Doctors! What do doctors know?
Shaman with a few shoddy chants and a saw. Do
doctors know this?" He kissed her. "Now look. Smile.
Come on."

"I'm fifty-two."

"Then we don't have any time to lose. Come on!" He
tried to pull her up and toward the couch. She shook
her head but laughed. "All right then." He sat down
beside her. "Tell me about your ancestors instead."

"Like what? They're all in the cemetery behind Town
Hall, I guess."

Rage beamed. "That's beautiful. Tell me all about
the past."

"Oh, I don't know. I think there's a book. My Aunt
Ramona knows." Tearful, Beanie put down the ham-

mer and strip of green cloth. "Richard, this is just wrong."

"Us? Don't be crazy. You know better."

"I *don't* know."

"Yes, you do." He took her hands in his. "Go back, talk to anybody you have to. I'll still be here. But Beatrice, darlin', trust me, fuck the brain."

"I'm scared. I'm scared if I go I'll lose you. And now I think I couldn't stand not to have you now that I know you are. If you're not with me, I won't be real to you."

"Are you kidding? Makes no difference, darlin', where you are, I'll think of you, night and day."

"Oh, Richard, you're crazy." Beanie stood up and smiled. "Why don't we make paella for lunch? Want to?"

"Love it," said the laughing poet.

CHAPTER
36

It was not merely that no one Walter Saar had ever loved had died; no one he had ever known had died. Those of his family who went before him went before he was born. The rest clung on. By the chance of circumstance, death had remained to him a literary condition. Never before had he experienced the incomprehensible though uncomplicated fact that someone with whom you'd been talking one morning might simply not be there the next, that someone could be unreachably, irrevocably absent. Dead.

After eluding the Thespian Ladies at the train station Wednesday night, Saar had hitchhiked all the way home and fallen diagonally into bed. Awakened by his familiars, hungover drink and memory, he'd thought

with a twinge of Oglethorpe. Had he not promised to
check on the old fellow's condition last night? The
headmaster had then groped his way from one handsome piece of furniture to the next, finally located his
desk, and called the hospital, which led him through a
series of switches until finally a nurse in Intensive Care
explained that she was sorry but the patient had died at
4:00 A.M.

"Are you sure?" She was. (Of course, what an
absurd question.) Where was the sister, Miss Oglethorpe? They had no idea. Mr. Oglethorpe was currently in the morgue. (Was it Archibald or Theobald
Oglethorpe? How cruel not to remember, when he
must have seen it written down hundreds of times.)
Saar had a drink. He had a shower. During breakfast
assembly he announced to his staff and students that
their teacher Mr. Oglethorpe had regrettably passed
away and that as headmaster he knew everyone would
be sorry to hear this because everyone remembered
with gratitude all Mr. Oglethorpe had done for Alexander Hamilton Academy through long devoted years,
and that everyone would want to consider some fitting
token to be chosen by committee, and that the guid-
ance counselor would now offer a brief ecumenical
prayer. One boy from Oglethorpe's homeroom (a
seventh-grader burdened with sensibilities that had led
him often to beg Saar to let him return home) began to
cry in loud snuffles. Everyone else fingered his silverware.

Saar then had a few more drinks before teaching the
Cavalier poets to his senior English class for, thank
God, the last time that year. Ray Ransom informed the
guffawing group that by "Gather ye rosebuds as ye
may" the poet meant "Rack up as many virgins on your
score pad as you can while there still are any." "In a
sense," sighed the headmaster, and let them go. He did
not feel very cavalier. It seemed unlikely, too, that
Oglethorpe had seized very many days, not even
pedagogically. Only in longevity had the old man

resembled Mr. Chips. Years from now, no one would
mention in a preface or speech that Archibald (or
Theobald) Oglethorpe's inspiration had made all the
difference. Saar stacked the smudged final essays. Well,
it was unlikely that anyone would mention Walter Saar
either. It was unlikely that anyone from Alexander
Hamilton Academy would ever write a preface,
though, unfortunately, most of them probably would
give speeches, if only to their employees. Saar went to
his rooms, put on a Mahler recording, had a few more
drinks, and smoked a dozen cigarettes.

In the parish office Father Fields was rummaging
through the rubble on his superior's desk, right on top
of which, Highwick had assured him, he would find "a
little outline of church finances," which the curate was
to "spiff up a bit" before they met with Ernest Ransom
and the rest of the vestry to explain that they needed
the roof money to repair the choir screen. Finally,
beneath birthday cards, old *New Yorkers,* and a rare
embroidered ecclesiastical stole that should have been
locked up with the other vestments, Fields found a
scrap of paper titled "Budget," in which annual
expenses were said to be "around $50,000,00," though
clearly the last comma had been a slip of a pen for a
decimal. As the curate stood to let one of the Rector's
cats back in, he saw, with a rush of adrenaline, that
Walter Saar was in the garden, looking around in some
confusion. Quickly, Jonathan pulled off his glasses,
which he wore while alone to rest his eyes from his
contact lenses. He ran his hands through his hair, down
his jacket, and over his shoes, and then called "Hello"
from the open door. Holding a ledger and financial
papers made him look, he hoped, adult.

"Ah, hello!" Saar came toward him, cool in fashionably crumpled summer clothes and dark, rich loafers
boasting the designer's signature in gold initials. But
Saar's face was splotchy red. "I wasn't sure where . . .

Didn't see anyone inside the church." A fit of coughing finished the sentence.

"Oh, I'm sorry, I—"

"I thought I'd—"

And so for longer than strangers would want to, or lovers need, they paused and echoed, ahed and ohed, stumbled their way through broken syntax into a clear resting place, grabbing as they went such flotsam as Father Highwick's being on the train, Evelyn Troyes's having been there as well, the rain's having ended, the flowers' having bloomed.

Finally Jonathan noticed that he was blocking Saar's entrance into the office. "Oh, I'm sorry, please. Come in."

"Can you spare a second?"

"Of course. You drove over from the academy?"

"Yes. Just have a few minutes. Duty screams."

"Is it, oh, I'm sorry, here, take this chair. Something about the choir? They're still meeting, aren't they, I mean this evening?" Ever since Saar's invitation on Monday to "play for him," after the practice session, Father Fields had, with growing anticipation, been rehearsing his best Bach all week.

"No, of course, yes, the rehearsal." Saar had forgotten, Fields realized, blushing. The headmaster suddenly uncrossed his legs and leaned forward. "Jonathan, I hate to be blunt, but have you got anything around here to drink?"

Panicked by the first half of this sentence, Fields was shocked as well as relieved as well as disappointed by its conclusion. Saar managed a wry smile. "I realize," he added, "the hour is early, the surroundings incongruous, and the request on the pushy side, but frankly, even a shot of the Communion wine would do."

As a habit Jonathan did not drink, but after having sherry in Saar's study, he had purchased a bottle of the same brand, gratified by the expense. It was now in the Waterford decanter that the Rector had been bequeathed by a Dixwell matron and had in turn given Jonathan. (The Rector gave everything away.) "I have some sherry in my cottage, I'll just run get it."

"But I'd love to see your place."

Mentally, Jonathan raced through his three rooms. His bed was made, his underwear was in the hamper, his dog-eared picture magazine *Sir Nude* he now kept locked (and why didn't he throw the thing away?) in his desk, ever since Father Highwick (who had no sense of private property) had rambled through his curate's possessions in search of shampoo. "All right, forgive the mess. It's just across the garden here."

"I'm probably keeping you from something celestial."

"No, nothing. Well, I have to pay a church call, but no special time." Unable to fit the key into the lock, Jonathan, embarrassed, took his glasses from his jacket pocket so that he could see the opening.

"Let me give you a ride then," offered Saar, trying not to analyze the fact that Jonathan's hand was shaking so that he seemed unable to get the key into the lock.

"Oh, no, thanks. There! Come on in. Walking is about the only exercise I get." This disclaimer was not precisely true, for Fields had a half-hour program of calisthenics that he did just before going to bed, both for his physique and as an anticoncupiscence measure. "I try to keep a little fit at least, walking."

"My dear man, you must hike around all day!" Jonathan blushed at this, and at the hyperbolic archness of Saar's eyebrow as the latter continued, "But why don't you come use the academy gym? Now, I go there at *least* once a year and tug at a barbell for five minutes, sometimes more. Your study? Charming!"

There were dinner parties (none in Dingley Falls) sufficiently open that Walter Saar, when passing around the aperitif of a gym joke, could offer quips on the secret life of a shower peeker or confessions of a public steam bather (the gaiety of gays being often, he knew, at their own expense—the cost of that "just a talent to amuse" to which alone Wilde and Coward would lay claim, their sung-for supper perfectly in tune), but such mock lechery, such parodic ogling of pectorals and penises could not be tried on Jonathan Fields, who had (thank God, thought Saar) no notion of the game's style. So the headmaster stopped talking, noticing when he did so that, probably as a result of his drinking since dawn, he had almost no sense of gravity (not a quip) and was in fact out driving illegally while both drunk and hung over and on the verge of slobbery tears.

The curate looked at Saar, leaning elegantly against the arm of the Edwardian love seat. A handsome man in handsome clothes who seemed to have the secret of how to hold his glass, cross his feet, look at a picture, light a cigarette as if the possibility that he could slop sherry on his shirt, expose a hole in the crotch seam of his pants, light his filter, or burn a hole in the couch (all of these, coincidentally, *faux pas* actually committed by Saar at some time or another) had not penetrated the man's perfect self-confidence. No, Saar sat there just as Jonathan, in daydreams, had often imagined his doing. But suddenly his face went wrong, the lines drew tight, and when he spoke the words were not at all those that Jonathan had often written for him.

"Did you know old Oglethorpe died early this morning?"

"No. No, I didn't. Oh, I'm sorry. Poor man." Jonathan's eyes closed, and he lowered his head for an instant. He's praying, Saar realized, surprised that he had never before consciously connected this beautiful young man with Christianity, though he *had* noticed his clothes. (Of course, he must actually believe . . . Naturally, he would pray.)

Saar waited, then said, "This is absurd, I know, but I'm afraid I'm rather, rather terrified by my response." He laughed quickly. "I never believed in death. I don't think anyone does." He drank a third glass of sherry.

It was so difficult for Jonathan to imagine the headmaster as anything but perfectly at ease that he did not at first hear the excessiveness of the laugh that followed Saar's saying, "Though I suppose all of us are scared to death of death."

The curate tried to mimic the wry smile. "I'm the opposite. It's life that terrifies me."

"That, too." Saar gulped down another glass. "But no one *believes* it. After all, it doesn't make the slightest bit of sense, does it, death? Not even the poets, much as they rant and wail, they don't believe it's true." He traced with his toe the pattern of cerulean flowers in the small rug in front of the couch. "It's just a horror story they read to scare the young and beautiful into surrender. Give *me* your virginity before the worms devour it." Saar's cheeks brightened and his eyes filled.

(I've never seen him like this, Jonathan thought. He's in pain, and he's come here, to me. The curate's body was tense with the carefulness with which he listened.)

Saar looked up at him. "The worms always win, don't they? In spite of swans and urns and nightingales and roses getting gathered. No matter what the color of your hair is. Despite all their raging against it, the poets are dead now, mute and deaf, dirt just the same."

Jonathan placed his silver candy dish beneath Saar's ash, but the headmaster seemed to have forgotten he was smoking. "Do you know Yeats?" Saar asked him.

"Not really. A little, we studied him, I mean. Did Mr. Oglethorpe teach Yeats?" (Why was Saar breathing like that? Was he going to cry?)

"No, well, I don't know. I was thinking about the poem about the swans. The offspring of those swans are swimming just where he said they would. I went there. But you see, I just don't believe he really thought a time would ever come when it wouldn't matter to him whether they swam there or not. Wouldn't matter what color somebody's hair was. Now he's dead—he warned us he would be. But even when he said it would happen to him, that was only because other poets who had said so really *were* nothing but dust then. And now the new ones will talk about him, because *he* really is dust now, and they think, in their heart of hearts, they'll never be. Never be nothing. And it comes to that nothing anyhow. All to that incredible nothing."

(He has no faith, thought Jonathan, surprised that he had never before considered Saar's religious beliefs or lack of them.) The headmaster's hand trembled as he poured another drink. He turned his head aside, and the curate went quietly into his kitchen, where he put on some water for tea. When he returned, Saar looked suddenly up into his eyes. Jonathan wanted to blink away the hurt exposed there, and the shame at being exposed, but he kept his eyes unblinking on the other man's. "So, Jonathan, you see, it doesn't do anyone any good to be a poet."

Silence moved with sunlight across the room. A curtain billowed, then flattened against the windowpane.

"But Yeats isn't nothing, isn't dust."

"Up in heaven with the swans, I suppose?" The headmaster shook out another cigarette.

"That's not what I meant. I don't know if heaven's 'up.' I meant, he's in here, in this room. You brought him." (Please, Jonathan prayed, let me be some little help this once, of all times, this time, please.) "Isn't that who Yeats was, really? What you keep alive?"

"What good does that do Yeats?"

"The good it does you."

Saar put the glass down on the floor and hugged it between his shoes.

"I probably won't remember this right," Jonathan said. " 'An aged man is like a tattered coat upon a stick unless soul clap its hands and sing, and louder sing for every tatter in its mortal dress.' "

Slumped over, the teacher ran his finger slowly around the rim of the glass. "But Oglethorpe was no

Yeats. I very much doubt he's done anything to warrant many postmortem visits."

"Besides this one, you mean?"

"Ah. Very good."

"We don't know, Mr. Oglethorpe didn't know, what he may have done, or even, you see, what he may do." The curate heard the kettle whistle.

Saar followed him into the kitchen. "Well, Oglethorpe was a harmless old fellow. Let's hope your Christ will open the gates of the kingdom for him."

"Oh, His gates are always open. But the kingdom's inside you. That's what makes it hard."

"Well, I'm afraid I don't know your book nearly as well as you know mine. And now I should apologize for sloshing my soul all over your study like this. Weeping into your rug like Little Eva over Topsy. *Was* that the name of her lover?"

"Please, let me fix you some tea."

"Very kind, but I have to get back. I was just passing by and thought I'd drop in and go to pieces."

Jonathan turned, realized he had never said "Walter," tried, couldn't, and called, "Mr. Saar."

His neck arched, Saar laughed. Tension left his face. "*Mr. Saar?* My God, am I that tattered a coat on a stick? *Please.* 'Walter.' Haul me back out of the tomb. 'Walter,' please! My God, I'm immediately rushing off to get my chest pumped and my hair dyed. Is it gray? I haven't looked since yesterday. Oh, thank you very much, I feel *so* much better, really." He stopped laughing and took Jonathan's hand with one of his. "Really. It was very kind of you." The other hand he moved quickly over the young man's hair and down the line of his cheek. "And about tonight. What about going to a party with me, after the rehearsal. Something or other at the Ransoms'. I never turn them down as my life is in the man's pocket. Might be pleasant. Why don't we go over there and appraise their furniture?"

"I don't know. I wasn't asked. I don't know them that well."

"Doesn't matter a bit, I doubt anyone does. Well, whatever you decide. Now, I should let you get back to work. *I* should get back to work. Frankly, the blessed fact that those hordes of junior Visigoths are actually going home Monday is almost enough to make *me* start igniting candles at an altar!"

The door closed, the car rumbled down the gravel drive. Jonathan stood motionless. Though Saar's fingers had barely brushed his skin, his face burned as if he had been slapped. He could hear his heart. The sound frightened him, and he hurried out of the cottage.

When the curate neared the haven of the apostate Ramona Dingley, he saw his spiritual charge hurtling in her wheelchair straight down her steep driveway toward the street. He rushed up the sidewalk to fling himself on the machine, but she managed her turn and shot past him. He noticed she was laughing.

"Miss Dingley? Miss Dingley. Are you all right?" Jonathan panted, his head bent and his hands on his thighs.

She spun around and putted back. "Perfectly. Oops, I think you dropped your glasses."

"Thank goodness. Oh, thank you. Your brakes failed? You were lucky."

"Lucky?" Miss Dingley arranged her white dress over her knees. "Ppht! I practice."

"On purpose? Really? Oh, I don't think I would if I were you."

"Probably not." She tapped his hand and grinned. "But it does bring the color up, don't it? Aha, here's Orchid finally." A red Firebird pulled up at the curb and Orchid O'Neal opened the side door. She handed Miss Dingley her cane, and then helped her to lower herself into the seat.

"You were going out then?"

"Now, Jonathan, don't tell me I forgot a date? Yes, I see I did. Back inside! Forgive me, my senility's acting up."

"Honestly, no. Some other time is fine. I was just coming your way."

She leaned on her elbow out the window. "You're such an awful liar, I can't help liking you, considering how good-looking you are. How are things?"

"Mr. Oglethorpe at the academy, did you know he'd died this morning?"

"Archie Oglethorpe? Thought *he* died years ago. Well, well, rest him. An atheist free thinker, Archie. Used to try to get Willie Bredforet to read Ingersoll. Useless, of course, to think you could get Willie to read anything. Not sure Willie *can* read. Well, well. We're dropping like leaves, us old shriveled ones. I heard the old nun passed away. The faithful and the faithless. Even-steven. God don't discriminate. I won't give you a lift. Walk do you good, a man your age. Exercise, find somebody, make love. Bring your color up, keep alive. Call me tomorrow then. Let's go, Orchid. And accelerate."

"Now, now, Miss Dingley." Her housekeeper frowned. The sight of Mrs. O'Neal with her flowered print dress, her gray hair pulled up in an old-fashioned bun, sunk in the red bucket seat with her plump hand on the floor stick, broadened Jonathan's polite smile into a grin.

"Good," said Ramona. "Laughter. Remember I told you, it's restorative. Like port." They roared away. Jonathan could feel the grin opening his face until he laughed aloud. He would right now walk around Elizabeth Circle and visit Mrs. Troyes, who had invited him over earlier to look at her vandalized patio, and who had also extended an invitation to treat him to supper. Perhaps he might have sounded brusque with her on the phone. He'd try to be helpful. Had he been helpful to . . . Walter? But Walter didn't need help,

not really. The curate was caught between two desires:
that he should be able to give this man something, and
that this man should never need to ask him for
anything.

CHAPTER
37

Unlike Tracy Canopy's trips to Vincent's tomb, Ramona Dingley's visits to the town cemetery were
custodial rather than communicative, and they were
limited to two a year. As individuals, ancestral Dingleys
were not exempt from Ramona's irony, but as her
family tree, they were dutifully tended by her with
respect. She was, after all, the last of her name. She
called herself the janitor of the past, while confessing
there was no earthly reason why she kept all the scraps
of refuse tossed by time into the bin of history. Among
these self-imposed familial responsibilities was the
maintenance of numerous Dingley graves. As she was
unable to persuade herself that any intimations of
immortality inscribed on the tombs were likely to prove
true, she assumed that whatever was left of her
relatives had been left right there in Old Town Burial
Ground, where now (along the paved back entrance)
she rode in her wheelchair accompanied by Mrs.
O'Neal on foot. In a hamper attached to the back of her
chair were bunches of summer flowers with which they
replaced the dry brown bouquets of last winter.

Everyone was there. Even, against their wills, Ramona's Catholic grandmother Bridget and visionary
father, Ignatius, both of whom had always disliked
being surrounded by Protestants. Everyone was there
except Ramona's uncle Charles Bradford Dingley IV,

misplaced in the second battle of the Marne, who was there only in granite, larger than life in dress uniform, hand on sword, naked Honor mourning at his feet. Actually, all the male Dingleys in the direct line had been lost at war, but only he had never been recovered and returned home. Ramona now distributed flowers among the heroes, from Elijah, lost in King William's War, 1689, and his son, Thomas Laud, lost in Queen Anne's War, 1710, to Timothy, lost fighting for his King, only a year after his estranged son Cutler died for the Revolution at the battle of Long Island. Pausing while Orchid pulled away weeds that covered the words, Ramona motored among the softening stones. Philip Elijah, lost under Perry at the battle of Lake Erie, father of Charles Bradford Dingley, lost under Zachary Taylor at Buena Vista. Charles Bradford II and Charles Bradford III, shot within feet and within hours of each other at Gettysburg. And so the old woman went along the lineal path, to Beanie's father, Charles B. Dingley V, lost in Hawaii, December 7, 1941.

"Bunch of idiots," Ramona told Orchid O'Neal, as she always did. "Walk down this path, and there it is, scratched into stone for you: civilization. Ppht! Well, Orchid, Jesus wept, but I suspect somebody was laughing."

They stopped at a small gray slab where Ramona's mother, Emily (1868–1910), lay with her infant son. "From earthly sorrow free / Called home to sleep with Thee."

"Poor woman," said her daughter. "Well. Well. Dingley. There's the whole batch addressed by that name still. Except for me. And I'm up to my knees in the dirt already."

"No such thing," said Mrs. O'Neal. "God above willing."

"Willing or not. Negotiate about the date. That's all."

They turned back, passing on their way the Dixwell

family plot, where, high on a slope above urns, angels, and marble blocks, glistened in the sun Vincent Canopy's multicolored metal and chrome monument, built from abandoned Buicks by Louie Daytona. Miss Dingley stopped her chair. "Never will understand why the overseers here didn't tell Tracy flatly to throw that junk in the town dump where it belongs, and then cover her husband with something decent. Come on, Orchid. Ransom Bank, now. Death and taxes this morning. All you can count on."

"Summer and babies," said Mrs. O'Neal.

"Pphht!"

Ramona waited on the sidewalk while her housekeeper climbed the steps of Ransom Bank to bring its president out. With some satisfaction the old woman surveyed from her wheelchair the town whose name she bore. No vandal had scrawled on the wood buildings or chiseled away at the stone ones. No natural disaster or economic blight had frightened the life out of her town and left it a ghost. The streets were clean, the green was green, people walked in and out of offices and stores. She nodded. Dingley Falls would last awhile longer, it would outlast her. She took some comfort in that. Given the world's limits, this little town was no worse than most places, and better than many. It had lived three hundred years, like the huge copper beech towering over the green that Elijah Dingley had planted when he founded the town. Elijah on his pedestal flecked his sun-dappled stone grin at her. All right, she agreed, three centuries was a drop in the bucket, but in the long run, so were the pyramids, so was the planet. Meanwhile, she, the last of the Dingleys, would leave the town behind her. It was something.

She spotted Winslow Abernathy as he walked, stooped and preoccupied, into the circle. "Winslow. Winslow!" He was waved over with the cane she kept folded on her lap. "What's this about you and Beanie? Sorry to hear it."

The lawyer frowned while smiling, a habitual gesture. "Who told *you?*"

"Half a dozen people. Don't say you're surprised."

"Just surprised it hasn't been announced on the radio." Winslow began fastening the button on his shirt pocket.

"Don't be an idiot. Well. Where'd she go? And what are you planning to do about it?"

"Nothing. But as a matter of fact she's in New York. I'd been really worried, of course, but she called late last night."

"And now?"

"Now?" He remembered Beanie had said he always fastened buttons on his clothes when he didn't want to communicate with her. He folded his arms.

"Still worried, I hope. Stand still, Winslow. You can spare a minute."

"Sorry, I didn't mean . . . Of course we're going to talk about things. She's taking a train back this afternoon."

"Going to *talk?* Not encouraging. What do *you* want. Want to talk?"

"Naturally, Ramona. There're a great many things Beanie and I need . . ."

"Shouldn't butt in. I'm aware of that. Old spinster, what do I know? Her and Sammy, though, only family I've got."

"Yes, I appreciate that. You don't have to apologize."

"Might be for the best anyhow, Winslow. True."

"What might be?" But then Orchid O'Neal returned, followed by Ernest Ransom's secretary.

"Mr. Ransom's engaged just now, Miss Dingley. May *I* help you?"

"No," replied the invalid. "Irene, you go tell Ernie to unengage himself because as much as I'd like to sit out here and get a tan, Orchid's corned beef is on the burner at home and I haven't the time. You remind him it was my family's dirty money pulled his family out of all those panics in the old days by the skin of their good-looking teeth. Remind him that bank wouldn't be there otherwise."

"He's in conference with Dr. Scaper, but I'll just see." Irene fled.

Ramona wheeled her chair around. "Don't look so disgusted, Winslow. Age has some prerogatives. Let me throw my weight around if I want to. Something the matter with Ernie's health?"

"Not that I know of."

"You know, somebody, I think Arthur, told me Otto wanted to have a conference with the selectmen, too. What's going on?"

"It's probably this new theory of his. I've got to get going, Ramona."

"Wait. What theory? Why don't I know about this?"

"Well, it's probably nothing. Some mysterious toxic substance or other he thinks is polluting Dingley Falls."

"What? Is he serious?"

"Well, he said he wanted to get a town meeting going to discuss it. He wants to bring in federal investigators. According to Arthur, now."

"Dingley Falls investigated? By Washington? Don't suppose Otto's going senile, do you? Hate to think so. Makes me wonder about myself in another ten years." And here Otto is, she thought, claiming the town's been poisoned. And here I am, driving out to look for atom bombs in a swamp. She shook her head. "Work's too much for Otto now. Five years now since that young Dr. Fredericks left him. He ought to get another partner. Did you hear how he lost Archie Oglethorpe?"

"Yes, afraid so. And apparently yesterday the delivery man collapsed at the post office and died before Mrs. Haig there could get help. Horrible thing for her to have to go through alone."

"Alf Marco? Sorry to hear that." She straightened

her back. "He wasn't sixty yet. Decent man. Well. Explains why my mail was late and most of it addressed to Evelyn Troyes. *Soap Opera News*. Intrigued me."

"I'd better get going then."

"Plan to change my will, Winslow. Want you to write it up. And you tell Beanie to use her head. No. Never mind. Give her my best."

At the post office Sammy Smalter found Judith Haig in black, seated behind her window. He offered his condolences about Alf Marco, then nodded to where, behind her, a sullen, overweight woman jabbed letters into pigeonholes as if they were knives. "They sent someone to help you?"

"Yes, from the Argyle main office. Mrs. Lowtry will replace me here as soon as we can manage it. I'm told there's some chance they'll close this branch entirely."

"Surely not. Ah, I dropped by because you mentioned yesterday trying to locate the Vietnamese girl who works . . ."

"Yes. Thank you. I got in touch with Miss Lattice."

"Ah, good. Pru had called me, in fact, well, to ask if I could give her anything to help the girl get some sleep. Hot milk and/or Scotch is what I always answer." He smiled. "Well, anyhow. If, I don't want to pry, but if there's any problem you're trying to help her with that I could be of assistance . . ."

"Thank you, but . . ."

"Please believe me that I'd *like* to, very much, if there is something."

"That's kind of you. But I'm afraid there's nothing really."

"Ah, well. Good. Please don't hesitate though, if something *should*, well . . . Back to work then." He tapped his hand on the counter. "Mrs. Haig. By chance, I spoke with Arthur Abernathy yesterday about getting something done about those dogs. In the meantime I'd be glad to furnish my yellow sewing machine again to give you a ride home."

"You're very thoughtful." Judith smiled, frowning. "But someone is picking me up. Mr. MacDermott's wife. Thank you though."

"Good. Well, if ever. I'm at your disposal."

Don't be, her eyes told him, please don't be. "Thank you. Good-bye then," she said.

"See you tomorrow. Good day."

Mrs. Lowtry came over to the window, gnawing dirt from beneath a fingernail. "That a dwarf that was talking to you?"

"I don't believe so." Judith turned her back and began to sort letters.

"Kind of turns my stomach, I can't help it. So do the ones that are, you know, all crippled. With the shakes. I feel sorry for them and everything, but it's just the way I feel. I guess I just can't help it. Just a natural response. See what I mean?"

"Yes. Our first delivery arrives here at nine-thirty, as I said. If you'll step back here with me, I'll show you how we've arranged the sorting."

Mrs. Lowtry decided Mrs. Haig was a cold fish.

The sounds of slamming doors bounced through the library. Coleman Sniffell at the periodical shelf disgustedly shut *Time* as he watched Lance Abernathy in tennis shorts stride up to the librarian at the main desk and shout, "Sidney! Get that lily-white ass in gear. Outside, man. Move! Drive you to the Club for a set, treat you to lunch, and spot you three games. Whaddya say?"

"Keep your voice down, how about?" whispered Mr. Blossom. "You know, I don't think I've ever seen you in here before, Lance. It's like somebody dropped a beach ball on a chessboard."

One tan hand on each end of his racquet, Lance swung it over his head. "I'd go nuts in here. Let's go."

"Thanks for the offer, but I have a job."

"What? I don't see you doing anything much. Come on."

"Sorry. Never can tell when the whole town could rush in here to check out *The Great Gatsby* because they saw it at the Hope Street Cinema last week."

"Yeah, I went. Bunch of junk. I didn't get the point of it all."

"Neither did the hero, that was the point."

"Huh? Oh. Never mind, listen, if it's no go, I'm gonna beat it. Maybe old Katie'll play with me."

"It's no go, Lance. Ask her. So, see you tonight over at her place, I guess."

"Right. I'm bringing a girl along."

"Never would have guessed. Please, don't slam that door."

"Hey, what a fairy." Lance grinned, his teeth twinkling like an advertisement. "Does Katie know what a fairy she's getting mixed up with?"

"*Omnia vincit Amor.*"

"What's that mean, winks at what?"

"It means the proof's in the pudding."

"Hey*heyhey!*"

The Vietnam war had come between Lance and Sidney—the former going to fight it to get out of law school, the latter staying in schools to get out of fighting it. For years they hadn't been able to speak without an argument over their nation's morality. Now that the war was over, they were more or less friends again as they had been since childhood, though for no other reason than that it was taken for granted that they were friends. It was one of those friendships with a life of its own, quite despite the taste, judgment, or desires of the two people involved.

The maroon Jaguar leaped around Dingley Circle. It flew past the pharmacy, where Luke Packer and Polly Hedgerow stood in the door. "Jeez." Luke whistled. "Look at that car!"

Polly frowned. "So what? What's he trying to prove?"

Abruptly, Luke agreed. "Yeah, some men feel like

they have to use a car or a gun for a phallic symbol.
That's one thing I like about Ben Rough's detective,
Roderick Steady. He just takes the bus."

In the center of the semicircular drive, gravel white
as a crescent moon in the lawn of the Dingley Country
Club, two black people stood beside an old Rolls-
Royce. One, Lance noticed, was female. She had a
very attractive body. "Hi there. Bill Deeds! What you
up to?" Lance flung his bare leg over the door of his car
and jumped out. "This your daughter? How do you do,
don't think we've met."

"Granddaughter. Ruth, this is Mr. Abernathy's
boy."

"Lance." Lance grinned. "Waiting for somebody?"
She was, he appraised, thirty at the most, really nice
outfit, lot of poise, that fantastic high rear end they all
have. "How about me?"

"Mr. Bredforet just stepped into the men's room,"
explained Ruth Deeds, who then got angry at herself
for avoiding Lance's eyes, then held his glance too
significantly, then got angry at herself for that. She
didn't have to hate him, she reminded herself. Just let it
ride.

Nice voice, thought Lance. Were there any rules that
blacks weren't allowed in the Club? Not likely, since as
far as he could recall there weren't any blacks in
Dingley Falls, except Bill Deeds. Of course, there were
a few in Madder, but nobody white in Madder belonged to the Club either. "Come on, Bill." He waved.
"Let's all go in and have a drink."

"My grandfather refuses to go inside. He's a snob."
Ruth Deeds smiled, and squeezed the old man's arm
protectively.

"He be coming right on out anyhow. Just showing off
for Ruth here, driving all over town. He better come
on, I got to get off this leg pretty soon now." Deeds
rubbed his calf.

"What's the matter with it? Let me see. Come on, Grandpa." The young woman bent down. Mournfully, Deeds pulled his pants leg up just above his sock, where a wide gash was sticky with pus. "This is infected." She frowned.

"Nothing to worry about. Dropped the clippers on it, that's all. Granddaughter's a doctor. Lives in Atlanta. Bossy," he explained to Lance with exasperated pride. "Doctor!"

"You ought to have some antibiotics."

"Girl. Don't you nag now. You supposed to be on vacation anyhow."

"Long stay?" Lance asked her. Jesus God, a doctor, a black female doctor! And she looked good enough to be a singer.

"No. Very short."

"Won't this place drive you nuts after Atlanta? Look here, Dr. Deeds. Ruth? Ruth. Hey, what kind of doctor?"

"Internist. Well, research. I work with chemical carcinogens."

"Sounds good to me."

William Bredforet, wiping his moustache with a finger, trotted down the steps. "I should have known. Look at that Lance already at point. Fine-looking woman inside the town limits less than half an hour, and you already got wind of it." He slapped Lance on the back.

Deeds sniffed at his employer. "I tell you what I got wind of. That's you. It wasn't no bathroom you went in there for. You went and had a drink."

"I did not."

"Yes, you did too."

"No, I didn't."

"Hear him lie, Lord."

"You think God's paying any attention to us?"

"He got His eye on the sparrow."

"Then He couldn't have seen me taking a drink."

While the two octogenarians squabbled back into the car, Lance winked at Ruth over the follies of the old. She did not respond. Nor did she wish to learn tennis, or take a drive around, nor could she easily tolerate the fact that he continued to grin like a cat at a mouse no matter how many offers she declined. Kept grinning as he held open the door of the Rolls-Royce for her. She ought to ask herself, she thought, why she disliked Lance Abernathy and yet liked William Bredforet, who was, if anything, more incorrigible, smug, sexist, a parasite of capitalism, and no doubt a racist as well. Was it only that the old man's lechery no longer held any sexual threat, or was it just the perversity of human attraction? She was, after all, also enjoying sitting alone in the back of a *limousine*. She, Dr. Ruth Deeds, political radical, social reformer, militant feminist. Something a lover had once said came suddenly back. She'd told him it was selfish of them to make love while the world was a mess, and he'd said, "Honey, you think the revolution's going to get here that much quicker because you won't take the time out to come?" Well, he'd been a sexist pig too and had cost her an A in microbiology. Dr. Deeds smiled at herself and tapped on the glass, and the chauffeur, nodding, drove out the gleaming drive.

CHAPTER
38

"Jesus bless," whispered Sarah MacDermott. "Who's that grouch you got in there with you?"

"Mrs. Lowtry." Judith put a finger to her lips. "She'll be taking over here."

"I hate to hear you say so, honey. And look at you here in black, just when you had enough problems of your own. If it doesn't rain, it pours. And anyhow, where is Hawk, what's the matter with that man? Joe's about to drop in his tracks, trying to do everything himself." Sarah popped her gum loudly. She took another piece from her green grocery smock, which she wore over a blouse and slacks printed to resemble zebra skins. "What's all this big secret Hartford investigation that's worth using up all his sick leave?"

"I don't know really. Just that it's taking longer than he thought. But he'll be home tomorrow sometime."

"I'll tell him straight to his face, it's criminal if you ask me, leaving you all alone after what you've been through. *And* Joe. That Mrs. Troyes on Elizabeth Circle had him over there at the crack of dawn because somebody pawed up her sweet petunias and took a knife to some fancy chairs that she just left out in her backyard, if you can picture that. Anyhow, what time is it?"

"Almost twelve. But that's horrible. How? Who did it?"

"Listen, if that's the only thing that woman's got to worry about in this world, who messed up her lawn furniture, well, Lord love her, and vicey versa. Well, I got to go, just came on lunch break to see how the services went. I wish I could have gone, you made it sound like it was real nice. Poor old Alf. Well, Joe and I are going to go look at that house again. 'Dream the impossible dream,' ta-da. How'd you say you were feeling?"

"Fine, really. Sarah, remember you were telling me about Maynard Henry's brother, the one who lives in Newton, Massachusetts?"

"You remember him now? Real good-looking, took algebra with us, sat in the back."

"Yes. Do you know, is he well off? I mean, reasonably."

"I guess so! He's in the insurance business. Arn was always the kind could sell a color television to a blind nun. Left Dingley Falls as soon as he got his arms loose from his graduation robe. And you know anybody that stayed that's worth a red nickel? Yes, last I heard he'd moved out of his duplex and built a real nice Colonial ranch."

"I spoke to him."

Sarah took off her orange harlequin sunglasses and stared until her friend dropped her eyes. "Judith Sorrow Haig. Tell me the truth. Are you getting yourself mixed up in that Chinkie's business? After I *told* you."

"Well, I know, but I felt I had to try to reach . . ."

A car horn barked three times. "On the Blessed Virgin! Joe won't believe you're telling me this! Honey, Hawk, your husband Hawk's the one that arrested Maynard in the first place, and what's more, Chinkie was already running off with Raoul. Oh, Joseph and Mary, that's Joe's horn, I've got to run. I want to hear all about this. I'll be here at five, and no buts, you're going to eat spaghetti with us."

As Mrs. MacDermott clopped in her white plastic sandals to the post office doors, William Bredforet opened them. The two started to pass, then glared at each other. Finally Bredforet nodded. "Yes," he said slowly. "At Pru's Tea Shoppe. You hit me with a tray."

Sarah puffed air up to her bangs. "And if I was standing up before my Maker and you tried any *more* funny business with me, you horny little sa-tire, and I had a tray in my hand, I'd hit you again!" She put on her sunglasses and swung open the door. "And every angel watching would let out a cheer."

Bredforet's face crinkled, his moustache curved up, and he laughed out loud. He was still chuckling when he reached the counter. "Hello there. A money order, is that something you still do here?"

"Yes, certainly. Just a moment."

William Bredforet kept staring at Judith until their eyes met; something in the other's face held for each of them a puzzling significance. It was something their eyes saw that their memories couldn't place. They had the same eyes, except hers were a slightly paler blue.

"Chin Lam sent you, huh? I told her no way I was going to deal with that dip public defender the state tried to fasten on me. She got you, huh?" Maynard Henry sat down, hunched forward in the starched blue shirt that stuck out in creases from his shoulders and arms. His eyes ferreted over Abernathy, over the summer suit, the watch, the faded calfskin of the old briefcase, gold-stamped with initials. Then the pale lashes twitched. "How? How'd she get you?"

"I haven't actually had an opportunity to speak with your wife yet," Winslow replied in his quiet, flat accent. "She talked with someone who then asked me if I would look into things." From his pocket he took an unopened pack of cigarettes, which he slid casually across the table toward the prisoner. "I could give her a message."

"Where's Chin? What do you mean, talk to who? Why didn't she come herself?"

"Isn't the best thing not to get her here, but you there?"

Henry pulled the pack toward him and lit a cigarette. He spit the smoke out.

Abernathy searched for his pipe. "Treating you all right?"

"Been in worse. Had an old colored nut in the cell with me, but they took him away this morning to run some psycho tests on him. He had me going up the wall for a while. He played the harmonica all the time."

"Must have been annoying."

"There was this dumb grit in my squad used to play, too. Used to get a cassette, play along with it, even carried it along on details."

"Yes?"

"Nothing. He tripped a wire one day, blew his leg off. Bled to death. Like a pig. Dumb grit." Henry jabbed the cigarette into the ashtray. "I can't pay you."

"Payment's not a problem now."

"That's a new one. Why not? It's a problem to me. I'm not asking for handouts."

"I understand that. You've made no arrangements for bail?"

"People want collateral. I don't own anything worth twenty grand."

"You have family?"

"Besides Chin? I got a brother. Leave him out of it. Sooner or later they got to bring me to trial, then I'll be out and it won't be because I went whining to my brother to bail me out."

Abernathy finally found his pipe and began to pat his pockets for tobacco. "First, you may not necessarily be acquitted. Second, trial isn't set until late July. You want to sit here till then? I should think your responsibility to your wife . . ." He paused, struck by the intensity in the man's face.

Henry pushed his hands on the table to shove his chair back. His wrist bones were a clean, scrubbed red below his cuffs. "Okay, okay, what's your deal?"

"No deal. Just some questions to start with." There was no answer. Locating the tobacco, Abernathy eventually got his pipe lit; he examined the lighter as he spoke. "Mr. Henry, I realize you've been through this story endless times, but bear with me. My understanding is that on the day of this incident, you thought your wife had left you for Raoul Treeca and so, when told that she had left, you pursued *her*. Is that correct?"

"Yeah. Sure." Disinterest closed around the voice.

"Or, you believed Treeca had, if not forcibly, then by misrepresentation, abducted your wife, and you attempted to stop *him*."

"Yeah."

"Which?"

"What's the difference? I should have blown the shithead away. He was scum."

"To establish your motivation, I need to know what you were thinking."

"I wasn't."

"You acted on impulse. All right. Now, did you know Treeca had stolen your trailer until you caught up with him on the ridge?"

"Yeah, the MacDermott kid told me."

"Told you what?"

Henry began to rub his palm roughly against his cheek, then up and down his leg. "He saw the beaner's truck with my trailer hitched to it."

"Saw Treeca. And your wife was with him? What did you think when you heard this?"

". . . Get him."

"Stop him. . . . What about her?"

"Nothing about her. Okay?"

"When you forced the truck onto the shoulder, you pulled your wife out. Then you struck her?"

"He just sat there. Drunk. He'd told her a bunch of shit about going to some fucking refugee camp, how the law said for her to show up there. She couldn't fucking understand. I mean, it's not her language, man. And he just sat there, after pulling that crap."

"But it was your wife you struck. . . . Did you mean to do it? . . . Did you know you were doing it? . . . All right, you don't know why. You were upset with her and relieved to find her at the same time, like a parent with a lost child. All right. . . . Did either of them try to explain their actions to you? Did you ask Treeca for an explanation?"

Henry's grin was derisive. "We didn't talk."

"You unhitched the stolen trailer, got back into your car. With your wife. You backed up, drove forward, and in so doing hit the rear side of Treeca's truck. Its front wheels slid over the edge of the ridge, and the truck turned over as it fell, injuring Treeca."

"How do you know all this?"

Abernathy tapped a thick manila folder that the district attorney's office had provided him. "Prosecuter lent it to me."

Henry smiled. "You make it sound a lot prettier than he did."

"Did you hit Treeca deliberately?"

"You could say so."

"I don't think I would, however. What was your motive in hitting his bumper? Were you trying to kill him?"

Henry's eyes sped back and forth, then fastened on the wall just above Abernathy's head. "It don't matter. He just kept *sitting* there and I wanted him gone."

"Then why did you climb down the slope to check him out afterwards?"

"Habit."

"Who called the ambulance? Didn't you?"

"No."

"Did you tell someone to?"

"No. I told some guy at the garage on Hope that Treeca was over the side of the ridge. If he called an ambulance, that was his business. Look, you said a *few* questions. I got to get back to the kitchen."

Abernathy folded his glasses carefully. "Mr. Henry. I'm not sure I understand your attitude. This is a serious charge, you have a previous record, both civil and military. Juries tend to think that . . ."

"Don't tell me about some sorry-ass jury." Henry's hand swooped at the cigarette pack and closed into a fist. "This is just between me and Hawk Haig. He wants me wasted."

"What do you mean by that?"

"He's been looking for a way. He figures he's found it."

"You're saying your arrest is some kind of personal vendetta? Some prejudice on Chief Haig's part?" Abernathy noticed with interest the surge of adrenaline in himself.

"You better believe it."

"Does that really make sense?"

Henry smiled, the first real smile, his face both bemused and tolerant, his voice soft and, strangely, Abernathy thought, sweet. "Hey, baby. Does it really make sense that Raoul Treeca wants this shit? Do you think he would have said *anything,* but it was all a lousy accident? His foot slipped and he gunned the truck and it went over the side and, tough shit, he busted his lousy legs? You think that dumb rockhead called Haig up at the station and said, 'I wanna press charges for aggravated assault, make it attempted homicide, and I wanna go to court'? *If* I cut the guts out of Treeca's sister and then fucked her corpse, maybe. Maybe he'd holler law. I doubt it. He'd just kill me. But you think he wouldn't *deny* he ever saw me, or that trailer, or Chin up on the ridge, if Haig hadn't gotten to him fast? It would never happen."

"I see. Do you know why Mr. Haig feels this way?" He already knew he believed Henry.

"What's the difference?"

"Practically speaking, perhaps you're right. Whether it's really between you and him or not, at this point it's also between you and the state."

Henry's eyes were bored again. "Sure."

Abernathy closed the notebook in which he'd been writing. "You're currently unemployed, but before that you worked for some time on the highway project north of Dingley Falls? And before that, you were in Vietnam?"

"Yeah. The war lasted longer than the highway."

"How long were you over there?"

"That much too long. Three tours. Khe Sanh was one of them."

"Marines. You enlisted?"

"Why wait?"

"My son's philosophy. He served in Vietnam."

"Why was that?"

"He was a pilot, stationed in Guam."

"Yeah." Amusement flicked past the pale eyes. "We used to see 'em fly over sometimes. Real pretty planes. He make it?"

"Oh, yes. He's home now."

"Most of them did. I was in Eye Corps. First Battalion, Ninth Regiment. Mean anything to you?"

"You had the worst of it."

"So I hear."

"Sure are a lot of folks taking an interest in that guy," said Sergeant Myers when Abernathy returned to the desk. "I told you Hayes was here, and now, awhile ago, we got a call from a lawyer up in Boston, saying he represented Henry's brother, Arn. Said he'd be here in the morning to arrange bail."

"My impression just now was that Mr. Henry had not been in communication with his brother."

"I bet Maynard made that pretty clear. No love lost there. But somebody's been in touch. Like I say, the bastard's got friends. Excuse me, but like you, Mr. Abernathy, must be a good ten years since we've seen you over here. I guess your clients aren't the kind that end up in the can. Money buys a lot of law."

Abernathy placed the folder back on the desk. "You share Anarcharis's view, Sergeant Myers. He said laws are spiderwebs, through which only the largest flies can break. The small are trapped and destroyed."

"Don't know about that. Do know crime's just like any other business. The little guy's the first to go."

"Not invariably. But, yes, more times than not. Well, in view of what you tell me, I'll assume this Boston lawyer will be responsible for the next step. Frankly, I can see no valid reason why Mr. Henry shouldn't be released at reasonable bail. There're no grounds to prove homicidal intent, in my view, and I can't imagine in Judge Farborough's either. The man's property was stolen. His wife virtually kidnapped."

"He's got a record."

"I read here he's also got the Bronze Star."

"Did you read where he was in the brig twice, a bar brawl where he chewed off another marine's earlobe? And a year later he takes a potshot at a *South* Vietnamese officer?"

"I read that that officer's ineptness had resulted in the death of one of Henry's squad members."

"Well, Jesus Christ, then I hope I never hand the guy the wrong stack of laundry!"

Abernathy took from a wallet of soft leather an engraved card. "Could you have that attorney give me a call in the morning?"

"Sure thing. Listen, Henry's been bugging me the last few days, asking where his wife is, why don't she come."

"Yes. He feels quite strongly about her."

"No fooling."

After Abernathy left, Fred Myers, fingering the rich paper of the card, considered briefly why the wealthiest lawyer in the area might have gotten himself involved in a squabble between two unemployed Madder hardhats. Could be Abernathy was bored clipping coupons, could be he had been born again, could be local politics. Or it could be blackmail, adultery, drug addiction, or sodomy. Nothing would especially surprise him. The sergeant went back to his Ben Rough paperback.

It was after one. Beanie had said the three o'clock train. He was already late for his appointment at The Tea Shoppe. If he went, he'd miss Beanie. The practical thing to do would be to eat in Argyle, then meet his wife at the train station. In the parking lot Abernathy stood irresolutely at the door of his son's Audi. Then he located the keys, got into the car, and drove back to Dingley Falls.

Judith Haig was still there. She sat in a corner table alone, her arms resting on the rose cloth, her hands folded. Sat in a black dress, iconic and alien, bordered by the white wall. He walked back to her table, and Judith raised her head.

"Mrs. Haig? I'm late, I'm afraid. My apologies. I hope I haven't inconvenienced you too much?"

"Not at all. Miss Lattice and I have been talking with Chin Lam. Mrs. Henry."

"May I?"

"I'm sorry. Please." Abernathy took the seat he had gestured toward. She lowered her eyes again and withdrew her hands from the table.

Then she looked back up at him, startled. "I'm sorry. It's just that I've been sitting here thinking about that girl's life. She's only nineteen. The things she . . ."

"I spoke with Mr. Henry, that's why I'm late." What should he tell her about that interview? That he felt strangely enlivened by it, thirty years younger? That he felt grateful to her, and to Henry, whom, in fact, he liked, strange as that thought was to him? Could he tell her all that? Yes. Strange that he thought he could.

"I wanted to call you," she was saying. "To tell you that, well, in fact, I called his brother in Massachusetts."

"Ah. I see." So she had done it.

"He said he has a lawyer."

"Indeed, he does, an efficient one. I'll speak with him tomorrow."

"I didn't realize I'd be putting you to so much trouble."

"No trouble. In fact, it's good for me; I've been away much too long. Honestly, I'm fascinated. I think Henry may refuse to deal with a lawyer hired by his brother. At any rate, you and I should certainly keep in touch about it. More coffee? Can you stay a bit longer?"

Miss Lattice, wiping her hands on a rose-ruffled apron, hurried to their table with a menu. "Winslow, hello, any news for us?"

"A little. Is Mrs. Henry free?"

"I'll just run get her. Have you eaten? Chin's made,

all on her own, a cabbage roll dish, with pork and crab. I tried it myself and it's really very good, wasn't it, Mrs. Haig? It's called *bajr cai nhor* or *bajr nai kor,* I think, or, well, never mind, but it *is* good."

Abernathy smiled. "All right, Pru. I'll try it . . . with a cup of coffee."

"Oh, Winslow, you should drink tea with it. Chin says."

He looked up at his hostess, her careful morning's hairdo now steamed into white wisps. "Fine, Pru. Tea then. And, Mrs. Haig, please stay for a cup of tea, won't you?"

"All right. Yes. Another cup, please. Thank you."

Walking past the windows of The Tea Shoppe on his way to his own store, Limus Barnum paused to see who was in there. His hands to the sides of his face to blind the sun, he watched the postmistress and the lawyer waiting silently for Miss Lattice to return. As he watched, a strand of Judith's hair came loose from its gold pin. She brushed it back behind her ear, but it fell forward again.

CHAPTER
39

Polly Hedgerow had biked to town from her private throne on the bank of the Rampage, where she'd left Anna Karenina in tears. Miss Dingley was to meet her and Luke Packer at the pharmacy. Next door, Mr. Smalter was having his regular three o'clock coffee at The Tea Shoppe. "Wait outside," Luke said. "I'll just go tell him I'm leaving."

His thin circle of yellow hair bent over a book he had propped up against the edge of his table, the druggist

sat alone across the room from where in a back corner
Mrs. Haig, all in black, sat with Mr. Abernathy. From
the window Polly watched Smalter look up, as if
relieved, to see Luke. He began talking to him. Then,
quickly finishing his coffee, he took his check to Miss
Lattice. He hesitated, Polly noticed, before waving at
Mrs. Haig, who nodded in return. Mr. Abernathy
twisted around in his chair, smiled, then leaned back
toward the postmistress. As Mrs. Haig listened to the
lawyer, her fingers moved slowly over a leaf fallen from
a vase on their table. She had beautiful hands. Polly put
her own in her jeans pockets. Not wanting Mr. Smalter
to know she had seen him trying to get Mrs. Haig's
attention, the girl stepped away from the window and
into the street, where she bent down to check the new
chain on her bike.

Through her wheel she saw the motorcycle speed
toward her from the end of Dingley Circle. She saw,
even from that distance, that Limus Barnum's eyes
stared straight into hers. Polly backed farther into the
street. She couldn't move away, she couldn't stop
looking at his eyes rushing at her. Suddenly she was
jerked up on the curb. Her glasses flew off. Then, with
a quick pat, Sammy Smalter let go of Polly's arm. He
stepped out in front of the motorbike and twisted the
handle. The throttle cut off.

"What the hell! You almost ran her down!" Smalter
snapped, while Barnum sputtered back at him, "That
stupid kid! Did you see that? Stepping in front of me!
Hey, what do you think you're doing? Leave that
alone!"

Luke picked up Polly's glasses from the street. "What
happened?"

She flushed. "I don't know."

Smalter kept his hand on the throttle. "I *said,* you
almost ran into this girl, Limus! The least you can do is
apologize. For Christ's sake, what's the matter with
you?"

Barnum's face was bloated with indignation, his scalp

wet beneath the thick coat of hair spray. "Get out of
here!" he snarled, and with a jerk pried Smalter's hand
off the handlebar. Then, open-palmed, he struck the
pharmacist in the chest, knocking him down into the
street. Smalter's head hit the curb.

"Hey!" Luke lunged at Barnum, who'd already
slammed down on the starter pedal. The cycle jumped
away.

"*Luke*. Never mind, come back!" Smalter scrambled
to his feet, red-faced. The elbow of his suit jacket was
ripped and his hand bloody. "Yes, yes, I'm okay," he
said impatiently, pulling away from Luke's hand and
turning to Polly. "Are *you* all right? Polly?"

"Oh, I'm sorry, thank you, yes. I guess I'm okay. I
mean, I didn't get hurt." Her cheeks and neck burned
with shame, for both herself and Mr. Smalter. She felt
close to tears.

The unfinished highway connector ran in glittering
asphalt straight into a wilderness of underbrush, where
it ended in weeds and dank, rotting leaves. The red
Firebird blistered there in the sun. Beside it, Ramona
Dingley sat in her wheelchair. She drank ale from a
bottle, stared into the dark forest, and thought about
the past. Nearby, under the shade of an oak, Orchid
O'Neal reclined, surrounded by her nephews' socks,
which she was darning to keep herself occupied.
Thursday was her free afternoon, and while she'd been
happy to oblige by driving Miss Dingley and the two
youngsters off to look for something in the woods, she
had to keep busy. She couldn't sit and think, hour after
hour, as her employer seemed content to do.

For a while Ramona, by mentally tracing memories
sixty years old, had followed Polly and Luke west
through the forest into the marshes, where often with
her aunt Camilla (Beanie's grandmother), she had gone
exploring. She had hunted for rocks and snakeskins,
birds' nests, fossils, Indian arrowheads, dead beetles,
deer tracks, minnows, beaver dams, and all other

treasure that forgotten land keeps safe. Before her
Dingley marriage, Ramona's aunt had been Lady
Camilla Upton. Wooed and won in that popular
alliance of the Edwardian Age, British breeding and
Yankee dollars, the athletic Camilla had come married
to Connecticut and had brought her favorite mount,
Big White, with her. At seventy she had been still
riding one of his descendants. Ramona recalled that
when Beanie Dingley shot up half a foot in the fifth
grade, everyone said Camilla's granddaughter had
inherited the Englishwoman's physicality and her ro-
bust good looks. They'd been passed down to Beanie
through her father, Chuck, who had distinguished
himself in the great game against Army his last year at
Annapolis. God knows, thought Ramona as she sipped
her ale, God knows Beanie inherited nothing from her
mother, May Rose, a Baltimore belle in despair at the
unlikelihood of a marriage between Beatrice and young
Ernest Ransom, whom the girl persisted in defeating on
the golf links despite her mother's predictions of
spinsterhood. How relieved May Rose had been when
Winslow Abernathy asked her (her husband, Chuck,
having died at Pearl Harbor) for Beanie's hand. So
polite. How fond she'd become of Ernest's quiet
roommate. Even if he had allowed Beanie to talk him
into an elopement. Well, Ramona now thought, nodding to herself with a smile, May had died in peace;
news of Beanie's bolting would never reach her up
there in the cemetery. And now it appeared that
Camilla's genes were still vaulting about with random
energy in that idiot Lance. Ppht! Miss Dingley pushed
her wheelchair to the very edge of the asphalt strip to
follow the retreating sun.

Waste, waste. What had all that absurd to-do about
the highway come to? She vaguely remembered Democratic editorials in *The Dingley Day* heralding a new
economic future for the town. She remembered being
bored by a long speech of Tracy Canopy's at a meeting
of the Republican Ladies or the Historical Society or

the Conservation Committee, where a petition was
signed to preserve Dingley Falls from the horror of a
new economic future. Then had come a spate of
muckraking and mudslinging which no doubt everyone
involved had enjoyed immensely. One day she'd asked
Ernest Ransom what had ever happened to the connector, but his answer, as usual, was no answer. Hard to
believe, though, that a man who still worked at his
grandfather's desk, who ate off his great-great-
grandmother's dishes, who kept solvent St. Andrew's
Church, the academy, the library, and the Historical
Society, that Ernest Bredforet Ransom would sell his
family's land to the government. True, Ernie had
always been a little mentally ossified, a truckler to
anything established, indeed a man with no more
ethical imagination than a park statue, but all the less
likely that he'd leave himself open to criticism by
allowing a bunch of Washington idiots to sneak in and
set up a missile site or anything else that might be
destroying the ecological balance or causing cancer or
pushing Dingley Falls way up on the Russians' hit list,
not right next door to the man's hometown. Of course,
it was possible that Polly Hedgerow was deluded, or
lying, or could have her head filled with thrillers, and
that they'd find nothing out there but an abandoned
hunter's shack.

The sun balanced on top of Wild Oat Ridge, then slid
behind it in a trail of orange and red streamers. Miss
Dingley glanced up at the scurrying colors. She
wheeled herself over to Mrs. O'Neal, who had now
finished all the socks and was letting out the cuffs on a
pair of boy's trousers. "Getting hungry, Orchid?
Famished myself. Let's open the hamper."

Mrs. O'Neal rubbed a numb ankle. She did not in the
slightest believe there was anything to be found beyond
the marshes except Bredforet Pond and was very
worried that the two teenagers might accidentally
drown in that. She was in most matters intimidated by
her employer, but about children, and how best to look

after their welfare, Mrs. O'Neal, mother of six, considered herself a far better judge than Miss Dingley, mother of none. "Well, maybe something's out there, and maybe something's not. Children are great talkers. I don't mean lying. But adding on."

"Oh, it's there," said the invalid firmly. "I knew this girl's grandmother."

In Polly's previous, solitary explorations she had entered the woods from the south and had hiked directly north. Now, following Miss Dingley's instructions, she and Luke found the old Indian path running west toward the marsh, the path Ernest Ransom had learned about from his father and his great-uncle William Bredforet. The path still left its impress on the land, but with each generation it yielded more footage back to the dark forest. Luke and Polly slipped in the damp undergrowth and had to crawl over fallen trees. They had talked only at the outset. Both exhilarating and hard work, the hike took their full concentration.

Finally, Luke asked if Polly hadn't invited Joy to come along. He had just been theorizing to himself that his fascination with Joy Strummer was no more personal than his fascination with the movies, and that his physical attraction to her was not even one particular to him, but a response publicly shared by all his male friends. Out of these thoughts, and a desire to push through the silence, and curiosity about what Polly felt regarding Joy, Luke had asked the question. But Polly was pained by an immediate assumption that Luke had accepted her invitation only in order to be with Joy. She didn't realize why she was pained, she just felt it.

Brushing past cobwebs that stuck to her hands, she shoved quickly through the low, leaf-heavy branches until Luke fell behind. She fantasized the three of them hiking in the dimness of the woods, Luke and Joy hurrying ahead of her, leaving her behind. She imagined coming upon them crouched at the base of a tree. She imagined them kissing and looking up at her. She thought of Sidney Blossom and Kate Ransom. She saw Limus Barnum's eyes, coming toward her, forcing her to share the knowledge that he had written the horrible letter. She began to run along the path; the compass hung around her neck kept knocking against her chest.

Seeing her running, Luke, excited, ran after her until he caught her by the arm. They both stopped, suddenly. He let go. Muttering, "Not much of a path, is it?," he unsnagged his pants leg from brambles, then held up a branch of briars for her to walk under. She had to pass under his arm, close by, brushing against him, pressed against a body alien in its male youth (thinner, harder than her father's body) and alien in its odor (like a secret escaped, objectionable and compelling). She became very aware of her own sweat, sticking her shirt back to her skin. The feeling had always been a clean, pleasant sensation. Now she worried that her sweat might have an odor, or might look "gross," as she would have said, and meant by it too unfeminine, too physical, too symptomatic of sex, that natural force overruning reason, which she had said would never have such power over her.

Luke had been startled by the physical shock that shot from where she pressed against him down his chest to his groin. It was her breast that had touched him. She had breasts beneath that baggy shirt. Her hair smelled like lemons. She walked on, he ducked and let the branch swing out. They went without speaking farther into the woods.

In the shadow of a rotted tree trunk they came upon the cigarette butt that Ernest Ransom had dropped there on Tuesday. And then finally they came upon the black strip of strange charred earth. Polly at first thought they had already reached the site of the government compound she was trying to find again, concluding that its buildings somehow had been incinerated. Luke at first thought of napalm. Neither thought of anything besides fire, not of blight and pestilence, of shallow beds beneath the strip in which were buried the discarded experiments of scientific research, lethal wastes working their way through the earth, leaving their impress on it. The boy focused his camera on the dead land.

For over an hour they trekked in the wet sedge beyond the end of the path. Marsh grass was sometimes as high as their waists, and Polly feared a snake might slither out at her unseen.

"Are we lost? How much farther?" Luke's tennis shoes were sodden and his jeans heavy with mud.

"I don't know," she confessed.

But her discovery was still there, just within the woods' edge, as if deliberately hidden from sight. The chain fence, the aluminum buildings, even the Coke machine, exactly as she had remembered them. Sunlight ricocheted off all the bright new metal like a hundred hurried messages reflected in Morse code. Luke shoved Polly down by the shoulder.

"I told you," she whispered. "What did I tell you?" They stared at the secret base. Nothing moved there except the sun.

Polly could hear Luke's breath as they passed Miss Dingley's binoculars back and forth. "It's too quiet," he said. "I don't think anybody's around anymore. But keep down, okay?" He pushed on her shoulder.

"What do you think, they're going to shoot us?" she sneered, annoyed at his assumption of command.

"I thought you said they had guns."

"I did. But there's no reason why they should use them on us."

Luke had a distrust of his government bred of his generation, and a style bred of movies. "Listen," he told her. "They just shoot. They don't ask questions."

"We don't even know who 'they' is."

"Listen, this place could be completely on the up and up, and you cross that trespassing sign there, and they could still shoot. They don't need a reason. This government's so paranoid, they have to make a big deal out of everything to puff themselves up."

"Oh, you got all that from Ms. Rideout in history."

She led him in a low crouch, stalking along the perimeter of the compound. She stopped, stood, pointed at a gray mound in the packed dirt clearing. A large German shepherd lay stiffly among spears of tree clubs. With the binoculars she could see that the dog's eyes were open and the tongue was swollen and bloody. Flies crawled on it. She felt fear like a rush of heat.

"Look at that window in the big building! It looks like it's all smashed to bits."

"This is crazy. I don't like it. They must have closed down."

"And just left all those new supplies sitting there in the dirt to rot? No way. Jesus, look. Look over there, no, by the door. It's another dog."

Polly took the binoculars. "Oh, jeez. It's dead too, isn't it?"

If Ramona Dingley had given the two young people not only the binoculars made by Dingley Optical Instruments, but one of the company's periscopes as well, so that they might have seen around the corner of the laboratory, they would have noticed Dr. Thomas Svatopluk sprawled beneath a tree. But, of course, their perspective was limited, and so they did no more than squat there, behind a hillock, and take pictures and wait for something else to happen. Nothing did. The few sounds of birds, leaves fluttering, the quick shudder of dried leaves as a squirrel raced over them, the whine of insects, sounds that had seemed so safe and full along the path here seemed sinister in their quietness. Buildings and motors required more noise to make sense.

"It's horrible here," Polly finally whispered. "Let's go."

"Yeah. Let's go." Luke pulled her up.

The flashes of sunlight had dimmed, fading from the metal buildings. When they reached the edge of the marsh, they turned back to see the gray glint of metal flickering from behind the trees. Luke shook his head in disbelief.

"I told you it was there," Polly said again.

In the Firebird Miss Dingley and Mrs. O'Neal sat with the windows rolled up. Gnats, mosquitoes, and moths crowded to swirl in the headlight beams. "Where are they? Where are they?" muttered the old woman. "Idiot to let them go off like that!"

"Yes, it's so dark, they might have fallen into the pond or been attacked by something wild, that's what's been worrying me."

"Orchid. Please!" Miss Dingley hit her thighs hard. "Absurd, crippled old busybody. Sometimes I think I have no more brains than the rest of the Dingleys. Me playing Hardy Boys with *their* legs." (God knows what was out there, a ring of car thieves, drug smugglers, a maniacal hermit, kidnappers and rapists.)

A sudden rap at the front window sent Mrs. O'Neal into a loud scream. Ramona flung open the door. "It's just them, it's them, Orchid, good God, calm down! You two! Get in before they eat you alive. Oh, my God, look at you! Are you all right?"

Luke and Polly huddled in the backseat. Their eyes, eerily light, looked fluorescent in their mud-brown faces. Their skin was blistered with scratches. "It got dark so fast," Polly mumbled. "And then we got lost." Her mouth was stiff with dried mud.

"Poor things, poor things," sighed Mrs. O'Neal.

Miss Dingley twisted around. "Was it there?"

"Yes." Polly nodded.

"Now, these children have to get some food in them, Miss Dingley. And some dry clothes, that's for certain, first things first," advised Mrs. O'Neal as she backed the Firebird into a careful three-point turn at the road's end.

"Have you got some water, or something you could give Polly?" Luke asked.

"Come on, I don't need anything, I'm okay," Polly was shivering.

"Here." Miss Dingley reached down into her hamper. "Here, Miriam. Luke. Giver her that." It was a bottle of port.

"It's not missiles," Polly said. "It is restricted. It's the federal government. Something's funny. There're dead dogs lying there. We took the pictures."

Enclosed in unbroken blackness, the car lights moved slowly along the silent expanse of an abandoned highway. The old woman who represented her town, both in her name and in her elective capacity, sat beside her driver and tried to decipher the meaning of what the girl and boy were telling her. She reminded herself that she was powerless even to get out of her car without the help of sticks and wheeled chairs.

CHAPTER
40

As people were beginning to remember, Beanie Abernathy was a woman who acted on her impulses. She did so again today by hiking to Grand Central earlier than planned and boarding the first train to Argyle. She arrived there nearly two hours before Winslow expected to meet her. Dingley Falls was seven miles away, the next bus wouldn't leave before 4:00 P.M., there was no answer at home or at the office, nor was Lance at the Club. Beanie ate a bowl of chili at the diner, then walked to the bar where on Monday she had sat with Richard Rage. She had a Scotch. Finally she phoned Tracy Canopy, who was happy to come get her, even when Beanie made it clear that she had not returned forever, but only for the day; even when she added that she preferred not to talk about her plans. She had made no plans.

"Yes, I understand." Tracy nodded as they drove back toward Dingley Falls. She did not understand at all actually; plan making was an integral and automatic part of her personality, and so she assumed that Beanie meant she had as yet made no full, no final, or no airtight plan, whereas Beanie meant just what she said. "We're very concerned, Beanie," Tracy went on, "and want what's right and *best* for you. My, I've been so worried, you can imagine. And Evelyn, we'll have to tell her right away that you're fine. You are, aren't you? Poor Evelyn, her patio, the vandalism I was telling you about, it's shattered her nerves. She's always been susceptible to the worst imaginings."

"But she didn't imagine this. Somebody did it."

"That's true. Really makes you wonder. My, here we are already. I'll just wait in the car, in case."

Seeing the Abernathy house, its lawn, the steps, the black shutters, all exactly the same when everything else had changed so much, was a shock to Beanie. She felt she no longer had the right to use her key. She pressed the doorbell, and when no one answered, she walked back to the car. So Mrs. Canopy insisted on driving her into town, where they parked (too far from the curb, Beanie thought without thinking, and then thought that she had always held Winslow's poor driving against him) in front of Limus Barnum's store, which was closed. "The point is," Tracy said, "you never know whether Mr. Barnum is going to be there or not. Or whether Prudence is going to be at The Tea Shoppe or not. Or Sammy at the pharmacy. Or anyone. And then the selectmen criticize all of us for not patronizing local businesses!"

The ladies walked to the little cream brick building that Dingley Falls's law firm shared with Dr. Scaper. Abernathy & Abernathy was open, but neither partner was in. The young secretary thought Mr. Abernathy, Sr., was already in Argyle.

"Oh, are you sure, Susan? I wanted to stop him before he left for the station."

"I haven't seen him since eleven this morning, Mrs. Abernathy. I had the impression he was going to Argyle right then. Gee. I could call . . ."

"Hello!" Otto Scaper squeezed through the door. "Beanie!" he yelled. "Hell's bells, you're looking nice and healthy. It sets me up to see you. Whole damn town's going under on me, one thing after another. I'm old, it's not fair. Tracy, hello there. What in hell's the matter with your hands?"

"I don't know! Oh. Clay."

"What?" He cupped his ear with his enormous palm.

"*Clay.* You know." She formed a pot in air.

"Oh. Looked like liver trouble from here. I gotta run." The doctor lunged at the secretary's desk and scooped up a pack of cigarettes. "Gimme these, okay? Thanks, beautiful, and I'll pay you back tomorrow. Now don't tell Ida you saw me smoking or she'll run out and buy me a damn book on how to stop. Is that a new hairdo? I like it. Well, so long, girls." Susan Packer was embarrassed, for it was not her hair style that was changed, but her hair color—from brown to strawberry blond. All day she'd felt like rushing home to dye it back or hang herself. Oh, she'd never find a husband in Dingley Falls! Beanie was thinking that Susan should have left her hair brown but cut it short. Tracy was talking now, suggesting that they drive back to Argyle. They were standing in the doorway of the office building.

"Maybe we'll pass him on the road. Really, Beanie, I swear, it's no trouble at all. I don't have anything to do. Not until five; it's only a quarter past three."

Beanie saw Arthur's green Audi drive into Dingley Circle. It stopped in front of the post office. She saw Winslow step out and open the door for a woman in a black dress. The two spoke for a moment, then he watched the woman enter the double doors. Beanie was trying to recall the postmistress's name when Tracy tapped her shoulder and said, "Oh, look, there's Winslow now, right over there."

The lawyer turned toward them. Startled, he stopped. Beanie came down the steps and hurried over to offer an explanation. "I took an earlier train," she said. "Tracy gave me a ride."

"Beanie . . ."

"I was worried you'd make a useless trip to the station."

They stood in the middle of the sidewalk. Abernathy squinted into the sun. "Tracy," he called. "Thank you for getting her."

Quickly Mrs. Canopy joined them to help out. "Oh, no trouble. I was just potting. See." She held out her hands with a laugh. "What a messy hobby! Otto thought I had some dread disease a minute ago."

"I'm sorry I inconvenienced you. I gave Pru a ride home," Winslow began to explain. He felt in his jacket pocket for his pipe. "She closed early. She and Mrs. Haig here at the post office, they're trying to help a girl who's working for Pru. Her husband's in jail." Abernathy took out his pipe, then put it back in his pocket. He buttoned all the buttons on his jacket, caught himself, and unbuttoned them.

"What a shame," said Tracy. "Oh, that pretty girl from Vietnam?"

"Yes. It's a bit complicated, I'm afraid." He turned to Beanie now. "Your trip all right, I hope?"

"Yes, thank you, fine."

Tracy looked noticeably at her watch. "I should hurry. I'm never prepared for that remedial class, no doubt make such a fool of myself. Beanie, you call me. Winslow, bye-bye." Mrs. Canopy hurried down the street to her car. At five on Thursday she taught remedial reading at Dingley Optical Instruments to a small group of factory workers who believed they could better themselves and stop being factory workers. As

Tracy got into her Volvo, she looked around. The Abernathys still stood on the sidewalk where she'd left them. Sun flamed in Beanie's auburn hair. With his hand Winslow shaded his eyes.

In her off-beige bedroom Mrs. Ernest Ransom was trying something new. She was a woman of education, one who was, if not before the times, then at least, she liked to think, not behind them. Indeed, her Sundays were spent keeping up with *The Times*, at least everything but the sports section, which she always folded like a giant napkin on the breakfast table beside Ernest's sculpted grapefruit. Current affairs rarely got past her.

All her life Priscilla Hancock had kept herself modern. As a teenager she'd been a fan of John Dos Passos, of Chanel, Picasso, the Lubitsch touch, and the Spanish Civil War. At boarding school she'd attended meetings to keep America out of the Second World War, then at Mount Holyoke meetings to help America win it. Always in the first wave, even in a backwater like Dingley Falls, Connecticut, Priss had timely taken up, among other things, theater of the absurd, Dr. Spock, Minimal Art, psychoanalysis, Ingmar Bergman, the sack dress, banning the bomb, modern dance, Antonioni, John Kennedy, Danish cookware, Ralph Nader, Mandarin restaurants, Pierre Cardin, solar energy, and belief in the guilt of Richard Nixon. The last a painful subject between herself and Ernest, who would not relinquish faith (in the office, and so of necessity in the man) until the resignation itself. Far, far later than Priss.

One wave, however, she appeared to have missed. The women's movement. It had rushed past her, gathering speed and volume until now she watched it smash into house after house, while she bobbed out at sea. Of course, she'd read de Beauvoir long ago, and all the others, more or less, and while what they said was no doubt true, wasn't it a bit beside the point, not to mention defensive? Mrs. Ransom was not one of those with a passionate capacity to inflame her bosom by pressing to it all the injustices ever committed against women since Eve thumbed her nose at a chauvinist God. When Kate Ransom read her mother anecdotes from the setbacks and humiliations endured by great women of the past and asked if the stories didn't make her want to "blow men's balls off," the answer was frankly, no, they did not.

The second wave, the militant bra burners, had amused, then irritated Priss, as had "hippies" in general. She could barely forgive Sidney Blossom for having once been one. As a group, they had struck her as not only unkempt and ill bred, but insolently naive. She quoted Molière: *"C'est une folie à nulle autre seconde,/De vouloir se mêler à corriger le monde."* There is no greater folly than the desire to dabble in reforming the world. And these dogmatic inarticulate innocents, handing out flowers one minute, throwing rocks the next, would no doubt have read that play and thought the misanthrope was a g.d. tragic hero. Here she and Ernest had been quite in agreement. The sixties had been a mistake. A loud, long, deliberate fart in a public place.

But women had swum out of the sixties. Now the very mainstream, in the buoyant camaraderie of their long-suppressed hatred for *everyone,* had paddled past Priss. Housewives in Little Rock had memorized ideological diatribes against their husbands, schoolgirls campaigned for the ERA, *Playgirl* magazine was in the Madder A & P, all the children were in day-care programs, and there wasn't a bra left to burn. That she was behind the times was a mortifying realization to Mrs. Ransom, but she faced the fact squarely after a catechism by Kate on *The Joy of Sex,* which their daughter had given her parents for their thirtieth anniversary. How often, Kate asked, did she "screw"?

When had she started? Was she multiorgasmic? Was she orgasmic? How often did she masturbate? When had she started? Had she ever had anal sex? Why did these questions make her so uptight? Why couldn't she be open and honest with her own daughter about desires that all women shared? Weren't they sisters?

"No, we are not," Mrs. Ransom had replied. "I have the honor of being your mother. Emerald is your sister."

"Yeah, crap, well, I can't talk to her. Do you know what she's doing right now? She's got olive oil on her hair and over that, aluminum foil, and she's got a face mask of honey and oatmeal on. I don't think Emerald even has a vagina. I don't think she even pees."

Kate's attitude had disturbed Mrs. Ransom. Then had come the obscene accusations made by the anonymous letter. Then Beanie's astonishing *cri de coeur* that she had "never felt like this before" Richard Rage. Felt like what? Priss didn't know whether she was orgasmic or not. Perhaps it would have been of some comfort to her to know that she had somehow managed to raise two perfectly, multiplicatively orgasmic daughters, to know that in fact at this very minute Emerald was lying with Arthur Abernathy on his sofa, where they had been having sex for four years. Lying with Arthur's hand in her lace panties and her hand around a handkerchief around his phallus. Shuddering from time to time, shaking off her climaxes like crinolines. But Mrs. Ransom had never asked about Emerald's sex life, or anyone else's. As for her own, there was little to say. Perhaps once a month now, Ernest pressed up against her after he turned out the light. He thrust his tongue in her mouth, then he massaged her breasts briefly, then he climbed on top of her and pulled down his pajama bottoms while she pulled down hers. Then he rubbed his penis against her crotch until it was fully erect. Then he or she or both of them positioned it to slide inside her. Sometimes it felt reasonably pleasant, other times decidedly less so. Certainly she did not writhe and moan, and frankly she found it farcical when actresses did so in films. No doubt, Ernest was not a very good lover. But did she want a good lover? And what would one be? In the past month she had begun to purchase magazines and paperbacks on the subject of her sensuality. They strongly advised her to cultivate autoeroticism, to practice it diligently. Finally she sent away for one of the vibrators that doctors in the field had recommended to women.

Now, behind the locked door of her bedroom, the house empty, Priss sat on the edge of her queen-sized bed with her purchase. She drank half a martini, then, after a deep breath, tugged her slacks, panty hose, and panties down to her feet. Should she take off her tunic and blouse? She decided not. Spreading her legs, she pressed the white plastic cone against her pubis and pushed the switch.

Nothing happened. Batteries had not been included. "This is g.d. ridiculous," muttered Mrs. Ransom as she hopped to her bathroom closet, where she removed the batteries from a portable makeup mirror. Seated on the toilet cover, she turned on the vibrator again. Her hand spasmed. Very gently she touched the tip of the machine to what the instructions called her climactic zone. The sensation resembled high E on a violin. She warmed the tip in her hand, then tried again, more firmly. Eventually the irritation faded. The whole area was numb. Leaning farther back, holding apart her labia, Priss eased the end of the vibrator into her vagina. The motor was quite hot now and she was slightly concerned about the possibility of its exploding inside her.

She caught a glimpse of her face, rather red, in the mirror that ran the width of the room above twin sinks. The outside wall of the bathroom had sliding glass doors that opened onto a fenced balcony, where one could sunbathe (Kate did so nude) and from which

Ernest had built a safety ladder in case of fire. Mrs. Ransom's eyes were drawn to the bamboo blinds lowered over the doors. Something drew her attention there. She looked back, then back again, then gasped. In a gap between the loosely woven slats, a pair of eyes stared at her. When they moved, she saw teeth flicker in a grin. She flung the vibrator at the eyes. It thudded on the safety glass. The eyes vanished. Simultaneously she heard someone driving into the garage on the other side of the house. On the balcony footsteps scrambled, falling down the ladder. There was a thud. A muffled grunt.

Mrs. Ransom pulled up her wad of clothes, then stood to listen. The only noise was the buzz of the vibrator. Then she began to shake. Her legs trembled as she walked to unlock her bedroom door. She lay down on the bed, got up. From the medicine chest she took a Valium, cut it in half with a fingernail file, swallowed the half with the martini on her night table, climbed back into the bed, and pulled the Marimekko coverlet around her. She was certain that the eyes were not those of anyone she knew well. That would have been worse.

"Your mother has a headache and won't be joining us for cocktails. Emerald, your Gibson. Arthur, one Scotch and soda coming up." Ernest Ransom mixed highballs at the ebony liquor cabinet. He had showered and changed from his suit to madras slacks and a yellow knit shirt. "So. To the end of another day, Arthur. How was yours?"

"Frustrating. I spent the public part of it going around in circles about when are we ever going to reinforce Falls Bridge. And the private part going around in circles with management at Optical Instruments. They don't need a lawyer over there, they need an Industrial Revolution." Arthur Abernathy hoped he had not previously made this remark, one of his favorites, to his future father-in-law. He had, however, and Ernest Ransom was thinking that Arthur was not going to get very far in politics until he learned to remember what he'd said to whom. "Yes, yes. Poor O.I." Ransom sipped his Scotch and soda. "It's a complete shambles now. But in your great-grandfather's day, remember, Arthur, O.I. was one of the major manufacturers of precision optics in New England. Telescopes, periscopes, everything, each one miles ahead of the competition in just plain quality."

"*Quantity* is the problem now, Mr. Ransom. They can't stay in business if they don't increase production, take some shortcuts on quality, and get the prices down. The Japanese are killing us."

"I don't know why in hell you and Winslow haven't sold the damn place to some conglomerate ages ago. Everything merges, Arthur, everything is drawn into the whole. Drink okay?" Ransom rattled the ice in his glass.

His future son-in-law smiled. "Could be, could be. But the thing is, Aunt Ramona holds as many shares as Mom does. I mean Mom could care less what we do, I mean she's always trusted our judgment, but you know how Ramona feels about the rest of the world coming into Dingley Falls *or* taking anything out of it. I just don't see her giving us her proxies to sell O.I." Arthur rattled the ice in his glass.

His fiancée, Ransom's daughter, had sat in a mauve satin armchair throughout their talk. She crossed her glossy legs and leafed through *Harper's Bazaar* and finished her Gibson. Emerald had heard both sides of the Optical Instruments conversation a number of times before.

From outside her sister, Kate, banged through the french doors into the room. "Hey. I hooked the speakers up next to the pool. Rock out!" She grinned and whipped her pelvis back and forth in a current dance. Arthur looked at the carpet.

"I don't know how the rest of Elizabeth Circle is going to feel about outside amplifiers," cautioned Mr. Ransom.

Kate shrugged. Slouching across the rug to a coffee table, where Wanda had placed a tray of hors d'oeuvres, she scooped up a fistful of cashews, which she tossed into her mouth as she spoke. "Okay, we'll keep it down. But crap, some nights I can hear those bullshit operas of Evelyn's up in my room with the window shut. Where's Mother?" She looked at Emerald, who shook her curls in the direction of the stairs. "Oh. Well, look," Kate said, with a glance at her father, "you guys are welcome to join in, Emerald. Arthur. No hard drugs, promise."

Emerald was not amused. Arthur offered to come, perhaps, sometime after dinner, which he had promised to eat at his father's house.

"Fine, nobody's coming till eight. Will you make me a Scotch, Daddy?"

"Scotch isn't a woman's drink. Why don't you let me make you a martini or something like that?"

"Crap Almighty, I don't believe it. That is so dumb, Daddy! Just never mind!"

"Well, I'm not sure you ought to talk like that. Anyone for seconds? No?" Ransom closed the cabinet. "Well, excuse me, then. I guess I'll go watch the news. Katie, you let me know when it's time to start the charcoal." He went into his library and wondered if his daughter was really angry at him. He didn't like to think so. But she flared up as if she hated him.

Kate smiled at the closing door. Then she said, "In five minutes he'll be asleep on the couch. He always is, and he always says he isn't." She ate three celery stalks stuffed with Boursin, opened the liquor cabinet, and poured herself a Scotch. "You know"—she grimaced— "I don't even much like this crap, and because of dumb remarks by chauvinist pigs like Daddy, I'm going to have to drink it forever."

Emerald Ransom stood to see herself in the coiled

gold mirror on the wall. With both hands she brushed her hair back off her bare shoulders. Arthur and Kate watched her. She was easy to watch. She was a woman at ease with her image.

CHAPTER
41

In Dingley Falls on Thursday evening, meals were being prepared—for the most part by women. At six Joy Strummer ate her pork chops under the constabulary eye of her mother. Though not at all hungry, she felt compelled to feign the ravenous appetite Mrs. Strummer associated with good health. Joy's plans were in jeopardy. Just before she'd announced the proposed visit to the library with Polly, Mr. Hedgerow had appeared at the screen door to ask them where Polly was. Joy's heart sank. If she weren't able to go to the party with Lance, she was going to double-*k*, kill Polly for disappearing. "Have some more stewed tomatoes, baby. Daddy, pass her the tomatoes." Joy's father handed the girl a bowl sticky with juice running over the sides. The red spoonful plopped onto her plate and seeped into the macaroni. Sweat drops formed a diadem across Joy's temples. She smiled at her mother.

At 6:15, in her Alice-blue dining room, Evelyn Troyes served *soupe à l'oignon* to Father Fields, with apologies that it was, of course, but a poor imitation of the onion soup she had so much enjoyed at Lasserre's in Paris. He apologized in return that his obligations to the academy choir that evening forced them to eat at such an uncivilized hour. The young curate was always enchanted with his hostess's culinary reminiscences, sometimes recounted in French so that he could

practice the language. He longed to travel to Europe
someday, to dine at the Savoy and stand before the
great cathedral doors of Chartres. Mrs. Troyes now
mentioned the *osso buco* they served at the Hotel
Danieli Royal. Was that Venice? Yes. In a rose sunset,
Jonathan saw himself walking through the Piazza San
Marco, with Walter Saar. Walking to dinner, and then,
and then . . . He blushed. "And once Blanchard and I
ate in the Tivoli Gardens, the most cunning way they
had of folding their napkins. Yes, the food was
delicious. And the Belle Terrasse, I think was it name.
Copenhagen, because I remember they sent up fire-
works after dark, and the sea there was such a blue,
just the color of your eyes. Blanchard was a great eater.
He adored food, I'm afraid, to excess, and brought on
his stroke. Very different from Hugo, who never
noticed if there were any food on the table or not, and
quite often there was not. Especially after Paris fell."
Jonathan hurried through his strawberries with a
feeling of goodwill: he had actually, and without
resentment, enjoyed listening to Mrs. Troyes talk.
Maybe God, after all, would enlarge his heart to make
room for others, as he daily prayed. It had been so
good of her to buy him that Rachmaninoff autograph in
New York. It was so awful of him to be thrilled by how
much it must have cost.

   At 6:30, in the shabby roominess of her kitchen,
Prudence Lattice cooked in a wok, which she had never
done before. Under Chin Lam's supervision the small
white-haired woman nervously poked a chopstick at
vegetables and pork slivers with a concentration so
intense that Chin laughed for the first time since she'd
come to work at The Tea Shoppe. Hearing the childish
giggle, Miss Lattice thought with a jolt of pleasure that,
if Chin were to live there with her, perhaps they could
do each other good. Then guilt snatched the thought
away. Did she hope that the girl's husband would go to
prison and leave her his wife? Did she think she could

fill her solitary old age by taking in this young woman like a homeless cat found outside her door? Really, thought Prudence, there was no excuse for such a selfish, silly fantasy. "Now, Miss Lattice, quick, all finished. Take off heat now. Yes, yes, yes. Doing *very* well!" Chin smiled, nodding, at the old woman, who, overcome with goodwill, turned to feed pork bones to the insatiable Night.

In Madder, at a round yellow vinyl-topped table, and at a card table, and in a high chair, the MacDermotts ate spaghetti off multicolored plastic plates. Judith Haig, guest of honor, had the sole china setting, from a service for eight depicting scenes of English country life, which Sarah was purchasing week by week from the A & P. "Anyhow, Monday I get the cups, and a week later the saucers. I told you you should have gotten in on it at the beginning. Well, the rolls are done, better late than never, here, Joe. Where in the world is Orchid? That's what I'd like to know, I don't know whether to let Jimmy eat her share or not. Just *one*, Eddie, just put that right back! 'Course, Judith, you can back-order any pieces you miss, and extras. Like I got the cream pitcher but then it's regular price. Jesus bless us, if you don't want the meatballs, Tommy, then don't eat them, but leave them on your plate. Did you hear me? All right, then, just get up from the table and go put on your pj's and get your homework done, excuse yourself to Judith. No, I don't hate you either. Joe, tell Tommy he has to, *Francis!* Stop teasing the baby! Oh, Jesus, Joseph, and Mary, I can't hear myself think!"

On High Street, Mrs. Mary Bredforet said to Dr. Ruth Deeds, "When Nancy's gone, we usually just walk across to the Prim and eat. I never did learn how to cook, I must admit, and William is so obnoxious if a dish happens to go a little awry." Mary poked dubiously at her boiled potatoes, as Ruth forked four charred steaks out of the broiler.

"I'm pretty bad myself." The doctor laughed. "I hate cooking. I'd even rather eat the mess they serve at the hospital. Some of the junk I munch on, I don't even want to think about what it's doing to my insides. But I love to eat; I'm just going to have to marry a gourmet, that's all."

A clump of cards in hand, Bredforet poked his head through the door, looked around, and said, "We should have gone out."

"Just a few more minutes," his wife vowed. The door swung shut. She sawed a head of lettuce into quarters and spooned mayonnaise onto each. The two women surveyed their handiwork. "It doesn't look very promising, does it?" sighed Mrs. Bredforet.

"Don't talk like that. They can take it or leave it," admonished Dr. Deeds. "If they don't want this, let them eat pizza. They're old enough to feed themselves. Men just pretend to be helpless."

Mrs. Bredforet giggled. "Why, yes! Let them eat pizza. Why, yes."

On Glover's Lane the Sniffells dined with the Hayeses, because the Hayeses had dined with the Sniffells in May. In the kitchen June Hayes leaned on the counter with her fingers pressed against her eyelids. Her little radio above the sink played the waltz from *Sleeping Beauty*. She turned it up as loud as it would go. Almost immediately her husband, A.A., slipped through the door and shut it quickly behind him. He snapped the radio off and caught her hand when she reached for the dial again. He felt a thick weight on his chest as he let his breath out before he quietly said, "Honey? What's going on? You've been in here ten minutes. Where's the dessert? They're just sitting out there. Okay, okay, I'm sorry I asked them," he hissed, "but I don't see how we could have decently . . ." Hayes set out coffee cups on a tray. "I'll take these out. Would you cut the pie?"

When Hayes returned, June still stood at the sink.

"June! Where's the pie?" He had thought his luck was going to hold. He had managed to bribe his son Charlie into taking his younger siblings out for hamburgers and a movie. He had gotten through the meal—Ida talked so much it didn't matter that June wouldn't open her mouth. He had almost made it. And now this.

She stared out at darkness. "There isn't any pie."

"What's that supposed to mean?"

"It was burned. I threw it away. . . . Don't give me that look of yours."

"What look?" Again Hayes let out all his breath. "How do you know how I'm looking? You've got your back to me. What look?"

"I don't have to see it, Alvis. The look of how it breaks your heart that I'm hopelessly insane." Her face squirmed in the distortion of fury. The Medusa, thought A. A. Hayes, was probably just somebody's wife. "June, please. Could we not get into this now? There are guests out there. Let's go back."

"You go. I'm not going to."

Hayes jerked open the freezer. "You *have* to," he said, but he knew she wouldn't. She might even start screaming. As always she had defeated him. Those who will not abide by the rules of the game cannot be beaten by those who do. The only alternative the latter have is to decline to play with them at all, and leave the stadium for good. That was not an option for Hayes. He spooned ice cream into bowls and took them with a smile into the dining room.

It was long after seven when Ramona Dingley returned Polly, with profuse apologies, to Glover's Lane. Around the Hedgerows' paint-cracked table Miss Dingley, Luke, Polly, and her father now sat among white opened boxes of giant pizzas, cans of beer, cans of Coke. Mozzarella stuck to their fingers, anchovies fell to the floor. "Ridiculous food. Marvelous, ain't it, Cecil?" Ramona asked happily. "I remember when I first saw one of those wonderful wretched

TV dinners. Always felt liberated eating out of cartons and cans. Nothing tasted better than chow mein in a cardboard container, except hot dogs in a napkin."

"If you think this is good," Luke told her, "it's too bad Mama Marco's closed for that funeral, because hers make these taste like a rubber tire."

"Pphht!" she snorted. "I see you two have ingested a tire and a half. While we old fogies babble away and pick at our crusts." There was a quarter of century between Cecil Hedgerow and his elderly guest, but she bridged the years with a wide grin. "Astounding. Look at those two, totally recharged after what they went through. Were we ever that young, Cecil?"

"Younger," replied the widower.

It was a pleasure to Miss Dingley to sit in this family kitchen, to watch (after her worry and remorse) the awesome regenerative capacity of the young. Fatigue and corruption simply washes off them, she thought. They recover. They forget. That's why they can bear to rush headlong into so much more of everything— including passion, hope, and grief—than anyone even only thirty could stand to risk.

It was 7:30 when Evelyn Troyes, after driving Father Fields up to the academy, knocked at her friend Tracy's door. Mrs. Canopy was embarrassed to be found in a butcher's apron, dining on prepackaged shrimp newburg still in its tinfoil square. She had her television set atop her dining room table, which, except for the clearing where she sat, was covered with newspapers, clay, paints, and a row of wobbly coffee mugs fresh from the kiln. "Oh, my, Evelyn, please pay no attention to this mess. Don't you look pretty! Is that a new blouse? I was watching the news. Funny how it can go on surprising you how horrible the news is. I really wonder what we're coming to."

"I'm so sorry to bother you, but I was feeling a little blue, sort of at loose ends," Evelyn aplogized. "But I'm probably intruding, aren't I?"

"You've always been such a ninny, Evelyn. Of course

you're not intruding. Do you think I have a lover hiding in the bathroom?" Mrs. Canopy made this joke in vigorous innocence; she had no desire for a lover, in the bathroom or elsewhere. But her friend Evelyn did harbor such longings, for herself, and—generously enough—for her friends. She would have been delighted had she glimpsed trousers slipping away up the steps. She was delighted, secretly, when in New York she had glimpsed Richard Rage kissing the inside of Beanie's wrist and palm, just as so long ago Hugo had kissed hers. Mrs. Canopy made coffee. Then she and her friend shared a box of Scottish shortbread as they watched a documentary on the invasion of privacy. Later, at Tracy's urging, Evelyn made a little clay ashtray and painted violets all over it. Loverless, they passed the time.

It was almost eight when Beanie cleared away stripped artichoke petals and the bones of Chicken Kiev. Dinner had been uncomfortably silent, her two sons and her husband murmuring from time to time into the quietness some talk of the world, of law, money, and sports. Arthur spoke to Beanie as if she were housemother of a fraternity he didn't particularly wish to join. Lance wouldn't look at her at all. Winslow thought that the situation was unfair to Beanie, but felt caught in it and unable to change anything. Beanie felt it had been a mistake to come to the house. Once there, she had been stung by her neglected duty, by the sight of the full laundry hamper, the illmade bed, the dust on her dresser, and the dried dirt in her plant pots. She (he) was low on butter and bread and out of milk. He (should she do it before she left?) ought to hire a house cleaner. It had been a mistake to prepare dinner, but everything in the refrigerator would have just gone bad if not used.

Now Lance shook his head at the offered coffeepot. "No, thanks, I guess I better shove off, going over to Kate's," he said to his place mat.

Beanie sat back down. "Lance, could you wait just a few minutes? And Arthur. I'm sorry, but we need to talk a little bit. Your dad and I. This evening we decided something and want you to know. Winslow?" She bit her lip and turned to him.

"Your mother," he said quietly as he folded his napkin, "and I have talked for a long time, and we've come to the decision, a painful decision, that it would be best"—he cleared his throat—"if we separated for a while."

Lance threw himself up from his chair. "Oh, Jesus God, Mom! What the hell!"

"Lance, sit down, please." Only Abernathy's eyes were angry; they were what Beanie called their "angry gray."

Lance leaned over the table "What are you trying to do, Dad? Did you tell her to go?"

"No," Beanie said. "Please, Lance. It was me, I felt, because of everything, you see, it would be the best thing. It's not just what happened . . . this week, but many things between, over a long time, I've tried to explain. Arthur, I know all this is horrible for you, with your wedding plans this summer, and I feel awful, but please try to understand."

"It's not for me to understand, Mother." Arthur folded his napkin. "That's for Dad to say."

Beanie stacked salad plates in front of her. In the silence she could hear Lance's breath grow louder and knew he was going to erupt now, just as he had when he lay kicking on the floor as a baby. "Are you going back to *him?*" His face lunged at her, red and twisted. "*Who is he?* I'm going to beat the shit out of him!" Beanie began to cry.

"All right, all right, that's enough." Abernathy stood.

"He's going to get his teeth shoved down his rotten throat! What the hell does he think he's trying to prove?"

Arthur stood as well. "Would you please shut your mouth?" He pushed his chair into the table. "You're upsetting Mom."

Lance flung his long, tan arms over his head. "Oh man, oh man! Upsetting her! You two are just going to sit around and let this guy get away with it. Aren't you? Just sit there sucking on your cheeks while some . . . *hippie,* some pervert, runs off with Mom! Jesus God, no way I can believe this is happening!"

"Do not yell at me, Lance." Winslow's voice had that stillness that Beanie dreaded. "It isn't your business to do anything. I know your mother appreciates that you feel strongly. But whatever choice she makes is hers to make. Whatever decisions she and I come to are between us. It simply is not your business."

"Well, fuck it. Just fuck it, that's all. She's out of her head. Why the shit did you make us come over here and go through this crap then?"

Her face watery with tears, Beanie looked up at the three men who loomed over her around the dinner table. She began to gather their silverware.

"Oh, Beanie, just leave it," her husband said. "For God's sake, just leave it."

"No. I'm all right. Please go on, I'm all right." She stood and took the dishes to the kitchen for the more than thirty thousandth time in her married life.

CHAPTER
42

The night was right, sweet smells of pink and plum flowers stirred in a warm wind, and in the looking glass of the Ransoms' heated pool the lights were bright. Boxes tacked to tree trunks made music. Desire twanged across Elizabeth Circle. The afterglow of charcoal smoldered in the grill while from kegs and carafes drink tumbled at a touch into glasses. At the shallow end of the pool Joy Strummer rippled small waves with her feet. From time to time she leaned forward to trail her hand in the darker water. The shimmer of her face floated there uneasily. Joy wore her black bikini for the first time and her hair loosely pinned. Coils of gold curled down to her neck. She had seen men notice her tonight. Among them was Sidney Blossom, who was thinking that the only achievement one can bring to a swimming party is the body. Maturity, wealth, talent, degrees, none, he noted (hiding his thin arms against his thin chest), can be worn on the flesh.

Earlier, while Joy tried to pretend to eat all her steak, she had overheard Kate whisper to Lance: "Are you out of your gourd? That's Bobby Strummer's *little* sister!" But Lance had replied, "So? Big deal." And even if the other guests had left her alone, still the place was the most beautiful she had ever seen, and Lance was better-looking than anyone else there could be in the world. Suddenly his head burst up out of the wet darkness at her feet. On his lashes water drops sparkled. She saw what he saw—that she was more

beautiful than anyone else there could be in the world.
"Hey, you! How you doing? Listen, I'm sorry I kept
you waiting so late. And I was in a lousy mood, too,
wasn't I? Okay? How you doing? I was driving like a
nut, wasn't I?"

"That's all right." She had never doubted, while she
had stood at the end of the lane waiting secretly, never
once doubted that he would come in the crimson
chariot and sweep her away. She had set aside his mood
as irrelevant to her and him. "Oh, that's all right." She
smiled.

"It was a nuthouse at home. Well. Hey. Now look.
I'm going to show off for you. Let's see if I can still cut
it." By his hands he sprang out of the pool. She
watched him walk to the other end. Water ran down the
curls of his hair, down the small of his back, down his
legs. From the top of the ladder he waved at her. There
was nothing else for either of them to notice but the
other's mysterious beauty.

To this party Kate Ransom had invited not only old
childhood friends stuck in Dingley Falls between spring
term and summer plans, but several young couples
sharing rented cabins on Lake Pissinowno whom she'd
met at the marina. Near nudity hastened acquaintance-
ship among the guests. Several, clustered in the middle
of the pool, chased a volleyball. A wave splashed
Arthur Abernathy's trousers as he sat in a lounge chair
next to Emerald and gazed glumly at his twin brother,
Lance, who now walked on his hands the length of the
diving board. Having known Lance for thirty-one
years, Arthur was no longer surprised to see him in a
mood so radically different from the one he'd been in
only two hours earlier. No longer surprised, but still
indignant.

Kate swam along the floor of the pool, grabbed
Sidney's trunks from behind, and tugged. When he
wrenched around, she kissed a spray of water into his
mouth. "You're too aggressive." He grinned. "Men
don't like it."

The accusation made Kate hostile, as she sometimes thought it might be true. "You ought to get a tan. Like that." She pointed up at Lance.

The librarian, though hurt, laughed. "I'd have to get a body like that first, wouldn't you say?" They watched Lance fly backwards off the board. Grinning, Kate floated against Blossom, pressed her hand against his crotch, and wound her legs around his. "I like your body better," she told him. It was a way of saying, "I like *you* better," which was true, though she did find preferable, as bodies go, Lance's. "I like feeling your hand there," he told her, which was true, though he would have preferred her slightly less rigorously athletic in her amorousness. Neither thought the other was (utterly) perfect, and each was beginning to look forward to telling each other so as the years went by.

Lance shot like a dolphin out of the pool, then crouched on the concrete beside his brother's lounge chair. "Hey, what went down after I left the house? Hi, Emerald, you're looking good. What's Mom up to?"

"She left."

"Are you kidding? Where?"

"Tracy Canopy's. She couldn't very well stay overnight with Dad now, could she? In the morning she's going back to New York."

"The hell you say."

Arthur helped his fiancée out of her chair. "I'll talk to you about this tomorrow, Lance, all right?" Emerald swirled her sweater in a perfect *farol de rodillas* so that it settled softly upon her bare shoulders.

"Very good," Walter Saar was saying to Priss Ransom, who had just compared the music coming at them from tree trunks in ever louder grunts to a recording of natural childbirth. Priss had sufficiently removed from her mind the sight of those horrible eyes spying through the bamboo shades to manage a brief appearance at the pool in order to greet her daughter's guests and check on the supply of refreshments. She was pleased to see the headmaster there, though surprised. She had thought of him as a member of *her* circle, and therefore anathema to Kate. "You're not swimming, Walter?"

"My dear, I prefer liquid down my throat, not up my nose."

"Refurbish your drink?" asked Mr. Ransom.

"Oh, thanks, Ernest. Besides, at our age, the most aesthetic thing we can do is keep our clothes on."

"*Our* age? How *galant.*" Priss smirked.

He knew he should offer her now a bite of candied wit, he even thought of a sentence, but he just didn't want to say it. "Priss, would you excuse me? Jonathan there looks a little lost." Father Fields, a sky-blue sweater over his clerical collar, stood, wineglass in hand, off by himself near the flowering azalea. He stared up at the stars.

"Is he praying?" asked Mrs. Ransom. "Don't tell me. You expect imminent death and keep a priest constantly at your side to sneak you into Paradise." She raised the arms of her white caftan in a parody of prayer.

He knew she was offering him another chance, but he didn't want it. He wanted very much to say, "No, he's my lover," just to see her face, but he didn't dare, and besides, it was not, technically, true. "I like him," Saar said. "He's very nice," and thought, That has to be the dullest remark I've made in years. "Ah. Thank you, Ernest; looks . . . very nice." (What was the matter with his tongue? Could it articulate nothing but "very nice"?)

"*Bien sûr.*" Mrs. Ransom smiled. "I'm sure he *is* very nice, and even if he weren't, *il est très beau, très beau. C'est vrai, monsieur?*" Her eyes looked at his for one interminable second, then Saar smiled, bowed, and walked away. (Hell. Goddamn her. But, all right, fair was fair, she'd let him know she knew and done it so that crystallized clone of the Successful American Male

had no idea what she was talking about. If anything had
"turned him queer," why not say it was the possibility
of turning, instead, into Ernest Ransom?) Now, what
was she going to do with the knowledge that the
headmaster of her son's school was "that way"?
Discounting its possible consequences (one word from
her and he would be fired tomorrow, with scant
likelihood of flattering recommendations), the question
of her power fascinated him, almost theoretically.
Suddenly Saar felt wonderfully free, triumphant over
shame. "Bored, Jonathan?"

"Oh, hi. No, not at all. It's a beautiful night."

Saar looked up at the sky from the curate's perspective. "Yes. It makes life down here look rather temporary, and generally silly." Light winked at him through
his ice cube. " 'Bright star, would I were stedfast as
thou art,' and et cetera. Yes, it's beautiful. However,
somehow *that*"—he pointed at a throbbing speaker on
a nearby willow—"does not sound capable of turning
the heavens in their spheres. Or, for that matter,
soothing the savage breast. Which calls to mind the
choir rehearsal. I think you did very well with that
phalanx of savage breasts."

"Really? I thought I was doing an awful job. I just
don't have enough authority. No matter what I said, I
couldn't seem to keep them in line. What's so funny?"

"My dear man, Attila couldn't keep those little Huns
in line the last week of school. Maybe if you'd simply
shot every tenth tenor, the rest would have paused to
consider. But, in the end, they outnumber us. Ah,
Jonathan, Rome always falls to the barbarian, and the
old to the young." Saar put his hand on the curate's, on
the pretext of removing his glass. "Now. I've done my
scrapes and curtsies here. Why don't we leave?"

"All right. Where shall we go?"

Saar very much wanted to say, "You could come
home with me." So he did, and watched the blue eyes
hurry back to the stars, pause there, then finally turn
toward his.

"I'd like to," Jonathan replied, his heart awed at his own bravery. "But let me say good-bye to Joy first."

Saar laughed. "Good-bye to joy? My God, if you think the prospect that gloomy, by all means let's stay here instead and watch that man, who, out of motives that I could never grasp, is repeatedly plunging backwards off that high board into that hard water."

"No, no." The curate grinned, relieved by levity. "It's a girl. Joy Strummer. I've gotten to know her parents a little because her old brother, Bobby, their son, has been reported missing in Vietnam for about two years now, and, well, I've tried to help them keep in touch with the government and, you know, see if we could learn anything about where he is."

"Don't you assume he's dead?"

"Oh, no. We assume he's alive. That's Joy over there in the pool. I'm kind of surprised she's here; she's awfully young. Over there." Saar followed the line of the curate's arm to a girl who stood, her hand raised in greeting, in the dark shallow water; a girl who looked, the headmaster said out loud, "Good God, like Aphrodite! Really!" But strangely, her beauty made him sad. He felt he wanted to wrap her in a warm covering, to cover such beauty and keep it safe. Such paternal impulses were new to him. And yet, of course, there was no shield behind which to preserve human beauty. No shield was strong enough. Keats ran in the teacher's mind still. "And Joy, whose hand is ever at his lips / Bidding adieu; And aching pleasure nigh, / Turning to poison while the bce-mouth sips."

Cecil Hedgerow kissed his sleeping daughter; she brushed her hand across her face and turned to the side. Alone downstairs he opened the violin case that sat atop Pauline's old upright piano, but before he could begin his evening practice, someone knocked at the kitchen door.

Jack Strummer wanted to know if Joy was upstairs with Polly. She had sneaked out of her room apparently, after her mother had forbidden her to get out of bed. "Jesus, Peggy's mad as a hornet. But I say, what the hell, let the kid have some fun. Just starting her vacation and all. You know Peggy. Not here, right? Bet you anything a bunch of them went up to the lake and all just like we used to."

Hedgerow was walking his neighbor across the backyard when his foot hit something thick and soft. Even as he was saying, "What in the world?" he had seen what it was. The little cocker spaniel's fly-buzzed body was lying in the unmown grass just where he had seen it this morning. "Jack, I'm afraid that's Joy's little dog."

"Oh, Jesus! Look there. Donny! Oh, Jesus, what happened? Poor little fellow. Joy's heart's going to be broken in two over this. You know how she loves Donny. Poor little princess. Look, I'll go get a box or something. Oh, Jesus. Sorry to bother you with this, Cecil."

At midnight the party had a great idea. It would go to the Ransoms' beach house on Lake Pissinowno, where it would not disturb Kate's parents—who had retired to their den—or their neighbors—Mr. Smalter had called twice. The party would go where it could build a fire, smoke pot, race naked into the glacial lake water, do whatever it wanted to do. What Kate wanted to do was make love on the pebbly beach. Sid didn't want to: "I'm not interested in anything that resembles pain," he told her. "Not even pleasure?" she asked, and grinned. "You don't understand. Orgasm is death's *doppelgänger*. Coming. And going. See?"

"Sounds Swedish to me." He grimaced. "Is it Ingmar Bergman?"

"Yeah. She says it to Humphrey Bogart in *Casablanca*. Ha. Ha. What's the matter with this car?"

"It's on orgasm's doorstep. Ha. Ha."

Behind Blossom's faltering VW, the party in a

caravan of cars crawled up High Street toward the lake. It passed the Bredforets' house, where Ruth Deeds lay awake, annoyed with herself for caring whether she was alone or not. Angrily she rustled her research notes on the harmful side effects of defoliants. The car passed the headmaster's house at Alexander Hamilton Academy, where Jonathan Fields was discovering that human communion could be fully as terrifying and as blissful as the divine, and where Walter Saar was discovering that in the awkward efforts of human communion there could be that same rush of divinity there was in music.

Left behind by the party at the pool's edge, Joy sat wrapped in Lance's sweater; it was warm against her shivering skin. Just before the party had had its great idea, Lance had asked if she'd mind if he was gone for a few minutes. He just needed to run across the circle to where his mother was staying and talk to her for a minute. But soon afterwards everyone else had all of a sudden decided to go, and though some had offered her rides, she had declined them. "Thanks anyhow," she had said, as she'd said to Father Fields and his friend. "I'm waiting for someone." She felt as if she might have been waiting a long time, but she was too intimidated to walk back to the enormous house that gleamed beyond the dark lawn in order to ask if Lance could be reached and brought to her. She'd wait here. The air felt too cold. She felt shaky and, hoping it would warm her, she slid back down into the pool water. Stupidly she'd forgotten to take off his sweater and was worried she had ruined it. Before he went, he had sat beside her and kissed her and said, "This sounds crazy, just these few days. I feel different looking at you. You know what I mean."

"Yes."

"I mean, it makes me wonder about just flaking around. And you're just a *baby*, that's what gets me. I mean when you look at me like that, I don't know what

I want to do, grab you, or push you away, or, Jesus
God, what! It gives me the spooks. You know what I
mean?"

"Yes."

Then he'd kissed her again and told her, "Don't
listen to me, I sound like a jerk. Just stay here. Okay?
How you doing?"

Yes, she would wait, because her body had chosen
him, elected him to be the vehicle of her rebirth
through new generations. She huddled down, shivering
in the dark water.

Ernest Ransom shuddered awake on the couch in his
library. Guests on a talk show had laughed into his
nightmare of soldiers lying in the surf near Caen in
Normandy. He turned off the television. Priss must
have gone to bed. The music was gone, there was no
noise at all coming from the pool. He looked at his
watch, but it was only 12:30. In the living room he
found Emerald and Arthur on the couch, examining a
catalog of bedroom suites. They told him they thought
the party had left together, not too long ago, to go do
something somewhere else. They didn't know what, or
where.

Closing the glass doors behind him, the banker
stepped out into the now chilly night. He walked
quickly along the flagstone path toward the trees that
hid the pool. His foot kicked a glass. There among
garden chairs lay plates, bottles, ashtrays, and records,
all strewn everywhere. That Kate! Just to run off and
leave this chaos! Leave half the lights on! Ransom
stepped around the pink flowering azalea and onto the
concrete.

In the shadows of the shallow end, something
luminous drifted against the side of the pool. He
thought someone must have thrown in a lounge chair.
Or a towel. He walked closer. Then he ran. He felt as if
his body were on fire. He could hear his own scream as

he jumped, already reaching for her in the water. His hand hit against her arm and the arm jerked and sank away from him. Not breathing, he bent under her floating body, lifted her up away from the water. Not breathing and his legs giving way uncontrollably so that he kept slipping under, Ransom turned her in his arms, turned her toward the light, and let her head fall back from his chest. Coils of wet hair sprayed across the face, and with strange whooping sounds that he didn't know he was making, in a panic he brushed the hair aside.

Ransom stood in the dark blue water, shaking, and rocked the dead girl in his arms. It wasn't Kate. It wasn't Kate.

CHAPTER
43

"Get that boy out of here, Ernie. Get him home. Is Winslow there? Goddamnit, just grab his arms!" Otto Scaper slammed shut the white ambulance doors into which two attendants had lifted the covered stretcher. Sirenless, it drove out of Elizabeth Circle, where lights now peered from house windows. "Hell! Okay, Lance! Okay, son! Okay!" The doctor pinned the young man's arms from behind and in his huge bear hug lifted him away from the Jaguar, the frame of which Lance was beating with his fists. Scaper held him like that (thinking that at any second his own dry old bones would snap in two) until he felt the other's muscles unclench. Then he spoke loudly into his ear. "You listen to me. You didn't do it. You didn't do it. Are you listening to me? Lance? There wasn't anything you could have

done. Now's the time to act like a man. You hear me?
All right. All right then." The voice softened to a
steady lull. "Okay. I'm going to let you go. There. Now
I want you to go inside with Ernie here and let him give
you a drink. Let me see those hands first. Goddamnit!
Ernie, tell Priss to get this bleeding stopped and put
something on the cuts. But this right one's gonna have
to be X-rayed. Okay, go on. And get out of those wet
clothes, Ernie."

Scaper watched Priss step away from the door to let
Lance and Ransom inside. Then he turned to the others
who still stood at the curb. "Arthur, I want you to take
Evelyn back home now. Limus, just go on home,
please. I don't know what in damnation you're doing
out riding around here on that motorbike this time of
the night anyhow. Everybody go on." The old man
stuffed his hands down in the pockets of the enormous
shabby bathrobe he'd grabbed when he'd run over
from next door as soon as Ernest Ransom had phoned.
Mrs. Troyes was in a bathrobe, too. She held the hem
away from the dew as she went away with Arthur
Abernathy across the lawn.

"Just a minute, Sammy." Scaper called back the
pharmacist, who wore a raincoat over his pajamas.
"Give me a match. Well, thanks for helping out. I
swear, some folks hear a siren and they act like they got
an invitation to a fair." Finally the doctor found a cigar
butt in his bag; he wiped it on his robe and lit it.
"Goddamnit to hell."

The two men stood beneath the stars. After a long
silence, Scaper threw the cigar into the gutter. "Well,
let me go check on that boy. You got any Seconal,
Nembutal, something?"

"At the pharmacy."

"What'd you say? Speak up."

"No. Not here. Ah, wait a minute. Priss Ransom
ought to have some Valium. I filled a prescription for
her yesterday."

Scaper spluttered his lips. "Doctors! All they can think of to do is drug out the fact that life hurts." He rubbed his ear behind the hearing aid. "Sure. Now I'll go on over to Glover's Lane and give that child's mother and father a couple of Valiums apiece, and then I'll tell them we got to drive over to the hospital now because your little girl that's not even twenty years old, that's always been just as healthy and pretty as a picture, your daughter's dead of a heart attack, and don't ask me to tell you why, because there's *no* reason. Just like Hanoi doesn't know and Washington doesn't know what in goddamn hell happened to your son, Bobby. Because there's no lousy reason in this world that makes any sense at all."

Smalter patted the doctor's immense arm. "Otto. She drowned. No one was there, and she drowned. Why do you say heart attack?"

"That child's been in swim camp up at the lake every summer of her life, and she didn't drown in any two feet of water!"

"People do. People get cramps. I'm sorry, but I don't understand."

"Hell! Hell! She was dead when she fell in. Hell's bells, don't tell me my business, Sammy. I know what I'm talking about. This is my responsibility, because I let all this go on too long now, and let people like A.A. and Ernie make me think I was off my rocker or something. I'm going to find that little girl's cocker spaniel tomorrow and run some tests on him."

Disturbed, Smalter looked up with alarm at the broad, crease-lined face. "I don't follow you, Otto. What are you talking about? What's her dog got to do with this? Look, let me go over to the Strummers' with you, all right?"

Scaper shook himself like a bear. "Naw. I'm going now. The fewer intruding the better. Lord knows I've had to say the words too many times in one lifetime. You know, I almost lost that girl's mother in a hard delivery the night she gave birth to Bobby. Listen, you want to help, go see what's keeping Winslow, tell him to come drive his boy over to the hospital. The poor dumb bastard's busted a couple of his fingers on that car hood. Okay, I'm going on over there. Tell Priss to give Ernie one of those Valiums, tell him to go to bed. Next time I tell him, and some others too, there's a serious problem in this town, I want them to think about tonight. Because something's going on, and I don't care if you think I'm nuts or not. I'm right." The old doctor stooped with a grunt to pick up his bag.

CHAPTER
44

No sirens had reached the shoulder of the highway, where Judith Haig sat knitting in one of the plastic-covered green plaid chairs that belonged to her husband's family room furniture. On the rug around her scraps of yarn lay in piles of different colors. It was late; Joe MacDermott hadn't driven her home until his TV show was over. Sarah and she had done the dishes together, then Judith had read to Francis, quietest of the MacDermott sons. He had wanted to sit on her lap until his mother explained that he was too heavy and Aunt Judith wasn't well. Mrs. Haig had been relieved. The boy's large, rimless spectacles reminded her of Sammy Smalter.

This scarf too was in some way connected with the pharmacist. Hadn't she been thinking about him when she began it? Perhaps, at Christmas, should she give him the scarf, just a token gift? No, what would someone think, offered such a ridiculous present, remnants knotted together, a scarf of scraps? It was nothing to give. His eyes were asking for gifts. She had none. She couldn't give him height, or health, or heart's desire. Mrs. Haig walked to her kitchen. Hours ago she had promised her husband not to forget her medication. John had called at midnight:

"Jude? Hi, honey, it's Hawk. Couldn't get you earlier. You had me a little worried so I called Joe. . . . Right. He said you'd been over there. . . . Right. That's what he said. That was real nice of them. You have a good time? Getting out of the kitchen for a while? . . . Good. Honey, you feeling all right? . . . Good. The thing is, Joe said something about how Sarah'd claimed how you'd let Maynard's wife, or whatever she calls herself, get you all upset about him being in jail. That's right where he belongs, and you just aren't in any condition . . . Oh. Oh. Okay. Good. Well, I figured. It just didn't sound like something you'd . . . Well, you know Sarah; you have to divide everything she says by ten. . . . Good. You're probably getting a little lonely on top of everything else, that's all. Been a rough week. I know. You sent some flowers to Mama Marco? . . . Good. Service all right? . . . Good, good. Well, I guess it's just the way things go, honey, just an act of God, poor old Alf, but you can't take things so much to heart. So, listen, I ought to be back tomorrow for sure, around suppertime. The reason I was calling, I've got some great news. Jude, I found it, I *think*. It was the old needle in the haystack, but I think I've hit the jackpot on that engineer's report. It was a fix, hon, and Ransom has got to have been in on it. . . . What? The highway, what do you think I'm talking about? You know, honey, I'm sitting on dynamite. I bet I could get myself *elected* on the ammo I've got now. I could end up in the State Assembly. I'm not kidding, you wait and see. Well, no sense talking about this business over the phone, long distance. I'll tell you all about it tomorrow. . . . Right.

So you better get in the bed. How's the house doing, no problems? . . . Good, Good." He sounded happy. She was relieved.

Judith had been married to John "Hawk" Haig for a long time. She didn't know him very well, though she knew him a great deal better than he knew himself. In high school she had gone out with him because he had been so baffled and unhappy and angry whenever she tried to refuse. As for Hawk, the fact that he had been taunted by his popular friends for being in love with Judith Sorrow was a fact of the same order as learning in his senior year that a damaged kneecap would cost him a college football scholarship, and therefore college. He felt sorry for himself on both accounts. Ironic that he, captain of his team and his class, who could have any girl in Dixwell High, had wanted the one, the only one perhaps, oblivious of, or indifferent to, his public desirability. As ironic as having his knee crushed because he stepped out of a friend's car just when some hot rodder didn't watch where he was backing up. Both were acts of God, punishments exacted (if not for personal sins—like self-abuse and skipping Mass—and Father Crisp had assured the young man they were not—then for the disobedience of Adam and Eve). What could he do but accept the facts?

As for Judith, she had married Hawk for the same reasons that she had dated him. If he had opened the door of his friend's car a moment earlier or later, she would not be Mrs. Haig now. For the football star, rich in collegiate fraternalism, would not have begged her. He would have forgotten Dingley Falls and Dixwell High and her. He'd now live, like Arn Henry, in a Colonial ranch in an executive subdivision with a wife who remembered her years in the sorority as the happiest in her life. He would not have gone to night school while working full-time, he would not still live in Dingley Falls, elected only to the office of police chief in a town where only stray dogs and adolescents required policing. He would not have been outdis-

tanced by lesser men of his class, not be in debt to
rumors of wealth that were canceled along with the
highway on which he might have driven himself out of
insignificance. His property was to have been his baby.
Judith and he had none. She had been relieved when
they were told their barrenness was her fault, not his.
Even so, he was baffled and unhappy and angry at this
latest act of God. Still, he loved his wife, Judith, though
he didn't know her well. He'd always secretly thought
that she'd be a perfect wife for a state assemblyman,
even for a congressional candidate. It was not merely
her beauty that impressed him. She had a dignity and
reserve that awed him. While it cost him comfort, ease,
and even—on the rare occasions when he pushed
against it—frightened him, he took pride in her distance. Her distaste for sex he took to be evidence of her
spiritual superiority; Judith had, after all, been raised
by the holy Sisters. Her passive remoteness in bed
assured him of her purity, fidelity, and indeed en-
hanced her desirability. So whenever Haig pictured his
wife to himself he imagined her not in any intimacy, but
seated, her hands folded, on a dais next to the podium
from which he was addressing his constituents. Only
rarely did the guilty fantasy intrude in which his wife,
sometimes dressed as a nun, was the victim of his sexual
assault.

As for Mrs. Haig, she had no such fantasies. She
tried not to imagine her husband at all, for doing so she
saw his face as the hot rodder's car ground his leg
against metal. She saw his face as he frowned, blood-
eyed, over a textbook at one in the morning, as the
doctor commiserated with their barrenness, as the
nurse pulled the curtain around his father's hospital
bed, as he told her they'd stopped the highway, and
with it his dreams. She did imagine what she might have
done if she hadn't committed the sin of will-lessness
that had led her to agree to marry him. She imagined
returning to the Sisters of Mercy. She imagined going
mad, muffling, behind quilted walls, the screams she

could not will herself not to hear. She imagined being killed by the dogs. And tonight, suddenly, to her confused shock, she found herself imagining what it might be like to be married to Winslow Abernathy. It must be, she thought, because he was coupled in her mind with the girl, Chin Lam, and with the visit to Dr. Scaper's, and so with the question of what troubled her heart—physically and really. The lawyer was a stranger who had involved himself, with kindness. By that kindness they were, in some peculiar way, joined. Behind the communication must lie some sort of unspoken knowledge he had of who she was, as well as her strange, unexpected sense that she knew who this man Abernathy was better than she knew John.

In her immaculate kitchen Judith took her pill, rinsed and dried the glass, then returned to her knitting. She wanted to think of Alf Marco, but she thought of Winslow Abernathy's life, of his ease with wealth and degrees, of his sons—one a lawyer like himself, the other remarkably handsome—she recalled someone laughing in an officer's uniform. The picture hurt her for John, who had neither sons nor ease. She imagined Abernathy's wife, Beatrice Dingley Abernathy, who received letters from charities and almost daily catalogs from fashionable stores. A handsome woman with a kind smile. She imagined her as someone rather like Rose Kennedy, who had once visited the Madder orphanage. Beatrice Dingley Abernathy. She must be the type of woman John would have wanted. A woman of gracious dignity, refined by breeding and education, mother of successful sons, benefactress of charitable institutions, a woman who with her husband had undoubtedly always done quiet good in the world, good like Abernathy's willingness to help Chin Lam Henry. Judith untangled a skein of green yarn. But the man's eyes in repose were heavy with a sad confusion, his hands moved uneasily, his mouth strained for composure. Winslow Abernathy wasn't happy. Why? She imagined a man so troubled by the injustice and misery others endured that no private joy could solace him. She imagined herself.

For Judith Haig imagined too much. The sorrow of the world arrested her heart as the concept of infinity arrests the mind. When Judith watched the news, she imagined each of the stories spilling over the frame of the lenses. Those who had worked a lifetime to own a house that fire or flood annihilated in an hour. "Insurance won't cover it, so I guess we're wiped out," they would say with nonchalant voices and baffled eyes to the television cameras. How could reporters bear to hear it? How could they bear to record the sobs of survivors of plane crashes still in flames; of widows of soldiers lost to war as the women sat politely in their living rooms, telegrams still in their hands; of parents of children that same day lost to disease, lost in hospital wards, in refugee camps, in hungry villages, lost in city streets? How could reporters bear to thrust a microphone up to the sorrow of the world and record its piercing, unending scream?

The Sisters of Mercy had always told Judith she imagined too much. They told her to be happy. They told her that being a Christian did not mean she had to suffer every pain ever felt by her fellow man. They said only Christ could bear to feel so much, and that He did feel it so that she wouldn't have to, so that she could be a happy child. Wasn't she young and healthy, well fed, warm, and graced with prettiness and a good mind? But she could not will herself to stop. They told her it was a sin to despair when God wanted her to rejoice in His gifts. They told her she made God unhappy, too.

Judith tied a piece of black yarn to the green. Then she heard her husband's clock over the family room fireplace, where electric logs glowed orange but never burned. The new old-fashioned clock beat three times into the silence. The bolt was locked, the chain was on. Judith turned off her lamp and forced herself to draw open the new drapes that covered the picture window of John's new house. High in the jet void around her, stars held their places, unmoved by the sorrows of the world. There was the bright star the Sisters had told her to wish on, when, like geese with wings spread, they had rustled on warm evenings down the corridors to bob good night beside each bed. Wish for God's grace and a good Christian husband.

And yet it couldn't be the wishing star that she saw now, Judith thought. In so many years the heavens had shifted. She had been a young girl then, when she had wished for her heart's desire. She had gone to sleep more easily, hours earlier, while Venus still brightened the summer night. While she dreamed that the mystery of her parentage would end happily ever after with the recovery of some beautiful mother and noble father, or the discovery of how the two had died together in some tragic, romantic way, leaving her the sole testament to their love. As she fell asleep then, sometimes she would imagine reunions; the faces of her parents faces of different men and women she had seen in Dingley Falls, or whose pictures she had saved from magazines.

In her prayers tonight Judith didn't wish for her own happiness; it was not something she expected to be given or knew how to want, though she knew (the nuns had told her so) that she had little justification for this failure of feeling. After all, she had never lived in a time, or at least not in a town, in which the streets were strewn with scab-oozing bodies everywhere struck down by plague. There were no rotting heads of those who had displeased arbitrary rulers shoved onto pointed sticks and stuck atop bridges. Never in the night had she or anyone she loved been carted off into slavery because of their color, or marched to the stake because of their faith, or herded to death because of their race. No child of hers had starved while she watched, no lover had been buried in dirt. She had known neither fire nor shipwreck nor earthquake. She had no enemies and could think of no one really that she herself even disliked, except perhaps the appliances store merchant

Limus Barnum, who stared at her surreptitiously with such ugly, naked feelings. She wanted to be able to wish for Limus Barnum's happiness, too, and told herself that she did so.

The star winked at Judith Haig's wishes and pulled a cover of clouds across its face.

CONCERNING SCENARIOS

Larger dramas than Dingley Falls's had their complications as well. The failure of Daniel Wolton and Bob Eagerly to return the helicopter (and pilot) to the U.S. Army post from which they had borrowed it eventually was reported to the chief warrant officer on duty there, who phoned his regimental commander in Transportation Corps, who wanted to know who the hell the jerks were who had taken the thing, and why didn't the CWO just send somebody to find them. Yes, sir, the chief warrant officer did understand that the army couldn't afford to misplace a helicopter that belonged to American taxpayers just because two birds wanted to go for a joyride in it, but, just a second, yes, here it was, a major general had requisitioned that machine for them.

The regimental commander eventually got in touch with the attaché of a major general of the Chemical Corps Division, who interrupted his employer's electronic tennis match with a next-door neighbor. The major general told his attaché to call G-2, the Intelligence Division.

Meanwhile, at army G-2, eyes-only letters were being eyed. On a captain's desk now was a memorandum from Daniel Wolton of the OSS requesting that all relevant material on one Operation Archangel be made available for immediate investigatory purposes. They found a memorandum from Robert Eagerly, White

House, requesting the same material, P.D.Q. Two memorandums, each a week old. The spotlight was on. What was the play?

"Never heard of it," said the intelligence captain.

"Oh, yeah, you know. Long time ago, that test lab, whatever it was, off in the boonies somewhere. I think it closed down," said another intelligence captain.

"I thought that was NIC. Wasn't that old Commander Brickhart's show?"

"Oh, hey, yeah. In Connecticut, wasn't it? But I think CIA was behind the scenes on that one, I don't think it was NIC," said the first, and slapped his thigh. The captains were secretly watching, without the sound, the Orioles play the Yankees on television.

But the phone rang. It was the major general of the Chemical Corps's attaché, who wanted to know if anyone in their theater of operations had any idea where in Connecticut Robert Eagerly and Daniel Wolton might have taken an army helicopter that the regimental commander wanted back, pronto. G-2 pieced the scene together and called OSS, who confessed that Mr. Wolton had failed to attend a dinner party in Georgetown, to the annoyance of his hostess, who had promised everybody that the bachelor Wolton would be there. Later that night G-2 reached Bob Eagerly's personal assistant while he was making love to his secretary in a Silver Spring motor lodge. He told G-2 that yes, Wolton and Eagerly had taken a jet to Hartford together yesterday afternoon.

The attaché had to interrupt the major general's pajamaed ride on an electric exercise bike because G-2 had called back: G-2 was now in a red-alert flapdoodle about that damn helicopter, as the major general later, back on his bike, yelled at his wife, over his motor, and her—she was shaving her legs at the time. He'd told them, sure, he'd gotten Bob Eagerly that helicopter; he'd done it because Eagerly'd said it was hush-hush, and he didn't want the White House officially written into the scenario, said it was just a check on a couple of characters in G-2, that's all. So that's why the general thought G-2 might have an inside line on the story, that's all. So that's why he'd taken the trouble to call them, just trying to help out, that's all. No, he hadn't known Dan Wolton was with Eagerly. No, he didn't know what they wanted the machine for. Bob Eagerly was a golf partner, that's all. Maybe they were shacked up with some broads in some cabin in the woods, wasn't Wolton big with the ladies? No, of course it wasn't funny if a White House aide and a senior official of the OSS disappeared while engaged in the performance of delicate duties. So what was so delicate? What was the score, the script, the scoop? What had they done, defected? Flown the damn helicopter to Moscow? Then G-2 hung up on him, or might as well have, the major general shouted at his wife. Sure, he added to himself, those two lucky stiffs were up to their necks in booze and hookers off in some hotshot hideaway right this minute.

Working long after hours, G-2 called the office of the inspector general, who called the office of the adjutant general, who was out on the Potomac asleep in an industrialist's sloop and could not be disturbed.

The next morning at a U.S. Intelligence Board meeting, a Colonel Harry of the DIA was called by an official of the OSS who wanted to know *re* code name Archangel, was there such a show on the road, and if so, where on the road was it? The colonel thought he could sketch that in for the official, as soon as he checked with his staff. Ten minutes later his staff lieutenant, a stern young woman who could not be persuaded to live for the moment, reported to Colonel Harry in his office at DIA headquarters. "Yes, sir. Code name Archangel. Immunodeficiency laboratory. Preliminary tests apparently were carried out but I can't give you any specifics. Top Secret classification. Initial funding in the area of two hundred M's plus, by DIT of CIA. Original coordinator appears to have been W. Derek Palter. You remember, he's dead now. They said it was suicide. Additional funding thought to be budgeted by Hector Brickhart at NIC in 1969, but there is no way to check their budget on miscellaneous expenditures. Staff, twenty. This is from memory, sir. . . . Yes, sir, we shredded our file on this two years ago. Your orders, sir. . . . No, sir, after the Pentagon Papers. You recall, sir, you said that we were to toss the gray area material overboard. You said the last thing we needed was the GRU to start hanging out our dirty laundry on the roof of the Kremlin. I believe I quote you, sir, that it was the CIA's you know what anyhow so let them get smeared with it and not us."

On his way to meet with an OSS official and a plans division official of the Central Intelligence Agency, Colonel Harry decided he had lost all desire to seduce his staff lieutenant and would from now on confine himself to professionals when he was not being faithful to his wife, which of course was his first priority.

The three officials met in the restaurant of the Hotel Occidental on Pennsylvania Avenue.

"Gentlemen, we have a problem," said Justin Tom, OSS.

Briefly they briefed one another. John Dick, DDT of CIA, opened with a review. Yes, apparently Archangel was still on the computer payroll. Its chief of staff, one Thomas Svatopluk, Ph.D., M.D., had been placed in charge (despite everything the FBI had dug up about him, including his hawking Communist newspapers outside his elementary school) and empowered to requisition supplies from private sources entirely at his discretion from an annual budget of $247,879.50, after, of course, the initial cost of his laboratory. Really, though, the whole thing was a farcically minor bit of business, a Punch and Judy show. Naturally, it might have slipped everyone's minds when briefing the White House, though, naturally, key people at OSS and at DIA had certainly been in the picture all along, and there was no use denying they had (no use, of course, denying it privately to him here). The point was that

CIA had had the impression that Dan Wolton was not, never had been, and never would be one of those key people at OSS, because he had always been on the enemy list as (1) anti-Pentagon, (2) a publicity hound, and (3) not a team player.

"Three," said Tom of Oss, "is truer than we realized, gentlemen. We have another problem. I had Dan's chief aide in on my carpet this morning. The little stool pigeon had enough savvy to lay it all out for me about his boss. Get ready for this. That prick Wolton is State Department! The whole lousy time he's been an OSS man he's been an INR man, too, A lousy double agent. How do you like that?"

They didn't like it. That the double-salaried Wolton should be leaking information about CIA operations to the Bureau of Intelligence and Research while masquerading as a loyal OSS liaison to CIA was double treason! Spying against his own country for his own country!

"So you let the bastard go through OSS files," sighed Colonel Harry, DIA.

Apparently they had. It was there in the OSS files, in fact, that Wolton had come across three increasingly outraged letters from Dr. Svatopluk about Commander Brickhart's Fascist interference with his operation, letters that apparently no one *but* Wolton had taken the time to take seriously. Not only taken the time, but taken the letters, too. The OSS Top Secret file on Archangel was empty.

"So you let the bastard go running to Eagerly," sighed Dick, DDT of CIA.

Apparently they had. But had the bastard kept running, had he raised the curtain over at the Oval Office, or at the Justice Department, or at *The New York Times*?

Apparently not, since not even CBS seemed to know about it. However, as Wolton would shove his mother out of the wings onto the floor of a carnival peep show if doing so would get him into the limelight, the odds were heavy that making a burlesque out of his country's national security would not give him pause. Well, should they wait for his move, or should they move in on him? Should they blackmail him, promote him, transfer him, assassinate him, subpoena him, haul him in on the carpet, or have his townhouse recarpeted free of charge? Should they deny everything, admit everything, beat him to the punch, or let him wear himself out on the ropes? Should they terminate both him and Eagerly? Should they terminate the operation since (a) everyone seemed to think it had already been terminated anyhow, (b) nobody seemed to know it had ever been started, (c) everyone seemed to think someone else had started it, (d) nobody seemed to know who, (e) nobody seemed to know what the operation was. However, the problem with ordering Svatopluk's operation inoperative was (f) nobody seemed to know where the man was, except that he was somewhere in Connecticut. Therein lay the gentlemen's problem. They couldn't simply go around knocking on Federalist doors in pretty little villages and asking the residents if they had happened to notice a CIA germ warfare lab anywhere in the vicinity.

After an interlude of gloom and tax-deductible seafood platters, Colonel Harry remembered his lady lieutenant's remembering that Commander Brickhart, formerly with NIC, was now president of ALAS-ORE Oil Company. They called Portland, who said to call Anchorage. One hour later the commander spoke to them from a CB radio in his skimobile:

"You dumb turkeys make me want to puke. You and your pansy pussyfooting around like a gaggle of gossipy old geese at a Weight Watchers meeting. Flushing this and faking that and dickering in embassy johns with Sony tape cassettes wired to your pricks. I'll tell you straight to your faces, you and all those Socialist fairies up on the Hill have cost us the goddamn ball game. Cuba down the drain. Chile down the drain. Spain, Portugal, Greece, Cambodia, Laos, Nam, the whole shithouse. Lost! The Reds are laughing their butts off at us. It makes me want to puke right here in God's pure snow!"

Yes, very well, they agreed, but hadn't he sometime ago inspected the site of a project coded Archangel, somewhere in Connecticut?

Damn straight he had inspected it. And that's just what he was talking about. After blowing close to half a million of NIC funds, that runny-nosed runt Svatopluk had had the balls to just stand there, picking boogers, and let the Commies call the U.S.A. out on strikes in Nam. But if they thought Svatopluk was going to shoot them the juice now, they had guano in their hulls, because he wouldn't let go of it even if he had any juice to shoot, which the commander doubted. And besides, it was too late anyhow, the winning streak was over. "Let's face it, we kissed it good-bye when we didn't keep going after Nagasaki, just keep on going and blow the Bolsheviks and the chinks right off the map, adios amigos."

Yes, no doubt, but could the commander remember exactly where Svatopluk was?

Hell, no, he'd tell them. In fact, he'd come show them how to shovel out from under the compost they were lying in. And it didn't surprise him one damn bit that they'd lost Operation Archangel since, as he'd just pointed out, they'd managed to lose South America and Southeast Asia, too. And since the spineless military didn't have the balls anymore to get out there and fight for what was ours, he'd turned in his uniform and joined forces with industry. "Because, you listen to me, boys, if we're not going to take it, we sure as hell better get in there and buy it, or let's face it, it won't be long before we end up with a bunch of Jap gooks running Detroit and a A-rab sliding his greasy butt down in the Oval Office." Then before they could properly thank him, Brickhart signed off. Off into an endless day the former naval commander raced, across a sea of snow to investigate reports that a Pakistani painter named Habzi Rabies was defiling the ALAS-ORE pipeline with Modern Art.

Back at the Hotel Occidental over too many mixed drinks, Tom, Dick, and Harry reviewed their reviews. Their conversation was not preserved, for each of the three (under the impression that at least one of the other two had a mike up his sleeve) had a scrambler in his pocket. As a result of their interference, a senator seated in the next booth was spared the embarrassment of rehearing some sybaritic suggestions he was making to a lovely undercover agent in the Treasury Department—which institution happened to be investigating the plump public servant's private investments. Down in the ladies' room with her fully bugged handbag, the lovely T-woman was chagrined to find on playback that she had recorded sweet nothings indeed, a dialog of woofs and tweets. She decided the senator was onto them and that he had a scrambler.

But as CIA, DIA, and DDT browsed over one scenario after another in search of the perfect play, Fate had already concluded the drama and dropped the curtain on Operation Archangel. Far from being at this minute off on their cans with the editor of *Time*, or even up to their necks in booze and hookers, Daniel Wolton and Bob Eagerly (along with the borrowed pilot) were over their heads in the deep water of Bredforet Pond. According to Eagerly's smashed Omega watch, they had been there since 1:33 A.M., Tuesday, June 1. There in the black, muddy stillness, tangled among algae and weeds, lay the carcass of a silt-covered helicopter, property of American taxpayers. Half out of its jagged hole floated dreamily in a Brooks Brothers suit Daniel Wolton, OSS, INR. His leg was hooked through a shaft of steel. Drifting against his Bond Street shoe was the swelling face of Bob ("Bucky") Eagerly. Around them darted the little fish and big fish that lived in the pond. A giant bass swam ponderously by. The minnows fled. The bass lumbered through the metal scaffolding over to the pilot's seat, veered away from the wave of a distended arm, and wriggled back into the inky depths.

Not far away, in a fenced compound beyond some marshes, scientific equipment lay gleaming in a laboratory beside an overturned counter. Sun glittered through a shattered window onto the shelves and counters and floor of broken glass. On that floor, like a yogi on a bed of nails, an ambitious young scientist lay on the jagged pieces of his final experiment. His eyes were red and his tongue was black. Throughout the compound, on floors, at desks, in bed, beside a Ping-Pong table, in front of a refrigerator, next to a sink, lay with protruding eyes and bloated black tongues a whole team of dedicated young men who had just perfected an irresistible, undetectable, instantaneous artificial pathogen, a Lethal Dose$_{100}$, a weapon flawed only, as Dr. Svatopluk had confessed to his Washington visitors before their departure, flawed only temporarily by its extremely short-lived effectiveness. For once released into the atmosphere, it killed everything within its immediate radius, but it was potent only for thirty minutes before structural decomposition took place. Svatopluk had been certain it would work. Sadly, as with many scientists before him, Truth had to suffice as its own reward.

But he had been right. Precisely at 2:07, thirty-four minutes after the tail rotor of an army helicopter had splattered Dr. Thomas Svatopluk against a tree trunk and smashed itself against a building (and approximately twenty-nine minutes after the excruciatingly painful, though rapid, demise of three biochemists, two microbiologists, two virologists, one geneticist, two pathologists, four lab assistants, three security guards, one cook, one handyman, one custodian, and two German shepherd dogs), Modified Q Fever No. 61 (New Q) suffered decomposition and left not a trace behind. There were the corpses, of course; Polly Hedgerow and Luke Packer had, on the following Thursday afternoon, seen two of the victims—the dogs—lying where murder had outrun them. But of the killer, not a trace was left of that chain of molecules.

And what of the chain of command? Could a jurist ever wind his way zigzagging like Theseus through the blind twists of a maze built to protect the vile secrets of a ruler's lust? Could he unravel a skein of tangled lines that would lead him from the lair of the monster straight back into the light of day? How could any thread possibly be brought out of that cave unbroken? Who could prove, who could believe, who could think to imagine a linked chain connecting a luncheon at the Hotel Occidental in Washington, D.C., with the body of a sixteen-year-old girl lying in an Argyle, Connecticut, morgue? Not even the links themselves. Not even the parents of Joy Strummer, in the maddest extremes of their grief, would believe that an adjutant general asleep on an industrialist's sloop in the Potomac was guilty of the murder of their daughter.

No. The Strummers felt guilty themselves. Lance Abernathy felt guilty, Polly Hedgerow felt guilty, to varying degrees every guest at Kate Ransom's pool party felt guilty. But how could any of those who knew Joy thread such a maze, when there was no Ariadne and when the door to the secret, as close to them as the marshlands north of their own hometown, was unknown not only to them but to those whom they trusted to protect Dingley Falls for them? The town doctor had not probed fast or far enough into deaths beyond his analysis. The town editor had not pursued the disconnected highway beyond a pro forma squawk of liberal outrage. The town police chief, while he had plunged into the labyrinthine caverns, had never raised his searchlight beyond his own outmaneuvered shadow. And the man selected by heritage and birth, by appearance, wealth, and congenial authority, to be the preeminent watchman over the town? The man whose flattering provinciality kept him home in Dingley Falls, for he modestly declined all suggestions that he seek public office? Was it likely that Mr. and Mrs. Strummer would charge Ernest Ransom with unpremeditated homicide? The banker might fault himself as careless with his pool, but careless with his country? No. The Bredforet land bequeathed him had been sold to a government whose purposes, unlike those of other nations, were—so Ransom had been taught to believe—all to the good. Only in such a country could one safely remain a private citizen. It was inconceivable that he should see a conspiracy linking the public good with the personal tragedy of a premature death in his Dingley Falls, indeed, horribly enough, in his own home.

And so there was neither guilt nor retribution nor even knowledge anywhere along the chain of command to connect those who had never heard of Dingley Falls with the death of Joy. At Transportation Corps, at Chemical Corps, at G-2, NIC, DIA, CIA, OSS, INR, NSC, on the Hill and in the House, there was nothing for anyone to wash his hands of. Nobody's hands were soiled. There were so many hands, no one even knew how many, or whose joined whose, or in whose hands the end of the thread was held. No one Daedalus has built, no one Theseus can brave the countless corridors of the maze.

The chain of command seemed even to its links to be a circle whose circumference was everywhere and whose center was the shifting, impenetrable cave of the hidden Minotaur, a fabled creation in whose murderous horror no one could sensibly believe. There is no one evil monster to slay. And if a virgin had walked into the labyrinth, who could ever prove that she had not died wandering lost there, had not drowned quite by accident in the great tortuous subterranean caves? The Minotaur deep in his own dreams had never known the human sacrifice was even there.

PART
Five

CHAPTER
45

Already burning, the sun seeped over the ridge that hid the marshland from Dingley Falls's view. In Madder stray dogs gathered to fight one another for scraps of garbage. They rooted in the battered tin cans that littered the trailer camp. When there was nothing left, they trotted away to find a place in the sun. The biggest dog carried a slab of stale, gnawed meat behind the cement blocks that held up Maynard Henry's now unguarded trailer.

What everyone called the trailer park was really a leveled field between Long Branch Road and Hope Street where the Lattice and Goff Chinaware factory had manufactured crockery from 1849 to 1929, when it went bankrupt, and where the empty building had stood from 1929 to 1959, when it was condemned and demolished. What everyone called Madder was really just the working-class section of Dingley Falls, just everything east of where the Rampage crossed under the bridge in the noisy waterfall that had given the town its name and its factories their first power. Just a late Victorian annexation of the brick blockhouses built by the Dingleys to house the men and women who came to work in the Optical Instruments factory during its Gilded Age, and the similar blockhouses built by Lattices and Goffs to house the men and women who came to paint the same patterns on eighty years of crockery, and the frame boxes built by men and women who left behind small farms to become small merchants, so that those who worked in the factories would be fed, clothed, fueled, furnitured, and, eventually, entertained. These men and women came to call their home "Madder" after the man who had ground telescope lenses for the Dingleys from 1862 to 1898, when, to the surprise of his opponent, he had left town to sit with the United States Congress for two and a half terms before his death. Everything southeast of the Rampage had been Lucius Madder's territory because he had fought for it, fought hooligans for the streets, Dingleys for a union, the state for a school, the church for an orphanage, the party for an election. Because it requires more people to work a factory than to own one, Madder had won the right to represent not only the Irish and Polish Catholics who had voted for him, but the Scotch-Irish-English Protestants over on Elizabeth Circle who most emphatically had not.

"Oh, that damn Luke Madder!" William Bredforet used to chuckle at his great-nephew Ernie. "Why, they say C. B. Dingley would puff up red as a gobbler's neck whenever he heard that man's name so much as mentioned. Luke Madder took the whole Dingley plant out once for fifteen weeks on some damn fool safety regulation. Oh, I remember hearing how sometimes Camilla had to get fat old C.B. saddled up quick so he could ride it off before he burst a blood vessel. Only way C.B. could get away from that man was to go try to sell his damn telescopes to Pershing and let the Kaiser's boys blow him to pieces in France. Left the plant to his boy Chuck, and I don't think Chuck ever set foot in it more than once a year for the Christmas party. Why, one time out in the duck marsh my dad and Luke Madder came to blows over President Taft. Well, Ernie, Luke, and Chuck, and C.B., they're all gone now. L and G Chinaware is shut down for good. Dingley O.I. might as well be. It's all gone now."

The descendants of most of the men and women who had come to work in the factories, who had christened their home "Madder's town," and then simply "Madder," had now moved to other homes and bigger factories. There were no longer any orphans in the old orphanage. There were only twenty trailers left in the trailer park, though that was enough for several Dingleyans to want the eyesore evacuated. There were not many inhabitants in the trailers, though there were enough to lead Hawk Haig to call the place a cesspool. Three years ago there had been more, construction workers who had been canceled with the highway and who, unable to find other work in Dingley Falls, had hitched their aluminum wagons to Mustangs, Pintos, and Mavericks and driven away. With wives, children, and in-laws, with broken-spring sofa beds, console televisions, cheap throw rugs, and nappy throw pillows, with velvet paintings of Christ or matadors or stags beside a mountain lake, with chipped plastic dishes, cracked plastic toys, ripped plastic chairs, torn plastic plants, with the chips, cracks, and tears of their lives patched with whatever mending materials the world and their wills provided them (the consolation of those TV consoles often foremost), they had moved out. Some, unable at the scramble of departure to locate dogs or cats—and short of space and food anyway—had left their pets behind, with other failures of the past. The dogs, herding into community, had survived, and bred, and now ran in the pack that so troubled Judith Haig's heart. The lean, restless dogs remained, long after their restless owners had returned to wherever they came from, or had gone on, westward, to whatever they thought they would find. Other highways to build, other land to connect.

A few stayed, including the Vietnam veterans Karl and Victor Grabaski, to take jobs building Astor Heights, the new development just south of Dingley Falls where Carl Marco was constructing traditional homes at old-fashioned prices as fast as he could. Building Cape Cods, Colonials, and saltboxes for those families, like the MacDermotts, who could afford to get out of Madder without having to leave town beneath the mattress tied to their car hood.

There were also two empty trailers in the park; one

was the old rusted teardrop model, where an elderly night watchman at Dingley Optical Instruments recently had been found dead in a cot whose gray sheets were gritty to the touch. The other, beside a brightly colored patch of garden, was the sparkling twenty-five-foot model that Maynard Henry had bought with most of the taxpayers' money he'd saved from three thrifty overseas tours. The rest of the money he'd blown on a week in a Taiwan whorehouse and on black market bargains on a digital watch, a tape deck, a kilo of grass, a carved ivory ball, and a suede jacket. What cash was left he'd shoved, with a grimace of disgust, into the hands of an old scarecrow woman who was squatting in a road near Dak To, brushing flies off a scrawny dead baby. He had subsequently regretted that such an impulse had seized him, since now he was a married man and could have used the money, which in any case had probably been stolen from the woman either before or after she too died. The money would have come in handy, for until his arrest made him a dishwasher for the state, Henry had been for the most part unemployed, a state highway cancellation. Unlike the Grabaskis, he had not found work in Astor Heights because Carl Marco, himself a veteran of an earlier war, would not hire anyone with a less than honorable discharge.

A third trailer, a double-width Silver Dream, was missing one of its residents. There were only five Treecas in it now, because Raoul was in the Argyle Hospital orthopedic ward with both his legs up on pulleys. He'd been laid off anyhow, so being laid up hadn't cost him a job. Raoul hadn't found work at Astor Heights either, because Carl Marco was an American and did not care for Puerto Ricans.

Carl Marco was a self-made man. He had made his father's tiny butcher shop into a supermarket that kept alive the best families in Dingley Falls. He had made his aunt's pastries into a catering service on call for Dingley Falls's best celebrations. He had made his mother's pasta into Mama Marco's Restaurant, where nearly everyone in town ate at least once a month (and Sidney Blossom ate twice a week). He had made Hedgerow Realty solvent by buying it, then hiring Cecil Hedgerow to sell real estate that no one knew Carl Marco owned. He had made his son, Carl, Jr., an ophthalmologist by whipping him through school, year by year. It hurt him that his brothers, the postman Alf and the gardener Sebastian, had not allowed him to make anything of them. It had been painful to see his own blood carrying the mail and carrying compost when the head of the family was perfectly capable of carrying his own blood. Had he not carried the family out of Madder on his shoulders? As soon as Carl, Jr., married his reception-ist, Marco would build them a house in Astor Heights, too. And houses for his girls. As he made money, Marco made plans.

He planned first regional, then national distribution for his mother's spaghetti sauce. He planned to build bungalows on the north arc of Lake Pissinowno on land that Cecil Hedgerow had finally finished buying for him, lot by lot. He planned to turn Lake Pissinowno into the Lake Tahoe of Connecticut, to turn Birch Forest and the marshland into a little subdivision. He believed that sooner or later Dingley Falls must become one more bedroom suburb of the great megalopolitan work force, as the panic to evacuate plague-ridden urban centers grew with the years. Like Pompeiians racing away from the tumbling lava, all those who could afford to flee would crowd the roads leading to nostalgic small towns, where to be mugged, robbed, raped, or taxed to death was only a future nightmare. As each town filled, emigrants would be forced to go farther and farther for refuge. When they reached Dingley Falls, Marco planned to be ready, with sliding doors to decks and Colonial porticos. In Astor Heights he awaited the evacuees, his gas lamp posts already flickering their old-fashioned welcome across yet un-seeded lawns.

But he was sixty. Realistically it was unlikely he
would live long enough to self-make all his plans. Look
at what had happened to Alf, his younger brother. So
Marco wanted to find someone who had wasted no time
making himself, to finish things in his stead. But the
only male of his four children had proved unsatisfactory; his brothers would give him no nephews. He'd
even briefly considered making Cecil Hedgerow his
partner. But unless his own blood gathered his harvest,
why had he labored? Why had he scrounged to grab his
share if there was no one of his own to share it with?
Besides, Hedgerow had been a Madder boy himself, his
mother had sewn other women's clothes. Marco wanted someone above such memories. And so his thoughts
pictured Lance Abernathy soaring high over the northern arc of Lake Pissinowno in a white Piper Cub.
Marco remembered the boy as a five-year-old kinetic
blur through the shining kitchen on Elizabeth Circle,
where, just starting out in the business, he had himself
delivered groceries to Mrs. Abernathy. Lance was a
Dingleyan, indeed a Dingley, a veteran, a sportsman, a
social socialite whom everyone seemed to like.

Marco believed he had the capitol to make Lance
Abernathy his. His eldest daughter, now abroad celebrating her graduation from the Rhode Island School of
Design, was as bright and gifted as she was pretty, and
as accustomed to the best as if she had never even
known where Madder was. Marco planned to ask
Lance to give Ilaina flying lessons when she returned
from Florence. She would become young Abernathy's
partner for life, and consequently so would Carl
Marco. It was time, decided the grocer, to put his house
in order. God had given him a warning, he reminded
himself as he straightened the CLOSED sign on Mama
Marco's Restaurant and wired the new black-ribboned
wreath to the outside of the door.

It was only 6:30 in the morning when he finished. By
seven he would be checking inventory in his office at
the supermarket. Dingley Falls would not stop eating

while he mourned his brother. Now, as he drove up
Three Branch, past his boyhood apartment, on his way
to Our Lady of Mercy to light the candle as his mother
had asked, Marco looked over at the spilled garbage
littering the trailer park. Something could be made of
that lot. Perhaps a plant to process an entire line of
Mama's products. He could even, he decided, as he
pushed a $10 bill into the church collection box beside
the red-bottled candles, he could even put a picture of
Mama's face on the red bottles of spaghetti sauce.
There she would be, smiling in row after row, millions
of smiles in thousands of stores, his blood from coast to
coast. At seven Marco stopped in front of the grimed
brick blockhouse where the MacDermotts lived without enough room, Sarah said, to wear out a crippled
ant. Her son, Joe MacDermott, Jr., was Carl Marco's
delivery boy. He'd decided to give the boy a ride to the
edge of town.

The MacDermotts were a working family. This
morning Tommy (thirteen) was already on the streets—
tubes of news, *The Argyle Standard,* stacked like organ
pipes in his bicycle basket. He had inherited his
position from Luke Packer. Eddie (fifteen) was an
usher at the Hope Street Cinema, which would be
closed for the next week, though Eddie had not yet
been told so. He had inherited his position from Bobby
Strummer, the owner's son. Jimmy (Joe, Jr., sixteen)
was already out making deliveries for Marco's supermarket. Joe, Sr., in Haig's patrol car, had already left
for the police station. Sarah, in a '68 station wagon that
burned as much gas, she said, as the Ku Klux Klan
raiding a minstrel show, was leaving her house at 8:30.
First she had to take Francis (seven) and Billy (three)
to her neighbor—who said she might as well watch two
more while she was at it, but who nevertheless accepted
a token subsidy to help make ends meet. Even so, they
rarely did. Neither did the MacDermotts', or anyone

else's in Madder. If, said Sarah, her own sister had not seen fit in her sunset years to go off and work her fingers to the bone for a dwarf in the mornings and a Frenchman's widow in the afternoons, then she could have left the kids with Orchid, which would have been a heck of a lot easier on everybody. But, of course, Orchid needed to make her own ends meet.

So today, as usual, Mrs. MacDermott was getting ready to drop off her sons at her neighbor's, her sister at Ramona Dingley's, and herself at the Madder A & P. The two women squeezed the two children into the front seat of the patched and spattered car, for its rear was stuffed with a set of secondhand garden furniture Sarah had bought at the Argyle Goodwill. She planned to put it out in her backyard as soon as she and Joe bought a backyard to put it in. She longed to see how it would look on the little patio of the little Cape Cod in Astor Heights that Cecil Hedgerow would give them a special deal on, if Ernest Ransom would give them a mortgage.

As Sarah drove off, Luke Packer bounded down the steps from the far end of the triplex where he lived with his parents and older sister. They were all working people. His sister, Susan, worked for Abernathy & Abernathy. His mother worked for Dingley Optical Instruments—what there was left of it. His father worked at the Dingley Club, where he prepared Bloody Marys for William Bredforet. Luke worked for *The Dingley Day* and the Smalter Pharmacy. He was on his way by bike to the drugstore now, a little early. He wanted to get ahead in the world. "Getting ahead" meant, to people who lived there, getting out of Madder. Getting as far ahead as you could meant going to California, as Sarah and Orchid's brother, and Orchid's children one by one, had all done; gone to where even if, as Sarah said, they couldn't find steady work, at least they could get nice tans. At least they'd gotten out, like Lucius Timothy Madder, who'd had the place named after him, because the men and women who worked in Madder's town had seen him leave it.

When she missed the light at Ransom Circle, Sarah MacDermott decided suddenly to be late for work in order to give her friend Judith a ride. She'd just go catch her at home before she left for the post office. Sarah didn't like the idea of Judith's walking into town when she might, for all anyone knew, have her stroke on the way and fall into the Rampage and get swept down the Falls before a soul could save her. So instead of turning onto Hope Street, she clattered over the old bridge up Goff, east on Route 3, where, between the marshlands on the north and the river on the south, the Haigs' new house thrust itself at the highway.

Jesus bless us, smack dab in the middle of pure nothing, out here with about one car an hour, if that, to look at out that big front window, and a dozen mangy squirrels, if that, to look at you through the back. And poor Judith lonely as Ruth in the wheat fields. What in the name of Mary and Joseph was the sense of getting out of Madder if all you did was build a brand-new good-looking house out where nobody but woodpeckers would ever look at it, and what's more, Joe said they could have had that garrison Colonial in Astor Heights for the exact same price? Anyhow, Hawk must have been out of his head. Which was funny since everybody'd voted him more likely to succeed than even Arn Henry; everybody'd always thought Hawk Haig would set the world on fire; every girl in the class had been green when he gave his ring on a chain to Judith Sorrow. Now it was enough to make the angels weep the Red Sea full of tears with pity to see Judith out here with heart trouble, and having to quit her job, and probably what destroyed her health in the first place was having to walk all that way to work and back, because she'd never had the nerves for driver's ed. And no babies, and a husband with a bad knee that wouldn't even come home after his own wife had to stand there and watch poor Alf Marco drop dead right in front of her eyes, if you can picture that. And now Joe said Hawk had started dropping hints about how he was going to resign from his job, because he had a scheme that was going to make him rich. What was he planning on doing—him and Judith collecting bags of nuts back there in the woods and selling them on the side of the highway? 'Course, if Joe got Hawk's job it sure would help make ends meet. It was criminal the way they couldn't seem to find two dimes to rub together at the end of the month. Not that it didn't make her sick to think that someday something awful might happen to Joe if he stayed in the police business. Her heart was in her throat the whole time she was watching those police shows on TV, the way they kept getting run down by bank robbers and machine-gunned by dope rings. Not that Ransom Bank had ever been robbed, or anybody in town ever run a dope ring (unless Mr. Smalter), but still. Look at that riffraff that lived in that trailer park, whiskey bottles poking out of their trash cans! Her boys were good boys, she thanked God, but if she didn't get them away . . . Riffraff like those Grabaskis and Raoul Treeca, and even Arn Henry's own little brother, Maynard, fighting over that Chinkie.

"Like she was Bathsheba naked in the tub, Lord love us."

As Sarah MacDermott had already dropped off her passengers, she was obliged to address this last remark to an empty car, unless she was talking to St. Christopher, whom she refused to take down from his chain on the mirror, no matter what the Pope said, it was better to be on the safe side. She turned into the Haigs' driveway. She would show Judith her garden furniture, that first purchase, even if secondhand, toward a new life. A life of lawns to sit in, and space to breathe in. A life quiet enough to hear herself think in. Sarah's grandfather had come to Connecticut from Donegal, where there had been space and quiet enough, but where half the roof of their stone cottage lay sinking into the wet earth of the yard, where they couldn't grow enough to eat and couldn't eat enough to grow. He had come to America, where he had at least had a whole roof over his head, even if fortune was less easy to find than song had promised. Sarah's father had been born and had died in Madder. His tiny liquor store had been swallowed by the Great Depression, like Jonah by the whale. Sarah's sister, Orchid, went to Dingley Falls every morning to clean other people's houses. Sarah was determined to go there for good and clean her own. She was determined to sit in a chair on earth that she owned.

She believed that in His own time, Christ the Savior would save the poor. He would march into the banks and flip over the money tables. He would flip the world over so that everyday people like Joe and her would come out on top. She saw no reason why death duties must be paid on the inheritance of the meek. Yet while she was certain that in Paradise the men and women of Madder would sit down with the angels and laugh, in the meantime she was determined to buy a house in Astor Heights. "Joe, if you ask me, God helps those who help themselves. And I know He's going to get me that Cape Cod with the patio, because He wouldn't have brought Grandpa all the way over here across the Atlantic Ocean and then just let the whole thing drop. And I believe in my heart that my daddy and mother are right up there, reminding Him, year in, year out, to bring this family one step further along to getting away from Madder."

CHAPTER
46

Out on the widow's walk of the tallest house in Dingley Falls, Ramona leaned with her cane against the white scroll railing. She could see over the top of Wild Oat Ridge, but there was nothing to see except haze settling on the forest. The invalid had been up since five, fiddling. Fiddling with boxes of possessions she kept meaning to pack up for the Thrift Shop, or for Orchid, or for whoever would take them. Fiddling with medications for her stomach, which had resented last night's unfamiliar pizza. Fiddling with her will and with theology.

Miss Dingley was furious with the Deity this morning. Like a thief last night He had left her future behind to snatch up instead the handsomer booty of a youngster's. If we had to go out at all, we should at least, she grumbled, leave in the order in which we came. But now even children were being pushed ahead of her. God was behaving like the body porter in a Japanese subway she had seen on television. He didn't seem to care whom He shoved through the snapping doors. Sammy's news about the girl's drowning had upset her more than she would have expected. What if it had been Polly Hedgerow? What if Luke had returned in the dark to tell her that Polly lay drowned in Bredforet Pond, because of an old woman's folly? No sense to say it couldn't happen, no doubt the Strummer girl's parents had thought the same. Hard to believe in something absurd as death happening to your own. But it happened all the time. Roof collapses on a school-

house. Camp bus plunges into a ravine. Sudden fevers.
Children gone in an instant while she lingered on and
on. Unfair. Unfair. What kind of game was God
playing? Fouls everywhere.

"Oh. Sammy. Startled me. Sorry. Made you come
all this way up. Breakfast ready?"

In his three-piece seersucker suit, Sammy Smalter
came to the railing to see the new day.

"Looks to be a scorcher, Sammy. Roast in that vest
and tie. Don't know why you bother. Nobody cares
anymore. Half the people appeared to be traveling in
their underwear last time I took a train into New York.
Whenever that was."

They went down in the elevator to Orchid O'Neal's
breakfast, served on a vast black mahogany table
designed, Ramona said, to seat twenty uncomfortably.
"Made up my mind. Now Sammy. If you're sure you
don't want any part of it, plan to talk to Winslow today.
Some coffee?" Here without preamble Miss Dingley
returned to a conversation about her estate begun in
1973, but, after seven years with his relative, Smalter
was generally able to decipher her terse code.

"Have you something in mind?" he asked.

The old woman rubbed her hawk's nose with the
edge of her cup. "Cecil Hedgerow's girl."

Smalter nodded slowly.

"Liked her grandma Miriam. Suspect I was jealous
of her mother; Pauline Moffat was a flower. Always
made me feel like a hulky Leviathan, beached and
flopping on the shore. True, Cecil's a quitter, but he's
had a hard time of it. I'm sure he's got nothing set
aside. Girl like that ought to have the best chance she
can. Ought to know what it is that's not worth having."

"Sounds reasonable."

"Odious to think of the government frittering my
money away on bombs. The Abernathys don't need it.
Arthur's got Emerald's money, and Lance ought to get
a job." She took three more pancakes and poured
syrup over them. "Don't say anything," she warned

him. "Why should I diet at my age? . . . And I'm too selfish for anonymity. My father, Ignatius, would have left the whole estate to a herd of Catholic lepers in Africa if Willie Bredforet hadn't threatened to have him committed. But few of us are saints."

Smalter smiled around his yellow pipe and puffed out, with smoke, another of his utterly ignored poetical quotes. "'No doubt there's something strikes a balance . . .' No, thanks," he refused offers of seconds.

"Much more disciplined than I am. Impressive, but don't gloat. So. What do you think of my plan? Plan to ship Polly abroad. Then put her in a good school. Sometimes wish I'd gone. Couldn't bear to be indoors long enough though. Ignorant now. So. Plan to leave Orchid a fat check. Plus her salary for life. Put the rest in trust, or whatever Winslow can figure out to keep the government off it. Give it to that girl. Why not? You agree?"

Mr. Smalter, polishing his spectacles on the wide linen napkin, wondered, bemusedly, if he shouldn't leave *his* money to Polly's friend Luke Packer. Then they could be shipped abroad together and both be sent to good schools. Smalter did not take very seriously Ramona's abrupt decisions about her estate. Past testaments had ranged from bequests to him and Lance, to Prudence Lattice, to a tennis camp, and to the Historical Society for the maintenance of the town green. He suspected she made these announcements to enjoy the pleasures of beneficence prior to death. "What about Cecil? Your taking charge of Polly's life because you've got the money to do a better job than he can might hurt his pride."

Miss Dingley shot backwards in her wheelchair to swoop the coffee urn off a mahogany sideboard. "Let's hope the man has more sense than to sacrifice his daughter's future on *that* altar!" She poured two cups. "Pride! *Pphht!* I'll tell him he's got a choice between my leaving it to Polly. Or to that American Nazi magazine that Barnum fellow used to try to get you to subscribe to. How's that? . . . Supposed to be a joke, Sammy."

Smalter put his glasses back on, looping the gold frames around his ears, and stared up at the invalid. "Sorry. I don't see the humor in mocking the fact that Cecil's mother was Jewish."

"Oh, stop moralizing. You think that's mockery? Sammy, you never could let yourself laugh at folks. Should, you know. Laugh at me, and yourself too. All of us and our antics must be pretty humorous to Somebody. Might as well go along with the joke." Miss Dingley threaded her napkin through its heavy silver ring.

"Some things don't lend themselves to laughter."

"You're a tad on the sanctimonious side, Sammy. So was your great-grandma Bridget. That same prissy, pursed-mouth look. For a parlormaid born in the slums of Limerick, Grandma was an odious priss at times."

Smalter's ears turned a dark blood red. Pushing the heavy chair in, he stood beside it and looked over at the woman he called "Aunt." She stared into her coffee. Finally a sigh rumbled through her lips. "Pay no attention, Sammy. Bad night for us both. I'm old. Mean. Angry I'm old. Impatient. Legs don't work. Hands can hardly unbutton my clothes. Be back in diapers soon. Have to hire a nurse to change them. Then you tell me the Strummer girl's gone." Ramona hit the arm of her wheelchair. "I'm here. She's gone. And that monstrous Almighty Idiot God . . ."

"Well." The little man placed his hand near hers on the table. "Ah, well, Ramona, what good does it do us to say there's no justice? What good?"

"What good? It's the *truth!* Oh, Sammy, Sammy, how can you of all people think otherwise?"

"Sometimes I imagine that it's gone beyond His capacity, that He's simply lost control."

"Why don't He admit it then? Let Him resign."

Smalter laughed. "For a woman who insists that God is merely a tyrannical male myth, you're a tad on the anthropomorphic side, Ramona." He tapped her hand quickly with his. "I'm off to work."

"Why do you go to that idiotic pharmacy if you're so rich?"

"Ask Emerson."

"Pphht! Who you going to leave *your* money to, Sammy, do you know?"

"I'm going to leave it to you. God's in no hurry to listen to what you're planning to tell Him; you'll outlive me by decades. But you're wrong, you know. You think you can subpoena the universe to answer your charges. But God's like the government. He can't be sued."

When he pulled the cord to turn on the stockroom light, Mr. Smalter found Luke Packer huddled on a footstool. Quickly the boy picked up a cardboard box and, with a muttered greeting, turned his back on the pharmacist. He moved like someone who continued to function after having, unawares, suffered a concussion. Immediately Smalter realized what he cursed himself for not having remembered earlier, that he had once seen Luke and Joy Strummer in conversation, and that the boy would have naturally been given the news. When he returned to the front of the store, he continued to curse—the fact that the girl had to die, the fact that Luke had to know and to come to terms with her death, the fact that anyone had to come to terms with death, whose terms were so unconditional and outrageous, the fact that everyone's body (whether beautiful like Joy Strummer's, or deformed like his own) was a rotting jail imprisoning, then killing, its captive. He cursed the fact that he was placed in a position of initiating a conversation in which he must comfort Luke. Such conversations struck him as inevitably awkward and embarrassing to both sides—"I'm deeply sorry"; "Thank you for your sympathy"—for they fell necessarily into rote memorizations like other polite forms of address. Smalter believed strongly in standard formalities, handcuffs on the flailing assaults of the savage heart. But good manners, he acknowledged, could not mix with the bluntness of death. He had nothing polite to say about such a barbarian. Still, he could not pretend to read a newspaper while he could hear, twenty feet away, the methodical stacking of supplies, the never interrupted movement with which he knew Luke was striving to hold off that old ugly fact that is so rightly antithetic and incomprehensible to the young. On the other hand, nor could he, railing against loss, rush back there, crush Luke in his arms, and soothe him with the salve of tears. Father Highwick could have, but Mr. Smalter could no more howl through the facade of his social self than he could have danced naked on Dingley Green. He found it difficult to go back into the supply room at all, but impossible, finally, not to. Luke, he knew, had too few words to understand, himself, much less to say, what he felt. Smalter had too many, and none would do.

"Excuse me. Luke? What say we let things go for the day and close up?"

Luke stacked one carton of mouthwash on top of another. "Okay. If you want to." He squared the edges precisely. "All right, just let me finish."

"Luke? I heard the news of your friend. . . . I'm deeply sorry, deeply sorry. I don't know what I can say." He placed his hand on the box on the opposite edge from where Luke tore at some loose tape.

"Thank you, Mr. Smalter." He had the defenseless smile of someone trying not to cry. "Kind of crazy, isn't it?" His eyes filled with the question, then wetness brightened their color, and he turned away to pick up another box. Smalter stared at it. Inside were twelve kits that promised to remove all signs of age from the buyers' hair. "Yes. It's kind of crazy."

"If you wouldn't mind though, you know, I think I'd like to keep working back here. If you close up. Would that be okay? I want to keep busy, I guess."

"Yes, that's always best."

The Tea Shoppe to which Smalter retreated was not

open. Its early hours, like his pharmacy's, depended on the proprietor's spirits or the weather. He walked on to *The Dingley Day,* where he interrupted A. A. Hayes in the compilation of a comparative list. "Do you know," said the editor, looking up at the door from his scratch paper, "that if I were Keats I would have been dead for twenty-three years? Alexander, fifteen. Christ, fifteen. If I were Martin Luther King, Jr., I would have been shot nine years ago."

"Pru's not open yet. How are you, Alvis?"

"Rotten. Now if I were Marx or Einstein, I'd have a whole lot of time left, not that it'd make a damn bit of difference. Some people make a *dent.* Not likely I'll be included in that number. What a pissass thing, Sammy. What a hell of a thing."

Smalter noticed Hayes's paper cup and bottle. "You mean Joy Strummer."

"She and my girl were in school together. All of us known her since we've been up here. I swear I'd get half a mind to take Otto seriously about this town being attacked by something, if the news from the rest of the world wasn't equally insane."

"Otto says she didn't drown. Is that what you mean?"

"Somebody killed her, I suppose."

"No. He says she had a heart attack."

"Oh, sure! I'm beginning to wonder if Otto ought not to be put out to pasture."

"It does happen."

"Doubt it makes a hell of a lot of difference to Jack and Peggy Strummer one way or another. 'Scuse me, how 'bout a drink?"

"It's a little early for me."

"After nine, isn't it?"

All at once there shot through Dingley Falls an extraordinarily loud noise. It sounded like a gun, which made absolutely no sense in such surroundings. Across the green half a dozen people, in static arrest, stared from the steps of the bank, from the library, and from the post office. The two men hurried out of Hayes's office and trotted down the sidewalk. The sound cracked around them again. They ran to Barnum's Antiques, Hobbies, and Appliances, where a shaded door said CLOSED. "Limus? Limus, are you in there?" Smalter rapped with his fist, then shook the door. Hayes ran around the side of the store, but the back was locked.

"Can you see up in that transom window?" Smalter asked.

Hayes jumped. "No. It's filthy. You think that ass has killed himself?"

"I'd be less surprised to hear he'd killed somebody else, all that neo-Nazi slime he reads."

"I didn't know there were any Jews in Dingley Falls *to* kill," Hayes said.

"Maybe you ought to kick the door in. It looks pretty flimsy."

"Well, I don't know, I hate to butt in. Hell. Here goes." But as the embarrassed editor swung his foot back, the door rattled, and in its crack Barnum's face glared at them.

"Hey! What do you think you're doing? Get the hell away! Were you trying to kick in my door?"

"What's the problem, Limus?" asked the pharmacist.

"You'll be the one with problems if you don't learn how to leave me alone. Trying to bust in here on private property. How come you got so much time to spend harassing me, Smalter? Why don't you go join a circus?"

"We heard a gun," Hayes said. "Somebody in there?"

"Me. I'm in here. I was cleaning my gun, okay? Any crime against that? It went off." Sun rushed in the crack so that Barnum's pale eyes kept blinking at them.

"Went off twice?" Smalter snapped.

"So what? I was checking it out. I got a license. Maybe I felt like doing a little target practice. It's my store, isn't it? If I felt like it, I could blow holes in every crummy piece of junk in here. How do you like that, huh?"

"Not if it disturbs other people," said Smalter. -

"So do something about it, if you think you can."

Hayes leaned over Smalter's head. "You didn't shoot yourself through the shoe again, did you?" He grinned broadly.

"Fuck you." Barnum slammed the door in his face and locked it.

The editor waved at the people across the green. "Everything's all right, y'all. Nobody hurt." Motion restarted.

Frowning, Smalter straightened his bow tie. "I dislike that man. I can't tell you how offensive I find him."

"Oh, hell, he's his own worst enemy, Sammy, don't let it bother you. I think he's nuts. His commercial was on TV last night, you know the one where he reaches out his hands into the camera like he was going to haul us right through it into his pocket? His eyes look like he's nuts with greediness! Then half the time he's got the damn store shut up. Mighty funny way for a man who says he's all business to run a business," Hayes added, as the two men returned to their own.

Orchid O'Neal found Miss Dingley at her desk in the parlor, beside her an elephant's foot wastepaper basket into which she dropped the paper waste of forgotten memorabilia. "Telephone, ma'am, it's the young priest, in a pitiable state."

Father Fields was in a pitiable state. Sin lay on him like slabs of stone. Before dawn he had awakened to find himself lying beside the naked body of Walter Saar. There rushed upon him the remembrance of pleasure. Pleasure ·he had dreamed of for years. Feelings too true to condemn. Doesn't God want us to be happy? he had kept asking himself as he drove the church Lincoln up Cromwell Hill Road and hoped no

one saw him go past at 5:00 A.M. Next he woke up
horrified in his narrow bed when he heard the long,
nagging honk of a car horn. It was 8:30! He'd missed
morning service! For the first time. Dear God, what
would the parishioners (though, thankfully, there were
only three at the most) think? What would the Rector,
what would God think? Heart pounding, Jonathan
rushed into his clothes, ran across the garden to the
vestry, pulled a surplice over his head, and raced down
the aisle to draw back the iron bolt on the doors. There
stood Mrs. A. A. Hayes in a pink sundress, looking at
his unshaved face and uncombed hair precisely as if she
had seen him last night through the window of the
headmaster's bedroom. Her son Charlie was a student
there. . . . Was it conceivable that she, an early riser
. . . The curate forced himself to be rational.

"It's just me." June Hayes frowned. "I was here a
little while ago, but I guess I must have just misunderstood your little notice up here about daily Mass, and
then I telephoned, maybe y'all should have the phone
company check yours, see if something or other might
be the matter with it. I feel awful dragging you out of
bed, but something's happened."

What had happened was that Peggy Strummer's
daughter had drowned last night in the Ransom's pool.
Mrs. Hayes said she'd recalled that Peggy had said how
grateful she was to Father Fields for his efforts about
Bobby, and so she thought, if he wouldn't mind, could
he follow her down to Glover's Lane as soon as
possible. Peggy was quite beside herself and they were
worried she might do something dangerous. This
hostilely explained, Mrs. Hayes hurried back to her car.

In a back pew of the shadowy church the curate
crumpled to his knees. How could that news be true,
and this building have any meaning? Joy? Why had he
left her at the Ransoms'? Why had he gone to Saar's?
How could he have done what he did there while she
was *dying?* If he had stayed, she might be alive. If he'd
only come home, he'd have been here if her parents

had needed him. Choosing himself, he had failed them all. How many had arrived to find the doors, the doors of the *church*, locked against them? Minutes passed and Jonathan fought to say, "Take her to Your peace, give her parents peace. Don't ask me to justify You. Just help me."

Miss Dingley told Orchid to get the car ready. The curate had called from the Strummers', where Dr. Scaper had given Mrs. Strummer a shot to make her sleep. Would she go see Polly Hedgerow? Because a woman might be better able to comfort the girl about her friend's death. Polly had refused to come out of her room, and her father had simply sat all morning in the kitchen drinking one cup of coffee after another, as if the pain of having to tell his daughter about Joy had dried his flesh away and left him dust. Miss Dingley said she would go at once.

As she waited in her wheelchair by the white frame fence at the foot of her lawn, she listened to an irascible cardinal. In the middle of her yard there was a Victorian birdhouse atop a pole; it was a replica of the ornate mansion behind it and was the size of a large dollhouse. The red-tufted cardinal chirped crankily out of a third-story window. "What do *you* want?" Ramona asked him. "A television set?" Ignoring his landlady, he flew off to attach himself like a cluster of dusty berries to the high shrubs that bordered Mrs. Canopy's white carriage house.

Next door to Miss Dingley's was Otto Scaper's house. Sebastian Marco sat there on the white wooden fence that ringed the doctor's huge old mulberry tree. The gardener sharpened his shears. "Mourning his brother, God bless him," sighed Mrs. O'Neal as they drove past. Next door, *The Argyle Standard* (left by the housekeeper's MacDermott nephew in the brass letter slot beneath the brass eagle knocker on the Ransoms' orange front door) fell out when Ernest Ransom opened the door. He had an American flag under the arm of his jogging suit. The eight orange-shuttered front windows gave the house an almost Caribbean air, like a Colonial hotel in the West Indies. How Ernie's wife talked him into allowing her to have those shutters painted orange, when they'd been black for two hundred years, was one of the mysteries of married life unfathomable, Miss Dingley concluded, to the unwed. Standing on the white wooden milk box, Ransom ran up a Bennington flag beside his door. A crescent of stars above the number 76 unfurled in pure bright color. Ransom set off jogging down his walk. I'm sure he thought about it, Ramona said to herself. And I guess he doesn't see any impropriety in going for a run the morning after a guest dies in his home. Well, but he's right. Life goes on.

Next door a newspaper was stuck in the brass ring in Evelyn Troyes's white front door that was set between two flat Doric columns to which two brass lanterns were attached. The lanterns matched the lamp on the post at the end of her lawn, up which now another of Mrs. O'Neal's nephews carried a cardboard box filled with Marco's groceries. "Your family appears to have staked out Elizabeth Circle as its territory. Isn't that another one of your nephews, with the groceries?" Ramona pointed at the jaunty teenager, who had left the radio on in his truck. The street music clashed with gleaming white brick and manicured lawns.

"They're good boys," vouched Orchid.

Out on Cromwell Hill Road, Ramona spotted two small women who walked a block ahead of the approaching car; between the two loped a huge black dog on a red leash. "Who's that with Pru? Stop. Blow the horn, Orchid. Pru! Pru! Want a ride? Take you to town. Who's this? Hush, dog! Nothing to get so fired about. Get down!"

Miss Lattice motioned Chin Lam to pull Night away from the Firebird's roaring noise and walk him ahead while she stepped to the window to speak with her old acquaintance. "Ro, dear. Good morning, Orchid.

Thank you, but we'll walk on. So short a way to bother. We were up at St. Andrew's earlier, but the doors were locked! Do you know why? Now, I'm afraid we're running very late."

"Who's this we? Who's that girl? What happened to her eye?"

"Her name's Chin Lam." Miss Lattice leaned into the window and whispered. "Oh, it's just a tragic situation, Ro. Her husband's in prison and Winslow's trying to get him out, though if he can't, really it might be for the best. He hit her."

"What?"

"Yes. Isn't it? I believe Mr. Henry tried to murder somebody. Chin, she's Vietnamese, but the nicest young girl you'd ever want to meet anywhere. There's no excuse to brood, but I had been very, very low about somebody's killing Scheherazade."

"What? Somebody killed your cat?"

"Winslow wasn't sure but I am. And I'd been so depressed about it is what I mean that having Chin with me has really been a help. But, of course, it's just for a few days."

Ramona was annoyed to find herself so thoroughly uninformed about her town. Obviously, she snorted to herself, she'd been out of touch the last ten years or so. And now! Folks trying to murder cats and each other, war refugees with bruised faces, children drowning, Beanie and Winslow quitting after thirty years, government compounds, Otto's theory that something, who knew what, was wrong with the very air or water or whatever. She was losing control of Dingley Falls. Perhaps while she sat crippled in her father's mansion, her birthplace, her namesake, her town, had gone as mad as the rest of the world. "Hideous to think of," she said aloud.

"Yes, isn't it? I feel so sorry for her."

"What's she doing here, Pru?"

"She came here after the war," said Miss Lattice, as though that were an explanation. "Now we simply don't have any idea what's going to happen. Mrs. Haig (you know, at the post office), really a very nice woman, I'd never actually known her except to say hello. Not at all what you'd think, given, well, years ago I did hear, I suppose it was Gladys Goff, that she was, well, a love child. No shame to her, of course. She's been kind about Chin. And so has Winslow."

Miss Dingley peered into the sun at the young Oriental woman who waited down the road with the German shepherd. "Handsome-looking. Work in your shop then?"

"Oh, she's doing wonderfully well."

"What about her own home? Got one, hasn't she?"

"Yes, but, well, Ro, she was out in that awful trailer park where my papa's plant used to be. All alone. Frightened to death. Anything might have happened to her. Of course, I don't have much to offer, but she's welcome to stay as long as she wants to. Really I just couldn't bear the thought of her going back there by herself. Not to Madder."

The two women walked into Dingley Falls with the large black dog. At the end of the green they saw Judith Haig in front of the post office, where she was attempting with some difficulty to attach the government flag to its pole. A breeze flapped the cloth around her legs, and breaking free of Miss Lattice's leash, Night raced at the moving colors. Judith froze, trapped in the cloth. "Night, come back here this minute! You, Night! You!" To her surprise, and possibly his, Prudence Lattice's frail peremptory voice stopped the dog; he wheeled around. "I go help," called Chin Lam. She ran to the post office in short, easy strides and caught up the fluttering corner that Judith had dropped. Together they raised the Bicentennial American flag over Dingley Falls.

CHAPTER
47

Everybody had always told Lance Abernathy that he was brave, and he had believed them. As a child he had never cried at shots, scrapes, or splinters, not at the dark, or a bully, or new classrooms, not even when he broke his collarbone trying to water ski off a pier at Matebesec Cove. While Arthur had vomited into the bushes after their father ordered them inside for a spanking (they had thrown Miss Lattice's Persian cat, Xerxes, into the clothes washer and watched him go mad with terror), Lance had laughed at the punishment. To be thrashed didn't frighten him, to be knocked to the ground and pounded in the kidneys on the football field didn't frighten him. Neither did marching to the headmaster's, taking a girl on a dare up to the parking lot beside the Falls; neither did dangling from a rope on the sheer side of a cliff, or swooping among thickets down a ski slope, or passing a bus on a hill in his Jaguar, or facing the cynical dean of his college, or flying through enemy flak high above the hazy, humid mountains of Vietnam. He'd met every challenge that centuries of his peers had devised to test him. He wasn't afraid to fight, drink, dive, speed, steal, flunk, screw, or, finally, and from eighteen thousand feet, kill.

Over the years of his developing manhood, Lance had collected the tokens of successful rites of passage. Black eyes, sprained ankles, broken arms and legs, suspended licenses, a pyramid of beer cans, lettered sweaters, stolen traffic signs, and, as he said, add it all up, more cherries than crabs. Here in his bachelor quarters, the second floor of the family carriage house, he lay among his relics. Chair lift tickets hung from his sky-blue parka like scalps. Bright strips of ribbon were pinned to his air force jacket. Citations for speeding decorated his walls. This morning he lay on the bed in his chieftain hut surrounded by testaments to all the exams he had passed: his old gold and tin and plastic trophies, his old medals and badges, and pictures of old girlfriends hanging like diplomas over his desk.

He lay and stared at his hand in its creamy plaster cast, and he confessed to himself that he was afraid to look at the faces of an unassuming middle-aged couple who were too frightened to ride in a plane, much less fly one. He was scared of a man who was in awe of Mr. Ransom, when Lance didn't hesitate to call the banker "Ernest" although (because) he knew it offended him. Scared of two people who could not bear to watch the war on television, much less fight or have their son fight, in it. He was afraid of Mr. and Mrs. Strummer, whom he had scarcely met.

What could he say to them? What could they answer? When someone in the squad lost a friend, you said, "Tough luck, man," or "Hey, listen, that's real bad shit," or "Let's go zap some of those little bastards for so-and-so," or, best, you just left the guy alone. But he couldn't walk into the Strummers' living room and say, "Tough luck, man" to Joy's father. There wasn't anything he could say. He'd just leave them alone.

Lance spun himself off the bed, his left arm raised. He pulled on Levi's and a T-shirt, slid his feet into loafers. He dumped drawers of socks, shorts, and shirts (put there by his mother) into a leather satchel. He scooped jackets and slacks from a closet, racquets and balls, rods and tackle from the floor. All of it he flung into the Jaguar. Its seats were already hot from the 6:00 A.M. sun. Then he strode across the damp lawn and eased open the back door of the big house, relieved to find his father still upstairs. A glassed-in summer room was green with flowering plants. Lance took to its round white table a quart of milk and six dinner rolls. Finally, in his father's study, he found paper and a pen and, while he ate, wrote for the first time in five years, "Dear Dad."

Thanks for getting me fixed up last night. Hand doing okay. What hapened got me down pretty bad. No way probally I can help here. Don't know what to do, accept get away for awhile and try to get my head together again. Would you do me a favor, and maybe send some flowers to her folks. Here's some cash. I'm going up to see Phil Lovell in Hyannis (from U. Mass. You met him.) I'll write. Thanks, Dad. I'm sorry about you and Mom. Hope it works out okay for you both. Take it easy okay. Lance.

He folded the paper, then, after pointing the pen a long time at a second sheet, wrote to his mother for the first time in two years.

Dear Mom. Sorry about last night. I was out of line barging into Mrs. C's. Tell her I apologise, okay? I found out something pretty horrible hapened at the party while I was gone. A girl drowned in the pool. She was my date. It's the worst thing I guess that's ever happened to me so I just honestly don't know how to cope with it, you know what I mean? I feel like I'm dead. I'm shoving off up to Phil's families' place and try to get my head together again. Maybe we'll go down to Gautamaula (sp.) Phil knows this co. that needs some guys who can fly supplies in and out for them. Maybe I'll try it. This girl's parents are the Strumers, over on Glover Lane, I don't know if you know them but maybe you could tell them how sorry I am. I wish it hadn't hapened, that's all. I'd give anything if I just hadn't taken her over there. Or I should have stayed, instead of acting like a jerk over at Mrs. C's and driving you up a wall. Mom, you know what I mean? I'm going to shove off now. I hope it works out so you and Dad can get back together. If that's what you want. You have to go with what makes *you* happy. But anyhow I love you. Take care of yourself. Lance. P.S. If you decide to go off, write me, okay, c/o Phil. P.S. I'm sure Dad does love you. You know, he's just so quiet. P.S. I love you more than anybody.

All he found in his wallet was a $20 bill. He left it on the table beside his father's note. The letter to his mother he pushed into Tracy Canopy's large black mailbox. It sat on a pole beside the white fence that bordered the clipped hedge that bordered the white house. Nothing stirred in all the white and green of Elizabeth Circle, for Lance had left before the hour of newsboys and grocery boys. Now nothing there but birds worked for a living. Nothing moved but light glinting on all the old brass, and a cardinal that hurried through the debris in Dr. Scaper's roof gutter like a shopper at a bargain basement sale, frantic with greed.

Crowded with sports clothes and the instruments of sports, the crimson Jaguar fled as silently as possible past the testing grounds of all Lance Abernathy's earlier triumphs, past the playing fields of Alexander Hamilton, past the courts of the Dingley Club, past Lake Pissinowno. If he could have brought back Joy by parachuting into an enemy fortress, or jumping his car over a chasm, or taking on, singlehanded, a dozen assailants large as Goliath, he would have done so, smiling. But Death would not fight with him, and there was nothing he could do about it. He had never been initiated into the kind of battle that Jack and Peggy Strummer now waged. Free of the town, the Jaguar leaped into speed as the sun rose bold and orange like an explorer's balloon above Wild Oat Ridge.

"Beanie, dear, I don't think you slept a wink. Go back to bed."

"No, I'm fine. . . . Do you have a sponge mop? Tracy, I'm sorry. Where's your mop? I could run over this floor a little."

"For heaven's sake, you make me feel slovenly, like I belonged in an Irish shantytown. Please, Beanie, go lie down."

"Am I bothering you?"

"Beanie, Beanie, of course not. Well, yes. I'm worried about you, that's all. Oh, all right, it's in the closet by the dishwasher." Tracy turned back to her secretary, where she was writing a letter to Babaha Tarook, who should be back in Lebanon by now. But she couldn't concentrate. What should she do with Beanie?

Last night from her own room Tracy had heard Lance say things to his mother that sounded like lines by one of the angry new lowerclass playwrights. Horrible things that had finally driven Tracy, trembling, into her robe, then down to the living room, where she told Lance flatly that he had both shocked and disappointed her. Then he had begun to say those things to *her*, his godmother, and the ultimate outcome was that she had been forced to show him the door, as the old melodramas used to say.

Afterwards, Tracy could not help but hear stifled sobs from her guest room until 3:00 A.M., when, at last, she'd fallen asleep, *Play It As It Lays* on her lap. At nine she'd waked to the sound of her vacuum cleaner; she'd dressed to the clatter of breakfast dishes downstairs. "Where in the world did you find all this stuff?" she asked Beanie as she surveyed her table neatly cleared of her pottery works and laden with what looked like the repast before a British fox hunt.

"Oh, in the refrigerator. And around. Hope you don't mind. . . . I didn't want to wake you."

Over zucchini omelets and ground lamb patties, the two discussed an idea of Tracy's that she had begged Beanie to sleep on. It was that Beanie and she should leave for England within the week. Having placed the ocean between herself and both Winslow and Mr. Rage, Beanie could better judge from this more remote perspective just what her decision should be. "I think we'd have a wonderful time, and you'd have a chance to see how you really feel."

Beanie frowned. "I know how I really feel. I don't see why people always think that if they get on a train or a plane and travel far off someplace they've never been, then all of a sudden they'll know what they feel. I already know exactly what I feel. I love Richard. What I don't know is what would be the fairest thing to do about it. I'm sorry."

Hastily Tracy corrected herself. "Yes, of course you know, but I meant, time lets things settle down. While you're gone, Winslow and the boys can adjust to the idea, before you and Mr. Rage . . ."

"Richard."

"You and Richard . . ." Mrs. Canopy realized she had no term for whatever Beanie and "Richard" planned to do. She didn't think they knew themselves. Marry? Become engaged? Live together? She decided on "Before you two locate yourselves."

Beanie stood by the bay window. She wore a pair of Winslow's old denim pants and one of Lance's cast-off shirts. Yarn held up her auburn hair. "Look." She pointed. "A cardinal. See? There on your carriage house. On the weather vane." She was thinking that to go with Tracy would be the easiest thing and maybe the best. Everyone, Winslow, Arthur, her friends, would say it was sensible, at least more sensible than moving in with Richard immediately. It would save Winslow shame, and herself shame. People would say the Abernathys had decided to separate for a while, and she had gone to Europe to see how she felt. And, honestly, she was frightened by what she had done, scared of what could happen to her if Richard should leave her in another week, scared of what could happen if he stayed forever.

"All right," she said. "Let's go soon."

"Oh, Beanie, you can't imagine how relieved I am to hear you make the sensible decision. We'll go as soon as possible. June can take over the Bicentennial Festival. We'll fly to London, see some plays, oh, the opera, the National Gallery. We'll, oh, my, yes, I know. We'll go to the Lake Country. Not London. You'll like it there, Grasmere, Windermere, it's so beautiful, and a lot to do outdoors. Should we ask Evelyn?"

Beanie watched the cardinal whir off the iron rooster atop the weather vane.

"Do you think it would hurt her feelings if we didn't? I guess it would. All right."

"She gets so lonely. Now you leave all the arrangements to me. I'm very good at that sort of thing."

"I'm going back to New York today. I'll tell you where to call me about the flight and all."

Mrs. Canopy put down the tray she had filled with dishes. "Is that wise?"

"I couldn't leave without seeing him again."

Mrs. Canopy examined her friend's face quizzically. "I guess I never felt that way," she confessed. "I suppose I might as well say even that I wasn't really what you'd call 'in love' with Vincent. Of course, I loved him. He was a wonderful man. Didn't you think so, Beanie?"

Beanie came to hug Tracy; only fleetingly though, for she was sensitive to her friend's discomfort with physical affection. "I liked him a lot. I liked his laugh."

"Yes. He was a sanguine person. I think he was probably happy, by nature. . . . Well, never mind. Here, now let me do these dishes."

"Tracy, just for three weeks. I mean, you stay as long as you like, and Evelyn, but I want to come back in three weeks. And the other thing, when we go, I'm going to ask you not to try to talk to me about what I've done, I mean try to make me change my mind. Because I won't, and you have to understand that."

Tracy took off her glasses. "Why, Beanie dear, of course. Of course it will be all right with me, whatever you do. Well, not if you stabbed someone to death or became a political terrorist." She laughed. Beanie didn't. It was one of the limits on their love that Beanie never joked. Tracy knew, however, that Beanie would not turn *her* away, even if she *had* murdered someone. Jokes were easier to come by.

For the rest of the morning, while Mrs. Canopy wrote some letters to her artists, Beanie had, as she put it, puttered around. She was regluing some loose tiles in the upstairs bathroom when someone knocked at the front door. It was Priss Ransom. She had telephoned earlier that morning with news of Joy Strummer, but Tracy had neither told Priss that Beanie was there, nor told Beanie about the tragic accident at the Ransoms' pool party. She had not understood Lance's involvement in the accident (his letter to his mother lay this minute in her mailbox) and had decided that Beanie had enough to upset her already without being told.

Priss was in what Beanie called her "too much mood." "Get me some coffee and a vial of morphine, will you, Tracy? I'm at my wits' end. It's been a g.d. nightmare. And then, Ernest! After keeping me up all night, so full of twitches and heaves I thought I was going to have to put *him* in a hospital, this morning he's merrily off on his jog, and merrily off to his bank, leaving me behind as frazzled as Lady Macbeth in a straitjacket." Mrs. Ransom sank carefully into the bent cane rocker.

"I can just imagine." Tracy nodded.

"I doubt it." Priss had picked up a thin book on the coffee table, a selection sent from one of the innumerable literary clubs to which Mrs. Canopy belonged. *Dangerous Constancy* was described as an "anthology of erotic verse by the best of the new New York women poets, frankly celebrating the pleasures of passionate promiscuity." Priss stared at the cover of bright-colored vulvas; her mind wandered, and as if conjured by her thoughts, Beanie appeared, clomping down the stairs, a hammer in her hand.

"Tracy? I think I've fixed . . . Oh. Prissie. Hi."

"What in h. are you doing here?"

Tracy hurried back from the kitchen. "Yes. Here's Beanie! She's staying with me. She came back to talk with Winslow."

Mrs. Ransom twisted around in the chair to look at Mrs. Abernathy. "Thank God. You've come to your senses. Where did you leave that ridiculous little man?"

"Do you mean Richard?"

"Was that his name?"

"Now, Priss, please." Tracy handed her the cup of coffee and shook her head surreptitiously. But Beanie walked around her to say to Priss, "You know his name is Richard. And I haven't left him anywhere."

"Oh?"

"I'm going back today."

"I see. And what does, is it Winslow, have to say about this remarkable news?"

Beanie opened her mouth, then slowly closed it. Ever since her childhood, the more hurt she felt, the less she could think of any words with which to say so. Tracy patted her arm. "Why, isn't that really a private . . . I don't think our Beanie . . ."

"I don't think our Beanie *thinks*. Now do you?"

"Priss!"

"If she had thought, just a teensy bit, I don't believe she would have behaved quite the way she has. Oh, put that g.d. hammer down, Beanie. You look like someone on a billboard stuck on top of a Russian factory. If she had *thought*, I don't believe she would have raised a son who has behaved the way he has either."

"What?" Beanie stuttered. "Has Arthur upset Emerald?"

"Arthur? There's nothing the matter with Arthur. Except his posture and his conversation. I'm talking about Lance. I'm talking about your son who brought a barely pubescent girl whom nobody ever heard of to our home, then merrily wanders off while she drowns in our swimming pool. And all he can think of to do about it is break his hand boxing with the hood of his g.d. car."

The hammer thudded on the rug.

"Really, Priss, I must insist." Tracy's cheeks were red as stop signs and signaled, in fact, exactly that. "Beanie, I didn't know Lance was involved, or I would have told you."

"Where is he?" whispered Beanie.

"*Qui sait?* No one's seen him; certainly not the Strummers, whom Ernest and I went to call on just now, under the impression that someone should offer them some explanation since they were not even aware that their child had been invited to our party. Just as I was not aware of it. Apparently, she sneaked out of her room." Priss lit a cigarette and took one of Tracy's pots for an ashtray.

Beanie tugged at Tracy's hands. "The girl's dead? Strummers? They have a girl? She died?"

Neither Beanie nor her friends knew the Strummers personally or socially. They knew the name. Priss had no idea, for example, that the Strummers' son, Bobby, had, four summers ago, taken her daughter Kate's virginity on her couch at the lake house. Their spheres didn't mingle.

Beanie ran toward the kitchen door. "I've got to find Lance and talk to him."

Through a stream of her smoke Mrs. Ransom called

after Beanie. "My dear, I'd say you were about thirty years too late."

"Oh, now, no." Tracy flushed scarlet. "Really, no. You can't talk to Beanie like that. You mustn't come in my house and be so cruel! What's the matter with you, Priss? Really, no."

The kitchen door slammed shut. Mrs. Ransom stood so quickly that the rocker flipped over behind her. Infuriated by the awkwardness, she jerked it up as she spoke. "And who in h. do you think *you* are to talk to *me* like that? I told that gallumphing imbecile the truth. You know it's the truth as well as I. So who in hell are you?"

Mrs. Canopy's square jaw jutted up, trembling at the cool, handsome face of her college idol. "Her friend," she said.

Mrs. Ransom blinked once, then smiled. "Thanks for the clarification, Tracy." She stubbed out her cigarette in the pot. "*A bientôt, or should I say adieu?*" She walked into the front hall. "Don't bother to show me the door, unless of course Beanie's moved it to a new location."

Alone, Tracy ran into her bathroom and sat down, shaking, on the porcelain head of Fidel Castro. She burst into tears. What had gone wrong with her world? What was everyone coming to? After thirty years she had loss Priss. But she couldn't allow her to talk so cruelly of Beanie. Undoubtedly the poor Strummer girl's drowning had driven Priss to the point where she didn't know what she said. "And here I sit, excited about other people's tragedies as if they were plays. Even looking forward to going to England, and having somebody to travel with, when it will probably break Winslow's heart. He may think I took Beanie's side against him. I suppose I did. But what should I do? It's her life, isn't it? And here, worst of all, I think I'm almost jealous of Beanie. Here she is, with children and a husband and now this man, too. Of course, she's so unhappy to have to hurt anybody, and I have a perfectly fine life, and friends. There's no reason to be envious. I suppose I should apologize to Priss. Oh, Vincent, Vincent, I wish I had you here to talk to sometimes. Sometimes I'm afraid I get a little lonely. Not that I have any right."

On the steps of the Ransom Bank Miss Dingley, sitting in her wheelchair in white linen skirt, blazer, and striped tie, conversed with the bank president. "No. Poor child. Wouldn't talk to me either. Can't say I blame her. Hope Cecil can pull himself together and give her some strength."

"I'm sure they'll work it out. Now, Ramona, I'm afraid . . ." Ernest Ransom put a foot on the first step.

"Saw Mary Bredforet at the hardware store. She said some idiot was shooting firearms off in the green here awhile ago. Where was John Haig?"

"A good question. It was Barnum, an accidental shot apparently."

"The man's dangerous. I want him charged."

"I'm afraid I'm in a bit of . . ."

Miss Dingley nudged Ransom toward her with her cane. "Don't fly off. Haven't said what I came to yet."

The banker smiled. Except for the pallid flush of a sleepless night, he looked, as always, perfectly fit and perfectly polite. "What can I do for you?"

"Not sure." She poked her cane tip at his chest and he stepped back. "What's going on out north of the marshland near the pond?"

A twitch flicked against his will in the corner of Ransom's mouth. "Excuse me?"

"Your grandfather Bredforet's land."

"What's the matter with it?"

"Asking you, Ernie." The old woman's cold hawk eyes held his as though he were a squirrel. "There's a military base up there." Ransom stared at her. "There's a government compound up there. You let those Washington idiots come piddling up here and start building nuclear bombs? In Dingley Falls?"

Ransom's laugh was slightly louder than was his habit. "Are you joking, Ramona? There's no missile sites anywhere around here."

"I wouldn't have thought so."

"It's crazy. Who told you this nonsense?"

"People have seen it."

"Who?"

Ramona paused, scrutinizing his face, before she answered. "Two young people. Went in along the old Indian trail. Took them there myself."

Ransom looped both hands through the back of his belt. He filled up his chest with air. "Now! Last time you were telling me there were flying saucers out in the marshland. Next, two kids say they see missile silos. Ramona!" He smiled indulgently.

Miss Dingley scooted her chair back so that she would not have to tilt her head up at Ransom. "Don't patronize me, Ernie. I'm not a fool. Tell me one thing, that's all I'm interested in. Did you stop construction on that highway connector because you knew there was something up there that no highway ought to be coming close to?"

"Good heavens, Ramona. You were one of the ones all up in arms about not wanting a major route coming close to town in the first place. Besides, don't be silly. *I* didn't stop the highway. Who am I? The commission in Hartford determined that . . ."

She waved away his words with her cane. "And you don't know anything about the federal government setting themselves up on Sewell Bredforet's property?"

Ransom hid his hands in the pockets of his blue blazer. His voice was kindly and tolerant. "There are no nuclear missiles out on that land, not as far as I know, and I would be flabbergasted to find out I was wrong. And if I *knew*, for a fact, that there was a clear danger to Dingley Falls from anything built on land I might have sold, I would not, as you seem to be accusing me, hide the fact from the town council."

Miss Dingley tried to move out of the sun so that she could study his eyes. But they looked as they always had since he was a child—a bland, attractive gray, innocent of irony. The eyes of a plodder, but so successful a plodder that there was no visible strain. As with his golf game, he had learned to work well with, and within, his handicaps. No, decided Miss Dingley, she was much brighter than Ernie, craftier, more capable of subtle maneuvers. No, he was not trying to mislead her. She snapped open the purse in her lap and took out of it a yellow canister of film. "Well, then. Find out if you *are* wrong. My friends took these." She handed him the film. "It's your land, Ernie. You have a right to know what's happening on it, and I think you'll be surprised. None of my business if you sell your own property. Long as it's legitimate. Far as I can judge, nothing the federal government's up to is likely to *be* legitimate, but, like I say, I admit to prejudice. But you wouldn't want me putting up a burlesque house next door to your bank. And I don't want somebody putting a pile of radioactive foolishness next door to my town. Shouldn't imagine you would either." She turned her eyes to the statue of Elijah Dingley in the town green. "Willie Bredforet always argued with me that I thought people who owned the land ought to give it all away, share and share alike. Always putting words in my mouth to rile me, just because I voted for Roosevelt against Hoover. Absurd, never thought such a thing. Be a fool not to believe in private property, capitalist like me. But I do think that people who own the land are responsible for it." She tapped his shoulder with the cane. "Let me know if you find out they *have* sneaked out there. Reprehensible. Government behaves like Italian gangsters. Gangsters behave like General Motors. General Motors behaves like the government. Can't tell them apart. Well, it's a question of the style of sin you're used to, ain't it?" She drove rapidly down the sidewalk, her back as straight as the trajectory of her wheelchair.

In one slow breath Ransom refilled his chest. Then he climbed the bank steps, one hand pushing against his weak leg. Seated in his private office, he opened his fist. The roll of film fell onto the desk. He pressed a button and asked his secretary to place a call to a Mr. W. Derek Palter of the Department of the Interior in Washington. Irene Wright asked if she could come in. "Could you sign these first, sir?"

They were interrupted by Mrs. Ransom, who didn't wait to be announced. She stood, sunglasses on, attired in a cream turban and a Pierre Cardin suit, with a travel bag over her shoulder.

"Hello, dear. Thank you, Irene. I'll sign these and bring them out." The Ransoms looked at each other until the door closed. "I thought you'd be resting," he said.

"I'm going away," she said.

"Where?"

"I don't know. The City. Mother's."

"Newport?"

"I'll take the Mercedes and leave the Saab outside for you. I feel like driving."

"When?"

"Now."

"Why?"

She sighed impatiently. "It's just been too much. One thing more and I'll snap. I have to get away for a few days."

"But. But, this is absurd. Don't you think we ought to attend the funeral? I realize we don't know them but we shouldn't give the impression . . . And Saturday, we'd planned on dinner with William and Mary and Tracy . . ."

His wife gripped her arms. "I cannot, I simply cannot abide the thought of another interminable evening a that ridiculous club with the same, same ridiculou people."

"What?"

"I feel like I've been trapped in a g.d. novel by
Somerset Maugham for thirty years!"

"Stop it, Priss." His wife's literary allusions in
personal conversation had always annoyed Ransom.
He didn't read.

All of a sudden Mrs. Ransom, quite remarkably,
screamed. It was not a loud or a long scream, nor was it
accompanied by any unseemly physical behavior, but
the banker was horrified, and frightened. "Priss. Priss.
Good gosh. Hold on." He stood up behind his desk.
"Admittedly you've been under a strain. But . . ."

"For God's sake."

"You're being silly." He waited until he saw that she
was herself again, but he remained standing. "Look.
Let's see. No, Sunday I have a vestry meeting." He
flipped over pages of a desk calendar. "Monday,
Tuesday. How about this? There's no point in your just
rushing off like this, all by yourself. I'll push my
vacation ahead. Tuesday, the two of us, well, Newport
if you like. Or the Cape. Or how about Hilton Head,
think it'd be too hot by now? But someplace restful. I
suppose I could slip away for a week."

Mrs. Ransom sat down in the chair where innumerable Dingleyans had sat to ask him favors. "Ernest,
that's sweet of you, but, frankly, chatting for seven
days with your golf caddy has never been particularly
alluring for me. I think, and it's in no way personal,
that I'd rather be by myself."

He came around the desk, stroking his Yale college
tie as if to comfort it. "Here. Sit down here. You're
upset. All this miserable business last night. Just try to
relax. Have you taken a pill?" She shook her head.
"You ought to go home, take a Valium, lie down for a
while. Where's Kate?"

"Who knows?"

"You two could play some golf or something. You
don't seem to spend much time together, and here
we've got her home for a change. Well, don't worry.

Look, Priss. Priss? Look, let's open the lake house, get
Wanda to go out tomorrow and fix it up, we'll spend the
weekend there, how would that be? Get some sun.
Then we could sit down and plan a really *nice* trip.
What about visiting the Mortons in Bar Harbor? Go
out on their sloop? You always liked Betsy."

"They're divorced."

"Oh. That's right. Stupid. Well, I bet I'll think of the
perfect thing. Don't worry. And `tonight, look, tell
Wanda to make something for the girls if they're going
to be there, and you and I will go to the Prim for
dinner. Or the Old Towne, we haven't been there for
ages. All right?"

Mrs. Ransom sat for a moment. She saw him glance
at the papers on his desk and knew it to be her cue. She
thought about saying good-bye and driving to Newport,
then she pulled her bag up over her shoulder. She had
never taken off her sunglasses. Now she realized the
office looked like a dim photograph. "All right," she
said. "I seem to be outbid. What time shall I say?"

"I don't know what you mean by 'outbid.'"

"Seven?"

"Fine," he said.

"Good," she said.

Mr. Ransom's secretary looked enviously at his
wife's clothing as Priss walked briskly past the tellers'
cages and out the doors of her husband's bank.

"Here. Just a second, Irene. Wait. You can send
these out." Ransom walked with her back into the
office, where he floated a hieroglyph of his name across
the bottom of six sheets of paper at which he no more
than glanced. Busy men must be able to trust those who
work for them. Had she been so inclined, Irene could
have led Ernest Ransom's signature, like a blind man's
hand, to sheets of libelous slanders, vast philanthropic
bequests, foreclosures, interestless loans to the indigent
unemployed in Madder. However, as she was neither
an ironist nor a revolutionary, none of this had ever
occurred to her. "On that call?" she said. "There is no

Mr. Palter with the Interior. There was a Mr. W. Derek Palter who worked there many, many years ago. But he transferred to the Central Intelligence Agency back in the sixties. I've been trying them all day, and *finally* somebody told me Mr. Palter had died overseas, I'm afraid. Should I try someone else with Interior? Sir, I'm sorry, should I try . . ."

"No. No, thanks, Irene. I had a question concerning this Mr. Palter in particular. It doesn't matter. Now. I think Carl Marco wanted to see me. Call and invite him to meet me for lunch at the Dingley Club, will you?"

She smiled. "He *is* going to get his loan then?"

Ransom smiled. "I think it would be hard not to admire a man like Mr. Marco. Coming so far, all on his own."

Irene thought it would be hard not to admire a man like Ernest Ransom. She thought him, in fact, perfectly wonderful, and often, when she returned home to her apartment in Argyle, she told her upstairs neighbor, Sally Rideout, that the bank president ought to run for the Senate or something. Ms. Rideout (Luke and Polly's stuttering history teacher at Dixwell High) agreed, saying businessmen ought to run America since the business of America was, and always had been, business. Irene (sadly enough, like so many of Ms. Rideout's students) failed to appreciate the teacher's ironic tone and took the remark as validation of her secret aspirations for her employer.

Mr. Ransom sat at his desk. He considered taking the roll of film to be developed at the Argyle Camera Shop, where he was, however, a frequent customer. Of course, he was certain (he was nearly certain) that there were no missiles on that property, but he was also certain (nearly certain) that whatever the compound did hold, it was best not photographed without permission. He put the film in his desk drawer. Then he took it back out and considered telling Walter Saar that he wished to make use of the academy's darkroom. Finally, Ransom walked to his window, from which he looked down at Dingley Falls. Across the green, where a large black German shepherd lay at the feet of Elijah Dingley's stone chair, the banker saw his wife. She stood in front of the broken window of *The Dingley Day*, where she seemed to be laughing at some remark being made to her by A. A. Hayes, who looked from a distance to be staggering drunk. Ransom did not care for the editor, but if Hayes could amuse Priss, all to the good. He did not like to see his wife unhappy.

He watched Ramona Dingley, followed by her housekeeper, motor her wheelchair through the door of The Tea Shoppe. Did Ramona plan to tell anyone about the roll of film? So what if she did? After all, he had not lied to her. His words had been carefully chosen, but there had been no direct lie. At the worst, at the very worst, thought Ransom, they had tested small arms, experimental conventional weapons out there. There was nothing nuclear going on. And even small arms was unlikely. The armed forces didn't hide in a swamp. Defense was nothing to be ashamed of. Even if it were (though it wasn't) a missile site of some sort, wasn't it the government's prerogative to protect national security, however it saw fit? That's what the government was there for. He stared at the green. Winslow Abernathy was coming out of his office; shading his eyes with his hand, he turned toward the post office. Ransom felt sorry for his old roommate. Life had treated Winslow shabbily: good family, but one that had lost its money in the Crash. Poor guy, never had had any funds for clothes or clubs, or even a good meal and a show their freshman year in New Haven. Always made up some excuse like the library when the other fellows started throwing out ideas for the evening. Never would take a little loan. Then after they enlisted, shunted off to float around in the Pacific for a few years. Now this, deserted by his wife, never really suited each other. Never would listen to reason about marrying Beanie. Must feel so humiliated now. And having a son like Lance. An irresponsible boor.

The banker shook his head at the lawyer's stooped-over walk, his hunched shoulders. Never would listen about regular exercise. Ought to take up golf. It wasn't too late.

As Ransom watched Abernathy tug open the post office doors he frowned at the sight of a fat, middle-aged couple (obviously from Madder; they looked like Puerto Ricans) coming out of the building. Probably went in there to pick up government checks that he had paid for in outrageous taxes. He supported, after all, his own family, and a dozen of theirs, of those too indigent to find jobs. Yet, of course, they all wanted houses and furniture and cars and everything else they could get. Where were they all coming from? They could flood Dingley Falls like a polluted tide. They should be sent back to Bridgeport or Springfield or wherever they came from. There was no room for them here. Yes, Uncle William was right. All the order was gone now.

Irene tapped at the door. "I'm going to lunch now. Mr. Marco will be there at one. I ordered the flowers. I spoke with Mr. Strummer. He asked me to tell you he's very grateful for all you've done. But he says he'll be able to manage, thank you anyway."

At The Tea Shoppe, where Chin Lam Henry served them clam chowder, Irene told her friend Sally Rideout that Mr. Ransom had offered to pay all the Strummer funeral costs, just because the tragedy had happened to occur in his house. How many men would think of being so considerate? She wanted to know why there weren't more people like Ernest Ransom in the world.

It was time for him to drive to the Club. Ransom looked at the thin gold watch his grandfather had given him. The office was quiet. He could hear the tick of time passed along through generations increasingly penurious of its expense. "There're only so many hours in a day," his father had warned him. "Stop wasting time," he now warned his children. Maybe it was silly to keep a pocket watch these days. No one wore them anymore. Ransom let it fall into the pocket of his gray trousers. He rapped the yellow Kodak tube against the windowpane. Suppose Priss, standing at the door of the Saab station wagon, looked up and assumed he was surreptitiously watching her. Instinctively he stepped back, though he knew she could not see him. He waited until her car was gone. Then he took the corner of the film and pulled, stretching out his arms until the black strip reached across the width of the sunny window.

CHAPTER
48

Amber gleamed in wood grain as sun splintered in the old glass. "Keep your wrist loose. Right. Right. Ah, too bad. Close though." In the billiards room of the Dingley Club, old William Bredforet was delighted to have someone to play with. Even a novice like Ruth Deeds, who confessed that she hadn't practiced once since he'd first taught her how as a child. There was rarely anyone to join him in a game these days. Place was practically deserted. Gloomy as the Tombs. He had particularly wished that somebody would be there today to register shock at his arrival with a young black woman, perhaps even to precipitate a scene in which Bredforet could display his chivalrous disdain of sexual or racial or generational bigotry. He felt this way even though he himself was on a membership committee whose entire principle of selection was bigotry, and even though he himself had blackballed Carl Marco (whom Ernie had put up, no doubt because Marco had at least a half a million in Ransom Bank) on the unspoken charge that Marco was, in his view, a loud-mouthed, ill-bred, ill-dressed dago. But no one had come into the billiards room to challenge Bredforet over Ruth Deeds. Everybody, he told his guest, seemed to have something else to do.

"Work for a living?" suggested Dr. Deeds.

"I suppose so," her host agreed. "Looks like it's come to that practically everywhere. Old British war chum of mine in Kent, Teddie Pratt-Read, last time I saw him he was slopping rubbish to a herd of giraffes out behind his family estate. Mary and I went over on some boring tour for the decrepit, and we escaped and dropped in on him. There he was, surrounded by zebras, and tourists riding up and down in golf carts snapping pictures of his dad's arboretum. His dad was Marquis of Thingamabob, I forget. Teddie came to the States back in the twenties and damned if I didn't catch him trying to get Mary to run off with him. There she'd be now, shoveling up giraffe dung into a pushcart. At least I don't have to worry that twenty tourists in bermuda shorts are going to open my bathroom door while I'm sitting in the tub." He reached for his Bloody Mary. "Your shot."

Ruth Deeds was looking at the empty leather chairs, the unread magazines, the vacant lush grass outside the window. "Why don't you open this club up? Look at all the nice things you've got just going to waste. There're a lot of people up at the lake all summer that would love to use the golf course and the bar and restaurant. You could take their money and set up facilities for local kids who can't afford things like tennis lessons or swimming. I bet you'd get a crowd in here."

"Expect we would." The old man smiled as he sipped his Bloody Mary.

"Well, why not?"

"It's a thought." (But it wasn't, really.) "Your go. Save my soul later. Try the five ball in the side pocket. There! Now the six."

"Damn it. I jerked."

"Now, you haven't told me, why did you leave Chicago? Get away from your folks? You know, I used to take the Santa Fe line out of there when my parents packed me off west in the summer. They claimed it was for my asthma, but the truth is they disliked all their children. Why'd you leave? Not a happy place to live?"

"No large city is a very happy place to live these days."

"True. Never could stand them myself. Except Paris, naturally. Most beautiful place in the whole damn world. Knows it, too. Multiplies itself with mirrors. Mirrors all over the place. Even in the subways. Everywhere you look, people admiring themselves in pieces of glass. Whole city's one great big dazzling reflection of itself. All the people in it blind as Cupid! City of lovers. Everywhere you look, couples going at it. You notice that?"

"Never laid eyes on the place. Oh, hell, I missed. Your turn."

"Never saw Paris?! I tell you what. I'll divorce Mary tomorrow. I don't think she'll notice. We'll fly to Paris together." Below his neatly combed white hair, Bredforet's eyes twinkled like blue gas flames on a stove. He spun his moustache. "Doctor can always find work in Paris. Half the women are pregnant, half the men have gonorrhea, all the rest have dyspepsia. You could support me, or I could support you, whichever makes you more comfortable."

Dr. Deeds pointed her cue stick at the man. "No, sir." She grinned. "I'm not going to be seen walking around Paris with you. Because when the revolution comes, you are going to end up with your head under the guillotine, irresistible as you think you are, because you are nothing but the decadent flowering of the whole capitalistic, imperialistic, chauvinistic system. And I'm going to be holding the basket when the heads fall. . . . Now, I mean that. That's the truth, I'll be on the barricades. Well, you win this round." Bredforet had neatly pocketed the six, seven, eight, and nine balls as she spoke.

"Child, have a heart. Don't be so bloodthirsty. I'm

tottering on the edge of the grave with Death booting me in the behind as it is. You'll win, sooner or later you'll win. Wait your turn." He unscrewed his pool cue and slid it into its leather case.

Behind the locked door of the cheerful blue rain shelter near the eighth green of the Club's golf course, Kate Ransom knelt between the legs of Sidney Blossom, who sat on a bench unhappily. His belt was unbuckled and his pants unzipped, and Kate's hand was inside his shorts where his penis shriveled away from her touch. "What's the matter?" she asked.

"I'm worried somebody's going to come."

"Oh, for crap's sake. It's a lot safer here than in the library."

He tried to smile. "Not very reassuring, considering what happened to us there," he pointed out.

She ran her fingers lightly down the organ's underside, then pulled the head out through his fly. "There's nobody on the whole front nine," she promised. "I checked the registration book."

"How do you know for sure?" He felt his penis stir on its own in the opening of his shorts as she stood now and, lifting off her white shirt, rubbed the nipples of her breasts. "How do you know someone won't, your *dad* won't, just decide on the spur of the moment to start out on the second round?"

"Daddy never does anything on the spur of the moment except fall asleep." Kate tugged now at his pants, pulling them down to his feet. "There, you see, it's chosen," she said and pointed down. She tossed back the unruly black curls that her mother continually told her to comb and lowered her head. After a few minutes, Blossom stopped her.

"It's just not going to work," he said. "It's not just that somebody might come in. I feel funny about doing it now." He explained that for them to make love the morning after someone had died, even if they had only known the girl by sight, seemed wrong. Sid was not a sophisticated man. Such an act struck him as disrespectful. He thought it likely that his feelings were stronger because he had felt so much hostility to Bobby Strummer when, two days ago, Kate had told him that Bobby Strummer had taken her virginity. He had taken an irrational dislike to Joy, when, at the pool, Kate had told him that Bobby had looked like a male version of his sister. And now Joy was dead. He told Kate he felt ashamed.

Kate, who had been last night far more upset by the news than Sid, felt differently. She had never known Joy; for that matter, she had never really known Bobby, but had simply chosen him as the most likely available candidate for the function he had been elected to serve. Yet the act done gave him (and his) a very real if mythic importance in her life. His being missing, his sister being dead, her own knowledge of that death when he had none and might be himself dead—she felt because of such things she had a responsibility to these two that she could not fulfill. "Please, Sid," she said. "Let's be close. I want to, *because* of what happened. I want things to be living, sort of to make up, you know, and sex with you makes me feel alive. Okay, please?" They looked at each other, the longest look they had ever shared. Then he kissed her. Stepping back, she slid out of her white shorts and underpants. He took her hands and kissed the palms. Straddled over the bench, she sat pressed against his chest, and when he unbuttoned his shirt, she rubbed her breasts in the hair between his nipples. His penis rose between them, pressing against her stomach. He bent and took her nipple in his mouth and moved his hands on her buttocks. She felt to him buttery soft and rich and smooth. Where her hands touched him he had goose bumps; everywhere her flesh touched, his was tingling. He held his hands in her hair and kissed into her mouth with his tongue while she helped him inside her. He wanted to thrust into every opening, through her, into her heart. He was coming too fast to try to wait. And then suddenly she came, too, her neck arched back. He thought how much like grief the look of her ecstasy was.

Almost at once she lit a cigarette.

"These post-coital light-ups." He grinned. "They showed you too many foreign films at Vassar." He re-dressed himself quickly. "You better hurry up before somebody opens that door."

"Crap, you are such a small-town librarian!" she told him. To his horror and delight, she ran outside, waving her arms over her head, then rushed back and slammed the door. "See." She grinned. "Did the state totter?"

"Yes," he said, "yes," and pulled her toward him, kissing her hair and neck. "Yes, it did. And the earth shook." The lovers laughed across the empty green, their silliness ignored by squirrels and birds, who had already mated and now had families to raise.

Sidney Blossom's lunch hour was at an end, without his having eaten lunch. At the door of his chipped, rusted Volkswagen bug the librarian waited until he was certain of his voice. "Kate? You said our making love makes you feel alive. Does it by any chance make you feel like getting married?"

She laughed. "Oh, Sid. Nobody gets married anymore!" She slapped his buttocks with her tennis racquet. "See you tonight at your place. Tell you what. We'll *pretend* we're married!" Laughing, he watched her scuffle away through the smooth white gravel. Her hair looked like clusters of wild blackberries. He was only thirty-two. He could wait forever.

A deathly presentiment had seized Priscilla Hancock Ransom and had grown, like a tumor, throughout the week, until now she felt the pain everywhere and unremittingly. Her life had slid away from her into the abyss. She had reached *la fin des bons vieux temps*. Accustomed since a précocious childhood to regard herself as a patrician of modernity, she felt today stripped of her titles and ignominiously drummed from

her station. Anonymous letters, her daughter, magazines—all accused her of superannuation. She, belle of
the *beau monde* of Dingley Falls's *bon ton,* was no more
than a *parvenu* as a modern woman. What she thought
risqué was passé, her chicness was senectitude. She
couldn't even masturbate, and even that shameful
failure had been witnessed by God knows who.

At the *kaffeeklatsch* of the women's movement, she
(upper crust of the upper class of Mount Holyoke wits)
was simply, glaringly, an *arriviste.* Even here in the
mental hinterlands she was blackballed by revolution-
aries. Here were Tracy and Beanie merrily reveling in
sororal bachelorhood like wassailing Maenads and
showing *her* the door! And why? Because she had
espoused the marriage vow and the duty of proper child
rearing. Life was ironic, as she'd always said. And that
g.d. Beanie, that nethermost plebe of the intellect, that
Brobdingnagian *haus* and horse *frau,* Beanie was the
modern woman! *Nouveau riche* in the riches of passion
with Rich Rage. It was Beanie who had flung the apron
to the hearth, defied censure for sensuality, put herself
before her husband and children, slept with a man, so
to speak, on the first date. It was Beanie who,
apparently, had no fear of flying at all. Mrs. Ransom's
world had flown off its axis. A reign of terror was upon
her. The revolution had struck down the aristocracy
and put peasants in the vanguard. The first had become
last, the last had become first. How should she put it?
She, a stylish forerunner of the first four hundred, had
been left in the dust by a Clydesdale mare.

That's how she should put it. Who should she put it
to? Certainly not Tracy. Tracy had made her choice and
chosen Beanie, who had never even heard of *Main
Street* as a girl, much less identified with its heroine (as
had Mrs. Ransom and Mrs. Canopy). Why in h., then,
was it Beanie who had eloped with a younger man to
make her bed among bohemian artists in Greenwich
Village? Why in h., then, was it Priscilla Hancock who
couldn't even insist on a weekend alone with her g.d.

mother in Newport, Rhode Island, where all she would
do anyhow would be to play bridge with seventy-year-
old widows whose rings hung loosely from their thinning fingers? If someone was God now, which she
doubted, it was probably Voltaire. She needed to talk
with Walter Saar. Wasn't he after all the mate of her
mind, the man whose company she most preferred in
all Dingley Falls? Even if he was (and he was—at least
she was modern enough to have noticed) a homosexual. Yes, she knew that beyond a shadow of a doubt, and
it had never crossed Tracy's or Ernest's (or, God
knows, Beanie's) minds. It would be tempting to tell
them, with sophisticated nonchalance, affecting surprise that they too had not simply assumed it. She could
not, however, take the risk. Her husband's sexual
mores were no more cosmopolitan than those of Calvin
Coolidge. If obliged to know of Walter Saar's practices,
he would feel obliged to arrange for Walter Saar's
dismissal. Then where would she be, especially now
that Tracy had proved a traitor? Without Walter, she
would go mad laughing alone in Dingley Falls. He was,
as well, the man with whom she had successfully bid a
grand slam, the man with whom she had commanded
the dance floor at the Club on New Year's Eve, the
most stylishly dressed, the most (he *was*, now that she
thought of it), the most handsome man in town. And if
he hadn't had the gall to be a g.d. queer, drooling over
that insipid Barbie-doll of a priest, she (now that she
thought of it) might have had a secret affair with Walter
Saar and lived in sensuous emancipation.

Priss flung open the doors of the ladies' locker room
at the Dingley Club. She hadn't wanted to lie down
with a Valium. She wanted to smack golf balls as hard
as she could. But the mocking wanton, Liberation,
chased poor Priss even into the sanctuary of the toilet,
for when she opened the stall, her daughter, Katherine,
looked up, startled, with one foot on the seat and one
hand extracting a diaphragm. "Oh! You scared the shit
out of me!" was the greeting her child gave her.

"*What* are you doing?"

"It was bugging me. I don't think I had it in right."

"Where did you get that thing?"

Kate held it in the hands that had once with wonder held up seashells. "At the health center. At Vassar. I wanted to get off the pill for a while."

These were breakers crashing over Mrs. Ransom. She closed the stall door, went to what had once been called the powder room, a room wallpapered with tiny pink roses, and sat down in front of the vanity table. She didn't feel very vain. Soon Kate reared over her in the mirror.

"Kate, are you sleeping with someone in town?" she asked the reflection.

"Sure. Sid," her daughter replied. "I thought you knew."

"At the *Club?*"

"Sure. Why? What's wrong with that?" As a defensive strategy, Kate assumed, first, innocence of her mother's disapproval, and, next, sarcasm. "Sex *is* legal, you know, or hasn't it been on the news yet?"

"Please don't be belligerent. And what do you think your father would say?"

"I don't think Daddy wants to know, or I'd tell him. It's his hangup, though, not mine."

"I won't pretend to follow that. Sidney Blossom?"

"What's wrong with Sid for crap's sake?"

"Somehow I can't see it, that's all."

"Nobody's asking you to."

Kate sprawled on a lady's lounge chair, her bare legs defiantly wide-flung. The two women glowered at each other.

"Kate. Listen to me. What are you going to do if you become pregnant?"

"I'm not going to get pregnant."

"Really? I can't share your confidence when you make remarks like 'I don't think I had it in right.' "

"Besides, so what? It wouldn't be the end of the world."

"For your father to find out you'd had an abortion?"

"I don't know whether I'd have an abortion or not. Maybe I wouldn't. It would depend."

"I don't believe that, even today, Vassar would let you back in the dorm next fall with a baby. Nor can I see you spending your life washing the windows of an abandoned train depot, living with Sidney Blossom in a backwater of civilization."

Kate was upset. She felt attacked in vulnerable positions, where she did not yet know herself how she felt. Her confusion made her even more combative. "Who's talking about my *life?*" she yelled, springing forward in the chair. "Besides, why shouldn't I? He's a great guy, for your information, if you'd take the trouble to notice."

"The world is at least sprinkled with great guys, some of whom must be a bit more interesting, not to mention solvent, than Sidney Blossom."

Kate jerked out of the chair. "Fuck. You live here. If it's such a craphole, why've you been here for the last forty or fifty years? I know it's not because you can't tear yourself away from Daddy either, because sometimes I think you don't give a crummy shit about him! Just because *you* married for money, or whatever it was, doesn't mean *I* have to!"

Mrs. Ransom looked up at the gilt-framed mirror. The girl, the woman, her daughter, glared at her, the blue eyes (like her husband's) bluer behind the narrowed black lashes; the brows tightened with anger. There was her own mouth, thin with anger, her own jaw thrust against her. Mrs. Ransom lowered her head to her hands. But how could she be crying when she didn't cry? Evelyn cried all the time, Beanie cried, even Tracy admitted to tears, but Priscilla Hancock, when looking life in the face, had always, always laughed.

As terrified as if she had been again a child who feared she had the power to kill, Kate stared at the turban bent toward the table. Then she rushed around the chair, fell to her knees, and hugged her mother's back. "Oh, God, I'm sorry! That was *rotten* of me. I didn't mean it. Mommy. I didn't even know what I was saying." She rocked her mother back and forth. "Mommy. Please. Please. I'm sorry."

Mrs. Ransom pulled back. Her nose was running. It was a sight so painful to Kate that she stepped away as her mother took from her jacket pocket a handkerchief monogrammed PHR and squeezed it to her nose. "You see," Priss said, "sometimes . . ." She blotted her eyes. "Sometimes anachronisms prove convenient." She waved the handkerchief. Kate smiled. Mrs. Ransom stood up and adjusted her turban in the mirror. "Even Gloria Steinem must have to blow her g.d. nose. Of course, perhaps she uses her hair."

"Oh, Mother! You always joke."

"Darling, if I didn't, I'd slit my throat. And then where would you be? *You'd* have to watch the inexcusably wide 'Wide World of Sports' with your father."

"The thrill of victory." Kate grinned, relieved. "The agony of defeat."

"Frankly," sighed Mrs. Ransom as she freshened her lipstick, "I never know which is which."

Coleman Sniffell was at his desk, trying with a pair of pliers to remove the twist-off top from a bottle of soda. His thumb was bleeding. He knew the sugar and artificial coloring inside were going to kill him if he ever managed to drink any of the garbage. He tore the clippings off his paper spike and jabbed it through the bottle top, then sucked. Then he took his sandwich out of its soggy bag. It was time for his habitual luncheon reverie. Sniffell used those blank moments when the brain is forced to fill itself *ex nihilo,* those confrontations with emptiness that come to everyone seated on the toilet without a book, or waiting for a bus or sleep or a watched pot to boil, to contemplate the murder of his wife, Ida. Entirely theoretically, of course, merely as a mental exercise, as some people work chess problems over a solitary meal. During the past twenty years he had poisoned her with untraceable salves applied by South American hunters to the tips of javelins, he had bumped her out of the head of the Statue of Liberty, he had shot, bludgeoned, run over, electrocuted, choked, mashed, and minced the unsuspecting Ida Sniffell, who stood convicted of optimism. As he now finished eating his sandwich and draining the brake fluid from the car just before his wife drove off in it over a cliff, Sniffell was interrupted by his boss, who brought layouts of the next *Dingley Day;* the lead page was black-bordered and a three-column box made this announcement:

We of *The Dingley Day* Wish to Express
OUR DEEPEST SYMPATHY
To the Families and Friends of
ALFREDO CESARINI MARCO
ARCHIBALD THEODORE OGLETHORPE
JAMES PRICE
JOY HELEN STRUMMER
SISTER MARY JOSEPH ZOLARINSKI

Their stories followed, under such headings as "Teacher at Alexander Hamilton Academy Since 1929 Expires in Argyle."

"How many piss-ass synonyms for *dies* are there?" asked A. A. Hayes as he spread out the page for Sniffell's perusal. "Look here, let's take Evelyn's story off one and put her on two, 'Police Seek Patio Vandal,' how's that? And what's this ad for Mugger-Buggers? What is that, is that real?"

"Absolutely. Limus Barnum ordered one; he showed it to me."

"A high-voltage hat pin?" He read, "'Afraid to go out, Afraid to stay home? Protect yourself, And whatever you own.' What is this? Electrocute trespassers?"

"More like a cattle prod. Some teenager in Argyle cleared over twenty-five thousand dollars last year on it. Invented it and sold it door to door. Now he's got mail orders."

Hayes sighed. "Now why can't *my* children show some of that kind of Yankee ingenuity?"

Sniffell pointed at the page. "Alvis, come on. What's this 'Ten Bloodiest Battles in American Wars'? Listen, don't put in another one of those lists. Nobody reads them." Hayes left with a shrug. Sniffell always grumbled about the lists, but secretly he liked them, believing that history should be showed up for the roll call of casualties that it had always been. On the other hand, this desperate, pitiful impulse of A. A. Hayes to rank chaos, to find an order of one through ten in the utterly random debris of civilization, was yet a further indication of how far from grasping cosmic absurdity the southerner was. Both men were collectors, but Hayes framed his signatures of the great in a symmetrical row around the walls of his den, and Sniffell pinned clippings of the unfortunate helter-skelter on a bulletin board. Sniffell made no evaluations of his findings, never attempted to choose the ten best or worst tricks played by the crazed and barbaric fates.

But Hayes had always been a list maker. Since childhood he had recorded errands, theories, heroes, habits to break, books to read, lives to live. He transferred to each new list the unaccomplished items on its predecessor. Over the years the gap between aims and execution had shortened as his desires dwindled. Later Hayes would find the yellow scraps of his forgotten "Things to Do, Be" in books or trouser pockets. He had long since concluded that he would never do or be anything but the out-of-shape editor of *The Dingley Day,* who smoked and went to the beach or the mountains for two weeks in the summer. He would never be any of those possible futures, a brain surgeon, trial lawyer, congressman, screenwriter, hitchhiker, prophet, millionaire, or enemy of the people, not a great editor, not a great lover, not a great sportsman, not, he concluded, a great anything. As he had told Sammy Smalter, he would leave no scratch on the tablets of history. He made lists of facts now. He and June could not get along. He would die. He would die from (1) a heart attack (smoking, drinking, no exercise, tension in the home), (2) cancer (smoking, southern diet, family history, tension in the home), (3) a car accident (poor driving habits, poor upkeep of a poor car, bad luck, tension in the car). At this point Hayes's personal lists were limited to modest aspirations: pick up carton of cigarettes, call printer's, June's birthday. But as the private lists contracted, the public ones grew. Into the lists that appeared boxed in *The Dingley Day* went all the ambition and idealism, the breadth and reach, displaced from his life. He made ruthless, sweeping decisions: the ten best books, movies, products, Americans, human beings. And the ten worst. He strode over history, awarded laurels, condemned to death. He posed questions in lists: Who really killed JFK, RFK, Martin Luther King, Jr., Malcolm X, Marilyn Monroe, Lindbergh's son, Howard Hunt's wife? He asked his readers if Sacco and Vanzetti were guilty. Was Anastasia shot? Who was Jack the Ripper? Did Jefferson have a black mistress? Was Hitler alive? Were the little princes really smothered in the Tower? Was Truman wrong to drop the bomb? Should Nixon have been brought to trial? Exactly when (for it must come) would all those "Looking Glass" planes, flying in circles over the Midwest since 1961, launch their nuclear missiles? Against whom? How long would that give us to compile our final lists, with whatever summations seemed fit? Was there a Holy Grail?

Nobody seemed to care. At least no syndications had ever picked up A. A. Hayes's lists. And no Dingleyan, except for the desperate Limus Barnum and the informative Tracy Canopy, had ever bothered to write an answer to his questions. In his list of military carnage, Hayes now scratched out Buena Vista and wrote in Hill 861 near Hue. Then, leaving Sniffell absorbed in an imagined effort to inject a syringe of herbicide precisely in the puncture hole where Ida Sniffell had just donated a pint of blood, Hayes walked over to the post office to buy some stamps so that he could cross at least that off his list.

At the post office this Friday morning Judith Haig had herself received a news item in the form of a letter from the headquarters of the postmaster general. It advised her that in the interest of saving the American taxpayers money (Hayes would have interjected that they were already paying the military well over $100,000,000,000 a year to defend their country, so it was quite true they could use a break), cutbacks in postal service would be necessary. As soon as the investigatory committee determined which branches were to be lopped off (and obtaining that information would cost the taxpayers half a million), the ax would fall on the unproductive. The postmaster wished the postmistress of Dingley Falls, Connecticut, to know that her office had been running at a loss for fifty years, that last year it had shown an income of only $7,719.31 ($844.65 of it came from Sammy Smalter) and an outgo of quite a bit more. This was no way to run a business. This was not what Benjamin Franklin had had in mind. In light of these facts, the situation would be examined. Unless the town could show just cause why their P.O. ought not to be closed, the P.G. would be obliged to erase Dingley Falls from his map and cancel its zip code. A rural route carrier from Argyle could deliver the town mail, and Dingleyans could buy stamps at the main office there, or wherever they happened to see any for sale.

This news bulletin Mrs. Haig had passed along to Arthur Abernathy's clerk at Town Hall, but she did not share it with the newsman. According to Hayes, nobody in Dingley Falls ever told him anything. Who, for example, was this fat female stranger behind the

P.O. counter informing him, "No space program stamps here. Got to go to Argyle, you want commemoratives?"

"Really? Y'all used to have them. Where's Mrs. Haig?"

"She can't help you. No commemoratives here."

Hayes heard low, murmuring voices. Emerging from the back office were Judith Haig and (to the editor's surprise) Winslow Abernathy. They appeared to be talking (to his greater surprise) about bail having been arranged for Maynard Henry. Hayes waved. They nodded.

As a stamp collector, the editor had been for years a regular customer of Mrs. Haig's, though they were not friendly. He suspected that she was the genuine omniphobic he suspected his wife, June, only pretended to be. Hayes recalled the night Limus Barnum had roused Glover's Lane by firing his Magnum pistol at his bedroom slipper while pursuing (he said) a burglar. At the shot June had spun, shrieking, out of bed and locked herself in a closet. What (wondered Hayes, watching the postmistress shudder as Abernathy stooped to retrieve his dropped briefcase), what would Mrs. Haig have done, shocked awake by a pistol shot? Gone temporarily insane? Why did women keep the pitch of life so high?

On the sidewalk in front of Abernathy & Abernathy, Hayes tossed four coughdrops into his mouth. "You representing the post office now, Winslow?"

"Pardon me? Oh, no, just relaying a message."

"Stop me if I'm butting in, but I thought I heard you talking about Maynard Henry. You know, I talked to the guy. He's nuts. Reminded me of a mistreated horse. Don't tell me you're representing *him?* I guess you knew he almost killed some poor Puerto Rican fellow. He didn't get out, did he?"

"Alvis, excuse me. I'm not representing him. But he didn't strike me as 'nuts.' How do you mean that? Violent?"

"For a start. He more or less told me he planned on killing the guy that put him in there. I sort of believed him."

"Well, he feels that he's been railroaded."

"How do you know all this?"

"He told me. I went to speak with him."

Hayes crunched up the coughdrops and lit a cigarette. "Mind telling me why?"

"Someone asked me if I would."

Hayes knew that that was the end of the information. Abernathy (who was the person closest in the town to what the southerner thought of as a friend) was not a person to share other people's news.

But Abernathy was no more reticent than most Dingleyans, who gossiped only within family fences or those made of historic social links. As an atheist, Hayes had no access to the one font of egalitarian gossip ever flowing from the lips of Father Sloan Highwick. For reasons of personal taste he could not join Limus Barnum, social voyeur and community spy, at his sweaty peephole. No, sighed the editor of *The Dingley Day*, as he looked in the broken window of his office and wondered how it might have happened, nobody ever tells me anything.

CHAPTER
49

Otto Scaper stomped across the front hall into the law office and winked at Luke Packer's sister, Susan, who appeared to be behind her desk but was really on a honeymoon in Martinique. For she was clandestinely reading a novel in which a beautiful, lonely, orphaned heiress had to choose among four handsome millionaires after sleeping with one on his yacht in Monte Carlo, with one in his penthouse suite on Sutton Place, with one in his Learjet over Stockholm, and with one in his diamond mine under Johannesburg. The heroine couldn't bring herself to choose among them until after she had modeled for some magazine covers, been caught up in a Third World revolution, been nearly raped by a guerrilla, exacted vengeance on the villain who had sold out her father on the big merger, and spent the night with a beautiful, lonely, famous Lesbian. Finally, on page 850, she had chosen the American. Abernathy's secretary sighed; perhaps she would have taken the Swedish industrial designer on the rebound, overlooking a penchant of his for prepubescent boys that was obviously intermittent anyhow, since no one had even known about it until page 790.

"Your boss in, honey?"

"Yes, sir." What a dull job. Of course Mr. Abernathy was in. What else would he be doing? Certainly not off entering the Grand Prix. She liked him, but couldn't imagine falling in love and having an affair with her employer, as in magazines executive assistants often went to New York to do. Susan Packer was a *Cosmo* girl, forced to live a *Saturday Evening Post* existence, but refusing to compromise life-style to life. She wore discounted versions of the most current fashions, she wore stylishly uncomfortable shoes, she awakened a half-hour earlier to force her hair and her face into modishness, and she did all this to walk to and from Three Branch Road in Madder and Abernathy & Abernathy in Dingley Circle, and to eat calorically counted lunches at The Tea Shoppe, and to sit behind her desk escaping to Martinique. There were only three men in the building where she worked: Winslow Abernathy, his son Arthur (whom she didn't even like and who was already engaged anyhow), and Otto Scaper, who was seventy-four years old and weighed three hundred pounds. "You women." He grinned.

"Always got your head in a book." At least, Susan thought, Dr. Scaper seemed to notice her sex, which was more than anyone else did.

The fat old doctor found Abernathy looking at a photographic triptych of Beanie, Lance, and Arthur. Each was fixed in black-and-white unease: the boys at thirteen in their Alexander Hamilton Academy blazers—Lance, tieless, his head cocked mischievously as a popgun at the photographer; Arthur, terrified into pomposity behind his middle-aged glasses. And Beanie, like a victim of lockjaw, searching for a person she doubted she'd find behind the camera. Scaper took his stethoscope from the pocket of a linen jacket that had probably once been white. Over Abernathy's protest he pressed the instrument to the lawyer's thin chest, then his back. "Just seeing how you're holding up, Winslow. Breathe in. Out. Again. Okay. Beanie's over at the Strummers' house, I don't know if you thought she'd left again or what. I didn't hear about *that* mess (you and her) until Arthur told me last night. Always thought Beanie had her feet on the ground. What do I know? Obviously nothing. Hold still." He grabbed up the thin wrist in his enormous paw and felt for the pulse. "She told me that poor jerk of a son of yours drove off without saying good-bye. Two broken bones in his hand!" He took Abernathy's blood pressure. "Whole town's falling apart. I've got to have some help, that's all."

"What are you doing, Otto?"

"I want you to take it easy, goddamnit. Try not to let things upset you. What's so funny?"

Abernathy sat down. He was too tired to feel the dislocations of his life with the seriousness they deserved. "What's funny? Nothing. I don't know. How are the girl's parents?"

"About how you'd expect. But they'll manage. Folks do somehow. Just don't you start feeling sorry for yourself and let that blood pressure go up. Hey, you got any cigars? Cigarettes? Hell's bells, there's just no justice, is there? My lungs are as sound as a bell and yours are a mess. *You* explain it!"

Across the hall, as she waited in Scaper's office, Dr. Ruth Deeds was eating potato chips and a Snickers bar. She was there because she had finally persuaded her grandfather to attend to his infected leg, which meant, in his terms, to go "see a real doctor." That his son's female child could command prescriptions from Smalter's Pharmacy or that he, Deeds, should go so far as to swallow any medication she did obtain was hardly likely. It was hardly any likelier that Otto Scaper, whose 1926 graduating class at the state medical school had included only males, would suspect that the Bredforets' chauffeur's grandchild was an M.D. At least he didn't think so until she declined to wait outside, until she peered around his arm as he felt the pus-inflamed wound, until in a carefully casual tone she remarked, "I'm a little worried about secondary septicemia. He's probably running a slight temperature; he wouldn't let me take it. But I'd like him to have something. Dicloxacillin maybe." She didn't look at Scaper's face. She was tired of seeing the shock.

Bill Deeds growled up from the examining table. "Ruth here's a doctor, lives down in Atlanta."

"Well, I'll be damned," Scaper replied.

Dr. Deeds was long accustomed to the ordeal of steeling herself for every first encounter with her professional colleagues. She had been the only black female in her medical school class and often felt that it might have been easier to work her way up through the ranks of the Ku Klux Klan than through such a self-centered, self-satisfied, self-aggrandizing clique of sexist pigs. Having endured everything from their sadistic jokes on the gynecology ward to the lowest salary in her department, she had come to expect the worst. Otto Scaper, however, now surprised her. He liked women and had outgrown his fear of them years ago.

"Why Atlanta? What's your specialty?" he asked.

"I'm at the Center for Disease Control there. Internist."

"Hell's bells! You busy this evening? Hold still, Bill. Thing is, maybe you're just what the doctor ordered. I'm pretty bamboozled about some symptoms I've been getting tied in with endocarditis on some patients of mine. Done much with heart disease?"

"Not really, Dr. Scaper. Most of my research's been with chemical side effects. Artificial carcinogens. Agent Orange, stuff like that."

"Don't say? Don't say? Don't believe in chemicals myself, Ruth. Ruth? My name's Otto. Anyhow, think you'd mind taking a look at some of my files, just for curiosity's sake? Why don't I bring them over to Willie's later on?"

"Well . . ."

"Those damn whippersnappers over at the hospital won't pay a damn bit of attention to me. Wouldn't surprise me if they thought I was daffy, or dumb as a skunk. You know how they can be. Think I'm making up problems that aren't there. But something's funny."

"Hey, listen, sure. I'll be glad to take a look."

Limus Barnum skulked close to the buildings and kept the huge black German shepherd in sight until it trotted away in pursuit of some other dogs. They scrambled up the hill beside the library whose summit was the town burial ground. All after some bitch in heat, Barnum concluded, and then asked himself, Who was this black bitch walking out of Scaper's with that toothless monkey of a chauffeur Deeds? Always honking his horn at cycles. Give a nigger a big car and . . . ! Who was she? Somebody forked out plenty for that outfit of hers. What was she doing in this junk town? Good ass. Tits too small. Snotty bitch. Looking at him like he crawled up out of a crack in the sidewalk. Good ass from the rear. But do it to a nigger? Must be smelly. Look at Hayes give her the once-over.

"Lime."

"How's it going, A.A.?"

"Fine."

"Look. About yesterday, the thing about the gun, okay? Look, that dwarf just rubs me the wrong way. He asks for it. No hard feelings, huh?"

"None."

"Pretty horrible about the Strummer girl."

"Yes. Horrible. Excuse me, got to get back inside, I'm expecting a call."

Sure he was. That lousy bastard, he didn't know who his real friend was. But when the time came, when the people of America finally woke up about what was going on in this country and turned to the party to put down the mugging and looting, the niggers and spics let loose by their Jewish money bosses and their Communist agitators, when the whole rotten roof fell in and the only thing between Hayes and death was the strong arm of good ole Lime, *then* he'd know who his true friends were. Look at that window. Still broken. How much was it going to take to show people they needed somebody tough to take over here? A lot of the work wasn't even his doing. Sure, he'd done Hayes's window, but who knew who'd got to the Troyes biddy's patio? He needed to do less and less. They'd better believe their precious Dingley Falls was crawling with vandals, like everywhere else.

Yes, horrible about the Strummer girl. Beautiful little girl like that destroyed because some rich SOB doesn't give enough of a damn about what goes on on his own property. Beautiful girl; hair like an angel. Yes, he ought to get a floral arrangement or something for the Strummers. Decent people, never knew what hit them. Lost their son to the lousy Communists and the government wouldn't do a thing about it. Pretty obvious that the recession had wiped Jack Strummer out with his movie theater. Way over his head. Pretty bitter about the way life's done a number on him.

Ought to take him over some of the literature. Give
him some answers. Show him what the party could do.

"How's it going, Coleman? Why doesn't the government take a little of our dough and air-condition this
post office? Like a sweat shop in here. Hey, let me give
you a hand with that. Quite a package. Typewriter?"

"That's okay, Limus. I've got it."

Don't kid yourself, Lime ole pal. They could have
bought one of *your* typewriters if they'd wanted to, if
they believed that shit about supporting your local
businessmen. But they got it in for me, that's all; simple
as that.

There she was. And there was that boy, Smalter's
pal; the punk that tried to start something about the
motorcycle. Was he trying to get her talking or just
buying some crummy stamps? What was it about her?
The Packer kid knew she had it, the way he was
watching her move. Lots knew. Her asshole husband
leaves town for a week, and lots start sniffing around.
Like Abernathy. His own wife gives him the brush-off
and runs off with some crummy hippie. Then he comes
panting first thing and invites somebody else's wife to a
lousy tea party at the Lattice biddy's. And women fall
for that pansy bullshit. That's what kills you. They
always do. And all the art-fart crap that goes with it.
They'll hold your dick under the table if they don't have
to know it's there. Just want to blab, blab, blab about
love, like their life depended on figuring it out. Just
want to be licked, and easy enough so they don't have
to know you're there. But not this cookie. They weren't
going to shove his nose in their goo and smother him.
No, siree.

But she was the real thing, wasn't she, locked away
behind those bars, white and pale, everything ironed
smooth and spotless. Not looking at him, keeping her
eyes down on the counter, waiting on other people,
never looking up over to his corner. But boy, you
better believe she knew he was there. She knew how

long, too. And there was not a thing she could do about
it. It was a free country, wasn't it? She was scared of
him, too. You could almost smell it. Sweat was popping
out across her nose. She couldn't keep from knowing, if
she was pure as an angel. She knew what she was doing.
Even if she covered herself with starch, she had skin
under there. Boobs with nipples and they got hard
rubbing on her bra. She had hair between her legs just
like the rest, and a hole up her, and probably stuck her
fingers up it every now and then even if she thought she
was the lousy Mother of God. Damn straight, she had a
belly and boobs under there, and her ass rubbing her
pants sweaty in this heat. It was all there, covered up
and behind those bars. She knew she was making it
happen. Rising up, hot, pushing on his pants. She could
see it, goddamnit, couldn't she? Hard as a fist, hard as a
gun, power over her, and there was nothing she could
do about it.

Mrs. Haig was very relieved when her replacement,
Mrs. Lowtry, finally returned from the "facilities" to
which she had excused herself half an hour earlier. The
appliance store man was still there by the table with his
postcards, but he wasn't writing. He made her feel the
way the dogs made her feel. Then doubt spun up
through her, and she worried that she would faint. Was
she insane? Why should Mr. Barnum, a successful
businessman, a former candidate for selectman, be
doing anything but what he seemed to be doing, writing
postcards? Why should she be so overwhelmed by
realities that were not real to other people, that other
people at least appeared not to notice? Always since
her childhood there had been this chasm between her
and others, her sense that they were feeling more (hurt
or anger or shame or torment) than they either actually
did feel or than they would admit to; this sense of a
wavery unreality somewhere, in herself or across the
chasm where everyone else seemed to be standing in

easy conversation as if they and the world were not mad
at all. Was it her or them?

The boy who had come just now to collect Mr.
Smalter's mail, was there hidden in his eyes, along with
a new sadness, a new anger at her, a relationship to her
that had not been there when he had said hello a few
days earlier? How could she know such things? Why
should she have to? At last Mr. Barnum was turning to
leave. Sarah MacDermott certainly wouldn't have been
intimidated by the man. Did that mean there was no
menace? Judith could never be certain if she misread
the rest of the world, or if everyone else either would
not or could not read as carefully as she did, or if they
read different books—as when she and her husband
watched television and he laughed at stories that left
her sick at heart.

Judith's temporary replacement, Mrs. Lowtry,
jammed her purse under her wide, pasty arm and, with
a jerk of her head at the clock, followed Mr. Barnum
into the street. Grateful to be alone, Judith tried to
calm herself after his intrusion by sweeping the floor of
her post office. Then she straightened everything,
locked her drawers and her safe. She went down the
steps to lower her flag. There was no breeze, and dusk
air held close the heat of the day. Nearby in the circle
two women parked in front of the cream brick building.
A large, vibrant woman got out of the car and went
inside. His wife, thought Judith. And Mrs. Abernathy's
friend would apparently wait for her in the car. The
postmistress turned so that she could fold her flag
without seeing into Winslow Abernathy's life or oblig-
ing him to deal with his life in her sight.

Mrs. Haig hurried back into her post office, closed
her windows, lowered her blinds, and turned off her
lights. She made the tasks last as long as possible, but
when the doors locked shut behind her, Abernathy still
stood with his wife beside the car. Mrs. Canopy still sat
inside it. Judith knew she could not simply remain

motionless on the steps, but nor could she force her body to walk past the couple. She must be insane; a week ago the man had barely spoken to her. Why should she feel so painfully deprived, so unwilling a witness at this scene of marital intimacy? The woman, his wife, reached out and enclosed Abernathy in her arms. He put his arms around her, too. They stood quietly, embracing each other, then his wife took his hands, squeezed them in hers, turned away, and got into the car. Her friend drove her quickly away out of the circle. The lawyer stood, not watching them, then—his hands feeling absently from one pocket to another—he turned back toward his office door.

Only when he was inside did Mrs. Haig feel free to pass his building. She hurried past it to The Tea Shoppe, which regularly closed hours earlier but was now unlocked. There were no customers there. Prudence Lattice was bent behind the counter, her hands in a steaming sink of cups and saucers. The picturesque ceiling fans did little with the heat but shove it at people, and the elderly shopkeeper had a worn, misty look. Conversation was awkward. Between Prudence and Judith there was only one connection, Chin Lam Henry, and Chin Lam was no longer there but was walking to the trailer park to search for the German shepherd, Night. At some point, unnoticed, the dog had vanished from the green where for most of the day he had lain in the shadow of Elijah Dingley's copper beech.

"Will she meet her husband there?" Judith asked.

Miss Lattice stacked cups as she dried them. She didn't answer for a moment, then spoke in evident discomfort. "Well, no, you see, Chin doesn't know when he'll be released."

"Oh, but I understood it was definitely to be this afternoon. Didn't Mr. Abernathy tell you?"

"Well, yes, of course, that is, Winslow did call me to say they'd arranged bail, but I haven't exactly had a chance to explain it to Chin, we've been so rushed, and then Night runs off!" Miss Lattice kept busy as she spoke. "And you see we'd already planned on our dinner for this evening and then I just didn't want for her to wait out there with no idea what might happen to her."

Judith was confused. "Perhaps I misunderstood. I had just assumed that she'd want to go to Argyle, or arrange to be at their home when—oh, watch out!" She reached across the counter at a cup that had slid from Miss Lattice's nervous hand. It smashed on the floor. "Oh, your cup, I'm sorry. It's broken."

The shopkeeper dropped the pieces into a trash basin. "Oh, it doesn't matter a bit." She smiled. In cups and saucers, if not in companionship, Prudence Lattice, heiress to a bankrupt china factory, would always be rich. The myriad crates of crockery that had escaped the liquidation of her father's substance were now in service to all Dingleyans who frequented The Tea Shoppe. Thus, chinaware supported the last Lattice still; no longer sold, but served to customers. It was the one commodity she felt she had in sufficient supply.

In the Bredforets' air-conditioned summer porch, Dr. Deeds was listening to Dr. Scaper describe his dilemma with a plodding voice and quick, irascible gestures. His dilemma was a similar peculiarity of symptoms among an increasing number of his Dingleyan patients. He told her first of the cluster of unconnected people, beginning with Vincent Canopy, who had died of some odd virulent strain of brucellosis. And how that series of deaths had been followed after a few years by periodic groups of other equally unsatisfactory terminal illnesses.

"All terminal illnesses are unsatisfactory," Ruth said. "All deaths are unnatural."

"You're young," he told her. "You'll feel different fifty years from now."

"I don't think so."

"I know you don't." But by unnatural deaths Dr.

Scaper meant a growing list of heart attack victims who were developing endocarditis much too rapidly to suit him. The town had lost more than twenty people in the past year, and at least five in the last five days.

"Heart attack is the biggest killer in the country," she said. She saw nothing unusual in the number of deaths.

But he told her that these heart collapse victims had symptoms that were more like those of viral infections: fevers, sweating, chills, malaise, headache, photophobia, prostration. Then all of a sudden their hearts gave out. The old doctor jabbed his finger through shelves of smoke stacked in the cooled air and cursed whatever was killing his patients. Finally he nestled his chins down on his chest and looked up at Ruth. "I never made any claims about diagnostic knowhow," he grumbled. "Was always the sort of fellow that just did the best I could for the patient there in front of me. But I've seen enough to know when something's way out of kilter. This Center for Disease place of yours is out of my league, I'm the first to admit it, so you tell me what you make of all this. Because I've got some good people I'm seeing right now, running these flu-type symptoms and crap showing up on lung X rays. So when I start picking up bad heart murmurs on them, hell's bells, I get scared I'm going to lose them, too."

Dr. Deeds had been leafing slowly through Dingleyans' medical charts, among them Judith Haig's and Winslow Abernathy's. Now, seated on the floor, her legs crossed yoga-style, she began to question Scaper, who slumped, fat and slovenly, in one of Mary Bredforet's cushioned wicker rocking chairs. "First of all," she said afterwards, "like I told you, this isn't really my field. But from what I can tell, I agree it looks peculiar. I mean it looks viral but doesn't seem to be contagious, at least it's not clear how. And you've got X rays indicating pneumonia, but then there's no record of really serious respiratory problems."

"Some of it looks like Rocky Mountain spotted fever, don't you think?"

"No rashes. But listen, it does sound like something like that, doesn't it? That's what I'm thinking. A rickettsia. You know, there're some guys at CDC, an epidemiologist friend of mine, we ought to let him take a look at some of this data."

"Why? You thinking something in particular?"

Dr. Deeds walked over to lean against the glass wall of the porch. Across the grounds her grandfather and Mary Bredforet stooped together in the humid heat, working their garden. She turned around, staring at Scaper as intensely as if she were about to answer a proposal of marriage, though in fact she didn't even see him. "Q Fever," she said.

"What?"

"Well, maybe not, but I know that sometimes, very rarely, but sometimes, *Coxiella burnetii* can spread through the blood to the heart. But endocarditis would be very uncommon. Q Fever itself's pretty uncommon. Nobody seems to know that much about it. Well, I don't know. There's a lot that wouldn't fit. I mean, Q Fever should respond to tetracycline. But you say you've tried several of them with no results. Which is weird. And your blood cultures are negative. But I still bet that's where we should start. Maybe it's some new strain of Q Fever. Maybe you're right, maybe it's being passed through pets." Dr. Deeds spread out the charts on the coffee table and began to read them again.

Dr. Scaper had only vaguely heard of the old strain of Q Fever, which had first been identified in Australia in 1937, long after he finished medical school. His ignorance surprised Dr. Deeds, and his willingness to confess it surprised her even more. They discussed all the other information there was to seek. Blood and sputum and stool tests and chick embryo cultures needed to be done so that specialists could look for what they'd been trained to recognize if they saw it, as

Dr. Scaper had been trained to recognize measles and whooping cough. Dr. Deeds argued with the old man that he should not yield to Jack and Peggy Strummer's refusal to have an autopsy performed on their daughter, Joy. It was crucial to examine the lungs and the heart valves; especially since complete autopsies had not been carried out on any of the similar victims.

But he said no. "The Strummers refused at the time, and they just aren't going to feel any different now. And I'm not about to browbeat them into accepting what feels to them like mutilating their girl."

Here the two physicians differed in their priorities. Dr. Scaper wanted not to lose Winslow Abernathy or Judith Haig or Sammy Smalter or anyone else in his care. Dr. Deeds wanted to discover the truth. As a child she had thrilled when Mary Bredforet had read her the stories of Florence Nightingale's ruthless courage, her willingness to toss overboard peace of mind, even lives, in order to ensure the safety of a voyage to the greater future good.

Finally Scaper agreed to drive her over to Glover's Lane so that she could talk with the Strummers herself. The couple heard her arguments politely, but they would not listen to reason. They apologized for their refusal, they asked forgiveness for the trouble they must be causing, then repeated mildly that they could not help how they felt.

Otto Scaper changed the subject. He cradled Peggy Strummer under his huge arm and asked about Joy's little golden spaniel. But the girl's father in his soft, dead voice said that Joy's spaniel's heart, like that of his mistress, had stopped. The Strummers, feeling guilty that they had denied the doctors their daughter, allowed them to dig up her dog to hand over to science.

Across the street A. A. Hayes, on his front porch jacking up a step with bricks, watched the bearish old physician, carrying a small bundle, get into his car with a young black woman. A private nurse for Peggy Strummer, Hayes assumed.

Back inside, hiding on the toilet under dinner was
ready, the editor found his clandestine place in a novel
in which a tough, cynical, idealistic loner had to choose
among facing a court-martial for helping a noble
German officer to escape, allowing Göring to succeed
in kidnapping Stalin, reconciling a breach between the
British and American high commands, or minding his
own business and finding somebody to love. Finally, by
page 420, he had done all four. Hayes grunted and
threw the book in the trash can. He pulled another off
the toilet bowl lid. A tough, cynical, idealistic loner was
going to rescue a brilliant female geneticist from a
Communist stronghold in the Alps. True, Hayes did
not find these stories very interesting. But he did prefer
them to his own.

CHAPTER
50

The first traders to invade the area set up their Dutch
posts along the Connecticut River from New Amster-
dam to Plymouth Colony and trafficked in the exchange
of trinkets for animal skins. They were pursued by the
English. Later the Irish came, and later still, French
Canadians. Then the Italians and Russian Jews, finally
blacks and Spanish speakers. Connecticut grew crowded and rich among the states. Maynard Henry's people
had made their homes here since the days of the Royal
Charter. They had never been rich, and they had felt
increasingly crowded. They were periodically resentful.
Maynard himself had no specific knowledge of his
American heritage, would not have known his grandmother's maiden name, or cared, or taken particular
pride in learning by how many generations his family

had been native-born. Yet it might be said that his blood insisted on his prior rights by rising up against the crowding trespasses of all later invaders than those pre-Revolutionary War ones who had spawned him. And this prejudice was in direct proportion to the chronology of the immigrants' intrusion: he had only the mildest instinctive antipathy to Joe MacDermott, whereas Raoul Treeca prickled his skin.

Henry felt not only trespassed upon but passed over by Carl Marco, who (objecting to his military discharge) had refused to hire him; not only crowded but crowded out by old Tim Hines, with whose refuge into madness he had been forced to cope. He sometimes felt that because of Hines's black brothers and Treeca's brown brothers, and all the people with names like Marco and Grabaski, and the rest, a man with a name like Maynard Clarence Henry could not find work doing construction in a rich state like Connecticut, but was forced to the degradation of accepting government handouts. As long as there had been room for everyone, everyone had been welcome, but America wasn't building many more Grand Central Stations or railroads from the Atlantic to the Pacific in 1976. It was not girding its loins with steel anymore, but tightening its belt. It was as big as it would ever be and could no longer take care of itself.

The public schools had taught Maynard that, apart from a little digging up the earth for iron and tobacco, Connecticut had by and large manufactured its wealth in the nineteenth century, when it filed more patents than any other state. Henry's people had helped the state grow rich. They had hammered together the hulls of the clippers that skimmed like eagles on the water out of the port of Mystic. They had turned the mills and laid the red bricks for factories where they, and their children, could labor to produce the weaponry invented by local geniuses like Eli Whitney and Samuel Colt and Oliver F. Winchester. Connecticut had thrived on the guns and ammunition that won the West, and on the artillery, submarines, planes, and helicopters that had made the world safe for those who had not been killed by (or in) them. Connecticut had helped to manufacture some of that advanced equipment that had taken Henry, the Grabaskis, Bobby Strummer, Juan Treeca, and the rest, into battle as the most expensively outfitted fighting force in the world.

Henry was thinking of that expensive abundance now, as he walked angrily along the highway from Argyle to Dingley Falls. Fields full of jet planes, mountains of M-16s. Everyone at the prison had been complaining of the heat today. Heat? He thought about standing off beside the roadway near Da Nang while somebody tried to fix an M-48 tank the V.C. had mined; a soldier near him had gone crazy with sunstroke. His flushed, dry skin having reached 109 degrees, he had collapsed into a coma and had died before the medics could land their helicopter, much less try to get his temperature down. They had said it was just as well; his brains had already burst. In the end the tank had to be abandoned anyhow. Like the rest. All that shining metal superfluity of affluence that by our willingness to spend it should have subdued any enemy, littered in the bright, hot orange and green landscape; machinery lost, thrown away, used up as fast as Connecticut, among other builders, could make it—as if shooting up useless flares in manic frustration, or firing clip after clip at dead Viet Cong out of the sullen boredom of despair would rid everyone of the war and so of guilt that much sooner. Henry had not known how many thousands of dollars it cost to support and supply him each day in Vietnam, nor would he have cared. It was all to him bullshit, a total waste. He still wore the boots. They had lasted.

As soon as released on bail arranged by his brother's lawyer, Henry had left to look for his wife, Chin Lam. There was no way to reach her except to find her. He had left on foot because his truck was parked at a station in Madder, and there was no one he cared to ask

to come get him. Besides, a seven-mile walk was
nothing to him. He moved without thinking. He wore
his boots and green fatigue pants and a white T-shirt
and carried a folded grocery bag packed with his other
belongings. The sharp, thin planes of his face (that face
that had reminded A. A. Hayes of the young male
invaders moving west to trade trinkets for land and
gold), the tan, creased lines, the hard mouth and
cold-colored eyes were tense with anger. Henry was
angry at everyone, at Hawk Haig and Raoul Treeca for
putting him in jail, at his brother, Arn, for buying his
way out, at his wife for not being there when he was
released, at Connecticut for stopping the highway that
paid his wages, at everyone who found jobs when he
couldn't, at prices for being too high, at himself for not
being able to make it and for being alive when so many
he had known briefly in the jungle had by the mis-
chance of standing so many feet to the front or rear or
side of him been blown away and burned away into
death. He was angry at the government for making him
a piece of that superfluity spent and discarded. Henry
took a cigarette from his pants pocket and lit it without
pausing in the rhythm of his march.

Tracy Canopy, returning to Dingley Falls from the
train station (where, with the brave smile of a mother
sending a daughter off to the Peace Corps in a jungle
someplace she couldn't pronounce, she had said good-
bye to Beanie), slowed her car when she saw the
hitchhiker, his arm patiently raised. Six years earlier, in
New Haven, Mrs. Canopy had been robbed of her
purse at knifepoint by a young hitchhiker, who had
then gratuitously hit her in the face with his fist.
Afterwards she had promised her friends never again to
pick up a stranger, even if he lay moaning in a ditch
beside the road, for muggers were known to play such
ploys upon the innocent. The problem was you couldn't
tell who anyone was from their clothes anymore: this
young man with his boots and funny pants could be a
state surveyor, or a hippie with a sack full of marijuana,

or he could have his bathing suit in that bag, or a lug wrench to crush her skull. No, pleasant as it was to meet the young and hear of lives so different from her own, she couldn't take the chance anymore. She remembered how the fist had hit against her cheek, and speeding up, she passed by Maynard Henry.

He was thinking that he would trade in his trailer, take the cash and his truck and his wife and leave Connecticut, travel to the Southwest where the money had gone. He'd settle things with Haig and Treeca first. If he had to, he'd jump his brother's bail. There were still jobs some places in America for a man who didn't mind hard work and high risks. He could pay Arn back in the end. But there was no way he was going inside that jail again. As he gestured his thumb at cars whooshing past him, Henry kept walking at a steady pace. If someone stopped, fine. If not, he'd be home in another hour. Henry had been trained, at considerable expense, to walk long distances efficiently.

Judith Haig stood in the trailer park and pressed her hand hard against the pain in her chest until it went away. She had forced herself to walk there from The Tea Shoppe. She wanted to find Chin Lam. For all her thoughtfulness, she could not have told herself why. Judith, because she was never insensitive to *what* she felt, or why she felt it. But the desire had been strong enough to overcome her terror of the place where the dogs lived. Now one of them, with a mammoth orange-brown head, lunged out at her as she went carefully past him, but he was roped to a junked car and jerked to a stop, whining. Two strays had jumped to their feet and started to trot toward her when a child running past kicked out at them until they retreated. The child ran on as if he had kicked out at air in a dance. Mrs. Haig did not see Chin Lam or Night anywhere in the area. It had been senseless to come. From what was she trying to protect Chin? She should leave. Coming from the trailers, she could hear the noises of air conditioners and televisions and babies and dishes, of men and women yelling angrily at children and each other. She could smell cooking grease.

A young boy and girl were walking toward her; each had an arm around the other and a hand in the other's front jeans pocket. Mrs. Haig recognized Jimmy Mac-Dermott. The girl, then, must be the Puerto Rican Sarah was so opposed to. Now, while the girl watched them with patient distrust, Jimmy pointed out for Judith Maynard Henry's trailer. The two teenagers in their flimsy, garish clothes looked very frail to her as, in rhythmic step like a dance, they moved away.

Sinuous autographs in wide curling colors had been scrawled along the sides of the trailer's new white siding. Crumpled beside a cinder block was a piece of paper the graffitist had torn with random destructiveness from the door. Judith did not see the paper, though if by chance she had, its message, in Vietnamese, would have meant nothing to her, or to anyone else in Dingley Falls except Maynard Henry and his wife, who had written it to let him know that if he did return, he should call her at one of two numbers, that of The Tea Shoppe or of Prudence Lattice's home. Despite the padlock, Judith knocked on the door. But when a dog's growl rumbled from somewhere beneath the trailer, she pulled quickly back and hurried away to Long Branch Road. From there she had intended to turn onto Goff, cross the bridge, and be home before dark to start dinner for her husband's return. Sarah MacDermott, however, carrying groceries up her front steps, saw her and called Judith over with the yelled demand that she explain what she was doing in the neighborhood. Knowing that Sarah was irritated by her interest in Chin Lam, Judith said merely that she was on her way home.

"Honey, from where? Fred's bar? Jesus bless us, you shouldn't be trooping all over Madder in this heat. Tell you the truth, when I first saw you, I thought you'd had a stroke and were wandering around in a daze. Here, would you just grab this bag for me so I won't have to make another trip? Judith, listen to me, don't ever have kids till they make it legal to kill them. My oldest son delivers groceries for a living, if you can believe that, and he trots right past me down these steps like he would have thrown a quarter in my tin cup if I'd had one to poke up in his face." Mrs. MacDermott butted the door open with her behind and held it for Judith. "Anyhow, he's not fooling me. I know exactly where he's rushing to. That little painted whore and him both are going to get hauled in to see Father Crisp and get the riot act read them, if not worse and he has to marry her. Sit down, have a Coke, how are you? I'm just so on edge about you after what happened to Alf and Sister Mary Joseph." On and on from there went Mrs. MacDermott with an exuberant necrology that included a fellow A & P clerk's sister, who had been born without either her arms or her legs from "thelidomide" and lived strapped to a tilting board in the family room. Like a Foxe's *Book of Martyrs* for the modern world, she detailed news of all the latest local sufferings, and not even after Judith had heard far too much about Jack and Peggy Strummer's private sorrows was Sarah willing to release her. "Besides, you know Bobby wasn't even really Jack's son because Peggy was married before. Used to live right here in Madder, I think he was an alcoholic, anyhow she dumped him. So Jack adopted Bobby. They both took after Peggy, Bobby and Joy, God bless her. Oh, he was so good-looking, well, you saw him. Sort of like a cross between Tab Hunter and Burt Reynolds. I used to keep my eye out for him when he was working at Hope Street Cinema, even if he was only eighteen or so, but still. You can't go to hell for looking. Anyhow, honey, have one of these beers before I drink them all, I already had two at Holly Brejinski's when I picked Francis and the baby up. I always did like Bobby, it gives me the creeps to think about him dead somewhere in a jungle or having bamboo shoots stuck up under his fingernails in a Communist prison camp. I don't know. He just had the build and that kind of sexy eyes that just about made me wet my panties. Well, Judith, you'll just have to excuse my expression, but between men and women these things are only natural."

As she spoke, Mrs. MacDermott continued to unpack groceries, set the table, boil hot dogs, broil frozen french fries, and arbitrate between sons who sporadically burst out of the TV room with legal briefs against their siblings. Between interruptions she pursued her conversation out of death and into sex; as a gossip, she necessarily discoursed on the great themes of life. Sarah was willing to confess to a lascivious nature. She attributed it to a polymorphous gluttony at the root of her personality, which made it impossible for her to get enough of anything (beer, TV, babies, parties, food, money, news), and sex was no different. No doubt she was a sinner, but she still loved the way it relaxed her after a long day. Yet despite her carnality, she had been completely faithful to Joe throughout their marriage except for one single "slipup," as she called it, for which she hoped Judith could forgive her, as Father Crisp had, though expecting Joe to was probably too much to ask, and so she'd kept it to herself, which she hoped Judith would as well. Promising to keep her friend's lapse secret (she had been subjected to this confession before), Judith ventured to suggest that Sarah might want to do the same; she didn't feel comfortable hearing such things.

"Honey, if I tried to bottle up everything the way you do, they'd carry me away in a straitjacket. But everybody's got to just live and let live. Because we're all the same, Lord bless us, when you get down to it. Not a one of us can poop with our legs crossed so tight it can't get out."

Mrs. Haig was spared any obligation to reply to this definition of humanity because the phone rang, and it was her husband, John, asking Sarah if she had his wife over there. He was home and wondered why Judith wasn't. He said he would come for her at once. "I started," said Mrs. MacDermott after Judith hung up, "to ask you both to stay for supper, but the pure and simple truth is I haven't got enough meat in this house to coax a starving tiger out of a burning building. Anyhow, you two haven't seen each other in a while, and I figure Hawk'd rather have you to himself tonight." Sarah rolled her eyes and waggled her eyebrows. Judith's blush flushed even the skin over her collarbone. "I'm sorry, Sarah, but could I use your phone for a minute?"

"Don't be sorry, be my guest." Sarah was spooning beans and french fries onto plates.

"Is this the only one you have?"

"Honey, how many do you need?"

"Just for a minute, I'm sorry, but could I ask if I could use it in private?"

Sarah stared at Mrs. Haig, then flipped off her stove burners. "Say no more." She grinned and backed out into the TV room with a tray of hot dogs.

Hot with embarrassment, Judith found Winslow Abernathy's home phone number. She noticed as she dialed that its four digits after the local exchange were the year of her birth. When Abernathy answered, she told him that perhaps it would be helpful to remind Miss Lattice that Chin Lam would need to make arrangements about meeting her husband. She told him again that she was grateful for his efforts on the girl's behalf, but that she herself would be unable to pursue the matter further because her husband had just returned home from an out-of-town trip. If he wouldn't mind she would call him at his office about the final outcome of the Henrys' difficulties and would prefer that he not call her at home. She hoped he would understand.

"Hawk's outside honking." Sarah popped her head around the door and saw that Judith had replaced the receiver. "Just like he did in high school, remember? I

remember once I was standing right next to you when
you asked him to never do it again. I really thought you
were going to lose your temper that time, 'course you
didn't, but still. Well, what can women do but grin and
bear it? Okay, well, tell him now he's back I'd like to
get Joe home at a decent hour. Honey, good-bye and
did I tell you, we're going to the lake tomorrow if you
feel like coming? You and little Francis could sit off by
yourselves somewhere and read. You know, that little
bookworm came right up and told me he wished he had
you for a mother, can you believe that?''

Sarah, back at work in her kitchen, wondered about
the telephone call. It struck her that she had never
known Judith to call *anyone*, much less demand privacy
to do so. Was she involved with someone? Oh, it wasn't
possible! Anyhow, how could she be having an affair
with a man and have to look up his number in the
phone book, which was still out on the counter? A man
whose name began with an *A* or a *B*. Over the gunfire
of the television and the clatter of her sons it had been
difficult to hear any part of Judith's conversation, not
that Sarah had listened, but she had caught the name
Chin Lam. What was it between Judith and Chinkie?
You'd think Chinkie was some long-lost relation the
way Judith was behaving! Well, Judith could act awful
frosty sometimes, so there was no sense in asking, even
after all the years of love Sarah had poured down on
her. And sometimes it just didn't seem worth it, so
much all give and no get. But it takes all kinds, that was
Mrs. MacDermott's motto, and what's more, who
knew what God was up to when He made some hearts
warm and some hearts cold? She had a very clear sense
that God approved of her persistent befriending of
Judith Haig. It was one of those kinds of accomplish-
ments, like missionary work or chastity, of which God
was said to be particularly fond.

The last purple had darkened Wild Oat Ridge to
indistinction and Dingley Falls lost its outline. Night

was only slightly cooler than dusk had been, outside was only slightly cooler than indoors. For years, however, the houses of Elizabeth Circle had been equipped to condition air to circumvent the vagaries of nature, and inside the brightly lit rooms there, residents moved at their ease. But the Abernathys' home had no air conditioners. The thought of having to keep her windows closed and having to smell machine-forced air for even such a summer night as this had been intolerable to Beanie. She could always, thought Winslow, endure a higher degree of reality than he could; for he had been forced to come outside to walk tonight, unable to function under the heavy weight of heated air that hung over his study. He wondered how he could have forgotten for so many years that he was a person who habitually took walks.

Winslow Abernathy, while entirely sober, was feeling light-headed. Wryly he considered the possibility that he had poisoned himself inadvertently in his novice but seemingly innocuous broiling of a steak and tossing of a salad. In his mood he decided that he, like a postman with special delivery news, would call on each of his neighbors in turn and preempt their speculations on his private life by declaring in their front halls that Mr. and Mrs. Winslow Abernathy wished to announce the separation of Beatrice Rose Dingley from Winslow Edward Abernathy on June 4. Private ceremony. No flowers. He was unaccustomed to behaving with public facetiousness, however dignified, and he attributed the desire now to joke with Elizabeth Circle to this odd light-headedness of his. His neighbors, he knew, would attribute it to the peculiar effects of grief on the unsuspecting.

But what was so peculiar was that the collapse of his marriage, while presumably unsuspected, had not, honestly (once he had been forced to take time to assess honestly his state of mind), had not seemed sudden at all. And more remarkably, had not seemed cause for grief. And most remarkably (unless his roughest digging had not been strong enough to pry loose hidden ore of suffering), his predominant emotion about the entire matter was that he was very proud and a little bit envious of Beanie for so clearly grasping the truth and acting upon it. This response to the abrupt adultery of his wife and her termination of their marriage after thirty quiescent years was, he thought, marvelously bizarre, but so absurd, even to himself, that he felt shy about sharing it, even with the wryest of his acquaintances, A. A. Hayes (who was too committed to the intolerableness of his own marriage to find amusing the buoyancy with which Abernathy watched *his* be torpedoed and sunk). Yes, he thought, the Hayeses kept themselves sensitive to life, and each other, by continually ripping the bandages off each other's wounds; they were unhappily married, far more so than the Abernathys. In fact, Winslow would not admit that he and Beanie had been unhappily married at all. He had been too civilized, and Beanie too good-hearted, for daily misery. Because, as Beanie had explained, unlike the Hayeses (who were fiercely monogamous in the intensity of their hate), she and Winslow had never been married at all. Yesterday she had sat with him in his study and had tried to explain to him why he felt less pain about what was happening than he thought he ought to feel.

It was not easy, she had said, but it is usually *easier*, to do the right thing, though it may seem, even for as long as thirty years, that it is easier not to. The Abernathys could have "easily" lived in pleasant accord until their deaths, except for the inevitable chance of Richard Rage, who had in a single day, and without intending to, made clear that the Abernathys were not living together at all, by reminding them that they were not touching, not seeing the other, that they had never been able to move into the other's world, though in the beginning both had been mesmerized by the very width of the chasm between them. So they had thought they lived easily together, only to find, when the chasm did split apart, how quickly everything could fall right. Like a painting, Beanie said, finally moved after hanging for years slightly too high on the wall, and suddenly you see that it's wrong and you change it. Like not consciously knowing you had been for a long while off balance in a plane until the wing tipped back and you were upright again and it felt right.

These were not the metaphors he would have chosen; still, he, with his more fugitive and cloistered virtues, stood in awe of Beanie's victory over language; less in awe of her courage in battling her way to Truth as her wrestling Truth down until it yielded her, like the angel yielding to Jacob, the words to explain its meaning. She who had actually once said she "hated" language. Yes, thought Winslow as he began to a second circuit of Elizabeth Circle, the situation was absurd. As a lawyer he would plead *non compos mentis*. Never had he loved Beanie more than today, when she had forced him out of his easy cell and into freedom, when she had released him from any obligation to love her at all. And so shocked had he been by the intensity of his affection, once he focused his attention—as he had not done for years—on who she was; so excited had he become about the reality of his regard, that he had nearly caught Beanie up in his arms and begged her to reconsider. But he hadn't done it, and in that fact, of course, the truth lay. Then briefly he had washed himself in warm tubs of pity that the actual process of their discovering themselves should cost him this new (this newly noticed) Beanie. But now he felt only light-headed, as if above the aching tiredness he had fought for weeks his mind floated, buoyant and marvelously detached from what must look to his neighbors like the stormy shipwreck of his life.

Winslow Abernathy chuckled aloud, though very quietly. He would not, after all, indulge in playing town crier for Elizabeth Circle. No one would believe him anyhow if he cried, "All's well." And the truth was he had no desire to make up something properly bereft to

say to them. Tracy he had already telephoned to thank
for her goodness to Beanie, and for the rest, he had no
comment. The lawyer chuckled, realizing he had
completed the circle of widely spaced houses twice
already, without noticing what he was doing. For years,
no doubt, he had not actually looked at the houses
surrounding his own. As Beanie, oddly, put it, he kept
his eyes on his brain. Evelyn Troyes, for example,
appeared to have a gas-flame lamp post at the end of
her lawn; had she always had it? He could hear
Evelyn's television, or record player, playing. What did
Evelyn do with herself, alone in that large, wasted
house? Why didn't she and Tracy both, and him too for
that matter, move in with Ramona and Sam Smalter,
plenty of room there, and give their houses to the
descendants of the Madder workers whose labors had
constructed and supported them? Or, for that matter
give it all back to the Indians, if any could be found.
How Arthur would bellow for his pilfered patrimony if
Winslow should simply sign over Dingley Optical
Instruments to the Algonquin tribe from which Elijah
Dingley had bought the land three hundred years ago in
exchange for glass beads, an axhead, and Agatha
Dingley's Dutch lace petticoat.

Abernathy waved at Mr. and Mrs. Ernest Ransom,
as with a honked greeting they pulled their Mercedes
out of their driveway and passed the pedestrian. Ever
since he'd known them, thought Winslow, the Ransoms
had dined out half the week and invited guests to dine
in the other half. Ergo, they hate being together in
private, or ergo, they love being together in public, or
undoubtedly endless other ergos that if he were interested in the Ransoms he would be interested in. He
noticed that Otto Scaper's lights were already out, and
then walked on around the curving sidewalk until up on
the hill from which Ramona's white Victorian mansion
looked down on its simpler Federalist neighbors, the
midget Sammy Smalter stood on the lawn so stilly that

Winslow was reminded of the plaster statues of Negro boys once used as ornamental hitching posts by Beanie's Baltimore mother, May Rose. It was another of those bizarre images attributable to his light-headedness.

"Outdoors too?" called Smalter in greeting. Abernathy could see the quick series of flaring red as Smalter puffed on his pipe. He began searching his pockets for his own.

"Yes. Rather muggy."

"Horrible. The whole sky feels like a steamy towel in a barber shop being lowered over your face."

"Yes, I suppose it does." Did it? How could it? What unsettling images Smalter evoked as a matter of course, as if his habitual frame of mind was as conceptually inebriated as Abernathy felt his own to be tonight. What a different way of seeing the world, to look at something *through* a simile rather than translating it into a simile after the fact. Very different from his perennial "it is as if" tactic in efforts to persuade Beanie to agree that he was right. And now, after all the verbal debates he was accustomed to winning both in his court and in his castle, he had been persuaded by Beanie that *she* was right, perhaps even right when she, absurdly, remarked, "I don't know if you'll want to, I mean take the time. It takes time to learn how you'd feel feeling in love, and you don't have to, Winslow, it doesn't mean you're wrong if you don't. But you could. But it would have to be a woman who *looks* like this statue to you." And she had put her hand on the head of Marcus Antistius Labeo, the Roman jurist.

What awed him about this remark was that he knew what she meant, even as he said he didn't. What struck him as remarkable was that while part of his mind was thinking what a ridiculous simile (for the chipped alabaster face was that of a sad, introspective, middle-aged man with pure, blind eyes and a too sensitive mouth; the nose was broken and the forehead balding), at the same time another part of his mind immediately, illogically, thought of Judith Haig. What was more remarkable still was that Beanie had then added, "Like the woman who runs the post office. She looks like that."

CHAPTER
51

The house of Mr. and Mrs. John "Hawk" Haig crouched beside the highway, an outpost on the watch for all those traders who were to invade Dingley Falls and make Hawk's fortune. Inside the house the Haigs sat like an illustration in their family room—he with the newspaper in his vinyl recliner, she with her knitting in her green plaid armchair, each with a coffee mug inscribed with their first names (gifts Haig liked to use because his sister had given them), both cooled by the air conditioning and lulled by the tick of the imitation antique clock. The evening so far had passed with less disjunction than Judith had expected. John was unusually talkative. He was disgusted by the possibility that Dingley Falls might lose its post office, and he was thrilled by his discoveries about the abandoned highway. Earlier in the evening he had been eager to lead her step by step through the maze where he had wound his way in Hartford, until, finally, when he was tangled in red tapes of confusion, a tip completely by chance had led him straight to the cache of hidden facts.

Somebody had been paid off to stop that highway connector. Somebody had been paid off to falsify that surveyor's report. Somebody had been paid off to negotiate the resale of that land. And Ernest Ransom, president of Ransom Bank, holder of the Haig mort-

gage, was up to his neck in the muddy waters of all
these payoffs. "And, Jude, I'm going to stir that water
up until the mud sticks on the faces where it belongs.
I'm not going to even bother with those jerk selectmen.
I'm going straight to the state attorney's office and press
charges for conspiracy to defraud the people of Connecticut. A shake-up like this is all I need to get my
name out there. So I can get a committee together and
they can start getting organized and soliciting contributions. So I can get a campaign going. I know, but that's
the thing about it these days. It takes a lot of money just
to buy yourself a chance to do something in this world.
All I want is my chance to show I can make just a little
bit of difference. Just a chance to make it. To matter,
that's the God's truth, hon, you know what I mean?
Hey, that smells great."

As he spoke, Haig had stood and walked to the
opening between the kitchen and the dinette. He was a
large man, bulkier than he had been as a youth, but still
muscular; by no means fat, just large. Most people
thought him a handsome man; some, in fact, thought
he looked better now than at eighteen, when his blond,
close-cropped curls and chiseled features and athlete's
body had seemed too perfect for down-to-earth manli-
ness. Now the hair was grizzled brown, the features had
broadened, the body had thickened. The bad knee
from the car accident had to be favored more, particularly when, as now, he was tired. Tonight, as his wife
had cooked, he had stood there with his weight off the
weak leg, still in his dress pants and suede boots and a
blue dress shirt, its collar loosened behind his tie. His
hands, raised over his head, pushed on either side of
the doorway. Judith was disturbed by the dark, wet
stains under his arms. His hands looked huge to her,
the fingers spread out, pushing against the walls. His
sleeves were rolled above his elbows, and muscles
twitched along the thick brown arms. "Well, more
later," he had said, then asked if he had time for a
shower, and she had nodded yes.

So dinner had been cooked and eaten under the protection of the post office news and highway news. Even ordinarily Mr. and Mrs. Haig were not at ease with each other. Whenever they were separated, the transition back to cohabitation was always clumsy. Hawk felt intrusive and Judith felt intruded upon. His voice and steps sounded to his own ears like a loud, hollow echo in the still house. He seemed to loom quickly and awkwardly there, out of proportion to the furniture. To her, his soiled clothes coiling out of the open suitcase on the bed were almost cause for panic. She had unpacked them and pushed them down into the hamper.

First evenings together were always difficult, but on this particular one Judith was constrained, as well, by the distance she had put between them through her unexplainable involvement with Chin Lam Henry and Winslow Abernathy. It was not that she had never kept secrets from John before. Her whole felt life was a secret, wholly unshared. Yet she had rarely, if ever— and she couldn't recall which, so devoid of significance had her actions been—falsified what she *did*. Now she had actively denied Sarah's report of her interest in the Vietnamese girl. Nor was she certain why she had felt it necessary to warn Winslow Abernathy against calling her at home, except she knew it was necessary that John not be challenged by so much as a thought that Abernathy presumed an interest in her—whether the thought were true or not.

After dinner the routine that kept them safe from intimacy had reasserted itself. Haig had announced his need to catch up, reclining, on the news of the world. She had saved the papers for him. From her knitting (the many-colored scarf she thought of as Sammy Smalter's was almost finished) Mrs. Haig looked over at her husband, now after a shower in a summer police shirt and trousers. His legs extended, longer than she had remembered them, out from the crackling newspaper. Inside the enormous socks his toes were moving.

He made continual tiny noises in his throat and mouth and with his fingers and by shifting his weight in the vinyl chair.

She felt an easing of pressure because it was almost nine o'clock; he would have to leave soon for the station to take over patrol until eleven. Then suddenly Haig flapped his paper shut and saw her looking at him. She lowered her eyes at once, but he came over behind her chair, stretching with a yawn to disguise his intent and awkwardness. Judith willed herself to relax as he put his hands through her hair, then onto her neck, and rubbed. Her head jerked slowly back and forth. Then the hands pressed on her shoulders, kneading them over and over in the same place. Then finally the hands slid down and pressed against her collarbone. Then they slid farther down and lay twitching against her breasts. It was to Mrs. Haig as if two large, pink baby animals of undefined and foreign species had crawled from behind the chair down to her bosom to try to suckle there. She took the hands away and held them.

He whispered, "Hey, honey, hey there," his breath slightly rasped, and came around in front of her, pulled her up by the hands, wrapped his arms around her body, and began to kiss her. The pressure of his lips strained her neck back, and his tongue was hard and jabbing inside her mouth. Her arms were crushed up between their bodies.

Her husband's action had not been unexpected by Mrs. Haig. Generally after such absences he expected them to do what he called "be together." In this case she was also aware that he felt he had been denied the previous three weeks by scrupulous sacrifice to her newly diagnosed illness. She knew he had asked Dr. Scaper just before leaving for Hartford whether, given her heart condition, the conjugal act could harm his wife, and the doctor had said no, there was no reason why it should. John had always kept an accurate record of the days lapsed between sexual relations. To repay these marital IOUs she had longer respites now than in the early years of their marriage. She had expected to be called to account tonight. But not this early; later, after they were in bed, where it usually began.

His hands were moving rapidly up and down her back; they pulled her hips toward him. She could feel the hardened lump and tried to twist to the side. "John," she said, and tried to push away from his chest with her hands, "it's nine o'clock."

Above her his neck and ears were flushed and his breath was loud. "Come on, hon, hey, come on."

"You told Joe you'd come to the station at nine. John. Please, John." The words were her only struggle to escape, though the wish to escape beat inside her like the flapping wings of an enormous bird panicked in a cage. "John, you told Joe."

He squeezed his hand around her waist and led her across the hall to the bedroom, where, without turning on the light, he pulled her down beside him on the bed, his weight forcing her next to him. Then pushing her backwards, he rolled on top of her, one leg wedging hers open.

"John. Please," she asked a final time.

"No," he said. "Now. Hon, come on, now. It's been almost a month. A month." He held her wrists down over her head. "I've missed my wife. Missed you, hon. You're still my girl." He was rubbing harder against her, then he rolled off and said hoarsely, "Take off your clothes and get under the covers, all right? I've got to wear these tonight, so I guess . . ." His voice trailed off. Standing beside her, he undressed like an athlete in a changing room, ignoring with silent circumspection a nearby body.

His wife had done as he had said. As his eyes adjusted to the dark room, he looked down at her; her eyes were closed, her arms beneath the sheet crossed over her breasts. He stroked his erect organ, then slid beneath the sheets.

When it was over, he pulled away immediately and showered once again. He returned to the bedroom in his shorts and a T-shirt, switched on the light, and slapped cheerfully at his stomach. "We're not so old," he said to his wife. She lay under the covering still, her face turned away from him. After he dressed, he sat beside her on the edge of the bed. "That's right," he told her. "You just lie back and get some rest. I'll let myself in, I'll be at the station really late, don't worry about getting up for me. Good to be back, Jude."

After she heard the car ignition, she pulled the sheet around her and, steadying herself for a minute by the bedpost, walked to the bathroom.

Maynard Henry had lost time. It had taken time to beat the padlock off his trailer with a rock. It had taken time, scattering to the floor the neat shelves of cartons and bottles, to find a can of strong cleanser so that he could scour the graffiti off the side of his trailer. It had taken time to search the area for his wife and his dog. Her balled-up note of explanation still lay in the dark dirt beneath the trailer where the graffitist had randomly thrown it. No one in the compound could tell him where Chin might be. Juan Treeca, Raoul's brother, had shoved their trailer door shut, cursing him in an endless stream of Spanish profanity that he couldn't translate. Henry walked back through the dark to his trailer, felt up along a closet shelf, and took down his service revolver. When the Treeca father jerked open his door again, Maynard shoved the gun in the old man's stomach. Then they told him Chin was not, and had not been, in their trailer at all. Mrs. Treeca, fat and proudly dressed, had shouted up at him, "You are free, and six weeks to come now Raoul must stay in that hospital. Who will pay? Ah, tell me who!" Henry had set her aside, firmly but without anger or even interest. He began to search Madder.

But no one was where he was supposed to be and that had cost Henry time. The man with whom he had left his truck at the station was out somewhere driving in it. Victor Grabaski, the only other person in town who might have taken her away, was not in his trailer, nor was Victor's cousin, Karl. Henry felt sunburned, grimy, hungry, and exhausted by frustration and alarm. Anything could have happened to his wife. She could be dead, or hurt, or lost and unable to explain herself. Any bastard could have told her anything. How could she tell the difference between what made sense in America and what didn't? It was possible that he had lost her for good, that the government had returned her to Southeast Asia as suddenly and as haphazardly as it had lifted her out of the panicked streets of Saigon and brought her, by chance, here to him. Anything could have happened to her because he hadn't been there to stop it. Because he had been tossed in the can by that bastard Haig, whom he'd like to kill with his bare hands.

Maynard Henry was a man of violent instincts whose outbursts, throughout his thirty-two years, had been matters for long, concerned discussion among first his family, then his teachers, and then his military superiors. All had judged him unmanageable in every cordoned area where they had had him in charge— playpen, playground, or combat zone. They judged him prickly, touchy, purposely unpleasant. Unlike his affable brother, Arn, he had made few friends. They said the marines would be the perfect place for him, since what he needed was straightening out, a firm hand, the goal of becoming a man. They thought he should be shipped somewhere (far from Dingley Falls, Connecticut) to get rid of all that young hostility and aggression. In 1965, when he was twenty-one, they sent him to the other side of the world to kill people. In 1970 he had come home, still a man of violent instincts. He had not been typically violent. Unlike many, he had not crawled out of that darkness mad. When his comrades in arms had whacked off the heads of Vietnamese, stuck cigarettes in their mouths, and photographed these trophies, he had responded with only a slightly heightened degree of the angry disgust with which he had regarded, for example, a black pimp in a peach and burgundy Eldorado, or a fatherly lecture by his brother Arn on how to make it in this world. Henry had not collected villagers' ears, but he had bitten off the earlobe of a fellow soldier whom he had attacked in a bar, and this ear, being an American ear, was more remarked upon in his battalion than those others.

The same passion that fueled Maynard Henry's choleric rages also ignited different kinds of turbulent urges in him, for he was susceptible as well to ungovernable fits of compassion, loyalty, and bravery in defense of others' safety or his own rigid principles. But he had almost no capacity to analyze or to adjudicate his emotions, and so when he lashed out at a beggar, he could not trace how pity beyond his control had triggered his rage.

For the past month the fulcrum of all the violent instincts, the eye of the still hurricane, had been his wife, Chin Lam. She had become the flame of his indignation toward his enemies and of his shame for having once been her enemy, of his anger for being left out and of his pride for taking his own way. He loved her fiercely. He ached to find her at once, but what he saw himself doing was shaking her until her neck snapped.

At the end of Long Branch Road Henry was standing, looking north across the small, turbulent Falls of the Rampage. On the other side of the river the shabby, red brick building that housed Dingley Optical Instruments was closed and dark. Dim shapes scurried across Falls Bridge. They were dogs, nearly a dozen of them, and as they raced at him now, he curled his palm around the .45 in the pocket of his nylon windbreaker. Then he recognized Night, his German shepherd, among the leaders and called to him with a whistle. The pack moiled around Henry's legs while he strapped his belt through Night's collar as the huge black dog leaped to his shoulders to lick at his face.

When they reached Ransom Circle, the dog began to

bark, scrabbling off to the right, toward Chin and the center of Dingley Falls, although Henry had turned left onto Hope Street. The two fought for control until, struggling against the dog's weight, the thin man stumbled. "You motherfucker cocksucker," he yelled, spitting out the curse as he yanked so savagely on the leash that the shepherd toppled for a second off balance. It yelped and then let itself be pulled along. Halfway through the block Henry reached down, rubbed the dog's head, and in a sweet, scratchy singsong said, "Hey, baby, it's all right, you all right, Night? You sorry-ass motherfucker, you all right? Where is she, boy? You know where Chin went? Thought you were going to watch out for her, you cocksucker, okay now, it's all right, we'll find her, don't you worry, you sorry-ass motherfucker, that's a boy, Night."

In 1974 Chin Lam's father (an eagerly corrupt petty bureaucrat) had chanced to do an army M.P. named Victor Grabaski a substantial favor involving the dismissal of certain potentially damaging legal charges about the trading of American blue jeans for opium. By chance Victor Grabaski had been in a position (near a helicopter) to return the favor a year later by shoving the just-orphaned Chin Lam to the front of a mob, then pulling her into the machine with him as it took off. She was transported eventually to California and finally (still in contact with Corporal Grabaski) to Connecticut, where two relatives of hers were thought to have escaped earlier. But by chance these people proved to be total strangers, with names confusingly identical to her aunt and uncle's—thereby misleading the Americans in charge of Vietnamese refugees, who had processed Chin. Her true relatives had been misplaced somewhere else in the United States (and were, in fact, managing a Burger King restaurant in Cincinnati). With the best will in the world, Operation Rescue and Resettlement, working in haste, was losing people right and left. Good Samaritans were running away with the homeless before they could be registered; childless couples were grabbing round-faced orphans right off the airline counters; needy hospitals were hauling away M.D.'s who would, as one administrator phrased it, "work like coolies for peanuts" as Americans opened their arms in this crisis, aroused to goodwill by the titillation of catastrophe.

Victor Grabaski, by default her oldest friend now, had finally arranged (through union contacts) for Chin Lam to be hired at Dingley Optical Instruments. But before she had to begin assembling binoculars (or repaying Victor in the currency he had slowly realized he preferred in exchange for his protection), Maynard Henry had seen her and begun precipitously to court her. When Grabaski had responded with a proprietary claim about the beautiful nineteen-year-old girl, Henry had broken a broom over Victor's back and kicked his cousin Karl unconscious while Chin Lam was running from the trailer to summon help for him.

They had married. On her part it was an act as full of meaning and as irrelevant as the act of a man falling off a cliff who grabs at the one hand reaching over the edge to him. Henry was her lifeline. Since they had been together, she had been equally terrified by the thought of his violence should she displease him and of her helplessness should he (who cared for her and spoke some part of her language) disappear. His arrest, for which she seemed to be responsible, had felt to Chin Lam so like another deadly fall through space that she had clutched again at the air above her and felt to her shock what Maynard had not wished her to find—other hands besides his own held out to her.

And now the thin, veiny hands of Prudence Lattice patted one of Chin's. In her living room the old woman sat beside the girl and promised her not only a livelihood but a home, should she, for any reason, ever require one. Miss Lattice had kept Chin safe for herself until after dinner. But then, prompted by Winslow

Abernathy's unexpected visit in the early evening while
Chin was out searching the neighborhood one last time
for Night, Miss Lattice had been forced by her con-
science to tell her guest that her husband would
probably be returning to Madder before morning. Yet,
she added, let Chin stay until he called her. He would
see her note. There was no need to go now. It was too
upsetting to think of her walking in the dangerous dark
to the trailer park, waiting in the dangerous dark for
someone. For someone, Prudence was thinking, like
Maynard Henry, whom she had never met, but imagined as a vague, violent shape, unpredictable, huge,
and menacing. Insistent on his own will, ravenous
with those impulses to seize and plunder and kill that
were ungovernable, and mysteriously male. Like her
brother, dead at war. Or the person who had murdered
Scheherazade. For it was inconceivable to Miss Lattice
that a woman would crush the head of a defenseless
cat.

CHAPTER
52

When he had killed the cat that way, he knew he was
losing control. He wasn't deranged. He didn't worry,
he said, that he would find himself stabbing nurses or
shooting down at passersby from the top of a tower. It
had been just a cat, a public nuisance that should have
been put to sleep anyhow. Still, something was wrong,
something was slipping out of place, out of line,
something was roaring up in him and pressing out the
reality of Limus Barnum, like suffocation by fire.

Up in his room where he kept things, Barnum sat in
his bathrobe, sweaty and cramped, in front of the

mirror. The robe was pulled open and underneath it he was naked. It was after eight. He was furious at the time it was taking him to masturbate. The erection Mrs. Haig at the post office had given him was still unrelieved. Livid with frustration, he flurried through more and more magazines of photographs. But whenever he got it back up, the man in the mirror paralyzed him. The eyes in the mirror were hateful and frightening. And yet he couldn't turn away from the mirror, for he had to be certain he would be seen.

The penis was limp again, chafed sore by now from being rubbed too long with panicked vigor. He felt a sudden vehemence swell up in him as if he would rip the flabby organ off and fling it away. Something had to happen. Whatever the problem, it was costing him too much time. He couldn't afford it. It had gotten out of hand. His life up in this room was seeping out under the door and following him into Dingley Falls. It wasn't that what he did in the room distressed him. All guys read pornography. And if you happened to be the kind of guy with a lot of sperm, you had to get it out of your system. As for his uniforms and fantasies, he did not analyze their rationality, and though he was aware of fear that he might be overseen and caught out, he did not translate this dread as guilt. Besides, everybody had a right to his own privacy. The world of the mirror was beginning to demand too much of him, that's all. He was losing control of the store. All his life he had made a good living, with no help from anyone else; but now he couldn't keep the store open. It had to be closed at odd hours because this other world was taking over.

When Limus Barnum examined himself in this way for possible psychic disturbance, he did so like everyone else, through highly selective lenses. For instance, from his perspective he saw nothing problematic in his Nazi party membership. In his honest opinion, and everybody had a right to his own opinion, the only salvation for America lay in its swift embrace of a

Fourth Reich against the Third World. In his honest opinion, America was not going to be strrong and clean until even in good places like Dingley Falls (which at least had not been overrun by niggers and spics like all the big cities) America got rid of the trailer park trash and Jews like Cecil Hedgerow, and intellectual left-wing faggots like Sidney Blossom, and freaks like Sammy Smalter, and women that wouldn't behave like women—rich bitches like Mrs. Troyes and pervert ballbusters like Mrs. Ransom with her plastic prick stuffed up her. Given these honest views, Barnum did not much brood over the reasonableness of his hostility toward his fellow Dingleyans. For example, the anonymous letters (which he thought he had started as a genuine political response by a concerned citizen to Dingley Falls's so-called leaders) had seemed cause for concern only when no one would acknowledge that they were being written. The silence of others had forced him to lie, to claim to have been threatened himself. Perhaps the letters had gotten a little out of control, but it had been just a joke, just something he had gotten into doing. There had been no chance of getting caught, and most of what he wrote was probably true anyhow. They had it coming for the contempt with which they belittled him by their bland, disinterested faces. He knew he was smart, picked up on things; caught, he said, vibes that others missed. He could see through them all so easily. Yet they never noticed how well he had read them over all these years. They had annihilated him by never noticing his hate. Nothing he did could slap the smiles off their faces.

That's what caused his rushing panic. Because it seemed that no matter how much he was pulled out of control—not insane, he said, just blowing his cool—they made no move to stop him. Because they were forcing him into exposure where his whole life could be ground to a halt, he could be thrown into jail and locked in a cell room. Because writing letters was one thing, or riding a motorcycle at a kike kid for a joke; but trespassing on Ernest Ransom's property, spying on his wife, or destroying other people's property like Hayes's window or that cat—that sort of stuff was out of line. Sure, it was important to teach Dingley Falls a lesson, but he couldn't bear the responsibility all alone. For the violence that must rivet the foundations of an American Reich a man needed comrades, battle brothers. Lime had too few to get his demands met. He had to communicate with his fellows through the mail, through magazines, through the mirror. They wouldn't read his newspaper, refused to have his news at the pharmacy newsstand or the library newsstand. The people in his life didn't like him, or didn't like him enough, or weren't the right people, or there weren't enough of them, or something was wrong.

How was he going to make it when he couldn't keep himself behind the counter of his lousy store? How was he going to make it when the dumb turkeys of this snotty town would rather have a lousy Jew selectman instead of him? He couldn't even make his lousy dick stand up. She had done this to him, safe there behind her bars, looking right through him like she blind, pretending not to know what she was making him do. Locked behind the brass grille of her counter, and married to the law, she thought she was safe enough to torture him. They were all like that, but it was mostly her now. That lousy bitch. She would not even look into his eyes.

Barnum pulled his robe closed. He locked up his room, dressed, locked his house, hurried to his garage, and pulled out his motorcycle. He had to go where he would be seen.

Sarah MacDermott popped her gum. "Joe, honey, slide over so Lime can sit down. Hard liquor? Take my advice, that stuff will rot a hole through your liver big enough to bury you in, believe me, I ought to know,

Lord love us, I come from a long line of dead drunks,
God rest them. I won't touch a thing but beer."

"How's it going, Joe? Hot enough?"

"Yes, Joe has practically got heat whatchacallit,
prostate. A man his size really suffers in this kind of
heat, don't you, honey? I told him, come on, we'll just
walk down to Fred's and cool off with a beer, because if
a fifteen-year-old boy can't even baby-sit his own little
brothers one Friday night in his lifetime, if you can
believe that, then I wish I'd had all girls, and I know
I've said so a thousand times. But it would have been
nice just once in a while to have pulled open a diaper
without getting a squirt in the eye. Excuse me, Lime.
Joe, tell Lime he'll have to excuse me. I'm just a little
bit snockered. Anyhow, it must be the heat. And all
those beers. But come on, sit down and join in, Lime.
'It's Friday night and I just got paid. Fool about my
money. . . .'" Sarah began to snap her fingers and
sing, grinning around the booth at her husband and at
their friend Wanda Tojek.

"Thanks anyhow, but I guess I'll just catch the
Yankees on the tube over there. Everybody take it
easy." With a nod at Joe MacDermott, Barnum walked
away. Why, he wondered, didn't MacDermott shut his
wife's mouth? A loud, foul-mouthed slut, talking about
her own son's sex organs, with her hand right there on
her husband's thigh. Bleached rat's nest coming out of
black roots.

The stocky merchant, dressed for his visit to the
neighborhood bar in his denim sports jacket, open
paisley shirt, and shiny tasseled loafers, jostled his way,
stiffly smiling, back to the counter. Fred Fry, owner of
the Madder tavern erroneously called Fred's Fries, or
Fred's, or Bar and Grill, had died in 1950, and
subsequent owners, striving for the veneer of a timely
prosperity, had updated the diner chrome, plastic, and
linoleum of Fred's era a dozen times since then. The
present owner had removed the overhead lights, installed fake dark walnut paneling everywhere, and

carpeted everything that wasn't paneled in cheap dark brown carpeting.

At ten o'clock Mrs. MacDermott was on the phone, standing where doors marked "Bucks" and "Does" on painted cutouts faced each other at the end of a dim corridor. Behind the one for men, Limus Barnum stood at the urinal. Three drinks in succession had left him with a frustrated sense of imbalance, but had at least relaxed him enough to relieve his bladder: what if his body should refuse to obey him altogether and stop functioning? He shook out the urine angrily. From outside the door Sarah MacDermott's voice yowled and screeched at him. Still here, wasting all this money on beer, half-drunk, when she claimed the whole time she could only pay thirty a month on that color Zenith. Sometimes he thought the Irish were as bad as the niggers. That trashy blouse she was wearing looked like she'd stolen it from one.

On the phone Sarah was telling Eddie that his father was on the way home because they had forgotten the wallet accidentally, so if the little ones were still awake or Eddie had let all hell break loose, he had better hide the traces fast before that door opened; and she hoped that his Aunt Orchid was being given some slight chance to sleep in peace. As she hung up, she turned and was face to face with Maynard Henry, who had waited, unnoticed, for her to finish. "Mary, Mother of God! You scared me to death!" Indignantly she refastened some bobby pins in her topknot, as if Henry had frightened them loose. "How in the world did *you* get here? You didn't escape, did you? Joe's nowhere around, and I hope you're not going to try to start something with him."

"I'm out on bail, no thanks to some I could name. Humped it from Argyle and I'm looking for Chin now. You know where she is?"

"Maynard, now be fair, Joe does his duty, that's all, just like any other man. You know Hawk Haig is his boss, and what's more . . ."

"I got no grudge against Joe. Where's Chin? My trailer had a damn lock on it. Some kid's marked some kind of shit mess all over it."

"Not one of my boys, I guess I would . . ."

Henry jammed his hands in his pockets; his eyes moved quickly to watch both of hers. "Listen to me," he said sharply. "I'm looking for my wife. Has Haig fixed it so she got sent away? Because if he has, you better believe it, I'm going to tear that cocksucker's guts out. Okay?"

Sarah puffed air up to her bangs. "Honey, talking like that is no way to make somebody want to tell you something. That exact same thing has always been your problem ever since you was little. Arn always said . . ."

His voice lashed out at her. "Will you cut the crap! Look, I've walked ten miles on no food. I want to find Chin, and I don't want to hear some dipshit crap about my fucking personality. I'm beat to shit."

"You see what I mean? Maynard, if you'd just hold your horses, maybe we could figure this whole thing out. Now, you checked everybody you know and nobody's seen her?"

Pushing out a breath of air like a swimmer, Henry leaned rigidly back against the corridor wall, his hand inside his pocket beating the gun against the side of his thigh. He held himself in check, waiting.

Sarah frowned as she thought, her arms folded over a sleeveless blouse of electric-blue nylon, a present from her sons. She peered around into the bar, then back at Maynard Henry. Finally she spoke. "I haven't seen her in ages and I don't think she's been in the trailer park since you got arrested, but you know that little lunch place next to the pharmacy on Dingley Circle? Well, she got a job there, just something temporary to tide things over in case, well, anyhow, you had to stay in Argyle or wherever. Of course, that doesn't help you now because The Tea Shoppe's closed, but still. That's what she's doing, and I don't want you to think she's been taken off."

"Where's she *staying?*"

"How should I know? She didn't come to me for help. But if you want my advice, because my motto is if somebody asks you for water don't give them vinegar instead, the only person I know of where Chinkie . . ."

"Her name's Chin Lam, okay? It's not Chinkie, it's not Chink. It's Chin."

"Maynard, you know I don't mean anything by it. It's just what everybody's gotten used to. Hi there, Doris, how they treating you, tips rotten as ever?" Sarah squeezed the arm of a waitress who passed them on her way to the toilet. "Anyhow, the only place I can think of where she could be staying is Judith Haig's house. I don't know if you remember Judith but she's Hawk's wife, now just calm down, now wait a minute, I wouldn't be telling you this if I thought you were going to break out in a rash about it, and what's more, Maynard, this is the pure and simple truth, Hawk had nothing to do with it, he's been out of town on business. Judith is my best friend and that's why I know about it. I know she was just trying to help because Chinkie went and asked her to."

"Bullshit. I don't believe it. Why should she?"

"I get the feeling Judith started feeling sorry for Chinkie, and she never had any kids of her own, and I guess she just took her in. Because the day after she found out about it, she started working on your case (now I'm telling you this in secret, Maynard, because I think you deserve it, but I'll kill you if it gets back to Hawk), but she was doing everything she could to help you, even going against her own husband, even calling Arn up in Massachusetts to come get you out, and I guess it worked, too. Jesus, Joseph, and Mary! Hey, what's the matter with you? Stop acting like a nut before they throw you out of here!"

Maynard Henry, cursing loudly against the Haigs' trespass on his life, had kicked out, in a sudden spasm, at the flimsy paneled wall. Behind it Limus Barnum felt the tremors of anger with a thrill.

Sarah's voice sharpened; she spun Henry away from the wall. "Jesus love us! If I let myself fly off the handle whenever I felt like it like you do, they'd have put me in a nuthouse years ago. Jesus! I'm trying to help you, and I have to look at enough temper tantrums at home without having to watch you have one at your age. Now you can think anything you want to, but it won't be true. If Chink, Chin, *is* staying out at Judith's, the thing for you to do, wait a minute, let me get a pencil, here, I'll write it down. . . . See you, Doris. Hon, Wanda's sitting over there by herself, would you tell her I'm in the can and I'll be out in a sec? Thanks. . . . is call her and tell her you're coming out there. And if you'll take my advice, you'll just thank her for trying to be a good neighbor and let bygones be bygones. Now, Hawk'll be at the station most of the night, that's why I say try her now. I'm not trying to make a big deal out of anything, but I wouldn't tell you if I didn't know he wasn't going to be there because I get the feeling you and Hawk had better keep out of each other's hair until everybody's cooled off. Just tell Judith you want to take Chinkie back home."

"Take her back home! This is fucking unbelievable! He throws me in the jug and his wife muscles in on Chin. Who the shit does she think she is? Fucking Christ? No way!"

"I'm not going to listen to you take the Savior's name in vain like that."

"Okay, okay, I'm sorry, it's nothing personal, okay?"

"Well, it really gets my goat. Now, do you want me to call for you, why don't I?"

"No. I'm going to take care of it."

"Well, Joe would kill me if he found out I told you, because you got to admit people got a right to wonder about you when you start going crazy and bulldozing Puerto Ricans down the side of a mountain; 'course it sounded to me like Raoul had it coming in the first place, but still. It makes it kind of hard for me to keep telling people, 'Oh, listen, his bark is worse than his bite' when they hear stories about you eating off ears."

Suddenly Henry smiled, shifting the bony surfaces of his face into the youth it had almost never revealed. It was that rare, oddly sweet smile that Winslow Abernathy had noticed in the visitors' room of the Argyle jail. "Hey," he said. "Thanks, okay?"

"Well, just don't yell at Judith like that. She'll drop dead. She's not used to it the way I am. The nuns raised her."

In the bathroom Limus Barnum still waited. He waited until after a long silence, then he slowly opened the door. On the shelf under the wall phone was a chewing gum wrapper with a number written on it. No one was in the corridor when Barnum dialed. The phone rang at least eight times, then a female voice, catching its breath as it spoke, said, "Hello?" Barnum said nothing. "Hello?" the voice repeated. "Hello? I'm sorry, is someone there? Hello?" Then she was silent. He waited. Each could hear the other's breath. Quietly he replaced the receiver.

After the artificial coolness of the bar, the heat outside felt briefly pleasant. Barnum could see Henry with his dog; the man walked slowly, almost as if he limped, and the two had not yet reached the end of the block. When he passed them, the large shepherd darted out at the motorcycle. Barnum kicked out at it as he sped away toward his house on Glover's Lane. There, stumbling through the small, dark rooms, he ran to his bedroom, felt under the bed, and pulled out his revolver. He fitted it carefully into his jacket pocket. If asked why, he would have explained, and believed, that the man now on his way to her house was a criminal. Everyone said he was violent, unmanageable, one of those whose mind had been lost in Vietnam, something that sounded like a rabid animal. Barnum believed that he was hurrying to see if Mrs. Haig needed to be saved. He was thinking that if he brought Henry in to Hawk Haig, it would foster a friendship between him and the

police chief. Haig had a lot of political influence locally
and it would be helpful to have the man in his debt. He
was thinking that Henry might get out of line and have
to be shot, and that if he saved her life by killing a
criminal, that would get him in good with everybody.
The scenario toward which he raced, rehearsing, was
vivid in his mind. But, in fact, all Barnum really knew
was that finally something was going to happen. He was
going to press his hand against life and feel that it had
the glaring intensity of the world in the mirror.

CHAPTER
53

Judith sat in the dark and waited for the phone to ring
again. Since the anonymous call she had sat, her legs
tucked up in the green armchair, with the lights off,
because it was more frightening to her to be seen than
not to be able to see. She continued to knit by feel,
soothed by the orderly sound. She had closed the doors
to the family room so that in less space she might feel
less vulnerable. One of her discomforts with her
husband's new house was that there were so few doors
to close; rooms gaped into one another as if their
occupants, smothering under the pressure of the low
ceilings and close, windowless sides, had snatched
sledgehammers and bashed down the walls. The living
room drifted into the dinette and so into the kitchen
and so onto the patio. Judith disliked being in the living
room because its size and its barren modernity more
radically exposed her and forced her to feel how
radically her body, like the tentacles of an oozy
jellyfish, held her trapped in its soft, defenseless flesh.

The family room could be closed, and was therefore her favorite.

Mrs. Haig had been trying to occupy her mind with meditations on her husband. It was only a little past ten, but she was already dressed for bed in a nightgown and bathrobe, for she had wanted to give herself time to fall safely asleep before John's return from the station. Then the phone call had come, and the still-heard sound of that breath so close to her ear, the threat of that intimate silence, had violated her escape and made sleep impossible. While waiting, then, she was finishing the scarf and thinking about her husband. She thought unhappily about him, with deep pity in her heart. He worked so hard to defeat failure, but felt himself defeated. This unnecessary house they couldn't afford, the unused furniture he had so carefully arranged according to the store display, the early morning and long evening hours he struggled to make the earth grow for him. Judith's heart swelled with sadness for John, because she could not love him as he deserved to be loved. Tonight had been horrible to her, more than it had been before, even more than in the early days of their marriage when she had been given instruction on how to will herself to love him. Why had he not cast her aside as barren, annulling the marriage? But he had never charged her with that loss of progeny. By choice, he would end his family with his life with her.

And yet she could not give herself to this man or be shared by him or accept his sacrifice. She could not will herself to let go of that consciousness of isolation that pulled her away. Now, had Mrs. Haig been a woman who sought the solace of a professional analyst, she might have been told by one that the problem lay in the poor quality of John's erotic techniques; another might have said that it should not surprise her that a woman of her sensibility could not give herself to so unconscious a man, a man so little aware of who she was that he had never realized that she had never given herself to him, and that his very happiness condemned him. She might have been told, had she chanced upon a different analyst, that her husband could never give himself to so uneasy, so forbidding, so ungiving a woman, that her unwomanliness unmanned him and that the fault lay with her father (whoever he was) or her nuns or some other secret yet undelved for. Or she might have been told it was a question of physical chemistry or of finding the Platonic other half that perfectly matched her incompleteness, that she had never been in love with John Haig and was now half in love with Winslow Abernathy, or that love was a myth and her career at the post office unfulfilling, or she might have been told a hundred other theories, all neatly fitted to the seams of her life. But Mrs. Haig had never brought her soul to any of those men of science who in her lifetime had grown rich in the fast-growth industry of female madness; nor had she consulted oracles in cards or looked for the fault in her stars or gone to the books that helped Ida Sniffell to help herself. Mrs. Haig had had only one counselor. He had told her years ago that she and John had been joined forever by God, and that she had no choice but to choose love.

While saying so, Father Crisp of Our Lady of Mercy in Madder had admitted to himself a conflict in dogma. Conjugal intercourse had a single purpose, procreation. Was Mrs. Haig not right then to take no pleasure in the act, since its sole pleasure, fertility denied, was therefore lust, a sin? Should he instruct her to honor her husband's desires, when those desires had been (through, however, no active fault of their own) altered from sanctity to sinfulness by the fact of the couple's sterility, or perhaps by their knowledge of that fact, or perhaps by their acceptance of that fact? For might not the desire nevertheless be holy, if in committing the act each *wished* to be creating life, whatever God chanced to do with those wishes? There were miracles. Had not life leaped in the ancient womb of Sarah? And perhaps, besides, she judged herself too harshly, for her husband by his confession seemed to feel no emotional deprivation. Should God ask for her husband more union than the husband asked for himself? Such speculations troubled Father Crisp, who was a warmhearted man continually balancing off the rights of his parishioners with the rights of God. Uncertain what to say through the velvet-curtained grille, the aged celibate had said only, "Marriage is a holy sacrament. You have made vows to God and to the church and to your husband. They must be honored. You must struggle with your heart and do your duty with good grace. You must pray for contentment. I know it seems hard."

Judith Sorrow Haig had struggled with her heart all her life. It did seem hard.

Darkness pulled around her like a shawl, she walked to the picture window and drew back the curtains. Haze hid the stars. The moon was luminous and full. Behind her, suddenly, the phone began to ring again. The loudness pierced her, though she had been waiting for it, and her legs almost gave way. Her hand tight on the curtain, she waited, listening as if the huge, splattering sound came from the man himself. She assumed a man. The phone kept ringing. Finally it stopped. She didn't move. Then it began again. What if it was John at the station? He would come home to find out what was wrong if she didn't answer. What if it were, for whatever reason, Winslow Abernathy? She jerked the curtain shut, ran, and holding her breath, lifted the receiver.

"On the Blessed Virgin, Judith, I figured you was dead. If I pulled you off the john, you'll have to excuse me, but listen, honey, did somebody call you a little while ago, maybe fifteen minutes?"

"Sarah! How did you know?" Judith sat down in the plaid armchair and turned on the lamp beside it.

"Now don't fly off the handle at me, but I told him the whole thing."

"What? Whom are you talking about?"

"Who, what? Maynard Henry. Didn't you just say he'd called?"

"No. I'm sorry, I don't understand."

"Well, he was supposed to. Never mind, I guess he's coming straight out there."

Judith squeezed the coil of phone. "Why should he be? Because of John? John's at the station. What is it you've told him?"

"Nothing. He's looking for Chinkie, and all I said was she was probably with you."

"Sarah! She's not with me. Why should you say such a thing?!"

"Well, what do I know? Anyhow, I figured she was. She was out there before, wasn't she, bothering you into getting all gaga about finding her a lawyer and who knows what else?"

"She's staying at Miss Lattice's on Cromwell Hill Road. Please tell him that right away. There's no need for him to come out here!"

"Honey, just calm down, I know what you're thinking. Hawk and Maynard ain't exactly what you could call madly in love."

"Tell him she's at Miss Lattice's, he could call there."

"Chinkie's getting pretty fancy-schmantsy, that's all I can say. I guess by next week she'll be living over on Elizabeth Circle and hiring Orchid to clean for her. Anyhow, the point is, seriously now, Maynard is trying to find her, and like I say, you did know where she was and that's why I told him you. So, if he shows up, because he may have already left and I don't know if he's got his truck or what, you send him back to town, and I'll tell him if I see him first. But I'm here waiting for Joe at Fred's. If you ask me, the less said to Hawk the better he'll like it, because what he don't know won't hurt him. The only reason I'm calling is I just figured with your nerves, if Maynard should try to spring something on you, with you out there alone in the middle of nowhere, we'd probably have to scrape

you off the ceiling and send the pieces to the nuthouse.
Anyhow, seriously, I know Maynard's got a lot of
strikes against him, but I think people should remember, and this will mean a lot to you, Judith, he lost his
parents young and Arn had to raise him, and just
between you and I, I sometimes got the intuition that
Arn didn't like him a bit, or vicey versa. But it's like I
used to say to Joe, 'Maynard's problem is his bark's
always been worse than his bite.' Now, Judith, *honey,*
is this true what Wanda says, they're planning to shut
up our post office like we all dropped dead?''

Fear of the unmet intruder blanketed Judith's anger
against Sarah MacDermott for instigating the intrusion.
Her first thought was to call John to come home, but
she could not bear, especially after the act that had
been committed just before he left, the shame of
confessing the extent of her involvement in arranging
the release of the very man she now wanted protection
from. Besides, even if Henry did come, she shouldn't
need protection; she would simply tell him where Chin
was and he would leave.

Judith dressed herself in what she had planned to
wear the next day. Then she opened doors. She turned
on lights. She turned on the television. A situation
comedy about treating wounded soldiers in the Korean
War laughed mechanically into the room. An unreal
audience guffawed as doctors ogled nurses. The sound
of their voices was no more human to her than the
sound of the air conditioner. Both were simply hums
between her and the noise that might, all at once,
shatter the silence. She sat back down and, knitting
again, tried to keep from listening to the night. To the
north there were sporadic rumbling tremors she took to
be thunder. Traffic on Route 3 seemed to her to be
heavier than usual, but she remembered that it was the
weekend and that it was summer and that therefore
people would be coming to the lake to spend all their
leisure quickly. She thought she recognized a loud
motor like Sammy Smalter's car, but the sound disap-

peared. Other cars hummed by softly. Finally she
finished the scarf of old scraps; having tied a last knot,
she spread it on her lap, folding and smoothing each
multicolored square.

As she moved, she could feel the discomfort left by
John's lovemaking. It was not the pain that distressed
her. It was that the pain made her conscious of the
literal breech in her defenses which kept her accessible.
As a young woman she had imagined sewing it closed,
despite the pain of the needle, so that she could feel
safe from the men who, nudging each other for
support, grinned out at her, whistling, from cars or
sidewalks. She had imagined walking encased in a steel
cage. She had imagined wearing the iron belt of chastity
in which medieval lords had locked their wives, or the
black habit of chastity in which the Sisters of Mercy
dressed. But but Sisters had told her she must wait until
she finished high school to make that choice, and by
then she had felt unable to refuse John Haig's proposal.
She had protected herself from male pursuit by being
taken by one male, who, divesting her of freedom, at
least locked out the others, at least as long as he stood
by the cell, and sometimes even his ring on her finger
worked alone as a talisman, held up like a cross at a
vampire, or a cloud obscuring the moon from a
werewolf's eyes.

Barnum snapped off the motor as soon as his
headlight beam exposed the location of her house, then
he pushed the bike along the highway's edge. Mountain
laurel grew in unchecked profusion down the side of
the Haig's gravel driveway. Having made sure, as he
inched around, that there were no cars parked anywhere, he dropped the motorcycle into the back of the
bushes. Hurrying off the gravel and onto grass, he
trotted, crouching, over to hide against the house's
shadows. The curtains of a big picture window were
poorly closed, so that, from where he squatted in John
Haig's methodical rows of flowers, he could see into the
room. Maynard Henry did not seem to be there, for,

framed in the narrow opening, she sat, alone, in a soft, pale blue garment, her hair pale gold under the lamplight. Motionless. He watched her begin to stroke something in her lap. He watched until his legs, stretched in a squat, began to tremble, until he was certain no one else was in the house.

Judith made herself breathe very carefully while the doorbell rasped at her. A shock rushed up, tightening around her heart, when, as she came down the hall, she saw that the chain was not on the latch. She tried to make her hand reach out, but was too embarrassed to be heard locking the door. She spoke behind it. "Yes?" There was no reply. She forced her voice louder. "Yes, please?"

"Mrs. Haig?" It was a male voice.

"Yes. Mr. Henry?"

"Look, could I see you a second, Mrs. Haig?"

The instant Judith turned the knob she felt the pressure waiting and the quick twist. The door pushed hard against her. Then someone was squeezing through it into the hall. He edged past her and shoved shut the door. He turned, and it was the man who came to watch her in the post office.

Neither moved from where they were when the few seconds of struggle (if indeed it had been a struggle— Judith felt it would be dangerous both to behave as though there had been one, and to behave as though there had not) stopped as abruptly as it began. Each stared at the other's eyes, trying to read there what was going to happen.

Then, suddenly smiling, he ignored the reality of her fear and spoke in a rush. "Hey there; Lime Barnum, you remember. Guess I startled you. Looks like I scared you out of your mind, huh? Sorry about that. I'm sure you're wondering what somebody's doing, dropping in on you this time of night. See, I heard about what was going on, there's this guy Henry who just got released on bail. I happened to hear word he might be coming out here to give you trouble. I thought somebody ought to get on the stick about it. I guess he didn't show, huh? Or maybe the two of you've already gotten in touch? That Oriental girl of his, I guess she's not staying here? Now I said to myself, Lime, somebody ought to keep an eye on Mrs. Haig. Guess you and I never got around to any official handshake, but we go back a long time, huh? I mean, fat chance I'd miss noticing somebody like you in this size town. Hawk's up at the station, huh?"

As Barnum spoke, smiling, his eyes raced to explore the house, while his head shook in slight spasms, buzzed by his thoughts. While he shoved through the door his sense of his power to frighten her both angered and thrilled him. At each step he took toward her, she moved backwards down the hall. She kept looking at his mouth and wouldn't raise her eyes back to his. Her hands were out in front of her, as if the urge swelling out from him impelled her backwards. No, it was as if the opening between her legs was compelling him toward her, pulling him down the corridor, trying to suck him inside a center that he imagined opening larger and darker like the pupil of the eye in the mirror.

He turned his eyes away from her panic and began to poke his head into the different rooms, checking windows, testing the back door. He looked in the entrance to the family room, then grabbed her arm and pulled her in there. He stood with her in front of the laughing television. "'M*A*S*H,'" said Barnum flatly. And for a few seconds he began automatically to watch it as if fallen suddenly into a trance. Then he led her across the hall into the living room, talking again. "I said, Hawk's up at the station, huh? Maybe he already took care of this guy. But if we had any kind of decent system in this country, guys like Henry wouldn't come waltzing out of jail ten minutes after they went in. Hey, nice." He nodded with solemn appreciation. The furniture was more impressive than he had made it in his fantasies. He began to walk around, picking up objects, sliding his hand along the cool, slick ceramic of the cone fireplace, pushing his fingers into the stiff, soft brown velveteen of all the sofa chairs and ottomans that fit together in what the ads called a living module. "Nice. Never had a chance to see your place before. Yeah, it looks nice. Doesn't look this big from the outside. I've ridden by here lots of times, stopped by just to take a look at your place, you know that?"

Barnum reached down between his legs and tugged at his pants. He noticed her eyes followed his hand down. So she knew she had gotten him hard, and maybe she would make it happen. Even now he could not tell what he intended to do. In his thoughts was the chance that she might just say, "Let me get you a cup of coffee, why don't I, and I'll give Hawk a call, he'll want to thank you for the warning," and that he might accept the coffee and they might discuss the Maynard Henry problem until her husband arrived. Or maybe she might ask him to wait and handle Henry himself. Barnum tried to imagine that she might suddenly come over and rub against him, overwhelmed by the sexual deprivation of her marriage. In his books women attacked repairmen, delivery boys, the sons of their neighbors. But he knew Mrs. Haig wouldn't. Even if she wanted to, she wouldn't let herself. "You know that?" he repeated, stepping in front of her. "Yeah, I've come by here lots; you'd be here, like they say, all by your lonesome. Guess maybe old Hawk doesn't give you enough of what a woman needs, being gone so much, does he, huh?"

Suddenly she covered her face with her hands. He could see her thin wedding band. Her hands were bigger than his wife's had been, and their shape and tint were different from hers, too. It shocked him that hands on women could be so dissimilar. His own wedding ring was still back in the top drawer of his dresser in a box with his cufflinks and tie clasps. The ring was hateful to him, but, still, gold was money. Her hair was gold.

"Hey, what's the matter? Look at me," he told her.

"Come on, you could be nice to me. How about that, come on."

But she wouldn't speak. Barnum pulled her hands away and saw the pupils contract, darkness receding from the blue. Excitement and fear spiraled up in him, each tumbling over the other to leap out of reach of his control. She shuddered when he moved his hands up to her hair. He stuck his fingers through her hair and jerked out the gold pins. Her eyes closed, but she didn't move. He was thinking that he had to keep hold, it still wasn't too late, that he'd be nuts to go ahead, that her husband would kill him. But he could just leave Dingley Falls, couldn't he? He could go tonight, just pack and pull out, hell with it all. What did he have keeping him here anyhow, in this little dump that nobody ever heard of where the snooty bastards wouldn't give him the time of day? But it wasn't like the other times now. It wouldn't be like quitting a job, grabbing a few bags, and getting on a bus. He'd lose it all, the store and house and all his things it had taken so long, working so hard with no help, for him to acquire. Like when that bitch took him for all he was worth. That bitch of a wife. This one was frightened, just like that bitch had been, finally; after his fist crushed into her nose, when her eyes had become for a second all pupil just before she screamed. Still, she'd stopped saying no, he couldn't, hadn't she? But if he did it to this one, that would be it, he'd lose everything.

Whenever he pulled a pin free, she shuddered, convulsing, as if he stuck needles into her nerves. Probably she wouldn't tell anyhow. She'd keep it quiet for her own sake. Besides, who'd believe her? It wasn't like he was some black teenager she could pin the rap on. He was a damn business leader in this town. Who the shit was she to say no? And maybe she really did want it, deep down. They all did, as long as they didn't have to admit it. Get those clothes off her and she was just like all the rest. Could be she didn't know what a good man was like; could be Haig couldn't get it up enough for her. He could show her what a man could do. But what if it got found out? Maybe he could blame Henry. MacDermott's wife had told Henry to come out here. He could tell this one he'd kill her if she ever said it was him and not Henry. He had an hour at least before Henry could get there. At least.

The hair fell around her shoulders, changing her into a stranger, a picture in a magazine. She wasn't inside her eyes. She'd gotten away someplace where he didn't exist. The eyes in the mirror were burning him like white-hot brands. He felt as if all his will had been sucked down into his penis and was pushing out now, strained against his pants. He had to take the clothes away and make her see it. "Look at me!" he snarled. The man in the mirror started to spin like a clock hand, and both his hands were pulling on the penis; the head of the penis was an eye. He wanted sperm to spurt out of the iris of the eye and then the whole mirror began to spin. "Look at me! *Look at my eyes!*" But her eyes squeezed shut. He slapped her across the cheek so that she lurched sideways, falling against the ottoman. "Don't think you can make me go away! Do you hear me?" Then he unzipped and opened his pants. It had happened, and now he couldn't stop. "Okay. There! Now, you look, you look now!"

He could see the print of his hand reddening her cheek. There were tears spilling out of her eyes, but she wasn't crying aloud. The only noise she made was a harsh breathing. Barnum had his hand on the gun in his pocket, squeezing it as he watched her; and when she still would not look, he pulled it out, pressed the muzzle next to her neck, and flipped her hair outward. He kept gulping so that he could breathe. "You listen to Lime," he said, himself listening to many years of books and magazines. "I'm not kidding. I don't want to have to kill you, so you look up here and see what ole Lime's got for you." He stuck the gun under her chin and tilted it.

"That's right, that's right," he whispered. Pulling up

his shirt, he thrust the purplish flesh out at her. "How
do you like that, huh? All of a sudden, you can see me
good. All these years you wouldn't look. Now it's too
late."

She twisted her back to him when he reached out,
but he wriggled his hand inside her summer dress,
sliding it under her slip and bra. He pulled hard on her
nipple, watching her eyes as she grabbed at his arm.
"Look. You better not. Don't make it hard. Because
you can get hurt really bad. Now you're going to have
to take off all your clothes for me. It doesn't have to be
bad; you could make it nice. Just cooperate, huh?
Otherwise, you're going to make me hurt you. Come
on, you knew all along, isn't that true? You've just
been waiting, you could feel it, you knew this was
coming; it goes way back, you and I, isn't that true?
You're no different from the rest, you're a cunt, so you
knew. Right? Say you're a cunt. Say it!" He swung the
gun.

"Please," she whispered.

The hand with the gun slammed against Judith's
cheek. Pain rose in her like the fright of a sudden fall,
but its cause seemed to be something happening far
away, or she was far away, safe somewhere, waiting
until this was over. She could see the arm shake and the
gun tremble, she heard the voice tell her again to take
off all her clothes or she would be hurt badly. She
understood the voice, she was aware that her hands had
begun to remove her clothes because her fingers could
feel buttons and hooks, but she was thinking that if she
could just keep from coming back, she would be all
right. She knew she could not make her legs run for the
door or the phone or make her voice try to talk to him.
Her mind kept sorting through, shifting contingencies,
gathering information should she need it. No knight
would come to her rescue if she screamed. She would
have to go through this. From across the hall the
television kept laughing as the flat, hollow voices
pretended to be real. Cooled air blew against her body,

and shame splotched her skin. She filled her head with the need to breathe carefully, to breathe away the panic that might attack her heart.

With a long, slow shudder, Judith unfastened her bra and let her arms fall. Her body stood motionless in front of him, limp and slightly shivering. Then the gun's coldness and the sticky heat of his hands started to move all over her, his fingers pulled at her breasts. She felt herself coming back and she fought against it, panting faster and making herself listen to the sound of her breath, not his. Fingers kneaded her skin, one pushed inside her, twisting. She was sweating, even in the mechanically cold air. Then she could feel his organ jerking between her legs. Nausea uncontrollable swelled up in her, and, bent double, she started to gag in quick, dry heaves. Already thrusting, he was shoving her down onto the flat expanse of ottoman and sofa. The stubbly velveteen prickled her back and buttocks. Her senses, despite her effort to escape them, were alive; her body had betrayed her. It had pulled her back inside it. She started frantically to will herself to disappear while he wriggled on top, but she could feel his fingers down there. Then the pressure started, widening, pushing. Suddenly lunging, he jabbed up through her and the pain was hot up her spine, with fragments bursting at the back of her head.

It was going on too long. Judith kept promising herself in a hypnotic litany, "This will end, this will end, this will end." She could not pull her mind away from what was happening there inside her. Her mind had not dulled sensation, but horribly focused and sharpened it; her senses so concentrated that time ballooned out of proportion, filling each inescapable instant. All his sad, false smells assailed her—the medicinal mintiness of his mouth, the raw, spicy odor of after-shave on his cheeks, and worst, the smell in the stiff sprayed hair, like plastic flowers too sweetly odorized. His face was too big, like the face in a magnified mirror that makes a moon surface of the skin. Only around the part of his body that flailed against her could she feel the heat and slipperiness of flesh. He still wore even his sports jacket, and his shirt, sweated through, stuck hideously wet against her breasts and stomach. She tasted the blood in her mouth from where she was biting her lip against the burn of his stabbing himself into her. He pulled her legs up, stretching them apart so that they hurt, as he kept slapping against her. Suddenly, he jerked out, but grabbed back at her to keep her down. He tore off his jacket and shirt.

From far off a loud crack of noise trembled through the house, but he paid no attention to it, and since the noise did not stop him, it was insignificant to Judith as well. All she could think was that it was unfair that everything required of her had been erased by his failure to finish, so that it had to begin again. For she could feel him between her legs yanking on the organ. Then it shoved into her and the pain started over again, on and on. Now she could feel the wet mats of chest hair and stomach hair that was alien to her, repulsive to her skin. She fought with careful breaths to climb up back safe into her mind. She thought about John, how his chest was smooth, how that first time on her wedding night the pain had surprised her but had still been less than she had expected and been led to expect; how she dreaded to feel that stiffened flesh poke at her in bed before she could sleep, so she would have to know that John wanted her to let him do it.

But how long had this been, a quarter-hour, an hour? With John it had always been only minutes, sometimes seconds, and she had taught herself even while he did it to disappear. Was this man different from other men, or was John? Judith could still hear the television; earnest voices made promises, feverish voices raved and sang about clean bodies, mouths, hair, sinks, toilets, windows, clothes, and on and on, spliced between the dirty news of the world. It must be, then, eleven o'clock. Why couldn't she faint? What held her here and wouldn't let her heart burst and kill her so that she could escape? Her hand, flung out, knocked against the cold metal of the gun. Why couldn't she make her fingers close around it? Why couldn't she pick up the gun and kill him, or her? She tried to remember what she had been taught in those tales the nuns had told to pose perilous dilemmas of faith. In them young girls were lashed, burned, raped, by atheist Orientals and Russians, and she recalled that it had been all right to deface yourself, ruining your beauty, to escape their lust, and it had been all right to be killed for your faith. For your faith. But for yourself? Or to kill? Or to kill yourself?

Sensation rushed back down to where the pain was. She could not stay away. And it kept on, labor until she whooped too for breath, her mouth gaping. And his huge face filled her vision, purplish and frenzied. Sweat drops and tears splashed onto her, then ran down her face, mixing with her own. His head banged into her shoulder, over and over, numbing at least that small part of her. She felt that they had dropped out of time, that this act would never end, but go on forever in tortuous incompletion, like the acts in hell.

Now, now, she begged, now let me go mad; now that it's happened, now that it's true. For everything that waited behind the glass had laid itself bare and proved itself as vile and scared and savage, as unjust and unjustifiable, as unloved and unlovable, as her heart had always known. Now that she had witnessed, now that she lay stained and bleeding in the shattered glass, why wouldn't God let her go?

But the man thrust frantic against her, sobbing now, his mouth sliding over her face and neck and breasts, sucking everywhere. And she wanted to plead, Just suck and be at peace. And she wanted to gloat, laughing, I'm barren so there is nothing you can do that can touch me finally. She was caught there now. His sweat, like vinegar, stung her eyes closed. His hands were desperate on her flesh, clasping and unclasping,

pulling her legs and hips against him. With panic she
felt that the penis was sliding away again and that he
could never finish. She looked up into his eyes. But the
eyes were glassy and emptied. "Move," he croaked at
her, and she was trying to move. Words gurgled
through saliva in his throat like a man choking on
blood. "Do it, make me come, do my balls, do it!" His
hand slipping in the \sweat of her hand shoved hers
down to where they joined and he squeezed her hand
around his testicles. She could feel heat and the sharp
prickle of hairs as he squirmed their hands down
between them until she wrapped her fingers around the
sac. A choked grunt at each thrust, he strained against
her, his face puffed up and purplish red. When she
lost hold of him, his hands clutched at her throat, and
she felt quickly to find him again just as it swelled upward, and he shuddered, moaning enough like John
for her to know that he had reached it, that they were
finishing it.

Now, she thought, I'm going to die now, because his
hands clamped, pushing on her throat as he jerked in
spasms above her. There was a swelling pressure inside
her head until blackness pushed at her eyes. But then
suddenly the hands twitched and fell away. His weight
fell away, and as it was lifted away from her, Judith
began to vomit. Compelled beyond the agony of having
to move in her nakedness, she ran, stumbling, already
heaving into her hands, got open the bathroom door
already leaning over, and retched into the toilet. But he
had followed her. He stood behind her while uncontrollably the last convulsions rose up through her as she
tried to make the toilet flush again and again. He said
nothing, but stood there rubbing the gun against his
thigh, only watched her as she pulled a towel around
herself. She reached, shivering with pain now, for the
pills above the sink, pills prescribed to keep her heart in
order. She noticed with a dulled astonishment that she
could stand there with him beside her and not go mad,
or die, or let her heart be killed; that between the death

of self and the vilest life, her body was choosing life for her.

She could even turn to him, seeing his eyes, and say, "Please. Just go now. Just leave." His eyes were glassy. She saw that hate and hurt were frozen on his face like the faces of the damned in a picture. But then slowly he began to grin, and the grin widened as his hand shoved inside his pants. Refusal like electric shocks vitalized her, so that she could push past him, running, out into the hall and toward the front door. And when he caught her, she was already kicking out at him. And when he touched her, she screamed, *"No! You can't!"* She hadn't known how hard the sound of the scream would tear up her throat. They fought as he hauled her through the entry of the family room, where from the television news of the world still babbled.

He caught at her hands. The nails were bloody. "It's gone too far now," he gasped with hoarse solemnity. "I can do anything. It doesn't matter what happens now." Shoving her back, he pushed his pants down. She could see the red flesh swell out at her. And rage at this violation of their contract, rage stronger than pain or pity or fear bellowed up and out of her in a growl that made him step back when she leaped at him, and bit his hand, and the gun flew to the floor.

She was still growling when, knocking her down, he grabbed at her foot and flipped her onto her stomach. Still growling, her head flailing back to bite at him, when, spreading apart her buttocks, he jabbed inside her. Still growling after her one shriek of pain so that she could not hear while he heaved out of his heart in senseless words the poisoned blood of his life. Still growling, spittle running from her mouth, when the crashing glass of the picture window flew splintering into the room and the German shepherd, Night, leaped through the hole.

CHAPTER
54

A soldier seeking revenge had been on his way to save Judith Haig. He was an unlikely cavalier, in quest of his own wife.

That sharp crack of noise, unnoticed by Barnum, had slapped at Maynard Henry, a half-mile back, with the impact of an explosion. He was coming west down over the top of the ridge when noise leaped into the sky with the old nauseating loudness he thought he'd have forgotten. With a volley of curses he flung himself over his German shepherd, pulling it, rolling with it over the slope of the highway shoulder. "Uncool." He chuckled softly. "Can't hack it, Night, you know, getting old. Fucking blisters. Right, should have waited to get the truck. Still the dumbest fuck around, just the way Arn always said."

From where the sound had come, some miles to the north, a pulsing spurt of fire jumped into the dark haze. Off beyond the marshland it spread over the sky like the bright orange, bright black of firefight, those school-made Halloween colors of Vietnam. The Halloween trick in Vietnam of that *whoosh*, that deep black smoke of napalm ballooning up in the jungle sun. Guys freaked under its spell. Too much power to get your hands on, it swept you up in it. But then guys went wild on gun-door fire too, coming down into an LZ to unload grunts or pick them up; a lot, dumb assholes, going back in zipper bags. Guys went wild with the noise and terror, spasming on the guns so much you couldn't tell if they were shooting or getting shot. The

birds flying the copters couldn't stand to touch the
ground, the ground could scarf you up so fast. It was no
place to be. And yet earth had saved Maynard Henry
once, easing him down in the orange monsoon ooze
when he had crawled, squirming, under sprawled
bodies to hide himself. Over him the bodies, wet and
warm like another layer of earth, had kept him alive
when death had passed over, its black muzzle rooting
for any who might have escaped, but missing him,
pressed into the mud. Lucky, he said, remembering.

Yeah, guys freaked on the ground. He could see the
face of one, a fat braggart child's face, the eyes crazy
with uppers and downers, telling him about a slope
female corpse, how "I propped her up and I spread her
gook legs and I got my whole clip off right up her gook
cunt. *Pow pow pow pow. Pow pow pow.*" And he had
pantomimed the shooting like a movie gangster. And
Henry'd seen guys taking pictures of each other
standing beside the corpses of women sawn in half.
Boys standing there with dead eyes and innocent
smiles. What purpose served by stopping one? Still, he
had; grabbing a skinny kid's camera once, slamming it
to pieces against a jeep fender. The kid had backed off
fast.

Dusky red rolled up over the sky. The woods behind
Wild Oat Ridge were now on fire. Without analyzing
the fire's cause, Henry automatically mapped its location as he loped down the steep graded road while
Night bolted ahead, then circled back, scout and flank.
Around a corner lights shone like steady fallen stars
near the side of the highway ahead. The ex-soldier
walked methodically on, limping now, noted peripherally the motorcycle shoved onto the purple flowering
branches, recalled peripherally the dipshit on a cycle
who had kicked at Night outside Fred's Fries.

Then as he came up the flagstone path to the large
ranch house, a woman's scream cried out at him,
savage. Henry rammed his shoulder at the front door,
already jumping from the step when it didn't open,

already running around the side of the house, with Night barking next to him, kicking Night down and pulling with both hands on the back sliding door. Then to the front again, to the large picture window, between the curtains a crack of light. On the floor somebody was on a woman. He had her on her stomach, her head crushed into the carpet; her legs were kicking and he was hurting her. From the highway Henry could hear sirens bleat, the noise still far away, coming toward him. He hauled a big, jagged flagstone out of the dirt and hurled it through the glass. Beside him, Night, wild, jumping.

With his wadded jacket, the gun in its pocket giving weight, he beat away the broken glass. Night leaped into the room. As Henry lifted his leg over the ledge, he saw the man, his face and torso clawed bloody, scrabble off the woman, his penis bobbing, coated and slimy, his pants bunched around his ankles, as he crawled for something on the rug. The woman wasn't Chin, but a blond woman older than Chin. Blood on the woman's mouth, blood on the insides of her thighs, blood on a nipple. Her cheek and throat, arms, thighs, discolored with bruises. He couldn't see Chin anywhere in the room. Then Night was growling; the man spun and had a revolver. The muzzle splatted a quick noise, and Night, already in the air, squealed, spun to the rug, twitching and yelping.

The man crouched there, his eyes dead and crazy, the gun pointed up at Maynard Henry.

"You *scumbag,*" Henry said tersely. "Stand up!"

Convulsive, moaning in high yelps, the man scurried to his feet waving the gun. "Get away, I'll kill you! I'm going to shoot! Get away! Get away! Goddamn you!"

But Henry simply shook his head as he walked forward and then grabbed Barnum's wrist and shook the gun to the floor. When Barnum lunged for it again, Henry kicked his hand away and, swooping quickly down, raised the gun himself. Without pause as Barnum kept grabbing for it he pointed the gun at

Barnum's naked crotch and fired, and without pause raised it to Barnum's naked chest and fired again, while astonishment, incisive, punctured the crazed blur of Barnum's eyes.

The body jumped backwards, falling. Blood, so red the man's auburn hair looked brown, pulsed out onto the stomach and thighs. Henry could hear Night's squeals and the groans of the woman who rocked on her knees beside the dog. A siren whooped, its loudness coming closer and closer until it was just outside the house. Finally it subsided in an abrupt whining halt. A light spun, flashing red through the window. Ignoring it, Maynard Henry bent down to Night, but the dog growled and bit at him; its whole side was torn open, soaked red.

"Fuck it," Henry whispered. He fired once, into the shepherd's head. Then the room was quiet. "Okay. Everything's okay now," he said to the dead dog. Still squatting, he turned to take Judith by the shoulders. "Tell me where Chin is. Is Chin here? Where is she?"

The woman's eyes, terrified, moved past his, came back, and looked for him as if she couldn't see him. "She's not here."

And Henry breathed out, weights pulled off his chest. From outside he heard, without registering it, a slammed door, footsteps running, and a man's voice yelling, "Jude! Jude!"

The woman was swallowing quickly and trying to speak again. "Miss Lattice first house Cromwell past Elizabeth, Chin Lam. Please. Help me. Please." Then she called, "John!," her body went into spasms, and she fell toward him, reaching for the towel next to her on the floor.

While Henry tried to pull the towel around her, a large shape loomed in the hole of the window and glints of silver flashed, a badge, a gun.

A voiceless howl twisted open John "Hawk" Haig's mouth. Driving to save his wife from fire, the police-man had heard three shots come from his home. The noise blew into his head and beat down reason. He was already insane when through the shattered glass he saw Maynard Henry's hands on the naked, bloody, motionless body of his wife.

Henry saw at once that it was too late to move, and he was knocked sideways by the shot before he heard it. A burn stung through his left arm as he waved yelling, "Hey, *no! Haig! Hold it! No!*" But Haig, his silent, piercing howl still unended, fired again. And then Henry, trained to kill rather than be killed, raised his arm with Barnum's gun still in his hand, fired, and the shape went away from the hole in the window, and the howling stopped.

As soon as Henry shot, he dropped the gun and crawled out through the window. But John "Hawk" Haig lay, face pressed against his careful earth and broken flowers, killed by a single trained bullet. "Fuck it, just fuck it!," the young thin man mumbled, shivering now in the wet T-shirt, as he bent to push his fingers against Haig's throat, knowing he would find no pulse.

Then she was running out the door, the towel around her. He jumped over the steps and led her back, his arms impersonal but shielding. Back in the hall, he let go.

"You his wife?"

She nodded, read the message of John's death in Henry's face, pressed her hands against her stomach.

"Listen, I'm sorry, but don't go out there, okay? He's gone. No, listen. I'm sure, honest, I'm sure. Hold tight. Nothing you can do." Then he went into the room where the blood of Limus Barnum soaked into the rug. With his thumb he lifted the eyelids. The dead eyes stared past him at some other horror, and the lips grinned a final smile.

As Henry snapped off the talking television, he saw the rivulets of blood running down his arm, so he grabbed a wool scarf off the armchair and wrapped it around the wound where a bullet had passed cleanly through his flesh. She was still nodding when he came back into the hall. "That one's dead," he told her. "Got a robe? Listen, you better get something on. You're okay. Listen." He kept talking to her as he moved through the house, his hand pressing against the scarf. On the bathroom door he found two robes; he brought her the woman's. Mechanically she put it on. As he opened closet doors, she watched him and tied the cord of her robe into knot after knot.

"Listen, okay? I'm going to take these blankets, okay?" He went back into the family room, then outside again, then he came back. They stood together in the hall by the open door. "Listen, I covered things up, okay? And I took the keys to that bike. Can you hear me? Look here. Are you all right? Look here." He shook her once by the shoulder. "Are you hurt bad?"

Finally she shook her head, still shivering, the click of her teeth audible.

"Okay. Now, try not to freak. Just keep breathing. Can you listen?" His frown was not as much angry as very impatient; he spoke in a hurried seriousness. "I'm going to call an ambulance to come get you, but then I'm going to get out of here. I gotta find Chin."

Dizziness swam over her eyes as she caught at his arm. But her hand slid on blood. Her eyelids started to twitch; her eyes rolled upward.

"Hey, lady. Hang on. Don't bum out now. You hear me?" He helped her into the living room but she pulled away, shuddering, when he tried to seat her on the velveteen sofa. He stood back. "I'm not going to do anything to hurt you. You understand?" He wound the scarf around his arm, tying it with his teeth. "I didn't come here to start shit, I was just looking for my wife. This is a bad scene. I'm sorry it got laid on you, but you saw, the minute the cop saw it was me, he tried to blow me away and I couldn't get him to lay off long enough to see what was happening. You see? It was just a damn motherfucker, just tough fucking luck. I know that's shit to you, but be sure you're clear on what's true, okay? Not that it'll help. They're going to fry me for this. So I gotta go right now 'cause I gotta see Chin before they grab me. Then you can tell them what you have to. I don't mean to stick you in the shit, but I got to have that little bit of time. Okay? Can you handle it?"

Judith raised her eyes to Maynard Henry's and studied them fixedly. He nodded at her. Then she could hear him telephoning. From the hall she watched him come out of the family room, something over his shoulder, her blanket. Judith stepped aside. The man walked, stooped, toward the door. The blanket began sliding, and the black German shepherd's head lolled limply against the thin white back, smearing the undershirt red.

Judith Haig stood in the door while Maynard Henry struggled to wrap the dog tightly in the blanket. With his belt and the chain left there, he managed to lash Night's body to the motorcycle. Then she went back inside the house, back into the family room. She pulled the blanket away from the body of Limus Barnum.

Outside the sky was livid now. Sweeping its blaze over the land, now climbing the ridge, fire scalded the clouds. The moon had fled. John "Hawk" Haig's new red brick ranch house that sat waiting to be connected to success now glowed with bright orange light. Of such force and so close was the fire that Maynard Henry, weaving dangerously up the steep grade of the ridge, did not hear above that terrible crackle the sound of a shot fired in the house behind him.

CHAPTER 55

Sirens screamed through Dingley Falls. From east and west and north as well men rushed to fight, then film, the fire. The *oogah-oogah* call to volunteer firemen summoned from the top of Town Hall. Among the volunteers, the selectman Cecil Hedgerow and Luke Packer's father, Jerry, already clung in careful nonchalance to the side of the bright polished truck. A co-fighter, Limus Barnum, had missed the rallying horn.

Except for William Bredforet, who paid no attention, and Coleman Sniffell, who wore wax earplugs to bed, and Mrs. Jack Strummer, who was sedated, and Sid and Kate, who were trying a new rear-entry position that required their full concentration, few Dingleyans were able to sleep through the noise of the battle. Winslow Abernathy in pajamas and robe was standing by his front window to watch the screaming red engines clatter past when he heard Prudence Lattice call his name as she hit at his door. In a panic of tears and agitation, the tiny woman told him that Maynard Henry, "that man," had barged into her home, set her aside, and taken Chin Lam. "His wife," the lawyer reminded Miss Lattice. But she shook her head, her fingers tremulous on his silk sleeve, and told him that Maynard Henry had not even allowed Chin time to pack her little suitcase. "Oh, Winslow, he was drenched in blood. He'll kill her, I know. She was just frightened to death."

With a stiff hug Abernathy assured the old woman that Chin Lam would not be hurt.

"How can you say that?" she sobbed into the robe.

And, of course, how could he be sure? Faith and truth need not necessarily coexist. While dread tightened on his heart, he rushed to his study to phone the police. An operator answered; neither Chief Haig nor his assistant were there. Had there been any accidents locally? he asked her. There was a major fire, she said, is that what he meant? What did he mean? Why did he think something had happened to Judith Haig, not to Chin Lam, but to *her?* He telephoned the Haig residence. The repeating ring infuriated him. His heart thudded absurdly against the bones of his chest, surely audible to Pru, who had followed him and who stood, baffled, fingers to her mouth.

"Pru, don't worry. Excuse me, I'm going to get dressed now. I'll look into this. I'm sure he's not going to hurt her, but, all right, thank you, excuse me." And he left his old neighbor there to find her way out or stay, as she chose. Upstairs in his room, where he pulled pants, shirt, and jacket on over his pajamas, Abernathy searched out the window for a plan? Absurd. He had just remembered that Beanie had taken her car, and a poet, to New York. Arthur had taken his car, and Emerald, to Litchfield. Lance, in his car, had sneaked out of town, probably to Gautamaula (sp.). And he, Winslow, apparently did not have a car of his own. A preposterous realization, but impossible to remedy after midnight. Whom could he ask? Not Evelyn, never get away; shouldn't involve Tracy; not Ernest; Scaper asleep; Smalter's light was on. He'd ask Sammy. Where were his shoes? Any shoes. He stumbled to dial his neighbor's number.

Smalter stood on the white rococo porch, car keys in hand, and watched Winslow Abernathy flap hurriedly across the landscaped grass of Elizabeth Circle. He began to talk while still in the street. "Very good of you, Sammy. Hope I didn't wake Ramona."

"Ah, you know better. She's up on that widow's walk gawking at the conflagration. Is that where you're going? I'm surprised at . . . what's the matter?" Smalter, his blue magnified eyes riveted on the lawyer's, suddenly felt the anxiety impatient in Abernathy's face and suddenly thought of Judith Haig alone in her house on the highway's edge.

"Ramona didn't seem to be feeling well at all earlier today when I brought the will by," the lawyer finished his sentence.

Smalter's hand, held out to offer the key, pulled back. "Winslow? What's the matter? It isn't Mrs. Haig? Has something happened to her? The fire's not all the way down to the highway, is it?"

More stunned at what he instantly sensed were Smalter's feelings about Judith Haig than at Smalter's eerie perception, Abernathy stared down at the midget a moment, then shook his head. "I don't know," he answered. "I want to go see." His hand was still extended.

Struggle was muted in Smalter's face. He remembered how he'd felt seeing Winslow and the postmistress sitting together in Pru's shop. Finally he gave a brisk sigh. "The pedals have been especially adjusted, you see, so you'll have to move the seat back as far as you can. I took my booster chair off. Unfortunately, Mrs. O'Neal has Ramona's car, or you could take that because I'm afraid someone as tall as you is going to look ridiculous folded up in this roadster."

Abernathy reached again for the key. "Oh, don't worry about that, Sammy."

"I don't," replied Mr. Smalter, leading the way up the dark brick walk to the Victorian carriage house.

With an enthusiastic sense of destiny, two young emergency van attendants (one of them brand-new at the job) jolted onto Route 3 toward what they assumed, from the fleet of fire trucks in the area, must be a major disaster on the order of a supersonic jet crashing on top of the house to which they had been directed by Maynard Henry's anonymous call. Slammed to a stop, the young men ran around an opened empty patrol car, its light flashing, and suddenly saw a woman crouched over in the yard beneath a huge broken picture window. They found her picking slivers of glass from the body of a dead policeman, whose head lay on the skirt of her robe.

Inside the house they found a male body sprawled naked except for the pants wadded around his feet. Bloody holes gaped in his groin and chest and face, three bright red-splattered openings in his flesh, and all around him the rug was sticky with dark stains. The younger attendant lurched back outside and vomited into a laurel bush. The older called the state police, as he was unable to persuade the woman to answer his questions about what he described to the patrol as looking like a double-murder gunfight over somebody's wife. Convinced that despite her bruised face and bloodstained robe the survivor was not critically injured, he simply gave her a shot to tranquilize her—not that she had offered the slightest resistance to anything they did, but lay, tightly wrapped, on the stretcher as they wheeled her into the van and screeched away. The new driver was worried that his partner might have seen him vomit; he feared too that he had sounded inanely naive with his "Gosh, I don't believe it, a shoot-out!" which he cursed himself for having exclaimed. He flipped on the siren and gunned the motor, forcing the car in front of him halfway onto the shoulder, then sped past with belligerent legality at ninety miles an hour.

Shortly before 1:00 A.M. the tiny bright yellow MG Midget was stopped by the roadblock set up on Route 3 to forestall locals and vacationers from driving up the ridge to sightsee. With some difficulty and more embarrassment, Winslow Abernathy, almost bent double, unraveled himself from the roadster, noticing as he extricated a leg that he wore no sock and that his pajamas showed below his pants cuff. The area looked like a battle station. With a group of men (among them the Argyle fire chief), Cecil Hedgerow stood bent over a car hood where a surveyor's map flapped up at the corners. For a wind had risen, after the still, sullen day, and now the fire licked south and westward, huge and hot even where they stood. "It doesn't look good," said Hedgerow, his own face singed and his hands white bandaged mitts. "It could head straight through Birch Forest and wipe out all those vacation homes around here." He swept an arm across the map to Lake Pissinowno. "Or worse, if the wind suddenly swings directly south, it's possible it could jump the highway and go down East Woods. Could get Dingley O.I. before the Rampage stopped it. Hell, it could go right into Dingley Falls. The damn thing was, nobody could get to it, it seemed to start out in the middle of nowhere!" And with disgust, he circled the area near Bredforet Pond.

Abernathy tried to fold his jacket up over his open shirt, through which his pajama top poked. "What about the Haig house?" he asked.

"Somebody told you what happened there? Unbelievable!"

"Tell me what?!" Terrified, he turned Hedgerow back toward him. "Cecil! What?"

And the selectman matter-of-factly (too exhausted for horror) explained that John Haig had been killed a few hours earlier, it appeared, at his house. So had another man, not yet identified as far as he knew. And Mrs. Haig . . . Abernathy's head was bursting against his eardrums . . . was in shock; Hedgerow didn't know how serious it was, but she was in the hospital, he thought, in Argyle. He did know there'd been a problem here between the fire department (who were considering water blasting or even dynamiting along that strip, should the wind turn the fire toward Dingley

Falls) and the state police (who didn't want anything destroyed that was possible evidence in the vicinity of possible homicides).

Abernathy left Hedgerow arguing that he could not let any more heavy fire equipment cross the rickety Falls Bridge, while the fire chief, more accustomed to disaster, accepted a Coke, yelled into his car radio mike, poked at the map with jabs of his finger, and posed for a photographer from *The Argyle Standard.* Word was that volunteer fire teams from three counties were working together to keep the situation under control. In addition, extra Madder volunteers (rounded up by Carl Marco, by whom most of them were employed) were up on the ridge wetting down the ground and trees and trying to clear a gap in the fire's path. It might work. And it might rain; the latest weather report gave a 50 percent chance of precipitation. And what you learn, the chief confessed to the reporter, after a life's experience, is that you never know what's going to happen and you better stop pretending you do.

Turned back by the roadblock, Winslow Abernathy (overaccelerating and popping the clutch) jerked the MG around, scraping the bumper of Ernest Ransom's Mercedes parked beside the road, and sped back through Dingley Falls. Racing back through a town that fire might raze. And though it bore his wife's name, had sheltered her family for three hundred years, and him and his for the last thirty of those, he was not thinking of Dingley Falls, but only of driving past it without getting killed. He felt that he looked like a clown in a tiny circus car, his knees around the steering wheel, as the yellow roadster motored, veering, loudly down High Street while emergency vehicles, rerouted from Falls Bridge, raced by in the other direction.

Sammy Smalter's car roared past Alexander Hamilton Academy, where Walter Saar and Jonathan Fields lay together a little less awkwardly than the night before. Past the Bredforets', where Mary stood by the street to watch the excitement while Bill Deeds warned her they should wake William and evacuate the house. It roared past Glover's Lane, where, seated on the toilet, A. A. Hayes was shocked by the changing times as revealed in his son's "girlie" magazine, as he himself had once called them; shocked by the erection the photos had given him; shocked by the unremembering innocence that allowed him even for a second to delude himself into supposing that his wife, June, would let him make love to her tonight if his life depended upon it. Feeling like a moronic teenager, he checked the lock sheepishly, then began to masturbate. No doubt, this was exactly why he could never get into the john; because that's what his sons Tac and Charlie were doing in here, and probably his daughters Suellen and little Vickie, too. By phone Hayes had already dispatched the annoyed Coleman Sniffell to go interview the fire fighters, but if the town started to actually burn down he was going to have to get involved himself. Funny to think of a northern town burning down while a southerner played with himself. Shocked, Hayes realized he was getting ready to ejaculate. He spun some toilet paper quickly off the roll.

The MG hurried past Elizabeth Circle, where Evelyn Troyes phoned Tracy Canopy to come help her make sandwiches to take up to the fire fighters. Past all the houses where Dingleyans stood in various stages of dishabille and watched from various vantage points as sulfurous clouds illumined by flames surged and swirled through a red sky. Up Cromwell Hill Road and on to Argyle. But all Winslow Abernathy could think of was the absurd notion that if Judith Haig were dying, he had only to get there in time to grab hold of both her hands and then he could pull her back, out of the arms of death. Wind gusted at the little car, swerving it and frightening him. He took a harder grip on the wheel.

Across the sky of Dingley Falls fire was blown in squalls. Up on her widow's walk still at 2:00 A.M., Ramona Dingley in her white cotton nightshirt leaned on her cane. She watched in horror as hundreds of trees burned, the trees of her past, her town's trees. At some point in her vigil she thought of the government base near Bredforet Pond that Polly and Luke had found out. Might it be consumed in this conflagration? But the young people had proof now; she would leave that work to them. As the blaze brightened, she could think only of Dingley Falls itself. Fire might destroy Dingley Falls. Three hundred years it had lasted, and now— under her protectorship—it might fall back to nothing. She, the last of the governors bearing the name Dingley, might be the one to lose the town. After all the lives that had built it; had lived and given birth and died in it; and all those still young who could wed its past to the future.

Tears squeezed from the old woman's eyes. She shifted her hands on two metallic canes that helped her support the useless legs and useless, sickly weight. Tendons and veins stood out on her hands. "You!" she said, her head tilted back to the bleeding sky. "Listen to me!" Wind stirred the short-cropped hair atop the hawk's face. "Not going to my knees. Never get up. But standing is hard and I'll do it. Here's a prayer. Don't say You knew You'd hear that word breathed by such a Thomas as I. I stand here to ask You. You save this town. Look what You've been doing here! To what purpose? Don't burn it. No bribe. Of what use an old soul like mine? Wouldn't give You my best years. Won't insult You by offering the dregs. I just stand here to ask You. Don't burn this town. Absurd, ain't it, me come to You? Here I am. Your serve."

She lost any sense of time there atop the white tall house. Her arms shook, rattling the canes. Spasms in her back jumped like current through her body. Her hands were numb now but still held to the cold steel handles. Then for an instant the air was still.

And then there came a rushing wind that blew over the sky like the foaming sea, and the wind parted the clouds. She heard the thunder, she saw the great arm of lightning point down at earth. Rain teemed out of the opened sky. And Ramona Dingley, shivering as water splashed down her face, lifted her head. "You!" she said. "Quite a trick, you ask me. Preposterous to believe You did it, of course." She smiled, her hand sliding from a cane. "But won't deny I'm impressed." She slipped down into the wheelchair and whispered, "Think You could ask Sammy to come up here?"

Inflamed by air, fire jumped up at the raining sky like little men furious at the gods, shaking their fists in vain. Water fell to earth despite fire and air. Thundering its arrival, rain washed over Dingley Falls. Rain filled the Rampage, tumbled down the Falls, lifted the old bridge like a reckless lover, and swept it away.

Rain fell like the tears of God's mercy.

Rain in unending ranks of seraphic soldiery seized each particle of the Archangel's weaponry and with iridescent wings beat pestilence back into the unresistant earth.

Rain saved the town, and the faces of those who fought the fire lifted, smiling like the faces of the faithful turned up to praise Creation.

CONCERNING DICTION

Thursday afternoon in a Hertz rental car, the intelligence officers Tom, Dick, and Harry cruised east along a Connecticut Interstate near a little private airport north of a little resort town called Dingley Falls. Once they discovered the low, leafy entrance to a dirt road dug some years ago down from the Interstate, down into woods to the south, it was not that hard to locate the secret base of Operation Archangel. Their rented

Mercury Marquis bounced like a rodeo ride, spun its wheels, lurched against trees, as they approached the secluded compound.

It was CIA assistant underdirector John Dick who smelled first the dogs, and then Dr. Svatopluk. Ants crawled all over a hand in which were clutched crumbs of what Dick thought must have been a sort of strudel. The Washingtonians identified the chief of staff by reading a plastic name tag pinned to Svatopluk's lab coat.

Inside a shiny building, where mums and marijuana twined around the door, the stench was worse, and the three civil servants did not attempt even a rough body count of all the young male bodies stretched in white on the plywood floors, helter-skelter, yet cosily near one another, some accidentally embracing. There was no need to confirm death, for the bloated limbs and bulging red eyeballs had already done that. The spies (who'd read a lot of spy stories but had always had cold war desk jobs themselves and had consequently never had a chance to see any action) stepped back at the sight and fled at the smell. Willy-nilly they gagged and, fearful of a radioactive plague for all they knew, raced, bumping, back to the airport motel where the Hertz girl expressed horror at what they had done in two hours' time to a beautiful Mercury Marquis with less than a thousand miles on it.

Tom, Dick and Harry rushed into a shower to scald off the chance of contamination. Their teenaged desk clerk, just on his way to a lunch break in the broom closet with the Hertz girl, thought he had walked into a trap of mad raping homosexual killers when three naked middle-aged men rushed him and offered him cash for his clothes. Their own were wrapped in the plastic shower curtain. The enterprising teenager charged them (on American Express) $50 each for what he could dig up, happily warning that it wouldn't be much.

Miserable in a booth at the motel's Round-Up

Restaurant, the three espionage executives sat shame-faced in ill-fitting and unwashed blue jeans, T-shirts, white socks, and (their own) expensive leather loafers. They were without their shorts and feeling very vulnerable. Brooding to and from the salad bar, they tried to come up with a game plan. Since, an hour after exposure, they appeared to show no signs of dropping dead from what was apparently a major flaw in Dr. Svatopluk's experiment, maybe they could still pull this mess out of the fire, or at least save their own balls from the shredder.

"Gentlemen, we have a problem," said Tom, sawing at his T-bone steak.

"Maybe Wolton and Eagerly killed them all," said Dick, swizzling his Scotch.

"Maybe they killed Wolton and Eagerly at the same time, don't forget that," said Harry, beating catsup onto his potatoes. "So I say, we go back, hold our noses, flip over the bodies, and check out the faces for Dan and Bucky. Because if they're out there somewhere and blow the lid off this thing, man, somebody's going to have to bend over and take the fall, and I for one am not about to take it in the shorts because the CIA's got caught again with its pants down."

"Go back? Are you kidding?" said Tom and Dick. But they were agreed that the problem wasn't going to disappear on its own. There was no New Left left to blame. Maybe they could dump it on black radicals, but after Watergate it would be a ballbuster to come up with a scenario that the press would buy. No, if it came out, there best bet was a solitary act of an isolated psychopath. But where would a psychopathic Svato-pluk have gotten all that government property? Because the computer had said he even had a navy cook and an army janitor. They ordered another round of drinks and three hot fudge sundaes and waited for help.

At last, at midnight the doors swung open and a man stepped inside. He was as hard-eyed and as bald as an American eagle. A little pudgy in the pot and splotchy on the hands and droopy by the jowls, but otherwise sound as a dollar. A big man in a Boy Scout scoutmaster's uniform.

Commander Hector Brickhart was a man of action, not thought. Urgently summoned, he had left his scout troop in mid-trip of their first shot at Mother Nature. Without taking time to change, he had hitched a ride from Alaska through a pal in SAC, had been flown into Boston, and had flown himself in a borrowed monoplane to the private airport north of Dingley Falls. He had been humping hard, he said, hotter than hell, to save the face of the nation by destroying this dumb base. "Now hear this, you three stooges. You're in here boozing on your fat butts, dressed up like a fairy chorus line of greasy hoods, but you don't know fuck about shit."

Impatiently, Brickhart heard the Washingtonians elaborate on the situation regarding Operation Archangel. In brief, there were bodies all over the base. They wanted them covered up. He told them, "Listen, boys, you're not thinking straight. If you look up your own asshole, there's just one thing you're going to see. Now forget trying to pin this on somebody else. This single-nut theory is junk and so's a feminist uprising. One thing you fellows never have understood is, if something's full of shit somewhere, and somebody's stuck in it balls deep, and that somebody's the U.S. of A., then you don't throw some fancy cover on top of him. You pull him out by the fanny! And that's what I'm here to help you bastards do." The commander would not, he said, hold a grudge against his country when the chips were down, even if that country had pensioned him off and disregarded every word of advice he'd ever given it since 1935, when he'd said, no bones about it, assassinate that goddamn Austrian paperhanger fast.

Okay, so there was a leak as big as a bull's pizzle in the Seventh Division Immuno-Deficiency Research Team, DIRT, and might as well shoot from the hip and call a spade a spade—DIRT was nothing but a goddamn germ warfare plant.

Well, said Tom, Dick, and Harry, it might be inappropriate to offer what were necessarily conjectures about the Svatopluk experiments; however, it could not be denied that whatever they were, any leakage about them could well be designed to embarrass the government at a most delicate juncture in current negotiations to agree on the language of a treaty one of whose provisos was to condemn all forms of biological antipersonnel software. And so the less said about the Svatopluk experiments the better. Brickhart replied that their agencies should have kept that in mind before they left a trail up to Svatopluk's ball park as wide open as an old whore's twat, and that personally he was surprised that a goddamn television camera wasn't sneaking in between his legs right this minute.

Brickhart outlined an offensive to which, after huddled conversation through the wee hours, the desperate civil servants agreed. At dawn on Friday, three army transport trucks (one carrying a dozen trained men perfectly equipped and outfitted to avoid infection) miraculously appeared on the Interstate north of Dingley Falls and rendezvoused with the Mercury Marquis at a rest stop. Roll out! waved Brickhart. Forward they bounced down the bumpy road to pick up the ball science had dropped. There at the compound, the gas-masked soldiers quickly, methodically, expensively, fumigated the area, collected all the bodies, zipped them up in surplus bags, and trucked them out. Back at the rest stop, the corpses were packed into a supply van to transport them to the Boston naval base where Brickhart had some pals. And from there they would be flown in a surplus plane out into the Atlantic to meet *en masse* legitimate deaths, when their plane would "crash" on its way to a military conference on Martha's Vineyard. "Happens all the time," Hector Brickhart had said, in reference to

planes lost at sea. "Well, not that often," said Tom,
Dick, and Harry, who thought he meant multiple
assassinations of American citizens by government
agencies.

The three desk men stood beside the van as the
plastic bags were carried by. A soldier unzipped
enough so that they could check the faces for the
features of Wolton and Eagerly. They found neither.
Except for one token black (the cook) and one token
Jew (the chief of staff), all the faces, behind the twists
of death, were young, bland, and hybridized Anglo-
Saxon, the purest strain that of the Tennesseean
janitor. The cook's bag was carried like a baby up to
the van by Brickhart himself. "I knew this boy," he
sighed, and showed the spies the wizened chocolate
face of a man at least as old as he was. "Cook on my
first ship. Isn't that something? In the Pacific. Used to
fry my steak just right. Lukewarm! Had an ensign on
that cruise, one of those Ivy League nervous nellies,
and every time I'd swab some bread around in that
steak blood, that ensign would turn puke green and
couldn't eat another bite. Sometimes, just to get at him
I'd take a big chew and let the juice run out of the sides
of my mouth. You know? This little black fellow here
always got a real kick out of it. The Japs got a lot of us
on that cruise." And the commander zipped up the
bag. It was tossed into the van.

The borrowed soldiers did not question the fact that
they were evacuating victims of a "freak chemical
accident," them dismantling the contaminated base—
that made sense to them. What they did question was
their sergeant's taking orders from a weirdo in a Boy
Scout uniform and from his three weirdo underlings
who were identically dressed as the late James Dean.
Commander Brickhart understood their unease and
told them, "Boys, your sarge here knows that your CO
wouldn't have sent you off in this goddamn heat to this
goddamn hole if he didn't know I either had a pretty
damn good reason for asking, or else I'd gone out of my

goddamn mind. So you do right by me and I'll do right by you. I know you're going to want to do your best, and you're going to want to do it fast! Fall out!" Because the commander had always said that while a British soldier would do his duty because he believed in duty, and a German soldier would do his because he believed in obedience, an American soldier did his duty if and when you persuaded him that the particular duty you wanted him to do was, according to his individual lights, worth doing, or that the particular officer he was doing it for was, in his personal judgment, somebody worth doing things for. His men, he was proud to say, had always liked him.

Taking apart the prefabricated base took much less time than it would have if things had been properly assembled in the first place. Walls came down at a tap. Despite heat and humidity, the shirtless soldiers worked with enthusiasm. Demolition had its peculiar carnal delights. Hastily they wasted a superfluity of scientific equipment for which Thomas Svatopluk (buying for the government) had been extraordinarily overcharged. Then they razed the lab and leveled the living quarters and wrecked the rec room. Into the trucks went the portables like the color TV, collapsible pool table, and Coke machine. What wouldn't fit into the trucks and wouldn't burn was lugged over to the big, murky pond nearby and chucked in. It all sank to the dark floor of the pond, like accidental offerings thrown to the monster down in the far depths, with its monstrous, single, round glittering eye of glass and the tentacles of arms and legs that waved loosely from its green metal body. Like household objects buried with Egyptian dead, typewriters, latrines, electric razors, and chess sets waited in the pond silt to accompany Wolton and Eagerly and their pilot into the Other World.

By the time the soldiers had destroyed the compound, the sun had seeped away, and, so said Hector Brickhart, a big white tit of a moon bobbed over their heads. The scientists' bodies were already on their way to accidental death in the gray Atlantic. The demolition team was dismissed with ribald good wishes for the evening. Now beneath the moon stood Brickhart with the exhausted Tom, Dick, and Harry. They stood ringed by a circle of the base's gasoline barrels, which they had collected and positioned along the perimeter of the compound. The barrels were stamped ALAS-ORE OIL CO. And at the base's center was raised a pyre of plywood and five years' worth of back copies of *Playboy* magazine. On top of these Commander Brickhart placed the chief of staff's framed diplomas (B.S. from Fairleigh Dickinson, Ph.D. from Rutgers University, M.D. from Harvard Medical School), along with a framed photograph of a younger Svatopluk, wiry-haired and blotto-eyed, in a line of scientists honored to shake hands with the fairy tale president, John Kennedy.

Finally, with a sprinkle of gasoline from a coffee can, the naval commander offered a short blessing, which the representatives of the secret services, who did not speak the language, heard with discomfort "Earth to earth, dust to dust, ashes to ashes. We brought nothing into this world and it is certain we can carry nothing out. That runt Svatopluk had a set of balls, I'll give him that. They weren't my shape of balls, but that's what makes the world go 'round. He stuck to his guns, the damn little kike, and my hat's off to him. He told me straight to my face, too, that maybe we didn't see eye to eye but he could appreciate my point of view."

(Dr. Svatopluk had said, "I don't make the mistake of assuming that because you are a bigot, a racist, and a war monger that you are *ipso facto*, if you know what I mean, a complete idiot, which may not be the case.")

"Still, the little prick never would slip me any of the stuff he was making up here in this two-bit operation of his. Otherwise we might be lighting matches on the fannies of slopes in Hanoi right this minute. But maybe not. Because, boys, I'll tell you what it is. This goddamn country never has had the balls to stick by its guns. I say let's shoot for the title if we're shooting for the title, and stop pretending the other guy pulled us into the ring and then got himself KO'd on our gloves when we stuck them out just to keep him from clobbering the referee. I say let's stop needing every country in the world to think we're better than they are and stop trying to make them say so by being just like us, or by God, if that's the way we feel, let's say so, and let's *make* them ours! But let's cut the crap. I say at our age it's time we stopped feeling as goddamn guilty as a virgin preacher that just fucked his first married parishioner. Because let's face it, we've fucked a hell of a lot including the British and the Indians and the Spanish and the Mexes and God bless us the Germans and those SOB Japs and screwed up bad when we stopped there and didn't go after the Russians, too. Because this is the *world*, and we got to make up our mind. It comes down to one thing. And that's all. And it's not any ideological crap or any economic crap either. It's when you get up on your back legs and you look the other guy straight in the face, which of you has got the biggest dick! That's right! That's the whole history of the world right there, and if you don't believe it, boys, don't start any fights. A lot of people think I'm a nut, but that's just because I plow the shit off the runway. I'm an American. I want to win! So let America ask herself, Are we going to do the fucking? Or are we going to be the one that gets fucked? And believe me, boys, we knelt right down and spread our cheeks so wide in Nam, I swear to God above, I'd be surprised if we could *ever* get it up again! But Svatopluk here, I know he'd say the same. He ran a tight ship. And so unto Almighty God we commend the soul of our brother departed, and we commit his body to the deep, now free from the deceits of the world, the flesh, and the devil. In hope of the Resurrection to eternal life when we all gather at the river, irregardless of race, creed, or color, and meet with our Savior in the sweet by-and-by. Amen."

And with a torch Commander Brickhart set the base on fire.

Throughout the evening as the four men ate a late supper at the Round-Up, off in the woods the strategically placed gasoline barrels ignited when the fire reached them and loudly exploded the flames forward. Microscopic particles of the unfinished Svatopluk experiments danced in the fire, swirling up into the atmosphere.

At the airport hangar, Brickhart bid *"adios amigos"* to the three government men, whom, in his contempt, he had called interchangeably by various combinations of their nebulous names. His CO pal who had lent him the demolition team had also sent, at the commander's request, a present, one that the old naval fighter had carried, in its straw-cradled crate, tenderly in his arms on the ride back down the bumpy road chased by fire. He took it from the car.

Now at eleven o'clock at night, his uniform muddy and sooty but his eyes still pure and blue as a frontier sky, Hector Brickhart gave thumbs up from the cockpit of his borrowed single-engine plane. Then, guided back to the base by firelight and moonlight, grinning and his heart in a dance, the commander dropped dead on target a little incendiary thermite bomb with a high explosive charge that shot fire roaring through the woods at a run. He did it for fun, for a last fling before returning to the deathly earnestness of business cartels that he didn't much understand and didn't much like. They spoke a different language. Not that he would have to put up with their crap much longer since apparently he was going to lose this goddamn sneaky war with cancer no matter how hard he fought. Still, he'd been lucky and lived a good long life and done the state some service, whether they knew it or not. And having loosed with that dangerous innocence so foreign to Thomas Svatopluk an instrument of destruction far more sophisticated than himself, that bomb he called his honey and his sweetheart and his baby, away Commander Brickhart flew into night.

On the land from which the secret of Operation Archangel was now being removed (along with abundant beech, birch, cedar, sycamore, and other natural things), there had once lived, in a harmoniously heartless life struggle, abundant deer, bears, wolves, foxes, otters, beavers, minks, raccoons, and other wild life that was, as William Bredforet used to say of the old great fortunes, "all gone now." Indeed their pelts had gone to make those fortunes in the shapes of hats, gloves, rugs, collars, and coats. Little but the unprofitable porcupine had not been stolen for a stole. The profligate rabbit had also survived, and the skunk, and the homely woodchuck. The human inhabitants of that time before Dingleys had been proud to own everything in sight (abundant Algonquin, Matabesecs, Mohegans, and Pequots) had been created with neither the strategic stench of the skunk, nor the reproductive stamina of the rabbit. So unlike those creatures, the Indians were all gone now, too.

Harried westward by westward movers founding little towns along the way.

PART
Six

CHAPTER
56

"There's been something the matter with Mrs. Haig's heart," Dr. Ruth Deeds explained to Chin Lam Henry outside the door to the hospital room. "That's why we have to have her here for a day or two, just to keep a check on her. But she's going to be all right. Which, really, is pretty fantastic considering the horror story that woman went through."

Chin Lam nodded politely. She had herself seen so many horror stories and had heard of so many others that in fact the sight of Mrs. Haig, alive with eyes and ears and all four limbs, propped up on snowy pillows with watchful attendants around her, was not especial cause for grief. And husbands were often killed. Bruises would heal. Chin had not been told of the rape, but rape was not uncommon, and after all not as bad for an adult woman as for a child, and not as bad when a single rapist, and after all there were far worse things than even rape. Some of them she had looked at. Mrs. Henry was not a particularly callous young woman, but her perspective had not been trained on the sanctity of the individual and that individual's right to freedom from violation and to freedom from misfortune, as had the perspectives of the Americans, Judith Haig and Ruth Deeds.

Last night at 1:00 A.M. (presuming upon, he said, his age and her youth), Otto Scaper had phoned Dr. Deeds to ask if she would save an exhausted old man's life by driving to Argyle to check on a patient they had just called him about. Because, he growled, if he didn't get a few hours' sleep tonight, she could have his office equipment tomorrow. Scaper had already brought Judith Haig's case to Dr. Deeds's attention as one of the victims of that unnatural heart trouble. When the woman doctor sleepily arrived at the hospital (in a borrowed 1947 Rolls-Royce), she found that Mrs. Haig had been brought into Emergency as a victim of shock and of "possible sexual abuse." The opinion of the young resident on duty was that Mrs. Haig was in a state of psychotic withdrawal. After visiting Judith, Dr. Deeds told the resident, with a little more stridency than she'd planned, that the woman was not psychotic, but that she had suffered a mild heart attack and that she had been raped, both vaginally and rectally, and that she had been severely beaten, and that if that was what he called "possible sexual abuse," she hoped it happened to him sometime. The resident shrugged. Women were hysterical and there was no sense in letting it get to you.

At the nurses' station Ruth shared a cup of coffee with a young RN, also black, who addressed her as "Sister." They talked about Judith Haig. Dr. Deeds was angry. In the Chicago years before she began to concentrate exclusively on research, she had seen a great many raped and beaten women brought into emergency rooms. She was inured to the sight, but not to the fact. "I don't want her to start thinking somehow it was her fault that whoever did this to her got killed, or that her husband got killed, because she got raped. It happens. She's got to get angry instead of ashamed. Right?"

"Right on, honey," said her sister, then looked at the chart Ruth was scribbling on and added, "Hey! You're a doctor! Right on, right on!"

By Saturday morning it was evident that Mrs. Haig was in no real danger of heart arrest. She was wheeled into a room across an opened curtain from a tired, affable woman close to her in age, who announced at once that though she had just lost one of her breasts, she felt confident that the doctors had caught the tumor in time and that she would be able to keep the other one. "Actually I don't know if one's better than none or not, it's hard to say. But staying alive, that's the main thing, isn't it?" she asked with an expectant nod.

Judith turned her head on the pillow and looked at the woman. "Yes, it is," she replied.

"My name's Betsy," said the woman, and burst into tears.

"I'm Judith," Mrs. Haig told her, and began to cry, too.

Those were the first words Mrs. Haig had spoken. When Dr. Deeds returned to check her at 10:00 A.M., Judith still had said nothing to the police about what had happened Friday night. All they had were two bodies, a weapon, and a few very rushed pictures of the room, taken under frantic circumstances while firemen hauled at the photographer's arms. Now a detective sat in the waiting room, waiting to hear what Mrs. Haig would say. She floated up out of sleep to see an attractive black female face with a wide halo of hair bent down over her. Dr. Deeds explained that she had been sent by Dr. Scaper to keep an eye on his patient, and that she had been there last night but Mrs. Haig had been under sedation.

"I'm all right now," Judith said.

The doctor's hands moved gently as she changed bandages behind the pulled curtain. "Are you doing okay here? Want me to try to find you a private room?"

"No, this is fine."

"Well, I don't see why you'll have to stay more than a day or two. We'll run some tests and let you rest and probably put you on a bunch of new medications. Now the problem is, I guess you know there's a cop waiting to talk to you?" Dr. Deeds smoothed the covers over Mrs. Haig, then stepped back, her hands stuffed in the wide white pockets of her jacket. "This is the last thing in the world you ought to have to talk to those jerks about. So don't you let them give you a rough time. You just tell them to buzz off. Or you send for me and

I'll be glad to get rid of them for you. They've been trained to kowtow to medical mumbo-jumbo. Promise? Okay. That's right, you get some sleep."

Judith with some effort murmured, "Thank you," touched her fingers to those of Ruth Deeds, then drifted back asleep before the door fully closed.

Without speaking, Polly Hedgerow and Luke Packer walked side by side along the rotary that circled the town green where Elijah Dingley sat, still laughing despite the disasters that had set upon his namesake. Under heavy rain and heavy traffic Falls Bridge had finally given way and tumbled down the waterfall, just as everyone had been predicting it would do for decades, and its splintered beams now bobbed in the Rampage. Carl Marco had already intimated privately to Arthur Abernathy, first selectman, his willingness to replace the loss with a modern bridge entirely at his own expense, a new old-fashioned Marco Bridge to welcome the world to Dingley Falls.

Apart from the bridge, Dingley Falls looked the same, but nothing was as it had been. Stores and offices wore mourning. Wreaths, donated by Carl Marco, marked the doors of the police station where death, passing by, had paused. At Arthur Abernathy's order, the flag of Dingley Falls's post office (which, the town was surprised to hear, it would soon be losing because the government was losing money on it), the flag that the postmistress had raised each work day for eleven years, had been lowered to half-mast for Police Chief John "Hawk" Haig. Luke and Polly walked slowly by Barnum's Antiques, Hobbies, and Appliances store. Though not empty, it was not open for business; police squeezed between the cluttered rows of dusty, broken things that Barnum had sold to vacationers. Next door, the Lattice Tea Shoppe was closed, and next to that Smalter's Pharmacy was also closed. Out-of-town reporters were lounging all over the front office of *The Dingley Day*. A man stood beside A. A. Hayes's desk and used his phone while the editor raised a paper cup to his lips.

In the cream brick offices shared by Dr. Scaper and Abernathy & Abernathy sat only Ida Sniffell (who had forced the old physician back home to bed) and Susan Packer (who told people that Abernathy, Jr., was at Town Hall dealing with the disaster, and that she had no idea where Abernathy, Sr., might be). A new postmistress and a new mail carrier were in the tiny office. The weekend volunteer librarian sat alone in George Webster Dixwell Library. And Ransom Bank was always closed on Saturdays. People milled around the circle as if expecting a parade. At one end of the green, teenaged boys tossed a football; at the other, small children fell into somersaults while their young mothers waited on benches. A couple in white took pictures of Elijah's statue.

Earlier in the morning, Luke had knocked on Polly's door and had said only, "Let's just go for a walk, all right?" And she had said only, "All right." Neither mentioned Joy. Upstairs Polly's father slept, mildly sedated for the pain of his burns. Cecil Hedgerow's hair was singed. His hands lay outside the sheet like two white boxing gloves someone had placed there in tribute. He deserved, he said, to sleep until noon. He was a hero. Dozens of hands had slapped his back and flashbulbs had popped spots in front of his eyes and a microphone had been nudged under his nose to find out how he had felt when his hair caught fire. "Hot-headed," he'd replied, with a sooty grin, and the little crowd that ringed the camera had cheered. Tonight when this moment was replayed on television, Democratic party people in the district would begin to wonder if Hedgerow, Dingley Falls's third selectman, might not be a possibility to challenge the incumbent Republican congressman, who, they said, was a sycophant with his hands in the pockets of local business and his head in a golf bag; another possible choice of theirs,

John "Hawk" Haig, was written off by the story of his tragic death on the same news program.

So the hero Cecil Hedgerow slept, his battle won. For Dingley Falls stood. The Federalist houses were not even seared. Around the town green the white brick and gray slate buildings looked much as they had looked last week, indeed last century, except for a fine drizzle of soot that was far less than what fell in pollution on most modern cities every day. Dingley Falls stood, saved by the work of men like Cecil Hedgerow and by four hours of torrential summer rain, but everywhere the town was in a buzz of shock. For north of the highway, geysers of smoke still steamed from the black wasteland that yesterday had been forest and marsh grass. Wild Oat Ridge was charred bare and looked to one Catholic reporter like Golgotha. Hawk Haig's house had burned. Live cinders blown by the wind had caught the roof on fire. Nothing remained but the blackened brick shell. But that was the only human structure lost, and, said the Argyle fire chief, people ought to thank their lucky stars. The little Rampage River had saved Dingley Optical Instruments, and so saved Madder. Westward, water in a storm of rain had battled fire past dawn, had held the line at the edge of East Woods and had defeated the flames before one touched Dingley Falls at all.

Still, Dingleyans were stunned. For not only had they suffered a major forest fire (and though the vacation cabins and the little airport north of the lake were intact, the mountain greenery looked so horrible that Bicentennial summer tourism was bound to suffer, too); they had also suffered on the same night a double murder of their police chief and an active local merchant. It was the worst thing that had ever happened to them. Naturally enough they had said the same of some dozens of earlier misfortunes, including severe winters, the spring the Rampage flooded, the Depression, and the riots when old Luke Madder had started a union strike in the otherwise gay nineties. But this was definitely the worst in a long time. Their privacy would be intruded upon by a scavenging pack of journalistic hyenas sent, wrote A. A. Hayes, to feed on their personal troubles, then haul the carcasses out into the Colosseum of the world for vultures to pick at.

Even by Saturday noon, Dingleyans were uncertain about the specifics of the calamities that had befallen them. Rumor had outraced fire and had burned up most of the town and killed half the citizens before the rain stopped. As for the gunfight murders, first it was thought that one or both of the Haigs had been burned to death in their house. Then the shooting news started. A burglar had shot both the Haigs, had shot just Hawk Haig, Hawk Haig had shot a burglar; Judith Haig had shot a burglar and/or had shot Hawk Haig. Limus Barnum had shot Hawk Haig. Hawk Haig had shot Limus Barnum. Limus Barnum had been Judith Haig's lover. Limus Barnum had come to fight the fire and had been accidentally shot by either Mr. or Mrs. Haig. Somebody else had shot all three. All three had been burned to death in the fire. Somebody else had shot Barnum and Haig and had wounded Mrs. Haig. Finally the word went out that Judith Haig had been raped. A few Dingleyans, of course, didn't care at all about any of it, and a few who scarcely knew the names of the principals cared with voracious hunger. A few had even fallen prey to still another rumor, that a maniac or something had poured a secret poison or something into the reservoir and that everyone in the town was dying, but this incredible tall tale caught the ears of only the most desperate thrill seekers and soon expired.

Most Dingleyans simply waited with some degree of curiosity for the evening television news to show them what had happened. Among that group were Polly and Luke, who could not help but find fire and fire trucks momentarily exhilarating, and who were programmed to find murder per se an even more thrilling disaster than fire, and who wondered what the firemen would say when they found the remains of the deserted base. But all this news stirred busily in the far distance, while three-dimensional and huge, the death of their friend Joy closed in on them like humid air that slowed their steps up Cromwell Hill Road.

Both tall, lanky, free-limbed, both in jeans, loose shirts, and jogging shoes, Polly and Luke were immediately, automatically labeled by passing motorists as generic American teenagers, indistinct as to age or social background or economic status, barely distinguishable by sex, pretty much warranted against fear and want, burdened largely only by their own almost limitless self-expectations and by the trials that adolescent flesh is heir to—acne, lust, emotional havoc, and other drawbacks to happiness from which the government, though it tries, cannot guarantee protection. Among those drawbacks, the dirty tricks of that foe to the free world, Death, rankled as injustice in the hearts of Polly and Luke.

As they scuffed past St. Andrew's Episcopal Church, Polly noticed Sebastian Marco at work again in the bright colors of the garden. Nearby a black Lincoln sat in the gravel drive, its trunk open. Father Highwick must be back from New York. With disgust Polly realized that thoughts of all the horrific news there was to tell the Rector had bubbled up in her at the sight, as if it was exciting that so much had happened while he was away. But of itself the bubble burst. She imagined someone who had been herself standing beside the red bicycle innocently bartering with Father Highwick the secrets of Dingley Falls. She could no longer be that person.

Before turning back, she and Luke walked as far as Dixwell High School. They peered into dark windows at classrooms left for the summer as though the students had just stepped outside into the hall. They found their history room, the podium still in place from which Ms. Rideout had made her valedictory speech with its stuttering confession that she could not cope with their abuse.

"If she thinks *we're* rough, why is she going to law school?" Polly said.

"She thinks we need more women in power. Women have to get into the same positions men are in. They should have the right to do what men do." Luke sat down on the steps of the school to pour gravel out of his shoe, while Polly did the same to hers.

"That's dumb," she said. "I don't think *men* should have a right to do what men do, much less the other half of the human race yelling they want to do it too. You know what I mean? Let's go home now."

"Hedgerow, that's not the point," began Luke, and then they both started to talk and were still talking when they reached Polly's house on Glover's Lane and still talking on the porch when her father, just awakened, appeared with his head wrapped in a bandage, like the flag bearer in *The Spirit of '76*, and said to his daughter, "I see life goes on, and if a hero can't sleep because his only child is outside yelling about how mean men were to poor Madame Curie, then it's too bad for the hero. So how about some eggs, you two? If life's going to go on, we might as well eat."

CHAPTER
57

Meetings of the Thespian Ladies Club were postponed until further notice. The president and the vice-president, Mrs. Canopy and Mrs. Ransom, were not speaking. The president and the chairlady of the refreshments committee (Mrs. Canopy and Mrs. Abernathy) were leaving in a few days for a few weeks abroad, without, however, the secretary (Mrs. Troyes), who had declined their invitation on the basis of other plans to which the president was not privy.

With Beanie out of town, with Priss out of touch, with Evelyn behaving in that sly, shy way she had when she was keeping secrets, Tracy Canopy was feeling a bit more lonely than she thought was good for her. Automatically she walked to the phone. The telephone cord was to her what the television cable was to her friend Evelyn—an umbilicus joining her to the life-sustaining world. For on it she daily called a "mayday" and was rescued from solitude. This morning she held the receiver like a lover's hand against her cheek. She spoke to a number of local acquaintances about the fire and murders, then, still unsatisfied, she began to make long-distance calls. To her travel agent, to her sister-in-law, to Beanie in New York.

Finally she called Bébé Jesus in Miami because she had been planning to write him to say she wished to buy the J. Edgar Hoover-in-tin wastepaper basket to go with her Castro toilet bowl. He had, amazingly enough, he admitted, already sold it. To a retired tax lawyer whose Palm Beach penthouse was, said the artist, "lousy like dee fleas on dee *perro*" with modern art, none of which was worth a spit. Still there was money in art, indeed *"mucho* moola in dees beesneece, *cara* Canôpy. But artist heeself, he geet *nada* dollair. Everybody reech, reech like puercos peegs selling, buying all dee art, while leetle artist, leetle *limosnero*, seeting out to freeze, even no coat to wear. Ees a good ting? I do not tink so." Mrs. Canopy did not think so either, though she felt obliged to inquire if it were really that cold in Miami this June, despite her willingness to allow artists that license to lie called poetic which in ordinary persons like herself she would have thought mendacity.

By coincidence, or the concentricity of design, Tracy was to enjoy a second communication from one of her artists that day, for shortly before noon, as she sat working on her accounts and paying some bills, she heard a noise that she thought was the garbage truck. But it was Louie Daytona, who drove one of the few 1949 Cadillac hearses still on the streets, and perhaps the only one with a cyclorama of the film *Quo Vadis* covering it from grille to fin, a mural that had been painted years ago by Daytona's friend Habzi Rabies. With a bleat of his horn, the sculptor kicked open the door right where a lion gnawed on the legs of a beatifically indifferent Christian starlet whose arms stretched up to the roof of the car and so on to heaven.

Mrs. Canopy ran out to greet her friend and hurry him inside. Louie Daytona was certainly handsome (as guests at the Harfleur film premiere on Wednesday had commented). Six months in prison had, if anything, improved a physique that was eminently visible in a tight-fitting blue jumpsuit that had belonged to a member of an Italian pit crew at Monte Carlo. That mechanic, like many other brief encounters of both sexes, had disappeared from Daytona's life and memory. The shirtless young man currently in his hearse, with his last-of-the-Mohicans haircut and his scar from ear to lip, did not look to Tracy's practiced eye like an artist, but rather (as she later told Evelyn) like a karate teacher who believed in Charles Manson; it was a remark she regretted not being able to make to Priss. Still, she greeted the gentleman politely. But he stared with sour blankness straight ahead, as if life were something rancid and far away.

"Hey, doll!" caroled Daytona, his arm flung around Mrs. Canopy as he walked her with his long-legged rumba into her house. "I don't call this civilization, you call this civilization? Where am I? Where'd you get this town? M-G-M? It's half burned down anyhow, did you know that?"

"But Louie, what are you doing here? And however did you find me in Dingley Falls? No, wait, but what about your friend, shouldn't we ask . . . ?"

"Nah, he can't switch onto that socialization scene,

you know what I'm saying? Just leave him sit, he'll be okay, he's out of his gourd."

"Well, if you're certain." She closed the front door behind them.

Daytona took his patroness by the shoulders. "Listen good. I'm about to blow you away, Tricia."

While not certain of the expression's exact meaning, Mrs. Canopy felt a surge of unease. Daytona was, after all, a former convict. Might he plan to harm her? Or perhaps to tell her that he had set fire to her Manhattan townhouse, just as his friend Habzi Rabies had burned up her lake cabin years earlier? Art was a very expensive hobby. "What do you mean?" she asked, jaw thrust up at him.

"They cut off your phone or what? I been trying to get you since last night. Then I just couldn't hold it in; I had to split and lay it on you right away."

"Lay what?"

"Jack! That's what! Lady, you are one rich dame!"

"Well, of course, I'm certainly comfortable, Louie, but, now, just a minute, couldn't I fix you a cup of coffee, and perhaps your friend out in the car would . . ."

"Yeah, well, I was nosing around, those extra bedrooms you got in the back of your pad."

"*Louie!* Those were locked!"

"Yeah, I know, but come on, Trina, this is big stuff, man. Catch me later with the lecture, okay? You know what's back in those rooms?"

"I certainly do. Personal belongings of my late husband's, and I feel that I must say . . ."

"I ain't talking about the clothes and junk, I'm talking *paintings*, couple *dozen* paintings, maybe fifty, you know what I'm saying? Leaning against the walls."

"Of course. They're just some things I bought from some artists a long time ago. Presents I picked out for Mr. Canopy over the years of our marriage, and I really don't think you should have gone . . ."

"Doll! Doll! You chose 'em yourself? Yeah? What'd

you pay for them? Nothing, just about frigging nothing, right? Hang on, Louie, don't space out! You know what you got there? You got de Kooning, you got Pollock, oh, *madre mia*, you got Jasper Johns and Rothko. Tracy, baby, listen to what I'm telling you! You're sitting on Lichtensteins, Rauschenbergs, Motherwells, Stellas, and I'm just talking Americans now. Yeah, well, you can nod, but, lady, you think what opening the door on an A-bomb scene like that could do to an acidhead like Louie here! You gotta put up a warning! Those are the Number One jammers, that's all. You got a big show, doll, and it's all prime time. They insured?"

"Well, yes, the whole house is insured, that is. I suppose you're saying that they appreciated then over the years?"

Daytona did a quick samba side step. "A million." He held up his hand as a pledge. "More. All I can tell you is, you got an eye! Millions. No hype, you with me?" He spun around on his way into her living room. "Now. I'm going to level with you. You been okay, you know; give me the pad, and bread. That's right, true, true, I mean it, you're okay, doll. So listen, I was about *this* far from pulling the hustle on you. I mean total ripoff. Me and that Guggenheim you're sitting on would have been *gonee*. But that's not my bag, Trixie."

"Tracy. You were going to rob me? Louie, you've surprised me! Really!"

"Yeah, well, what can I tell you? Let me give you some free advice, Mrs. C., no jazz. Don't ever trust a sculptor. Don't trust a painter or a writer and don't even *talk* to musicians. Because we are desperate folk, lady, and we're working for a mean fuck of a master, you know what I'm saying?"

"You mean Art."

"You got his name. So, okay, it's a horse race, but look at you. You got in for a buck and you come away with a bundle. You don't need the jack, put those things in a museum, get a good tax man to work on it with you. Oh, when I opened that door! Bootiful!

Bootiful! I cried, I'm gonna tell you that, I cried." On his dancing way to the mantel to see his friend's canvas, *Fingerpaint on a Widow's Fur*, over which he shook his head, Daytona swooped a book off the butler's table. "Hey, I know this guy. Nice guy. Real nice." In his hand was Mrs. Canopy's copy of *Poetry Sucks!*, on its back cover, the laughing, tawny-bearded author, Richard Rage.

"Oh, my, *is he*, Louie? Is he nice?" She caught the sculptor's arm. "If you don't mind, I have the most *vital* reasons for wanting to be sure. Do you think he's a good man?"

Daytona looked down, puzzled at the round, earnest, bespectacled eyes. "Hey now, doll. Sure thing. They don't make 'em any nicer. Him and you got something on? Small world."

Scarlet, she shook her head vigorously. "No. No. Nothing like that."

"Yeah, well, you couldn't do better if you go that route. Guy's just not very smart, that's all. Brains ain't everything, you with me?"

Mrs. Canopy gave him her valiant smile and nodded yes.

Flurrying past the hearse, Evelyn Troyes was slipping through Tracy's white picket gate to see if she should phone the police for her friend, when coming toward her in the arms-swinging, finger-snapping, hip-sliding step that had made him king (and queen) of Manhattan discos strutted Louie Daytona, and Evelyn's heart stopped at the sight. At the sight of those black satin curls and molten blue eyes, at the dark arrow of hair pointing down from the bare chest into the half-zipped jumpsuit, down to the plump bulge between legs moving toward her. Mrs. Troyes's lashes fluttered and so did her knees. Hugo Eroica, all those years ago! That first time in the conservatory practice room when he had set aside the violin and taken up her. When he had moved her hand down that arrow of hair and over that bulge. His *batocchio*, they called it in private. And

hers, *campanella*, the bell. They had hidden everywhere—in his study, friends' homes, cars, parks,
hotels, and finally across an ocean to Paris—so that
Hugo and she could touch. A beautiful man. Had he
not been killed, he would have come back to her, she
believed that. Who cared for what mistaken cause he
had been silly enough to run away and fight? A
beautiful man.

"Evelyn! This is Louis Daytona; I don't think you
met on Wednesday. He's here on a business matter.
You remember he did Vincent's statuary for me, and
we're just going to have a look at it before Mr. Daytona
and his friend there have to leave. They're on their way
to Texas, it seems. Was there something you wanted?
Evelyn?"

"Ah. Oh, I'm so sorry, ah, Tracy, but have you any,
ah, ah, any . . ." Mrs. Troyes seemed unable to force
her eyes away from the sculptor. "Any, *merde!* Ah, oh,
olive oil?"

"I have no idea, but help yourself, I'll be right back."
Tracy was going to punish Evelyn just a little bit for
being so secretive about not coming to England with
her and Beanie. "Louie, shall we?"

"With you, doll. Nice 'ah meet yah," he said to Mrs.
Troyes, and winked. She floated into Tracy's house.

As they climbed to the top of the town burial ground,
Mrs. Canopy and Mr. Daytona saw a young couple in
white photographing *Victory over Death*, Louie's abstract expressionist rendering from rendered Buicks.
He didn't like it anymore. "That's a piece of junk," he
told the admirers, but they, moving away, shook their
heads in affable disagreement. "That's not art." He
confessed to his benefactress that he'd been wrong in
what he'd said to her on Wednesday. Hab *did* have
something going for him on the pipeline. It was time to
stop messing in the minimal and the personal and the
farcical Marxical. They'd all gone wrong, back the last
ten years, jumping off the bandwagon and then barfing
on it. All that pop and op and color field and do your

body, like dumb old Porko Fulawhiski sticking a knife in himself for a couple of photographers from small-time newspapers. No, Habzi was leading the way, like always. It was time to go public and monumental and stoic heroic. And he, Louie, was on his way now with a commission to do in Carrara marble *The Siege of the Alamo*, double life-size, in the mall of a Houston shopping center. He and New York were splitting up, so he would just say "So long" for a while, and here was the key to her townhouse, and believe it or not, the furniture was still in it. And maybe they never got around to making it, but she was okay. And before she could stop him, he kissed her.

"You treated me right. I won't forget ya, Trudie."

"Tracy."

"Yeah. Well, time to play on down to Lone Ranger land. *Louie, Louie, can* you *take* it? I'm gonna rodeo on Michelangelo!" And in a disco beat the handsome sculptor shimmied down the incline of tombstones and spun with a kickout into his hearse.

CHAPTER
58

The only time Winslow Abernathy knew of when his death was an imminent possibility (no doubt there had been countless near car crashes, viral epidemics, black widow spiders that he had never noticed) had been a sunny Pacific afternoon when a kamikaze crashed into the foredeck of the battle cruiser on which he served as ensign, the plane exploding just far enough from where he sat reading Livy not to kill or even maim him but to knock him through space so that somehow, a second after he turned a page, he was dangling, arms around a

broken metal beam that stuck out over the churning
ocean miles below. For minutes, hours, days Abernathy clung there, arms and legs locked on the beam—as
he'd never been able to do in gym class—until someone
helped him back onto deck, where flames and smoke
and screaming men blurred. Only then had he realized
that not only was he bleeding, but, worse, he'd lost his
glasses when struck. The odd part was (he couldn't be
sure, of course, but it had seemed to him) that while
hanging there like a monkey, literally clinging to life, he
had been able to see perfectly well without his glasses.

This kamikaze experience had been so abruptly
extraordinary, so discontinuous with the life of Winslow Abernathy, that he attached to it no personal
meaning—except that he still ducked in a sweat at the
sight of low-flying planes. But Saturday at 5:00 A.M. he
thought of it again, for life, after simply leaping the last
thirty years forward, had flung him through air again
out to that same precarious clarity suspended over
chaos. He was too old for it, he told himself, lying
awake at 5:00 A.M., exhausted and unquiet. But in fact,
even young, he'd had no desire to live life at the peak:
more than one social event a weekend depleted his
small store of extroversion. How long could he keep
holding on now as loud debris flew past and waves
snatched up at him? How long could he see without his
glasses? Beanie had left minutes, hours, years ago?
Lance hurt, the girl's death, fire, when? And the rest?

Last night. Abernathy thought back again to where
he had brought Lance twenty-four hours earlier, the
fluorescent corridor of the hospital emergency entrance
glowing an evil absinthe green. Where everything was
clean but looked dirty. People, mostly poor, lethargic
on benches, some with heads in hands, wills yielded to
the wait, submerged in pain or fear, as blank-eyed as if
they waited for buses. Down the corridor came five
people, a family, awkwardly clinging together even as
they walked. All were crying, the males without a
sound, as behind them a doctor tried to herd them

along while appearing to comfort them. As they passed, the man supporting the loudest weeping woman turned his own teary eyes, embarrassed, from Winslow. Even now, thought the lawyer, even in the midst of death, he is ashamed to be exposed in the weakness of grief, in his failure to keep the woman from tears. But hadn't Winslow, too, feared women's tears?

Tonight at the nurses' station when he had arrived after 1:00 A.M., a woman nearby, manic and noisy, had heard him asking for Judith Haig. Under the lights her hair was lime yellow around the enormous green plastic curlers. She was a woman in her early forties who wore a boy's lettered football jacket, a black and white housecoat, and straw sandals. Eyes puffed red, tears running from her nose, she introduced herself to him as "Judith's best friend." He was repelled, then disgusted by his snobbery. Surely Mrs. MacDermott had a right to claim friendship. More than he. Who was he to Mrs. Haig?

"Of course you don't know me from Adam, but somehow I got this intuition from what people in town have said about you that you'll stick by Judith. I've been sobbing my eyes out ever since Joe told me (my husband, Joe, Chief Haig's second in command). I said to him, Joe, that poor thing has had nothing but misery since she was left on the church stoop to freeze or live as God saw fit. And now this! Poor, poor Hawk. Voted most likely to succeed. We were all green with envy. Oh, you have to excuse me. Please. *Oh, poor, poor thing!*"

Abernathy took her to one of the hard plastic couches and sat with her and waited, nodding, until she collected herself.

"I'm sorry, Mr. Abernathy, but it's only human. I got to tell you something, you being a lawyer, and you advise me what you think. I haven't said a word to Joe either, and what's more, won't either, until I can talk to Judith. Blessed Mary, pray for her in her hour of need.

This is all my fault! Oh, Jesus love me oh, please, here I go again, just excuse it, Mr. Abernathy, just a sec, I'm okay. Slobbering all over you. The thing is, nobody knows what really happened out there. But I got to tell you there's a chance that Limus Barnum didn't come till later and, because it was *Maynard.* Yes. Maynard Henry. I sent him out there to get Chinkie! Just shooting my mouth off. But I don't know if he ever went, and that's why I don't dare to say anything to Joe until Judith comes to, saints look over her, because there's no sense kidding ourselves, if Maynard's name gets into this after what him and Hawk have said about each other, poor Maynard won't have much more of a chance of getting out than Hitler in a synagogue. But I'll say this, if the little bastard did that to Judith, then God have mercy on him because I'm going to have trouble doing it myself."

Did what to Mrs. Haig? Strange that she came into his thoughts, as well as his speech, so formally, as "Mrs. Haig," though she came there a constant and intimate visitor.

And then Mrs. MacDermott told him what had been done to Mrs. Haig. And then after he lied, claiming to be the patient's legal counsel, they let him see her for a minute. Rape. The vestal skin bruised. Eyelids swollen, specks of dried blood in the smooth, muted hair. Yes, sexual assault and battery, confirmed the young woman doctor, a Dr. Deeds. Rape. He backed away from the foot of the bed, back into the hall. Then by rote he began to ask the physician where, and when, and who, and how ask why? And as they spoke he sensed as if against his skin the heat of Dr. Deeds's growing hostility. Certainly he imagined it, for how could Dr. Deeds read and diagnose and judge his yet uncharted response?

The friend, Mrs. MacDermott, sat on the couch, legs crossed, cigarette in hand, Kleenex to her nose. She had said she thought it was Maynard Henry! Had Henry done it? That bitter young man suddenly connected to his life; that man who had brought Judith Haig to him, and whom she had sent him to defend. That hard, innocent, threatened, and threatening man whom he had defended already to A. A. Hayes. Had he been wrong? Had Henry done it? No! Impossible he had so misjudged the man.

Through a sudden burst of rain, Abernathy hurried back to the tiny yellow roadster. As he drove, dangerously skidding on the wet highway, driving by faith for the most part, for the thundering rain made it impossible to see, he tried with a sense of its vital urgency to analyze his response before he reached the Madder trailer park and Maynard Henry. First shock, denial, nausea, and fury too quickly mixed for analysis. Then, with the whole force of his consciousness, the want to will it away. He did not want her to be raped. No other fact in his life had been as simple, as absolute, as that, as uncluttered and unmodified by qualifications and compromises and recognitions of ambivalences; not even his abrupt desire to marry Beanie. No fact but the will not to let go of that broken beam hanging above the Pacific. And how *easy* holding to that beam had been compared to what Judith must have felt. Water streaked down Abernathy's face. He put his hand to the canvas top, then to his eye. "Know what you *feel*, Winslow!" Beanie had told him. Yes, they were tears. *Had Henry raped her?*

It would be better to think. He should think. It hadn't been Henry, but the other man. Limus Barnum, had the doctor said? Or perhaps there had been no other man involved but her husband (there was no way to know, she had made no statement yet). But would it be easier or worse if it had been her husband? But why hadn't her husband stopped the man then? Incontrovertible proof that Haig was unworthy. Good God, thought Winslow, what kind of man am I? Gloating at the failure when Haig had probably died in her defense. Gloating at the death? No, no. Intolerable that any man, enemy or not, should die so. Was it intolerable? Not Haig, but what of the man who did that to her? Could he bear not to murder such a man? Not to crush his head to bleeding broken bone and pulp? *Had Henry done it?*

Yes, but that's why there was law, impersonal, impassionate, above revenge—or should be, or could be. But what about the blood in her hair?

And she, she, damn it, why? Just when his soul had seen her, to lose her! Lose her? How was she his? How had he lost her? Wasn't she alive? Abernathy envisioned an illumination, white and leaf gold. Hideously from behind the parchment red stain bubbled the vision. Why hadn't she stopped it? Why had she let the vision be ruined? Could she not be vestal guardian of her own temple? Mustn't she have in some way (titillation, fear, kindness, hostility) encouraged the rapist? Nothing like that could ever have happened to Beanie! Or Tracy. Or Priss. Impossible. Perhaps Evelyn.

He caught himself and fought back his anger at her. Weren't even strong athletic women raped, too? And old decrepit women, and girl children? Must there be something in every female psyche that solicited rape? And if that something were their fear, had they not every right to be afraid? Were victims to be charged not only as accomplices, but as sole perpetuators of the crime, as if the victims of theft should be condemned for being robbed? If even he, mildly, obediently marshaled through life by women, if even a male like himself felt males to be so irredeemably impelled by lust that law itself was not strong enough to contain them, then surely women were right, and only their instinct to create life must keep them from withdrawing into Amazonian fortresses of civilization, from which they would emerge merely long enough to be impregnated among the savages.

But, no, it wasn't that bad. Who were all these rapists? He didn't know any. How many men could there be under such compulsion, such unbearable hatred of women? Or fear, It must be fear really. The disenfranchised preying on those more disenfranchised than they. But what if the victims were the monster? In his office (days, weeks, years ago) he had pledged himself to take up her quest, to help Maynard Henry. Dear God, now he himself may have helped the animal who had ravaged her to escape its cage. *Had Henry done it? Had he?* But he had believed Henry about Treeca and about Haig! What if Haig had been right? Why, damn it, had she ever gotten herself involved in this? If only the Vietnamese girl hadn't come and asked. Oh, "if only," absurd! If only America had never gone to Vietnam so that Chin Lam would have never been evacuated, so Henry never would have married her and Treeca would never and I would never and Judith Haig would never!

He had thought his life's work would be in defense of the disenfranchised. Instead he had defended money. His wife's. But could he ever had defended, anyhow, anyone who claimed an "irresistible" impulse to defile another human being? He who had difficulty believing in madness. He who had always responded to his son Lance's claims that he could not help his outbursts against his mother or his brother with disbelief: "Are you so weak that you cannot command your own will? Society will not tolerate this kind of indulgence in barbarism. I certainly will not tolerate such behavior toward your mother." Always Beanie had said, "Oh, Winslow, he doesn't mean it." Always Lance had thrown up his hands and soon enough flown off to war where they tolerated barbarism perfectly well. Could Lance have raped someone? Could any of Winslow's own peers, Hayes, Ransom?

No. He didn't know any rapists. No, not even in war. Of course, all the stories about the Germans, Japanese, Italians. Terrible stories about the Russians as they advanced on Berlin. Even rumors about some few Americans, no doubt true. But he had honestly known no one. There had been brothels at shore leave, of course. He himself had gone only once; it was not worth it to him. But clearly it had been to many other men. Could he rape? He honestly did not think it possible. Had he ever once in his life imagined raping? But surely that sole fantasy did not inscribe him in his heart of hearts a rapist, any more than a woman who fantasized being raped secretly wished really to be assaulted.

Of course, he had never asked Beanie if she fantasized rape. He had never asked her if she feared the possibility of actual rape. It just didn't seem likely; she was so unafraid of anything physical, so much less afraid than he. But how could he know? He had never asked Beanie how she felt about much of anything, or heard kindly her inquiries about his feelings, or cared to hear about the intensity of hers. Yes, and he had missed the births of his sons, and done too few dishes, and shared in too few "real conversations," and no doubt did wish the sexes separate in soul as well as body, did wish women to feel and believe and soothe and bless and nourish and be without need to prove, did wish them to stop the rape of the world with all the hundred graces of the soul that women now announced they were unwilling to feel alone. And if he did wish women to keep safe for men (and despite them) that temple of grace, no doubt this desire for segregation was as sexist as racial segregations more beneficial to one race than the other were racist. And no doubt he proselytized with himself on women's rights while slipping off a beam above the churning sea only because there was this *fact* that he could not get around. Someone raped her. Terrorized her, entered her, hurt her, violated her, violated her, violated . . . and the noise of the windshield wipers brought Abernathy back.

Rain in a torrent as loud as hail on the hood flooded the highway. Blinking their lights, other cars had pulled onto the shoulders to wait. But he found that by sticking his head out the window he could gauge the road well enough to stay on it. As he bounced over the peak of Cromwell Hill Road, he glimpsed still going on in the northern sky the hissing battle of fire and rain. The MG fishtailed when the lawyer, accustomed to power steering, jerked to the right onto Goff Street. His heart still in a thud, he drove straight into the muddy field of the trailer park. Here, as throughout Dingley Falls, lights blazed despite the hour, for many of the citizenry were still up on Route 3 with the fire. Mrs. MacDermott had given him lengthy instructions. Nevertheless he wandered through the mud for a while among the trailers before he identified Maynard Henry's. And more time went by as he waited, beaten by the rain, on the steps before he saw the lights come on in response to his pounding against the metallic door. Abernathy planned to be judicious.

"Stop that! What do you want?" snapped a voice.

"It's Winslow Abernathy. Let me in!" Henry's belligerence had outraged him, and when the door opened, Abernathy pushed inside, already yelling, "Tell me! Judith Haig! *Yes or no! Did you rape her?*" His voice astonished him, and he tried to lower it. "Just yes or no!" Finally, he had not prepared what he would do if the man confessed, or lied, but he was sure he would know a lie from Maynard Henry. Careful not to blink, he waited, watching, noting without thought that Henry, barefoot, shirtless, had hurried into pants to answer the door, that on his upper arm was a thick bandage; noting that Henry was thinner and not as tall but far more muscular and, of course, younger, better-trained. When Henry started to turn away, Abernathy jerked him by the shoulder, then raised his fist. *"Did you?"*

"*Hey, man, no way!* Okay?" Henry cupped his palm over the fist and moved it aside. "The answer's no. No, I didn't rape nobody. Okay? Now, got any more questions? Then when you get around to it, you can tell me what you're doing busting in here laying rape on me! I oughta knock you through the wall!"

Slowly the lawyer nodded. Bands loosened around his heart. Henry was telling the truth. But he also already knew about Mrs. Haig. His voice was strained, his eyes restive. He was not a man to manage deception with ease.

Gradually now the trailer came into focus in Abernathy's consciousness. Its furnishings were as sparingly and as carefully arranged as the contents of a teepee or a Kansas sod house. On hooks and shelves and cabinets the few items (like a row of cooking utensils or a stack of a half-dozen tape cassettes) sat immaculate and symmetrically positioned. But there were also rush mats on the floor and bright colored pillows on the drab couch. There was a lavishly whorled and sinuous white dragon on a parsons table beside a vase of dried pussy willows. Next to the couch near a ball of ivory was propped a photograph of Henry and his wife, Chin Lam, standing stiffly side by side, he in a dark suit slightly too short, she in a cheap American dress. His eyes suspicious of the photographer, her fingers tight around his arm.

Abernathy looked at the closed door. "Your wife is sleeping?"

"Yeah."

"You found her at Pru Lattice's."

"What business is it of yours? You know what I wish? I wish people would leave my wife alone!"

"Miss Lattice mentioned that you were bleeding." Abernathy pointed at the bandage.

"Yeah. I was. Look, you want a towel or something? You're dripping on my floor."

Abernathy stepped back onto a doormat. "Understand. I've got an investment in you. I don't want you in trouble that's not yours."

Henry snorted. "Meaning I got enough of my own to hang me."

"I don't know. A Mrs. MacDermott told me she advised you to go to Mrs. Haig's earlier tonight to look for your wife. I'm now giving you the information that two homicides took place there sometime before midnight. Two men were shot to death; one of them was Police Chief Haig. Mrs. Haig suffered assault." Abernathy could see no change in Henry's face; indifference masked it. "Mrs. MacDermott told me . . ."

"You know what's the problem with women? They talk too much."

"Told me she hasn't made known your conversation with her, not even to her husband. She realizes, as I'm sure you will, that if possible, it's best left quiet. Given your upcoming trial and your quarrel with Mr. Haig, which seems to be fairly common knowledge, I quite honestly would hate to have to take your case to a jury if there were *any* hard circumstantial evidence to tie you to this crime."

Henry, hugging his hurt arm, sat down in a black cloth director's chair beside the dragon. He put his hand on it, then looked up at the lawyer with a derisive grin. "No shit," he said. "They'll fry my ass."

"Look here, you're going to have to talk to someone sooner or later, so why don't you talk to me? If you like, hire me for a dollar right now. Everything you say will be privileged. How involved are you in this? Because let's not waste time pretending you don't know what I'm talking about. What happened out there?"

Henry's eyes whirred up at the tall, thin man whose pajama cuffs clung to his hands beneath the soaked summer jacket, water dripping from his glasses and from the gray strands of hair matted on his forehead. "What does *she* say?" he asked Abernathy.

"Who? Mrs. Haig?"

"Yeah. What does she say happened?"

"She hasn't said. She's under sedation."

"You ask her. Tell her I said ask her first."

Abernathy shook his head. "Good God, man! Help me out. I'm asking you! What happened to your arm? Is there a bullet in it?"

"You think I'd sit around and leave it in there to

gangrene if it was, after how I've seen them sawing arms off? Look, I know you think I'm dumber than shit, but maybe I'm not that dumb."

"What happened to your arm?"

"Why don't we just say my dog got out of hand and bit me? How's that?"

"For what? A reasonable statement? All right. The truth? I don't know yet." He could see that the younger man's eyes were scared, though the mouth was hard and the voice angry. "You going to tell me?"

"No way. You talk to the lady first. Then you come back, talk to me. I'm still around, I'll talk. That's it, only offer. Look, mister."

"My name's Abernathy."

"You guys can't force me to play your game anymore. Why should I play if I can't win? Nothing personal, just fact."

Abernathy stared back at him, his hand in his pocket feeling the pipe. "I'll tell you what's *fact*. I can have you picked up right now as a suspect, or at the least material witness. Or I can wait. I'll wait on one condition; no, two. One, you're still here tomorrow. Two, do you have a gun? If so, give it to me. Joe MacDermott could show up here any minute with a warrant."

Henry shook his head, but slowly pulled himself to his feet, went over to his closet, and reached for something. It was a .45 government issue service revolver. Abernathy took it, surprised by the familiarity of the weight, parenthetically noting that the design had changed since 1944. He sniffed the barrel and after a fumble, let Henry pull the clip for him.

"Hasn't been fired. Okay?"

"Do you have a license for this?"

"How about my enlistment papers! Naw, okay, I brought it home in my bag. Hey, what the fuck? Did that gun just get to be yours? You don't take a man's gun. Come on, give it back."

Abernathy turned angrily at the door. "Look here. This is not Da Nang and it's not Dodge City."

"Don't kid yourself."

"Listen to me, Maynard. Don't *you* kid yourself. The law has no interest in your sense of injury or in your righteousness. And it has no tolerance for the sort of personal violence you appear to have resorted to all your life."

"Is that so? I thought it really got off on my violence. You know, like, let's hear it for the Green Berets."

"Something else you better understand. It can slam you in jail for life, even if you're right. Even if! So you don't kid yourself, Maynard, and if you don't want people to think you're stupid, don't behave as if you were. Because you're not. If MacDermott comes, go with him, keep your mouth shut, and call me." Abernathy pushed against the wind until the trailer door flung open.

"Okay, okay," yelled Henry after him, annoyed at how the lawyer made him feel that maybe he had some slight chance. "Fuck it," he reminded himself, and pulled the door shut.

The little wheels of the MG roadster spun furiously, and futilely, in the mud of the swampy lot. Abernathy found in a trash bin a pizza box to wedge under the back tires. Gears screeching, he managed to rock the car out of the mud hole, only to have it stall in Ransom Circle. When an effort to restart it flooded the engine, the lawyer, drenched, mud-splattered, walked home. There from his window he noticed lights still burning on all floors of the Victorian mansion across the circle. So before changing he telephoned.

"Sammy? Winslow. It looked as if you were up. I thought you'd want to know. There was an incident. Unconnected to the fire. Mrs. Haig was assaulted. They've taken her to the hospital. She'll be all right. Haig and another man, it appears to be Limus Barnum, were killed. You know, the man with the appliance store. Sammy? Sammy?"

"Yes. I'm here, sorry. To the hospital. Sorry. Winslow, can you . . ."

"She'll be all right. I saw her. I'm afraid your car stalled; it's locked on Ransom Circle."

"Winslow, can you come over here? I wasn't going to call until morning but since . . . Ramona's been asking for you, about whether her will's been finalized. I know the time. But she caught a very bad chill. I found her on the floor of her widow's walk, soaked through. Otto's here now. For some reason I went to check." Smalter spoke quietly and from far away, as if he spoke in a dream.

And so last night at 5:00 A.M., Winslow Abernathy was awake, thinking about the kamikaze plane that had cometed into his life some thirty years ago. He lay naked across his bed, too tired to shower or to search for pajamas. The lawyer tried to keep his eyes closed, but every few seconds, minutes, hours, they sprang open again. Slowly night became morning by fading the black sky to a gray sheet streaked diagonally by lines of rain. On his stomach, back, side, legs bent, stretched, scissored—all positions maddened him with an exhausted impatience. He could not numb his mind. This wasn't what life was like, certainly not what his life was like. Life was not one of Evelyn's grand operas. Life was a soap opera, a rerun of "Search for Tomorrow," interminably paced and imperfectly performed. It was a story in which one could expect to live moderately happily (at any rate, as an affluent American male) for a moderate numbers of years, touched by a moderate number of losses, moderately spaced over those years. Yet here was Winslow Abernathy hurling through his life with the velocity and the faith (and no doubt the fate) of a kamikaze pilot.

What in God's name was he trying to prove? That if his thirty-year wife could run off with a poet, he could, before the week's end, outdo her in audacity by involving himself with a troubled married woman whose husband was murdered a few days after Winslow met her, possibly by her rapist, possibly by a new client of his (an unemployed ex-con ex-marine out on bail for aggravated assault)? Because yes, he was involved with Mrs. Haig, whatever that was supposed to mean. It was absurd. Did he expect her to listen to his suit before they buried her husband and marry him the day he could divorce his wife? When Mrs. Haig did not (as that woman at the hospital had put it) know him from Adam! But that wasn't true. She knew him as well as he knew her. She felt as he felt. He could see that she did. What *was* this new sense he had that he could read unspoken truth everywhere he looked? It was absurd. He couldn't see without his glasses. Life wasn't like being blown across the foredeck of a battle cruiser by an exploding airplane. At least it was not like that until the instant when it became like that, when the plane crashed, or they told you you were dying, or the woman was raped, or the car hit you, or the baby was born, or you fell in love. Hours, days, decades passed. And finally, unable to sleep, he got out of his bed.

By 7:00 A.M., when north of Dingley Falls smoke of the fire still wisped in clouds against the clouds, Winslow Abernathy was showered, shaved, and dressed. By eight he had finished breakfasting with Prudence Lattice (at her request), had conferred with Sammy Smalter about Ramona's condition (unchanged), had called a garage to repair (unnecessary) and deliver the MG to its owner, and had (with a note pinned to his front door) stolen his son Arthur's Audi, to which he still had a key. By nine he was out on Route 3 in conversation with police detectives who were rummaging among the ruins of the Haig house. By ten he was in further conversation with other detectives who were rummaging through stacks of neo-Nazi literature in Limus Barnum's store. By eleven he was walking down the hall in Argyle Hospital as Chin Lam Henry came out of Judith Haig's room. He asked Mrs. Henry to wait for him in the cafeteria, explaining that as he'd be going to Madder shortly to speak with her husband, he could offer her a ride while she answered a few questions for him. Then he knocked on Mrs. Haig's door.

By noon he was eating chili in the hospital cafeteria. By 12:25 he was driving back north from Argyle, his hands so casual on the steering wheel that no one would ever suspect that this moderately attired, middle-aged man, his thinning hair neatly combed, his glasses firmly in place, was clinging to life suspended over a foreign sea and convinced that he enjoyed, miraculously, perfect sight.

CHAPTER
59

"Do you know the Book of Kells?" asked Walter Saar over orange juice in his study. "To paraphrase them, Jonathan, life is not linear. Not causal. Not, pardon me, straight. Look at us here, idiotically enamored, in the midst of slapdash, heartbreaking mayhem, and all those flukes will loop into our lives, and we have looped into each other's, and altered everything, including the future. Croissant? Frozen, I fear, but my country right or wrong."

"Thank you. The Book of Kells?" asked Father Fields.

"Yes. Those stir-crazy Irish monks have scribbled the truth around their capital letters. Life twists and turns, rebounds on itself, loops out, slides back, heads everywhere and nowhere, and is inextricably *connected*. It is their slightly crazy Gaelic way of showing life can be lovely, but honey, you sure can't see where it's going."

Youth triumphant over lack of sleep in his clean blue eyes, the curate looked past the French coffeepot at the beautiful bloodshot eyes of the headmaster. "I can see where I want it to go," said Jonathan shyly.

Saar smiled slowly, then he stood to clear the table. "But you are, by medical report, bland as a bat. And so am I. And so is love. Because I confess, somehow I have trouble envisioning Ransom and his fellow trustees seeing our His and His towels hanging in the master's john. Nor can I imagine the academy permitting me—assuming now that the Reverend Highwick failed to notice—to commute to classes from our little cottage at St. Andrew's, where of course Ernest Ransom also rules among the moneychangers. It seems to me that our best bet is to draw straws as to who will seduce Ernest Ransom, then we can all keep our jobs and live happily ever after."

Jonathan laughed, pleased that Saar assumed a commitment between them, even for the purpose of demonstrating its impossibility.

Saar raised his coffee cup. "'Ah, love, let us be trite with one another, for the world which seems to lie before us so' et cetera 'hath really neither joy, nor love, nor light, nor certitude, nor peace, nor help for pain.' Absolutely true!" insisted the headmaster, full of joy and love and certainty and peace. "Still, I think it was tacky of Matthew Arnold to be so negative on his honeymoon. But then the Victorians were like that; they all resembled their furniture, earnest and massy and flaccidly muscular, like Robert Browning's thighs."

Jonathan put his fingers to Walter's lips. "We don't have to be trite."

"How about trite and true?" said the irrepressible Saar, who was nonetheless sincere. Indeed, far readier, terrified though he was of the danger, to leap from the sea cliffs into love than was Jonathan Fields, who saw no dangers and did not think he was terrified of the ocean at all but rather of standing alone on the ledge.

In the handsome Ransom home, order, though under the sword, still sat on the throne. As the help

(Wanda Tojek) rested on weekends, Saturday meals were served by Mrs. Ransom, and she served cereal for breakfast. Mr. Ransom ate his in the presence of a morning newspaper, over which he superimposed certain of his personal preoccupations. One of these was the land that had just been burned to ashes. Of course, it wasn't his property, and of course, whatever the owners had built there (if anything) had clearly been removed (or destroyed), since none of the fire fighters had reported finding anything (or anyone), and of course, that was all to the best. The compound of buildings that he himself had seen years ago (or had he? After all, long ago. A nightmare? A mirage?) could not then have been whatever it was that Ramona's two "young people" claimed to have photographed. So the base (or whatever) had been removed, just as he had supposed. And what if it *had* still been there, anyhow? There was certainly nothing illegal about it! His children's generation had tried to poison his mind against his government, whereas his was the best government in the world. Had it not saved the world only thirty-some years ago? Of course, the less government the better. It had no business in business, of course, or in the rights of individuals to bear arms or to bear children (certainly should be illegal to abort them and ask the government to pick up the tab!), and other rights, and so on, as long as order was preserved. Nor should the majority bed and board the so-called underprivileged, who were sure, as soon as they were rested and fat enough, to bite the hand that fed them! But social security was one thing, national security another. Ridiculous! The middle-class children of the last decade, with their middle-aged gurus, had, to put it bluntly, tried, well, to unman their founders. Here in this Bicentennial summer, this wonderful country was ashamed of who it was, suspicious even of what was no more than self-preservation! Ridiculous! Didn't know what they were saying!

With such annoyance, Ernest Ransom argued his

way through the editorial pages of the morning *Times*. The banker (decorated for gallantry in the last just war, recipient of a silver star and the Croix de Guerre) grieved that his nation, which had once driven triumphant through the streets of the world, puissant in its virtue and honorable in its preeminence, was now stripped of its rank, mocked, harried at home, and despised abroad. He closed and tersely folded his paper, then felt for his coffee. His wife moved the cup into his hand.

"Oh," he noticed. "Where's Kate?"

"Is that a joke? It's only nine o'clock. All I ask of Kate and Emerald is that they wake up in time for dinner. If she came home at all. Do you want to know what I think? Kate's going to marry Sidney Blossom."

"Don't be silly."

"All right."

Folding his napkin and kissing his wife, Ransom rose from the table. He was dressed in a gray linen suit with a yellow shirt and a gray tie with tiny red crossed gold clubs on it that Arthur Abernathy had given him last Christmas, when Emerald had given him an oil painting of herself done from one of his photographs, and Priss had given him a five-band portable radio for the boat, a digital watch pen, a monogrammed robe, a nautical brass shoe horn, a gold-plated badger shaving brush, and a case of Scotch; and Kate had given him a baby cherry tree for his garden (with a card saying, "Daddy, Don't read anything into it! Kate"), three books on the forced resignation of the former president, and a pair of boxer shorts on which were printed Wall Street ticker tapes (he had never worn them).

Though the bank would be closed today, the banker would be in it. He would also be meeting for lunch with some town leaders at the Dingley Club to discuss what steps to take—for example, about the influx of newsmen—in the aftermath of the fire and the "gunfight murders." But he would not be meeting with John "Hawk" Haig to discuss the highway cancellation so

many years ago (a meeting that Haig, in a mysterious
and offensively threatening tone, had insisted on Friday
evening when he had phoned), for Haig had died
tragically, so the first selectman Arthur Abernathy
announced in the press release, died in defense of his
home as a man, and in performance of his duty as an
officer of the law.

"Oh," noticed Mrs. Ransom. "Have a good day."
Her husband left the glassy gazebo of their spring-
green breakfast nook, and she (already dressed for her
tennis lesson two hours later) sat back, lean and sharply
tan, to keep up with *The Times*.

CHAPTER
60

Dingley Falls had not been so communally aquiver in
ages, as now over the gunfight murders. The fact that
the town had almost burned down quickly dulled in
comparison. Indeed, since no one had been killed by
the fire, visiting newsmen ignored it completely, except
as a background to death when television reporters
stood on the charred grass in front of the skeleton of
the Haigs' home and talked of the tragic site of the
Gunfight Murders.

Of course, it happened to be the case that the forest
fire was covering up a much bigger story than the one
that had taken place in John "Hawk" Haig's red brick
ranch house. But Dingleyans blamed the blaze on a
bolt of lightning; that is, on God or chance, depending
on their point of view. No one absorbed in the
fascinating horror of local killings had the foggiest
notion that the federal government was slipping away
undetected after having, over seven years' time, coolly

murdered (simply in order to learn how to do it better) at least fifty human members of the surrounding community, and who knows how many other mammals, before God or chance, butting in, murdered the murderers.

Had the two-man staff of *The Dingley Day* been told that in their very front yard Operation Archangel had, in the name of national security, come, killed, and vanished without a trace, while all Dingley Falls sat inside staring at Limus Barnum's face on their television screens, A. A. Hayes would have called the news "ironic," and Coleman Sniffell would have called it "typical." But suppose even that such news had filtered into town from elsewhere; suppose even that they had heard proof of viralogical testing in some other town in Connecticut, reports of fatalities from mysterious infectious disease. The local scandal of the Haigs and Limus Barnum still would have loomed more luridly for Dingleyans. Suppose even that an ambitious scandal tracker from a national syndicate, or a bounty man from a national network, uncovered the facts; that someone with the valor of Theseus and Daedalean brains slithered through the meandrous maze, seized the monster, slew it, held up its squirmy hydra heads, and cried, "Look! Evil!" Yes, the hounds of the press would have come on a run, and at first, everyone, outraged, would have shaken his fists at the government or shaken his head at human nature or voted out the current party, and sooner or later forgotten about it, as Dingleyans had forgotten the abandoned highway. As their fellow countrymen had forgotten countless other high and secret crimes committed against them by their government, and by big businessmen busily making business big.

The gunfight theory first announced by the police hypothesized that Limus Barnum, having abandoned his motorcycle (which three teenagers had pulled from the Rampage below the Falls), had walked to the Haig house, assaulted Judith Haig, been surprised in the act by Hawk Haig, who, coming to rescue his wife from the fast approaching fire and unable to get into his chained house, had broken through the window and fired at Barnum, precipitating the gunfight. This theory was discredited when it was learned that while Haig's gun had been fired several times, it was bullets from *Barnum's* .357 Magnum that had killed both men. There was one bullet in Haig's heart. There were three in Barnum's body. Fortunately, the police's sole witness, Mrs. John Haig, was able to dictate to her lawyer an alternative theory that fit the facts.

That afternoon, Winslow Abernathy returned to the trailer park, where he spent a little time in conversation with some of the residents before he knocked on Maynard Henry's door again.

"Hello, Maynard. I gave your wife a ride back from the hospital just now. Nice of her to be concerned enough about Mrs. Haig to pay a call."

"Yeah. I guess. Where is she?"

"Actually I asked her if I might speak with you privately. She said to tell you she'd be in the A & P."

"Okay, okay, come on in."

Maynard Henry wore a long-sleeved sweatshirt now, but he had on the same pants as last night and hadn't shaved. The wheat-colored hair was dirty; it lay flat on the narrow skull. In his eyes was the panic that his pacing tried to assuage. The eyes were bleary as though he hadn't slept. "What's going on?" he snapped. "MacDermott never showed. No cops all morning. You saw the lady?"

"Yes. So did your wife." Abernathy walked past him into the room.

"Yeah. She talk to you?"

"Yes. How's your arm?"

"Fine. Better. You talk to the cops already? What are they going to do?"

"May I ask something first? What about your dog? Where is it?"

"He's dead. I had to kill him." Henry kept his eyes

on the window as he said this and spoke without
inflection.

"Really? You shot him?"

"Yeah."

"I see. He must have hurt you quite badly then. I
mean, some of your neighbors happened to mention to
me that you were very devoted to the dog. You killed
him?"

"Cut the shit and let me have it, what's gonna
happen here? You talk too much."

"Like women. Will you sit down for a second?"

Henry flung himself into the black cloth chair. The
lawyer cleaned his glasses with a fresh handkerchief.
"About an hour ago," he began quietly, "Mrs. Haig
talked with me and asked me to make a brief statement
on her behalf to the police, which I did. In it she
positively identified *her* assailant as Limus Barnum."

"She told you I never did a thing to her, right?"

"Yes. Right." He was watching Henry's eyes." "Yes.
She told me you came there sometime close to ten,
asked for Chin Lam, and she told you Chin was at Pru
Lattice's." Abernathy crossed his arms over his chest.
"And she told me that you left immediately upon
learning where your wife was." The lawyer watched
Henry's head jerk up and saw the eyes widen before the
mask hurried over them.

After a silence, Henry muttered, "So how'd they get
shot, the two guys you said before? Haig, her husband,
who's she say shot Haig?"

"Yes, that is the question, isn't it? Mrs. Haig says
that Barnum shot and killed her husband, who was
firing on him through the broken picture window."
Abernathy turned to look down at the dragon on the
table. "Her statement is that then she, struggling with
Barnum for the gun, and convinced that he intended to
kill her as well as her husband, shot Limus Barnum
herself."

Henry sucked in air with a soft hiss.

The lawyer nodded. "Yes." They were quiet. Then

Abernathy buttoned his jacket. "The gun went off three times. Face, chest, and groin." He could see the mask jerked off Henry's eyes, and in them pure surprise. The look terrified him, snatching at his own suppositions. Had she actually done it? For the surprise was not feigned, unlike the clumsily professed ignorance in the young man's earlier question. No, impossible that she had murdered. But something was wrong. He went on. "Since Mrs. Haig is presumably the only witness and the only surviving participant and since the premises have been destroyed by fire, her testimony will be almost the sole basis of any official account of this incident. Unless, of course, there should happen to be contradictory evidence. But the police have no reason for thinking there is. On the other hand, quite honestly, Maynard, a few questions *have* occurred to *me*. Private speculations." Abernathy waited while Henry took his cigarettes and matches from the table that held the ivory ball and wedding picture. "Would you be interested? Well, indulge me, anyhow. While I realize he would have wanted to approach the house quietly, I find it odd that Barnum would leave his motorcycle behind on the highway, with the key in it, and yet there seems to be no key among the effects on the body. The police assumed some joyriders took his bike, drove it around, and then pitched it into the Rampage. Perhaps. That's a fairly long walk from the Haigs' back into town. Isn't it?"

Henry shrugged, his eyes intent on the lengthening cigarette ash.

"Well, but you've probably done a lot more walking than I have. Did you walk out there when you went to look for Chin Lam?"

"Took my truck." Henry's eyes were fixed on the ash.

"Ah. Funny, I didn't notice a truck here by the trailer last night. Well, I've been told I'm not very observant. I was thinking that if you had walked home, you would have undoubtedly passed Barnum on his way to the house. And then, you see, you could have cleared up whether he was on foot or on the cycle. So. That's one thing that bothers me. And, I don't know, a couple of other things. One is that Mrs. Haig says she phoned for the ambulance. I think that shows remarkable presence of mind for someone in the condition she was in. But I chanced to locate on the phone this morning the operator who took that call, and oddly enough she thought the voice was that of a man. Of course, she admitted she easily could be mistaken."

Neither spoke for a while. The ash fell into Henry's palm. Finally he jerked his head toward the couch. "Look. Sit down. No reason to stand." With a nod the lawyer sat on the couch, his arm touching the bright silk pillow. "Okay," Henry told him, his voice low. "Let's say it goes down this way. What happens next? She don't have to stand trial, does she? I mean if Barnum killed her husband . . . Okay, look, say she took back what she told you, any way to keep this rape shit out of it, if, say, she wasn't the one that, you know?"

"No, I don't know. But no. There's no way not to have the assault brought out in testimony, it's already part of the statement, on medical record. That's the whole point. Her assault is the crime that precipitated the deaths. *Isn't* it? Maynard?"

"Yeah. Sure. But why drag it up?"

"You mean to save her embarrassment?"

"So what happens? I mean, she says the scumbag raped her and she blew him away before he blew her away. So she has to stand trial, or what? I mean, I'd say the creep got justice, man."

Abernathy found his pipe. "Yes. I realize you think so. I disagree. Private execution is not justice. It's revenge."

"Private, public. What's the difference besides twelve guys do it instead of one, and the TV cameras are there to watch them fry you?"

Abernathy reached into his jacket pocket and took out the .45 service revolver. "What if I judged you as you judged him?"

Henry stared back at him. "Go ahead."

"I couldn't."

"Yeah. We're different. I do all the shit work." He reached over, took the gun, and set it on the table beside the dragon. "If she sticks to this, would the fucks take her to trial? Is that what you mean, testify?"

"No. It won't go to trial. As presented, it's clearly self-defense. A woman trying to stop a rapist who is shooting at her husband, a police officer. No. No grand jury would indict her. It won't go beyond the coroner's inquest. But even at the inquest she will have to testify under oath."

"Meaning?"

"Meaning, as her attorney, I've naturally advised Mrs. Haig that perjury is a crime. Of course, as a believing Catholic, she would already consider it a sin, wouldn't she?"

"Come on, Abernathy!" Anger climbed through frustration in Henry's eyes. "What are you getting at?"

"Just letting you know a bit about Mrs. Haig. You don't know her well, I understand, though Chin Lam asked her for help when Haig had you jailed. That bothers you, doesn't it? You don't want any help, and you don't want Chin Lam to want any, except, of course, yours. But you don't want to be indebted, do you? I certainly can't blame you. I never had the courage either; I mean, to let myself feel connected." Abernathy pulled the silk pillow up onto his knee and felt the threaded design. "Well, but 'what am I getting at?' I don't know Mrs. Haig that well myself, to be honest. For example, this morning I posed to her the hypothetical situation that you had come to *her* defense and that therefore she felt indebted to you, so much so that in order to protect you she was prepared to lie in order to assume responsibility for what happened out there."

Henry, both feet in a rapid, nervous tap, watched Abernathy furiously.

"I posed to her, what if you had actually arrived during the assault. That *you* had been the one who struggled with Barnum and shot him, after he had already killed Haig. Or that it was you Haig fired at (one bullet hitting your arm), and that you shot back in self-defense, after Haig had killed Barnum. Private speculations. I posed the possibility that Mrs. Haig feared that if you (husband of the young woman to whom she feels such a commitment), if you came to trial, circumstances might lead to your unjust punishment. She told me no. She told me that she took no responsibility that was not hers, and that the truth was that Limus Barnum was responsible for her husband's death and that she had shot Limus Barnum." Abernathy set aside the pillow and stood. "Well, you see, I don't know her well. I would have thought it would be impossible, psychologically, for a woman like Mrs. Haig to, in your phrase, blow a man away with a gun like that, nor merely once, but *three* times. Or that she would protect a man who had killed her husband."

"People do what they got to do."

"Yes. That's exactly what Mrs. Haig told me."

"What?"

"We are all capable of anything. It's just that our lives are stuffed inside so much padding that most of us never have to find it out."

"I guess." Henry stood also.

"All right, Maynard. For now, let it go at that." The lawyer picked up the wedding photograph, looked at it, then took the ivory ball in his hand. Inside the ball a world had been marvelously carved. He turned it as he spoke. "A detective will come to interview you. Be civil. You drove to Mrs. Haig's at Mrs. MacDermott's suggestion. I'll assume you tried to call her first but found the line continually busy. You asked for your wife, left, drove back, saw no one. Period." He set the ball back on the tabletop and, with Henry behind him, walked out of the trailer past the small garden patch, still muddy from the long rain.

"Look," said the younger man. "What are you doing all this for?"

"I don't know, Maynard. I haven't decided."

"Well, what's it going to cost me? What if it's too much? Let's get clear." ·

"I don't know that either. But I can think of two things to start with. That, of course, you'll stick around for your hearing on the Treeca assault. And the other is to point out that Chin Lam genuinely appears to enjoy working with Pru Lattice, and that it means a lot to that really very kind, and rather lonely, woman to have your wife's friendship. I'd just point out that your trying to protect Chin Lam from life . . ."

Henry banged his fist into the side of the trailer. "Forget it, man! If I owe you, you own me. Listen, you could start here and lay any kind of trip on me you felt like. How 'bout I do some supposing now! How 'bout this? How 'bout you're so pissed because *you* weren't the one that blew Haig and Barnum away! How 'bout this supposing? You're *glad* the dudes got wasted! Not just the scum either, but her old man! But you're gonna blackmail *me*, man? I'm gonna owe *you?* Forget it!"

Flushed pink, Abernathy nodded. "That's right, Henry. You'll have to be indebted. Just like everybody else. Just like me. And you'll have to trust me, won't you?"

"How do you know so much anyhow? What makes you so sure what happened out there?"

"Oh, I *don't* know. A million things could have happened. For one, you and Mrs. Haig might have arranged the whole thing in order to murder her husband. Or you might have assaulted her yourself and intimidated her so she won't confess it. You might have killed both men in cold blood and started the fire to cover up the evidence."

"Oh, fuck you. You know that didn't happen."

"No, I don't. I just have to trust you, don't I?"

With a snort, Henry walked toward the trailer, then turned back at the cinder-block step. "Hey. Abernathy. Suppose I told you I didn't have anything to do with what happened out there? Just like the lady said. I came and I went."

The lawyer took off his glasses and rubbed the bridge of his nose. "Then I suppose I'd tell you to make very certain that no one ever investigated the death of your German shepherd and that no one ever located the grave and that no one ever noticed that the bullet in his body came from a gun belonging to Limus Barnum. Naturally, these are only suppositions. The bullet may have passed *through* his body. Though it's a bit more distance to travel through than the outer flesh of an arm, isn't it?"

One boot up on the makeshift stoop, his tall, rangy body a sharp line against the metal silver of the trailer, Maynard Henry looked across at Abernathy, and then his uneven features smoothed into that sudden, strange, sweet, and painfully innocent smile. "Hey, man. You tell the lady, well, something. Okay?"

Abernathy nodded.

Then Maynard Henry raised his index finger like a gun, tipped it in salute against the edge of his brow, and went back inside his mobile home.

CHAPTER
61

Chilly in the gray gloom, Luke waited while each of the three men, silent and static on the grass, tapped the white balls into the cup (Marco overshooting twice), and then Arthur Abernathy replaced the jaunty flag numbered 18.

"Mr. Ransom? I'm sorry to bother you, but they told me you'd be finishing up here. Could I talk to you a second?"

The other two men stopped behind him as Ernest Ransom, polishing the head of his putter with a chamois cloth, answered, "Of course."

"My name's Luke Packer. My sister Susan works for Mr. Abernathy there."

Behind Ransom's back, Arthur nodded a confirmation.

Luke nodded at Carl Marco as well. "The thing is, Miss Dingley told me she gave you a roll of film. As a matter of fact, it was mine, and if it's no trouble I'd like to get it back. She's gotten pretty sick, I guess, so I didn't want to bother her with it and so I came out here."

"Go ahead, you two, I'll catch up." Ransom waved his companions on. Obediently they headed toward the clubhouse, hunchbacked under their heavy bags. The banker frowned, then smiled at the lanky young man whose hair was, he thought, still slightly too long for propriety, but not as bad as it could have been (he thought with a shudder of Sidney Blossom a few years ago). "Now. Luke? Yes, Luke. I'm sorry, I do recall now that Ramona handed me a roll of film or something recently with some cockamamie tale attached to it."

"It was true."

"Naturally with real problems like the fire on my mind, I'm not sure I remember what she said about it." He returned the putter to the soft leather bag, slung the bag onto his broad, cashmered shoulder, and walked past Luke, adding, "At any rate, I'm sorry, but I'm afraid I threw it out."

Stunned, Luke didn't move until Ransom was almost at the Club steps; then he ran after him. "Mr. Ransom! Just a second. You see, I took some pictures on that roll. They were mine. There's, well, there *was*, a kind of hidden compound out on your land, and Miss Dingley didn't think you knew about it, and it must have gotten burned up last night, but it doesn't make sense because nobody's mentioned it since the fire, so I really want to get those pictures developed! Mr. Ransom?"

At the doors the banker paused, his smile patient. "Wish I could help you. I'm sorry, Luke, I hadn't realized the film belonged to you. Ramona gave it to me. She's an old woman, and pretty sick now, as you know. Once in while she gets carried away with some silly ideas; you know how women can get." He widened the smile briefly. "I just didn't take her seriously. You understand."

"Don't you care if they put stuff up on your land?"

Ransom allowed mild impatience to tighten his voice. "I don't know who 'they' are supposed to be, or what you mean by 'stuff.' Now Luke, don't get involved in things that don't concern you and in business matters that you couldn't possibly be expected to appreciate."

"But that roll of film was my private property!"

The banker's smile twitched, but stayed in place. He reached into his back pocket for his wallet. "Yes, I'm sorry, but there's nothing I can do about it. Now, if you'll excuse me, I'm in sort of a hurry. Here. This should replace the cost of the film." He handed Luke a $5 bill.

The boy followed him into the lobby, but Ransom disappeared by a door to the locker room marked "Members Only."

In the empty Club bar Luke found his father, the bartender, by the color television switching channels from a motorcycle race to a baseball game to a karate match. "What are you doing here? Something the matter, Luke?" Jerry Packer turned off the set and returned behind the bar, where he began polishing glasses. Luke was embarrassed for his father, for the not unusual mix of shame and pride that made Jerry Packer not want his family to see him at work, or those he worked for to see him with his family. "Something wrong?" meant "Why else are you here?"

"No. Had to see somebody about some pictures. Just thought I'd say hi."

The father was caught between the wish to have Luke gone and the desire to do something for him. He said, "You eaten? I could go to the kitchen, get you a nice club sandwich."

"Sounds great." Luke stood by the entrance where he could see the locker room door.

"Well, probably you oughta get back though, Mr. Hayes'll be waiting though, huh?"

"No, not really. Well, you know, if you don't want to bother the kitchen, Dad, I mean, you know, I'm not really that hungry."

"I'll get you the sandwich."

When Jerry Packer returned to the bar, he was dismayed to see his son in an apparent argument with a member, not merely a member but one of the overseers. Ernest Ransom, a piece of money in his hand, looked flushed and annoyed, a look the bartender had never seen on his face. He wondered if Luke could be doing something so horrible as soliciting (what? magazines? charitable contributions?) in the Dingley Club. But then Ransom was saying, "Bothering an ill woman is going to do you no good and possibly do her harm. Now I don't know how I can impress this on you, but the film is gone. Any installation that may or may not have been there would be perfectly legitimate and none of your affair, and this whole thing is ridiculous. I'll have to ask you to stop bothering me."

Packer hurried over. "Something the matter? Anything wrong, Mr. Ransom?"

Ransom stuffed the $5 bill back into the pocket of his kelly-green cotton slacks. "No, no. Everything's fine, Jerry. Scotch and soda, please."

Luke, crimson-faced, left the room. His father, still holding the plate with the huge club sandwich on it, did not call him back.

CHAPTER
62

Peter Dingley, the Puritan father of Elijah, the founder, had fled England to escape religious persecution at the hands of Thomas Laud, Archbishop of Canterbury. Elijah was no Puritan, and as if to make of his only son a testament saying so, he named him Thomas Laud Dingley. And so began that generational battle waged down three centuries of Dingley firstborn males, a battle in which rebellion against the father continued a familial (and national) tradition of theological revolt. For if the father were High Church, the son was sure to be Low, or Higher still (a few, in fact, vaulting up into Catholicism, a few slipping off the ladder of faith entirely). Thus, Thomas Laud, in spite of his name, was very Low, and his son, Timothy, consequently, very High, and he it was who had ordered from England in 1740 not only the organ (the cost of whose annual upkeep was higher than Jonathan Fields's salary), but the rosewood confessional that still stood in its somber niche at the rear of St. Andrew's (High) Episcopal Church. There, for an hour on Saturday, Father Highwick kept up the old-fashioned tradition of private confession, cheerfully absolving the half-dozen elderly lady sinners who brought him their meager culpabilities, spiced with town gossip, week after week.

Now Prudence Lattice, in tears, amazed him. To her old sins of staying, in her view, too slothful, too envious, too full of self-pity, still unable to stop depending on medication to stave off depression, still unable to give up her silly dreams or her gothic romances, still terrified of her death, and now of poor Ro Dingley's too—along with all these sins, which he promptly forgave her—she was now torn between her awful desire to see a man arrested for murder so that his wife would come live with her, and her awful desire to stay loyal to Winslow Abernathy even though Winslow appeared to be trying to hush up the bloody crimes of this awful man, Maynard Henry, by telling her it was just his dog he'd killed! And why kill Night? So shocked was the Rector (who had missed everything while away in Manhattan), so shocked and so eager to hear her story, that he leaned around his side of the ornate booth, popped his head through her velvet curtain, and exclaimed, "Pru! Good gosh! Poor thing! Now start again and don't leave anything out! Now don't judge Winslow, whatever you do. I'm sure it's all for the best. And let's not judge this horrible killer either. I admit it sounds grim. Shot two men, a woman, *and* a German shepherd? Oh, not a woman! Pru! I don't know what to say, but let's remember, judge not, cast not the first stone. Oh, yes, *sorry, Jonathan!* Shhh! Pru, they're practicing for tomorrow, just beautiful! So we'll have tea, oops, stupid chair out in the middle of nowhere!" He called a loud apology up the long aisle to the nave. "*Yes, sorry, Jonathan, stupid chair!*"

Contrapuntal to Pru Lattice's secular tale came

sacred melodies from the Alexander Hamilton Academy Choir rehearsing the Gloria from Ralph Vaughan Williams's Mass in G Minor. Close to setting, the sun had finally shown itself. Dusky yellow light came slanting through the western window's triptych of Christ risen and crowned in heaven. The schoolboys, aged ten to sixteen, squirmed in their stalls like piebald colts, some in blazers, some in sweatshirts, some in windbreakers stamped *A.H.A.*, some in striped polo shirts, none motionless, until Jonathan Fields, medieval in the skirted cassock, clapped his hands over his head. Charlie Hayes stepped forward with a smaller boy beside him. They began again. In a back pew Walter Saar heard the harmonious sound with astonishment, whole like the sweet, unending note of a seraph's trumpet heralding some quiet, eternal triumph. All those adolescent faces uplifted (those "in" mingling with those "out," no cliques but those of pitch), all those voices the headmaster knew from experience to be infinitely capable of lies, boasts, bigotry, curses, hypocrisy, hate, sniveling cowardice, and smug stupidity—all tuned to that key, together in the perfection that is music's alone, and that Saar in his rasher moments told himself was a more intense pleasure than sex. *His* boys (his gobbling, stuttering, hee-hawing, farting, cacophonous boys) were making that faultless sound.

Saar started to hyperventilate, and then he burst into tears. Mortified, he pretended to sneeze convulsively in order to camouflage this preposterous breakdown. It was the church, he told himself. He had always known churches to be dangerous places. He had always intelligently avoided them. Yet here he was, absurdly falling in love with not only a Christian but a priest (and if the truth be known, he would have to say, a mediocre musician, ignorant as a babe of the world of the arts, really not terribly bright, and almost totally devoid of erotic technique); here he sat, in love with such an idiot (not to mention its being homosexual, and a damn waste of time and shame to have to hide it, and still probably—if the country continued to slide back down into the pit of conformity it had briefly pulled its head above in the last decade—probably lose his job); here he sat, in love with this man. Here he sat, badgered by music, importuned by an optical illusion, stained through glass, of haloes goldening the heads of his urchins. Music swells, sinner falls to his knees, he'd seen it in a hundred movies called *The Robe*. A shoddy gimmick.

And high above the choir screen, over their heads, the huge gilded crucifix; Christ in careful realism, larger than life, carved and hung there. My God! thought Saar, as he felt his friend Mr. Hyde puff up in his breast. Why not gild the gas chamber then? Why not paste precious stones on an electric chair and hang *it* up over the altar! What a hideous, slimy, lurid symbol for a religion to exalt—a machine of public execution! My God! Gibbon was right, Voltaire, Nietzsche, Marx, who else? Well, whoever, they were all right. (Hadn't he heard that Nietzsche had ended up hugging an overworked cart horse, blubbering tears all over its scrawny neck? But, wait, hadn't he gone senile from syphilis by then? Yes!) Yes, they were right. Saar felt the impulse rise to spring up from his seat, up into the air, and haul Christ down from that Cross, hurl Him down to the floor of the church. How dare He hang there as if it were all that simple! His mere six hours of suffering to compensate for the slow, wasting agony of all the ages! His scourging and short walk to death to make up for it all! Millions had died more mercilessly mocked, in greater thirst, in greater fear, in greater pain, unsolaced by faithful tears, not to mention resurrection. How dare He hang up there and claim He paid the cost of one child, panicked for breath, dying in a terror of incomprehension while his parents power-lessly watched. Oh, naturally it appealed to the blind and the halt (halted by misfortunes mental, physical, or otherwise), naturally it was the perfect tool of oppression. It meant nothing and everything, a potboiler of paradox. God born in a manger (every child a movie star), riding to glory on an ass, betrayed with a kiss, savior to whores and drunks and other flashy types, crowned with thorns. Have your king and eat him, too. It was a wonder it wasn't already a TV series. Hyde started laughing while Saar cried.

The choir faltered. Jonathan stopped them with a wave. "No, no, this is tricky. Now listen again." He ran over to the organ and played a melody with one hand, beating time with the other, singing the words with wide contortions of his mouth. "*'Laudamus te, benedicimus te, adoramus te.'* All right? Try it. Ready?"

A more horrific urge seized Walter Saar. He was entirely sober, yet he held with both hands to the sides of his seat, so strong was the sensation that if he let go, he would be bodily pulled through air, as if by wires attached to the Cross, and sprung against the body of Christ. Compelled to throw his arms around Christ's neck, his legs around Christ's hips, to kiss the worm-eaten wooden lips, to thrust his finger in the sword hole, his tongue in the nail holes, to rub his sex against the body of God here in the sanctity of the church before the world to make a fool of this long-suffering Christ. For what, cackled Mr. Hyde, could Christ do, perfect Love that He was, hung above everyone else, but accept the embrace with open arms? His arms were open to every sinner. They were nailed open.

"*'Tu solus Dominus. Tu solus altissimus.'*"

"Just once more, Jordan, okay?" Jonathan said to the small boy beside Charlie Hayes. Oh, God! Saar choked. Naturally, the only little black boy in the whole damn school, and there he is stage center, voice like an angel, grinning part and parcel of this conspiracy of coincidental significance designed to choke me up! Oh, God, I'm a sentimental jerk! Bring on Dilsey and Tiny Tim and let them sing a duet of "Ave Maria"! Let Little Nell and Little Eva play harps and the deaf Beethoven conduct!

"Yes, wonderful, now everyone."

"'*Jesu Christe. Cum Sancto Spiritu in Gloria dei Patris. Amen.*'"

"Young man? Excuse me, young man? Can I help you? Are you ill?" Prudence Lattice put her hand on the blue chambray shirt. Walter Saar was bent over in the pew, his head to his knees. He lifted his face to see a shimmery blur of a small, birdish, elderly woman. "No," he mumbled, hands and face covered with tears. "Thank you. I'm not ill."

"Oh. Good." She smiled. "You're just crying. Good. I thought maybe you'd had an attack or something. Music often makes me cry. It just gets so big inside you, you're not big enough for it, and out it comes in tears. Do you know what I mean?" She shook her head, fumbling through her purse. "You young people. None of you ever have any handkerchiefs. Never plan to cry, I suppose. Or catch colds or perspire or have anything go wrong. Oh, I guess I was just the same. Here we go. You take it. Yes: There."

"Absurd. So sorry. Can't imagine what. Feel a perfect fool."

"Oh, that's all right. That's what church is for. No, no. You keep that. I have lots at home. People give them to you for presents when they don't know what else to do, and, well, over the years they add up."

CHAPTER
63

Ramona Dingley was very ill, but though her voice had lost all volume, it persisted adamantine as she refused to be tormented or distracted by something as morally irresponsible as a hospital at so morally serious a moment in her life as her death.

"Sammy, hell's bells," growled her physician, "leave her alone. If she doesn't want to go, don't nag her. They can't do anything for her anyhow."

"There's no hope then?"

"Didn't say that. I learned my lesson years ago when she got over that heart attack to stop forecasting Ramona's demise. All I'm going to say is that if a woman her age and in her condition chooses to stand out seminaked all night, she's not doing much to help her odds."

"It's not funny, Otto."

"Oh, Sammy, listen, I know, I know. Why don't you go take a walk, go get a drink. There's nothing you can do here. Orchid's sitting in there; I'm going to sleep. Either take a sleeping pill or take a stroll. Go on, go on."

Smalter walked westward among the pine groves and orchard and meadow that lay picture-book perfect between Elizabeth Circle and the silken river Rampage. Through the pines on the far bank a plum and lavender sky pinked the water. Slowly, thumbs hooked in the pockets of his seersucker vest, puffing on his pipe enough to keep it lit, the pharmacist took his prescribed

619

stroll north along the side of the Rampage and
wondered how Ramona felt, what it would be like to be
Ramona now. As he passed under a low willow branch,
he patted the bark with his hand. Boys, when he was
young, had swung out on the branch and dropped from
there naked into the river to swim. And once or twice,
in the coldest winters, when the Rampage was safely
frozen, older boys had brought their jalopies onto the
ice to race them. Children had skated. Ramona had
skated, too, a grown woman, astonishing him with her
sudden leaps and turns. Smalter recalled hearing as a
child that a young couple, sweethearts, people called
them, had fallen through the ice and drowned. For
weeks he'd waked with nightmares of their swimming
down the black river under ice, pushing up against the
dark cold, searching for the jagged hole of light they'd
fallen through. His parents had thought he was dreaming of his operations.

"Hi, Mr. Smalter." It was Luke's voice. In a bend a
few hundred feet ahead, Luke and Polly sat quietly by
the bank, Polly in a huge tree trunk hollowed into a
seat. From a distance they looked like a Winslow
Homer painting. Close up, they looked thinner to the
pharmacist; their eyes different.

Smalter nodded and stood beside them for a while.
Then he said, "I told Ramona that you'd dropped by
earlier, Polly, but Dr. Scaper thinks it'll be better in
general that she not have any visitors while she's feeling
so weak." (Miss Dingley had in fact said to Smalter,
"Tell her, don't come. Could pontificate. Be pleasant.
Deathbed advice. Young heiress. Tears and gratitude.
Won't indulge myself. She's seen enough dying. Tell
her I liked her. Right off the bat. Tell her, don't waste
my money. Don't be an idiot. Don't forget, love too,
some point along the way.")

"I hope she's better. Is she?" the girl asked.

"About the same, I'm afraid. I'll keep you in touch,
Polly. Luke. See you soon. Don't stay out here too
late." Frail and urban among the pines and weeds and

brambled thickets of berries, Smalter walked on north, following the river.

The two young people were quiet until he was out of sight, then they returned to what they'd been talking about before he came. Polly said, "I bet we could tell Mr. Smalter about it, I bet he'd help. He could talk to Dr. Scaper. Listen, if Miss Dingley dies, we still can't let it drop about what we saw, okay? I just wish we had those pictures."

"Don't worry. I'll get them. It's just a matter of time."

They were quiet again. Sky and water faded together into night's monochrome.

Sammy Smalter didn't drink, had no taste or tolerance for alcohol, and so on the rare occasions when he ordered, ordered quixotically by title such concoctions as Singapore Slings and Jack the Rippers. Returning from his walk by way of The Prim Minster, he stopped to have a Bicentennial special, "The Valley Forge," which appeared to be grain alcohol poured over a tall glass of crushed ice with a Betsy Ross flag stuck in it. At Glover's Lane he stopped to visit A. A. Hayes. He found the editor, drink in hand, seated in the dark on his porch steps, a southern custom the expatriate clung to, though none of his neighbors had adopted it. On Hayes's house was a placard modeled facetiously on Ernest Ransom's. It read, "Built 1948."

"Sit down, Sammy, I'm all alone. And how am I? Tight as a tick. And how do I feel about life? About like Moby Dick. I mean the whale, not the book."

"Mind company? You were reading."

"Just a piece of junk." Hayes held up a paperback, *Heather Should Have Died Hereafter* by Ben Rough. Smalter said nothing. The two men, moonlit, sat on the steps, and Hayes having pressed a glass on the pharmacist, they shared a bottle.

Around them Glover's Lane was quiet. The Strummers had closed their house and gone to upstate New

York, where Jack's parents lived. They would bury Joy there in her father's family plot. Lights were on in the Hedgerow home. Luke Packer sat in the living room with Polly watching the old Capra movie *Mr. Smith Goes to Washington* on television. Evelyn Troyes sat in the kitchen watching Cecil Hedgerow sip the soup she had made him. He held the spoon carefully in his bandaged hands. They talked about violin music. Limus Barnum's house was dark. On Glover's Lane no one was outside except the editor and his guest.

Finally Hayes spoke. "How much more can we take? Can you believe that about the poor Haigs? Awful." He drank again.

"Yes."

"You know, Lime was a creep, but I never figured he'd ever *do* anything. Just a bunch of hot air. I actually used to theorize about him a lot. Boy! So much for my theories. He came into the *Day* all the time, wanted us to be friends. Just wanted a friend. Poor creepy son of a bitch."

"He wanted you to become a Nazi."

"Aw, who took that seriously?" Hayes took Smalter's lighter to light a cigarette. "Poor old Lime. 'Spend time with Lime, and spend less.' You know, really, what was he? Like he said, a guy that worked hard, paid his own way, never had it easy, felt pushed around, put down, not too special, not too successful; devoid of charm, or family, or grace, or much luck, or even the trust, much less affection, of most people around him. All the grudges and frustrations and that piss-ass unarticulated unhappiness of the vast silent majority."

"If you're writing his obituary, Alvis, don't forget to mention he assaulted a woman and shot her husband to death. Your poor son of a bitch."

"Aw, what do you know?" slurred Hayes loudly. "Get off your high horse, Sammy. Who knows what happened out there?" He offended the midget, who set down his drink, which Hayes (entirely unaware of Smalter's response to his tone) immediately refilled. Then he patted Smalter on the back and spoke warmly. "I like you, Sammy. Always have."

Smalter tugged at his boy tie, shook off the affront as alcoholic and not personal, picked up his glass, and took a drink. "What is this?"

"Scotch."

"Isn't it a tad on the bitter side?"

"Tad on the cheap side. Keep drinking, won't matter in a while. Sammy," Hayes said solemnly. "I had a dream last night. You'll appreciate it. I dreamed Richard Nixon was King Lear. He was running crazed and half-naked in the rags of that black three-piece suit of his. Roaring up and down a deserted beach at San Clemente howling things like 'Take physic, pomp!' But Nixon's not crazy like Lear. He's only crazy like the Pentagon and Exxon."

"Sane."

"Right. Have some more."

"Ah, well, just a bit. How much is enough?"

"I don't know yet. Ask me twenty years from now. Sammy, that's the point. If Nixon would go crazy, he'd be great! What we need in this country is some tragic heroes. Know what Coleman said? Said there weren't any in America, not even Lincoln when Booth shot him." Hayes staggered to his feet and shook his glass at the stars. "No heroes! But it's not because there's no throne to fall off. Sammy, it's because we don't believe in the Fall. America elected to escape Original Sin. No last act. That's why. If the land gives out in Tennessee, why, the grass is always greener on the Great Divide. Right? Sammy, my friend, if Adam and Eve had been Americans, they would have left the Garden of Eden in a covered wagon, yelling, 'Yippy-ki-yi-yay! Move 'em out!' They would have settled down west in Babylon and started writing their memoirs and going on shows telling what it had 'done' to them to be pushed out of

Paradise. Not After the Fall. After the Shove! That's
our philosophy. Yep, and they would have gone into
analysis and 'fixed' their heads."

"Alvis. Excuse me. Could you point me toward your
toilet?"

"Shit. Are you going to throw up?"

"No. Of course not."

" 'Cause do it out here on the grass. Okay, okay, it's
straight back, down the hall on the left. For God's sake,
don't do it on the rug. She'll kill me."

When Smalter returned to the porch, the editor was
smoking two cigarettes, one in his mouth, one in his
hand. He was already talking and, from all Smalter
could judge, may never have stopped. "Imperfectibility
is un-American, so's unhappiness." Hayes burped.
"We won't admit we're flawed, or handicapped, we
won't even be inconvenienced! Old age is un-
American. Poor refuse to be poor; minorities insist on
the rights of majorities. Cripples protest a lot of steps."

"I don't much like a lot of steps myself," threw in
Smalter, easing himself up into a porch rocker. "I
gather you're saying the former president is not tragic
because he doesn't sense that he was wrong. And this is
a national trait."

"Well, don't make it sound so dumb. Think about it,
Oedipus didn't call a press conference and announce,
'Listen, Jocasta and I made a few mistakes, so you're
throwing me out. Well, you won't have Oedipus Rex to
kick around anymore.' No, he said, 'Look, I was
wrong, I was blind but now I see.' See? Tragic heroes
accept the imperfectibility of man. Human character,
human destiny."

"It would seem so. How can you drink that stuff like
it was water?"

"Sammy, if you were southern, you'd understand me
better, but you Yankees never knew what it was to be
defeated. You learn there's no place left to go. The
puny little confines of human nature have you all
fenced in. No amount of overreaching is going to work.

Not over the gate of that sadist, that usurer God Almight, Jahweh, Lord of Lords and Lord of Flies. You know that? You don't know that. *I* know that. You don't know that." Hayes's head kept shaking mournfully.

"I thought cursing the gods was only supposed to make matters worse."

"Nope, we won't accept our Fall. Won't do it. Nope. You know that?"

"Yes, love it or leave it. America's a romance, Alvis. That's all. Wonders of the newfound land, and man. Rebirth. Like the phoenix rising."

"Think the South will rise again, Sammy? It will, you know, you wait. Never should have lost," mumbled Hayes. "Damn Gettysburg. Damn." The word was a long, drawled sigh. "Ever heard Lee's farewell to his troops? Let me get it. Now there's a hero!"

Smalter rocked out of his chair and sat Hayes back down. He had often before heard the editor, intoxicated, on the true cause, course, and consequences of the War of the Confederacy. "Look." He pointed. "Police."

A patrol car had turned into the street and parked next door. Hayes quickly hid his bottle behind the shrub bordering the porch steps. "God, Alvis, you *are* paranoid," whispered Smalter. They watched Joe Mac-Dermott, in uniform, lead two policemen, one with a camera, into the house of Limus Barnum. Lights came on, first floor, then second. Hayes stumbled down his steps and across the lawn, Smalter behind him.

"Alvis, wait. You think you ought to?"

"Freedom of the press," the editor said, then belched loudly.

Barnum's house was full of things. Old and new furnishings, dozens of electrical appliances. A set of encyclopedias and framed prints of the Impressionists in textured cardboard were among the hundred curiously impersonal artifacts, things chosen because they were the things the world told him to choose. Ordinary things. Hayes and Smalter stared, nevertheless, because the possessions of those separated from the rest of the world by the fame of fortune or misfortune or by a madness to create or destroy seem to take on the mystery of their owners' secret, whether the secret is one of glory, or horror, or death. Ordinary objects seem granted the significance of talismans. And once granted, of course endowed.

But on Barnum's top floor there were possessions perhaps less ordinary, perhaps less ambiguous as clues to the secret of their owner than all the things collected downstairs. They were certainly more personal things, at least in the sense that none of the men who looked at them now had been meant to see them. In the opened door Smalter and Hayes stood, staring. Joe MacDermott by a closet held up a Nazi military jacket with bewildered dismay in his bland face. Shoddy pictures torn from magazines, the articles known as sexual "aids" and those designed for sexual "discipline," cheap, false-colored, shiny plastic and rubber objects flashed stark bright with the hissing eye of the policeman's camera.

Hundreds of dollars in self-improvement equipment lay on the floor, instruments for all the muscles of the body. And prominently in the center of the room was a full-length mirror hung on swivels inside a heavy, ornate wooden frame; its feet were clawed balls, and an eagle was carved into the top piece. The glass of the mirror had been smashed. The photographer with a grin drew the attention of MacDermott to a picture taped to the wall of a man forcing a bound woman to fellatio him.

Smalter felt angry and ashamed of his sex, ashamed of himself and the money he made with cheap, false books about quick guns and fast women. He felt sad about the human race, sad and sick at heart. Looking at the mirror, he thought of the words Ramona had said to him jokingly last night. "Deathbed advice, Sammy. Listen. Get a big mirror. Take off your clothes. Stand there. Laugh. Come too, stand beside you, if I could walk. Am I saying words? Can't hear. Nod. Good. All these years. Same house. Not true aunt. Should have had sex. Why not? Curiosity. Now, never know. Missed it. Old woman, but as a favor you could have. Too late now. Don't be so prissy. Blushing. Shame, ain't it? Laugh."

"Oh, Lord," said Hayes, shaking his head at the room where Limus Barnum had spent that time that others did not care to spend with him. "Poor creepy bastard."

Smalter took Hayes by the arm and led him home. Brushing his hand through his wreath of hair, he said, "Ah, well, Alvis, you see even in the land of romance, sometimes character *is* destiny. Sadly enough. Go to bed now."

CHAPTER
64

Tracy Canopy's television set was tuned to the Argyle news on which was now being shown a clip of the sooty Cecil Hedgerow talking authoritatively into the camera while, somehow, beside him Evelyn Troyes gazed admiringly up. Behind them the woods were burning. Tracy ate a late dinner absentmindedly alone. She could rarely remember, once she'd thrown out the aluminum containers, what it was she'd had for dinner. She was not, like Evelyn, like Beanie, a creature-comfort creature at all. Not a sensualist. Not, she supposed, if certain sorts of things were meant by it, a terribly womanly woman. Thus, to be absolutely honest, she was happier now than during her homely childhood, when she had been for the most part

frightened or frustrated, happier than during her plain
adolescence, when she had been continually baffled
and humiliated, happier than in her severe young
matronhood, when she had been at least partially
conflicted and restricted. Now, finally, at fifty-two,
Tracy Canopy was free. Never again would she be
caught between the shame of having her pigtails yanked
and the shame of not having them yanked. Never
again, to escape pity and censure, need she submit to
the rituals of being whistled at (or not), being asked out
to be whiskered across the face and squeezed elsewhere
(or not), of being given away, a raffle prize, in a church,
then carted off to the deflowering like Anne Boleyn (or
not). Free from the urge to give birth, and from months
calendared by blood, Tracy Canopy felt free as a
butterfly after a clumsy crawl as a caterpillar and a
long, will-less, squishy passivity in the marriage co-
coon.

No doubt it was a matter of metabolism or hormones
or genes or diet or morphology. Look at Beanie. Or
Evelyn, confessing that she "longed to have a man."
"Longed"? What did that mean? The way Evelyn had
oohed and aahed all her life over men, had even at six
delighted in getting her hair yanked, had even at
fourteen secretly fashioned in an attic room a shrine to
Charles Boyer, with candles burning before his photograph. And still now in that gush over Louie Daytona,
or even the selectman Cecil Hedgerow last night at the
fire. Well, Evelyn was up to something moony and
hidden again. Something like the shrine or her running
off, unwed, with Hugo Eroica. But that was Evelyn.
Tracy wouldn't press her. She'd wait. In good time
Evelyn would come to her with a confession.

Yet Priss would not. Absentmindedly sipping tea in
which the bag still sat, turning the liquid to tannic acid,
Tracy puzzled now over a moral dilemma. On the one
hand, she believed that Priss had been in the wrong,
speaking so unfeelingly to Beanie, and to her; but on
the other hand, should she cast Priss aside for that

offense? For she knew that Priss would be unable to ask forgiveness, might even want to but simply would not be capable of taking that first step, any more than someone whose legs were broken could climb a mountain. And yet Priss would miss her; her absence would become gradually a more conscious irritant in Priss's daily activities. This Tracy knew from their past quarrels. She suspected, in fact, that there was a way in which Priss, who seemed to care for so little, was more in need of Tracy, than she of Priss. Well then, what was there to do but move the mountain over to Mrs Ransom? Mrs. Canopy decided to go up and speak to her friend tomorrow after church, seeking her out, but matter-of-factly, so as not to embarrass her. A neutral topic. Well, she would think of one. Then from England she'd write (as she always did—quatrains on postcards: "Wish you were here in Windermere / Except the rotten weather's dreary. / Beanie climbed mountains, while I, I fear, / Soon quit because I'd gotten weary. Love, Tracy"). Then when she returned to Dingley Falls, life between them would take up its old dance, discord forgotten though not formally forgiven.

Tracy would call to inquire about Ramona once more, then she really should get to bed. There were a million and one things she needed to do before Tuesday when her trip with Beanie would begin. Not that she held out much hope that this excursion to the Lake District would save the Abernathy marriage, though it should help temporarily to save its face. For people could be snide. Well, Beanie was Beanie. And why assume that someone doesn't know what she's doing if she says she does? If Beanie chose to leave a snug lake to dive headfirst into the raging ocean, then no doubt the landlocked, the high-grounders, for whom even the most shallow pond was too wet (and oh, my, Vincent, I hope I was not really an awful disappointment, because we were very good friends, weren't we?), then all those scared of drowning should admit, "I am out of my element and ought not to judge what certainly looks like the most terrifying folly from back here, high and dry on the shore."

In their off-mauve living room the Ransoms were trying to decide what to do for dinner. Meanwhile cocktails were being served. Ernest, in sailing blazer, served a martini to his wife, in caftan, and a Scotch and soda to himself. Arthur Abernathy, in suit and tie, was invited to serve himself as he awaited Emerald, who was up in her room engaged in those somnambulistically serene rites known in the family as "Emerald's getting ready." Kate, in shorts and a T-shirt stamped "Women Belong in the House . . . and the Senate," served herself a Scotch and took a glass of wine to Sidney Blossom, who had surprised her by showing up in what looked like a starched shirt. Blossom was at the piano in the corner, forcing himself to work to win the Ransoms' affection, though he didn't especially want it; or at least their tacit tolerance of him as the future kinsman he intended to become. While ten years ago Sid had been thrust into moral absolutism by the strategies of the revolutionary times, and had thus earned Kate's parents' nervous enmity as a "protester" and a "freak," he was by nature a pragmatist. What he wanted was Kate. Kate was connected to a family. Best all around if relations with the family were as near cordiality as goodwill could make them. Rummaging through the piano seat, he found a book of Cole Porter songs inscribed "Priscilla Hancock." He flipped it open and began "Begin the Beguine."

If Emerald ever appeared, she and Arthur would be dining with acquaintances in Argyle. Kate and Sid would be eating at Mama Marco's. The Ransoms, senior, were at somewhat looser ends. Neither felt tonight like another trip to the Prim or the Club or the Old Towne, or a drive elsewhere, or a show, or much of anything. Priss had tried unsuccessfully to stir up two players for bridge. Evelyn had never answered. Finally

Walter Saar had, explaining he'd passed the afternoon at St. Andrew's listening to the choir rehearsal and was now unfortunately in bed with, he said, a sudden attack of something he must have picked up there. "Not the curate?" she had queried lightly, and he had managed a laugh, and she had laughed back, and they had arranged to be partners at the Club's duplicates tournament the following Friday. Mrs. Ransom decided it would probably be pleasant to share with Saar private innuendos about his illicit perversity. Naturally they'd never mention it directly; she would never "know" he was homosexual, but they would play with knowledge as with cards. She liked him better than ever. Still, what were she and Ernest going to do this evening?

"Why don't you pick up a couple of grinders and go bowling?" suggested Kate.

"Take your legs off the arm rests, dear," her mother replied.

"Tell you what, I bet we could get Sloan. And Tracy. Play a few rubbers," Ransom urged politely. (He actually would have preferred to watch television.)

"Sloan doesn't play bridge."

"Oh. Sorry. Are you sure?"

"Yes. He plays Hearts and, I believe, Go Fish."

Sid gave an appreciative chuckle and swept into a medley from *Kiss Me, Kate*. Kate looked at him with alarm and returned to the magazine she was reading.

Ransom passed his wife a smoked oyster on a cracker. "Well, the Rector said he was preaching tomorrow anyhow. Probably burning the midnight oil."

"Not unless he's making soap," replied Priss. Sid chuckled again. She took her martini to the coiled gold mirror, where she brushed back a short lock of hair and thought again that perhaps she should salt and pepper her hair, like Ernest's. She said over her shoulder, "Really. When is your vestry going to admit that Sloan Highwick ought to retire?"

"That's true." Arthur Abernathy nodded.

"Really. He's becoming senile. The man's mind is like a Dr. Seuss book."

"Oh, don't be silly, Priss. Sloan's always been like that."

"Is that a defense? Ernest, you yourself told me when you met his mother that she was certifiable."

"What's that got to do with it?" asked Ransom, refurbishing his drink.

"Listen to this!" Kate mumbled from her book. "'Resolved, that the women of this nation in eighteen seventy-six have greater cause for discontent, rebellion, and revolution than the men of seventeen seventy-six.' Susan B. Anthony. And here we are, with *another* hundred years of crap dumped on our heads!" She threw the magazine on the floor and yelled, "And where's the fucking revolution for *us?*"

"Kate! Hold on, now! I don't think that's the right kind of language for you to . . ."

"Oh, Daddy! You know, I bet if a truck ran over me and I were lying on the sidewalk dying, and I said, 'Oh, fuck it, Daddy, I'm dying!' you'd say it wasn't the right kind of language to use."

Around Ransom's mouth the skin turned white. "Don't talk about your dying like that."

"See!"

Ernest Ransom took his drink, told everyone to help themselves to his liquor, said he hoped he would be excused, and, retired to his den.

"Oh, shit! Now I've hurt his feelings." Kate went over to the piano, where Blossom was tinkling through "Miss Otis Regrets." She pummeled him on the back, the gesture somewhere between a massage and an assault. "I feel like I ought to stick a dollar in your glass," she told him. "What is this, cocktail hour at the Ramada Inn? What are you playing this junk for?"

"I for one happen to be enjoying it," said Mrs. Ransom from her plum wing chair. "Porter's my favorite." Sid slowed seductively into "It's All Right with Me."

Finally the double glass doors opened, and there stood Emerald, ready. Her glossy black curls were blown into perfect disorder. Her lips and fingernails and toenails and blouse were red, her scarf and skirt were white, her blazer and her sling-back open-toe pumps were blue, as if she had been decorated to commemorate the Bicentennial year. Pierced through her ears were tiny ruby hearts. Perfectly she waited.

"If Daddy were in here, he'd take a picture of you," said Kate. All Emerald's life people had been taking pictures of her. Now she always seemed to expect it.

"You look lovely, dear. Have a good time," her mother told her.

"Have a nice evening," Arthur told Mrs. Ransom.

The couple went to the door. Then Emerald paused, turned. She raised her hand, diamond twinkling, and said, "Ciao."

"Ciao!" called Sid Blossom with a friendly wave, and swooped into "What a Swell Party This Is."

CHAPTER
65

In the fold-out bed beside Chin Lam, her sleeping head pressed in the crook of his neck, her arm across his thin chest, Maynard Henry lay awake and concluded, after a series of speculations, that his luck, bad as it had been, could have been worse. These speculations did not question the justice of what he had elected to do to Limus Barnum, or had been forced to do to John Haig, any more than he would have brooded over whether or not he should have killed a spider that had bitten him, or deflected a rock thrown at his head.

But Maynard Henry did have a few theories about

what had happened since the shooting; about, for
example, the feelings about Judith Haig that had
motivated Winslow Abernathy to protect (and then to
blackmail) him. Yet some of Henry's conclusions were
based on false premises. It was not true that Judith
Haig had told the lawyer everything, and that she and
Abernathy were conscious conspirators. She had told
him no more than he had repeated to Henry. Also false
was the younger man's immediate assumption, when
told that a bullet had been fired into Barnum's face,
that Judith had held the gun there and squeezed the
trigger in violent revenge, in uncontrollable disgust and
despair. He understood the phenomenon, having seen
other corpses shot at, but he thought the less of Judith
Haig for doing it. Such vengeance was not clean, so he
judged.

Henry was frustrated. He didn't understand her code
of debt and payment, and his ignorance tilted him off
balance. What equaled what? What kind of woman
would shield a man who had killed her husband
(though by chance misfortune)? Unless she wanted her
husband killed. Or was his causing Haig's death
justified by his executing the rapist for her? An
exchange of necessities? He wanted to know if he and
Mrs. Haig were even. If she sent no bill, that would
make it harder.

The flat disc of the moon, a hunter's moon, came like
a watch light through the small window and whitened
the slender arm that, enclosing him, moved with his
breath. The wound from the bullet ached, but he could
not turn away without moving her aside. Henry's legs
were too long for the cheap, thin mattress; his feet had
always hung over the edge, and Night had often
startled him by licking them. Now Maynard Henry
curled himself against Chin Lam, bending his legs
toward her.

The sheets on Judith Haig's bed were white and mild
as milk against her skin. She had let the weight of her

head sink into the pillow; it felt tender. Judith had been washed by nurses with warm, easy hands and dressed in the open nightgown. Now, unmedicated, she lay, drowsy, in the dark room. After the clatter of the day, silence in the night-lit corridor was slumbery and peaceful. Beyond the curtain her neighbor, Betty, slept with soft, regular snores. Judith held a piece of cloth against the white blanket and touched it with her fingers as if it were an infant creature of some sort. It was the scarf she had knitted over the past week from scraps of yarn. Brought to the hospital, placed in her hands by Chin Lam Henry, the returned scarf was, Judith knew, the wordless statement of Chin's understanding and gratitude. Neither had needed to say anything to translate its message.

The wool strip now looked nothing like the bright, scattered, multicolored threads, the scarf of scraps that Maynard Henry had snatched up from Judith's chair to press against his wound. Last night Chin Lam must have soaked the wool in chemicals to bleach the blood away. Now the stains flowed into a pattern, for the scarf was one pastel flow of delicate hues run together. Judith liked the way it looked.

She was thinking, waiting for sleep, about Winslow Abernathy, who had sat with her again this afternoon, coming back to tell her of Maynard Henry's response to her statement about the shootings. He had told her also, suddenly, of his separation from his wife. He had told her, in a rush, how he felt. The pretense about Henry was like a barred window between them, she felt. She'd thought she was being kind, not telling him she planned to testify to a literal, though not a spiritual, lie by saying Barnum had killed John. She'd thought it was unkind to burden Winslow with that guilty knowledge. Now she was the unkindness in separating him from a burden that was a gift as well. She would ask him to share it. As she had chosen to share Maynard Henry's act.

Not that Judith Haig ever would have herself killed

Barnum, or approved Henry's doing so. But she had taken from the nuns' teaching the outmoded idea that the purpose of punishment is to redeem the offender's soul through the cleansing of penance. She did not think of punishment either as unnecessary or as a salve or recompense to the victim. Consequently, to murder a murderer was not in her philosophy, whether the murdered were Limus Barnum or Maynard Henry. Yet at the heart of her protection of Maynard Henry lay not merely her Christian condemnation of retaliatory justice (as Abernathy surmised), not merely her fear that prejudice would falsely punish Henry if he were brought to trial (as Abernathy surmised). At the heart lay her knowledge that she could not disconnect herself from Maynard Henry.

Outside, trailed by stars, the moon floated by. Mother moon and all her bright pretty children, the nuns had said. And Judith had prayed to the moon for her own mother to return and claim her as her own. Now she looked at her watch, then pulled herself on her side and reached for the telephone. Winslow Abernathy's number was one she was easily able to remember, though she had never dialed it but once, for Dingley Falls had but one exchange, and the last four numbers were the year of her birth.

He said that he could sleep now. Judith knew that she too could sleep. She wondered at the strange peace she felt. It was not that her bruises and lacerations and her strained heart no longer hurt, but that she had taken in the pain like cold air into the lungs so that pain itself was restful. It was not that, but how oddly untroubled her heart was, how unafraid. There was the difference. She was no longer afraid. Nor was this lack of fear simply knowledge that she had now suffered as much terror, as much loathing and loss, as bullying life had to threaten. Not simply that, tortured, she had been willing to leap off the precipice into madness and had fallen, still unbroken, into the sea, where she floated sane and whole. Not simply that she had begged death to carry her down, drowning knowledge; or that he had, for an instant, held her in the dark water, then pushed her painfully back to air; though all were undoubtedly true. And doubtless she would be told that this peacefulness was the anesthesia of shock; that she was still too stunned for wild grief. And yes, she knew there was much yet to feel about John, about the sad, chance waste of his death, much yet to forgive herself and him about the fearful waste of their marriage. She knew, too, that what she had felt during the assault and the killings lived still unordered inside her and could never be wholly excised; that from time to time memory would spring open the unlockable gate, and shame or pain or rage or grief would leap up in her thoughts like the dogs of her imagination.

Yet Judith knew that she was not stunned by shock. This peace that made no sense was not stupefying, but was clear and clean and light. She had let go of all she had lost, and so let go of cowardice as well. The world was oddly upside down. The violation of her self, the defilement of her body, were unrelieved horrors to her. Dr. Deeds had not needed to warn her. Judith did not lacerate herself, or think she deserved what had happened to her. And still, out of the violation, her heart had been freed, as if immersion in dreadful polluted water could clean. She had fallen into the filth beside those other drowners she had always pitied. But the world was upside down, and in falling through its glass dome, she had fallen, stained clean, down into life.

Her hands resting on the scarf—her colors, worn on the arm of the stranger who had gone into battle her liege man—Judith Haig closed her eyes and fell asleep.

CHAPTER
66

Judith and Maynard and Chin Lam slept. But it was not yet midnight on Saturday night, and most people, to whom what had happened to Judith Haig was just a story, were still awake.

At night when the gusty flotsam of life had settled, and the ghosts of the day sprang up grinning in the windows unseen, the readers of Dingley Falls read on. They read not merely to keep their eyes lowered so that they wouldn't see the goblins, not even if they thought of themselves as refugees from their own lives, or thought of their books as evacuation routes. As did A. A. Hayes, who had fallen asleep in his armchair finally, with one of Ben Rough's little escapist mysteries beside him, with melted ice from his glass spilling into the rug as his hand relaxed, and around him on the walls the signed names of famous men. Or old Prudence Lattice and young Susan Packer, who were turning over (with that quick, unsatisfying unconsciousness with which the overweight eat) pages of the same sugary romance. No, Dingleyans were reading because, unlike God and unlike the periscopes made by Dingley Optical Instruments, they could not see around corners; because from any one perspective life is so much less full than fiction and so much more painful. Safe in fiction, they were testing their hearts.

Some Dingleyans read not for delight but for instruction, as Evelyn Troyes now read sheet music for voice and violin lent her by Cecil Hedgerow. As Ida Sniffell now sat in bed underlining inspiration in *Like Your*

Life! while in the kitchen her husband, Coleman, read, with gloomy satisfaction, the artificial ingredients on a can of just-spread sandwich spread. For instruction, Dr. Deeds (escaping the endless gin game between her grandfather and William Bredforet) read what little the Argyle Hospital library had to offer on the collapse of the heart. Ruth had disappointed Dr. Scaper when she'd told him it would be impossible for her to extend her vacation beyond Tuesday. She promised to keep in touch, to pass on, when he sent them, his patients' files and the results of the dog's autopsy. She advised him, however, to request an official investigation by epidemiologists from state or federal agencies. Meanwhile, she'd talk with her colleagues. Of course, she reminded him, the experts might find a perfectly obvious explanation. There might be no new disease at all. And even if there were, to isolate a rare factor like a variant Q Fever might take months, might take years; would take money, might never happen; an antibiotic might never be found. So much depended upon the haphazard coincidence of skill and luck. But she could not promise to stay, or to come back. In all honesty, she didn't think she'd want to come live in Dingley Falls to inherit his general practice. In all honesty, she preferred the frontier campfire to the bedside lamp. He told her, "Keep us in mind, quarter of a century or so from now. Come back, see if you don't feel different."

At midnight, high in the hawk's nest from which for so many years she had sat brooding over her town, Ramona Dingley lay encased in the clear plastic oxygen tent in the middle of her massive mahogany four-poster that her father, Ignatius, had inherited from his mother, Bridget. Ramona's eyes were closed, her breath a soft sigh. Around her sat Orchid O'Neal, and a hired nurse that Sammy Smalter had insisted upon, and the druggist himself, and Father Jonathan Fields. Orchid was telling her beads, the nurse was working a crossword puzzle, Jonathan was repeatedly reading to himself the Visitation of the Sick. From time to time he

looked over at the old woman. At one point her eyes
flicked open, caught his, and then (or at least so it
seemed to the curate) she winked at him. Of course, it
might have been an involuntary twitch, but in memory
Jonathan always preferred his interpretation. He had
winked back and broadly grinned.

On the other side of the room, near the bureau
crowded with her trophies, Ramona's closest friend,
her kinsman Sammy, sat holding his book of Browning
persistently before his eyes until he could compel
himself to see the words. Daily for most of his life
Smalter had relentlessly trained his will to let go,
without a futile and so unseemly struggle, of unfulfill-
able desires. He had let go of the love of Judith Haig
without ever thinking it could be his. He had lost her
again, to Winslow Abernathy. He knew this with all
certainty, whether the two yet knew it or not; for love,
though its eyes are seeled, swoops down like a falcon,
unerringly on the heart. Yet Judith's assault by the
unforgivable Barnum, and her near death, in some
ways as painful to him as anything in his life could be,
Smalter had borne without a sign. Or so he thought;
though both Judith and Winslow, and even Polly
Hedgerow, had seen that he loved her.

This afternoon Smalter had gone briefly to the
hospital with flowers, had expressed briefly his sympathy to Mrs. Haig, had tapped briefly her hands as he
left, and when she placed her hand briefly on top of his
had allowed himself to think no more about it than he
could bear; just as, when he lost Ramona, the closest
person to his heart, he would risk missing her no more
than he could bear to. Now the pharmacist forced his
eyes to reread the first line of poetry on a page he had
stared at for hours, to reread it again and again until the
words came into focus.

In bed Winslow Abernathy did not see the words on
his page either. That carried on such fragile wings,
Judith Haig had passed over death was also the subject
of his thoughts. That, and planning how to tell her

tomorrow that she didn't need to share with him the literal facts of what had really happened at John Haig's house beside the highway. Winslow would say to her that the gift lay in her desire to tell him. He would say that he with fear and happiness accepted that gift. But he would explain that he had taken vows to the principle of the law, and that if the *words* were spoken to say that Maynard Henry had violated the law, then Winslow would have to act on those words. If the words were not spoken, he could not, of course, hear them. Winslow smiled at this legalistic threading of his moral maze; the technique was one learned from reading Thomas More. Hand resting on the book that moved gently on his thin chest, Winslow, falling down into sleep, smiled too at the fact that he knew just what he felt. The technique, he acknowledged, was one he had learned from listening to Beatrice Dingley.

Far from Dingley Falls, surrounded by dozens of library books on American history, Richard Rage stared at a scratched-out scribbled page. On it were written the first lines of the long poem about Beanie's family line, the poem with which he would hand their child an inheritance:

> *Harried out of their land by Laud's command,*
> *By gaudy strictures on the heart of faith;*
> *Borne westward on a wave of protestations,*
> *They set up their arks in a somber sea*
> *And started to sell us America.*

Sleepily, he kept looking at the words while he ate his eraser. It was hard work being a poet with traditions. Rich yawned, scratched his tawny gold beard, and wriggled his toes against Big Mutt at the foot of the bed. Then filled with thanksgiving, he hugged his muse. She had fallen asleep already and happily he joined her.

Beanie was dreaming of Rich jouncing down the

sidewalk with their little daughter high above the
blurred crowd, laughing in the crook of his shoulder at
the silly jingle of his song. And then in her dream the
sidewalks raised up and floated off like ghosts, and
grass long buried stirred again out of the earth. And
then she was the little daughter high in that safe crook
of frail bone and flesh. And the red-gold sweet swirling
hair was her father's, and the rumbling sound of song
was his voice, at her command rolling his eyes as he
sang, "The choo-choo train that takes you / Away from
me, you'll never know how sad it makes me. / Toot-
toot-tootsie good-bye / Toot-toot-tootsie, don't cry."
And they jounced across Dingley Green until they fell
laughing beneath the mammoth copper beech that was,
he told her, their "family tree," planted long ago by
the man whose statue sat in the stone chair nearby.
A family tree that flamed in the fall with the generous color of the Dingleys' hair, a tree whose roots
reached for three hundred years down toward the
earth primeval.

Beanie always remembered of her father, first his
tawny hair, and next the sound of his voice singing
through her childhood. "I Want to Be Happy." And
"Barney Google." And when he drove her, shy and
teary, to boarding school, he sang "When You Wish
upon a Star," while in the backseat her mother kept
repacking all of Beanie's new bags and telling her to do
a hundred things that had she been a southern belle,
and half a foot shorter, she might have been able to do.
And Beanie had always thought, that sad December in
1941 after her father had been killed at Pearl Harbor,
how much her dad would have liked the new song,
"White Christmas," which all the people of Dingley
Falls gathered to sing together around the town tree
that stood without lights that year, and in the next few
dark years of the war. Stood with only a gold star at its
top, like the gold stars in the windows of more and
more houses in Dingley Falls and Madder. A tall native
spruce that grew not far from where Elijah Dingley had

planted his copper beech and blessed it with a long laugh and a short prayer: God keep us in health and heart. God keep us in bread and ale. God keep us at home and out of the hands of the godly.

Whenever Rich sang, Beanie would think of her father and of those singers standing together on the Dingley Green in the cold night of that Christmas, 1941, when America with its smug and warm, silly heart joined a world at war for what it promised was the last time.

In celebration of the town's rescue from fire, song and laughter kept local bartenders busy everywhere except at the Dingley Club, where only a few people played bridge. But at The Prim Minster, a piano and a banjo came free with drinks. At reopened Mama Marco's, pizzas spun in air and beer whizzed into jugs, while on the record player Mel Torme sang as loudly as he could. Noisiest of all was Fred's Fries, where the Grabaski cousins fought each other, and a local rock band, with Tony Treeca on drums and Jimmy MacDermott on lead guitar, fought hard against conversation. Most of the attempted talk was about the fire, and about Cecil Hedgerow's valor. Some Madderites went so far as to say they'd like to see Hedgerow running the town, making something useful of it, bringing it jobs, getting its highway connected to the world outside it, stirring things up like in the stories of the old days when Congressman Luke Madder had been alive.

At home Sarah MacDermott was also thinking, parenthetically, of Cecil Hedgerow, but in tears. Sarah, in her robe of black zigzags on cheap white nylon, sat on a child's plastic chair beside the lower bunk of her little Francis, who kept having nightmares no matter how much she loved him. Mrs. MacDermott was crying because it looked as if finally, after three generations, an O'Reilly would own land in America. She, Sarah O'Reilly MacDermott, could bring her family out of Madder and set them down on garden furniture on the

patio of that little Cape Cod through which Cecil
Hedgerow had often walked her. Right there on Pilgrim
Boulevard in Astor Heights. But what horror entangled
this gift of a lifetime! Joe, now acting police chief,
would beyond doubt be officially appointed to that post
at the town meeting called for next week. And his
salary would rise so that the bank could not refuse them
the mortgage. And so the dream of her heart's
preeminent desire was to come true, but at, God bless
him, poor Hawk's expense. Poor Hawk's big salary was
going to make *their* dreams come true, not his. While
he lay all alone in the cold ground, with his beautiful
house that he never should have built out in the
wilderness burned to a crisp over his corpse. And worst
of all his beautiful wife, that if Sarah could trust her
intuitions hadn't even loved Hawk in the first place for
some reason, his poor dear wife lying in her hospital
bed, snatched right out of the grim jaws of death not a
moment too soon after being dragged through hell on
earth, and what's more, no home or husband to go
home to, and the post office itself shutting down even if
Judith had the strength to get her old job back which
she didn't. And even though Judith had told her this
morning that Maynard hadn't done it, and had even
held her hands and said, "Sarah, stop saying this was
your fault. It wasn't." Still, Mrs. MacDermott would
never get over this in a thousand years, and that's what
she'd said to Chinkie in the A & P today, and at least
Chinkie'd had the human feelings, even if she was an
Orientaler, to say she was grateful for what Judith had
tried to do to get Maynard out of jail. No, she'd never
get over it in a million years. But what can we do but
grin and bear it? First thing to do was get Judith well,
and then move her in with them. Orchid could make
room, until they got the new house, which would really
be part Judith's anyhow, if you looked at it that way.
And then time would just have to heal all wounds. And
God's good mercy. And Sarah, weeping, took from her
pocket a bunched strip of toilet paper, blew her nose as

noiselessly as possible, and kissed her sleeping son. Well, Jesus bless us; Hawk voted most likely to succeed, and Judith, best-looking. Well. Sarah vowed to go first thing in the morning to early Mass, to ask the Blessed Virgin to whisper in God's ear a special word of kindness for her best friend, Judith Haig; and at the same time, if it didn't sound too awful, special thanks for getting her that little Cape Cod with the patio, for bringing her out of Madder and into the promised land of property she could call her own.

Mrs. MacDermott's spiritual adviser, Father Patrick Crisp, was also thinking tonight of Judith. He had visited her this evening at the hospital, where he had chastised a reporter who had sneaked into her room with a tape recorder to ask what it felt like to be raped and lose her husband. Father Crisp had known Judith since the year of her birth. That is, the year she was found by the then young priest beneath a Station of the Cross at the Church of Our Lady of Mercy. It had been beneath the Station depicting Simon the Cyrenean's carrying Christ's Cross for him that the mother (perhaps consciously, more likely by the divinity of coincidence) had put down her burden in its cardboard box. This girl, Judith's mother, left Dingley Falls the next day, Holy Saturday, and went to Ontario, where she married an older man for whom she had cared as a practical nurse, and after he died, had married again, and had had other children. No one in town knew the parentage of Judith Haig, whom the nuns took in. The old town librarian Gladys Goff, neatly stitching together her genealogical quilts of the best families, knew nothing of wholly private connections and would not have sewn in such names if she had. For Judith's mother had herself been illegitimate, the only child of a Madder factory girl whom one of the sons of one of the daughters of Charles Bradford Dingley III had seduced at the Optical Instruments factory where the young man was then the young girl's supervisor. And so by birth, though not by title, Judith's mother's maternal grandmother had been that housekeeper, that Irish parlormaid named Bridget Quin, for whose bridal gift the asthmatic and uxorious Charles Dingley III had built, to his mother's fury, that huge, white Victorian wedding cake of a house where Sammy Smalter now sat beside his kinswoman, Ramona Dingley, last to live by that family name the whole town shared. As a child Judith had imagined being plucked from the orphanage by a noble inheritance, like the heroines of romance. It had never happened. She would never inherit a family name or a family past. Still, she had inherited her mother's height and figure. She had inherited her father's arresting good looks, particularly the remarkable gas-flame blue of his eyes. For Judith's father was William Bredforet.

But Father Crisp and the Sisters of Mercy, knowing of her only that she shared those original parents shared by everyone, named her Judith Sorrow: Sorrow for her situation, and Judith for that Apocryphal widow who defeated the army of Nebuchadnezzar by herself cutting off the head of his general, Holofernes. They named her that; then told her to be a good, obedient girl; then fed her, clothed her, and taught her what they knew. Still, she had in these last five years hardly attended Mass at all. Poor child, sighed the old priest, inching his hips over to escape the spot where a spring poked up in his lumpy mattress. Poor child. Pray God this tragedy isn't the last straw for her, and she turns her face entirely away from His loving kindness, unreconciled. Why in the world had God tried this particular child in this particularly horrible way? And conscientiously attempting to discover the answer to this question, Father Crisp fell asleep.

His Anglican brother, Father Sloan Highwick, had gone to bed hours earlier, without a single word written on his Whitsunday sermon. For more than forty years of Saturday nights, Highwick had said that he probably should jot down some notes in preparation of his pastoral duty, but somehow he never did it, finally relying on his general maxim that it was all to the glory of the Lord anyhow, whatever we do.

He slept and was joined one by one by other Dingleyans as night moved across all the round earth, until only one light burned high above the little town, shining from the window where Ramona Dingley lay, watched over by Orchid and Sammy and Jonathan. And the light kept darkness away until the Morning Star came and found it burning.

nobody on his precinct means that there is all to the can't
of the Kane dullness, whatever it was.

The West End was jomed brief in the top office
ghiplwate as night packed around the noise aroll
until a whole light burned high above the Kane racing,
shining from the window where Bannus Dusky let
forward over he David and feature and a matter.
And the light kept burnmg away until the Morning
Star came and failed the sky.

PART
Seven

CHAPTER
67

Father Highwick drew to a close:

"And finally, dear friends, on this Whitsunday feast let us remind ourselves of these three or four great truths. Truly God is no great respecter of persons. For He rains on all alike, and of course is more often sunny, we mustn't forget, though from down here it may seem a bit gloomy, or even splashes and no umbrella; for He told us after what happened to poor Noah that He would never flood us out again. And he's kept that promise like the True God He is. And yet, though all the same we're none of us alike, as we heard in today's Epistle, ah, sorry, yes, um, here it is: 'For to one is given by the Spirit the word of wisdom; to another the word of knowledge,' and it goes on and on, we might say, to butcher and baker and Indian chief, or anything we like; rich, poor, Christian, or apostle or rather apostate, male or female, married or monosexual. To God these little differences of opinion are nothing. Nothing. And so no matter what we do, my friends, it's all to the glory of the Lord. Which is my second point. And which is why, isn't it, that when after that glorious moment when Peter was enjoying a little picnic lunch up on a friend's roof and he fell asleep from the heat and the dust of the day, God came down to him in a great, huge, snowy white sheet so big its corners were the ends of the world, and God said to him something like, 'Peter. Why don't you let the Gentiles come and join in as well as the Jews, and don't hold a bit of surgery (that only half the population was getting anyhow, now that I think of it) against the whole rest of

the world.' Which is why, after that, on Pentecost the
apostles began with no planning ahead to speak in
tongues so all the multitudes were amazed and understood every word of that gibberish just as if it were
English. Whether they were Parthians or Moabites and
I think some Romans were there and Cappadomians
and all those other little countries that are all over the
Holy Lands. And I know that there are a few denomi-
nations who even in this day and age have continued to
see fit to have convulsions and babble away for all
they're worth, I'm sure with the best intentions in the
world, but I really think we needn't go to that length
here at St. Andrew's in order to find words to wonder
at the wonderful works of God. Of which we ourselves
are surely the wonderfulest, or most wonderful, of all.
Think of all those people together talking away in a
great hubbub, not the Tower of Babel now, but a
babble of Good News. For what is the Good News? I'm
reminded that our curate, Father Fields, whom we've
been so proud and happy to have with us this last year,
told me, I think, that 'gossip' and 'gospel' meant the
same thing. Or perhaps that wasn't it. I see Jonathan
laughing there! I know, it was that 'gossip' means
'kinsman'! Yes, and so does 'kind.' And that's my
fourth point. Kindness and kinship. If someone, our
parent or child or friend or whoever, asks any one of us
for bread, will we give him a stone? Or if fish, will we
give him a serpent? Let's remember to ask, 'How much
more shall your Heavenly Father give?' And if we can
listen so happily to a song—I know at least personally I
love to sing, though I've been told I can't carry a tune
at all—then perhaps what sounds like babble to us
sounds to God with His great universal ears like
sublimest music! My friends, it is not the letters, or the
language, of the words, but their spirit.

"Trust in the spirit of the words no matter if they
make no sense. In the Pennsylvania town where my
mother grew up, a church minister kept calling for God
to strike with lightning an apparently (I was too young

to know myself one way or the other) salacious and evil beer hall that was too great a temptation to the poor thirsty miners. And lightning did strike it, and there it was burned to ashes. And the beer hall owner hired a lawyer, and he sued the minister. And the minister laughed and said, 'Don't be an idiot.'

"But God is an Idiot. I mean, God is an idiot to the wise. And who do you suppose was saved? The wise minister? Or the poor beer hall manager? Well, let's hope they both were. But our Savior will always leave the fat sober sheep in the pen and go out in the dark of night to search for the one little drunken ewe that has wandered off and toppled into a ditch. And if Christ will stoop down in that ditch, let's try not to mind too much the mud on our knees. Or stand above and pitch down rocks. Or walk away and say, 'I don't understand what you're saying. We don't speak the same language.' Because the same heart beats in every human breast. And so, sixth but last, my good neighbors. This has been a horrible week. With this awful fire. And I don't think I can remember quite so many sorrowful deaths in so short a span since we lost that June so many of our good boys overseas fighting Hitler because there comes a point when you have to. Some of you have come to me and said that saying that death has no dominion since Christ died does not help the hurt. So I would say, well, I remember my mother told me often, 'Sloan, never grab a rose.' Of course, perhaps she meant because of briars, but we could say that our loved ones are all roses, and we only kill them when we won't hold open our hands, and their deaths only hurt us when we clutch. So in the name of the Father and the Son and the Holy Ghost. Next week will be much better. It always is. Such is Life. Amen."

Prudence Lattice listened with affection to Father Highwick's sermon, though he had told the congregation the story of the beer hall many times before. For some odd reason she was having strange, sudden pains in her chest, and then a jabbing, funny kind of pain running down her arms. Don't be melodramatic, she told herself. These last few days have you all upset; put it out of your mind. And quickly she rummaged through her purse to find a dollar before Ernest Ransom reached her back pew with the gold plate. And as the offertory was collected, the Alexander Hamilton Academy Choir, celestially scrubbed and robed, sang "Gloria" as well as they could. And Mass was said. And Communion offered. For some odd reason, Prudence Lattice was having difficulty straightening up. Alone in the pew in front of her she noticed the attractive young man, the academy headmaster, to whom she'd given her handkerchief on Saturday. She tapped his shoulder, and when he jerked around, she whispered, "Excuse me. Will you be taking Communion?"

"No, ah, no, not at all. Came to hear the choir. My boys. Not a member."

She tapped his shoulder again and whispered, "Excuse me. I'm sorry to bother you, but I have this funny stitch in my side for some reason and can't seem to get going by myself. Could I ask for your arm so I could take Communion? Would you mind?"

What could he do? Refuse her? Walter Saar slid out of the pew and helped the tiny elderly woman out of hers. Together they started down the aisle, then stood at the back of the line of communicants who were waiting, Saar was thinking crimson-faced, to gobble God like piglets at a sow, shepherded there by their babbling pastor.

There at the rail the congregation knelt, different sizes and colors and ages all scrunched together as the smiling Father Highwick and the serious, radiant Jonathan walked among them offering a corpse's body and blood as gifts, Walter told himself as he felt the slight weight of the woman lean into him. Some at the rail he recognized. Mr. and Mrs. Ernest Ransom were handsome even from the rear. Beside Priss, Tracy

Canopy, and next to her the emaciated wraith of what looked like the sort of old derelict Walter suspected he would someday become if he didn't stop drinking, an old man with matted hair and no socks, and next to him the huge bulk of Otto Scaper, and next to him two teenagers, one blind, and next to them Walter walked slowly beside the bent figure of Prudence Lattice, just as Priss Ransom, starting to stand, nearly stumbled back to her knees at the sight of him. For as Walter attempted to disconnect himself from her arm, Prudence plopped down onto the purple cushion and pulled him down with her. Toward them came the Rector with the silver cup of wafers and behind him the curate with the gold cup of wine. Above them was the larger-than-life crucifix and in front of them was the choir, singing, and, no doubt, staring at their headmaster. Everyone else along the rail was reaching out, and suddenly Walter Saar, the color of the cushion and feeling a perfect fool, said out loud, "Oh, what the hell!" and reached out his hands, too.

THE PEOPLE
(in alphabetical order)

THE TOWN

Beanie Dingley Abernathy	A Juno-esque heiress to what is left of the Dingley fortune.
Winslow Abernathy	Beanie's husband, a lawyer.
Arthur Abernathy	Their stolid son and Winslow's law partner; Dingley Falls's first selectman.
Lance Abernathy	Arthur's good-looking fraternal twin; an amateur tennis player.
Limus Barnum	Unsavory owner of local antiques, hobbies, and appliances store.
Sidney Blossom	Town librarian and former hippie.
William Bredforet	Roguish octogenarian; Ernest Ransom's great-uncle.
Mary Bredforet	His wife.
Tracy, *Mrs. Vincent Canopy*	A perky widowed patroness of the arts; Beanie's childhood friend.
Father Patrick Crisp	Elderly Catholic priest at Our Lady of Mercy in Madder.

655

Louie Daytona	Gorgeous bisexual sculptor and ex-convict befriended by Tracy Canopy.
Bill Deeds	The Bredforets' cranky eighty-year-old black chauffeur.
Dr. Ruth Deeds	His granddaughter, an eager young internist at the federal Center for Disease Control, a Marxist feminist.
Ramona Dingley	Tennis champion of 1927, town selectman, wry caretaker of the past, invalid seventy-three-year-old distant relative of Beanie.
Jonathan Fields	Exquisite, diffident curate at St. Andrew's, Dingley Falls's Episcopal Church.
John ("Hawk") Haig	Police chief; a big, handsome man in his early forties.
Judith Sorrow Haig	His wife, a beautiful woman with a heart condition; postmistress of Dingley Falls.
A. A. Hayes	The alcoholic editor of *The Dingley Day*, southern expatriate, sardonic failure.
"Junebug," Mrs. A. A. Hayes	His migraine-prone wife.
Tac and Suellen Hayes	Two of their children.
Cecil Hedgerow	Widower; third selectman, unenthusiastic realtor.
Polly Hedgerow	His sixteen-year-old daughter, a bookworm, gossip, and sleuth.
Maynard Henry	Unemployed construction worker, Vietnam veteran.

Chin Lam Henry	His nineteen-year-old wife, a Vietnamese refugee.
Father Sloan Highwick	Affable sixty-six-year-old Rector of St. Andrew's.
Mrs. Highwick	His mother, a senile painter.
Prudence Lattice	Lonely spinster in her sixties, owner of a tea shop that has fallen on hard times.
Joe MacDermott	Hawk Haig's assistant.
Sarah O'Reilly MacDermott	His wife, gabby, ebullient cashier at the Madder A & P, mother of five boys, self-elected best friend of Judith Haig.
Alf Marco	Dingley Falls's colorless postman.
Sebastian Marco	His younger brother, a moody gardener.
Carl Marco, Sr.	Their older brother, a self-made Madderite merchant, tract developer, aspiring philanthropist.
Carl Marco, Jr.	His son, a muscular ophthalmologist.
Sgt. Fred Myers	A desk clerk at the Argyle jail, a philosopher.
Orchid O'Neal	Sarah MacDermott's widowed older sister, a house cleaner.
Jerry Packer	Bartender at the Dingley Club.
Luke Packer	His seventeen-year-old son, a bright, restless film buff.
Susan Packer	Luke's older sister, secretary to Abernathy & Abernathy.

Richard Rage	Lascivious avant-garde poet.
Ernest Ransom	The most influential man in Dingley Falls, the meticulous, methodical president of Ransom Bank.
Priss, *Mrs. Ernest Ransom*	His chic, satiric wife; college friend of Beanie and Tracy.
Emerald Ransom	Their eldest child, a practiced beauty.
Kate Ransom	Emerald's younger sister, a Vassar senior long wooed by Sidney Blossom.
Ray Ransom	Their son, a braggart.
Walter Saar	Headmaster of Alexander Hamilton Academy, a sleek, witty, aesthete homosexual secretly possessed of most of the old-fashioned virtues.
Otto Scaper	Fat, gruff physician in his seventies.
Sammy Smalter	Town pharmacist, a midget.
Coleman Sniffell	Assistant editor of *The Dingley Day*.
Ida Sniffell	His mercilessly cheerful wife; Dr. Scaper's nurse.
Jack and Peggy Strummer	Nice people.
Joy Strummer	Their beautiful blond teenage daughter, Polly's best friend.
Wanda Tojek	The Ransoms' maid.

Evelyn, *Mrs. Blanchard Troyes*	Wispy, lovely widow of a French industrialist, childhood friend of Beanie and Tracy.
Irene Wright	Ransom's secretary.

OPERATION ARCHANGEL

Comdr. Hector Brickhart	Former USC tackle, warrior in the Pacific, chief of naval intelligence, now on the board of ALAS-ORE Oil.
Bob ("Bucky") Eagerly	Public relations expert on White House staff.
Thomas Svatopluk, *M.D., Ph.D.*	Brainy, arrogant East European biochemist, chief of staff of Operation Archangel.
Daniel Wolton	Professionally moral Boston Brahmin; INR spy on OSS.
Justin Tom	Government official with OSS.
John Dick	Government official with CIA.
Colonel Harry	Government official with DIA.